The Venus Throw

G·K
Hall
&Cº

To Rick

CONTENTS

CHRONOLOGY

Listed below are some significant events preceding the action of *The Venus Throw*, which begins in mid-January, 56 B.C.

90 B.C.
Gordianus in Alexandria.

80 B.C.
King Soter of Egypt dies; succeeded briefly by Alexander II, then by Ptolemy Auletes. Sulla dictator in Rome; Cicero's first major speech, in defense of Sextus Roscius; the events of *Roman Blood*.

76 B.C.
Appius Claudius (father of Clodia and Clodius) dies.

75 B.C.
First senatorial attempt to act on the alleged will of Alexander II bequeathing Egypt to Rome.

72 B.C.
Second year of Spartacan slave revolt; the events of *Arms of Nemesis*.

68 B.C.
Clodius incites mutiny in Lucullus's army.

65 B.C.

Crassus as censor makes a foiled attempt to declare Egypt a tributary province of Rome.

63 B.C.

Cicero's consulship; the events of *Catilina's Riddle*. Caesar and Pompey attempt to exact Egyptian tribute with Rullan Legislation, foiled by Cicero.

62 B.C.

Clodia's husband Quintus Metellus Celer governor of Cisalpine Gaul. Clodius disrupts the celebration of the Good Goddess.

61 B.C.

Clodius tried for the Good Goddess scandal and acquitted.

59 B.C.

Caelius prosecutes Antonius (Cicero defending). Caesar as consul arranges for King Ptolemy to be recognized as "Friend and Ally of the Roman People" in return for thirty-five million denarii. King Ptolemy raises taxes in Egypt, angering the populace. Clodius becomes a plebeian in order to run for tribune. Clodia widowed by the death of Quintus Metellus Celer.

58 B.C.

Clodius tribune. Cicero forced into exile (March). Roman takeover of Egyptian Cyprus. King Ptolemy flees to Rome.

57 B.C.

Cicero returns from exile (September). Caelius supports Bestia for praetor. The delegation of one hundred Alexandrians, headed by Dio, arrives in Italy.

At dice I sought the Venus Throw.
Instead: damned Dogs — the lose-all low!

PROPERTIUS, *Elegies*
IV, vii: 45–46

We've all *heard* about Alexandria, and now we
know about it — the source of all trickery and
deceit, where the plots of all the mimes come from.

CICERO, *Pro C. Rabirio Postumo*, 35

Democritus disapproved of sexual intercourse as
being merely the act whereby one human being
springs from another — and by Hercules, the less
of that the better! On the other hand, sluggish
athletes find that sex rejuvenates them; sex can
relieve hoarseness, cure pain in the loins, sharpen
eyesight; sex can restore mental balance and banish
melancholy.

PLINY, *Natural History*,
XXVIII, 58

PART ONE

NEX

CHAPTER ONE

"Two visitors at the front door, Master." Belbo looked at me from under his brow and shifted from foot to foot uncertainly.

"Their names?"

"They wouldn't say."

"Familiar faces?"

"I've never seen them before, Master."

"Did they say what they wanted?"

"No, Master."

I pondered this for a moment and stared into the flames of the brazier.

"I see. Two men — "

"Not exactly, Master . . ."

"Two visitors, you said. Are they both men or not?"

"Well," Belbo said, wrinkling his brow, "I'm pretty sure that one of them is a man. At least I think so. . . ."

"And the other?"

"A woman — I think. Or maybe not . . ." He looked thoughtfully but without much concern into the middle distance, as if trying to remember what he had eaten for breakfast.

I raised an eyebrow and looked beyond the flaming brazier, through the narrow window and into the garden, where the statue of Minerva kept watch over a little fishpond. The sun was beginning to lower. Days in Januarius are all too short, especially for a man of fifty-four like myself, old enough to feel the cold in his bones. But the daylight was still strong enough to see clearly, certainly clearly enough to tell if someone at the door was male or female. Was Belbo's sight beginning to fail?

Belbo is not the cleverest of slaves. What he lacks in brains he has always made up for with brawn. For a long time this hulking mass of bulging muscles and straw-colored hair has been my bodyguard, but in recent years his reflexes have grown noticeably slower. I had thought I might be able to start using him as a doorkeeper, reasoning that his long service at my side would enable him to recognize most of my visitors and that his size should intimidate those he didn't. Alas, if he couldn't even tell the difference between a man and a woman it would hardly do to have him answering the door.

Belbo ceased to ponder the middle distance and cleared his throat. "Should I show them in, Master?"

"Let me see if I understand you: two strangers of indeterminate sex, who refuse to give their names, have come to call on a man with a lifetime's worth of enemies, here in the most dangerous city in the world. Show them in, you ask? Why not?"

My sarcasm was apparently too subtle. Belbo

nodded and left the room before I could call him back.

A moment later he returned with my visitors. I stood to greet them, and realized that Belbo's eyes were indeed still sharp, probably sharper than my own. Had I seen this couple across the street or walking through the Forum, I might have taken them to be exactly what they appeared to be, a rather small young man with delicate features, dressed in an ill-fitting toga and wearing a broad-brimmed hat (despite the less than sunny weather), and a much older, much larger woman wrapped in a stola that modestly covered her from head to toe. But on closer inspection, there was something amiss.

I could see nothing of the young man's body, obscured as it was by the loose folds of his oversize toga, but his face was not quite right; there was no sign of a beard on his cheeks, and his soft, beautifully manicured hands moved with a delicacy that was not masculine. Also, instead of lying flat around his ears and the back of his neck, his hair appeared to have been pushed up under his hat, which meant it must be unusually long. The color of his hair was odd as well — dark at the roots, but turning blond where it was tucked up under the brim of his hat, which he declined to take off.

As for the woman, a woolen mantle draped over her head obscured much of her face, but I could see that her cheeks had been painted, and not too expertly, with a rose-colored blush. The wrinkles of her neck hung down in folds considerably looser than the folds of the stola that strained to contain her bulk, especially around the middle. Her shoulders seemed a bit too broad and her hips too narrow. Nor did her hands seem quite right, for Roman matrons take pride in keeping their flesh as pale as possible, and hers were dark and weathered as if by many years of exposure to the sun, and while any woman vain enough to color her cheeks might be expected to take good care of her fingernails, those of my visitor were ragged and bitten down to the quick.

The couple stood mute beside the brazier.

"I understand that you've come to pay me a visit," I finally said.

They merely nodded. The young man pursed his lips and peered at me, his face stiff. The old woman tilted her head so that the brazier lit up her eyes. Between lashes stained black with antimony I saw a flash of apprehension.

I waved to Belbo, who fetched a pair of folding chairs and placed them opposite my own.

"Sit," I offered. They did, demonstrating even more clearly that things were not what they seemed. The wearing of the toga is an art, as is the wearing of the stola, I imagine. From their manifest awkwardness it seemed highly unlikely that the little man had ever worn a toga before, or that his companion had ever worn a stola. Their clumsiness was almost comical.

"Wine?" I offered.

"Yes!" said the young man, sitting forward, his face suddenly animated. His voice was high and somehow too delicate, like his hands. The old woman stiffened and whispered "No!" in a hoarse voice. She nervously fiddled with her fingers, then bit at her thumbnail.

I shrugged. "For myself, I feel the need of something to stave off the chill in the air. Belbo, ask one of the serving girls to bring some water and wine. And something to eat, perhaps?" I looked inquiringly at my visitors.

The young man brightened and nodded eagerly. The woman glowered and struck at his arm, making him wince. "Are you mad?" she whispered gruffly. I thought I detected a slight accent, and was trying to place it when I heard her stomach growl.

"Yes, of course, exactly," the young man muttered. He too had an accent, faint but vaguely eastern. This was curious, for only Roman citizens wear the toga. "No food, please," he said.

"How unfortunate," I said, "for we have some very good must-cakes left over from breakfast this morning, flavored with honey and pepper in the Egyptian style. My wife comes from Alexandria, you see. I spent some time there myself as a young man — oh, that must have been over thirty years ago. The Egyptians are famous for their soft breads, as I'm sure you know. My wife says it was a baker at the mouth of the Nile who discovered the secret of leavening and dedicated his first loaf to the great Alexander when he founded the city."

The woman's mouth began to twitch. She pulled

at her mantle to shade her eyes, but I could feel her gaze on me as hot as the flames of the brazier. The little man's face lost its animation and turned stiff again.

Belbo returned with a small folding table which he set between us. A serving girl followed with three cups and two ewers, one of water and one of wine. The girl poured wine into each cup and then departed, leaving it to me to apportion the water. "For myself, in the cold months I take it almost straight," I said, leaning forward and adding only a splash of water to the nearest cup. "And you?" I looked at the young man. He held up his forefinger and pressed his thumb against the furthest joint. "A knuckle's worth of water," I said, pouring, then looked at his companion. "And will you join us after all?" She hesitated, then copied the little man's gesture. Again I noticed her bitten nails and the sun-weathered flesh of her hands.

"You won't regret it," I said. "This comes from my private stock. I still have some jars of wine remaining from my brief tenure as a farmer up in Etruria a few years ago. It was a very good year — for the wine, anyway." I handed them each a cup. Before I could pick up my own, the woman quickly put hers down and reached for mine. "I changed my mind," she whispered hoarsely. "Less water will suit me. If you don't mind."

"Of course not." I picked up the cup she had abandoned and held it before my lips, pretending to savor the bouquet. She watched me intently and put her cup beneath her fleshy nose, sniffing at it cautiously with no pretense of enjoyment, waiting for me to take a sip before she would do the same. It was an absurd moment, like a scene in some hackneyed comedy, except that had we been on a stage the audience would have hooted at us for playing our parts too broadly.

At last I put the cup to my mouth and drank, letting the red wine linger on my lips for a moment before licking them clean, to show her I had swallowed. Only then did she sip cautiously from her cup. Her companion, having watched this interchange as if awaiting permission, put his cup to his lips and drained it. "Excellent!" he exclaimed, his voice slipping into a higher register. He cleared his throat. "Excellent," he said again in a voice that was deeper but still distinctly feminine.

For a moment we sipped our wine in silence, listening to the crackling of the brazier. "You seem cautious about stating your purpose," I finally said. "Perhaps you could begin by telling me your names."

The little man looked at the woman, who then turned away from the flames and hid her face in shadow. After a moment the little man looked back to me. "No names," he said softly. "Not yet."

I nodded. "As you wish. What do names matter, anyway? Names are but a cloak, a garment which men put on and take off. A disguise, if you will. Don't you agree?"

The little man looked at me with gleaming eyes — was he intrigued, or had he simply drained his cup too quickly? His companion kept her face in shadow, but again I felt the heat of her gaze. "A *name* is not the same as a *thing*," she finally whispered.

I nodded. "So I was taught long ago — when I lived in Alexandria, as a matter of fact. And yet, without names, we have no way of discoursing with one another about the things those names represent."

The woolen mantle nodded gravely up and down.

"A thing is called one name in Greek, another in Latin," I said. "The thing remains the same. That which applies to things must also apply to persons. King Ptolemy of Egypt, for example, is King Ptolemy, whether we give him the Greek title *basileus* or the Latin title *rex*."

The figure in the stola drew a sharp breath and seemed on the verge of speaking, but held back.

"So it is with the gods themselves," I went on. "Romans call the father of the gods Jupiter; Greeks call him Zeus. 'Jupiter' is an onomatopoeia for the sound of lightning striking the earth, while 'Zeus' captures the sound of a thunderbolt cutting through the air. Thus do names convey to the ear what the eye and the soul of man perceive, however imperfectly."

"Exactly!" whispered my visitor. The head tilted to reveal the eyes, which were fixed upon me with the excitement of a teacher who hears his pupil repeating back to him a lesson learned long ago but never forgotten.

"Still, names are not things," I said, "and while the study of names may fascinate us, it is the study of things, or more precisely our human perception of things, which must occupy anyone who cares to discover philosophy. For example: I see the flame in this brazier, yet how do I know that it exists?"

The little man, who had availed himself of more wine during my discourse, laughed out loud. "Simple — put your hand into the flame!"

I clucked my tongue disapprovingly. "You must be of the Epicurean School, if you believe that by sense perception alone we can determine the actuality of existence. Epicurus taught that all sensations are true; still, the fact that *I* am burned by the fire should be no proof to *you* of its existence, since you would feel no pain."

"Ah, but I would hear you scream."

"Perhaps; but there are those who can endure such pain without screaming. If I didn't scream, would the fire be any more or less real? What if I did scream, and you happened to be deaf and looking elsewhere — would I still have been burned? Then again, if I were to scream, and if you were to hear me, you still would have no way of knowing whether my pain was real or a sham."

"You seem to know a lot about such things," said the young man, who smiled and took another sip. I noticed he had spilled a bit of wine on his toga.

"A little. Philosophy is the creation of the Greeks, of course, but a Roman may attempt to comprehend it. My old patron Cicero made himself something of an expert on philosophy, to help his oratory. From the Skeptics he learned that a proposition is always easier to disprove than to prove — a useful thing for a lawyer to know, especially if he has no scruples about defending guilty men."

I took a long sip of wine. The mood in the room had changed completely. My visitors' frosty suspicion had melted into trust. The comforting cadence of philosophic discourse was familiar ground, as I suspected it would be.

"But just as a name is not a thing, so *appearance* is not *existence*," I went on. "Consider: two visitors come to my home. At first glance, they appear to be a man and a woman, and this is clearly the impression they wish to give. But on closer scrutiny this is only an impression, not the truth; thus do my senses tell me and my powers of logic deduce. Questions follow: if the man is not a man, and the woman is not a woman, then *what are they?* Who are they? Why do they wish to be perceived as something they are not? Who are they trying to fool, and why? And why do they come to the house of Gordianus the Finder?"

"And do you know the answers to all these questions?" rasped my visitor in the stola.

"I think so, to most of them, anyway. Though some things about your companion still puzzle me . . ." I looked at the little man, who smiled in a way I couldn't account for, until I realized that he was smiling not at me but at someone behind me.

I turned to see my daughter, Diana, in the doorway.

Her posture was tentative, as if she had merely paused to have a look into the room and would move on at any moment. She wore the long-sleeved gown that children of both sexes wear, but at thirteen she was already beginning to fill the garment in ways unmistakably feminine. Her dark blue gown merged with the dimness of the hallway, so that her face, lit up by the brazier, seemed to hover in the air. Her skin, which had the creamy texture and the rosy glow that my visitor's painted cheeks so crudely mimicked, made the darkness of her long eyelashes and her thick eyebrows all the more pronounced. The flames caught the highlights of her long black hair, which was parted in the middle and fell down her shoulders. Her brown eyes peered at us curiously and with a hint of amusement. How like her mother she had always been, and how more like her she became every day! Sometimes it seemed to me that I had nothing to do with creating her, so completely was she cast in Bethesda's image.

She smiled faintly and began to move on. "Diana," I called, "come here for a moment."

She stepped into the room, wearing that mysterious smile she inherited from her mother. "Yes, Papa?"

"We have visitors, Diana."

"Yes, Papa, I know. I saw Belbo let them in

at the front door. I was on my way to tell Mother, but I thought I'd have a closer look first."

"A closer look?"

She gave me a bemused, exasperated look, such as Bethesda gives me when I belabor the obvious. "Well, Papa! It's not every day that a eunuch and a man dressed as a woman come calling on you, is it?"

She looked at my visitors and smiled sweetly.

They didn't smile back, but instead looked glumly at each other. "I told you that the pretense was worthless. Even a child saw through it!" grumbled the old man in the stola, no longer disguising his voice or his Alexandrian accent. He wearily pushed back the mantle from his head. His silver hair was pulled back from his face and knotted at the back of his neck. His forehead was wrinkled and covered with spots. The folds of flesh hanging from his chin quivered and he suddenly looked ridiculous, an unhappy old man with painted cheeks and painted eyes.

The eunuch in the toga covered his mouth and giggled tipsily. "But you look so pretty in makeup!"

"Enough of that!" growled the old Egyptian. His mouth settled in a deep frown and his jowls drooped as he stared bleakly into the flames, his eyes full of despair.

CHAPTER TWO

"This is my daughter, Gordiana, whom we call Diana." I took her soft, smooth hand in mine. "Diana, we are honored by the presence of Dio of Alexandria: philosopher, teacher, esteemed member of the Academy, and currently the chief ambassador to Rome from the people of Egypt."

With the unstudied dignity of a distinguished man used to being formally introduced and hearing his titles recited, Dio stood, clasping his hands before him, pulling his shoulders back. His self-possession seemed peculiarly at odds with his strange costume; with his painted face and his feminine garments he looked like the priest of some eastern cult — which was precisely what his companion turned out to be.

"And this," said Dio, gesturing to the little eunuch, who likewise stood, though a bit tipsily, "is Trygonion, a priest at the Temple of Cybele here in Rome."

The eunuch took a little bow and pulled off his hat, from which tumbled a mass of pale yellow hair. The color was a bleached, unnatural shade of blond. He ran his fingers through his hair and shook his head to untangle the curls.

"A philosopher . . . and a gallus!" Diana said

wonderingly. The last word gave me a start. *Gallus* is the Latin term for a castrated priest of the Great Mother, Cybele. All the galli are foreigners, since by law no Roman can become one. The word is pious in the mouths of the goddess's adherents, but others sometimes use it as a vulgar epithet ("You filthy gallus!"); the idea of men becoming eunuchs, even in the service of the divine, remains foreign and repulsive to most Romans. I couldn't remember ever having taught the word to Diana, but then she is always coming out with things I never taught her. She learns them from her mother, I suspect.

"Yes," Dio said ruefully, "puzzle that, Gordianus: what could a philosopher and a gallus possibly have in common — the man who lives by reason, and the man whose life is the surrender of all reason? Ha! Circumstances make strange bedmates. The more desperate the circumstances, the odder the bedmates." He cast a sidelong, gloomy glance at the eunuch, then suddenly looked doubtful. "I do not intend this metaphor literally, of course. You do have this phrase in Latin, yes? About circumstances and bedmates?"

"Something close enough."

He nodded, satisfied that he had made himself understood. His Latin was in fact impeccable, though his accent was distinctly Alexandrian, with the particular inflections of those born in Egypt whose ancestry and primary tongue are Greek. Hearing him speak freely, I now recalled his voice from many years ago. It had grown coarser with age, but was undeniably the same voice I had listened to so attentively on the steps outside the temple of Serapis in Alexandria when I was a young man, eager to learn all I could about the world. Dio's voice took me far back in memory and far away from Rome.

Introductions finished, we sat, except for Diana, who excused herself and left the room, no doubt to go tell her mother.

Dio cleared his throat. "You remember me, then?"

"Teacher," I said, for that was what I had always called him in Alexandria, and it now felt awkward to call him by his name, though I was long past the age of deference, "of course I remember you. You'd be a hard man to forget!"

"I had thought, after so many years . . . And then, when they told me your name, how could I know for sure that it was the same Gordianus whom I had known so long ago? To be sure, the name is unusual, and also they seemed to think that you had been to Alexandria as a young man, and what they said of you sounded like the tree that would have grown from the sapling — this expression you have also, yes? And I have used the correct tenses? Good. Still, with so much danger around me, so many betrayals — you understand why I could not come to you openly? Why I hesitated to reveal myself to you? Why I had to be suspicious even of your very fine wine?" He looked at me uneasily and chewed a fingernail. "Even when I saw you, I was not quite sure that you were the Gordianus I had known in Alexandria. Time changes us all, and you wear a sort of disguise as well, you know."

He gestured to something on my face. I touched my chin and realized that he meant my beard.

I smiled. "Yes, I was clean-shaven back then. Alexandria is too hot for beards, and I was too young to grow a decent one anyway. Or do you mean all the gray among the black? Gray hair and wrinkles are a kind of involuntary disguise, I suppose, worn by anyone who lives long enough."

Dio nodded and studied my face, still trying to decide whether he could trust me. "I have to be very careful," he said.

"Yes, I know something about your situation," I said. "Your journey from Alexandria, the attacks on your entourage after you landed down in Neapolis, the threats against you here in Rome, the fact that the Senate looks the other way. There's plenty of talk in the Forum these days about what people call 'the Egyptian situation.' "

"Still, how did you guess it was Dio?" asked the little gallus, pouring himself another cup of wine. "Our disguises got us safely through the streets. Granted, they may be less convincing at such close quarters — "

"Yes," said Dio, "how could you possibly have known it was me? Surely you didn't recognize my face, hidden in shadow and painted like a woman's, and after all these years. And surely it was not my voice, for I tried to speak like a woman and as little as I could, and you have not heard me speak for so long."

"Teacher, I'm not sure exactly why you've come to see me, but I assume it has something to do with the reputation I've made for myself: Finder, I'm called. I knew who you must be almost at once. If I couldn't figure out as small a thing as that, coming to see me would be a waste of your time."

"Elucidate," said Dio, in his expressionless teacher's voice.

"Yes, make yourself clear!" laughed the little gallus, lifting his wine cup and shaking out his bleached curls.

"Very well. That you were not what you wished to appear was immediately evident to me, as it was to Diana, and even to Belbo, my doorkeeper."

"What gave me away?" said Dio.

I shrugged. "Little things. Who can list all the differences between the ways that men and women walk and talk and hold themselves? An actor on the stage can convincingly portray a woman, but an actor trains for the task. To simply paint your face and put on a stola is hardly an impersonation."

"Then the pretense was not at all convincing? Be specific! I have to know, because if I cannot succeed with this disguise, then I must find another. It could mean the difference between — between life and . . ." He bit at his fingernails again, but finding nothing left to gnaw at, pulled nervously at the wrinkles that hung from his neck.

"Your fingernails gave you away, for a start.

Roman matrons make a ritual of their manicures."

"Ah!" He looked at his nails with disgust. "A terrible habit. It's come back to me only since I arrived in Italy. I cannot seem to stop myself."

"You might grow back your nails, but your hands would still give you away. Such brown, weathered hands — no Roman matron has hands like yours, and neither does any citizen of standing. Only slaves and farmers have such hands — or visitors from foreign climes where the sun stays hot all year long and burns everyone brown as a nut, from King Ptolemy down to the lowest field slave."

"Ptolemy!" Dio spat the name.

"Yes, I saw your agitation earlier when I spoke his name, which gave further confirmation to what I already suspected: that Dio of Alexandria had come to pay me a visit."

"But you still haven't explained how you came to have such a suspicion in the first place," said the gallus. " 'Elucidate!' " he quipped, mimicking Dio.

"By steps, then: My visitor is dressed as a woman but is not a woman. My visitor must be a man, then, with a reason for concealing himself — I confess that I overlooked the possibility that either of you might be a eunuch. A man in trouble, perhaps in danger — that seemed likely from your nervous mannerisms and the fact that you refused any food, despite the fact that your stomach was growling. From your brown hands and your accent, I knew you must be foreign."

I shrugged. "But there's a point where explaining the discrete steps in a logical progression of thought becomes too tedious to bother with — would you agree, Teacher? Like asking a weaver to explain how a tapestry was made by taking it apart thread by thread — what a mess you'd have! Suffice it to say that given what I had already deduced, the supposition leaped to my mind that my visitor must be Dio of Alexandria. I've heard of your plight; rumor says that you've been hiding in private houses here on the Palatine Hill; suddenly it occurred to me that this foreign stranger with a desperate demeanor might be Dio. To test the possibility, I felt you out. I spoke of philosophy, my days in Alexandria, King Ptolemy. Your reactions confirmed my suspicions. This is not philosophy or mathematics, Teacher, but I think you must see how my mind works, and how I have put to use the ways of thinking which you taught me long ago."

Dio smiled and nodded. How curious, that in the fifth decade of my life I could still be warmed by the approval of a teacher I hadn't seen and had scarcely thought about for thirty years!

"And what about Trygonion?" Dio said.

"Yes, what did you make of me?" asked the little gallus, his eyes sparkling. (I say '*his* eyes,' though many people, perhaps most, would say '*her* eyes'; as often as not, eunuchs are referred to as females, which seems to please them.)

"I confess, Trygonion, that you stumped me.

I knew that you weren't what you pretended to be, but I got it wrong. I assumed you must be a young woman in a toga and hat, trying to pass herself off as a man."

The gallus threw back his head and let out a throaty laugh. "A logical balance, I suppose, for those who think of things as one or the other: a young woman in a toga, to match an old man in a stola!"

I nodded. "Exactly. The expectation of symmetry seduced me into error."

"So you took me for a woman!" said Trygonion, sitting low in his chair and fixing me with a feline gaze. "Who did you think such a woman might be — the philosopher's slave, his daughter, his wife?" He reached over and stroked the top of Dio's wrinkled hand with his fingertips; the philosopher made a face and drew back at the touch. "Or his Amazon bodyguard, perhaps?" Trygonion laughed.

I shrugged. "Your features and your voice confused me. Eunuchs are rare in Rome; I overlooked that possibility. I saw that you were unaccustomed to wearing a toga, as might be expected of a woman — but also of a foreigner. I did notice your accent, but it's faint, and not Egyptian; Phrygian, I assume, now that I know you're a gallus. Your Latin is almost that of a Roman. You must have lived here a long time."

"For ten years. I came to serve at the Great Mother's temple here in Rome when I was fifteen, the very year that I consecrated myself to her worship." By consecrated, Trygonion meant castrated; Dio winced. "So, the gallus proved a harder riddle to solve than the philosopher," the little priest said, looking pleased with himself.

"As is only logical," said Dio irritably, "given that philosophers strive for lucidity, while the priests of Cybele make a religion of mystifying the senses."

"And yet our host's young daughter perceived the truth at a glance," said Trygonion.

"A beautiful girl," said Dio softly, wrinkling his brow.

"Such insight on the part of a child seems almost preternatural, don't you think, Gordianus?" Trygonion looked at me shrewdly. "Perhaps your daughter is a witch."

Dio scowled and shifted uneasily, but I decided to indulge the gallus's sense of humor rather than take offense. "Diana's mother grew up in Egypt, which has many eunuchs. Diana was born with Egypt in her blood, so I suppose she knows a eunuch when she sees one. I'd like to take credit for her cleverness, but certain insights definitely come from her mother."

"Perhaps they are both witches," said Trygonion.

"Enough of your rudeness," growled Dio. "These galli think they can say anything and behave however they choose, under anyone's roof. They have no shame."

"That's not all we lack," said Trygonion with a straight face.

Whatever the source of her insight, Diana had also put her finger on the more perplexing mystery that lay beyond the thin disguises of my guests: what were they doing together? It was clear that they had no love for each other.

"If you've had enough wine," I said, knowing that Trygonion had drunk more than his share while Dio had barely touched his cup, "and if we've talked enough of your disguises, perhaps we should speak of more serious things. Why have you come to me, Teacher, and what do you want from me?"

Dio cleared his throat. "You spoke a moment ago of what you Romans call 'the Egyptian situation.' I take it, then, that you know of the false will of King Alexander, the schemes of Caesar and Pompey to get their hands on the wealth of Egypt, the wholesale murder of my colleagues who have come to seek justice from the Senate of Rome — "

I raised my hand. "Perhaps you should begin at the beginning and explain to me each step that brought you to my door. But to start, I want only the simplest answers to two simple questions. First: why have you come to me?"

Dio looked at me for a long moment, then gazed into the flames of the brazier. His voice trembled. "I have come to you because there is no one else in all Rome to whom I can turn for help, no one else I can trust — if indeed I can trust even you."

I nodded. "And second: what do you want from me, Teacher?"

"I want you to help me to — " He choked on the words. He turned his gaze from the brazier to me, so that I saw the flames dancing in his eyes. His jaw quivered and the fleshy folds of his neck shook as he swallowed hard. "Help me. Please! I want you to help me to . . ."

"To help you do what?"

"Stay alive!"

CHAPTER THREE

With his great mane of dark hair, his towering physique (not yet gone to fat), and his amiable manner, the philosopher Dio had been a conspicuous figure in the Alexandria of my youth. Like most of the upper class of Egypt, Dio was of Greek blood — with a touch of the Scythian, he had claimed, to account for his height, and a bit of the Ethiop to account for his dark complexion. He had been a familiar sight on the steps of the library attached to the Temple of Serapis, where philosophers met to debate one another and instruct their pupils.

As a young man I had ended up in Alexandria after a long journey and had decided to stay there for a while. That was where I met my future wife, Bethesda, or more precisely, where I purchased her; she was a slave offered for sale at the great slave market, very young and very beautiful. (And a troublemaker, the auctioneer had begrudgingly admitted, which was why I was able to afford her; but if what she gave me was trouble, I only craved more of it.) Thus I passed the hot Alexandrian nights in a haze of lust; and during the day, while Bethesda kept herself busy in my shabby little apartment or went to the market, I gravitated to the library steps and sought out Dio. I was no student of philosophy — I lacked the money for formal education — but it was a tradition among Alexandrian philosophers to engage common men in conversation from time to time, at no charge.

Now, thirty years later, I could recall only bits and pieces of those conversations, but I vividly remembered how Dio had fanned my youthful passion for truth into white-hot flames with his rhetorical conundrums, just as Bethesda had fanned my other passions. In those days I had everything I needed, which for a young man is not much: an unfamiliar city to explore, a partner in my bed, and a mentor. We do not forget the cities, or the lovers, or the teachers of our youth.

Dio was attached to the Academic school. His mentor was Antiochus of Ascalon, who in a few years would become the head of the Academy; Dio was one of the great philosopher's leading protégés. In my ignorance I once asked Dio where the Academy was, and he laughed, explaining that while the name originated from a specific site — a grove near Athens where Plato taught — it applied nowadays not to any particular place or building, but to a discipline, a school of thought. The Academy transcended borders; kings might be its patrons, but they had no hegemony over it. The Academy transcended language (though of course all great works of philosophy, including those of the Academics, are written in Greek). The Academy embraced all men, and yet belonged to none. How could it be otherwise with an institution dedicated to discovering fundamental truths?

How does a man know what he knows? How can he be sure of his own perceptions, let alone those of others? Do the gods exist? Can their existence be proven? What is their form and their nature, and how can men discern their will? How can we determine right and wrong? Can right action lead to an evil result, or wrong action to a good outcome?

To a young Roman, barely twenty, in an exotic, teeming metropolis like Alexandria, these were heady questions. Dio had studied them all, and his quest for knowledge was a profound inspiration to me. Dio was hardly more than ten years my senior, but to me he seemed infinitely wise and worldly. In his presence I felt quite out of my depth, and I was immensely flattered that he would take the time and effort to explain his ideas to me. Sitting on the steps of the library while his slaves shaded us with parasols, we would discuss the differences between intellect and sensation, range the senses in order of reliability, and consider the specific ways that men depend upon logic, smell, taste, sight, hearing and touch to make sense of the world.

Thirty years had passed. Dio had changed, of course. He had seemed old to me then, but now he truly was old. The mane of dark hair had turned to silver. His belly had grown big and his skin had grown loose and wrinkled. But his broad back was unstooped. Unused to having his arms covered, he pulled up the sleeves of his stola to reveal a pair of muscular forearms as brown and weathered as his hands. He looked as healthy as myself, and given his size and robustness, he was probably stronger.

You'd be a hard man to forget, I had told him. Now, as he implored me to help him stay alive, I almost said, *You look like you'd be a hard man to kill.*

Instead, after a considerable pause, I changed the subject. "What I find surprising, Teacher, is that you should remember *me* after all these years. I was your pupil only in the most casual way, and my time in Alexandria was relatively brief. After I left, I heard that your mentor Antiochus succeeded Philo as head of the Academy; your life must have become very busy after that, conversing with kings, playing host to diplomats, advising the great and powerful. How curious, that you should remember making the acquaintance of a footloose young Roman who liked to loiter on the library steps, eavesdropping on the discourses of his elders and occasionally daring to converse with them."

"You were something more than that," Dio said. "You say that you would be a poor Finder if you could not deduce the identity of a visitor like myself. Well then, what sort of philosopher would I be, if I could not recognize and remember a kindred spirit when I met one?"

"You flatter me, Teacher."

"I most certainly do not. I never flatter anyone, not even kings. Not even King Ptolemy! Which is one reason I find myself in this terrible state."

He smiled weakly, but in his eyes I saw the haunted look of a man oppressed by constant fear. He stood and began to pace nervously around the small room, hugging his arms to his chest and shaking his head. Trygonion sat with folded hands and watched him with a curious expression, content to be silent.

"Do you remember the things we used to talk about on the library steps, Gordianus?"

"Only bits and pieces, I'm afraid. But I remember your eloquence when you spoke of perception and truth, of how the teachings of Plato and the Stoics had been clarified rather than refuted by the Academy — "

"Is that what you remember? How strange! That's not at all what I recall of our conversations."

"But what else was there, except talk of philosophy?"

Dio shook his head. "I don't remember talking of philosophy with you, though I suppose I must have. All those abstract fancies and high-minded ramblings — how pompous I must have seemed to you!"

"Not at all — "

"No, what I remember are the stories *you* told, Gordianus."

"What stories?"

"About your adventures out in the great world! About your long, roundabout journey from Rome to Egypt, and your visits to the Seven Wonders along the way, and your exploits in Alexandria.

How dull my own life seemed by comparison. How old you made me feel, as if life had passed me by! While my colleagues and I lounged under parasols, debating good and evil, you were out in the streets, encountering good and evil in the flesh, taking part in the whirling drama of life and death. Who was I to speak of discerning truth from falsehood, when sitting beside me on the steps of the library was the young Roman who had solved the riddle of the cat murdered in the Rhakotis district, which caused half the populace of the city to riot?"

"You remember that story?" I said, amazed.

"I have never forgotten it! Even now I can close my eyes and hear you telling the tale while philosophers and shopkeepers gathered around to listen in awe."

"The killing of a mere *cat* caused the city to riot?" Trygonion turned a heavy-lidded, dubious gaze at each of us in turn.

"You obviously have never been to Alexandria, where cats are gods," said Dio curtly. "Only a few years ago a similar incident occurred. The culprit was a Roman, or so they said. But given the political climate in Alexandria these days, any pretext will do to stir up the mob to chase a Roman through the streets, cat killer or not." He stopped his pacing and took a halting breath, then another. "Do you think we could retire to another room? The brazier is too hot. The air grows stuffy."

"I could call Belbo to unshutter another window," I suggested.

"No, no, perhaps we could step outside for a moment?"

"As you like."

I led them into the garden. Trygonion made a show of shivering and hugging himself, flapping the folds of his toga in an undignified, decidedly un-Roman fashion. Dio studied the fishpond with an abstracted air, then gazed up at the darkening sky, took several deep breaths and resumed his pacing, which brought him to a startled halt before the statue of Minerva. The virgin goddess held an upright spear in one hand and clutched a shield in the other. An owl perched on her shoulder and a snake coiled at her feet. The whole statue was painted in such lifelike color that the goddess seemed to breathe and gaze down on us from beneath the visor of her crested helmet.

"Magnificent," he whispered. Trygonion, loyal to the Great Mother, gave the goddess of wisdom only a cursory glance.

I stepped alongside Dio and gazed up at the statue's familiar face. "The only female in the place who never talks back to me. But then, she never seems to listen to me, either."

"She must have cost a small fortune."

"Probably, though I can't tell you the cost. I gained her by inheritance, more or less, like the rest of this house. The tale of how that came to pass would fill a book."

Dio surveyed the portico that surrounded the garden, clearly impressed. "Those multicolored tiles above the doorways — "

"Fired by artisans in Arretium. So my late bene-factor Lucius Claudius once told me, when I was merely a visitor here."

"And all these finely carved columns — "

"Salvaged and brought up with great difficulty, so I was told, from an old villa at Baiae, as was the statue of Minerva. All are of Greek design and workmanship. Lucius Claudius had impeccable taste and considerable resources."

"And now all this is yours? You've done well for yourself, Gordianus. Very well, indeed. When they said that you lived in a fine house here on the Palatine, I wondered if it could be the same man who'd led a wanderer's life in Alexandria, living from hand to mouth."

I shrugged. "I may have been a wanderer, but I always had the humble house of my father to come back to here in Rome on the Esquiline Hill."

"But surely that couldn't be as fine as this. You have prospered remarkably. You see, I judged you rightly when I met you long ago in Alexandria. I have known many wise men, philosophers who crave knowledge as other men crave fine wines or sumptuous clothing or a beautiful slave — as a glittering possession that will bring them comfort and earn other men's esteem. But you sought after truth as if you wished to marry her. You yearned for truth, Gordianus, as if you could not live with-out breathing her perfume every morning and night. You loved all her mysteries in equal measure — the great mysteries of philosophy as well as the practical mystery of discovering the killer of an Alexandrian cat. To search for truth is virtue. For your virtue the gods have rewarded you."

I could think of no response but a shrug. In the thirty years since I had last seen Dio I easily could have died a hundred times, for my labors had often brought me into danger, or I could have fallen into ruin like so many other men. Instead I owned a fine house on the Palatine and counted senators and wealthy merchants among my neighbors. Dio's explanation of my good luck was as reasonable as any other, though it seems to me that even philosophers cannot say what causes Fortune to smile on one man and show spite to another. Watching him resume his fitful pacing, I couldn't help thinking that Dio, for all his years of devotion to finding the truth, had the haggard look of a man whom Fortune had abandoned.

It had been some time since I had conversed at length with a philosopher. I had forgotten how much they loved to talk, even more than politicians, and not always to the point. We had rambled far from the purpose of Dio's visit. It was beginning to grow chilly in the garden.

"Come, let's go back into the house. If the brazier is too hot, I'll have the serving girl bring you some cool wine."

"Heated wine for me," Trygonion said, shivering.

"Yes, more of your very fine wine," Dio murmured. "I'm quite thirsty."

46

"Hungry, as well?" I said. My own stomach rumbled.

"No!" he insisted. But as he stepped through the doorway he tripped and stumbled, and when I reached out to steady him I felt him trembling.

"When did you last eat?"

He shook his head. "I'm not sure."

"You can't remember?"

"Yesterday I dared to take a walk outside, disguised as you see me now, and bought some bread in the market." He shook his head. "I should have bought more to eat this morning — but of course someone could have poisoned it while I slept . . ."

"Then you've eaten nothing at all today?"

"The slaves tried to poison me at the last place I stayed! Even at the house of Titus Coponius I can't feel safe. If one man's slaves can be bribed to kill a houseguest then so can another's. I eat nothing unless I see it prepared with my own eyes, or unless I buy it myself in the markets where it could not possibly have been tampered with."

"Some men have slaves to taste their food for them," I said, knowing the practice was especially common in Dio's Alexandria, where the inbred, rival monarchs and their agents were forever attempting secretly to do away with one another.

"Of course I had a taster!" said Dio. "How do you think I escaped the attempt to poison me? But the problem with tasters is that they must be replaced, and my stay in Rome has exhausted my resources. I don't even have money to make my way back to Alexandria once the weather

47

warms and the sailing season begins." He stumbled again and almost fell against the brazier.

"But you're faint with hunger!" I protested, gripping his arm and steering him toward a chair. "I insist that you eat. The food in my house is perfectly safe, and my wife — " I was about to add some extravagant estimation of Bethesda's culinary skills, but having just been praised as a seeker of truth I said instead, "My wife is not at all a bad cook, especially when she prepares dishes in the Alexandrian style."

"Your wife cooks?" said Trygonion. "In such a grand house as this?"

"The property's more impressive than my purse. Besides, she likes to cook, and she has a slave to help her. Here she is now," I added, for in the doorway stood Bethesda.

I was about to say more by way of introduction, but the look on her face stopped me. She looked from Dio to Trygonion, then back at Dio, who in his faint seemed hardly to notice her, then at me, all with a scowl that after thirty years of living with her I could not account for. What had I done now?

"Diana told me that you had visitors," she finally said. Her old Egyptian accent asserted itself and her tone was even haughtier than usual. She scrutinized my visitors so harshly that Trygonion nervously dropped his eyes, and Dio, finally taking notice of her, blinked and drew back as if he had looked into the sun.

"Is something wrong?" I said, secretly grimacing

at her with the side of my face. I thought this might make her smile. I was mistaken.

"I suppose you want to eat something," she said in a flat voice. The way she twisted her mouth would have spoiled the looks of a less beautiful woman.

Ah, that was it, I thought — she'd been in the doorway longer than I'd realized and had overheard my qualified endorsement of her culinary skills. Even so, a mere lifting of her eyebrow would have sufficed to express her displeasure. Perhaps it was the fact that I had packing to do for a trip the next day and was leaving the work to her while I entertained visitors in my study — and dubious visitors at that. I took another look at Dio, with his rumpled stola and clumsy makeup, and at Trygonion, who played with his bleached hair and nervously fluttered the folds of his toga under Bethesda's harsh gaze, and saw how they must appear to her. Bethesda acquiesced long ago to the parade of disreputable characters through our house, but she has never hidden her disdain from those she dislikes. It was clear that she thought very little of the Egyptian ambassador and his companion.

"Something to eat — yes, I think so," I said, raising my voice to capture my visitors' attention, for they both seemed spellbound by Bethesda's stare. "For you, Trygonion?"

The little gallus blinked and managed to nod.

"And for you, too, Teacher — I insist! I won't allow you to leave my house without taking some

49

food to steady you."

Dio bowed his head, looking tired and perplexed, trembling with agitation and, no doubt, hunger. He muttered something to himself, then finally looked up at me and nodded. "Yes — an Alexandrian dish, you said?"

"What could we offer our visitors? Bethesda, did you hear me?"

She seemed to wake from a daydream, then cleared her throat. "I could make some Egyptian flatbread . . . and perhaps something with lentils and sausage . . ."

"Oh yes, that would be very good," said Dio, staring at her with an odd expression. Philosopher he might be, but hunger and homesickness can addle the mind of any man.

Suddenly Diana appeared at Bethesda's side. Dio looked more confused than ever as he gazed from mother to daughter. Their resemblance is striking.

Bethesda departed as abruptly as she had appeared. Diana lingered for a moment and seemed to mimic her mother's scowl. The longer I live with a woman the more mysterious the experience becomes, and now that there are two of them in the household, the mystery is doubled.

Diana turned on her heel and followed her mother with the same quick, haughty stride. I looked at my guests. In comparison to comprehending a woman, I thought, comprehending another man — even a philosopher in a stola or a gallus who had given up his sex — was really not so difficult.

The serving girl brought us wine and some crusts of bread to stave off our hunger until the meal was ready. A chill had crept in from the garden, so I called on Belbo to stoke the brazier while I closed the shutters. I glanced outside and saw that twilight had descended on the atrium, casting the face of Minerva into inscrutable shadow.

With more wine in his stomach, as well as a bit of bread, Dio at last found the fortitude to recount the events which had reduced him to such a state of uncertainty and fear.

CHAPTER FOUR

"Best to begin at the beginning," sighed Dio, "insofar as that's possible with such a twisted tale. You know something of the story already — "

"Refresh my memory," I said.

"Very well. All my life, Alexandria has been in constant political upheaval. The members of the royal Ptolemy clan wage unending warfare against each other. For the people of Alexandria, this has meant bloody massacres and crushing taxes. Time and again the people have risen up to drive ruler after ruler out of the capital. One Ptolemy goes into exile, another takes his place — I won't recite the list. Whoever is winning occupies Alexandria, with its great granaries and royal treasury. Whoever is losing flees to Cyprus and plots his return. Fortunes reverse and the rulers change places, while the people endure. I forget which Ptolemy was on the throne when you were in Alexandria, Gordianus — "

"Alexander, I believe."

"Yes, that's right; a couple of years later he was chased out of the city by an angry mob and died in suspicious circumstances. Then Alexander's brother Soter took the throne. Eight years later Soter died, leaving no legitimate sons. That was twenty-four years ago."

Dio put his fingertips together. "The only legitimate male heir of Ptolemaic blood was Soter's nephew, named Alexander like his father. He happened to be residing here in Rome at the time of Soter's death, under the dictator Sulla's protection; this is where Rome first enters the story. Backed by Roman diplomacy — and by funds borrowed from Roman bankers — Alexander II returned to Egypt to claim the throne. To do so he had to marry his aunt, Soter's widow, because she refused to step down as queen. Marry her he did — and summarily murdered her. The queen had been well liked. Her death ignited the fury of the mob."

"The same mob which rioted over the death of a cat?" Trygonion sniffed. "I shudder to imagine what they did over the murder of a popular queen!"

"You anticipate the story," said Dio, slipping into his lecturing voice. "Alexander II then announced a rise in taxes so that he could repay his Roman backers. That was the final spark. Nineteen days after he ascended the throne, the new king was dragged from the royal palace and murdered by the mob. They tore him limb from limb."

It was tales such as this which Romans like to cite to make themselves feel proud of the relative civility of our republic. As a young man I had admired the Alexandrians' passion for politics, though I could never accustom myself to their propensity for sudden, extreme violence. Alexandrian healers peddle a poultice with the Egyptian name "cure-for-a-human-bite-which-draws-blood," and most households keep a supply on hand — a fact which says much about the Alexandrians.

"Now we come to the beginnings of the current crisis — the Egyptian situation, as you call it, Gordianus. After the brief and inglorious reign of their cousin Alexander II, two of Soter's bastards came forward to press their claim for the throne."

"Brave men!" quipped Trygonion.

"One bastard took Cyprus. The other took Egypt, and has since reigned for twenty years — proof that a man can keep himself on a throne without possessing a single kingly virtue. His full name in the Greek" — Dio took an orator's breath — "is Ptolemaios Theos Philopator Philadelphos Neos Dionysos."

"Ptolemy, God: Father-Lover, Brother-Lover, the New Dionysus," I translated.

Dio curled his lip. "In Alexandria, we simply call him Ptolemy Auletes — the Flute-Player."

"The Piper!" Trygonion laughed.

"Yes, King Ptolemy the Piper," said Dio grimly, "whose only known accomplishment is his skill on the flute, which he loves to play day and night, sober or drunk. He stages choruses in the royal palace and plays the accompaniment. He debuts his own compositions at diplomatic dinners. He organizes contests and pits his talent against common musicians. How did Egypt ever deserve such a ruler? He epitomizes and exaggerates all the baser qualities of his decrepit line — indolent, self-indulgent, luxury-loving, licentious, lazy . . ."

"He should have been a gallus rather than a king," laughed Trygonion.

Dio looked at him sidelong. "I am compelled to agree with you."

"I remember something Cicero said about him in a speech," I said. " 'Nearly everyone agrees that the man who occupies the throne of Egypt today neither by birth nor in spirit is like a king.' And there are those who say the Piper's reign is illegitimate and always has been, because of a will that was made by his unfortunate predecessor."

"Ah, yes, and there you put your finger upon the heart of the matter," said Dio. "Shortly after the death of Alexander II at the hands of the mob, from the very start of King Ptolemy's reign, a rumor began to circulate to the effect that Alexander II had left a will, bequeathing all of Egypt to the Senate and people of Rome."

Trygonion raised his eyebrows. "A splendid prize! The granaries! The treasure house! The crocodiles! But surely no one could believe such a tale. Such generosity is preposterous."

Dio sighed, exasperated. "You show your ignorance of both politics and history, gallus. Preposterous as such an idea may be, it is not without precedent. Attalus of Pergamum bequeathed his kingdom to Rome over seventy years ago; it became a province of the empire and to this day supplies the people of this city with subsidized grain. Forty years ago Apion left Cyrene to Rome; Apion was a Ptolemy and Cyrene was once a part of Egypt. And less than twenty years ago Bithynia was left to Rome by its last king."

"But why would any king do such a thing?" asked Trygonion.

"To save his country from the bloodshed of a disputed succession; to spite his presumptive heirs; to protect his people from being conquered by rival kingdoms even more oppressive than Rome; to bow to the tide of Roman expansion." Dio sighed. "In my lifetime, Rome has gained Pergamum, Cyrene and Bithynia by inheritance, and Pontus and Syria by conquest. Two years ago Rome seized Cyprus without a skirmish; King Ptolemy's brother committed suicide. Rome has overrun the East. Of all the kingdoms that grew out of the empire of Alexander the Great, only one remains: Egypt."

"And now the rumors are circulating again, about a will made by Alexander II bequeathing Egypt to Rome," I said. "King Ptolemy's sleep must be uneasy."

Trygonion nodded sagely. "I wouldn't care to be the slave who has to change his bed sheets."

"Vulgar, vulgar," Dio muttered through clenched teeth. "Rome now dominates the East. This is a fact which no one denies. But the people of Egypt demand a ruler who will resist that domination. Our land was ancient beyond imagining even before Alexander the Great came and founded Alexandria. The kingdom he established flourished with beauty and learning while Romulus and Remus were infants suckling the she-wolf. We have no need of Roman ways or Roman government. But instead of standing firm against Roman domination, King Ptolemy quivers with fright and offers whatever concessions are demanded of him. The people of Alexandria demand that he redeem Cyprus from Roman rule and restore it to the kingdom; instead he plays host to the Roman commissioner sent to plunder the island. To quiet talk about the alleged will, he gives a 'gift' of thirty-five million denarii to Caesar and Pompey, so that Caesar can bribe the Roman Senate and Pompey can pay off his own troops. The bill is passed along to the people of Egypt in the form of higher taxes. Our taxes go directly into the pockets of Roman senators and soldiers — we might as well be a Roman province! And what does King Ptolemy receive in return? A tentative acknowledgment by the Roman Senate of his legitimacy as king, and a plaque set up on the Capitoline Hill, inscribed to the honor of Ptolemaios Theos Philopator Philadelphos Neos Dionysos, 'Friend and Ally of the Roman People.' To be a friend and ally is all very well, but to pay for the privilege he bleeds his own people white with taxes. The people's anger finally drove Ptolemy to flee the city, fearing for his life. He fled all the way here to Rome, where Pompey put him up in a great rambling villa with a vast household of slaves to serve him."

"For thirty-five million denarii, he should expect such royal treatment!" said Trygonion.

Dio scowled. "He spends his time practicing his flute and drafting letters to the Senate begging them to restore him to his throne against the wishes of the Egyptian people. But it is too late for that. His daughter Berenice has already been named queen of Egypt."

"A woman?" said Trygonion, who seemed genuinely intrigued.

"It was not my choice," said Dio hastily. "Philosophers have influence in Alexandria, but so do astrologers. It was the star-gazers who insisted that the time is right for a woman of the Ptolemaic line to rule Egypt."

"It strikes me that you may be too hard on King Ptolemy, Teacher," I said cautiously. "All his life he's seen kingdom after kingdom swallowed up by Roman imperialism, sometimes by war, sometimes by statecraft. His position has always been precarious. He must know that he's kept his throne this long only because the Romans can't settle among themselves who should reap the rewards when Egypt is taken over. I know something of these matters, Teacher. A man can't live in Rome and be entirely ignorant of what goes on in the Forum. During Ptolemy's reign there have been several attempts by the Senate to act on the alleged will of Alexander II and to stake a Roman claim on Egypt. Only the Senate's internal bickering and rivalries have prevented those attempts from being carried out. During Cicero's consulship, I remember, Caesar and Pompey tried to put themselves on a board of governors to oversee the takeover of Egypt; Cicero killed the legislation with one of his brilliant speeches by claiming, in so many words, that Caesar and Pompey would ultimately make themselves kings. Now Caesar and Pompey have taken to extorting money directly from King Ptolemy."

Agitated, Dio began to speak, but I held up my hand. "Hear me out, Teacher. If Ptolemy bends to Roman wishes so that he can stay in power, even if he pays for the privilege with silver to keep the Romans at bay, how can you fault him for that? So far, by one means or another, he's kept the Romans from moving into Alexandria and taking over the imperial palace. That indicates to me that King Ptolemy must possess more diplomatic expertise than you give him credit for."

"He bends too far for the Romans," said Dio sternly. "What does it matter whether they conquer us outright, if they can use King Ptolemy as their private tax collector to drain our lifeblood?"

"Perhaps; but I think I see a contradiction, Teacher. Why do you resist Roman rule if you despise your own rulers so very much?"

Dio sighed. "Because, ultimately, the Ptolemies rule over Egypt by the will of the people. When they rule badly, the people rise up and cast them out. When they rule tolerably, the people tolerate them. Such a system may lack the perfection of Plato's ideal republic, but it suits the people of Egypt and has done so for hundreds of years. On the other hand, if Egypt should become a Roman province under the sway of a Roman governor, its people will become mere vassals of Rome, and we shall have no say at all over our destiny. We shall be drafted to fight in wars that are not of our choosing. We shall be forced to abide by laws dictated to us by a Senate of wealthy Romans who live too far from Alexandria to hear the complaints of its people. We shall become just another outpost of Rome's empire, watching our wealth become Roman plunder. Our statues and carpets and paintings will decorate the houses of Rome's rich; our grain will fill the stomachs of the Roman mob, and you can be sure that any payment will be far less than fair. Egypt is a great and free nation; we will not become minions of Rome." Dio took a deep breath. A tear glinted in his eye, and the gravity of his expression was oddly heightened by the feminine cosmetics that colored his weathered, wrinkled face. The absurdity of his costume could not disguise the depth of his emotion.

"But this is all academic, if you'll pardon the pun," said Trygonion blandly but with a twinkle of mischief in his eyes. "If the former king, Alexander II, really did leave a will bequeathing Egypt to Rome — "

Dio exploded. "No one in Egypt believes in the validity of the so-called will, because no one in Rome is able to produce it! The will of Alexander II is a fiction, a fraud, a pretext for the Roman Senate to go meddling in Egyptian affairs, a device to make whoever rules Egypt grovel at their feet. 'You may hold sway for the moment,' they say, 'but you cannot be legitimate without our approval, and you can never be anything but an impostor, for Egypt was left to us by our puppet Alexander II and we may choose to exercise our hegemony at any time.' They wave an imaginary scrap of parchment in the air and call it a will. King Ptolemy was a fool to play along with such a lie. 'Friend and Ally,' indeed! The plaque on the Capitoline should read, 'Piper and Puppet of the Roman People.' "

"But now you've replaced the puppet," I said.

"The Piper has been booed off the stage!" cried Trygonion.

Dio clenched his teeth. "The crisis which revolves around Egypt's throne may be a matter of amusement to you, gallus, but to the people of Egypt I assure you it is not. Roman diplomats and merchants in Alexandria seldom go out of doors these days, for fear of being torn apart by the mob. Rabble-rousers make speeches against Roman greed, and even my fellow philosophers neglect their teaching to engage in heated debate about the Roman threat. That is why I came to Rome, heading a delegation of one hundred Alexandrians: to demand that the Roman Senate stop meddling in Egyptian affairs and to ask for their recognition of Queen Berenice."

"I see a contradiction, Teacher," I said quietly. "To request the Senate's approval of your new monarch implies, in itself, that the Senate has a right to meddle in your affairs."

Dio cleared his throat. "In philosophy we seek the ideal. In politics, as I have learned to my bitter enlightenment, we seek whatever accommodates.

So it was that I came to Rome at the head of the delegation of one hundred. So many distinguished voices, we thought, simply could not be ignored, even by your lofty senators. And that is where this despicable farce turns to tragedy!"

He put his hands to his face and suddenly began to weep, so profusely that even Trygonion was stunned. Indeed, the little gallus seemed deeply moved by the old philosopher's tears, biting his lips in sympathy, pulling at his bleached hair and rubbing his hands together in agitation. I have heard that the galli, cut off from the circle of earthly passion, are given to sudden transports of extreme and inexplicable emotion.

It took Dio a moment to compose himself. The fact that a philosopher of his stature should have lost control and given vent to such an outburst, even briefly, testified to the depth of his despair.

"This is how it was: we landed down in Neapolis at the very end of the autumn sailing season. I had friends there, members of the Academy who offered us lodgings. That night, men armed with knives and clubs came crashing into the houses where we were staying. They upturned furniture, set curtains afire, smashed priceless statues. We were roused from sleep, dazed, barely able to fend them off. Bones were broken and blood was spilled, but no one was killed, and the attackers escaped. The assault put such fear into some of our party that a few set sail for Alexandria the next day."

Dio stiffened his jaw. "The attacks were well

organized and planned in advance. Do I have proof of King Ptolemy's complicity? No. But one need not see the sun to deduce its presence by the casting of a shadow. The midnight attacks in Neapolis were engineered by King Ptolemy, have no doubt. He knew that we were coming to dispute his right to the throne. His agents were ready for us.

"After that we moved on to safer quarters in Puteoli, to regroup and plan our strategy for approaching the Senate. We stayed closer together and guarded ourselves at night, but we made the error of thinking that we would be safe walking in the town forum in broad daylight. One afternoon a group of fifteen men, led by one of my Academic colleagues, Onclepion, went out to buy provisions for our journey up to Rome. Out of nowhere they were set upon by a group of small boys who began to pelt them with stones. The boys shouted curses. When passersby stopped to ask why, the boys told them that the Alexandrians had been defaming the honor of Pompey and his troops with vicious slanders. Some members of Onclepion's group, simply to protect themselves, began to shove at the boys and tried to drive them off by throwing stones in return. One of the boys suddenly screamed, clutched his head and collapsed in the dust — or feigned collapse, as I suspect, for I'm told that his body was not found afterward. The crowd that had gathered was sparked into a frenzy, and soon a mob of grown men and women had joined the boys to stone the Alexandrians, who found themselves surrounded on three sides and trapped against a wall. Have you ever witnessed a stoning, Gordianus?" Dio shuddered. Beside him, the little gallus shivered in empathy. "Thirteen of them were killed that day, stoned or trampled to death. Only Onclepion and his slave managed to escape. Onclepion boosted the slave onto the top of the wall, and the slave managed to pull his master after him. But Onclepion was blinded in one eye, and his slave lost several teeth.

"That was the outrage at Puteoli. More men deserted the delegation that night, until only sixty of the original one hundred remained. I thought it best to head immediately to Rome, before some further incident occurred. The trip was not easy. The oxen we hired to pull our wagons fell to their forelegs just outside Capua and died with blood-flecked bile pouring from their mouths — poisoned, I had no doubt, since they all died in the span of an hour. More of the delegation deserted.

"Halfway to Rome, we stopped to spend a night off the Appian Way at an estate owned by my acquaintance Palla. It was a rustic house in the woods which he kept for hunting boar, simple and without luxuries but with provisions for a great many visitors. Palla himself was absent, staying at one of his villas north of Rome, but his slaves had been told to expect us. To accommodate us all, they crowded our sleeping couches close together, blocking the hallways. That very nearly proved disastrous.

"It was a scream from Onclepion that woke me

in the night. At first I thought he cried out in pain, because of his ruined eye. Then I smelled the smoke. It was only by the will of the gods that no one was burned alive that night, for the doors had all been blocked from the outside by handcarts, the type that slaves use for trundling bales of hay. The building quickly filled with smoke. We at last managed to break through one of the doors. The cart blocking it had been loaded with heavy stones! Somehow, we all escaped into the woods, where we stood and watched as the house was consumed by flames. I have never known such fear as I knew that night, for at any moment I looked for King Ptolemy's henchmen to descend on us from out of the woods, forcing us to choose between being hacked to death or fleeing back into the burning house. But the attack never came. Why should King Ptolemy mount a full assault, when a handful of agents can set a fire and possibly kill everyone at once? Especially if they have the help of someone inside."

"Then you think that Ptolemy had agents within the delegation?"

"From the beginning! Oh yes, I have no doubt of that, ashamed as I am to say it. How else could his men have known which houses to attack in Neapolis? Or known when Onclepion's party was setting out for the market in Puteoli, so as to set the little boys upon them? How else did someone poison the oxen's water trough that morning in Capua, without anyone taking notice? King Ptolemy has ruled Egypt these twenty years by bribery, treachery and terror. His agents know how to use the weak and silence the strong.

"On the morning after the destruction of Palla's house, beside a stream in the woods, and with Palla's slaves keeping watch for an attack I still dreaded might come, I called a meeting of the delegation. I expected some desertions, but I was shocked at how few decided to continue on to Rome. Only fifteen! Even Onclepion joined the ranks of those who made up their minds to turn back that morning. I told them that they would find themselves trapped for the winter in Puteoli or Neapolis, unable to find ships to carry them home, for the sailing season was over. But they would not be dissuaded. Once King Ptolemy saw that they had turned back from Rome, and no longer intended to address the Senate, he would stop his attacks against them — so they reasoned, and no argument from me could change their minds. Onclepion even engaged me in mock debate over the matter. I was appalled at the tawdry way he excused his own cowardice with sophistry. Even more appalling was the fact that after our debate was over, five of the men who had originally stood by me that morning claimed to have been won over by Onclepion's eloquence and joined the deserters!

"Only ten then remained of the one hundred who came from Alexandria to confront the Senate, armed with righteous indignation and the certain favor of the gods for a just cause. Attended only by our slaves we made our bedraggled way to

Rome. There was no grand entrance for us! Instead we slunk through the gates like thieves, hoping to escape notice. We dispersed ourselves about the city, staying with friends and acquaintances; many turned us away, when they learned of the tribulations we had brought upon our hosts in Neapolis and Puteoli, and the destruction of Palla's property! Meanwhile, we petitioned the Senate for an audience — but the Senate answered us with silence."

He turned toward the brazier and stared into the flames. "What a winter! No winter in Alexandria was ever so cold. How do you Romans stand it? I cover myself with blankets at night and still I can't stop shivering. What misery! And the murders . . ."

He began to shake and couldn't seem to stop.

"Shall I call a slave to bring you a blanket?" I said.

"No, no, it's not the cold." He hugged himself, and at last managed to take a deep breath and stopped shaking. "During those terrible days in Neapolis and Puteoli and on the road, I kept one thought in my mind: *When we reach Rome,* I told myself, *when we reach Rome . . .*

"But you see, there was a fallacy in my reasoning, for I never really finished that thought. When we reach Rome — then what? Did I tell myself, When we reach Rome, there shall be only ten of us left? Did I ever think that the Senate would snub us, and refuse even to hear me? Or that there would be still more treachery and betrayals, until I would lose my faith even in the men I most trusted when we left Alexandria? Or that we would be murdered one by one, until only a handful remained — by the very fact of their survival, traitors and tools of King Ptolemy? Do you understand what has happened to me, Gordianus?" He held out his hands in a gesture of supplication, and on his face I saw the full measure of his despair. "I left Alexandria full of worry but also full of hope. Now . . ."

"Murders, you said. Here in Rome?"

"Yes. At least three since we arrived. We all stayed in different houses, under the roofs of men I thought we could trust. I feared another full-scale attack, you see, until I realized that Rome is Rome, not Neapolis or Puteoli. Even King Ptolemy would never dare to stage a massive assault or manufacture a riot in the shadow of the Senate. The men who rule Rome tolerate such flagrant crimes at a distance, but not in their presence. No foreign king could be allowed to stir up the masses or set fires or practice open warfare in Rome itself."

"You're right. Senators reserve those privileges for themselves."

"So the king changed his tactics. Instead of trying to kill us all at once, he turned to assassinating us one by one."

"By what means?"

"Quietly. By poison. Suffocation. Stabbing."

"With the complicity of their hosts?"

Dio paused. "Perhaps. Perhaps not. Slaves can

sometimes be bribed or blackmailed. But masters can be bribed or blackmailed as well, especially when the pressure comes from the kind of men allied with King Ptolemy."

"Men such as Pompey?"

He nodded. "And I suspect there are respectable Romans — perhaps even senators — who are not above committing a murder or two to gain Pompey's favor or repay some debt they owe him."

"Be careful, Dio. So far you've accused your own king of being behind this slaughter. Now you're implicating a man who happens to be Rome's most beloved general and very possibly her future dictator."

"I tell you, these are the men behind the killings. King Ptolemy is not even in Rome any longer. He's retired to Ephesus for the winter, leaving everything in Pompey's hands. And why not? Pompey has as much to gain as Ptolemy if the king can keep his throne, so Pompey has continued the attacks against the delegation. Since we arrived in Rome, his agents have snuffed us out one by one."

I shook my head. "You admit that you have no proof of your allegations against King Ptolemy, Dio. Do you have proof of what you say against Pompey?"

He glared at me and was quiet for a long time. "A few nights ago, in the house of Lucius Lucceius, someone tried to poison me. Do you want proof of that? My slave died horribly, writhing and gasping on the floor, only moments after tasting a portion of soup that was served to me in my private room!"

"Yes, but — "

"And my host, Lucius Lucceius, despite his knowledge of philosophy, despite the disdain he espouses for King Ptolemy, is Pompey's friend."

"Do you know where the poison came from?"

"Earlier that day, a certain Publius Asicius paid a call on Lucceius. A handsome young man — I happened to see him as he was leaving the house, and I asked Lucceius his name. That night, my slave was poisoned. The next morning, after I fled from Lucceius's house, I made some inquiries about his visitor. They say this Publius Asicius is a young man of easy morals who indulges in poetry and wine and dabbles in politics with no fixed agenda, willing to do anything to curry the favor of anyone who can advance his career."

I sighed. "You have just described a whole generation of young Romans, Teacher. Many of them may be capable of murder, including, quite possibly, this Publius Asicius. But mere proximity to the scene of a crime is not — "

"Asicius is also said to be in debt to Pompey, for some very large loans which the general made to him."

"Still . . ."

"You see, you have no rejoinder for that, Gordianus. The chain goes back to Pompey and thence to King Ptolemy."

"Your host, Lucceius — did you confront him

70

with your suspicions?"

"Even as my taster lay writhing on the floor! I insisted that Lucceius come and witness the atrocity himself. I demanded that he find out how the soup had been poisoned."

"What was his response?"

"He pretended to be appalled, of course. He said that he would interrogate each of his household slaves himself, and torture them if necessary. Perhaps he did, or perhaps not. I left the next morning, desperate to be away from the place. I told Lucceius that I would be staying at the house of Titus Coponius, but he has made no effort to contact me."

Trygonion, who had been silent for a while, cleared his throat. "Having escaped alive from the man's house, perhaps you would have been wiser not to tell Lucceius where you were headed next." The gallus made a wry face and seemed to be in a mood to cause trouble again, but what he said made sense.

"Am I then to behave like a fugitive or a criminal?" demanded Dio. "Skulking from shadow to shadow, hoping no one sees me, praying that the world will simply forget my existence? Already I put on this absurd disguise to go out during the day — is that not shame enough? I refuse to vanish altogether. To do so would give King Ptolemy unconditional victory. Don't you understand? I am all that remains of the delegation of one hundred who came to speak for the people of Alexandria and their new queen. If I allow fear to turn me invisible and mute, then I might as well never have come to Rome. I might as well be dead!"

With that, Dio gave another shudder and began to weep again. I watched him fight back the tears and struggle to compose himself. Over the last months he had endured much misery and seen unspeakable tragedy, and for all his travails he had nothing to show but bitterness and shame. I was awed by his perseverance.

"Teacher," I said, "what is it that you want from me? I can't force the Senate to hear your demands. I can't make Pompey waver in his support of King Ptolemy. I can't resurrect the dead, or redeem those who betrayed you."

I waited for Dio to answer, but he had not yet composed himself, so I went on. "Perhaps you wish for me to ferret out the truth, so that justice can be done. That's why men usually come to me. But you seem satisfied that you already know the truth. I'm not sure what good it will do you. That's the odd thing about truth, how much one craves it, yet how useless it often is. If you're thinking of bringing charges of murder against King Ptolemy, I'm not sure that a Roman court has jurisdiction over a friendly foreign monarch; I am sure that nothing could be done without the Senate, and we know that you can't rely on them. If you're thinking of bringing a charge against Pompey, then I would advise you to think again. Pompey has enemies, to be sure, but not one of them would be willing to attack him openly in a court of law, no matter how compelling the evidence. Pompey is much too strong."

I wrinkled my brow. "Perhaps it's this Publius Asicius against whom you want to bring charges, for attempting to poison you. If he did put Lucceius's slaves up to it, then you might have a case, provided that Lucceius is not the creature of Pompey that you suspect him to be, and is willing to let his slaves testify against Asicius. Such a trial might be useful. This Publius Asicius can't be too important if I've never heard of him, and that means he might be vulnerable. A trial against him could draw attention to your cause and elicit sympathy. Even so — "

"No, Gordianus," Dio said. "It's not a trial I seek. Do you think I expect justice from a Roman court? I come to you seeking merely to save my own life, so that I can continue with my mission."

I bit my lip. "Teacher, I can't offer you accommodations under my roof. I can't guarantee your safety, for one thing. While I place great trust in my household slaves, this house would hardly be secure against assassins as determined as your enemies appear to be. And then there's the danger to my own family. I have a wife, Teacher, and a young daughter — "

"No, Gordianus, I don't ask to spend a single night under the roof of your splendid house. What I need is your help in deciding whom I can trust and whom I cannot. They say you have ways of finding the truth. They say you have a sense for it, as other men have a sense of smell or taste.

73

You say that truth is often useless, but it might save me now. Can I trust my new host, Titus Coponius? I met him in Alexandria. He is wealthy, educated, a student of philosophy — but can I entrust my life to him? Will he betray me? Is he another of Pompey's tools? You must know how to find out such things."

"Perhaps," I said cautiously, "but the task is more complicated than you may realize. If only you had come to me wanting to recover a stolen ring, or trying to find out whether a rich merchant did or did not murder his wife, or seeking to trace the origin of a threatening letter. Such mysteries are simple, and relatively safe. But to ask the kinds of questions you would have me ask, of those who would know the answers, would almost certainly attract the attention of powerful men . . ."

"You mean Pompey," said Dio.

"Yes, perhaps even Pompey himself." I nervously tapped at my chin. "I would hate for you to think me a coward, Teacher, afraid to move for fear of offending powerful men. In years gone by, I've dared to beard a few lions when the cause demanded it. Sulla the Dictator, for one, when I looked for the truth behind the murder of Sextus Roscius. Marcus Crassus, when he sought to slay a whole household of slaves. Even Cicero, when he grew reckless with power in the year of his consulship. Fortunately, so far, I've never crossed paths with Pompey. I don't wish to do so now. As a man grows older, and presumably wiser, he grows more cautious."

"You won't help me, then?" The despair in his voice made me feel a prickle of shame.

"Teacher, I can't. Even if I were eager to do so, it would still be impossible, at least for a while, because I'm about to go on a long trip. I leave at dawn. My wife has been busy all day packing my things . . ." I paused, surprised at how hollow my words sounded. What I said was true, and my trip had been planned for a long time. Why did I feel as if I were making excuses?

"Then you cannot help me," said Dio, staring at the floor.

"If the trip were less important," I began, and shrugged. "But it's to see my son Meto. He's been serving under Caesar in Gaul. I haven't seen him for months. Now he's at Caesar's winter quarters in Illyria, hardly close but considerably closer than Gaul, and he may be there for only a short while. I can't miss the chance to see him."

"I see," said Dio.

"In other circumstances, I would recommend that you pay a call on my elder son, Eco. He's twice as clever as I ever was — but he's coming with me to visit Meto. We'll both be gone until at the least the end of the month, perhaps longer. The uncertainties of traveling in the winter, you understand . . ." Again, the words sounded hollow in my ears. I shifted uneasily in my chair, and the room suddenly seemed hot. "Of course, after the trip — that is, when I come back to Rome . . ."

Dio fixed me with a gaze that pulled at the hair

on the back of my neck. I had seen such a glassy stare only in the eyes of dead men, and for a moment I was so unnerved that I couldn't speak. I cleared my throat. "When I come back to Rome, I'll be sure to send a messenger to you at the house of Titus Coponius — "

Dio lowered his eyes and sighed. "Come, gallus, it's time to go. We've wasted our time here."

"Hardly wasted, if that smell is what I think it is," said Trygonion cheerfully, as if oblivious to what had just passed between Dio and myself. A moment later a serving girl passed in the hallway carrying a tray of food, followed by two others who carried little folding tables.

We retired to the adjoining dining room, where we each reclined upon a couch. The folding tables were placed before us. Bethesda appeared, with Diana following after her, but they did not join us. The two of them made a point of carrying in the first course and serving it themselves, ladling the first portions of the lentils with sausage onto the plates of my guests, then onto mine, and then watching while we each took a bite. Under their scrutiny, the philosopher, the gallus and I nodded and made noises of approval. Satisfied, Bethesda and Diana retired, leaving the service to the slave girls.

Miserable and desperate as he might be, Dio was also a very hungry man. He swallowed great spoonfuls of food and called to the serving girl for more. Beside him Trygonion ate with even greater relish and an appalling lack of manners, using his thumb to push food onto his spoon and popping his fingers into his mouth. Barred from the ecstasies of sex, the galli are said to be notorious gluttons.

CHAPTER FIVE

Midwinter night descended on Rome, cold, clear and still.

Once my guests had eaten, they quickly departed. Telling his tale had exhausted Dio. Stuffing his yawning belly had made him sleepy. He was ready for an early bed. Smarting from a twinge of guilt, I almost relented in my earlier refusal to put him up and was ready to offer him a bed, if only for the night; but Dio with a few curt words made it quite clear that he was set on making his way back to the house of Titus Coponius. If he was sharp with me, how could I blame him? He had come to seek the help of an old acquaintance and was leaving empty-handed. Desperate men — even philosophers — do not accept rejection graciously.

I insisted that Dio take Belbo along to see him safely home. This seemed the least I could do. Trygonion hid his long hair in his hat and adjusted his toga, Dio covered his head with the mantle; again they became impostors at Roman manhood and womanhood. Under cover of darkness they departed as they had come.

Having dispatched my guests, I was faced with the chore of finishing my packing for the trip to

Illyria to see Meto. Bethesda had done much, but certain preparations can be made only by the traveler. With the short winter days allowing less daylight for travel, I planned an early start and so had hoped to be abed early, but the preparations kept me up until midnight. It was just as well; once I finally did crawl into bed I couldn't sleep, thinking about Dio and his plight. I reached out to touch Bethesda's shoulder, but she turned away from me, peeved about something.

As I pondered the strange visit, it occurred to me that there were some things I had neglected to find out. Someone had recommended that Dio come to see me. Who? And what was he doing in the company of the little gallus? The two of them seemed like oil and water, and yet Dio obviously trusted Trygonion enough to go out with him in disguise.

Ah well, I thought drowsily, these questions could wait until I returned from Illyria and saw Dio again. But as soon as this thought crossed my mind, I remembered the look I had seen in the philosopher's eyes — the look of a man already dead. I gave a start and was suddenly wide awake.

I turned on my side and reached for Bethesda. She exhaled noisily and pulled away. I called her name softly, but she pretended to be asleep. What had I done wrong? At what had she taken offense? A bit of moonlight strayed onto the bed, illuminating her hair. She had rinsed it with henna that morning, to give it luster and to cover the gray. The smell was familiar, comforting, erotic. She could have helped me to fall asleep, I thought, but she seemed no more willing to comfort me than I had been willing to help Dio. I stared into the tangle of her hair, an impenetrable forest, pathless and dark.

I tossed and turned and at last rolled out of the bed and onto my feet. I was already wearing a long tunic to keep warm. I stepped into my shoes and reached for a woolen cloak.

Out in the atrium, beneath the shadowed gaze of Minerva, I looked up at the firmament of bright twinkling stars. The air was cold and clear. I studied the constellations, and to tire my mind I tried to remember all their names, both Latin and Greek, which I had learned when I was young in Alexandria: the Great Bear, which Homer called the Wagon and others call the Seven Ploughing Oxen; the Little Bear, which some call the Dog's Tail; the Goat, which some say has the tail of a fish . . .

Still I couldn't sleep. I needed to walk. A few circuits around the fountain in the atrium was hardly enough to drain my restlessness. I walked to the front door and unbolted it. I stepped over the threshold and onto the smoothly paved street.

At night, the Palatine is probably the safest neighborhood in Rome. When I was a boy, it was as mixed as any other neighborhood in the city, with rich and poor, patricians and plebeians all crowded together. Then Rome's empire began its great expansion, and some families became not merely wealthy but phenomenally so, and it was the Palatine, with its proximity to the Forum and its elevation above the less wholesome airs of the Tiber and the cramped valleys, which became their neighborhood of choice. Over the years tall tenements and cramped family dwellings were torn down block by block, and in their places were built great houses separated here and there by strips of green and little gardens. There are still humble dwellings among the mansions on the Palatine, and occupants who are far from wealthy (I'm proof of that), but by and large it has become an enclave of the rich and the powerful. I live on the southern side, just up the hill from the House of the Vestals down in the Forum. In a circle of no great circumference around my house — hardly further than an arrow's flight — I count among my neighbors Crassus, Rome's wealthiest man, and my old patron Cicero, who the previous September had made a triumphant return from political exile and was busy rebuilding the house which an angry mob had destroyed two years before.

Such men own bodyguards — plenty of them, and not merely brutes but well-trained gladiators — and such men demand order, at least in their immediate vicinity. The roving, drunken gangs of troublemakers who terrorize the Subura at night know better than to bring their rowdiness to the Palatine. Rapists and petty thieves practice their crimes in other places on more vulnerable prey. And so, after dark, the streets of the Palatine are quiet and mostly deserted. A man can take a brisk stroll up the street on a chilly winter's night beneath a waxing moon, alone with his thoughts, and not fear for his life.

Even so, when I heard the sound of drunken voices approaching, I felt it prudent to conceal myself until they passed. I stepped back against a wall, beneath the deep shadow cast by the branch of a yew tree. I was just across the street from a venerable old three-story tenement at the end of my block. The place was exceptionally well built and well maintained, the property of the Clodii, an ancient and distinguished patrician family. It had withstood the changes on the Palatine, and was still divided between shops on the ground floor and apartments above. The whole of the middle floor was rented to Marcus Caelius, the young man who had embroiled me a few years before in Cicero's battle of wits with Catilina. It was his voice, together with another, that I now heard approaching from the eastern end of the street.

I stayed hidden in the shadows. I had nothing to fear from Caelius, but I was in no mood for company, especially drunken company. As he and his friend drew closer, careening up the street, I saw their shadows first, cast before them by the moonlight like spidery, elongated wraiths. They walked with their arms around each other's shoulders, twisting this way and that, laughing and conversing in shouts and whispers. It wasn't the first time I'd chanced to see Marcus Caelius coming home in such a state. Not much more than thirty years old and uncommonly good-looking — remarkably handsome, actually — Caelius was of that particular class of young Romans whom Dio had spoken of that afternoon when he described Publius Asicius, the man he suspected of trying to poison him: charming, quick-witted young men with good backgrounds but uncertain prospects, notorious for their complete lack of scruples, witty and well educated with a taste for hard drinking and scandalous poetry, affable, ingratiating, and never under any circumstances to be trusted. Caelius and his friend were probably returning from a late-night party at some fashionable house nearby. The only surprise was that they hadn't brought a young woman or two with them, unless, of course, they were satisfied to make do with each other for the night.

They stopped in the street before the entrance to Caelius's private stairway. Caelius banged on the door, and while they waited for a slave to come open it I overheard some of their drunken conversation. When I heard Caelius say the name "Asicius" I gave a start. Probably, I thought, I merely imagined it, putting it together from a sigh and a hiss; I had just been thinking about Dio's description of Publius Asicius, and so had the name in my mind. But then I heard it again. "Asicius," Caelius said, "you ass, you very nearly flubbed it this time as well! Two disasters in a row!"

"Me?" cried the other man. I couldn't see him well for the darkness, but like Caelius he appeared to be tall and broad-shouldered. His words were slurred, some shouted, some muttered, so that I could catch only fragments of what he said. *"I'm not the one who . . . you neglected to *tell* me that we'd have to . . . and then, to find . . . *already!* . . . and the look on his . . . oh go on, off to Hades with you, Caelius, along with that pitiful Egyptian . . ."

The door rattled and opened. Caelius and his friend moved to enter simultaneously and bumped into each other. Something clattered on the pavement; moonlight flashed on steel. Caelius turned back, stooped down and picked up the dagger that had been dropped. That was when he looked up and saw me in the shadows across the street.

He squinted drunkenly and turned his face sidelong, trying to decide whether I was a man or merely a shadow. I held my breath. He stepped slowly toward me, holding the dagger in his hand.

"Where in Hades are you off to now?" moaned Asicius. "Come on, Caelius, it's cold out here. You said you'd warm me up!"

"Shut up!" Caelius whispered hoarsely. He was halfway across the street, staring straight at me.

"Caelius, what — is someone there?"

"Shut up, Asicius!"

The night was so still I thought they might be able to hear the pounding of my heart. Caelius's dagger glinted in the moonlight. He stepped closer and tripped on a paving stone. I flinched.

"It's only me, neighbor," I said, through gritted teeth.

"Only — you, Gordianus!" Caelius grinned and lowered his dagger. I sighed with relief.

"Who is he?" demanded Asicius, swaggering up

behind Caelius and reaching inside his tunic. "Trouble?"

"Oh, probably not," said Caelius. In the moonlight, with a smile on his lips, he looked like Apollo done in white marble. "You're not looking for trouble tonight, are you, neighbor?"

"Out for a walk," I said. "I leave on a trip tomorrow. I can't sleep."

"Cold for a walk, isn't it?" said Asicius.

"Not too cold for you to be out," I said.

Asicius growled, but Caelius slapped him on the shoulder and laughed. "Go home and get some sleep, Gordianus! Only people up to no good are out at this time of night. Come on, Asicius. Time to warm you up." He put his arm around his companion's shoulder and drew him back to the doorway. They disappeared inside and the door slammed shut.

In the stillness of the night, through the closed door, I heard their muffled voices and the clump of their heavy footsteps on the stairway. These sounds quickly faded, and the empty street seemed almost preternaturally quiet. The cold suddenly penetrated my cloak, making me shiver. I walked back to my house taking quick, careful steps. Everything was bland oyster-white and fathomless black shadow. Cold moonlight had turned the world to stone.

I slipped back into bed. I might have stayed awake for a long time, staring into the darkness above, but Bethesda rolled toward me and snuggled against me, and I fell asleep almost at once.

As planned, my son Eco came calling before day-break. Belbo brought horses from the stable, and the three of us set out through the quiet gray streets of the waking city. We took the Flaminian Way and passed through the Fontinal Gate, leaving the dangers and deceits of the city behind us, at least for a while.

CHAPTER SIX

The journey was without incident, except for a brief but wave-tossed crossing from Fanum Fortunae, at the terminus of the Flaminian Way, across to the Illyrian shore. In winter there are only a handful of boatmen who will ferry passengers across the Adriatic Sea, and on this trip we discovered why, for we very narrowly escaped a sudden squall that easily could have sent boat, Belbo, horses, Eco and myself to the bottom of the sea.

Before we left Fanum Fortunae, I had insisted on visiting the famous grounds consecrated to the goddess Fortune and leaving a few coins at her temple. "Better spent tipping the boatman," Eco had muttered under his breath. But after surviving the wet, windy crossing, it was Eco who suggested we give thanks at the nearest temple of Fortune. Pounding rain turned the wooden roof into a drum. Inside the rustic little temple incense swirled, coins jangled, and the goddess smiled, while the trembling in my knees and the queasiness in my stomach gradually subsided.

With our feet back on solid ground, even the arduous, rain-soaked journey up the rugged coastline and over the windswept hills to Caesar's winter quarters seemed like a holiday.

After he became a soldier in the legions of Gaius Julius Caesar in Gaul, I didn't see my son Meto for months at a time, though we conversed often by letter. This was fortuitous in a way that I could never have foreseen.

Meto's letters came to me by military messengers. This is a common way to send all sorts of correspondence, since only very wealthy men can afford to have slaves merely for the purpose of carrying letters, while military messengers range far and wide throughout the empire and are more reliable than merchants or pleasure travelers. Letters leaving Caesar's camp, as it turned out, were not entirely private; the messengers who carried them usually read them to make sure that they contained no compromising information. One of Caesar's most trusted messengers, impressed by Meto's style and observations, passed a copy along to one of Caesar's most trusted secretaries, who thought it worthwhile to pass it along to Caesar himself, who then moved Meto out of the tent where he had been ordered to polish newly minted armor and into the commander's staff.

Between conquering Gaul and vying for control of Rome, it seems that the great man finds time in his busy schedule to keep a minutely detailed journal. While other politicians leave their memoirs as monuments to posterity, Caesar intends to distribute his (so Meto suspects) as a tool in his election campaigns. The people of Rome will read of Caesar's extraordinary skills of leadership and his triumphs in spreading Roman civilization, and then rush to support him at the polls — provided, of course, that things continue to go as Caesar wishes in Gaul.

Caesar has slaves to take his dictation, of course — Meto says the commander often dictates while on horseback riding from camp to camp, so as not to waste time — and he has slaves to assist in the collation and compilation of his notes, but as my own experience has often borne out, the rich and powerful will make use of other men's talents wherever they find them. Caesar happens to like Meto's prose style — never mind that Meto was born a slave, received only sporadic tutoring in mathematics and Latin after I adopted him, and has no experience at practicing rhetoric. Ironic, too, is the fact that Meto, who chose to be a soldier against my wishes, now finds himself a tent-bound literary adjutant instead of a sunburned, wind-bitten legionary. It would be hard, I imagine, for one of his humble origins to rise much higher, with so many patricians and sons of the rich vying for honor and glory in the upper ranks.

Which is not to say that he no longer faces danger. Caesar himself takes extraordinary risks — this is said to be one of the keys to the hold he has over his men, that he faces the enemy alongside them — and no matter what his day-to-day duties, Meto has seen plenty of battle. His role as one of Caesar's secretaries simply means that during quiet times, instead of building catapults or digging trenches or making roads, Meto labors over his commander's rough drafts. Just as well; Meto was never very good at working with his hands or his back. But when the crisis comes and the enemy must be faced, Meto puts down his stylus and takes up his sword.

Meto had plenty of hair-raising tales to thrill his older brother and set his brooding father's teeth on edge. Ambushes at dawn, midnight raids, battles against barbarian tribes with unpronounceable names — I listened to the details and wished I could cover my ears, as images ran riot through my head of Meto in hand-to-hand combat against some hulking, hairy Gaul, or dodging a rain of arrows, or leaping off a catapult consumed by fire. Meanwhile I watched him wide-eyed, at once amazed, appalled, proud and melancholy at how thoroughly the boy had vanished and the man taken his place. Though he was only twenty-two, I counted a few gray hairs among the shock of unruly black curls on his head, and his jaw was covered with stubble. His speech, especially in the excitement of recounting a battle, was salted with crude soldier's slang — could this really be the boy whose prose Caesar found so admirable? Relaxing in his quarters, it was Meto's custom to wear the same garment day after day, a dark blue, much-washed woolen tunic. I raised an eyebrow at his slovenliness but said nothing, even when I noticed the numerous murky spots, large and small, which stained the fabric in various places. Then I realized that the stains were clustered where his armor joined and around the edges of his leather coat. The spots were bloodstains, made where the blood of other men had soaked through his battle gear.

Meto told us of mountains he had crossed and rivers he had forded, of Gallic villages with their peculiar sights and smells, of Caesar's genius at outwitting the tribes and putting down their rebellions. (Much of the commander's behavior sounded like gratuitous cruelty and base treachery to me, but I knew better than to say so.) He confirmed that the Gauls were uncommonly big, many of them veritable giants. "They think of us as a midget race, and make fun of us to our faces," he said. "But they don't laugh for long."

He was eager for news of Rome. Eco and I shared with him all the gossip we could remember, including the latest maneuvers regarding the Egyptian situation. "Pompey and your beloved commander seemed to have matched scores in the latest round," Eco noted, "extorting equal hoards of silver from King Ptolemy in return for bribing the Senate to smile on his claim to the Egyptian throne. It's Crassus who's been left out."

"And what does Crassus need from Egypt?" said Meto, who had his own reasons to dislike the millionaire quite apart from his loyalty to Caesar. "He's rich enough."

"Crassus will never be rich enough for Crassus," I said.

"If he wants to keep his hand in the contest," said Meto, absently reaching for his short sword and fiddling with the handle, "Crassus will need to wrangle another military command from the Senate and score some victories to impress the people. Silver buys votes, but only glory buys greatness." I wondered if these words came from Meto himself or from Caesar, whose finances become more precarious even while the list of his conquests grows longer.

"But Pompey has pacified the East, and now Caesar is pacifying Gaul," said Eco. "What's left for Crassus?"

"He'll simply have to look further afield," said Meto.

"Well, Egypt is as far as I care to cast my thoughts," I said, and proceeded to relate what I had learned from Dio on the night before I left Rome. From his proximity to Caesar and his staff, Meto already knew a little about the murders of the Alexandrian envoys, but had not realized the scale of the scandal. He seemed genuinely appalled, and I found myself wondering how someone who had become so inured to the carnage of battle could be alarmed any longer by mere murder. The thought made me uneasy, as I suddenly felt the growing distance between Meto and myself. Then, as I continued to describe the peculiar circumstances of Dio's visit and my guests' absurd disguises — the philosopher as a woman, the gallus as a man — Meto burst out laughing. His laughter encouraged me to pile on more details, which made him laugh all the harder. Suddenly the stubbly jaw and the bloodstains faded from my sight. The harrowing tales and the crude soldier's slang were forgotten. I saw the face of the laughing little boy I had adopted years ago, and found what I had come searching for.

As it turned out, Eco and I were gone from Rome for almost a month, and did not return until after the Ides of Februarius. First a snowstorm detained us. Then I fell ill with a cough in my chest. Then, just as I was well enough to travel, Belbo fell ill with the same complaint. While some men might scoff at postponing a trip to coddle a slave, it made no sense to me to go traveling over dangerous back roads with a sick bodyguard. Besides, I welcomed the excuse to spend more time with Meto.

On the way back, we happened to cross the Adriatic using the same intrepid boatman and in the same boat as before. I had no trouble getting Eco to pause for a few moments in the temple of Fortune before we set sail. Happily for our crossing, the sky was clear and the waters were calm.

Back in Rome, Bethesda seemed to be in considerably better spirits than when I had left. Indeed, her attentions to me on the night of my return could have stopped the heart of a weaker man. Once there had been a time when a month's separation was enough to build our appetites for each other to a ravenous pitch; I had thought those days were long gone, but on that night Bethesda managed to make me feel more like a youth of twenty-four than a bearded grandfather of fifty-four. Despite the aches and pains of the previous days' long hours on horseback, I arose the next morning in excellent spirits.

As we ate our breakfast of Egyptian flat bread and millet porridge with raisins, Bethesda caught me up on the latest gossip. I sipped at a cup of heated honeyed wine and listened with only half an ear as she explained that the miserly senator across the way was finally putting a new roof on his house, and that a group of Ethiopian prostitutes appeared to have taken up residence at the home of a rich widower who keeps an apartment up the street. When she turned to affairs down in the Forum, I paid closer attention.

Bethesda had a soft spot for our handsome young neighbor Marcus Caelius, the one whom I had run into on the night before my departure. According to Bethesda, Caelius had just finished prosecuting a case which had set the city abuzz.

"I went down to watch," she said.

"Really? The trial, or the prosecutor?"

"Both, of course. And why not?" She became defensive. "I know quite a lot about trials and the law, having lived with you so long."

"Yes, and Marcus Caelius is exceptionally good-looking when he gets himself all wound up with an exciting oration — eyes flashing, veins bulging on his forehead and neck . . ."

Bethesda seemed about to respond, but thought better of it and stared at me straight-faced.

"A prosecution," I finally said. "Against whom?"

"Someone called Bestia."

"Lucius Calpurnius Bestia?"

She nodded.

"You must be mistaken," I said, with a mouth full of millet.

"I think not." Her expression became aloof.

"But Caelius supported old Bestia for the praetorship last fall. They're political allies."

"Not any longer."

This was entirely credible, given Caelius's reputation for fickleness, both in love and politics. Even when he was publicly allied with a candidate or cause, one could never be quite sure of his real intentions. "On what charge did he prosecute Bestia?"

"Electoral bribery."

"Ha! In the fall he campaigns for Bestia, and in the spring he tries the man for illegal campaigning. Roman politics!" I shook my head. "Who defended?"

"Your old friend Cicero."

"Oh, really?"

This added a new wrinkle to the matter. Marcus Caelius had made his entry into public life as Cicero's pupil and protégé. Then, during the turmoil of Catilina's revolt, he parted ways with his mentor — or perhaps he only pretended to do so, in order to spy for Cicero. Throughout that tumultuous episode, Caelius's real allegiance remained a mystery, at least to me. Afterward, Caelius left Rome for a year of government service in Africa. On his return he seemed to have left the camp of his old mentor for good, going up against Cicero in court and actually getting the better of the master orator. Later, when the Senate exiled Cicero and his enemies went on a rampage and destroyed Cicero's beautiful house on the Palatine, it was my neighbor Marcus Caelius who came knocking at my door with the news — complaining that the windows of his apartment afforded no view and asking if he could watch the flames from my balcony! The way the lurid glow danced on his handsome face, it was impossible to tell whether Caelius was appalled or amused, or perhaps a little of both.

After much political wrangling, the Senate had recalled Cicero from exile, and he was back in Rome. His house on the Palatine was being rebuilt. And now, according to Bethesda, he had again matched wits in a court of law with his one-time pupil Marcus Caelius.

"Well, don't keep me in suspense," I said. "How did the case come out?"

"Cicero won," Bethesda said. "Bestia was acquitted. But Caelius says the jury was bribed and vows that he's going to prosecute Bestia again."

I laughed. "Tenacious, isn't he? Having once defeated Cicero in court, I imagine he simply can't stand being bested by his old teacher this time. Or did a single speech not suffice for Caelius to adequately slander Bestia?"

"Oh, for that purpose I think the speech did very well."

"Full of venom?"

"Dripping with it. In his summation Caelius

brought up the death last year of Bestia's wife, and the death of his previous wife before that. He practically accused Bestia of poisoning them."

"Murdering one's wives can't have much to do with electoral bribery."

"Perhaps not, but the way Caelius brought it up, it seemed entirely appropriate."

"Character assassination," I said, "is the cornerstone of Roman jurisprudence. The prosecutor uses any means possible to destroy the accused's reputation, to make it seem more likely that he's committed whatever crime he's accused of. It's so much easier than producing actual evidence. Then the defender does the same thing in reverse, accusing the accusers of various abominations to destroy their credibility. Strange, to think that once upon a time I actually had a certain amount of respect and even admiration for advocates. Yes, well, I've heard the rumors that Bestia did his wives in. Both died relatively young, with no preceding illness and without a mark on them, so naturally people say he poisoned them, though even poison usually leaves some evidence."

"There wouldn't have been much evidence if it was done the way that Marcus Caelius implied," said Bethesda.

"And how was that?"

She sat back and cocked her head. "Remember that this was said in a court of law, before a mixed audience of men and women alike, not in a tavern or at one of his orgies. Marcus Caelius is a very brazen young man." She did not sound wholly disapproving.

"And a brazen orator. Well, out with it. What did he say?"

"According to Caelius, the quickest of all poisons is aconitum."

I nodded. Many years of investigating the sordid means of murder have given me some familiarity with poisons. "Aconitum, also called panther's-death, harvested from the scorpion-root plant. Yes, its victims succumb very quickly. But when swallowed in sufficient amount to cause death, there are usually noticeable reactions in the victim and plentiful evidence of foul play."

"Ah, but according to Caelius, the poison was not *swallowed*."

"I don't follow you."

"According to Caelius, if aconitum touches a woman's genitals, she will die within a day."

I raised an eyebrow. Even with all my experience of poison, this bit of information was new to me, and I was not sure I believed it. "What Caelius says is possibly true — though I'm inclined to wonder how anyone could ever have discovered such a curious thing. But then, I suppose there's not much that Marcus Caelius doesn't know about female genitalia."

"Ha!" Bethesda's eyes sparkled. "Even Cicero didn't come up with that one."

I turned up my palms to show modesty. "So, Caelius accused Bestia of having poisoned his wives by . . ." I left the sentence unfinished. There seemed no delicate way to complete it.

"He did not accuse Bestia outright. Having stated the properties of aconitum, and having worked himself up to a feverish pitch, Caelius pointed his finger at Bestia and shouted, 'Judges, I do not point the finger of guilt — I point *at the guilty finger!*' "

I choked on a mouthful of porridge. "Outrageous! Just when I was beginning to think that Roman orators had degraded their craft to the lowest level of indecency and bad taste, along comes a new generation to push the limit even further. Oh Minerva," I added under my breath, glancing out the window at the statue in the garden, "preserve me from a day in court! 'I point at the guilty finger.' Ha!"

Bethesda sipped from her cup of honeyed wine. "Anyway, Bestia was acquitted, finger and all."

"I suppose Cicero made a stirring speech for his defense."

She shrugged. "I don't recall."

Cicero's speech would probably have made a greater impression on her, I thought, had the man delivering it been as young and good-looking as Marcus Caelius. "Fortune smiled on Lucius Calpurnius Bestia, then."

"Though not on his wives," said Bethesda dryly. There was a flash of something like anger in her eyes, but then a smile crept across her lips. "Speaking of young Caelius reminds me of another bit of gossip from the Forum," she said.

"Also involving Caelius?"

"No, involving his landlord."

"I see. And what fresh outrage has Publius Clodius perpetrated now?" Clodius owned the apartment building down the street, the one in which Caelius had his lodgings. In his mid-thirties and a patrician of impeccable lineage, Clodius had made himself much feared in recent years as a rabble-rouser and exploiter of populist resentments. It was Clodius, as tribune, who had masterminded the Roman takeover of Cyprus in order to finance his scheme to pass out free grain to the people of Rome. Once friendly to Cicero, he had almost single-handedly engineered Cicero's exile and was now his archenemy. His political tactics were crude, relentless and often violent. Just as men like Caelius were pushing the boundaries of oratory in the courts, men like Clodius were pushing the boundaries of political intimidation. Not surprisingly, the relationship of the two men went beyond that of landlord and tenant. They had become frequent political allies, and they shared a personal bond as well. It was well known that Caelius was the lover, or at least one of the lovers, of the rabble-rouser's widowed older sister, Clodia.

"Well, I didn't witness the incident myself, but I heard about it at the fish market," said Bethesda, practically purring. "It seems that Pompey was down in the Forum, arriving with his retinue at some trial or other that was about to begin."

"Could this have been the trial of Pompey's confederate Milo, for breach of the peace?"

Bethesda shrugged.

"With Clodius acting as prosecutor?" I added.

"Yes, that was it, because Clodius was there with a large retinue of his own, made up of some very rough types, apparently."

To describe Clodius's notorious gang of troublemakers as "rough" was to understate the case. These were strong-armers of the lowest order, some hired, some obligated to Clodius for other reasons, some voluntarily in his service to sate their appetites for violence.

For a man like Clodius to be prosecuting anyone for breach of the peace seemed ironic, but in this case the charge was probably justified. The accused, Milo, had his own rival gang of ruffians ready to rampage through the streets supporting whatever political cause their master happened to favor at the moment. Where great men like Pompey, Caesar and Crassus contested one another in exalted spheres of financial and military prowess, vying for mastery of the world, Clodius and Milo struggled with one another for immediate control of the streets of Rome. The greater powers allied themselves with these lesser powers for their own purposes, and vice versa. At the moment, Milo was Pompey's enforcer in Rome, so Pompey was obligated to speak in Milo's defense. Clodius, whether acting for Caesar or Crassus, or entirely on his own, appeared to be badgering Milo chiefly to get at Pompey. Clodius seemed determined to undermine Pompey's attempts to take control of the notorious Egyptian situation . . .

This chain of thoughts caused me to remember my visit from Dio the previous month, and I suddenly felt uneasy. "By the way," I said, "do you remember the odd pair who visited me on the day before I left for Illyria? I was wondering if you had heard from them, or if you knew — "

Bethesda gave me her Medusa look. Her anecdote was not to be interrupted. "There was a great crowd gathered for Milo's trial, too many to fit into the open square where it was being held, so the mob spilled out into the nearby streets. When Pompey appeared, there was much cheering from the crowd. You know how the people adore Pompey."

"The Conqueror of the East."

"Exactly. But then Clodius appeared atop some high place and began shouting to the mob below, which was apparently packed with his supporters. Most people were too far away to hear what he was shouting, but whenever he would pause the mob below him would cry out with one great voice, 'Pompey!' Even those too far away to hear Clodius or even see him could hear the name of Pompey being shouted in unison. It was like a slow chant: 'Pompey!' A pause. 'Pompey!' A pause. 'Pompey!' Well, apparently Pompey heard his name being called, for they say he pricked up his ears and broke out in a broad grin, then changed his course and began making his way toward the shouting, thinking he was being lauded by the crowd."

"A typical politician," I remarked, "beating a path toward his adoring supporters like a calf heading for the teat."

"Except that this milk was sour. As he drew

closer, the smile vanished from Pompey's face. First he saw Clodius, pacing back and forth atop the ledge, addressing the mob below and clutching himself with laughter whenever they responded with the cry of 'Pompey!' When Pompey drew close enough, to hear what Clodius was shouting, he turned the color of a hot flame."

"And what set Pompey's cheeks ablaze?"

"Clodius was posing a series of questions, like riddles, over and over, and the answer was always the same — 'Pompey!' "

"And what were these questions?"

"Like his friend and tenant Marcus Caelius, Clodius is a very brazen man . . ."

"Please, wife, no false modesty. I've heard you blast dishonest vendors in the market with curses that would make even a man like Clodius blush with shame."

"You exaggerate, husband."

"Only slightly. Well?"

She leaned forward. "The chant went something like this:

What's the name of the general who's generally obscene?
Pompey!
Who peeks up his soldier's skirts when they're marching on parade?
Pompey!
Who makes like a monkey when he scratches his skull?
Pompey!"

This last was a reference to the great commander's habit when deep in thought of scratching the back of his head with his forefinger, and was innocuous enough, though with a bit of pantomime I had no doubt that Clodius could make it quite scathing. The other riddles were typical invective of the sort that might have been directed at any politician or general. All in all, such doggerel was pretty tame stuff, and hardly in a league with Caelius's quip about Bestia's guilty finger. But then, Pompey was not as accustomed as other politicians to the free-for-all of the Forum. He was used to being obeyed without question, not to being insulted in public by a Roman mob. Generals make thin-skinned politicians.

"But in the end," said Bethesda, leaning forward and lowering her voice, "it was Clodius who got the worst of it."

"How did that come about?"

"Some of Milo's men heard the shouting and came running. Soon there were enough of them to drown out Clodius and his gang. Their chants were positively shocking."

"Oh, probably not all that shocking," I said, idly shaping the last of my breakfast porridge into little peaks and valleys, feigning indifference.

Bethesda shrugged. "You're right, they weren't really shocking at all, since one has heard all those rumors before. Though I imagine hearing them chanted by a mob in the Forum must have made even Clodius squirm."

"What rumors?" I said, giving in.

"About Clodius and his older sister. Or half sister, I should say."

"Clodius and Clodia? Oh, yes, I've heard whispers and a few nasty jokes. Never having met either of the doubtless charming siblings face to face, I wouldn't presume to second-guess the secrets of their bedchamber. Or bedchambers."

Bethesda gave a delicate snort. "Why Romans should make such a fuss over relations between a brother and sister makes no sense to me anyway. In Egypt, such unions began with the gods and have a long and sacred tradition."

"No such tradition exists in Rome, I can assure you," I said. "What exactly did the mob chant?"

"Well, it started with something about Clodius selling himself to older men when he was a boy — "

"Yes, I've heard that story: when their father's early death left them in financial straits, the Clodii boys rented out little brother Publius as a catamite, and with considerable success. It could all be a spiteful lie, of course."

"Of course. But the chant went something like this:

Clodius played the girl
While he was still a boy.
Then Clodia made the man
Into her private toy.

And then more of the same, only more and more explicit."

"The Greek vice, coupled with the Egyptian vice," I observed. "And easterners complain that we Romans aren't versatile in matters of sex. How did Clodius react?"

"He tried to keep up his chant against Pompey, but when Milo's men began to drown him out, he disappeared pretty quickly, and not with a smile on his face. The chanting finally broke into a scuffle between Milo's and Clodius's gangs."

"Nothing too serious, I hope."

"Not serious enough to disrupt the trial."

"Probably only a few heads split open. And how did the trial turn out? Was Milo acquitted or found guilty of disturbing the peace?"

Bethesda looked at me blankly, then shrugged. "I don't recall. I'm not sure I ever heard."

"Probably because no one cares a whit. What they all remember and what they'll keep talking about is the scandal of Clodius's reputed incest with his sister being shouted aloud in the Forum. What's the difference in their ages — five years? Well, the widow Clodia does have a reputation for liking younger men, like our neighbor Marcus Caelius. I wonder what *he* thinks of having his lover's alleged incest made into a ditty by the mob?"

"Actually, Caelius and Clodia are no longer lovers, and Caelius isn't on such good terms with Clodius anymore," said Bethesda.

"How could you possibly know that?" I shook my head in wonder. "You haven't been slinking off to some of these wild Palatine Hill parties, mixing with the sophisticated young set in my absence, have you?"

"No." She leaned back on her couch with a smile and luxuriously stretched her arms above her head. The gesture was unabashedly sensual, evoking memories of the night's pleasures, as if to demonstrate that despite my teasing she would indeed fit in quite well at a Palatine Hill debauch, were she not so acutely aware and protective of her hard-won role as a respectable Roman matron.

"Or has young Caelius been confessing the secrets of his love life whenever the two of you happen to meet in the street?" I said.

"Not that either. But we have ways of sharing what we know."

" 'We'?"

"We women," said Bethesda with a shrug. She was always vague about her network of informants, even to me. I had spent a lifetime ferreting out secrets, but Bethesda could sometimes make me feel like an amateur.

"What caused the parting of the ways," I asked. "Surely sophisticated lovers like Clodia and Caelius don't abandon each other over trifles like infidelity or a bit of incest."

"No, they say it was — " Bethesda abruptly frowned and creased her brow.

She was teasing me again, I thought, trying to add suspense to the telling. "Well?" I finally said.

"Politics, or something like that," she said hastily. "A falling out between Clodius and Caelius,

107

and then trouble between Caelius and Clodia."

"You're well on the way to making a poem, like the mob in the Forum: Clodius and Caelius, and Caelius and Clodia. You need only insert a few obscene verbs. What sort of falling out? Over what?"

She shrugged. "You know I don't follow politics," she said, suddenly fascinated by her fingernails.

"Unless there's a good story involved. Come, wife, you know more than you're telling. Must I remind you that it's your duty, indeed your obligation under the law, to tell your husband everything you know? I command you to speak!" I spoke playfully, making a joke of it, but Bethesda was not amused.

"All right, then," she said. "I think it was something to do with what you call the Egyptian situation. Some falling-out between Clodius and Caelius. How should I know anything about the private dealings of men like that? And who should be surprised if an aging whore like Clodia suddenly loses her charms for a handsome young man like Caelius?"

I had long ago learned to weather Bethesda's moods, as one must weather sudden squalls at sea, but I had never quite learned to comprehend them. Something had set her on edge, but what? I tried to recollect the phrase or topic that had offended her, but the sudden chill in the room numbed my mind. I decided to change the subject.

"Who cares about such people, anyway?" I

picked up my empty cup, twisted my wrist to set the dregs aswirl, and stared into the vortex. "I was just wondering a moment ago, about those odd visitors I had on the day before my trip."

Bethesda looked at me blankly.

"It was only a month ago. You must remember — the little gallus and the old Alexandrian philosopher, Dio. He came seeking help, but I wasn't able to help him, at least not then. Did he come calling again while I was gone?"

I waited for an answer, but when I looked up from my cup I saw that Bethesda was looking elsewhere.

"It's a simple enough question," I said mildly. "Did the old philosopher come asking for me while I was gone?"

"No," she said.

"That's odd. I thought that he would; he was so distraught. I worried about him while I was away. Perhaps he didn't need my help after all. Have you heard any news of him, through your vast network of spies and informants?"

"Yes," she said.

"And? What news?"

"He's dead," said Bethesda. "Murdered, I believe, in the house where he was staying. That's all I know."

The swirling dregs in my wine cup slowed to a stop, the porridge in my stomach turned to stone, and in my mouth I tasted ashes.

CHAPTER SEVEN

It was not until several days after my return to
Rome that I found time to write a letter to Meto.
I recounted to him the events which had transpired
in my absence — Cicero defeating Caelius in the
trial of Bestia despite the accusation of "the guilty
finger" (the perfect anecdote for Meto to share
with his tentmates!), Pompey's embarrassment on
his way to Milo's trial, the obscene chant about
Clodius and Clodia.

Since I had made such a story of Trygonion's
and Dio's visit when I saw Meto in Illyria, I felt
I should let him know what had become of the
philosopher. Merely a matter of keeping him informed, I told myself, as I began setting down
the words. But as I wrote, I began to realize that
telling the tale was in fact my chief reason for
writing the letter. Dio's murder had left me with
a nagging sense of guilt, and writing down the
gory facts for Meto's perusal, painful though it
was, somehow eased my conscience, as if describing an event could mitigate its awfulness.

When it comes to correspondence, I am not Meto;
my prose will never capture great Caesar's admiration. Nonetheless, I will copy down a bit of what
I wrote to Meto on that last day of Februarius:

Also, son, you will probably remember the tale I told you about my visit from Dio, the philosopher I once knew in Alexandria, and the little gallus named Trygonion. You laughed when I described to you their absurd disguises — Dio dressed like a woman, and the eunuch in a toga trying to pass himself off as a Roman.

The sequel, I fear, is quite the opposite of funny.

What Dio dreaded came to pass, only hours after he left me. That very night, as I was making ready for my journey to see you, Dio was being viciously murdered in the house of his host, Titus Coponius.

I learned the bare fact that Dio had been murdered from Bethesda on the morning after my return to Rome. She claimed to know no details at all. Bethesda took a disliking to Dio the instant she laid eyes on him, and you know how she is — from that moment on he might as well not have existed; even her appetite for gossip seems unstirred by his murder. I had to discover the details for myself, posing discreet questions in the proper quarters. This was not difficult, though it took some time.

It seems that there had been a previous, failed attempt to poison Dio. He mentioned this to me himself on the night of his visit. Apparently some slaves of his previous host, Lucius Lucceius, were suborned (doubtless by agents of King Ptolemy) to poison Dio's food, but succeeded instead in killing his sole remaining slave, who had taken on the role of food taster. Dio fled from Lucceius's house to that of Coponius.

It was from the house of Coponius that Dio came to call on me, and to ask for my help. If only I had offered to let him spend the night in my house! But then his assassins might have done their bloody work here, under my roof. I think of Bethesda and particularly of Diana and I shudder at the thought.

Poison having failed, Dio's enemies resorted to less subtle means. After leaving my house, Dio returned to Coponius's as quickly as he could — darkness had fallen and Dio feared the streets, even disguised as he was and with Belbo along for protection. As for Trygonion, Belbo says that he went along as far as Coponius's door and then went his own way, perhaps returning to the House of the Galli, which is also here on the Palatine, close by the temple of Cybele. No one seems to know much about this gallus, and no one can explain to me his relationship to Dio.

What follows is secondhand information, some of it thirdhand — which makes it gossip, really — but I think it's reliable.

Back at Coponius's house, Dio shut himself alone in his room, refusing to take any dinner. (He had already eaten at my house, and was very fearful of being poisoned.) The household of Coponius retires early, and soon after dark everyone was abed except the slave who had been posted inside the front door to keep watch through the night. At some point (before midnight, according to the watchman) there was a noise from the back of the house, where Dio was quartered.

The watchman went to investigate. Dio's door was locked. The slave called his name and rapped on the door. Finally the slave pounded so loudly that Coponius himself (in the bedroom adjoining) was awakened and came to ask what the matter was. At length the door was broken down and Dio was discovered on his sleeping couch, lying on his back with his eyes and mouth wide open, his chest pierced by gaping wounds. He had been stabbed to death in his bed.

A window in the room opened onto a small courtyard. The shutters of this window were open and the latch had been forced from outside. The killer or killers apparently crept over a high wall, skulked across the terrace, broke into Dio's room through the window, murdered him, then skulked away.

The killer or killers escaped unseen.

It was a wretched end to a distinguished life. That Dio foresaw his destruction and spent his final days in a city far from home, dreading every shadow, casts an even gloomier pall over his fate. That he came to me, asking for my help on the very day of his murder, fills me with agitation. Could I have prevented the deed? Almost certainly not, I tell myself, for the men who wished to see Dio dead have resources far beyond anything I could forestall. Yet it seems a cruel jest of the gods to have brought him back into my life after so many years and then to have snatched him away so violently. I have seen much carnage and suffering in my life, yet it never becomes easier to bear. It only becomes harder for me to fathom.

Now every member of the embassy which arrived last fall from Alexandria has been murdered or has fled back to Egypt or has otherwise vanished from sight. (The few still in Rome, I am told, have either pledged their allegiance to King Ptolemy or been bribed to keep silent; no doubt some or all of them were the king's spies from the beginning.) The people of Rome should be ashamed that such an atrocity could occur not just in Italy but in the very heart of the city itself. To be sure, there are those who say that Dio's murder is such an outrage that the Senate will be shamed into taking some action to punish his slayers (if not King Ptolemy, then at least his henchmen). The Senate may even move to repudiate the king and recognize Queen Berenice, which was the object of Dio's mission. While he lived, the Senate would not even allow him to officially address them, but in death Dio may yet achieve what he desired: an Egypt with a new, independent ruler.

Can justice follow upon a tragedy such as Dio's murder? Considering the state of Rome's courts and the persons whose interests are at stake, I strongly doubt it. But I refuse to brood overmuch concerning this matter. Had I accepted Dio's commission to expose his enemies, I might now feel some obligation to pursue the matter of bringing his killers to justice. Fortunately, my rejection of his commission was explicit. I told him that I could not help him and gave him a good reason. My conscience is clear. The task of finding the blade which drew Dio's lifeblood, and punishing the hand that wielded it, does not fall to me.

Whatever happens next, it will not involve me, and for that I am glad.

Rereading that letter now, I see that my statements regarding the circumstances of Dio's death are marred by a number of errors, some of them quite significant. But no statement was more in error than the final one, which I read now with a shudder of amazement. How could I have been so blithely, smugly unforeseeing? What a perilous world we move through, like men blindfolded. The past and future are equally obscure, and broad daylight can hide as many dangers as the landscape of the night.

PART TWO

NOXIA

CHAPTER EIGHT

Almost a month passed before I had occasion to write to Meto again.

To my beloved son Meto, serving under the command of Gaius Julius Caesar in Gaul, from his loving father in Rome, may Fortune be with you.

I write this letter on the twenty-ninth day of Martius, an uncommonly warm day for so early in the spring — we have thrown open all the windows and the afternoon sunshine is hot on my shoulders. I wish you were here beside me.

Alas, you are not. Nor are you safely at ease in Illyria, where I last saw you. I learned in the Forum of your sudden move to Gaul not long after my visit. They say that Caesar was called to put down a revolt by some tribe with an unpronounceable name — I won't even try to spell it. I presume that you have gone along with him.

Take care, Meto.

Given your movements, I have no way of knowing if my letter of a month ago has reached you, or will reach you after this one, or will

119

ever reach you at all, but since one of Caesar's message bearers (a young soldier who has carried my letters to you before) is about to leave for Gaul and says he will take along a letter from me if I can finish it within the hour, I am writing very quickly and will simply give you what news I can, even at the risk of conveying events that make little sense for lack of context. (Don't show this letter to your commander, please. I fear that a man who dictates his memoirs on horseback would hardly accept being rushed as an excuse for fashioning such awkward sentences.)

Hopefully, you did receive my last letter, and so you know of the murder of Dio. I scoffed at those who said Dio's murder was too big a thing to go without consequence and that the scandal would result in someone being punished, but it seems that I was wrong and they were right, up to a point.

The scandal has been enormous. Dio was even better known and more highly regarded than I had realized — or did murder make a martyr of him and render him larger and more beloved in death than he was in life? For a man who is now spoken of in such tones of awe, he was certainly treated very shabbily in the final months of his life, shuffling from one reluctant (perhaps treacherous) host to another, expending his resources until his purse was empty. The senators who now speak of Dio as a second Aristotle and weep at the mention of his name are the same men who refused to allow Dio to speak in their chambers not long ago.

(I've suddenly remembered that old conundrum, which Dio posed to me as a young man in Alexandria: Is it better to be beloved in life and despised after death, or despised in life and revered after death?)

So the debate in the Senate over the Egyptian situation grinds on, freshly fueled by this shameful outrage. Meanwhile a charge of murder was recently brought against one Publius Asicius.

I must say that I was not surprised to see Asicius accused of Dio's murder. Dio himself suspected this young man of being involved in the failed poisoning attempt at the house of Lucius Lucceius, and told me as much when he visited me. On the very day that Dio's food taster died of poison, Asicius had paid a visit to Lucceius. By itself, this is a merely circumstantial connection. But then, after Dio left my house, and probably not long after he was stabbed in his bed, I happened to encounter Asicius and our neighbor M.C. in the street, and while I overheard them say nothing directly incriminating, the circumstances, at least in retrospect, struck me as highly suspicious.

So when I heard that the charge had been brought against Asicius, I felt greatly relieved, thinking that if he was guilty, then perhaps the whole ugly truth would be given a chance to come out — and without having to become involved myself. (I imagine you sometimes feel the same relief in your work for Caesar, when an odious task is unexpectedly accomplished without any effort on your part, as if some friendly god had decided to do you a favor.)

But the gods can be fickle with their favors.

Who do you think stepped forward to defend Asicius? Yes, the best defense advocate in Rome, our old friend Marcus Cicero.

When I heard that news, my hope abruptly dwindled. Many things may happen in a trial where Cicero is one of the advocates, but the emergence of the truth is seldom one of them. If justice triumphs, it happens in spite of Cicero's smoke and mirrors, and will have nothing to do with whether or not the truth was spoken.

They say that Cicero and Asicius were both away from Rome, down the coast, when Asicius was arraigned — Cicero in Neapolis, Asicius across the bay at his family's villa in Baiae. To discuss the case, Asicius went to fetch Cicero and took him back to Baiae in his magnificent litter. Well, not *his*, exactly, but a litter lent to Asicius by — can you believe it? — King Ptolemy.

(The complicity is absolutely damning! You would think that a man accused of murdering King Ptolemy's enemy would hide his connections with the king rather than flaunt them, but like most men of his generation, Asicius can't seem to resist any opportunity to show off.)

The litter was an enormous eight-man affair,

elaborately decorated (Egyptian litters make the most elegant Roman conveyances look plain) and attended by no fewer than a hundred armed bodyguards, also lent to Asicius by King Ptolemy. (If the king supplied the bodyguards for Asicius's physical defense, who can help but conclude that it was also the king who hired Cicero for Asicius's legal defense?) Can you see it in your mind — Cicero and Asicius discussing the upcoming murder trial while they proceed along the shore borne aloft in a litter, lolling about in Egyptian luxury with a hundred swordsmen in their train?

I missed the trial; a relapse of the cough which plagued me in Illyria kept me from venturing down to the Forum. Bethesda went to watch, but you can imagine the sort of report she came back with — I was informed that Asicius is quite good-looking, if a bit wasted and pale (Bethesda has heard that he drinks to excess); that Asicius's friend, our handsome young neighbor M. C., was nowhere in sight; and that Cicero was as long-winded and boring as ever.

And oh, yes, that Asicius was *acquitted* of murdering Dio.

I now regret having missed the trial, for I should like to have heard with my own ears the evidence presented. But I do not regret having missed whatever devious conjurer's tricks Cicero used to distract, disorient and ultimately persuade the judges. I don't need the aggravation.

So, for better or worse, the matter has come

to a conclusion. Poor Dio shall go unavenged, but his legacy may yet prevail —

I lifted my stylus from the parchment, distracted by a knock. I turned in my chair and saw Belbo in the doorway.

"The messenger's come back, Master. He says he must have your letter now if he's to take it for you."

I grunted. "Show him in. No need to make him wait in the hallway." I returned to the letter.

I must close abruptly. Caesar's message bearer has returned.

I have foolishly spent this precious hour recounting Forum gossip and left myself no time to speak of family matters. Know that all is well. Bethesda is as always, and Diana becomes more like her mother every day (more beautiful, more mysterious). Eco continues to prosper, though I often wish I could have taught him a less dangerous trade than his father's, and his beloved Menenia has proved herself a woman of surpassing patience, especially in bringing up the uncontrollable twins. Imagine having *two* four-year-olds squabbling and stubbing their toes and catching colds. . . .

I must close. The messenger has entered the room and stands before me, glancing over his shoulder at the statue of Minerva in the sun-filled atrium, tapping his foot impatiently.

Take care, Meto!

I dusted the parchment with fine sand, then pursed my lips and gently blew the sand away. I rolled the parchment, slipped it into a leather jacket and sealed the cylinder with wax. As I handed it reluctantly to the messenger, thinking of things left unsaid, I took a closer look at the man. He was dressed in a soldier's regalia, all leather straps and clinking steel and blood-red wool. His jaw was stiff and his countenance stern.

"How old are you, soldier?"

"Twenty-two."

Meto's age exactly; no wonder the fellow looked to me like a child playing soldier. I studied his face, searching for some sign of the horrors he must have beheld already in his young life, and saw only the bland innocence of youth framed by a soldier's helmet.

His stern expression abruptly softened. He looked puzzled. I realized he was staring beyond me at someone in the doorway.

As I swung about I heard Belbo bluster, "Master, another guest — I told him to wait in the foyer, but he's followed me anyway — "

At first I hardly saw the visitor blocked as he was by Belbo's bulk. Then he slipped into view, and what he lacked in stature was more than made up for by the gaudy splendor of his garb. He was covered from the neck down in a gown of vibrant red and yellow. Silver bracelets dangled from his wrists, a silver pectoral with glass beads hung from his neck, and his ears and fingers sported silver rings. His cheeks were painted white. On his head was a multicolored turban, from which his bleached hair hung down in wavy tresses. The last time I had seen him he had been dressed in a toga, not in the vestments of a priest of Cybele.

"Trygonion," I said.

He smiled. "You remember me, then?"

"I do. It's all right," I said to Belbo, who continued to hover uncertainly, ready to interpose himself between the gallus and myself. Belbo could easily have lifted the little priest over his head and could probably have snapped him in two, but he kept his distance, afraid to lay his hands on a holy eunuch. Trygonion had slipped into my study without missing a step, while a man three times his size blustered for him to stay back.

Belbo gave the gallus a disgruntled look and withdrew. Behind me I heard the clearing of a throat and turned to see the soldier slipping my letter into a leather pouch. "I'm off, then," he said, nodding to me and then looking at the eunuch with a mixture of curiosity and distaste.

"May Mercury guide you," I said.

"And may the purifying blood of the Great Goddess spring from between her legs and wash over you!" added Trygonion. He pressed his palms together, making his bracelets jingle, and bowed his head. The soldier wrinkled his brow and hastily moved to depart, uncertain whether he had just been blessed or cursed. As he moved to slip out the narrow doorway, he turned sideways to avoid touching the eunuch, but Trygonion deliberately shifted his stance so that their shoulders brushed, and I saw the soldier shudder. The contrast was striking, between the stern, virile young Roman in his military garb and the diminutive, grinning, foreign-born gallus in his priestly gown. How odd, I thought, that the larger, stronger one, trained to kill and defend himself, should be the one to shiver in fear.

Trygonion seemed to be thinking the same thing, for as the soldier stomped down the hallway the eunuch looked after him and made a trilling laugh. But as he turned back to me his smile quickly faded.

"Gordianus," he said softly, bowing his head in greeting. "I am again honored to be admitted into your home."

"It would seem I had little choice over whether to admit you or not, considering how giants give way before you and soldiers flee in panic."

He laughed, but not in the trilling way he had used to mock the soldier. It was a throaty chuckle, such as men exchange over a witticism in the Forum. The gallus seemed able to change his persona at will, from feminine to masculine, never seeming wholly one or the other but something which was neither.

"I've been sent to fetch you."

"Oh?"

"Yes, imagine that — a priest of Cybele, dispatched like a messenger boy." He cocked an eyebrow.

"Dispatched by whom?"

127

"By a certain lady."

"Does she have a name?"

"Of course she does — many names, though I'd advise you to avoid the more scandalous ones and call her by the name her father gave her, unless you wish to have your face slapped. That is, until you get to know her better."

"What name is that?"

"She lives here on the Palatine, only a few steps away." He gestured toward the door with an ingratiating smile.

"Still, before I go off to see her, I think I should like to know her name and what business she might have with me."

"Her business involves a certain mutual acquaintance. Two mutual acquaintances, actually. One living; one . . . dead." He looked coy, then somber. Neither expression seemed quite genuine, as if he had exchanged one mask for another. "Two mutual acquaintances," he repeated. "One, a murderer — the other, the murderer's victim. One who even now moves through the Forum, laughing with his friends and flinging obscenities at his enemies, while the other moves through Hades, a shadow among shadows. Perhaps he will meet Aristotle there and debate him face to face, and the dead can decide which of them knew more about living."

"Dio," I whispered.

"Yes, I speak of Dio — and Dio's killer. That's the business I've come about."

"Whose business?"

"The business of my lady. She has made it her business."

"Who is she?" I said, growing impatient.

"Come and see. She *longs* to meet *you*." He raised an eyebrow and leered like a pimp procuring for a whore.

"Tell me her name," I said slowly, trying to keep my temper.

Trygonion sighed and rolled his eyes. "Oh, very well. Her name is Clodia." He paused, saw the expression on my face, and laughed. "Ah, I see that you've already heard of her!"

CHAPTER NINE

On our way out, we passed Bethesda and Diana in the hallway.

"Where are you going?" Bethesda cast a chilly glance of recognition at Trygonion, crossed her arms and gave me the Medusa look. How could such a woman ever have been anyone's slave, least of all mine? Diana stood alongside and slightly behind her mother. She too drew back her shoulders and crossed her arms, affecting the same imperious gaze.

"Out," I said. Bethesda's arms remained crossed; the answer did not suffice. "The gallus may have some work for me," I added.

She stared at the little priest so intently that I would hardly have been surprised to see him turn to stone. Instead, he smiled at her. The two of them seemed impervious to each other. Trygonion was not intimidated; Bethesda was not charmed. "You'd better take Belbo with you" was all she had to say before uncrossing her arms and proceeding down the hallway. Diana followed, mimicking her mother's movements with uncanny precision — I swung around and tickled her under her arms. She let out a scream of laughter and ran forward, stumbling into Bethesda. They both turned and looked back at me, Diana laughing, Bethesda with one eyebrow raised and the merest hint of a smile on her lips.

"Take Belbo!" she repeated before turning her back and walking on. Now I understand, I thought: she remembers Trygonion from his visit with Dio, she knows about Dio's murder, and now, seeing me leave with Trygonion, she fears for me. How touching!

The three of us — the gallus, Belbo and myself — stepped out into the bright afternoon sunshine. The warmth in my study had seemed mild and the air sweet, like early springtime; here in the street, the sun had heated the paving stones and the air was hot. Trygonion produced a tiny yellow parasol from the folds of his robe, opened it up and held it aloft.

"Perhaps I should have brought my broadbrimmed hat," I said, squinting up at the cloudless sky.

"It's only a short walk," said the gallus. "Straight ahead for a block or two, then off to the right."

We walked up the street and passed the apartment building where Marcus Caelius lived. The shutters of all the upper-story windows were closed, despite the heat. Could he be sleeping, at this time of day? What a life!

The building was owned by the rabble-rouser Publius Clodius; now I was on the way to see his sister. What a small town Rome is, I thought, and growing smaller with each passing year. I had never met either of the notorious Clodii. They were distant cousins of my old patron Lucius Claudius, but our paths had never crossed. That had suited me. In recent years I've grown increasingly selective both of those I choose to help and of those I choose to offend. From what one heard about them, Clodia and Clodius were the sort it was best simply to avoid.

An obscure citizen lamenting the theft of his family's silver; an old acquaintance threatened by anonymous letters; a young wife unfairly accused of adultery by her vindictive mother-in-law — in my semiretirement, these struck me as the sort of people to whom I should lend my expertise. Men who deal in raw power, who control vast networks of secret operatives, who dispatch strong-armers to crush their opponents — the Pompeys and King Ptolemies of this world — these struck me as men I should take extreme care to avoid offending, even if it meant passing up the chance to help an old friend; even though it had meant turning my back on Dio of Alexandria.

Now I found myself on the way to the house of Clodia, supposedly to discuss some matter relating to the murder of Dio, following a priest of Cybele carrying a bright yellow parasol through the sunny streets of the Palatine. The gods delight in surprising men with the unexpected — and are notorious for the cruelty of their mirth.

Clodia's house was situated at the end of a little cul-de-sac off a quiet lane. Like the houses belonging to most patrician families, it looked old and showed an unassuming face to the street. The windowless front was stained with a muted yellow wash. The doorstep was paved with glazed red and black tiles. Twin cypress trees framed the rustic oak door. The trees soared to a great height; I had often noticed them from the balcony at the back of my house, but had never known exactly where they were located. Like the house, the cypresses had obviously been there for many years.

The slave who answered the door was a burly young man with a neatly trimmed black beard and bushy eyebrows that grew together above soulful brown eyes. He opened the door only halfway and smirked when he saw Trygonion. He hardly looked at me or Belbo. "She's gone out," he said, crossing his arms and slouching against the door frame.

"Gone out?" said the gallus. "But I only just left her, to go fetch this fellow."

The doorkeeper shrugged. "What can I tell you? You know how she is."

"But she knew I was coming straight back," said Trygonion in a petulant voice. "Where has she gone?"

"Down to the river."

"What, to the markets?"

The slave narrowed his eyes. "Of course not. You know she never goes to the public markets anymore. Afraid Milo's men will be there to start up the chants about her. Pretends she doesn't care, but you know how she hates that." The slave arched his right eyebrow, which created a striking effect, since his eyebrows were joined. "She's gone down to her place on the Tiber. Said it was the only spot to be on a beautiful day like this. 'Everyone will be at the river,' she said. Looking to catch an eyeful, I imagine — the swimmers." A sudden twitch at the corner of his mouth turned into a smile, as a hand belonging to someone hidden behind the door slipped across the gap and made its way onto the slave's backside. The visible patch of wrist moved in a sinuous fashion, like a wriggling snake. The young doorkeeper gave a ticklish start and flexed his muscular forearms. "She should have taken me with her," he sighed, "but I'm managing to stay busy."

"Did she leave any word for me?" asked Trygonion, exasperated. "She must have!"

From just beyond the door I heard a woman's laugh, then a smiling face appeared, pressed cheek to cheek with the burly doorkeeper. "Don't worry, she didn't forget you," the woman trilled. Her voice had a cultured accent and her chestnut hair was extravagantly put up, though a few stray tendrils had escaped the pins and combs. The lines around her eyes and mouth had been skillfully softened with makeup, but I could see she was no longer young. "Barnabas is teasing you! Aren't you, Barnabas? Wicked!" She playfully bit the slave's ear.

Barnabas laughed brusquely and jerked away, freeing his ear from the woman's gleaming white teeth and his buttocks from her grip. "Off with you, then!" she said, laughing and snapping her fingers. "Go on! I'll tend to you later." She growled deep in her throat and clicked her teeth. The door slave departed.

"It's a Hebrew name, you know," she said, turning back to us. "Barnabas, I mean. Clodia says it means 'consolation.' She should know!" The woman laughed, and I caught the smell of wine on her breath.

"What did Clodia say about me?" demanded the gallus.

"About you, Trygonion? Hmm, well, we all know where your name comes from, don't we?" She looked at him knowingly.

"Never mind!" snapped the gallus. "What did she say before she left?"

The woman's expression soured, undoing the illusion of her makeup. "Oh, all right, then. She said she simply couldn't stay indoors for another instant, and she's been dying to get down to her place on the river for days, so she told Chrysis to call for her litter bearers and pack up a few things and off they went in a cloud of dust. She asked me to come along, but I told her I was too, too despondent and in great need of *consolation*. Ha!" She barked out a laugh, showing perfect white teeth. "So, since I was staying, Clodia asked me to please give you a message if you should happen to come around, to tell you that you and your" — she looked at Belbo and me blearily, as if noticing us for the first time — "your friends, or whatever, should trot down to the river and meet her there. Is that clear enough?"

"Yes, thank you," said Trygonion curtly. He turned around and hurriedly strode away, taking the longest steps his short legs would allow.

"Cut off their balls and see what pests they turn into," the woman muttered between clenched teeth. She shrugged and slammed the door.

"Horrible woman!" Trygonion said as Belbo and I caught up with him.

"Slow down," I complained. "Who is she?"

"Just a neighbor. Nobody. A cousin or something. I don't have money for a litter, do you? I suppose we can walk."

Which we did. As we made our way down the western slope of the Palatine, through the cattle markets, across the bridge and up the west bank of the Tiber, at several points I considered telling Trygonion that I had changed my mind and was turning back. What was I doing, after all, coming at the summons of a woman I had happily avoided until now, to discuss a matter from which I had deliberately distanced myself? Blame it on Cybele, I thought, as I followed her priest, his parasol held resolutely aloft.

It is a sign of wealth and good taste to own a green patch on the banks of the Tiber. Such estates are something of a cross between a park and a garden; the owners call such grounds *horti*. There is usually a structure of some sort — sometimes no more than a rustic retreat with quarters for the groundskeeper and a few guests, sometimes a whole complex of buildings. The grounds themselves are often a mix of wilderness and cultivation, depending on the size of the property, the owner's proclivities and the gardener's skill; patches of tall grass and woodland may be interspersed with rose gardens, fishponds, fountains, and stone-paved walkways adorned with statuary.

Clodia's horti were unusually close in. A hundred years ago, the property must have been well out in the countryside, but the city had greatly expanded since then. It was an enviable location for a piece of riverfront property and must have been in her family for generations.

The impression of great age was reinforced by the grounds themselves, which on such a warm, windless day had the feeling of a place where time stopped long ago. The immediate approach was a long, narrow lane bordered by sprawling berry bushes which met overhead, shading the way. This tunnellike path opened onto a broad field of grass kept closely mown by a pair of goats which bleated at our approach. Facing the meadow and perpendicular to the river, which was almost entirely obscured by an intervening stand of dense trees, was a long narrow house with a red-tiled roof and a portico running along the whole front. The open meadow was as private as any walled garden in the city, for the view on all sides was shielded by tall cypress trees and majestic yews.

"She won't be in the house, but I suppose we can take a look all the same," said Trygonion.

We crossed the meadow and stepped under the shade of the portico. Trygonion rapped on the nearest door, then pushed it open and stepped over the threshold, beckoning to Belbo and me. Each room of the long house opened onto the next, and every room had its own door onto the long portico, so that one could walk from end to end of the house either along the shaded outdoor walkway or through each room in succession.

I could tell at once that the house was empty. It had the feeling of a place left unoccupied all winter, which had not yet been brought back to life. The air was still and cool inside, the walls and the sparse furnishings exhaled a slightly musty odor, and every surface had a thin coating of dust.

We followed Trygonion slowly from room to room as he called Clodia's name. In some of the rooms, dropcloths covered every object. In other rooms the cloths had been pulled away, apparently quite recently, for they still lay carelessly crumpled on the floor. Having acquired a furnished house on the Palatine, I know a few things about furniture. The pieces I saw in Clodia's house on the Tiber were of the sort which fetch astonishing prices at auction nowadays, especially among our burgeoning empire's new rich who have no such treasures in their obscure families — sleeping couches saved from the flames of Carthage, their plush cushions so faded that the exotic patterns can barely be made out; gilded cabinets and trunks with massive iron hinges of a sort no longer made; ancient folding chairs that the Scipios or the Gracchi brothers might have sat on.

There were paintings as well, in every room,

and not theatrical wall paintings such as are fashionable among the wealthy nowadays, but portraits and historical scenes painted in encaustic on wood and mounted in elaborate frames. These were darkened by age, their smooth surfaces covered by a skein of very fine cracks. Collectors set great store by these qualities, which time alone creates and which cannot be mimicked by human artists. There were also tiny sculptures mounted here and there on pedestals, none of them taller than a man's forearm, in keeping with the small scale of the rooms, and all of rustic subjects to match the rustic mood of the place — little statues of Pan and Silenus, of a slave boy pulling a thorn from his foot, of a wood nymph kneeling on a rock.

We came to the end of the house and stepped back onto the covered portico. Trygonion peered toward the woods on the opposite side of the meadow, where I could see nothing. "No, she wouldn't be over at the kitchens or the slave quarters or the stable," he said. "She's down by the water, of course." We set out across the meadow again, toward the grove of trees along the river. In their shade, we came upon a statue of Venus — not a small, decorative object like those in the house, but a magnificent, towering bronze upon a marble pedestal. The goddess looked out on the water with an expression of almost smug contentment on her face, as if the river flowed merely to give music to her ears, and the city on its further bank had been erected for no

139

other purpose than to amuse her.

"Extraordinary," I whispered. Beside me Belbo stared up at the statue dumbly, a look of religious awe on his face.

"Do you think so?" said Trygonion. "You should see the one at her house in the city." He turned and walked on, humming a hymn to Cybele. His mood seemed to lighten with each step that brought him closer to the river, and to the red and white striped tent pitched on the bank.

We stepped out of the trees and into the sunlight. A mild breeze stirred the lush grass. The tent stood out in dazzling relief against the bright green grass, the darker green of the river beyond, and the glaring azure sky above. Its fine silk panels shivered in the delicate breeze. The red stripes wavered like slithering snakes against a field of white, then, by a trick of the eye, the illusion was reversed and the stripes became white snakes against a field of red.

From somewhere I heard the sound of splashing, but the tent and the high trees on either side blocked my view of the river.

"Wait here," said Trygonion. He stepped inside. A little later he stuck his head out the flap. "Come in, Gordianus. But leave your bodyguard outside."

As I moved toward the flap it was pulled aside by an unseen slave within. I stepped into the tent.

The first thing I noticed was the scent, a perfume I had never smelled before — elusive, subtle and intriguing. The instant I first smelled it, I knew

I would never forget it.

The red and white silk softened the bright sunlight, filling the tent with a warm glow. The panels facing the river had been rolled up, letting in the view and framing it like a picture. Sunlight danced on the green water and cast lozenges of light into the tent, where they flitted and danced across my hands and face. I heard the sound of splashing again and now I saw its source, a group of young men and boys, fifteen or more, who frolicked in the water just beyond the tent. Some of them wore bright-colored scraps of cloth about their loins, but most were naked. Beads of water clung to their sleek flesh; in the sunlight they glimmered as if chased with jewels. When they moved into the shade beneath trees they became dappled, like spotted fauns. Their splashing caused the lozenges of light to dance wildly inside the tent.

I walked toward the center of the tent, where Trygonion awaited me with a beaming smile on his face. He stood beside a high couch strewn with red and white striped pillows, holding the hand of the woman who reclined upon it. The woman was turned so that I could not see her face.

Before I reached the couch a figure suddenly appeared before me. She looked hardly older than a child but wore her auburn hair coiled atop her head and was dressed in a long green gown. "Mistress!" she called, keeping her eyes on mine. "Mistress, your guest is here to see you."

"Show him to me, Chrysis." The voice was sultry and unhurried, deeper than Trygonion's but

141

unmistakably feminine.

"Yes, Mistress." The slave girl took my hand and led me before the couch. The smell of perfume grew stronger.

"No, no, Chrysis," her mistress said, laughing gently. "Don't put him directly in front of me. He's blocking the view."

Chrysis tugged playfully at my hand and pulled me to one side.

"That's better, Chrysis. Now run along. You, too, Trygonion — let go of my hand, little gallus. Go find something for Chrysis to do up at the house. Or go look for pretty stones along the riverbank. But don't let one of those river satyrs catch either one of you or who knows what might happen!"

Chrysis and Trygonion departed, leaving me alone with the woman on the high couch.

CHAPTER TEN

"The young men you see in the river wearing loincloths are mine. My slaves, that is — my litter bearers and bodyguards. I let them wear loincloths here at the horti. After all, I can see them naked anytime I wish. Also, it makes it easier for me to pick out the others. Any young Roman worth being seen naked knows that he's allowed to come swimming along my stretch of the Tiber anytime he wishes — so long as he does it in the nude. They come down from the road along a little pathway hidden beyond those trees and leave their tunics hanging on branches. At the height of summer on a hot afternoon there are sometimes more than a hundred of them out there, diving, splashing each other, sunning themselves on the rocks — naked by my decree. Look at the shoulders on that one . . ."

I found myself staring at a woman of no few years — knowing that she was about five years older than her brother Publius Clodius, I calculated that she was probably forty, give or take a year. It was hard to say whether she looked her age or not. However old she looked, it suited her. Clodia's skin was certainly finer than that of most women of forty, the color of white roses, very creamy and smooth; perhaps, I thought, the filtered light of the tent flattered her. Her hair was black and lustrous, arranged by some hidden magic of pins and combs into an intricate maze of curls atop her head. The way that her hair was pulled back from her forehead gave emphasis to the striking angles of her cheekbones and the proud line of her nose, which was almost, but not quite, too large. Her lips were a sumptuous red which surely could not have been natural. Her eyes seemed to glitter with flashes of blue and yellow but mostly of green, the color of emeralds, sparkling as the sunlight sparkled on the green Tiber. I had heard of her eyes; Clodia's eyes were famous.

"Look at the gooseflesh on them!" She laughed. "It's a wonder they can stand to go in the water at all. The river must still be frigid so early in the year, no matter how warm the sunshine. Look how it shrivels their manhoods; a pity, for that can be half the fun of watching. But notice, not one of them is shivering. They don't want me to see them shiver, the dear, brave, foolish boys." She laughed again, a low, throaty chuckle.

Clodia reclined on her divan with her back against a pile of cushions and her legs folded to one side beneath her. A long stola of shimmering yellow silk, belted below her breasts and again at her waist, covered her from her neck down. Only her arms were naked. Even so, no one could have called the costume modest. The fabric was so sheer as to be transparent, so that it was hard to tell, in the glittering light from the sun-spangled river, how much of the sheen of her contours came from the shiny silk and how much from the sleek flesh beneath. I had never seen a dress like it. This must have shown on my face, for Clodia laughed again, and not at the young men in the river.

"Do you like it?" She looked steadily into my eyes as she smoothed her palm over her hip and down her thigh to the bend of her knee. The silk seemed to ripple like water before the advancing edge of her hand. "It comes all the way from Cos. Something new from a famous silkmaker there. I don't think any other woman in Rome has a dress like it. Or perhaps they're like me, not quite brave enough to wear such a garment in public." She smiled demurely and reached up to the silver necklace at her throat. She spread her fingers, and I could clearly see, thanks to the transparency of the silk, that while she rolled one of the lapis baubles between her forefinger and thumb, with her little finger she delicately stroked one of her large, pale nipples until it began to grow excited.

I cleared my throat and glanced over my shoulder. The young men in the water were now throwing a leather ball back and forth among themselves, making a game of it, but every now and then they shot glances toward the tent. No wonder they had come to the river on the first warm day of the year, I thought. They came to look at her no less than she came to look at them. I cleared my throat again.

"Is your throat dry? Did you *walk* all the way from the Palatine?" She sounded genuinely curious, as if walking for any distance outdoors was a feat she had watched her litter bearers perform but which she had never attempted on her own.

"Yes, I walked."

"Poor dear, then you *must* be thirsty. Here, look, before she left, Chrysis put out cups for us. The clay pitcher holds fresh water. The wine in the silver decanter is Falernian. I never drink anything else."

The vessels were set on a little table beside her. There was no chair, however. It appeared that visitors were meant to stand.

My mouth was in fact quite dry, and not entirely from the heat of the day. Clodia's cup was already full of wine, so I reached for the pitcher of water and poured myself a cup, drinking it slowly before I poured myself another.

"No wine?" She sounded disappointed.

"I think not. It's bad for a man my age to drink wine after exerting himself in the heat of the day." If not bad for my bowels, I thought, then bad for my judgment in such company. What would the transparent silk dress begin to look like after a cup or two of strong Falernian?

"As you wish." She shrugged. The silk pooled above her shoulders, then rippled like a sheet of water over her breasts.

I finished the second cup of water and put it down. "There was a reason you sent the gallus for me?"

"Yes, there was." She turned her gaze from me and fixed it on the young men in the river. I

146

watched her eyes flit back and forth, following the leather ball. Her face remained impassive.

"Trygonion said it had something to do with Dio."

She nodded.

"Perhaps I should close the tent flaps," I said.

"Then what would the young men in the river think?" The idea of scandal seemed to amuse her, as did my growing consternation.

"If we need a chaperon, call back your hand-maiden."

"*Do* we need a chaperon?" The look in her eyes was unnerving. "You obviously don't know Chrysis; she would hardly qualify for the role."

"Trygonion, then."

At that she laughed aloud and opened her mouth to speak, then thought better of it. "Forgive me," she said. "When I have business to conduct with a good-looking man, I like to indulge in a little teasing first. It's a fault of mine. My friends have learned to overlook it. I hope that you'll overlook the fault as well, Gordianus, now that I've confessed it."

I nodded.

"Very well. Yes, I wanted to consult you regarding the untimely death of our mutual friend, Dio of Alexandria."

"Our *mutual* friend?"

"Yes, mine as well as yours. Don't look so surprised, Gordianus. There are probably a great many things about Dio that you didn't know. For that matter, there are probably a great many things about me that you don't know, despite all you may have heard. I'll try to be brief and to the point. It was I who suggested to Dio that he should go to your house to seek your help on the night he was murdered."

"You?"

"Yes."

"But you don't know me."

"Even so, I know of you, just as you undoubtedly know of me. Your reputation goes back a long way, Finder. I was a girl of seventeen, still living at home, when Cicero made such a splash defending that man accused of parricide. I remember my father talking about the case for long afterward. I didn't know of the role you played until many years later, of course, when I learned the details from Cicero himself — how Cicero loved to rehash that old case, again and again, until his triumph over Catilina finally gave him something even bigger to crow about! Cicero used to speak of you often to my late husband; on a few occasions he even recommended that Quintus seek out your services, but Quintus was always stubborn about using his own men for snooping and such. I shall be honest with you: Cicero didn't always speak highly of you. That is to say, from time to time when your name was brought up, he sometimes used words that should not be repeated aloud by a respectable Roman matron such as myself. But we've all had our fallings-out with Cicero, have we not? The important thing is that even when he was infuriated with you, Cicero always made

148

a point of praising your honesty and integrity. Indeed, when Quintus was governor up in Cisalpine Gaul, Cicero and his wife Terentia came for a visit, and one night after dinner we all played a game of questions and answers; when Quintus asked Cicero what man he would trust to tell the truth, no matter what, do you know whom he named? Yes, Gordianus, it was you. So you see, when Dio asked us to whom he might turn for help, the name of Gordianus the Finder came to my mind at once. I didn't know at the time that you and Dio already knew each other; Trygonion told me about that after their visit to you."

"I suppose I'm flattered," I said. "You know, then, that I met Dio in Alexandria, years ago?"

"Trygonion explained it to me."

"But how is it that *you* knew Dio?"

"Because of his dealings with my brother Publius, of course."

"What dealings?"

"They met shortly after Dio arrived in Rome. The two of them had much to talk about."

"I should think that Dio and Publius Clodius would have had a hard time finding common ground, considering that it was your brother who engineered the Roman takeover of Egyptian Cyprus."

"Water under the bridge, as the Etruscans say. Far more important to Dio was my brother's opposition to Pompey. Publius offered Dio a much-needed ally in the Senate. Dio offered Publius a means to cheat Pompey of his ambitions in Egypt."

"And your place in all this?"

"There's something about sharp-witted older men that I find simply irresistible." She gave me another of her unnerving looks.

"And what did Dio see in you?" I asked bluntly.

"Perhaps it was my well-known love of poetry." Clodia shrugged elegantly, causing the sheer silk to catch and drag across her nipples.

"If you and your brother were such great friends and supporters of Dio, why didn't he stay at your house where he'd be safe, instead of moving from one dubious host to another, staying barely ahead of his killer?"

"Dio couldn't stay at my house for the same reason that you may not lower the flaps of this tent, Gordianus. A man and a woman together, you understand. Dio's position with the Senate was precarious enough without having it further eroded by sexual innuendos. Nor could he have stayed with Publius; imagine the rumors that would have set off, about the Egyptian trouble-maker hatching plots with the famous rabble-rouser. Notoriety exacts a price. Sometimes our friends must stay at arm's length, for their own good."

"Very well, Dio was your friend, or ally, or whatever, and you sent him to me for help. I had to refuse him. A few hours later he was dead. You and your brother didn't do a very good job of protecting him, did you?"

Her lips tightened and her eyes flashed. "Nor did you," she said icily, "who had known him

150

far longer than I had, and whose obligations must have run far deeper."

I winced. "Just so. But even if I had agreed to Dio's request, I would've been too late to save him. By the time I woke up the next morning — no, even before I fell asleep that night — he was already dead."

"But what if you had said yes to Dio? What if you had agreed to begin looking after his safety the next morning, helping him decide whom to trust and whom to fear? Wouldn't you have felt some obligation after his death, to try to bring his murderer to justice?"

"Perhaps . . ."

"And do you feel no such obligation now, simply out of respect for an old friendship? Why do you hesitate to answer?"

"Doesn't everyone know who was behind Dio's murder?"

"Who?"

"King Ptolemy, of course."

"Was it King Ptolemy who slipped poison into Dio's soup in the house of Lucceius? Was it Ptolemy himself who stole into Dio's room and stabbed him to death?"

"No, of course not. It was someone acting on the king's behalf — "

"Exactly. And do you feel no obligation to see that this person is punished, if only to give solace to Dio's shade?"

"Asicius has already been tried for the crime — "

"And acquitted, the swine!" Her eyes flashed.

"Nemesis will have to deal with him in her own fashion. But there's another man, even more culpable than Asicius, who has yet to be brought to justice. You could help, Gordianus."

Though there was no chance that the men in the river could overhear, still I lowered my voice. "If you mean Pompey — "

"Pompey! Do you think I would send *you* against Pompey? That would be like sending a one-armed gladiator into the arena to take on an elephant." Her laughter was like sand in my face. "No, Gordianus, what I want from you is very simple, and well within your capabilities. How many times have you investigated the circumstances of a murder? How many times have you helped an advocate find evidence that would prove a man guilty or innocent of such a crime? That's all I want from you. I'm not asking you to topple a king from his throne or pull down a colossus. Only help me bring down the wrath of the law on the man who killed Dio by his own hand. Help me punish the cold-blooded killer who plunged a dagger into Dio's breast!"

I expelled a heavy breath and turned to stare at the sunlight on the river.

"Why do you hesitate, Gordianus? I'll pay you for your labors, of course, and generously. But I expected you to leap at this opportunity, out of your respect for Dio. Is his shade not whispering in your ear even now, pleading for vengeance? He asked for your help once before, while he was still alive — "

"These days, in a case such as this — in a matter of murder — I usually defer to my son Eco. He's younger, stronger, quicker. Those things often matter when the stakes are so high. Sharp ears and eyes can mean the difference between life and death. An old fellow like myself — "

"But your son never knew Dio, did he?"

"Even so, I think it's Eco you want."

"Well, never having seen him, it's hard for me to say whether I would want him or not. Does he look like a younger version of you?" She looked me up and down, as if I were a slave on the auction block. I bit my lip for having mentioned Eco, imagining him in my place, alone with such a creature. What was I thinking, recommending him to her?

"Both of my sons are adopted," I said. "They look nothing like me."

"They must be ugly, then," she said, affecting a frown of disappointment. "Well, then, you're the man I want, Gordianus, and there's no way around it. Will you help me or not?"

I hesitated.

"For Dio's sake?"

I sighed, seeing no way out. "You want me to find out who murdered Dio?"

"No, no!" She shook her head. "Didn't I make myself clear? We already know that. What I need from you is your help in collecting evidence to convict the man."

"You know who murdered Dio?"

"Of course. You know him, too, I'm sure. Until a few days ago, he lived just up the street from you. His name is Marcus Caelius."

I stared at her blankly. "How do you know that?"

She leaned forward, absently running her hands over her thighs. The movement pressed her breasts together and caused the sheer cloth which outlined her nipples to shimmer. "Until recently, Marcus Caelius and I were on rather intimate terms. He and my brother were also close. You might say that Caelius was almost like a brother to both of us."

The way she said it, the implication was vaguely obscene. "Go on."

"Not long before the poison attempt was made on Dio in the house of Lucius Lucceius, Caelius came to me asking to borrow a considerable sum of money."

"So?"

"He told me he needed the money to pay for some games being held in his home town, Interamnia. Apparently Caelius has an honorary post on the local council there. In return, there's an obligation to help pay for local festivals; that's the way Caelius explained it to me, anyway. It wasn't the first time he asked to borrow money from me."

"Did you always oblige him?"

"Usually. You might say I had developed a habit of indulging Marcus Caelius. He always repaid me, but seldom with money."

"Then how?"

"With favors."

154

"Political favors?"

Clodia laughed. "Hardly. Let's just say that I had an itch and Caelius knew how to scratch it. But I'm digressing. As I said, the sum of money he asked to borrow was rather large — considerably larger than he'd ever requested before."

"Enough to pay for an awful lot of scratching," I said.

Her eyes flashed. "Why, yes, perhaps that's what I was thinking when I foolishly agreed to give Caelius the loan. Afterward, I became apprehensive, and made some inquiries. Imagine my displeasure when I discovered that the games at Interamnia are held in the autumn, not the spring. Caelius's pretense for the loan was a complete fiction."

"He would hardly be the first young man to lie to a beautiful woman to get her money."

Clodia smiled at this, and I realized that I had called her beautiful without even thinking; I had meant to say 'an older woman,' surely. The flattery was all the more sincere for being spontaneous, and I think she sensed this.

Her smile faded. "I believe Marcus Caelius used the money to obtain poison and then to bribe one or more of Lucceius's slaves to try to kill Dio with it."

"You said it was a large sum of money."

"Poison isn't cheap; the stuff has to be reliable, and so does the person selling it. Nor is it cheap to bribe the slaves of a rich master to commit such a crime." Clodia spoke with authority, as if she had personal knowledge of such matters. "The connection occurred to me only later, after Dio was dead. Little things — the tone of Caelius's voice and the look on his face whenever the subject of Dio arose, cryptic comments he would make, my own intuition."

"These are hardly evidence."

"Evidence is what I want from you, Gordianus."

"Whatever the truth of the matter, it wasn't the poison attempt that killed Dio. What about the stabbing?"

"Early on the evening of the murder, Caelius was at my house, which isn't far from that of Titus Coponius, where Dio was killed. Caelius was carrying a knife, concealed inside his tunic."

"If it was concealed, how — "

"I assure you, nothing on Marcus Caelius's person was hidden from me that night," she said with a brittle smile. "He was carrying a dagger. He was also nervous and fretful, in a state such as I had never seen him in before, and drinking more than was good for him. I asked what was wrong; he said there was an unpleasant task ahead of him, and that he would be relieved when it was done. I pressed him to tell me what it was, but he refused. You men, with your little secrets. I said, 'This unpleasant task which you dread so much — I hope it's not the task I asked you here to perform.' 'Of course not!' he said, and proceeded to demonstrate as much. But our lovemaking that night was a disappointment, to say the least. Caelius was about as effectual as one of our shriveled friends in the river today. Later, when his friend Asicius came by to collect him, Caelius was eager to leave. Well then, I thought, let the boys go off and play with each other. A little later that night — only moments after the two of them left my doorstep, I imagine — Dio was stabbed to death."

I paused for a long moment before speaking, puzzled not by the details of Clodia's story but by her whole manner of speaking. I had never heard a woman talk of her sexual relations in such frank terms, and with such acid in her voice. "You realize that everything you've told me connecting Caelius with Dio's murder is merely circumstantial."

"Then here is another circumstance: the next night, when Caelius came calling on me, he brought me a little gift — a silver necklace with lapis and carnelian baubles — and boasted that he could now repay every sesterce of the money he had borrowed from me."

"And did he repay you?"

She laughed. "Of course not. But from the way he talked, I had no doubt that he had come into some money. He had performed his task, you see, and been handsomely paid off."

"Is this merely your assumption?"

Clodia wasn't listening. She stared at the roof of the tent, remembering. "Our lovemaking that night was quite the reverse of the previous evening. Caelius was a veritable Minotaur — horns rampant, eyes aflame, his flanks glossy with sweat . . ."

I opened my mouth to speak, but before I could interrupt her it was done for me by the approaching sound of a man's laughter, deep and throaty, accompanied by splashing footsteps. Clodia snapped out of her reverie and sat forward on her couch. On her face was a look of pure joy.

I turned to see a man taking high steps through the shallows along the riverbank, striding toward the tent. Like the other men in the river he was naked. The light of the lowering sun glittered on the water behind him, casting him in shimmering silhouette; beads of water on his shoulders and limbs sparkled like points of white flame outlining the dark mass of his body. As he emerged from the river he raised his hands and pressed the water from his hair, showing the sleek muscularity of his shoulders and arms. On dry land his stride became a swagger, and though his features were still shadowed in silhouette, I could see the flash of a broad smile on his face.

"Darling!" The word emerged from Clodia's lips like a breath made audible, as uncalculated as a moan or a sigh. There was no pretense or teasing in her voice, no slyness or innuendo. She sprang from the couch to meet the man as he stepped into the tent. It was hard to say which of them looked more naked, the sinewy, long-limbed man wearing nothing but beads of water, or Clodia in her gown of transparent yellow silk. They em-

158

braced and kissed each other on the mouth.

After a moment Clodia drew back and took his hands in hers. Where her gown had become wet from being pressed against his body, the silk was even more transparent and was molded to her like a second skin. She turned her head, saw me gaping and laughed. The man did likewise, as if he were her mirror image.

"But darling," she said, squeezing his hands and giggling like a girl, "why didn't you simply come in through the tent flap? What on earth were you doing out in the water with the others? And when did you join them? How could I not have noticed?"

"I only just arrived," he said, with a laugh deeper than Clodia's but uncannily similar. "I thought it would be fun to slip in among your admirers and see if I could attract your notice. Which I didn't, apparently!"

"But I was distracted, darling, by something very important!" She nodded toward me and affected a sober expression. The teasing tone had returned to her voice. She was performing again, but for whom? "It's about Dio, darling, and the trial. This is Gordianus, the man I told you about. He's going to help us punish Marcus Caelius."

The man turned his beaming smile on me. I recognized him now, of course. I had seen him at a distance in the Forum on many occasions, haranguing his mob of followers or keeping company with the great powers of the Senate, but never naked and wet with his hair slicked back.

How very much like his sister Publius Clodius looked, especially when one saw the two of them together, side by side.

CHAPTER ELEVEN

"I remember something you used to tell me, Papa, when I was starting out on my own: 'Never accept a commission without obtaining some sort of retainer, no matter how small.' " Eco cocked his head and gave me a penetrating look.

"What is your point?" I said.

"Well, when you left Clodia's horti this afternoon, was your purse heavier than when you arrived?" This was his way of asking if I had accepted Clodia's commission to investigate the murder of Dio — how typical of Eco to get directly to the heart of the matter!

Despite the summerlike warmth of the day, darkness had fallen early; it was still the month of Martius, after all. By the time I left Clodia's horti, shortly after her brother's arrival, the sun was already sinking, turning the Tiber into a sheet of flaming gold. It was twilight by the time Belbo and I reached home, trudging back across the bridge, through the shut-down cattle markets and back up the Palatine. Night fell, with a slight chill in the air. After a hurried meal with Bethesda and Diana, despite the tiredness of my legs I again set out with Belbo across the city to take counsel with my elder son.

We sat in the study of the house on the Esquiline Hill, which had once been my house and my father's before that. Now it belonged to Eco and his brood. His wife Menenia was elsewhere, probably trying to put to bed the squabbling twins, whose high-pitched screams of laughter occasionally rent the cool evening air.

I had just described to Eco my interview with Clodia, up to the arrival of her brother and my departure shortly thereafter.

"When I left the lady's horti," I said, "my purse was *substantially* heavier."

"So you did accept her commission?"

I nodded.

"Then you do believe that Marcus Caelius murdered Dio?"

"I didn't say that."

"But you'll be looking for evidence to convict him."

"If such evidence exists."

"Clodia's reasons for suspecting him seem to me tenuous, at best," said Eco. "But then, you've begun investigations with less to go on and still managed to dig up the truth."

"Yes. But to be honest, I'm a little uneasy about the whole affair."

"I should think so!"

"What do you mean?"

"Well, Papa, everyone knows that Caelius and Clodia were lovers. And Caelius and Clodius are political allies and drinking partners, or used to be. For that matter, there may have been something more than friendship between the two of them. Or the three of them, I should say."

"You mean the three of them in one bed?"

Eco shrugged. "Don't look surprised. A woman like Clodia — well, you said yourself that there wasn't a piece of furniture in the tent except for her couch."

"So?"

"Papa! You assumed that you were meant to stand. From what I've heard, the woman is more hospitable than that. If there was no chair, only a single couch, perhaps that meant that you were invited to *recline*."

"Eco!"

"Well, from the dress you say she was wearing — "

"I should have been less descriptive."

"You should have taken me along with you. Then I could have seen for myself."

"You're well into your thirties now, son. You should be able to think of something besides sex."

"Menenia never complains." He grinned.

I tried to make a grunt of disapproval, which came out sounding more like a hum of curiosity. Eco had chosen a black-haired beauty not unlike Bethesda for his wife. In how many other ways was she like Bethesda? I had wondered about this from time to time, in the perfectly natural way that a man of my years ponders the younger generation and their goings-on. Eco and Menenia . . . naked Clodius and his sister in her transparent gown . . .

At just that moment, one of the twins let out a scream from elsewhere in the house. I was jolted from my reverie, rudely reminded that physical pleasure can have consequences.

"We stray from the subject," I said. "I told you I felt uneasy about accepting this commission from Clodia, and you said, 'I should think so.' "

"Well, it all seems rather unsavory, don't you think? Perhaps even suspicious. I mean, there's an odd smell to it. Look, Papa, all you really learned about Caelius from your interview with Clodia is that he borrowed some money from an older, richer woman — under false pretenses, to be sure — and failed to repay her. Oh, and that he happens to carry a knife on his person, which is technically illegal inside the city walls but done by most people with any common sense these days. Until very recently these two were lovers, and now she's after evidence to convict him of murder. What are we to make of that? Caelius was her brother's confidant, and now the two Clodii accuse him of being a hired assassin for King Ptolemy, or for Pompey, which is the same thing. Why, Clodius is Caelius's landlord — Caelius lives in that apartment just up the street from you."

I shook my head. "Not anymore. Clodius kicked him out."

"When?"

"A few days ago. I didn't know about it until today when Clodius told me himself — standing there naked in the tent, dripping wet, nonchalantly discussing his real estate with me. Funny, the gallus and I walked by the place on our way to Clodia's house and when I saw that all the shutters were closed on such a warm day, I thought Caelius must be inside sleeping off a hangover. Instead it turns out that the apartment is empty. Caelius has gone back to live at his father's house on the Quirinal Hill — where he'll undoubtedly stay, until his trial is finished."

"Then they're definitely bringing charges against him?"

"Oh yes, charges have already been filed. But *not* by Clodius."

"Then by whom?"

"Can you guess?"

Eco shook his head. "Marcus Caelius has too many enemies for me to hazard a guess."

"The charges were filed by the seventeen-year-old son of Lucius Calpurnius Bestia."

Eco laughed and mimed with his outstretched arm. " 'Judges, I do not point the finger of guilt — I point *at the guilty finger!*' "

"So you know that story?"

"Of course, Papa. Everyone knows about Caelius accusing Bestia of poisoning his wives. I only regret that you and I were gone visiting Meto when that trial took place. I heard about it second-hand from Menenia."

"It was Bethesda who told me about it. Well, it looks as if Bestia may soon exact his revenge on Caelius."

"Has the date for the trial been set?"

"Yes. The charges were actually filed five days

165

ago. Given the customary ten days allowed for the two sides to prepare their arguments, that puts the beginning of the trial only five days from now."

"So soon! You don't have much time."

"Isn't that always the way? They come to us thinking we can pull evidence out of thin air."

Eco cocked his head. "But wait, you're saying the trial will start two days after the Nones of Aprilis. If it goes on for more than a day it would overlap with the opening of the Great Mother festival."

I nodded. "The trial will go on despite the holiday. Lesser courts are suspended during the festival, but not the court for political terrorism."

"Political terrorism? Then it's not a simple murder trial?"

"Hardly. There are four charges against Caelius. The first three accuse him of organizing the attacks on the Alexandrian embassy — the midnight raids in Neapolis, the stoning in Puteoli and the fire at the estate of Palla. I'll take no part in investigating those matters. My only concern is the fourth charge, which relates directly to Dio. It accuses Caelius of attempting to poison Dio at the house of Lucceius."

"What about the actual murder, the stabbing at Coponius's house?"

"Technically, that's also included. But Publius Asicius has already been acquitted, and the prosecution is wary of trying to prove the same case against Caelius. Instead, they want to concentrate

166

on the earlier poisoning attempt. Of course, I'll find out what I can about the stabbing at Coponius's house, as a corroborative detail."

"And to satisfy your own curiosity."

"Of course."

Eco pressed his fingertips together. "A politically charged trial, held during a holiday when Rome will be packed with visitors, with Cicero's estranged protégé as the accused and a scandalous woman in the background — this could turn into a spectacle, Papa."

I groaned. "All the more reason for my misgivings. All I need now is for some of Pompey's or King Ptolemy's strong-armers to come banging at my door, warning me to back away from the investigation."

Eco raised an eyebrow. "Do you think that's likely to happen?"

"I hope not. But I have a bad feeling about the whole affair. As you said, there's an odd smell to it. I don't like it."

"Then why not back away? You don't owe Clodia any favors — or do you? Are you telling me everything that happened in her tent today?" He affected an insinuating smile.

"Don't be absurd. I owe the woman nothing but the retainer I left with. But I do feel an obligation."

He nodded. "To Dio, you mean."

"Yes. I refused him to his face when he asked me for help. Then I talked myself out of going to the trial of Asicius — "

"You were sick, Papa."

"Yes, but was I *that* sick? And then, when Asicius was acquitted, I told myself that was the end of it. But how could it be the end, with no one convicted of the crime? How could Dio be at rest? Still, I managed to shun the obligation I felt, to shove such thoughts to the back of my mind — until yesterday, when the gallus arrived to bring me face to face with my own responsibility. It was Clodia who summoned me, but it wasn't only her."

"Her brother Clodius as well?"

"No, I mean to say that those two are only the agents of something larger. It begins with Dio, but where it ends only time will tell. Some greater power seems determined to pull me into this matter."

"Nemesis?"

"I was thinking of another goddess: Cybele. It was one of her priests who accompanied Dio to my house, and the same priest who came for me yesterday. Do you think it's only a coincidence that the trial will be held during the Great Mother festival — the celebration consecrated to Cybele? You know, it was one of Clodia's ancestresses who saved the statue of Cybele from being lost in the Tiber when it was brought from the East long ago. Do you sense the link?"

"Papa, you grow more religious as you grow older," said Eco quietly.

"Perhaps. More fearful of the gods, anyway, if not more respectful. Leave them out of it, then.

Say that this is merely between myself and the shade of Dio. My sense of obligation runs deeper than my misgivings."

Eco nodded gravely. As usual, he understood me completely. "What do you want from me, Papa?"

"I'm not sure yet. Perhaps nothing. Perhaps only to listen to my doubts, and nod if I say something that remotely makes sense."

He took my hand in his. "Tell me if you need more than that, Papa. Promise me."

"I promise, Eco."

He released me and sat back. From elsewhere in the house I heard one of the twins shrieking. Surely it was time for them to be in bed, I thought. Through the gaps in the shutters I could see that the world outside was dark.

"What does Bethesda think?" said Eco.

I smiled. "What makes you think I told her anything?"

"You must have told her something when you ate dinner with her tonight."

"Yes — a somewhat expurgated version of my visit to Clodia's horti."

"Ha! Bethesda would have appreciated the detail of the naked bathers, I think." Eco laughed.

"Perhaps, but I left them out of it. Just as I left out the description of the dress which seems to have intrigued you so much."

"I think it intrigued you first, Papa. And Clodius's emergence from the river, as naked as a fish from the sea?"

"Omitted — though I did leave in the siblings' embrace."

"And their kiss?"

"And the kiss. Well, I had to give Bethesda *some* grist for gossip."

"And what does she think of the accusation against Marcus Caelius?"

"Bethesda stated quite flatly that it was absurd."

"Really?"

" 'Impossible!' she said. 'Marcus Caelius could never have committed the crime. The woman is defaming him!' I asked her upon what she based her opinion, but the Medusa look was the only answer I got. Bethesda has always had a weakness for our dashing young neighbor. Or ex-neighbor, I should now say."

"She'll miss having him living just up the street."

"We shall all miss the occasional spectacle of watching Caelius stumble out his front door in the middle of the day with tousled hair and bloodshot eyes, or seeing him carouse through the street with a prostitute from the Subura, or hearing his drunk friends recite obscene poetry from his window at night — "

"Papa, stop!" Eco choked with laughter.

"It's no joking matter, I suppose," I said, suddenly grim. "The young man's whole future is at stake. If he's convicted, the best that Marcus Caelius can hope for will be a chance to flee into exile. His family will be shamed, his career ended, all his prospects ruined."

"It hardly seems punishment enough, if he's guilty."

"*If* he's guilty," I said. "Which it's up to me to find out."

"And if you find that he's not guilty?"

"I'll report that to Clodia."

"And will that make any difference to her?" said Eco shrewdly.

"You know as well as I do, Eco, that Roman trials are only incidentally about guilt and innocence."

"You mean that Clodia may be more interested in destroying Caelius than in punishing Dio's killer?"

"That thought has crossed my mind. A woman scorned — "

"Unless it was *she* who scorned *him,* Papa."

"I suppose that's one of the things I'll need to find out."

"If you believe the rumors, Caelius wouldn't be the first man she's destroyed," said Eco. "Though I suppose exile and humiliation are more merciful than poison."

"You refer to the gossip that she murdered her husband three years ago."

He nodded. "They say that Quintus Metellus Celer was healthy one day and dead the next. They say that his marriage to Clodia was always stormy — and moreover that Celer and her brother Clodius had become fierce enemies. The rift was ostensibly over politics — but what man could abide having a brother-in-law for a rival in his bed?"

"But which brother-in-law was the usurper —
Clodius . . . or Celer?"

He shrugged. "I suppose that was up to Clodia
to decide. Celer was the loser; he lost his life. And
now Caelius? Perhaps any man who comes between
this brother and sister is risking more than he
realizes."

I shook my head. "You repeat these scandalous
charges as if you knew them to be true, Eco."

"Only because I think you should consider very
carefully what sort of people you're dealing with.
You've made up your mind to go through with
this, then?"

"To try to find the truth about Dio's murder,
yes."

"Under Clodia's auspices?"

"It was she who hired me. Circumstance led her
to me — circumstance, or Cybele."

"But the political danger of associating yourself
in any way with Clodius — "

"I've made up my mind."

He stroked his chin thoughtfully. "Then I think
at the very least we should review what we know
about these Clodii, before you go off pursuing their
interests or pocketing any more of their silver."

"Very well, what *do* we know about them? And
let us be careful to separate fact from slander."

Eco nodded. He spoke deliberately, carefully
framing his thoughts. "They are patricians. They
come from a very old, very distinguished family.
They have many renowned ancestors, many of
whom served as consuls, whose public works are

scattered all over Italy — roads, aqueducts, temples, basilicas, gates, porticoes, arches. Their relatives are intermarried with families of equal stature in such a tangle that even a silkmaker could never unravel all the threads. The Clodii are at the heart of Rome's ruling class."

"As fractured and at odds with itself as that class may be. Yes, the respectability of their ancestry and their connections is beyond question," I agreed. "Though one always has to wonder how the rich and powerful became so in the first place."

Eco shook his finger at me. "Now, Papa, you've already bent your own rule — mixing facts with innuendo."

"Facts only," I conceded. "Or at least, anything not a fact must be clearly identified as hearsay," I amended, realizing that it might otherwise be impossible to talk about Clodia and Clodius at all.

"Well then," Eco continued, "to begin with, there's the spelling of their name. The patrician form is Claudius, and their father was Appius Claudius. But Clodius and all three of his sisters changed their spelling of the family name to the more common form some years ago, with an *o*, not the posh-sounding *au*. That must have been when Clodius decided to cast his lot as a populist politician and a rabble-rouser. I suppose it helps to give him the common touch when he's consorting with his hired strong-armers and brick throwers, or canvassing for votes among those who live off the grain dole he established."

"Yes, but what advantage does it give to Clodia?" I wondered.

"From your description of the goings-on at her horti this afternoon, I'd imagine she craves the common touch as well. Gossip, I confess!" Eco hurriedly added, as I raised a finger.

"Another fact, then," I said. "They're not full-blooded siblings."

"I thought they were."

"No, Clodia is the eldest of the lot, and she had a different mother from the rest. Her mother died giving birth to her, I believe. Soon after, Appius Claudius married his second wife and sired three boys and two more girls, the youngest of the boys being Publius Claudius, now Clodius. Clodius must be about your age, Eco, thirty-five or so, and Clodia is about five years older than him."

"They're only half siblings, then," Eco said. "So any copulation — conjectural or otherwise — would be only half incest, I suppose."

"Not that such a distinction would matter to anyone this side of Egypt," I said. "Actually — more gossip — one hears that Clodius has been the lover of all three of his sisters, the two full-blooded, younger ones as well as his big sister Clodia. Just as one hears that Clodius was groomed as a catamite by his older brothers when he was a boy, to sell his sexual favors to wealthy rakes."

"But I thought Clodius and his family were wealthy to begin with."

"Fabulously wealthy by our standards, Eco, but not by those of their peers. During the civil wars, when Clodia and Clodius were children, their father Appius was on the side of Sulla. When Sulla's fortunes ebbed, Appius had to flee Rome for several years. His children had to fend for themselves in a city full of enemies. Clodia, the oldest, was barely into her teens. It can't have been easy for those children. Those were hard years for everyone." This was something I hardly needed to tell Eco; it was in those years of chaotic civil strife that his own father had died and his mother had been reduced to such poverty that she eventually abandoned him to fend for himself in the streets, until I took him into my home and adopted him.

"When Sulla eventually triumphed and became dictator, Appius Claudius returned and for a short while thrived. He was elected consul in the year that Sulla retired. Then he took his reward, a provincial governorship — of Macedonia, I think — where he could bleed the locals for taxes, collect tribute from their chieftains and thus provide his sons back home with silver to start their political careers and his daughters with dowries. So it goes for a Roman with a successful political career. But not in the case of Appius Claudius. He died in Macedonia. The taxes and tributes were collected by his successor, and the only thing the children of Appius Claudius got back from Macedonia were the ashes of their father. They must have gone through a bad patch after that. They were never so poor that they dropped from sight, but one can imagine them scrimping and cutting corners to keep up appearances — the kind of petty humiliations that privileged patricians find so galling.

"And without a father in the house, the children must have made their own rules. Did young Clodius and his sisters carry on like rutting sheep without a shepherd to separate them? I don't know, but growing up in a turbulent, often hostile city with their father absent for years at a time, and then losing him while they were still quite young, must have brought the siblings close together — perhaps uncommonly or even unnaturally close. And while I seriously doubt that young Clodius was ever a prostitute in the strictly commercial sense — that kind of talk reeks of slander — given the circumstances, it's not hard to imagine him using whatever attributes he possessed to curry favor with those who could help him and his brothers get ahead. It's also not hard to imagine that there were those who found him desirable. Even now Clodius still has the look of a boy — sleek-limbed, slender-hipped, broad-chested. Smooth skin. A face like his sister's . . ."

"Yes, I was forgetting that you've just seen him naked," said Eco, raising his eyebrows.

I ignored his teasing. "The third name attached to their branch of the Claudian line is Pulcher, you know — 'beautiful.' Clodius's full name is Publius Clodius Pulcher, and his sister is Clodia Pulcher. I don't know how far back the name goes, or which of their ancestors was vain enough to add it, but it certainly fits the current generation. Pulcher, indeed! And yes, I speak advisedly, having just seen both of them naked, or near enough

— fact, not gossip! You know, I can well imagine that there are those, having seen the two of them together, who rather like to picture Clodia and Clodius making love, whether it's true or not."

"Papa, your eyes are glazing over!"

"They most certainly are not. But never mind all that. Everyone knows that the Clodii are good-looking, and everyone suspects that they both have far too much sex for anyone's good. What else do we know about them? I think the first time that I ever heard of Clodius was when he acted as a prosecutor in the trials of the Vestal Virgins."

"Ah, yes, when he accused Catilina of seducing the Vestal Fabia."

"But when both Catilina and the Vestal were acquitted, things got so hot for Clodius in Rome that he had to flee down to Baiae until the furor cooled down. He burned his fingers on that one. I don't suppose he was even twenty at the time. I could never make out what his object was, except to stir up trouble. Perhaps he wasn't quite sure himself, just testing his powers."

"The next thing I remember about him happened a few years later," said Eco. "Something about stirring up that mutiny among the troops."

"Ah, yes, when he went off to serve in the East as a lieutenant under his brother-in-law Lucullus. Clodius styled himself as the soldiers' champion. They were already dissatisfied with the way Lucullus was driving them from campaign to campaign with no end in sight and no sure prospect of a reward, while Pompey's troops were already receiving farms and settlements for fewer years of service. Clodius made a famous speech to the troops, saying they deserved more from their general than the chance to lay down their lives protecting his personal caravan of camels laden with gold. 'If we must never have an end to fighting, shouldn't we reserve what's left of our bodies and souls for a commander who will reckon his chief glory to be the wealth of his soldiers?' "

"Papa, what a head you've always had for remembering speeches, even those you've heard only secondhand!"

"Such a memory is as much a curse as a blessing, Eco. Anyway, you can see that Clodius was a rabble-rouser even then, making himself the advocate of the masses against their rulers, setting himself up in opposition to the status quo. No wonder he switched to the plebeian form of his name."

"And then more scandal," said Eco. "The affair of the Good Goddess."

"Yes. Was it only six years ago? Ironic that the man who started out by prosecuting a Vestal Virgin and her alleged lover should have gotten himself into such a sacrilegious scandal. The hearsay — gossip, not fact — was that Clodius was carrying on with Caesar's wife, Pompeia, but Caesar had caught on and set his mother to watch Pompeia like a hawk, so that it became impossible for the lovers to meet. Never one to let his appetites be denied, Clodius concocted a scheme to reach Pompeia. He decided to sneak into the women's festival of the Good Goddess, Fauna, which was being held that year in Caesar's house. No men allowed, of course. How could Clodius get in? By dressing up as a woman! Imagine him all fancied up as a singing girl in a saffron robe with purple hose and slippers — I wonder if his sisters helped dress him up."

"Perhaps it wasn't his first time in a stola," said Eco.

"I suppose he couldn't resist the idea of taking Pompeia in Caesar's own bed, with Caesar's own mother and scores of other women chanting and lighting incense in the next room. I wonder if Clodius planned to keep his stola on while he did it?"

"Papa, I object! You're letting your lurid imagination seduce you into accepting hearsay, and then compounding the slander."

"Granted, Eco. I shall try to get back to the facts. The story goes that Clodius almost pulled it off. In the haze of the incense and the confusion of the chanting and dancing — who knows what sort of rituals these women engage in behind closed doors? — Clodius managed to make his way into the house and to find one of Pompeia's slave girls, who was expecting him. She went to fetch her mistress, but when she failed to return, Clodius became impatient and started wandering through the house on his own, staying out of the light as much as he could, observing the proceedings."

"Wouldn't you love to know what he saw?"

"Wouldn't every man, Eco? But it was Clodius's

bad fortune to be spotted by another serving girl, who saw his hesitant manner and innocently asked him who he was looking for. He told her he was looking for Pompeia's serving girl, but he was unable to disguise his deep voice. The girl let out a shriek. Clodius managed to hide in a storage room, but the women lit torches and searched the house until they rooted him out and drove him into the street."

"Well," said Eco wryly, "if nothing else, Clodius disproved the old superstition we all learned as boys, that any man who witnesses the secret ceremonies of the Good Goddess will be instantly struck blind."

"Clodius could still see, granted, but he might have wished to be struck deaf, so as not to hear the clamor he set off. The women went home and told their husbands, and you know how men are with gossip. By the next morning, the scandal was the talk of every tavern and street corner in Rome. The pious were outraged, the impious were amused, and I have no doubt that some from both camps were more than a little envious. The matter was much talked about for a season and then put aside for months, until some of Clodius's enemies decided to bring him to trial for sacrilege.

"At the trial, Clodius claimed that he was innocent and that the women were mistaken, because during the festival of the Good Goddess he had been fifty miles from Rome. Clodius and Cicero were still on friendly terms back then, and when the prosecution called Cicero to testify, Clodius expected him to back up his alibi. Instead, Cicero dutifully affirmed that he had seen Clodius in Rome on the day in question. Clodius was infuriated. That was the beginning of the bad blood between them."

"But Clodius was acquitted nonetheless," said Eco.

"Yes, by a slim majority of the fifty-odd jurors. Some say there was outright bribery by both sides; others say that the jurors simply voted along political lines. At any rate, Clodius was vindicated and emerged stronger than ever. He became bolder about using the street gangs he had been organizing to swell his retinue and intimidate his enemies. As for Caesar, the cuckolded husband, his only response was to divorce Pompeia, even though he publicly insisted that nothing untoward had occurred between her and Clodius. When the paradox was pointed out to him — why divorce Pompeia if she had been faithful? — he said, 'I have no doubt whatsoever about her fidelity, but Caesar's wife cannot be tainted even by suspicion!' Well, Caesar can't have been too offended by Clodius. The two of them have turned out to be close allies."

"As demonstrated by the way Caesar helped Clodius get his tribunate."

"Exactly. Clodius wanted to be elected tribune, but was barred from doing so, since it's a strictly plebeian office, off-limits to patricians. What was Clodius's solution? With Caesar pushing the paperwork, he managed to get himself adopted by a plebeian almost young enough to be his son, and so got himself officially enrolled *as a plebeian* — which outraged his fellow patricians and delighted the mob, who elected him tribune. At last Clodius was a commoner in fact as well as in name."

"I see a pattern," said Eco. "If a man can't witness the rites of the Good Goddess, Clodius will make himself a woman. If a patrician can't run for tribune, then Clodius, who has the most patrician pedigree in Rome, will make himself a plebeian."

"Not a man to let himself be stymied by technicalities," I agreed. "During his year as tribune he managed to get a lot done — introducing a grain dole to please the mob, arranging for the Roman takeover of Egyptian Cyprus to pay for the dole, and passing a law to send Cicero into exile."

Eco nodded. "But now Cicero is back in Rome, and Clodius's ally Caesar is off conquering Gaul. The big political issue of the moment is the Egyptian crisis, which brings us up to Dio's ill-fated mission. If we believe Clodia, Clodius made himself a friend of poor Dio before he was killed — and now they want you to find evidence against Clodia's lover Marcus Caelius to convict him of the murder."

"An admirable summing up," I said. "I think we've managed to sort out a few truths from the slanders and come up with a few conclusions about Clodius's character, though I'm not sure where it all leaves us. I haven't changed my mind. In the past I've worked for men whose means and morals were at least as questionable as his. I see no point in refusing a commission from Clodius if it leads me to the truth of Dio's murder."

"What about Clodia, then?"

"What about her? All right, let's take a look at Clodia. The same rules: truth only, except for gossip identified as gossip — though I think the rule will be even harder to observe with Clodia than with Clodius. I think we've probably *heard* more about her and *know* less. But I'll begin. She was the first child of Appius Claudius, raised by a stepmother among younger half siblings — did this circumstance make her stronger, more responsible, more independent? Mere speculation. We do know that she married young, before her father died and left the family in financial straits, so she managed to bring a good dowry to her marriage with a cousin, Quintus Metellus Celer — which may help to explain her independence when it came to butting heads with her husband over family squabbles and political differences. In any dispute, even with Celer, she appears always to have sided with her siblings."

"The Clodii against the world?" said Eco.

"It sounds admirably Roman when you put it like that. Could all those rumors of incest merely reflect the jealousy of less beautiful, less beloved outsiders? Why not give Clodia the benefit of the doubt, and put down the rumors of her adulteries and incest to malicious tongues?"

"You're the one who spent the afternoon at her

horti, Papa, watching her ogle naked men."

"Yes, well, it's true that she doesn't do much to stamp out the lies about her, if they are lies. And there's no doubt that her marriage to Celer was stormy. There are plenty of witnesses to that, including Cicero, who used to be their frequent houseguest back when he was on friendly terms with the Clodii. But it should count for something that despite their troubles, Clodia and Celer did stay married for twenty years — "

"Until Celer mysteriously died three years ago."

"Yes, well, we've already talked about the rumor that she poisoned him. It's worth noting that no one ever brought charges against her, as someone in Celer's family might well have done, had there been any evidence. Any time anybody notable in Rome dies of anything but an accident, there's someone who'll say it was poison. Just as there are those who will always whisper that any exceptionally beautiful woman — or man, for that matter — is a whore. While we've both heard plenty of rumors, when it comes down to it, we don't really *know* very much at all about Clodia, do we?"

Eco leaned back and pressed his fingers together. "I think, Papa, that you are letting the transparent yellow gown cloud your better judgment."

"Nonsense!"

"It covers your eyes like a veil."

"Eco!"

"I'm serious, Papa. You told me to be honest with you, so I will be. I think that Clodia is probably a very dangerous woman, and I don't like it that you're working for her. If you must do so, for Dio's sake, then I hope you'll see as little of her as possible."

"I've already seen quite a bit of her."

"I mean what I say, Papa." There was no levity in his voice. "I don't like it."

"Nor do I. But some paths a man must walk, taking whatever ways are opened to him by the gods."

"Well," said Eco with an edge in his voice, "I suppose a religious argument can put an end to any discussion."

And if it didn't, then what happened next did, for at that moment two tiny human missiles came hurtling through the room like fireballs hurled from a catapult. One chased the other at such a speed that I couldn't tell which was the pursuer and which the pursued; I often found it hard to tell the twins apart even when they were standing still. At the age of four there was not much to distinguish them. Gordiana (whom Meto had called Titania from birth, because she was so big) was perhaps slightly larger than her brother Titus, but the two of them were dressed for bed in identical, long-sleeved tunics that went down to their ankles, and they had the same long, golden locks — a legacy from their mother's side of the family, which was perhaps why Menenia had so far refused to clip a single curl.

Never slowing down, the two of them tore across the study and disappeared into the next room. A moment later their mother followed after them. She seemed quite calm and was even smiling.

"Are you men finally finished with your serious discussion?" she asked. Menenia comes from a very old plebeian family, as respectable as it is obscure. Some of her ancestors managed to obtain the consulship hundreds of years ago; that will always count for something, but it hardly puts food on the table. Still, Eco was lucky to make the match, considering his adopted father's far less distinguished ancestry, and Menenia herself is above reproach in every way, the model of a Roman matron. She even knows how to handle her mother-in-law with effortless tact; I only wish that I could do as well at staying on Bethesda's good side.

"Yes, wife," said Eco, "I believe we're done with discussing life and death and justice and the gods, and other such trivial matters."

"Good. Then perhaps you both have a moment to spare for your offspring. The only reason the twins have been flying about in such a frenzy is because they refuse to go to bed without a last chance to say goodnight to their grandfather."

"Well, then, make them wait no longer," I said, laughing, and before I had a chance to brace myself, out of nowhere two fair-haired fireballs came hurtling straight toward my lap.

The hour had grown late; Bethesda would be expecting me home. I said a quick farewell to Eco and Menenia and finally extricated myself from the surprisingly strong grips of Titus and Titania

— no easy task, for each took hold of one of my hands and refused to let go. When I yelled for Belbo to come help me, I was hardly joking.

Belbo and I made our way down the Esquiline Hill beneath the light of the waxing moon, back through the Subura, where the streets were busy even at this hour, and across the Forum, where the temples were quiet and the broad, moonlit squares almost deserted. Above our heads the cold sky was full of stars. As we passed the House of the Vestals I shivered and pulled my cloak more tightly about my throat, thinking it was the night air seeping into my bones.

Just beyond the House of the Vestals, near the steps of the Temple of Castor, we turned sharply to the north, onto the broad footpath called the Ramp, the best shortcut from the Forum up the steep face of the Palatine Hill to the residential district. The Ramp is well traveled, but even in daylight it can seem secluded and secretive, hemmed in at its lower portion by the stony base of the Palatine and the high rear walls of the House of the Vestals, and shielded along both sides of its upper course by close-set rows of cypress trees. At night the Ramp is a place of deep shadows, even when the moon is full. "The perfect place for a murder," Bethesda had once exclaimed before turning around in midcourse and refusing ever to take the path again.

I felt another sudden chill and knew that it had nothing to do with the night air. We were being followed on the path, and not by chance but stealthily, for when I signaled Belbo to stop, I heard behind us the faint sound of footsteps that stopped a moment later. I turned and peered down the mostly straight path but could make out no movement among the dense shadows.

"One man or two?" I whispered to Belbo.

He wrinkled his brow. "One, I think, Master."

"I agree. The footsteps stop all at once, without any shuffling or whispering. Do you suppose the two of us have anything to fear from one man, Belbo?"

Belbo peered at me thoughtfully. A bit of moonlight illuminated his furrowed brow. "Not unless he has a friend waiting at the top of the path, Master. That would make it even odds."

"And what if he has more than one friend up there?"

"Do you want to turn around, Master?"

I peered into the darkness below, then into the shadows ahead. "No. We're almost home."

Belbo shrugged. "Some men have to go all the way to Gaul to die. Others can do it on their own doorstep."

"Just keep your hand on the dagger inside your tunic, and I'll do the same. Keep to a steady pace."

As we neared the top of the path I realized what a perfect place of ambush it would provide. Once upon a time I could take the steep path without missing a breath, but not any longer; a winded man makes an easy target. Even Belbo was breathing harder. I listened for the steps behind us, or for any sound from ahead, but I heard only the beating of my heart and the rush of air in my nostrils.

As we neared the top of the Ramp the cypress trees thinned on either side and the way opened up, dispersing the shadows with moonlight and allowing glimpses of the houses up ahead. I could even see a bit of the roof of my own house, which made me feel at once reassured and uneasy. Reassured to be so close to safety, uneasy because the gods sometimes resort to the most appalling ironies in discharging the fates of mortals. We were almost clear of the path but there were still plenty of shadows where any number of assassins could be concealed. I steeled myself and peered into the pockets of darkness.

At last we stepped from the Ramp onto the paved street, only a few doors from my house. The way was clear on either side. The street was deserted and quiet. From an upper story nearby I heard the quiet singing of a woman crooning a lullaby. All was tranquil.

"Perhaps *we* should play ambushers," I whispered to Belbo after I caught my breath, for now I could hear the sound of our follower's footsteps approaching. "If someone is after us, I should like to have a look at him."

We drew back into the shadows and waited.

The footsteps grew nearer, until at any moment the man would catch up with us and emerge into the moonlight.

Beside me Belbo gasped. I stiffened, wondering what was the matter.

Then Belbo sneezed.

It was only a partial sneeze, for he did his best to stifle it, but in the stillness it might as well have been a thunderclap. The footsteps stopped. I peered into the darkness and was able to discern the man's vague outline, a silhouette among mottled shadows. From his posture he seemed to be peering back at me, trying to make out where the sneeze had come from. An instant later he vanished, and I heard footsteps running down the Ramp.

Belbo gave a jerk. "Shall we go after him, Master?"

"No. He's younger than us — probably a lot faster."

"How do you know?"

"Did you hear him breathing hard?"

"No."

"Exactly. Neither did I, and he was close enough that we would have heard, had he been winded. He has strong lungs."

Belbo hung his head, chagrined. "Master, I'm sorry I sneezed."

"Some things even the gods can't stop. Perhaps it was for the best."

"Do you really think he was following us?"

"I don't know. But he gave us a scare, didn't he?"

"And we gave him a scare!"

"So perhaps we're even, and that's the end of it," I said, but I felt uneasy.

We walked hurriedly up the street to my house.

Belbo rapped on the door. While we waited for the slave to open it I pulled him aside. "Belbo, whether we were followed or not — don't mention this to your mistress. No need asking for trouble. Do you understand?"

"Of course, Master," he said gravely.

I thought for a moment. "And don't tell Diana, either."

"That goes without saying, Master." Belbo smiled. Then his jaw suddenly began to quiver and his face contorted. I gripped his shoulder, alarmed.

Belbo threw back his head and sneezed again.

CHAPTER TWELVE

The next morning I rose early, ate a frugal breakfast of honey and bread, offered my beard to Belbo
for a trim (I trust no one else to use anything
sharp near my neck), donned my toga, since I intended to pay some formal visits, and stepped out
of the house. The fresh, dewy air was bracing;
the lingering chill of the night was tempered by
the morning's warm sunshine. I filled my lungs
with a deep breath and headed up the street with
Belbo beside me.

The Palatine seemed to me particularly lovely
that morning. Of late, whenever I left the immediate vicinity of my house, I had been struck by
how dirty and grubby so much of Rome had begun
to seem, especially the Subura with its brothels
and taverns and foul-smelling little side streets,
and the Forum with its toga-clad hordes of politicians and financiers going about their frenzied
business. How much more pleasant the Palatine
was, with its shaded, well-paved streets, its quaint
little shops, orderly apartments and handsome
houses. One could breathe in such a neighborhood,
and walk even in the busiest part of the day without
knocking elbows with a hundred rude, shoving
strangers.

I had gotten used to living in a rich man's neighborhood, I realized, and the adjustment had not been difficult at all. What would my father say, who had lived all his life in the Subura? Probably, I thought, he would be proud of his son's material success, however unconventionally I had acquired it. He would also probably remind me that I should keep my wits about me and never be deceived by appearances. The rare and beautiful things that wealth and power can buy are often only decorations to conceal the way that such wealth and power were attained. Yes, a man can breathe freely on the airy, spacious Palatine — and a man can also stop breathing. Something more awful than knocking elbows with strangers had happened to Dio. The quality of a man's bedsheets counts for nothing if his sleep is forever.

The way to the house of Lucius Lucceius took us past the apartment building from which Marcus Caelius had recently been evicted. As we passed I paused to take a look. Not only was the upper story deserted, but a sign had been painted in handsome black letters on the corner of the building:

FOR SALE BY OWNER,
PUBLIUS CLODIUS PULCHER.

Beneath this was a drawing of some sort. I stepped across the street for a closer look and saw that it was a crudely rendered graffito showing a man and woman entangled in sexual intercourse. At first glance, it struck me that their positions were absurdly acrobatic; on closer examination I decided that they were physically impossible. Running from the woman's gaping mouth was a scrawled caption, with almost all the words misspelled:

THERE'S NOTHING LIKE
A BROTHER'S LOVE!

The artist was too poor a draftsman to have captured any recognizable features, but I had no doubt whom the copulating figures were meant to represent. The graffito had probably been left by one of Milo's rabble, I thought, though Clodius and his sister had plenty of other enemies. Considering the misspellings, the vandalism could hardly be attributed to Marcus Caelius. Or could it? Caelius was wickedly clever enough to deliberately disguise his handiwork as that of a lesser intellect.

Belbo and I moved on. After numerous twistings and turnings down smaller side streets we reached the house of Lucius Lucceius. As befitted the domicile of a wealthy and respected senior senator, it presented an irreproachable facade. The only ornamentation was the massive wooden door, which looked very old and was carved with elaborate swirls and bound with massive iron clasps that had the savage look of the finest Carthaginian handiwork. It was not unlikely that the door had been brought back from the sack of Carthage itself;

I have seen many such trophies in the homes of those whose families conquered Rome's rivals. Belbo, unawed by its history or design and seeing only a door, knocked upon it.

It was quickly answered by the door slave, with whom Belbo exchanged the requisite formalities. A moment later I was admitted into the foyer, and then into a sparsely furnished study. The walls were decorated with Carthaginian war trophies — spears, swords, pieces of armor and even a pair of elephant tusks. The white-haired master of the house sat before a table littered with scrolls, styluses, wax writing tablets and bits of parchment.

"I can allow you only a moment," he said, without looking up. "I know who you are, of course, and I can guess what you're doing here. There's the chair. Sit down." At last he put down the scroll over which he had been poring and squinted at me. "Yes, I remember your face. First time I saw it was when Cicero pointed you out to me in the Forum — must have been fifteen years ago during the trials of the Vestal Virgins. Damned Catilina, corrupting a Vestal and getting away with it! It was I who prosecuted him for murder, you know, the year before he staged his little uprising. Didn't win that case, did I? Probably would have been better for everyone concerned if I had, Catilina included — he could be off somewhere enjoying his exile right now, buggering all the pretty boys in Massilia or wherever. By Hercules, you look fit! I'd have thought you'd gotten as old as me by now!" With that, Lucius Lucceius smiled broadly and pushed himself from the table. He was a remarkably ugly man with great bristling eyebrows and an unkempt mane of white hair.

He leaned back and rubbed his eyes. "Need a break anyway. Working on my history of the Carthaginian wars. Great-great-great-grandfather helped Scipio Africanus put an end to Hannibal, left the family a pile of scrolls nobody's read in years. Fascinating stuff. When I've finished writing it I'll browbeat all the friends and family into buying copies. They won't bother to read it, but the work keeps me busy. Gordianus, Gordianus," he mused, staring at me and wrinkling his brow. "Thought you were retired, not even living in Rome anymore. Seems somebody told me you'd left it all for a farm in Sicily."

"Etruria, actually. But that was a while ago. I've been back in Rome for several years now."

"Still retired?"

"Yes and no. I take on simple cases now and then, just to keep myself busy. Rather like you writing your history, I imagine."

From the flash in his squinting eyes, I saw that Lucceius took his role as historian more seriously than his self-deprecation indicated. "So," he said curtly, "Cicero has sent you around to collect my statement. Afraid it's not ready."

I stared at him blankly.

"Well, so much else to do," he said. "That is why you're here, isn't it? This business about young Marcus Caelius being brought to trial by those rascals claiming he tried to do in Dio?"

"Yes," I said slowly. "That is why I'm here."

"Surprised me — well, surprised everybody, I imagine — when I heard that Cicero was going to handle the boy's defense. Thought those two had fallen out for good, but there you have it. Things get dicey and the naughty schoolboy goes running back to his tutor. Rather touching, really."

"Yes, it is," I said quietly. Was it really possible that Cicero had taken on Caelius's defense? The news was startling, but made perfect sense. Cicero had successfully defended Asicius, probably to please Pompey. Pompey would be pleased to see Caelius acquitted as well, and Cicero was the man to do it. As for the feud between Caelius and Cicero, the same pragmatism that can make friends into enemies in the blink of an eye can do the reverse as well. "So your statement for Cicero isn't ready yet?" I said.

"No. Come back tomorrow. Actually, surprised he sent you to fetch it instead of that secretary of his, the one who picks over all the tiny details."

"Tiro?"

"That's the one. Clever slave."

"Yes, well, I suspect Tiro will be the one who comes to collect your statement eventually. But as long as I'm here, perhaps I could ask you a few questions."

"Go on."

"About Dio."

He waved his hand. "It will all be in the statement."

"Still, perhaps it could save us all some time — you, me, Tiro, Cicero — if you could give me an idea of what exactly will be in the statement."

"Just what I told Cicero. Dio was my houseguest for a while, and then moved on. As simple as that. All this nonsense about poisoning — 'Nasty rumors spread like olive oil, and leave a stain like red wine.' "

"But there was a death in this house, wasn't there? Dio's slave, his taster — "

"Worthless slave died of natural causes, and that's the end of it."

"Then why did Dio move on to the house of Titus Coponius?"

"Because Dio was frightened by his own shadow. Saw a stick on the ground, swore it was a snake." Lucceius snorted. "Dio was as safe here as a virgin in the House of the Galli. That's the beginning and end of it."

"And yet, Dio believed that someone in this house tried to poison him."

"Dio had no damned sense. Look what happened to him at Coponius's house, then tell me where he was safer!"

"I see your point. You were good friends, then, you and Dio?"

"Of course! What do you think, I'd ask an enemy to sleep under my roof? He'd sit here during the day, where you're sitting now, and we'd talk about Aristotle, or Alexandria, or Carthage in the days of Hannibal. Gave me some good ideas for my history." Lucceius looked aside and bit his lip. "Wasn't a bad fellow. Sorry to see him go. Of course he did have some nasty habits." He smiled grimly. "Picking the fruit before it's ripe and all that."

"What do you mean?"

"Never mind. No point gossiping about the dead."

" 'Picking the fruit . . .'?"

"Liked them young. One of those. Nothing wrong in that, except a man should keep his hands off what belongs to his host. I'll say no more." From his face I could see that he meant it.

"You said that Dio's slave died of natural causes. What killed him?"

"How should I know?"

"But a death in the house — "

"The death of a slave, and another man's slave at that."

"Surely someone noted the symptoms."

"What do you think, I summon a fancy Greek physician every time a slave has a stomachache? Slaves take ill every day, and sometimes they die."

"Then you can't be sure that it wasn't poison. Dio thought so."

"Dio thought lots of things. Had quite an imagination — made a better philosopher than historian."

"Still, if someone in the household could tell me exactly how the slave died, what he complained of before the end — "

I was stopped by the look on Lucceius's face. He stared at me for a long moment. His bushy eyebrows gathered above his squinting eyes. "Who sent you here?"

"I'd rather not say."

"Wasn't Cicero, was it?"

"I come as a friend of Dio's."

"Meaning that I wasn't? Get out."

"My only interest is discovering the truth about Dio's death. If you were truly his friend — "

"Get out! Well, go on. Up! Out!" Lucius Lucceius picked up a stylus and waved it like a dagger, glowering at me as I stood and walked to the door. I left him bent over his scrolls, muttering angrily to himself.

The slave who had shown me in was waiting in the hallway to show me out, but before we reached the foyer a formidably large woman stepped into the hallway and blocked our path.

"Go on, Cleon," she said to the slave. "I'll show the visitor out myself." From the tone of her voice she was clearly the mistress of the house, and from the slave's obsequious manner as he backed away I gathered she was not the sort of Roman matron who allowed her slaves much latitude.

Lucceius's wife was as ugly as her husband, though she looked nothing like him. Instead of bristling eyebrows she had only two lines painted above her eyes. Her hair might have been as white as his, had it not been dyed red with henna. She wore a voluminous green stola and a necklace of green glass with matching earrings. "So, you're

Gordianus the Finder," she said abruptly, appraising me with a caustic gaze. "I heard the slave announce you to my husband."

"What else did you hear?" I said.

She appreciated my bluntness. "Everything. You and I should talk."

I looked over my shoulder.

"Don't worry," she said, "no one eavesdrops on me in this house. They know better. Come this way."

I followed her into another wing of the house. I might as well have entered another world. Where Lucceius's study had been an austere museum of war trophies and musty documents, his wife's quarters were flamboyantly decorated with intricately embroidered hangings and precious objects of metal and glass. One long wall was painted to show a spring garden in bloom, all pale greens and soft pinks and yellows.

"You deceived my husband," she said wryly.

"He thought I came from Cicero. I didn't contradict him."

"So you merely let him believe what he wanted to believe. Yes, that's the best way to handle Lucius. He wasn't intentionally lying to you, you know. He's convinced himself that nothing untoward took place in this house. Lucius has a hard time dealing with the truth. Like most men, most of the time," she said under her breath. She walked about the room, picking things up and putting them down.

"Please, go on," I said.

"Appearances matter more than facts to Lucius. To have had a houseguest poisoned under his roof, or even a houseguest's slave, is unthinkable to him. So it simply never happened, you see. Lucius will never, ever admit otherwise."

"But such a thing *did* happen?"

She stepped to a small table covered with a number of identical clay figurines. They were about the size of a child's fist and brightly painted. She picked one of them up and idly turned it over in her hand. "Who sent you here asking questions?"

"As I told your husband, a friend of Dio's."

She snorted. "Never mind. I can guess who sent you."

"Can you?"

"Clodia. Am I right? Don't bother to answer. I can read your face as easily as I can read Lucius's."

"How could you possibly guess who hired me?"

She shrugged and twirled the little clay figurine between her forefinger and thumb. It was a votive statue of Attis, the eunuch consort of the Great Mother, Cybele, standing with his hands on his plump belly and wearing his red Phrygian cap with its rounded, forward-sloping peak. "We have ways of sharing what we know."

" 'We'?"

"We women."

I felt a prickling sensation in my spine, a sense of having had the same conversation before — with

Bethesda, when she told me that Clodia and Caelius were no longer lovers, and I asked her how she could possibly know such a thing: *We have ways of sharing what we know.* For an instant I had a glimmer of insight, as if a door had been opened just enough to let me catch a glimpse of an unfamiliar room. Then she started to talk again and the door was shut.

"There's no doubt that Dio's slave was poisoned. You should have seen the poor wretch. If Lucius had kept his eyes open instead of looking away when the man was dying, he might have a harder time making that glib pronouncement about 'natural causes.' But then Lucius has always been squeamish. He can write his little accounts of women being spitted on stakes and children being chopped into pieces at the fall of Carthage, but he can't stomach watching a slave throw up."

"Was that one of the symptoms?"

"Yes. The man turned as white as marble and went into convulsions."

"But if the slave was poisoned by tasting food intended for Dio, how did the poison get into the food?"

"It was put there by some of the kitchen slaves, of course. I think I know which ones."

"Yes?"

"Juba and Laco. Those two fellows were always up to something. Too smart for their own good. Had fantasies of buying their freedom some day. Juba must have sneaked out of the house that afternoon, because I caught him sneaking back in, and when I questioned him he tried to get out of it by playing stupid and spouting a lot of double-talk, the way slaves do. He said he'd gone to the market to fetch something, I don't remember what, and even held up a little bag to show me. What nerve! It was probably the poison. Later I caught him whispering to Laco in the kitchen and I wondered what they were up to. They're the ones who prepared the dish that killed Dio's slave."

"Dio told me your husband had a visitor that day."

"Publius Asicius. He's the one who was later accused of stabbing Dio at Coponius's house, though they couldn't prove it at the trial. Yes, he came by to visit Lucius at just about the time Juba must have been sneaking out. But I don't think Asicius delivered the poison, if that's what you think. He didn't go near the kitchen slaves."

"But he could have been here as a distraction, to keep your husband busy while Juba sneaked out of the house to get the poison from someone else."

"What an imagination you have!" she said wryly.

"Where is Juba now? Would you let me speak to him?"

"I would if I could, but he's gone. Juba and Laco are both gone."

"Gone where?"

"After his taster died, Dio was quite upset. He screamed and ranted and demanded that Lucius determine which of the slaves had tried to poison him. I pointed out the suspicious behavior of Juba and Laco, but Lucius wouldn't hear of any suggestion that there was poison involved. Even so, a few days later he decided that Juba and Laco — trained kitchen slaves — would be of more use doing manual labor in a mine. Lucius owns an interest in a silver mine up in Picenum. So off the slaves went, out of reach, out of mind."

She held up the clay figurine of Attis and stroked it with her forefinger. "But this is the most curious fact: when Lucius made his pronouncement about sending Juba and Laco to Picenum, they suddenly offered to buy their freedom. Somehow, from the few coppers Lucius gave them every year to celebrate the Saturnalia, the two of them had managed to save up their own worth in silver."

"Was that possible?"

"Absolutely not. Lucius accused them of pilfering from the household coffers."

"Could they have done that?"

"Do you think I'm the sort of woman whose slaves could steal from her?" She gave me a look calculated to make a slave soil himself. "But that was the explanation Lucius decided on, and nothing will ever sway him from it. He took the silver away from them, sent them off to an early death in the mines, and that was the end of it."

"Where do *you* think the slaves obtained the silver?"

"Don't be coy," she said. "Someone bribed them to poison Dio, of course. Probably they received only partial payment, since they didn't finish the job. If I were the master of this house I'd have tortured them until the truth came out. But the slaves belong to Lucius."

"The slaves know the truth."

"The slaves know something. But they're far away from Rome now."

"And they can't be compelled to testify anyway without their master's consent."

"Which Lucius will never give."

"Who gave them the silver?" I muttered. "How can anyone find out?"

"I suppose that's your job," she said bluntly. She walked back to the little table and replaced the clay figurine of Attis. I drew alongside her and studied the tiny statues.

"Why so many, all alike?" I asked.

"Because of the Great Mother festival, of course. These are images of Attis, her consort. For gift-giving."

"I never heard of such a custom."

"We exchange them among ourselves."

" 'We'?"

"It has nothing to do with you."

I reached to pick up one of the figurines, but she seized my wrist with a startlingly strong grip.

"It has nothing to do with you, I said." After a moment she released me, then clapped her hands. A girl came running. "Now you had better go. The slave will show you out."

CHAPTER THIRTEEN

The easiest route to the house of Titus Coponius, where Dio had died, took me back the way I had come. Passing the former residence of Marcus Caelius again, I noticed that the FOR SALE announcement was untouched, but the obscene graffito beneath it had already been daubed over with paint. Clodius's henchmen could be accused of many things, but not idleness.

Titus Coponius saw me at once, and soon I was seated in his study with a cup of wine in my hand. If the study of Lucius Lucceius was a hoary homage to the conquest of Carthage, the study of Titus Coponius was a tribute to the enduring triumph of Greek culture. Black-on-red drinking cups, too ancient and precious for use, were displayed on shelves. Small statues of the great heroes and busts of the great thinkers were displayed on pedestals against the walls. A pigeonhole scroll case was full of cylindrical leather slipcases, and on the little colored tags hanging from each cylinder I glimpsed the names of the old Greek playwrights and historians. The room itself was impeccably appointed, with high-backed Greek chairs and a Greek carpet with a geometrical design, all harmoniously in proportion to the space they occupied.

Coponius was a tall man with a long rectangular face and a handsome nose; even seated he had an imposing air. His hair was clipped short and was very curly, black on top but gray on the sides. His clothing and manner were as elegant as the room in which we sat. "I suppose you've come about Dio," he began.

"What makes you think so?"

"Come now, Gordianus. I know you by reputation. I also know that Bestia's son has brought charges against Marcus Caelius for trying to poison Dio, among other things. It hardly takes a philosopher to figure out your reason for coming to the house where Dio died. What I don't know is who sent you — Bestia's boy for the prosecution, or Caelius for his defense."

"Neither, actually."

"Now that's a puzzle."

"Not to everyone, apparently," I said, thinking of Lucceius's wife. "Does it matter who sent me, so long as I seek the truth?"

"Most men have some ulterior motive, even in seeking for truth. Revenge, vindication, power — "

"Justice. For Dio."

Coponius put down his wine cup and folded his long, elegant hands in his lap. "Some day, when we both have a great deal more time, we should discuss that word, 'justice,' and see if we can come up with a mutually acceptable definition. For the short term, I assume you mean you seek the truth in order to identify Dio's killer. A straightforward enough ambition — but I don't think I can help you."

"Why not?"

"I can't tell you what I don't know."

"Perhaps you know more than you realize."

"A conundrum, Gordianus?"

"Life is full of them."

Coponius contemplated me with a catlike gaze. "As I understand it, the charges against Caelius involve attacks on the Egyptian entourage on its way to Rome, and an alleged attempt to poison Dio at Lucceius's house. What happened in this house isn't even cited in the formal list of charges."

"Technically, it is. But the prosecution intends to concentrate on the attempted poisoning, and use the actual murder of Dio as a corroborative detail."

"Then you do come from the prosecution." Coponius gave me a brittle smile. "Don't misunderstand. I don't mind you coming around asking questions. I went through all this before, when Asicius was prosecuted. I shared all I know with both sides, and in the end I helped neither. The simple fact is that the killers left nothing behind to give themselves away. Asicius was prosecuted on hearsay, not evidence. Yes, 'everyone knows' that he was somehow involved, just as 'everyone knows' that King Ptolemy must be at the back of it, but the proof was never put forward, and you won't find it in this house."

"Still, I should like to know what happened here."

Coponius took a sip of wine and turned his catlike gaze on me again. "I knew Dio in Alexandria," he finally said. "A few years ago, my brother and I spent some time there. Gaius, always the practical one, was interested in studying the financial workings of the grain markets. I found myself drawn instead to the steps of the library at the Temple of Serapis, where philosophers discussed the very things we're talking about — truth, justice, conundrums. That was how I met Dio."

"That was how I met him as well," I said.

Coponius raised an eyebrow. "You knew Dio in Alexandria?"

"Briefly, and long ago. I was quite young. My instruction from Dio was strictly informal."

Coponius understood at once. "Ah, you were one of those young men too poor to afford an education who linger on the steps hoping to catch the eye of one of the philosophers. Mendicants for wisdom, Dio called such young men."

"Something like that."

"There is no shame attached to such begging. The more one must struggle for wisdom, the more honor attaches to its attainment. My relationship with Dio was more formal than yours, I imagine. By the time I met him he had been elevated to the highest ranks of the Academy, and seldom appeared on the steps of the library; it was only by chance that I happened to meet him there. I invited him to dine on several occasions with Gaius and myself at the house we had rented in the imperial district. Dio knew all the Greek thinkers by heart. He could discourse for hours on the laws of perception and rational thought. Gaius would yawn and go to bed early, but I would stay up until dawn listening."

"Your brother doesn't care for philosophy?"

Coponius smiled. "Not particularly. But Gaius and Dio managed to find common interests. I was the one left out when the two of them went looking for adventure in the Rhakotis district." He raised a suggestive eyebrow.

"Dio never struck me as particularly adventurous."

"Then you didn't know him as I did, and certainly not as Gaius did."

"What do you mean?"

"Dio was considerably older than my brother and me, but he still had appetites. Rather strong appetites, actually. He enjoyed showing Gaius what he called 'the secrets of Alexandria.' "

" 'Picking the fruit before it's ripe,' " I said to myself.

"What?"

"Something that someone else said about Dio."

"Ripeness is a matter of taste. With Dio it was more a question of bruising the fruit, I would say."

"I don't understand."

Coponius fixed me again with his feline gaze. "There are those who would say that Dio's particular appetites were a flaw in his character, a sign of some imbalance in his humors. I myself have never been a slave to the flesh; my life is of the mind, and this seems to me ideal. Given my temperament, I'm often tempted to pass judgment on other men's weaknesses, but for friends I forgo such judgments. We must remember that while Dio's blood was Greek, his spirit was Egyptian. These people are more worldly than we are, earthier, in many ways cruder and more primitive. They make greater allowance for things we might consider out of bounds. On the one hand, Dio was a paragon of logic and reason; but on the other, he could release himself into a state of ecstasy beyond reason. If his pleasure sometimes depended on acts which you or I might consider to be cruel or excessive — "

"I don't understand."

Coponius shrugged. "What does it matter? The man is dead. His teachings are his legacy, along with his efforts on behalf of his countrymen. Few men can claim as fine a monument." He stood and began to slowly pace, running the palm of his hand over the tops of the busts that lined the wall. "But you came to talk about Dio's death, not his life. What is it you want to know, Gordianus?"

"I already know the bare facts of the murder — what everyone knows, as you say. But water from the mouth of the spring is freshest. I want to hear whatever you or anyone else in the household can tell me about the exact circumstances of that night."

"Let me think back . . ." He paused before a bust of Alexander. "I was here in my study when Dio came in that evening. I had just finished eating my supper, alone, and had come here to do some reading. I heard a couple of the slave girls tittering out in the hallway. I called them in and asked them what they were laughing at. They said that my houseguest had come in dressed as a woman!"

"Hadn't he worn the same costume before?"

"Apparently so, slipping in and out of the house without my seeing him, accompanied by that little gallus who was always visiting him. Dio behaved very secretively in this house. He kept to his room with his door locked. He wouldn't even join me for meals. When he asked to stay with me, I had hoped that the two of us would share some civilized conversation as we had in Alexandria, that we would dine together and discuss philosophy or politics. I was rather disappointed at his aloofness, and a little irritated."

"He was a very frightened man."

"Yes, I realized that. Which is why I stayed out of his way. If he wished to hide in his room all day, or slip in and out of the house without telling me, I decided to say nothing. I wish now that I had somehow taken steps to intervene, though I'm not sure what I could have done."

"Dio was a hunted man. You must have known he was in terrible danger."

"Of course. That's why I kept a watchman posted inside the door every night. Even so, I never imagined that anyone would actually break into this house and commit such an atrocity. It seemed unthinkable."

"Would you show me where this unthinkable thing occurred?"

Coponius led me down a long hallway to the back of the house. "The watchman was posted in the foyer at the front of the house. When the assassins broke into Dio's room, he didn't hear it. I myself was sleeping in the room next door and heard nothing."

"Did Dio cry out?"

"No one heard him if he did."

"Would you have heard him?"

"I was sleeping, as I said, but I should think a scream would have awakened me. The walls aren't that thick. On other nights I was able to hear — well, never mind."

"You were about to say something?"

"This is the room." Coponius pushed opened a door and gestured for me to enter.

It was a small room, sparsely furnished with a sleeping couch, a chair, and a couple of small tables. A carpet covered the floor. Metal hooks were mounted in the walls for hanging clothing and lamps.

"How did the assassins get in?" I said.

"Through that window, by the couch. The shutters were drawn and latched, I'm sure. Dio would have seen to that, if only to shut out the cold. The latch has been repaired, but you can still see where the wood was splintered when the shutters were forced open."

"Was the old latch made of bronze, like this one?"

"This is the very same latch, hammered straight by a smith and reattached in a different place."

"This seems to be a rather strong latch. I should think that forcing it from the outside would have made some noise."

"I suppose."

"A considerable noise."

"It couldn't have been that loud — "

"Perhaps not a loud enough noise to awaken you in the next room, or even to be heard by your watchman at the front door, but surely loud enough for Dio to hear if he was lying on this couch."

"You might think so, yes. But as I told you, no one heard Dio cry out. I suppose he was a very sound sleeper. Or perhaps the breaking of the latch didn't make as much noise as you seem to think."

"We could argue the point forever," I said. "Or shall we make an empirical test?"

"Do you mean — ?"

"If you'll let me."

Coponius shrugged. "Go on."

I unlatched the window and stepped through it, into the courtyard beyond, which was surrounded by a high wall. Inside the room, Coponius latched the shutters. I pushed on them, testing their strength, and realized it would take a considerable effort to force them open. I looked around and spotted a loose stone. Clutching it in my fist, I struck a hard blow against the shutters. With a sound of splintering wood the shutters flew open and the metal latch went flying across the room and landed on the carpet.

I climbed through the window. "Tell me, was the broken latch found across the room like that, lying on the floor?"

"Why, yes. I'm sure of it. I remember, because when I came into this room I stepped on the latch and cut my bare foot."

"Then we can assume that the shutters were forced open with at least as much force on that night, and must have made as much noise. I would say that was noisy enough to wake anyone in this room."

"Yes," Coponius agreed, fretfully tapping his forefinger against his lips.

"And yet, Dio didn't cry out."

"Perhaps he was awakened from a deep sleep, unable to comprehend. Or perhaps he comprehended only too well and was paralyzed with fright."

"Perhaps. Was his throat cut?"

"No. All the wounds were in his chest."

"How many wounds?"

"I'm not sure, exactly. Quite a few."

"There must have been a great deal of blood."

"Some blood, yes."

"A struggling man, stabbed repeatedly in the chest — the room must have been covered with blood."

Coponius wrinkled his brow. "When we came in the room, it was very dark, of course. The slaves held lamps. Shadows swung all about. I remember seeing blood — I don't know how much. Does it matter?"

"Probably not. You don't still have the sleeping

tunic Dio was wearing, or the cushions he was sleeping on?"

"Of course not. They were burned."

I looked around the room, imagining Dio on the couch, silent, terrified, being stabbed repeatedly in the chest. Somehow the image did not make sense. "Your watchman finally did hear something, and came to investigate."

"Yes."

"Would you let me speak to him?"

"Of course." Coponius summoned the slave, a sturdy young Greek named Philo, who looked keen enough. I asked him exactly what he had heard on the night that Dio died.

"A noise, coming from this room."

"What kind of noise?"

"A banging kind of noise."

"Not a scream, or a moan?"

"No."

"Splintering wood, cracked hinges?"

"No, more like something being knocked onto the floor."

"When we came in," Coponius interjected, "everything was in disarray. The tables were upended, the chair on its side. The scrolls Dio kept by his bedside were scattered about."

"When you heard the banging noise," I said to Philo, "how quickly did you come?"

"Right away. I heard more noises while I was running down the hallway."

"How did you know where the noises were coming from?"

"As I got closer I could tell that they were coming from inside this room."

"So you tried to open the door?"

The slave hesitated. "Not right away."

"Because you were frightened?"

"No . . ."

"No? I would have been. It takes nerve to open a door with strange sounds coming from the other side, especially in the middle of the night."

"I wasn't scared. Excited in a way, my heart beating fast, but not scared."

"Then why didn't you try to open the door, Philo?"

"I called out Dio's name instead."

"Did he answer?"

"No. There was another banging noise."

"Then you tried the door?"

"Not right away . . ."

"What were you waiting for?"

"For them to finish!" Philo said, exasperated.

"To finish killing Dio?"

"Of course not! For Dio to finish his business, if that's what he was up to." The slave made a face and looked away. "The master knows what I mean."

I looked at Coponius, who looked back at me blandly and pursed his lips. "Philo means that such noises could have meant something besides . . . danger."

"Danger to Dio, anyway," said Philo under his breath.

"That's enough, Philo," said Coponius sharply.

"Get back to whatever you were doing."

The slave left us. I turned to Coponius. "These noises — "

He sighed. "Shortly after Dio came to stay here, he — how shall I say this? — he appropriated one of my slaves for his own use."

I nodded. "The last slave he owned had died tasting his food."

"That's not what I mean." Coponius shook his head. "He was a troubled man, in great distress. If ever a man needed something to take his mind off his problems, it was Dio. There was a young serving girl who caught his eye. He decided to make use of her. For his pleasure. He used her almost every night."

"With your permission?"

"I was never asked, actually. It was presumptuous of Dio to simply take what he wanted, to be sure, but under the circumstances I decided I would be a selfish host if I withheld the use of a slave from a guest, especially since I had no plans to use the girl myself, at least not in that way."

"I see. Then Philo thought he might simply be hearing the sounds of Dio using the girl."

"Exactly."

"All the bumping and thumping — surely you heard it, too."

"Eventually it woke me. At first, I made the same assumption that Philo made. 'At it again!' I thought. I shut my eyes and tried to get back to sleep."

"Did Dio always make so much noise?"

"Not always."

"What on earth would he do to the girl?"

"I hardly see how that's any of your business, Gordianus. I've been indiscreet in telling you as much as I have. May Dio's shade forgive me. I begin to grow tired of this interview — "

"But eventually Philo realized that something was terribly wrong," I said, pressing on.

"Yes. When the bumps and knocks stopped, things got a bit too quiet. He called out Dio's name, louder and louder — I could hear him calling, so Dio should have been able to. I could also hear him rattling Dio's door, which was locked, of course. I got up then and told Philo to fetch some others. They brought torches and together managed to break down the door. Inside we found the shutters open, the room a mess . . . and Dio dead on his couch."

"And the slave girl?"

"She wasn't in the room at all, as it turned out. She was in the slaves' sleeping quarters."

I walked to the window and peered out. "How did the assassins get onto the terrace in the first place? It seems to be surrounded by a high wall."

"They must have scaled it. They couldn't have come in the front because of Philo, and the side walls were set flush against the houses on either side. The wall enclosing the little courtyard out back runs along a little alley. There's a gate in the wall, but it was securely locked. They had to have climbed over from the alley."

I nodded. "It's a high wall — too high for a man to climb without help, I should think."

"Do you want to test that as well?" Coponius raised an eyebrow.

"No. I think we can assume that there were at least two assassins, to help each other over the wall. Did your neighbors see anything?"

"None of my neighbors can see into the courtyard behind the house. The alley is practically unused. I doubt that anyone could have seen anything, unless they happened to be standing on a rooftop, which would have been unlikely on a chilly Januarius night. Besides, if anyone had seen something, I'd have been told. I'm on good terms with my neighbors. They were all quite upset by the murder."

I walked about the room, idly tapping my forefinger against the metal hooks set into the walls. "So the slave girl wasn't with Dio when the murder occurred?"

"As I told you, she was asleep in the slave quarters."

"Could I talk to her?"

Coponius shook his head. "Not possible."

"Why not?"

"I sold her to a slave dealer here in the city."

"Was there something wrong with her?"

Coponius hesitated. "After the use Dio made of her, she was no longer suitable to serve in my house."

"You don't mean she was crippled?"

"Of course not. Oh, a few strap marks and

bruises, perhaps, but nothing that wouldn't fade with time. Possibly a scar or two, but nothing that would show unless she was naked. Nevertheless, she was damaged property. It simply wouldn't do to keep her in the household; much better to pass her on. I'm sure some other master will find her suitable — perhaps even find her value enhanced by the instruction Dio gave her." He shrugged. "I never intended for the girl to become a pleasure slave, but it must have been the will of the Fates."

"Or of Dio." My mouth was dry.

"The subject is distasteful to me," said Coponius. "Indeed, this whole conversation has begun to tire me. I should think that you've already found out more than you need to know."

"More than I intended to, anyway."

"Then perhaps you should be going. Here, I'll summon a slave to show you out." He clapped his hands.

The slave who came running was Philo. Coponius didn't notice. Having dismissed me, his mood abruptly darkened. He didn't even bid me farewell as he walked to the window and gazed out at the sunny courtyard, idly fingering the newly broken latch with one hand.

In the foyer I put my hand on Philo's shoulder and drew him aside. "The slave girl we were talking about — what's her name?"

"Zotica. But she's not here anymore."

"I know. Your master sold her to a dealer. You wouldn't know which dealer, would you?"

The slave hesitated, scrutinizing me. He peered

222

up the hallway and bit his lip. "The master sold her to a man down on the street of the Scythe-makers," he finally said. "I don't know his name."

I nodded. "Let me make sure I understand: when you broke into his room and found him dead, Dio was alone. Zotica wasn't with him."

"That's right."

"What about earlier that night?"

He looked at me and then peered up the hallway again. "Oh, all right, why not tell you? She's gone now, anyway, the poor child. Yes, Zotica was with Dio earlier that night. He came in wearing that ridiculous outfit, dressed up in a stola, if you can believe it, and in a foul mood, even fouler than usual. He snapped his fingers at Zotica and told her to come tend to him in his room. 'To help him take off his makeup,' quipped one of the other serving girls. 'No, just to help him take off!' said one of the others. They were always mean to Zotica because she was the youngest, and the prettiest, but I think they were also glad that Dio had settled on using her instead of them."

"So Dio went to his room and took the girl with him."

"Yes, but later he must have sent her away."

"Why do you say that?"

"The rest of the household had gone to bed. I was standing watch at the front door. I heard something in the hallway and went to have a look. It was Zotica walking up the hall, away from Dio's room. She was naked, clutching her gown and hiding her face in her hands, sobbing."

"Clutching her gown? Why wasn't she wearing it?"

"Why do you think? I figured the old man had ripped it off of her and torn it too badly to wear. I asked her what was wrong, but she just shook her head and ran toward the slave quarters. I figured he'd finished with her early, and been even rougher than usual."

"How long was this before the noise you heard later, when the assassins came?"

"Oh, quite a while before."

"But when you heard those noises and went to investigate, you told me you thought they might have been the sounds of Dio and Zotica . . ."

He shrugged. "I thought she might have slipped back into his room. But she hadn't. When we were breaking down the door to Dio's room, Zotica was off in the slave quarters with the other girls. There's no question about that. She woke some of the slaves with her weeping when she came in, then kept them awake with her sobbing, even when they threatened to beat her. There's no doubt that she was with the other slaves when Dio was stabbed."

"Still, I should dearly like to have a talk with her. Tell me, when you broke into the room, what exactly did you see?"

Philo was thoughtful. "Chair and tables overturned. Window shutters open. Dio on the couch, dead."

"How did you know he was dead?"

"The look on his face!" Philo turned pale, remembering. "Such a look — his eyes and mouth wide open with a look of pure horror, as if he'd seen the face of Cerberus himself."

"Pure horror — and yet you never heard him cry out?"

"Never."

"But to have such a look on his face, he must have known he was under attack, he must have felt the blows. Why did he not scream?"

"I don't know. I only know I never heard him."

"Did you see the wounds?"

"Very clearly. I helped undress him later, when the men from the necropolis came to take him away."

"How many times was he stabbed?"

"Six or seven times, I think. Maybe more. All in the chest, close together."

"How close?"

He held up his palms side by side. "Two hands could have covered the wounds."

"But surely he thrashed about. A frightened man startled from sleep, horrified. He's stabbed the first time — surely he cries out. Surely he thrashes and twists to avoid the next blow."

"Perhaps his arms were held down and his mouth was covered."

"How many men would that take?"

"The room was a mess. Perhaps there was a whole gang of them milling around in there."

"Perhaps. I suppose there was blood everywhere, on the walls and carpet?"

Philo wrinkled his brow. "Not really."

"And the sleeping tunic he wore — that must have been soaked with blood."

"Around the wounds, yes."

"But not — "

"Philo! I thought you were showing Gordianus to the door." Coponius appeared at the far end of the hall. He crossed his arms.

"Yes, Master!"

"There was something I forgot to ask him," I said. "Just a small detail — "

"*Farewell*, Gordianus."

I took a deep breath. "Farewell, Titus Coponius."

Belbo was waiting for me outside the front door, sitting in a patch of warm sunshine. Together we took a silent walk through the streets of the Palatine, breathing in the smells of midday cooking, listening to the noises that echoed up from the Forum. I walked merely to walk, with no particular goal. I needed to think.

I was beginning to discover a side to Dio that I had never guessed at. This disturbed me. I had also begun to piece together the sequence of his final days and hours. The gory drama of his death seemed forthright enough; it only remained to determine who had broken into his room that fateful night. Yet I could not put aside a nagging feeling that something was very, very wrong.

CHAPTER FOURTEEN

"The girl is important. I'm not sure how, but I can't help thinking so."

"What girl?" said Eco.

"The slave girl, Zotica. The one Dio was . . ."

"Important?" said Eco. "But how? If she'd been in the room when the killers broke in, she'd be a witness, though I doubt they would have left her alive. Unless of course she was in on their plan, in which case they'd have had no need to break in the shutters — she'd have let them in. But then they'd have broken the shutters and killed her anyway, to keep her from talking . . . but all this takes away from what we know, which is that the girl was *not* in the room when Dio was killed."

"Still . . ."

I had finally tired of walking and thinking and had gone home for something to eat, to find that Eco and his family had dropped by. While the women and children visited in the garden at the heart of the house, Eco and I sat in the little atrium just off the foyer, basking in a narrow shaft of warm sunlight. I told him all I had learned that morning from my visits to Lucceius and Coponius.

"It's too bad that Cicero's entered the picture,"

said Eco. He shook his head. "Imagine, Cicero taking on Marcus Caelius's defense, after the bad blood between them!"

"There's a lot at stake," I said. "The charges are serious — serious enough to send even a brash fellow like Caelius running back to his old teacher. I'm sure Cicero made him promise to be a good boy from now on and always support the status quo. It must have been quite a coup for Cicero, bringing the errant sheep back into the fold."

"And, provided Cicero gets him off the hook, Caelius will get a chance to betray his old mentor all over again," observed Eco.

I laughed. "Exactly. I suppose the two of them deserve each other."

"Still, too bad it's Cicero for the defense. Even if you do find compelling evidence against Caelius — "

" — Cicero will probably make it go up in a puff of smoke while he takes the judges down some completely irrelevant path to Caelius's acquittal. Yes, I was thinking the same thing myself. Having worked for Cicero, we know just how thoroughly unscrupulous and damnably persuasive he can be. It's not much fun, being on the opposing side."

Eco closed his eyes and leaned back against a pillar, letting the sun warm his face. "But the really bad news is about the slaves in Lucceius's kitchen being sent off to work the mines in Picenum. If Lucceius's wife is right, those two are at the very heart of the matter. If they were bribed to administer poison, they must have some idea of who paid them, or should at least be able to yield up a clue. They're the link in the chain, the ones you need to go to next. But there they are, away up in Picenum, and no matter what they know, it doesn't sound like Lucceius would ever let them testify."

"Yes, it's frustrating. But I suppose someone could trek up to Picenum and try to get at them. Even if they can't testify, they might lead us to someone who could."

Eco half opened one eye and peered at me sidelong. "I have no pressing business for the next few days, and it's always nice to get out of Rome. Just say the word, Papa."

I smiled and nodded. "Perhaps. I suppose it is the next logical step. Still, I keep thinking about the girl . . ."

"The girl?"

"The slave girl, Zotica. I should have a talk with her. She might know something."

"I'm sure she knows a great deal, Papa. But do you really want to hear it?"

"What do you mean?"

Eco peered at me shrewdly, narrowing his eyes in the bright sunshine. "Tell me, Papa, do you want to talk to this Zotica to find what she knows about the murder, which is probably nothing — or do you wish to talk to her to satisfy your own prurient curiosity about the things that Dio did to her?"

"Eco!"

"If she told you that her treatment from Dio was not nearly as cruel as you've been led to think, you'd be relieved, wouldn't you?"

I sighed. "Yes."

"And what if the opposite happened? What if the things that Dio did to her were quite as appalling as you fear, and even worse? I know how you felt about Dio, Papa — the way he died, the fact that he came to you for help. But I also know how strongly you feel about those who abuse slaves in such a fashion."

"Coponius may have been slandering Dio," I said.

"It hardly sounds like it. From the way you tell it, Coponius talked about Dio's bedroom habits only reluctantly, and he was more embarrassed than judgmental, as if he was telling you that Dio was flatulent or snored. And what about the slave, Philo? He told the same story."

"Slaves like to gossip as much as their masters." I shook my head. "I don't like having my memories of Dio tainted by hearsay."

"Ah, but from the girl's lips it wouldn't be hearsay."

"So you think I want to find this girl for no other reason than to put my mind at rest about Dio?"

"Isn't that it, Papa?" His sympathetic gaze made me feel suddenly unsure of myself.

"Partly, yes. But that's not the only reason," I insisted. "There's something else, something I can't quite put my finger on."

"Another intuition from the goddess Cybele, guiding you on?"

"I'm serious. I can't help but feel that this Zotica knows something, or did something . . ."

"Or had something done to her," said Eco under his breath.

"Eco, you said I could call on you if I needed help. This is what I want you to do: find this slave dealer on the Street of the Scythemakers. Find out what became of Zotica."

"Are you sure, Papa? It seems to me that my time would be better spent trying to contact Lucceius's kitchen slaves. And if I'm to do that, I should get started. It will take me a day to get to Picenum, another day to get back, plus the time spent there. Since the trial is only four days away — "

"No, find out about the girl first. You can get started this afternoon. It's too late to leave for Picenum today, anyway."

Eco shook his head at my stubbornness. "Very well, Papa. I'll go and see if I can track down this Zotica for you. If her story is awful enough, I suppose it may save me the bother of needing to go up to Picenum."

"What do you mean by that?"

"Well," Eco began, but he was interrupted.

"If Dio was such a bad man, why are you bothering to find the person who killed him, anyway?"

"Diana!" I turned and saw my daughter standing in the doorway.

"Can't I come and be with you, Papa?" She walked to me and took my hand. Her long straight hair glittered blue-black in the sunlight. "The only thing Mother and Menenia talk about is the twins, and all the twins want to do is pull my hair and scream in my ears. They're such little monsters! I'd much rather be with you and Eco."

"Diana, why did you say that?"

"Because the twins *are* monsters — Titania is a harpy and Titus is a cyclops!"

"No, why did you say what you said about Dio? No one said he was a bad man."

Diana looked at me blankly.

"I think," said Eco, "that someone has been eavesdropping, and for quite a while."

"No I haven't!"

"It's a very bad habit, Diana, especially when your brother and I are discussing business."

"But I told you, I wasn't eavesdropping." She stepped back and crossed her arms, and gave me her version of the Medusa look.

"Diana . . ."

"Besides, Papa, isn't eavesdropping what you and Eco do for a living? I don't see why you should pick on me for doing it, even if I was, which I wasn't."

"It's a matter of showing respect to Papa," said Eco.

"No one in this house seems to have any respect for me," said Diana. "Whenever the monsters come over I might as well be made of stone." She turned and left the room.

"My, my," said Eco. "Is that what it's like to have a thirteen-year-old daughter in the house?"

"Just wait," I sighed.

"Perhaps you've been ignoring Diana."

"I probably have. She's becoming difficult."

"It was the same with Meto, remember?"

"It started later with Meto, and that was different. That I understood, whether I liked it or not. But with Diana, I don't understand. Not at all. She's the only one of you who's actually of my own flesh and blood, but sometimes I think Bethesda created her all by herself."

"She's more like you than you realize, Papa."

"Yes, I'm sure you're right." I tried to remember what we had been talking about, but found myself musing instead on the scent of jasmine that lingered in the warm air. Diana had recently begun to use the same fragrant oil that Bethesda used to scent her hair, just as she had begun to occasionally use her mother's jewelry and scarves. I closed my eyes. I breathed in the fragrance; it might have come from either of them. Diana was becoming so much like her mother . . .

I was interrupted by the sound of a cleared throat. I opened my eyes, blinking at the bright sunshine. "What is it, Belbo?"

"A caller, Master. The little gallus again. He says that you must come with him at once."

"Come with him?" I turned my face back to the sun and closed my eyes again. My legs ached from too much walking. The sunshine was making me sleepy.

"Yes, you must!" piped a familiar voice. I opened my eyes to see Trygonion slipping past Belbo into the atrium. His silver bracelets jangled

233

and glittered in the sunlight, and his red and yellow robes were dazzling. Eco raised his eyebrows. Belbo stamped his foot in frustration.

"Clodia needs you," said Trygonion. "At once! It's a matter of life and death!"

"Life and death?" I said skeptically.

"And poison!" said Trygonion, exasperated. "The monster is planning to poison her!"

"Who?"

"Caelius! Clodia!"

"Trygonion, what are you talking about?"

"You must come at once. There's a litter waiting outside."

I wearily got to my feet.

"Do you want me to come with you, Papa?" said Eco.

"No. I'd rather you got started finding Zotica."

"Take Belbo with you, Papa."

"No need to take along that hulking brute," said Trygonion. "You'll be in the litter. It's well guarded."

"Shall I tell Bethesda you'll be back for dinner?" said Eco, raising an eyebrow.

"Bait me all you like, Eco. I'm not letting you come along," I said. His laughter followed me out of the atrium.

The litter in front of my house was far more impressive than I would have expected even Clodia to send for a mere hireling. The box was draped with red and white striped silk, like Clodia's tent on the Tiber. The poles were of polished oak, borne aloft by a team of bare-chested slaves with oxlike shoulders, dressed in white loincloths and thick-soled sandals. Every one of them was blond — Scythians, perhaps, or captured Gauls from Caesar's conquests. I had seen them before, among the young men cavorting in the river at Clodia's horti. A small retinue of bodyguards stood behind, probably recruited from Clodius's gang. I didn't like the looks of them, which meant they had the right look for a bodyguard.

Trygonion snapped his fingers. With well-practiced efficiency, the bearers lowered the box. A slave put down a block of wood so that we could step inside.

I gestured for Trygonion to enter but he shook his head. "I have business elsewhere. Go ahead, climb in!"

I stepped onto the block and parted the curtains. A mélange of exotic scents issued from within. Jasmine was among them, along with frankincense and sandalwood and more elusive scents — Clodia's smell. The inner draperies were of some heavy, opaque fabric, making the interior of the box seem very dark after the bright sunlight of the street. I was already inside, settling back against the cushions and being lifted aloft, before I realized that I was not alone.

"Thank you for coming." A hand touched my arm. I sensed her presence, smelled her scent, felt the warmth of her body.

"Clodia!"

She stirred beside me. Her leg brushed against mine. She laughed softly and I smelled her breath, warm and moist against my face and vaguely smelling of cloves.

"You sound surprised to see me, Gordianus."

"I thought the litter was empty." As my eyes adjusted to the dimness I saw that there was yet another occupant. Across from us, settled against the cushions at the front of the box, was the auburn-haired handmaiden, Chrysis. She smiled and nodded.

"A woman learns early never to step into a litter without knowing who's inside," said Clodia. "I should think men could profit from the same rule, though the danger may be different."

The ride was impeccably smooth. I parted the nearest curtain and saw that our pace was very quick. From behind us I could hear the sound of the bodyguards trotting to keep up.

"We don't seem to be headed toward your house, Clodia."

"No. What I have to tell you is best discussed away from curious ears." She saw me glance at her handmaiden. "Don't worry about Chrysis. No one is more loyal than she." Clodia extended her leg and touched her bare foot against the slave's. She leaned forward, as did Chrysis. When their faces met Clodia gave the girl a kiss upon the forehead and gently stroked her cheek.

Clodia leaned back. I felt her warmth next to me again. "It's too dark," she murmured. "Chrysis, beloved, open the inner curtains."

The slave girl moved nimbly about the compartment, pulling back the heavy inner curtains and tying them to hooks at each corner. The box remained private, concealed by the translucent red and white striped curtains, which wavered in the breeze. The sounds of the street rose and fell as we swiftly passed by. From time to time the chief of the litter bearers whistled to signal a turn or a stop or a change in pace, but the box never pitched or swayed. A lethargic sense of luxury crept over me, the feeling of being borne effortlessly aloft in a private world from which the squalor of the street was excluded.

The sudden, unexpected nearness of Clodia's body was intoxicating. She was so close that I could see her only in sidelong glances, never all at once; like an object held too close before the eyes, she dominated my senses even while she eluded them. In the filtered glow of sunlight through silk curtains, the flesh of her arms and face appeared as smooth as wax, but radiant with an inner warmth. Her stola was as transparent as the one she had worn before, but was of a different shade, a creamy white the exact color of her flesh. As we passed through dappled patches of sunlight and shadow, the illusion that she was naked was sometimes uncanny, until she moved, whereupon the dress moved with a life of its own, as if the shimmering fabric, provoked by her touch, sought to caress all the hidden places of her body.

The box was suspended so as to stay level when the poles were tilted, but I could tell when we began the sharp descent down the western slope of the Palatine toward the Forum Boarium. The noises from outside grew louder as we passed through the great cattle market. The congested streets forced the bearers to come to numerous stops, and the smells of roasted flesh and live beasts for sale intruded on Clodia's perfume. The spell within the box slackened. I felt as if I were waking from a dream.

"Where are we going?" I said.

"To a place where we can talk privately."

"To your horti on the Tiber?"

"You'll see. Tell me what you discovered today."

As we passed through the cattle market, and then through a gate in the old city wall and into the Forum Holitorium, the great vegetable market, I told her what I had learned at the houses of Lucceius and Coponius. My account was more businesslike and circumspect than the one I had given Eco; she was not paying me, after all, to look into Dio's sexual habits.

"You see why it would be difficult to pursue the charge against Caelius for killing Dio," she said. "The crime couldn't be proved against Asicius, and probably can't be proved against Caelius, though everyone knows the two of them were accomplices. The attempted poisoning is the key. But you're right, Lucceius will never allow his slaves to testify. He'd have them put to death first, rather than lose face at a public trial. What a hypocrite! A true host would want to see a crime against his guest avenged, rather than pretend it never happened." She stirred beside me, and it seemed to me that her body had grown warmer. "I wonder if we could somehow trick Lucceius into selling the two slaves to me?"

"Possibly," I said. "Not likely."

"Then I could compel them to testify. The court would insist that their testimony be extracted by torture, of course, which would take it out of my control . . ."

"Am I here to discuss strategy? Trygonion acted as if there was some terrible crisis at hand. Something about poison . . ." I parted the nearest curtain a bit to catch a glimpse of the marketplace. Vendors were selling plucked chickens and bundles of early asparagus.

Clodia put a finger to her lips. "Almost there."

A few moments later the litter stopped. I thought we had merely come to another congested spot until I felt the box being lowered and Chrysis sprang up to open the outer curtains. She produced a hooded cape which she deftly draped over her mistress as Clodia stepped out of the box. I stayed where I was, uncertain whether I should follow. We appeared to be at the southwestern foot of the Capitoline Hill, on the fringes of the vegetable markets, still very much in the heart of the city. What sort of privacy could such a spot offer?

Chrysis sat back against the cushions. She smiled and raised an eyebrow. "Well, go on! Don't be shy. You won't be the first man to pass through those gates with her."

I stepped from the litter. Covered by her cape, Clodia was waiting, and at my appearance she turned and walked quickly to a high brick wall which appeared to enclose a corner of land against the craggy base of the Capitoline. There was a wooden door in the wall, for which she produced a key. The hinges creaked as she pushed the door open. I followed her inside and she closed the door behind us.

All around us were sepulchers of weathered marble, adorned with plaques and inscriptions, carved tablets and statues. Cypress and yew trees reared up from the jumble of marble. The brick wall shut off the teeming city behind us. The sheer base of the Capitoline loomed before us, with blue sky above.

"There's no more secluded spot anywhere in the city," said Clodia.

"What is this place?"

"The ancient burial ground of the Claudii. It was granted to us back in the days of Romulus when our ancestors moved to Rome from the Sabine lands. We were enrolled among the patricians and given this parcel, just outside the old city boundaries, to be our family burial ground. Over the centuries it's become filled with shrines and sepulchers. Clodius and I used to play here as children, imagining it was a little city all to itself. We hid from each other in the sepulchers and walked down the pathways in make-believe processions. The sepulchers were great palaces and temples and fortresses, and the pathways were broad avenues and secret passages. I could always scare him, pretending to raise the lemures of our ancestors." Clo-

240

dia laughed. "Five years is such a difference be-tween children." She pushed the cape from her shoulders and carelessly laid it atop a stone bench.

The westering sunlight, reflected off the stony face of the Capitoline, cast a faintly orange glow over everything, including Clodia and her shim-mering stola. Trying not to stare, I found myself pondering the wall of a nearby tomb, on which a carved tablet depicted the stained and weathered faces of a husband and wife long dead.

"Then, when I was older, I would come here to be alone," Clodia said. She walked among the monuments, running her hands over the pitted stone. "Those were the bad years, when my father was always away, either exiled by his enemies or off fighting for Sulla. My stepmother and I didn't get along. Looking back now I know that she was sick with worry, but then, I couldn't stand to be in the house with her, so I would come here. Do you have children, Gordianus?"

"Two sons and a daughter."

"I have a daughter. Quintus always wanted sons." There was an edge of bitterness in her voice. "How old is your girl?"

"Thirteen. She'll be fourteen in August."

"My Metella is just the same! Just beginning that difficult age, when most parents are glad to shuttle a girl off into marriage so that she can be-come someone else's problem."

"We've made no plans yet for Diana."

"She's lucky to be home, and lucky to have a father there. Girls need that, you know. Everyone always talks about boys and their fathers. It's only the male children anyone cares about. But a girl needs a father as well, to dote on her, to teach her. To protect her."

She was lost in thought for a long moment, then seemed to wake to her surroundings. She smiled. "And of course, when I got a little older still, I brought boys here. My stepmother allowed my brothers to do whatever they wished, but she was strict with her daughters and with me, or tried to be, though it brought her nothing but grief. Oh, there was many a secret tryst in this place, beneath these trees, on that very bench. Of course, all that ended when my father betrothed me to cousin Quintus," she said glumly.

"And now that you're a widow, do you still bring suitors here?"

Clodia laughed. "What an absurd idea. Why do you ask?"

"Something Chrysis said as I was leaving the litter."

"Naughty Chrysis. She was teasing you, I'm sure. Oh, I suppose the gossips say such things about me — 'Clodia meets her lovers at midnight in the Claudian graveyard! She drags the young men into the sepulchers and deflowers them while her ancestors gasp in shame!' But these days I really much prefer a couch and pillows. Don't you?" She stood sideways and turned her face to look at me straight on. The reflected sunlight seemed to turn her stola to a thin mist that clung to her naked flesh and could have been dispelled

242

with a puff of breath.

I looked away, and found myself nose to nose with a stately basrelief of a horse's head, the ancient symbol of death. Death as departure; death as something more powerful than man. "You were going to explain this talk of poison."

She sat on the bench, using her cape for a cushion. "Marcus Caelius is plotting to murder me before the trial."

She allowed this statement to reverberate for a moment, then went on. "He knows that I have evidence. He knows that I'm planning to testify against him. He wants me dead, and if he had his way, I'd be joining the shades of my ancestors before sundown tomorrow. Fortunately, the slaves whom Caelius thought he could seduce have remained loyal to me, and have informed me of his plot."

"What plot?"

"This very morning Caelius obtained the poison he plans to use. He bought a slave to test it on. The wretched man died in horrible agony while Caelius watched. It took only moments. Caelius wanted a quick-acting poison, you see, and had to make sure it would do the job."

"How do you know this?

"Because I have spies in Caelius's house, of course. Just as he thinks he has spies in mine." She stood up and began to pace. "This was his plot: to have a friend of his meet some of my slaves tomorrow afternoon at the Senian baths and hand over the poison to them, whereupon they would bring the poison home and Chrysis would put it into my food. His agent approached the slaves yesterday, including Chrysis. The slaves pretended to agree, but instead they came to me and told me everything."

"What made Caelius think he could suborn your slaves?"

"Marcus Caelius used to be a welcome guest in my home. He got to know some of the slaves, including Chrysis, rather well — well enough, I suppose, that he thought he could sway them with promises of silver and freedom if they would help him murder their mistress. He underestimated their loyalty to me."

I stared at her, trying to decide whether I should believe her, and found myself studying the shape of her body instead. I shook my head. "So the plot has been uncovered. You've nipped it in the bud. Why all this secrecy? Why tell me about it at all?"

"Because Marcus Caelius doesn't know that his plot has been spoiled. He thinks my slaves have agreed to follow his orders. He still plans to go through with it. Tomorrow afternoon, his agent will arrive at the Senian baths, carrying the little box of poison. My slaves will be there to receive it from him — along with witnesses. We shall seize the poison, expose the agent, produce the evidence in court, and add another count of attempted murder to the charges against Marcus Caelius."

"And you want me to be there?" I said.

She drew close to me. "Yes, to help seize the

poison. To witness everything that happens."

"Are you so sure you can trust your slaves, Clodia?"

"Of course."

"Perhaps they're not telling you everything."

"We all have to trust our slaves in the end, don't we?"

"Then why have you brought me here, away from your house, away from your bodyguards and litter bearers, where even Chrysis can't hear?"

She lowered her eyes. "You see through me. Yes, I can't be certain. No one can ever be certain of anything in this world. Yes, I'm a little frightened — even of my slaves. But for some reason I trust you, Gordianus. I imagine you've been told that before."

With her head bowed and her eyes lowered, I noticed the remarkable line of her eyebrows, like the wings of a bird in flight. Then she turned her face up and all I could see were her deep, luminous green eyes.

"Clodia, you asked me to find evidence that Marcus Caelius tried to kill Dio. Whether you're pursuing this matter for the sake of justice, or for political gain, or simply to hurt Caelius, I don't know, nor do I really care. I agreed to take part for one reason: to do what I can to put Dio's shade at rest. This warfare between yourself and Caelius — broken love affair, festering hatred, whatever — is of no concern to me."

She stepped even closer and looked steadily into my eyes. I felt the heat of her body, as I had felt it in the litter. Her eyes seemed impossibly huge. "Love and hatred have nothing to do with it. Don't you see, Gordianus, it's all tied to Dio's murder. That's why Caelius wants to kill me, not because I loved him once and don't anymore, but because I'm trying to prove what he did to Dio. That's why I want you to go to the Senian baths tomorrow, to help foil his plot against me and expose it for all of Rome to see. This is all a part of the case against Caelius, which is the only way to bring Dio's killer to justice."

I stepped back from her. "The Senian baths," I said ruefully. "I suppose I could do with a hot plunge. At what time?"

A smile barely registered on her lips. "I'll send a litter to take you there tomorrow afternoon. Chrysis will go along, to give you more details on the way." She picked up her cape and handed it to me, then turned so that I could drape it over her shoulders. She leaned back, barely pressing her body against mine. "Oh, and tonight I'll send over the silver you may be needing."

"Silver for what?"

"To buy those two kitchen slaves of Lucceius's, of course, the ones who took part in the plot against Dio. That is, if you're able to track them down. You'll need ready silver if you're to buy them from under the nose of Lucceius's foreman at that mine up north, or bribe him into letting you have them. How much silver do you think that would take? Well, let me know before we part, and I'll send it to you tonight."

"I'll send back a receipt with the same courier," I said.

She pulled the cape about her neck and smiled. "No need for that. I'm sure you'll return any silver that's still unspent after the trial. You see, Gordianus, I really do trust you."

"Would you mind if we took a little side trip?" said Clodia, when we were back in the box and aloft.

"As long as I'm back in time for my dinner," I said, thinking of Bethesda.

"It will take only a few moments. I have an urge to go up on the Capitoline, just to take in the view. The air is so clear today, and the sun will be setting in the west." She nodded to Chrysis, who stuck her head out of the curtains and gave instructions to the chief of the litter bearers.

We passed back through the vegetable and cattle markets, crossed the valley between the Palatine and Capitoline hills, and entered the Forum. The day was waning, but a glimpse outside showed me that the squares were still thronged with men in togas going about their business. I appreciated the privacy of a closed litter — how else could a man cross the busiest spot in Rome side by side with a scandalous woman, without anyone seeing him?

Clodia's entourage did not go unnoticed, however. At one point we crossed paths with some of Milo's gang, who must have recognized the distinctive red and white striped curtains of the box.

"Bring out the whore!" one of them shouted.

"Are you in there with her, Clodius?"

"Wet the bed again and gone running to your big sister?"

"She'll kiss it and make it all better!"

"Or bigger!"

There was a sudden jolt as the litter came to a halt. From outside we heard more obscene taunts, then the sounds of a skirmish. The moment had a peculiar, nightmarish quality; inside the box we were hidden, but also blind to the outside world, so that the obscenities seemed to come from disembodied voices and the scuffling noises were all the more alarming, their causes unseen. I heard the slither of steel pulled from scabbards, then more shouts. Beside me Clodia's body seemed to radiate heat. I glanced at her face, which remained expressionless. I thought I saw her ears turn red, but it might have been a trick of the light within the box.

The litter began to move again, then abruptly stopped.

"Turn it over!" someone shouted.

"Make a bonfire of the bitch!"

Staring straight ahead, Clodia reached for my hand and squeezed it. I gritted my teeth and sucked in a breath. From outside came the sounds of clashing steel, along with yells and grunts.

Finally the litter began moving again and rapidly picked up speed, leaving a chorus of obscene taunts behind us. Clodia stared straight ahead. Gradually she relaxed her grip and let go of my hand. She let out a barely audible sigh, then gave a start when a gruff voice called her name from outside.

"The chief of the bodyguard," she said to me, regaining her composure. She pulled back the curtain. A straw-haired gladiator with a crooked nose trotted alongside the litter.

"Sorry about that," he said. "Nothing to worry about. They got the worst of it. Milo's men won't try a stunt like that again anytime soon!"

Clodia nodded. The man grinned, showing rotten teeth, and Clodia let the curtain drop.

We turned sharply to the left and then to the right again, going up the long steep ramp that ascends to the summit of the Capitoline.

We passed by the chief monuments, the Auguraculum and the great Temple of Jupiter, and headed past the Tarpeian Rock to the less built-up southern end of the hill. The litter came to a stop. Clodia donned her cape and we stepped from the box. The spot was deserted and silent except for the sound of wind in my ears.

The sky above us swirled with the orange and purple clouds of a spectacular sunset. The Tiber was a sheet of gold and the whole western horizon was aflame. "You see?" said Clodia, wrapping herself in her cape. "I knew it would be marvelous!"

I stood beside her, staring at the sunset. She pointed at something directly below us. "If you look straight down, over the edge of the cliff, you can see just a bit of the brick wall that closes off the Claudian burial ground, where we were. You see, there? And just beyond that, the Temple of Bellona, built on the same parcel of land by one of my ancestors, the Appius Claudius who was victorious against the Etruscans two hundred years ago. Instead of holding a triumphal parade, he built a temple at his own expense and dedicated it to the war goddess Bellona, and gave it to the people of Rome to be his monument. Sulla was especially fond of Bellona, you know. He gave her credit for his victories. I remember him once telling Father, 'Thank your ancestor for me, the next time you talk to him, for building Bellona such a fine place to live here in Rome.' "

She smiled and turned her back on the sunset, walking slowly until she came to the opposite side of the hill. Across from us the Palatine loomed with its great jumble of rooftops. A little more to the south the view opened up. In the valley between the Palatine and the Aventine hills lay the vast expanse of the Circus Maximus with its long racetrack. Clodia pointed to the regions beyond. "Over there the Appian Way begins, and runs south all the way to Campania and beyond. And there, crossing the Appian Way, joining the wall for a stretch, is the Appian aqueduct, which has been bringing water into the city for almost three hundred years. These works are the legacy of my family. And those men in the Forum dare to call me such names!"

She stared at the view for a while, blinking as if the wind had blown dust in her eyes, then looked over her shoulder. A stone's throw away was the southernmost of the temples that crowd the Capitoline. "I need to go inside, just for a moment," she said. She strode toward the temple steps and left me behind, wondering whether I had just seen a patrician's pious desire to burn a bit of incense for her ancestors, or a woman's need to hide a sudden burst of tears.

The litter bearers rested. The bodyguards threw dice. Chrysis remained within the canopied box. I shuffled about the paved square in front of the temple, staring at the flagstones. Suddenly I realized which temple it was, the Temple of Public Faith, and remembered the inscription that had been added some time ago to the marble parapet in front of the building.

The inscription wasn't hard to find. In the fading light I read the chiseled letters with a feeling of odd detachment:

PTOLEMAIOS THEOS PHILOPATOR
PHILADELPHOS NEOS DIONYSOS
FRIEND AND ALLY OF THE ROMAN PEOPLE

When all else was said and done, King Ptolemy was the reason behind everything: Dio's journey to Rome and his gruesome death, the Egyptian machinations of Pompey and Clodius and the rest of the Roman Senate, the impending trial of Marcus Caelius. But as the philosophers point out, the single trunk of a tree, so clear to see at its base, becomes increasingly obscure the farther one proceeds into the branches.

I didn't have to look up to know that Clodia had finished her business in the temple and was silently descending the steps toward me. I smelled her perfume.

CHAPTER FIFTEEN

I stepped from Clodia's litter onto the street in front of my house just as the last of the day's light was retreating from the rooftops into the ether. The red and white striped litter departed. The stamping feet of Clodia's bodyguards left a haze of dust in their wake, which made the empty, twilit street even murkier. I rapped on my door, but Belbo was slow in opening it.

Some apprehension — a tap on the shoulder from Fortune, as they say — caused me to glance over my shoulder.

Across the street I saw the figure of a man. He wore a toga, and from his pose he appeared to be standing still and watching me. I turned and rapped on the door again. I tried the latch, just in case the door might have been left unbarred. It had not. I looked over my shoulder again.

The figure had moved closer, into the middle of the street. In the dimness and dust I could make out nothing but a silhouette.

Where was Belbo when I needed him? *No need to take along the hulking brute,* Trygonion had told me when I left the house. *You'll be in the litter. It's well guarded.* Now I found myself alone on my own doorstep, without a bodyguard, without

253

a weapon. I rapped on the door again, then turned to face the man. If I was to be stabbed, I'd prefer to look him in the eye rather than have my back turned. Of course, the man was probably just some passing stranger, I told myself, even as I went through the catalogue in my mind of all those who might want to put a stop to any further investigation into the murder of Dio — King Ptolemy, Pompey, Marcus Caelius, Clodius's enemy Milo, whose gang had just threatened Clodia in the Forum — men notorious for using whatever means were necessary to snuff out their opposition.

The figure drew nearer, taking halting steps. It was the way he walked that frightened me. If he knew me, why didn't he simply walk up to me, or call my name? If he was merely passing by, crossing the street on his way to some destination, why did he approach in such a hesitant fashion?

I suddenly remembered the stalker who had followed us up the Ramp on the previous night, the figure who had abruptly turned and fled back into the darkness.

"Citizen," I said, finding my voice. "Do I know you?"

A puff of wind caused the dust that hung in the air to swirl and disperse. Somewhere far above the earth a bit of cloud caught a dying ray of light and cast a faint glow into the gloomy street, and I caught a glimpse of the stranger's face. Surely not an assassin, I thought. Not with a face like that . . .

Still, my heart began to pound in my chest.

The door rattled. From inside I heard the sound of the bar being lifted. The door swung open and I quickly stepped back, colliding with something and turning to see Belbo smiling down at me sheepishly. "Sorry to take so long, Master. The mistress insisted that I come help her — "

"Never mind, Belbo. Do you know that man?"

"What man, Master?"

The figure had vanished, as quickly and surely as the dust in the air swirled and vanished at the least puff of wind. I peered up and down the street.

"Who was it, Master?"

"I don't know, Belbo. Perhaps nobody."

"Nobody?"

"A stranger, I mean. A man who just happened to be passing by. No one at all."

Even so, later that night I found myself remembering the young man's face — a dark, gaunt face with a scraggly beard and piercing eyes. It was a face marked by some terrible catastrophe, with the kind of look one sees on men of a fallen city, numb with despair except for eyes suffused with a hopeless longing too poignant to bear. The memory of it made me shiver. It was not a face I would care to see again.

I was in time for dinner. Bethesda received my compliments on her ragout of lamb with lentils with a barely perceptible nod and commented that Diana had done most of the cooking.

A courier from Clodia arrived some time later,

bearing the silver she had promised. She must have counted out the coins herself. They smelled faintly of her perfume.

As we prepared for bed, Bethesda asked me how my work was going. Suspecting that Diana had reported everything she had overheard me discussing with Eco, I gave as perfunctory an answer as I could without telling an untruth.

"And what did that woman want with you this afternoon?" she said, unbelting her stola.

"She wanted to hear what I had to report." I said nothing about the alleged new poison plot or Clodia's scheme to send me to the Senian baths.

"That woman has sent you down the wrong path, you know."

"The wrong path?"

"Going after Marcus Caelius."

"But Bethesda, 'everybody knows' that Caelius is involved."

Bethesda let the stola fall and stepped out of it, standing nude for a moment. "You tease me by pretending that I would believe a thing simply because it's gossip. Why? Because I'm a woman? You're the one paying heed to gossip." She reached for her sleeping gown and pulled it on. I tried to imagine her in a gown made of transparent silk from Cos. Bethesda saw the look on my face and softened a bit. "You have no reason to suspect Caelius, only that woman's word for it. It would be a terrible thing for a young man to be punished for a crime he did not commit."

"And if he did commit the crime?"

She shook her head and began to pull out the various pins and clasps that held her hair up. She sat down in front of her mirror at the little table that held her boxes of cosmetics and unguents, and began to brush her hair. She seemed a little surprised but made no protest when I took the brush and began to do it for her. Nor did she protest when I put down the brush and ran my hands over her shoulders, then bent down to press my lips to her throat.

We made love that night with a heat that staved off the chill in the room. I tried very hard not to think of Clodia. I might have succeeded had it not been for her perfume. It had permeated my clothing and my skin. It had gotten onto my hands from touching her silver and thus onto Bethesda. The smell was faint, elusive, insidious. As soon as I would forget about it, lost in the tangle of Bethesda's hair, there it would be again, filling my head and conjuring up images beyond my control.

The next morning Eco came by with news of the slave girl Zotica. The previous afternoon, while I had traversed the city in Clodia's litter, he had made his way to the Street of the Scythemakers and located the slave dealer.

"Zotica is no longer in Rome," he said. "The dealer claims he tried to place her in a rich man's household, figuring he could fetch the highest price by returning her to the type of place she came from. But apparently the marks on her body were a little more apparent than Coponius let on. Nobody wanted her for a serving girl or a handmaiden. The man ended up selling her to another dealer who specializes in pleasure slaves."

"So she ended up in a brothel?"

"Maybe, but not in Rome. The second dealer hemmed and hawed and held out his hand for some coins and finally remembered that he had her sent with a consignment of slaves down to an establishment in Puteoli."

"I'll repay you for the bribe, Eco. Meanwhile, what do you think it would cost to buy such a slave girl?" I produced the little bag of silver that Clodia had lent me.

"Considerably less than that," said Eco. "Where did it come from?"

I explained.

"Clodia is a sharp woman," he said. "More and more I long to meet her. If only my father didn't keep getting in the way."

"Clodia could eat us both for breakfast, suck out the marrow and turn our knucklebones into dice without batting an eye."

"That might be a memorable experience."

"I advise you to stick with Menenia, and also to stick to the subject."

"Then I'll say it again: Clodia is a sharp woman. It's a clever idea, trying to buy those slaves from under Lucceius's nose. Of course, a fellow could get killed trying to do something like that."

"You needn't worry about it."

"Papa, I was joking. Of course I'll go up to

258

Picenum to see if I can find these slaves, and find out what they know. And if it's at all possible, I'll bring them back with me for the trial."

"No, you won't."

"Papa, you're not thinking of doing it yourself?"

"No."

"Then it's up to me. I dread the saddle sores, but Menenia has a treatment for that which I'll look forward to."

"No, Eco, you won't be going up to Picenum. But you can get just as saddle-sore riding down to Puteoli and back."

"Puteoli? Papa, surely you don't want me to go chasing after Zotica instead of finding the kitchen slaves who may hold the key to everything? There's no way that I can do both. Picenum is north, Puteoli is south, and the trial starts in three days. I'll barely have time to get to either of those places and back. It's one or the other."

"Yes. Well, then, it's Zotica."

"Papa!"

"Eco, you must do as I ask."

"Papa, you're letting sentiment cloud your judgment."

"Sentiment has nothing to do with it."

He shook his head. "Papa, I know how your mind works. You think for some reason that it's up to you to redeem this slave girl. Very well — but there'll be plenty of time for that *after* the trial is over. Right now it's those two slaves up in Picenum that we need. That's a dubious enough prospect, given all the complications that could

259

arise, but at least it makes sense. At least it wouldn't be a waste of my time."

"So you think you'll be wasting your time if you go down to Puteoli to find Zotica and find out what she knows."

"Yes, a terrible waste of time, considering how little we have. What could this Zotica possibly know about Dio's death?"

"Find her for me, Eco." I placed the bag of silver in his hands. "Here, I'll prove to you that sentiment has nothing to do with it. If the girl knows nothing, if she has nothing to tell us about who killed Dio, then don't bother to buy her. Leave her where she is. But if she does have something to say, buy her and bring her back with you."

He bit his lips and tossed the bag from hand to hand. "Not fair, Papa. You know that I'll buy her no matter what, to please you."

"As you think best, Eco. Only I'd suggest that you get started. The days are still short, and you're missing the best hours for riding."

In the afternoon a litter came for me, just as Clodia had said.

It was a considerably less conspicuous affair than her grand litter with its red and white canopy. This litter had plain woolen curtains and was just big enough for two people to sit face to face. Belbo joined the handful of bodyguards while I climbed into the box and sat opposite Chrysis, who stared back at me with an enigmatic smile on her face, idly coiling her auburn hair around a forefinger. I found myself thinking that she could not possibly be as young and naive as she looked. The litter rose in the air and began to move.

"So," I said, "exactly what is it that Clodia wishes me to do at the baths today?"

Chrysis stopped playing with her hair and ran the forefinger over her lips as if erasing her smile, leaving an even more enigmatic expression on her face. The gesture reminded me of her mistress.

"It's very simple. Almost nothing, really. You're to wait in the changing room. One of Clodia's men will find you."

"How will I know him?"

"He'll know you. Now, Caelius's agent, the man who's bringing the poison, is named Publius Licinius. Do you know him?"

"I don't think so."

"No matter. Clodia's man will point out Licinius to you when he arrives."

"And then what?"

"Caelius's scheme calls for Licinius to pass the poison to one of Clodia's slaves. But as soon as Licinius hands over the box of poison, some of Clodia's friends are going to seize him and make a public scene. They'll open the box to show everyone what's inside. Then they'll twist Licinius's arm until he confesses what he was up to and who sent him."

"Why should he confess?"

"Some of Clodia's friends are very good at twisting arms. I mean that literally." Chrysis laughed at her own wit.

"What am I to do? I'm a finder, not an arm-twister."

"You're there to witness what takes place."

"Why?"

"Clodia says you have a reputation for being a good observer."

We took a winding path down the eastern face of the Palatine and were soon in the square in front of the Senian baths, jostling for space with all the other litters. "I'll wait here," said Chrysis. "Bring me news as soon as anything happens. And don't do anything naughty with the other boys."

"What do you mean?"

"Please! We know the sort of things you men like to do with each other in the baths." She raised an eyebrow, recalling another of Clodia's gestures.

"Are all the slaves in your mistress's household as insolent as you?"

"Only her favorites." When Chrysis giggled she looked even more like a child.

I walked up the steps, signaling for Belbo to follow.

I paid the attendant in the foyer, who handed Belbo a towel. We walked down a hallway and into the long, narrow changing room with its elaborately coffered ceiling and rows of wooden benches. Patrons came and went in various stages of undress. A number of fully dressed slaves stood idly about, alone or in small groups, waiting while their masters took their plunges. Whenever the heavy wooden door to the bathing rooms opened, from beyond came echoes of conversation and laughter and the sound of lapping water. The distinctive odor of the baths washed over me — a mixture of sweat and steam accented by the tang of wood smoke from the furnaces, with a musty hint of mildew.

I loitered for a bit, waiting for someone to approach me, then began to feel conspicuous in my street clothes. I took off my tunic and handed it to Belbo, who found an empty niche for it among the cubbyholes that lined the walls. I lifted my arms and Belbo wrapped the towel around my waist. I slipped off my shoes and let out a little sigh as my bare feet touched the floor, which was heated to just the right temperature by the hot-water pipes underneath.

"I know that sigh!" said a voice beside me. "Like a poem: the sound a man makes the moment his bare toes settle onto a heated floor."

I turned my head and barely nodded, thinking the man was simply another patron. Then I saw his face.

The look of despair was gone, replaced by a sardonic smile. It was a handsome face despite its gauntness and the scraggly beard, but there was a keenness about his brown eyes that made them hard to look into.

"You were outside my house last night," I said.

"I suppose I was."

That explained it, then — he was Clodia's man, the one I was to meet. Still, why had he followed me up the Ramp and then run away? Why had he lingered outside my house the night before, and then vanished without introducing himself?

"The Senian baths are still the best in Rome," he said, toweling his damp hair. He was naked and still wet from the hot plunge, with wisps of steam rising from his flesh. His limbs were slender and his chest narrow. There was no fat on him at all. I could have counted his ribs and tapped a drumbeat on his hip bones. "They keep the cold water cold and the hot water piping hot. It's close by the Forum, so there's always someone interesting to talk to. But it's not too far from the Subura, so there's usually a bit of trash about to liven things up. Like that lecherous serpent Vibennius."

"Vibennius?"

He nodded toward the opposite side of the room. "See those three fellows over there? Vibennius is that rakish-looking fellow with the fleshy rope hanging down to his knees, leaning against the wall with his arms crossed and nothing to hide. Busy Fingers, he's called, for more than one reason. Look at that smarmy expression on his face — you can tell he's up to something rotten. That's his son, the young fellow with the remarkably hairy buttocks, leaning over at the bench taking off his shoes. Have you ever seen such a woolly bottom? Really, it makes me queasy to look at it, like a beard growing at the wrong end. Appropriate, I suppose, since he uses the hole down there like a mouth. From the way he's flexing and wriggling his buttocks, you'd think he was chewing on something tough. That's obviously what that third fellow has on his mind, the bald sap sitting there on the bench staring at Junior's hairy rear end with that slack-jawed expression. I don't see the point of the towel on his lap, do you? It's not hiding what's on his mind. Like a soldier at attention in a tent! Do you suppose the sap is waiting for a kiss from Junior's bearded lips?"

I looked at the stranger beside me, trying to make out his expression — disdain, amusement, envy? Whatever, his preoccupations seemed far removed from our immediate reason for being at the baths, and I was about to say so, when he gripped my arm and nodded intently. "See there, Junior's finished undressing. He bends over to pick up his shoes — well, really, he might as well make himself into a hairpin. Now he unbends, picks up his clothes, turns to the wall. Do you suppose he really has to stand on tiptoes like that to reach the cubbyhole, or is he just showing off his shapely thighs? The bald sap certainly appreciates the show — oh, Eros, he's actually groping himself! Look at that smirk on Papa Vibennius's face. Now Junior regally strides toward the door to the tubs, arching his shoulders, thrusting out his backside, walking just a bit on tiptoe — could an Egyptian catamite do it better? Sure enough, the sap takes the bait. He's on his feet, heading after those hairy buttocks like a hound trailing a rabbit. He's at the door; he's through the door. And now look at Busy Fingers!"

While we watched, Vibennius looked discreetly right and left, uncrossed his arms, turned around and began rooting about in one of the cubbyholes.

"Oh really, this is too much!" The man beside me threw down his towel and strode across the room. I followed, with Belbo trailing behind.

The man walked up behind Vibennius and tapped him on the shoulder. Vibennius gave a start and swung around with a guilty look on his face.

"Still up to your old tricks, Busy Fingers? Robbing randy bathgoers while your boy leads them on a chase?"

"What?" The man was dumbfounded for a moment, then flashed an uncertain smile. "Catullus! What in Hades are you doing here? I thought you were off playing imperial governor somewhere."

"Somewhere, yes, and sort of. A year in Bithynia under Gaius Memmius was quite enough. I thought he was going to make me rich, but Memmius just took me along to read my poems to him. Couldn't blame him for craving a touch of culture; Bithynia's a hellhole. Couldn't wait to get out of the place; came back early, as soon as the weather allowed. It's so good to be back in a truly civilized place like Rome, where a fellow's likely to get robbed while lusting after a pair of hairy buttocks."

"What are you talking about?" Vibennius giggled nervously and looked about, shifty-eyed.

"Vibennius, you disgust me. For Cybele's sake, leave the poor sap's things alone. What did you expect to find that would be worth taking? His smelly loincloth?"

"Catullus, you jest. I was just looking to make sure that my son put his shoes away. Oh, but that explains it — I must have gotten mixed up. I've been looking in the wrong niche. I wondered why everything looked so unfamiliar!"

Catullus laughed scornfully and shook his head. "Vibennius, I should report you to the management. But they'd probably cut off your busy little fingers and throw them in the furnace, and then we'd all have to suffer the stench. Why don't you go see what your boy is up to? Then the two of you can pull your other bathhouse trick."

"What do you mean?"

"You know, the one where Junior finds a dark corner and grabs his ankles to lure the unsuspecting sap, and as soon as he's got him in a death grip with that bearded mouth, you sneak up behind and start goosing the fellow with your busy fingers, loosening him up for what's to come."

"Catullus, you slander me!"

"On the contrary, Vibennius, your 'massages' are quite famous."

Vibennius crossed his arms and looked smug. "From your foul mood, I'd say you could use a good 'massage,' Catullus."

"Get closer to me with that ugly thing, Vibennius, and I'll tie it in a knot."

"And what if the rope isn't slack enough for tying?" Vibennius smirked.

Catullus stepped toward him. I retreated toward Belbo, expecting blows. Instead Catullus grinned. "Oh, Vibennius, it *is* good to be back."

Vibennius opened his arms. "You wicked goat, how we've all missed your sharp tongue," he said, embracing Catullus and slapping his back.

I blinked, not sure what to make of this display, then gave a start when a hand touched my shoulder. "Gordianus?" said a voice behind me.

I turned and saw the vaguely familiar face of a burly young man with a neatly trimmed beard and soulful brown eyes. It was the way his eyebrows grew together into a single line that jarred my memory — he was the slave who had answered Clodia's door. He stood before me fully dressed and slightly out of breath. "Barnabas," I said. "Hebrew for 'consolation.' "

"That's right." He nodded and lowered his voice. "Chrysis said you were already here. Publius Licinius is on his way now, with the box."

I frowned. "You're the one I'm supposed to meet?"

"Yes."

"Then who — ?" I turned toward Catullus and caught just a glimpse of his enigmatic grin before Barnabas pulled me back and hissed in my ear. "Licinius just walked in! Come with me." He took me by the arm and led me across the room with Belbo lumbering behind. "In the green tunic," Barnabas whispered.

The young man did look familiar, though I had never met him — I had seen him in the Forum, and walking through the streets of the Palatine in the company of Marcus Caelius. He was nervously glancing from side to side and fiddling with something in his hand.

"We part now," whispered Barnabas. "Just stand aside and watch. Make sure you keep your eyes on the pyxis!" By this he meant the tiny box Licinius carried in his hand, one of those elaborately decorated containers with a hinged lid and a latch, so favored by ladies for keeping their powders and unguents — and by poisoners for keeping their poisons. The pyxis Licinius carried appeared to be made of bronze with raised knobs and inlays of ivory. He turned it over and over in his palm.

Licinius spotted Barnabas and sighed with relief. He stepped forward to meet the slave, but Barnabas signaled with a nod that they should withdraw to a corner of the room. As Barnabas turned, his eyes very briefly met mine, making sure I would follow. I glanced over my shoulder, wondering where Catullus and Vibennius had got to, but I couldn't find them in the throng of clothed and naked flesh. The dressing room suddenly seemed to have gotten considerably more crowded.

Barnabas arrived at the corner and turned. Licinius reached him and began to extend his hand, obviously eager to pass along the pyxis. Then the mad scramble and the shouting began.

Since I had arrived in the changing room I had been studying the crowd, trying to spot Clodia's arm-twisters. I had marked down several likely candidates, judging by their brawniness, and sure enough, these were among the men who suddenly rushed Licinius. But there were more of them than

I would have expected, at least ten. Among them, to my surprise, was the busy-fingered Vibennius.

They moved to apprehend Licinius the moment the pyxis changed hands, but their timing was premature. Someone shouted an instant too early, or someone bolted toward the box before he should have, or perhaps Licinius was simply so nervous that he froze in midtransaction and panicked before the box reached Barnabas's hand. Whatever the exact sequence of events, the pyxis was never handed over. It remained in Licinius's possession as he wheeled about in alarm and began to dodge and dart around the room, slipping through the grasp of his would-be captors. I caught a glimpse of his face and thought I had never seen a man who looked so much like a rabbit, and a frightened rabbit at that. But the pyxis remained tightly grasped in his white-knuckled grip.

The brawny arm-twisters would have made persuasive captors, but what they had in muscle they lacked in agility. Arms closed on empty air as the rabbit scurried by. Heads banged together as Licinius slipped through their pincers. It was like a comic scene performed by mimes, but more elaborately choreographed than anything I'd ever seen on a stage.

The rabbit made for the main exit, but the way was blocked.

"Hand over the pyxis!" someone shouted.

"Yes, the pyxis!"

"Hand it over!"

"Poison! Poison!"

The bystanders witnessing this spectacle wore various expressions of confusion, outrage and mirth. Some seemed to think it was merely a game, while a few scrambled for safety under the wooden benches. In the throng I spotted the sharp-tongued Catullus, who watched with wide-eyed surprise.

Licinius, unable to get out through the blocked entrance, wheeled about and headed for the un-guarded door into the bathing rooms. Just as he reached it, the door was opened by an old man draped in a towel. Licinius knocked him to the floor. With a great whoop, Clodia's arm-twisters followed, leaping over the old man like hounds over a log.

"Damnation!" muttered Barnabas as he rushed by me, grabbing my arm.

We followed in the rabbit's wake, past a giant tub full of shouting and laughing bathers. One of the arm-twisters had fallen on the wet floor and kept slipping as he tried to get up. We angled past him and ran through another door into the innermost room, where the air was thick with steam from the hot pool. Confusion reigned as a tumult of splashing and a chorus of shouts echoed through the dimly lit room.

"Block the door! He'll try to slip back out!"

"Poison!"

"Don't let him throw the pyxis into the pool!"

"Did someone say 'poison in the pool'?"

"Poison? Let me out!"

There was a great deal of running and slipping and colliding as the arm-twisters tried to find

Licinius. Some of them stepped into the piping-hot pool with hisses of discomfort and poked about.

"He must be here!" said Barnabas. "The door's blocked and there's no other way out."

"Of course there is," I said, pointing to a dark corner. "The door to the furnace room."

Barnabas groaned and ran to pull the door open. Sweltering air poured out from the dark passage beyond. Barnabas took a few hesitant steps, tripped against something and let out a gasp. "Hades! A corpse!"

There was something in the darkness at his feet, but not a corpse, unless corpses have two heads and writhe about.

"Get lost!" moaned one of the heads.

"Go find your own!" wheezed the other.

Barnabas gave a start. "What — ?"

"It's woolly-bottom and the bald sap!" I said.

This meant nothing to Barnabas, but he caught on quickly enough. "Did someone else pass this way?"

"Yes," gasped one of the voices. "The idiot stepped on my hand! He'll have passed through the furnace room and be out in the alley by now. So — if you don't — mind — "

Barnabas groaned.

The writhing figures on the floor thrashed, gasped and bleated in ecstasy.

I pulled Barnabas back into the bathing room and shut the door behind us. Now the farce had everything, including a climax.

PART THREE

NOX

CHAPTER SIXTEEN

Chrysis fretted all the way back to Clodia's house. She insisted that I come along to explain what had happened. I think she was afraid to break the bad news to her mistress alone.

The litter bearers turned down the little cul-de-sac, with the bodyguards and Belbo following behind, and deposited us in front of the house. Belbo and I waited on the red and black tiled door-step, looking up at the towering cypress trees on either side while Chrysis rapped on the door and then clutched my hand to draw me inside. Belbo followed.

"What do you mean, she's not here?" I heard her say to the slave who opened the door.

"She's gone off," said the old man. "I don't know where."

"For what? For how long?"

He shrugged. "Nobody tells me anything. But — "

"Surely she didn't decide to go down to the Senian baths herself," mumbled Chrysis, nipping at a fingernail. "No, she would have seen me. Unless we passed each other on the way. Oh, Attis!" Chrysis made a little yelp of frustration. "Wait here," she called to me as she disappeared down a hallway. "Or in the garden," she added, waving

275

vaguely toward the center of the house.

While Belbo stayed in the foyer, I walked through the atrium beyond, down a wide hallway, through a colonnaded archway and finally down a short flight of steps into the open air and sunlight. The garden was square, surrounded by a covered portico. There was a low platform at the opposite end, which appeared to be a stage, for behind it was a wall painted with a jumbled cityscape, like a theatrical backdrop. In front of the platform there was a small lawn with room for several rows of chairs. At each of the four corners of the garden were cypress trees, taller than the roof. In the center of the garden was a small fountain with a statue of a naked Adonis. Bronze fish beneath his feet emptied water into the pool from their gaping mouths. I walked closer to have a look at the mosaics that lined the bottom. Beneath the splashing water the images of dolphins and octopi quivered against a shimmering field of blue.

The Adonis was captured in the act of kneeling — knees bent, upraised palms extended, his face turned upward with a radiant expression. It was obvious to whom he was showing obeisance, for on the stairway which I had just descended, atop a high pedestal looking out over the whole garden, was an enormous bronze statue of Venus, even more magnificent and more opulently detailed than the one which decorated Clodia's horti on the Tiber. The goddess was naked above the waist; the folds of cloth gathered about her hips seemed frozen in the act of fluttering to the ground. The curves of her body were sumptuous, and the painted bronze gave the illusion of pliant flesh, but the size of the statue was out of scale, disconcertingly large, more intimidating than beautiful. Her hands were captured in gestures of eloquent tenderness, more motherly than erotic, but this was at odds with her face, which was strangely impassive, severe in its beauty. Her unblinking lapis lazuli eyes stared down at me.

As I stood before the fountain, studying the Venus from Adonis's point of view, I began to notice the echoing sounds of chanting and music from somewhere nearby, rising and falling and obscured by the splashing of the fountain, but now growing abruptly louder and faster. I heard the piping of flutes, the rattling of tambourines and the jangling of bells, along with a strange ululation that was nothing like normal singing. I thought I heard words, but the splashing fountain kept me from making them out. The music grew louder, the tempo accelerated. I stared at the face of Venus. The longer I looked into her lapis lazuli eyes the more it seemed as if the statue might actually move or speak. She blinked — or I blinked — and I felt a sudden tremor of apprehension. I was not alone.

But it was not the goddess who had joined me. The voice behind me was decidedly masculine. "They're at it again!"

I turned around to see a man on the low stage, dressed in a toga. He had been naked the last time I saw him.

"Every year it's the same." Clodius shrugged and made a face. "If I were Clodia, I'd complain, but I suppose my dear sister is too fascinated by the galli to want to stop their fun. And it *is* only once a year."

"What's only once a year?"

"The Great Mother festival, of course. The Temple of Cybele is just over there," Clodius said, pointing behind him. "The House of the Galli is right beside it. For days before the festival they practice, practice, practice. It all sounds hopelessly wild and discordant to a Roman ear, doesn't it? And the singing — hardly better than screaming. But then, I'd scream too if they'd cut my balls off." He hopped off the stage onto the lawn and sauntered toward me. "You know, it's absurd, but I've forgotten your name."

"Gordianus."

"Oh yes. Clodia's new man, the one to get the goods on Marcus Caelius. Been busy?"

"Busy enough."

"Clodia's not here at the moment. Some errand or other. The door slave should have told you. He's getting old."

"He did say something, actually. But Chrysis suggested I wait here."

"I see. Oh, that's right, today was to be the little drama down at the Senian baths. How did it go?"

"That's why I came. To tell Clodia."

He stared at me with green eyes uncannily like those of his sister. "And? What happened?" When

278

I hesitated, he scowled, which made his face impossible to read. Was he feigning boyish petulance, or showing genuine anger? The scowl did nothing to spoil his good looks; it merely rearranged them. "Oh, I see," he said. "You're here to report to *Clodia,* not to me. She said you were the loyal type. Rare enough in Rome these days. But my sister and I have no secrets from each other. No secrets at all. And I should hope you have nothing to hide from me, Gordianus. I've certainly hidden nothing from you." He gave me a knowing look. When I said nothing, he laughed. "That's a joke. About what I was wearing the day we met." He shook his head. "She also said that you have no sense of humor."

"You seem to have discussed me at length."

"My sister likes to get my opinion of the men she's dealing with. She could use some advice! Clodia hasn't always exercised the best judgment, choosing whom to trust. As in the case of Marcus Caelius, which brings us back to the Senian baths. How did it go? Here, we'll sit on the bench in the shade, and if we're lucky Chrysis will come walking by and I'll send her for some wine."

As we sat I noticed that another man had stepped onto the stage, a giant whose face glinted like a broken shard of ebony in the sunlight. He leaned against the painted wall with his arms crossed, watching us from a distance. He was incredibly ugly, with a bullish neck and enormous arms. Beside him Belbo would have looked like a child. He curled his upper lip in a snarl that made my blood turn cold.

Clodius saw my reaction and glanced over his shoulder. "That's the Ethiop. Clodia gave him to me last year. Goes everywhere I go. Keeps an eye on me. The loyal type, like you. A couple of months ago, one of Milo's men came up to me in the Forum and waved a knife at me. He never saw the Ethiop coming — don't let his size fool you, he's fast as lightning. The Ethiop grabbed the fellow from behind and broke both of his arms, just like that." Clodius snapped his fingers twice. "No one's threatened me in the Forum ever since. But don't worry, he's completely harmless to my friends. Oh, that noise! If those galli aren't mad already, they'll surely drive each other crazy by nightfall. Can you imagine being in the same room with them? What sort of goddess would want to go into a temple with such a racket going on? Now, about the baths . . ."

I told Clodius about the farce I had witnessed. He listened in silence, making expressions of disgust and amusement. "So Licinius got clean away?" he finally said.

"Yes."

"And the pyxis with him?"

"I'm afraid so."

He sneered. "I wish I'd been there. I'd have grabbed Licinius by the balls and squeezed until he croaked out everything he knew. Then I'd have stuffed the poison down his throat, pyxis and all. Hung the corpse up by the heels and dragged it into the trial that way — an exhibit for the prosecution! You want evidence, Cicero? Here's our evidence!"

Up on the stage, the Ethiop heard the anger in his master's voice and looked at me as if mulling over which arm to break. I shifted uneasily on the bench. "I suppose your sister will be quite displeased."

Clodius's demeanor changed in the blink of an eye. He laughed. "Don't count on it. She adores a bit of drama, you know. Loves comedy even more. Well, just look at what she's done to this garden. Made it into her private theater so she can bring in mimes from Egypt to amuse her friends, and host recitals for whatever poet has caught her eye lately. No, once Clodia has thrown a priceless vase or two across the room and given a few slaves a good beating, I think she'll see the humor in it. Well, look who's here — and just when my throat was getting dry."

Chrysis appeared at the top of the steps, beneath the Venus. When she saw us she began to turn back, but Clodius clapped his hands and waved her over.

"Chrysis, darling, bring us some honeyed wine — I'm in the mood for something sweet. And perhaps some dates. And some of those little seed cakes that Clodia's cook always keeps in the kitchen. Will that suit you, Gordianus?"

I nodded.

"Will that be all?" said Chrysis, lowering her eyes.

Clodius growled. "Don't tease me, little one."

"I don't intend to tease you," said Chrysis, keeping her head bowed.

"Harpy! Go on and fetch the wine, before I grab you and ravish you right here, in front of the guest. Or better yet, I'll put the Ethiop to the job and Gordianus and I will watch while the two of you make a baby up on the stage." Chrysis turned pale and quickly departed. "So young," Clodius murmured, gazing after her. "That auburn hair, that pale flesh. Delicious — I should like to pour honeyed wine all over her and lick it up. But Clodia forbids it. Won't let me touch the girl. I suppose she thinks it would spoil her. Or maybe Chrysis is in love with another of the slaves; Clodia is sentimental that way. Anyway, I keep my hands to myself. My sister and I always respect one another's property."

I noticed that the chanting of the galli had stopped for a moment. Suddenly it started up again with shrill piping and a clashing of cymbals. Clodius made a face. "Well, I suppose we can somehow work around the loss of the pyxis," he said, gazing abstractedly at the statue of Adonis. "This crazy attempt to poison Clodia is just further corroboration of the charge that Caelius tried to do the same to Dio at Lucceius's house. He used Clodia's money to buy the poison and bribe Lucceius's slaves, she came to suspect him, and now he's trying to stop her from telling what she knows by poisoning *her*. A reckless, desperate man — that's the picture we'll paint for the judges. Clodia says you've tracked down some slaves that Lucceius has hidden away in a mine somewhere."

"Perhaps."

"Didn't she give you some silver, in case you're able to find these slaves and buy them?"

"That was mentioned," I said uneasily. "It may not yield anything worthwhile."

"It had better. We need stronger evidence. It's our job, you see, Clodia's and mine, to get the goods on Caelius concerning the poison attempt on Dio. Others are concentrating on the crimes Caelius perpetrated against the Egyptians on their way up to Rome. Let's hope they've come up with something stronger. Witnesses! That's what we need. Credible witnesses — we could walk through the Forum right now and find ten men who'd swear to Caelius's guilt, but they'd be about as reputable as a drunken general; bad witnesses merely water down a good oration. The strongest thing in our favor is the thought that's on everyone's mind: if Marcus Caelius didn't murder Dio, who did?"

"I've been pondering that myself."

"We don't want the judges to ponder too much. They might come up with someone else!" Clodius smirked.

"You don't believe Caelius is guilty?"

"Of course I do," he said sharply. "You really don't have a sense of humor, do you?"

"How is it that you're both involved in this affair, you and your sister?"

"We each have reasons to want to see Marcus

Caelius get what he deserves. As do you."

"I?"

"Caelius murdered your old teacher. Isn't that why you're here? Your reason is personal, like Clodia's. Mine is political. Each has his own incentive. What do the judges care?"

I nodded. "What I mean is, do you and your sister do *everything* together?" The double meaning struck me as soon as I spoke, which was too late to call back the words.

"I believe that our wine and seed cakes have arrived," said Clodius.

Chrysis descended the steps bearing a tray, followed by another slave who carried a folding table. While they set the food and drink before us, the chanting from the House of the Galli stopped for a moment, then resumed at a different pitch and tempo. The priests were singing a new song, if indeed the keening noises constituted a song.

Clodius sipped from his cup and looked thoughtful. "I never drink honeyed wine without thinking of the bad old days."

"The bad old days?" Clodia had used a similar phrase.

"After Papa died. The lean years. We were expecting him to come home from Macedonia with wagons full of gold, and instead he left us saddled with debts. Well, that sort of crisis can happen even in the best families. A good thing in the end: it sharpened our wits. You do what you must. You prove to yourself that you can get by on your own, and you're never afraid of the world again.

It made us closer; we learned we could depend on each other. Clodia was the oldest, and the keenest. Like a mother to the rest of us."

"You already had a mother."

"Clodia was closer than a mother. At least to me she was." He gazed into his cup. "But I was talking about the honeyed wine. We were poor, you know, but the dinner parties never stopped. That was our investment in the future, those dinner parties. My sisters needed husbands. My older brothers needed to launch their careers. And so the dinner parties, every night. For the guests, honeyed wine. But not for us. Into our cups the slaves would secretly pour the cheapest wine. We drank it with a smile. The guests were fooled, and never knew that we couldn't afford honeyed wine for everyone. That was excellent training for a career in the Forum, learning to put on a pleasant face even when something disagreeable is going down your throat."

He put the cup to his lips and drank. I did the same. "The wine is excellent," I said. "But if your sister isn't here, there's really no reason for me to stay."

He shrugged. "She may come back at any moment."

"Where is she?"

"Probably gone to her horti, or off to visit someone. She took Metella with her."

"Her daughter?" It seemed hard to imagine Clodia as a mother, or to imagine what her daughter would be like.

"My dear niece. Willful, like her mother. But also beautiful, like her mother. And she adores her uncle."

"Like her mother does?"

He took a bit of seed cake. "Perhaps not quite that much. Damnation, they've started singing again!"

"I think I'm getting used to it," I said. "There's one phrase they keep repeating that's rather pretty. There, that's it." The music floated above our heads.

Clodius laughed and shook his head. "Watch out, or the next thing you know you'll have a strange urge to run off to Phrygia to have your balls lopped off." He poured himself another cup and insisted on pouring another for me.

The wine spread through me with a delicious warmth. "As long as I'm here, there is something I should ask you," I said.

"Go on."

"A few days ago I was out after dark and noticed someone following me. I think I spotted the same man outside my house last night, and today he spoke to me at the baths. I'd decided he was one of Clodia's men, but then found I was mistaken. Would you know anything about it?"

"About a man following you? No."

"You seem to be rather protective of your sister. I thought perhaps — "

"That I'd have you followed, to investigate my sister's hireling? Don't be ridiculous. I offer Clodia advice when she asks for it, but she deals with whomever she chooses. I have no control over her associates, friends or lovers. What did this fellow look like?"

"Young — not quite thirty, I'd say. Medium height. Slender, dark. A scraggly beard, but he's just back from a trip; maybe he was at the baths to have it shaved. Good-looking, in a hungry sort of way. His eyes — there's something sad about them, almost tragic. But today at the baths he seemed anything but sad. Sharp-tongued."

Clodius looked at me curiously. "Did he tell you his name?"

"No, but I overheard someone call him — "

"Catullus," said Clodius.

"How did you know?"

"There's only one: Gaius Valerius Catullus. So he's back already?"

"His friend at the baths said something about him returning early from a government post out East."

"I knew he'd hate it. Catullus loves Rome too much. Those country boys always do, once they've gotten a taste of the big city."

"He wasn't born in Rome?"

"Hardly. From some backwater up north; Verona, I think. Clodia met him the year Quintus was governor of Cisalpine Gaul and they were stuck up there."

"Then there *is* a connection between Clodia and this man Catullus?"

"There used to be. That was finished before Catullus left Rome last spring. Finished on Clodia's side, anyway. You think he was following you?"

"Yes. Any idea why?"

Clodius shook his head. "He's a strange one. Hard to make out. No interest in politics; thinks he's a poet. Clodia thought so too; half of his poems were about her. Women love that sort of crap, especially from fools like Catullus. The sort who bleeds from love; a walking hemorrhage, and bitter about it too. I remember him reciting from this very stage one summer night, standing where the Ethiop is standing now, with the beautiful young poets and their starry-eyed admirers gathered around, crickets chirping, moon above. He'd lull them with words like honey, then stir the pot and show them the worms at the bottom. Self-righteous, foul-mouthed, long-suffering. He even made one about me."

"A poem?"

Clodius's jaw tightened. "Not much better than the doggerel Milo's gang comes up with, and considerably nastier. So he's back? Clodia will hear from him soon enough, I imagine. If you catch him following you again, my advice is to give him a good blow to the jaw. He's no fighter. His tongue is his weapon. Good for making insults and poems, and not for much else, according to my — according to those who have reason to know. Look, this little bit of food has only made me hungrier, and the sun's getting low. I'm not leaving until I see Clodia. Stay and haye a proper dinner with me."

I hesitated.

"I told you, she may show up at any moment. She'll want to know exactly what happened at the baths, from your lips. If I try to tell her, I'll either get angry and choke or else laugh in all the wrong places."

Slaves came to clear away the wine and cakes. I asked one of them to fetch Belbo from the foyer. He came lumbering down the steps, peering up at the monstrous statue of Venus with a proper expression of awe. Then he spotted the Ethiop across the way. The two of them flexed their shoulders, dilated their nostrils and exchanged suspicious glances.

"Yes, Master?"

"Take a message to Bethesda," I told him. "Tell her I'll be dining elsewhere tonight."

"Here, Master?"

"Yes, here, at Clodia's house." I winced, realizing how it would sound to Bethesda. If she only knew that I was dining alone with another man to the sound of singing eunuchs, with a giant Ethiop playing chaperon!

"And then shall I come back, Master?"

Before I could answer, Clodius raised his hand. "No need, Gordianus. I'll see that you get home safely."

He gave me a cool look, challenging me to show distrust. I shrugged and nodded. "No need to come back afterward, Belbo," I said. "I'll find my way home."

Belbo cast a final suspicious glance at the Ethiop, then turned, craning his neck to take in the full, frightful splendor of the Venus as he walked up the steps.

Twilight fell. With a mad crescendo of tambourines and shrill piping, the chanting of the galli abruptly ceased. A serene silence followed.

"Well," said Clodius, "I suppose even eunuchs have to eat. It's a warm night. Now that the racket's over, shall we stay in the garden to eat?"

Couches were brought, along with lamps. The dinner was simple but exquisite. Clodia's pleasures apparently included those to be had from owning a fine cook. It was a meal to be eaten slowly and savored, accompanied by leisurely conversation.

"The galli!" said Clodius, sipping noisily at his fish soup. "What do you know about the cult of Cybele, Gordianus?"

"Not a lot. I sometimes see the galli in the streets on the days of the year when they're allowed to go begging in public. I've heard the invocations to Cybele at the Great Mother festival. And of course I've met your sister's friend Trygonion. But I've never heard anything like the music I heard here this afternoon."

"The cult has been in Rome a long time, yet most people don't know much about it. It's an interesting story, how Cybele first came to Rome."

The wine and food had put me at ease. I was almost able to forget the glowering presence of the Ethiop, who stood cross-armed on the stage and watched us eat. "Tell me."

"It happened back in the days when Hannibal

was rampaging through Italy, and no one could drive him out. The College of Fifteen Priests consulted the Sibylline Books, and found an oracle: if an invader should take root in Italy, the only way to expel him would be to bring the Great Mother goddess to Rome from her shrine in Phrygia. At that time King Attalus ruled Phrygia, and happened to be our ally. Still, the goddess herself had to be consulted. When her Phrygian priests put the question to her, she shook the earth and told them, 'Let me go! Rome is a worthy place for any deity!' So King Attalus agreed to make a gift of the statue of Cybele, along with the great black rock which fell from the sky at the dawn of time and first inspired men to worship her."

"How do you know all this?" I said.

"Gordianus, you impious man. Don't you know that I'm a member of the College of Priests? I'm privileged to look at the Sibylline Books. I sit on the committee that regulates the galli and the worship of the Great Mother. Which is fitting, since there's a family connection going all the way back to Cybele's arrival in Rome."

"You mean the tale of Claudia Quinta," I said.

"You know the story?"

"Only vaguely, and never as told by one of the great woman's descendants."

Clodius smiled. "The ship bearing the sky-stone and the statue of Cybele arrived at the mouth of the Tiber and sailed inland to Rome, attended by great crowds along the riverbank. But when the ship pulled alongside the dock to unload its divine cargo, it sprang a leak and began to founder. The dignitaries on the dock were thrown into a panic. Just imagine: a group of politicians out for a day of impressing the masses suddenly find themselves in the midst of a catastrophic omen — the Mother Goddess sent to save Rome from Hannibal is about to sink into the Tiber! More honeyed wine?"

"Not for me."

"A bit more, surely." He gestured to one of the slaves to fill my cup. "Anyway, it was my ancestress Claudia Quinta who saved the day. Only the purest virgins and most upstanding wives were allowed to welcome the Great Mother to Rome, and there had apparently been some grumbling about letting Claudia Quinta take part in the ceremony. Something about her loose morals and the bad company she kept — does this sound like someone we know? But that day she was vindicated. She stepped forward and seized the mooring rope, and miraculously the ship began to rise again. Thus Cybele showed her divine approval of Claudia Quinta. The pious say this proved her purity. Of course, when you actually picture the scene — a woman reaching out and grasping a slick rope, the big boat bobbing up like a swollen wineskin — well, Claudia Quinta must have had an amazingly skillful touch.

"The mud-spattered sky-stone and the statue were unloaded from the ship and cleaned up — the ritual bathing of the statue is still a part of the annual festival. The Temple of Cybele was built here on the Palatine and dedicated with great

292

ceremony, with Claudia Quinta as the guest of honor. Just as the oracle had promised, Hannibal was driven from Italy. And today, generations later, we have to put up with the singing of the galli here in Clodia's garden!

"What must they have thought, our staid, dour ancestors, when they got their first look at the Phrygian priests who arrived with Cybele, with their outlandish costumes and jewelry, their long bleached hair and high, lisping voices? Or when they saw how the priests worshiped Cybele, with whirling dances and wild frenzies, and secret ceremonies in the middle of the night? Or when they learned that the consort of the Great Mother was a beautiful, castrated youth called Attis? Not the kind of consort to give a female much pleasure, I should think. Perhaps Cybele prefers a woman with a skilled hand, like Claudia Quinta. I prefer Venus myself. There's no ambiguity about what Venus wants from Adonis, is there?" He gazed up at the towering statue. "When they got a taste of what the Great Mother's cult was *really* like, our stern, stiff-jawed ancestors must have felt rather queasy.

"But then, Rome has a way of gobbling up anything that lands on her plate and shitting it out as something acceptably Roman — art, customs, habits, even gods and goddesses. That is Rome's genius, to conquer the world and adapt it to her convenience. The cult of Cybele was simply cleaned up for popular consumption. The Great Mother festival is just like every other festival, with plays and chariot races and animal shows in the Circus Maximus. None of those inscrutable rites that Cybele's followers practice in the East — ecstatic riots by worshipers in the streets, all-night vigils of men and women together in the temple, the chosen faithful crawling through tunnels that drip blood. We Romans don't care much for that sort of thing, whatever the religious pretext. And no mention, ever, of Attis! We'd rather not think about the castrated lover. So the official celebration of Cybele became another chance for state priests and politicians to put on plays and circuses for the people. Of course, what the galli and their inner circle of worshipers do behind closed doors is another matter . . . Oh, I don't believe it!"

With a shiver of tambourines, the music had recommenced.

"They must have finished their dinner and now they're at it again," said Clodius glumly. "Do you suppose they eat like normal men?"

"Trygonion showed a hearty appetite the night he ate at my house."

"When was that?"

"When he came with Dio, asking for my help. The night of the murder."

"Ah, yes. When he talked the poor old man into playing dress-up with him. Clodia told me about it. Dio, going out in a stola — it's too painful for me to imagine. That's Trygonion, longing to be something he's not and pulling others into his fantasy world."

"The gallus seems to have a curious relationship with your sister."

Clodius smirked. "Another example of Clodia's questionable judgment. Like Catullus, like Marcus Caelius."

"You're not saying that she and Trygonion . . . ?"

"Don't be stupid. But in some ways he's no different from the men who've come and gone in this house with their balls intact: they all let Clodia treat them like slaves — for a while, anyway. We haven't seen much of Trygonion lately. He's busy preparing for the festival with the other galli. That might be him we hear now, blowing on his flute." He frowned. "You don't suppose Clodia could be over at the House of Galli, concocting some sort of entertainment for her party?"

"Her party?"

"Clodia always throws a party on the eve of the Great Mother festival. It's the first social event of the spring. Three nights from now."

"But that's the opening day of the trial."

"Purely by coincidence. One more reason to celebrate, if all goes well. This garden will be full of people, and up on the stage — well, every year Clodia has to outdo herself. Maybe this year Trygonion will play his instrument for us." He laughed crudely. "I won't be able to come. I got myself elected aedile this year, so I'm in charge of overseeing the official events of the festival — too busy for pleasure. I'll probably have to miss the trial as well. Too bad. I should like to watch Caelius squirm. I love a good trial." His green eyes glittered. In the lamplight he looked uncannily like his sister. "I even enjoyed my own trial. You remember that, don't you, Gordianus?"

"I wasn't there," I said cautiously. "But I think that everyone remembers the Good Goddess affair."

He drank deeply of the honeyed wine. "From that ordeal I learned three things. First, never trust Cicero to back you up. Stab you in the back, more likely! Second, when bribing a jury, account for a comfortable margin of victory. You'll sleep better the night before. I did."

"And third?"

"Think twice before putting on women's clothing, for whatever reason. It did me no good at all."

"It did Dio no good either," I said.

Clodius made a dry little laugh. "Perhaps you have a sense of humor after all."

The older I get, the more easily I fall asleep without meaning to.

At the end of our meal Clodius got up, saying he had to relieve himself. I relaxed and closed my eyes, listening to the chanting of the galli. The pleasing phrase I had heard before recurred, and I followed it along until it seemed that I was floating on the strange music, rising above Clodia's garden, levitating face to face with the monstrous Venus, then flying even higher. Rome was a toy city beneath me, moonlit, her temples made of little blocks. The music rose and fell, and I was carried along like a bubble on a wave, like a feather in a mist, until someone whispered in my ear: "If Marcus Caelius didn't murder Dio, *who did?*"

I woke with a start. The voice had been so clear, so close, that I was puzzled to find myself alone. The lamps had died. The sky above was spangled with stars. The garden was dark and quiet, except for the soft splashing of the fountain. Someone had put a blanket over me.

The blanket smelled of Clodia's perfume.

Too much honeyed wine, I thought. Too much rich food. Yet I felt clear-headed and refreshed. How long had I slept?

I pushed away the blanket. The night was too warm for it. I stood, stretched my arms and looked around, still not quite certain I was alone. But there was no one in the garden, except for the suppliant Adonis and the towering Venus, huge and black in silhouette. Her eyes glittered dully in the starlight. Again I had the unnerving feeling that the statue was about to come to life. I shivered and was suddenly eager to leave the garden.

At the top of the steps I paused to quietly call out — "Clodius? Clodia? Chrysis?" — but no one answered. The house was absolutely still. I might have been in an empty temple, shut up for the night. I walked through the hallway and the atrium, into the foyer. Surely there would be a slave at the door, perhaps the same old man who had let us in that afternoon.

But the slave at the door was Barnabas, fast

297

asleep. He sat on the floor, leaning against the wall, his head tilted back so that by the faint starlight which seeped in from the atrium I could see his face with its joined eyebrows. There was something gathered about him on the floor, a puzzling shape which I slowly realized was the body of Chrysis, asleep with her head nestled on his lap. In the utter stillness I could hear their quiet breathing.

Clodius had promised to see me safely home, which I took to mean an escort. It was only reasonable that I should wake Chrysis or Barnabas and tell them what I needed. But their repose was so perfect that I feared to move, not wanting to disturb them.

A hand touched my shoulder. I turned and stared into the darkness. The Ethiop was so dark that for a moment I couldn't see him at all.

"My master said I was to take care of you if you woke up," he said, with an accent I could barely understand.

"Clodius is still here?"

The giant nodded.

"And Clodia?"

"She came, while you slept."

"Perhaps I should see her before I leave."

"They've gone to bed."

"Are they asleep?"

"What difference does that make?" By the faint light, I couldn't tell whether the giant was grinning down at me or gritting his teeth. The garlic on his breath was overpowering. Gladiators and strong-armers eat it raw to give themselves strength.

He unbolted the door and swung it open, letting it bang against the sleeping figures on the floor with a smirk of disdain. Chrysis let out a sleepy whimper. Barnabas grunted. "Poor excuse for a door slave," the Ethiop sneered. "She's too soft on her slaves. Well, go on. I'll be right behind you."

"No," I said. "I'll go alone." The man made me uneasy.

The Ethiop crossed his arms and looked at me grimly. "The master gave me specific orders."

"I'll see myself home," I said. It was suddenly a battle of wills.

At last the Ethiop made a face of disgust and shrugged his brawny shoulders. "Suit yourself," he said and closed the door on me.

It was such a short way to my house, and the night was so silent and so deep, surely there was nothing to fear.

CHAPTER SEVENTEEN

Rome slept. The great houses and apartment buildings of the Palatine were dark. The streets were silent, except for the sound of my own footsteps. What was the hour? Dusk and dawn seemed equally distant, like opposite shores impossible to make out from the middle of a vast, black sea. I felt utterly alone, the last man awake in Rome.

Then I heard footsteps behind me.

I stopped. The footsteps stopped a heartbeat later.

I took a few steps. The footsteps behind me resumed.

Gordianus, I whispered to myself, you've finally done it, taken the final risk of a lifetime full of foolish risks. You've fallen into the lazy habit of relying on Fortune's favor, always assuming that the goddess will make allowances for your foolishness and shield you at the last moment because the singular drama of your life for some reason intrigues her and she wishes it to continue. Now Fortune's interest has waned; she's turned her attention elsewhere for as long as it takes to blink an eye, and you will be snuffed out, removed from the world's story for good.

A part of me believed this and steeled for the

worst. But another part of me knew that it was impossible for me to die just yet, and merely gave lip service to the possibility, to let Fortune know that I wasn't taking her for granted, and to gently remind her she had better do something, and quickly.

The footsteps behind me speeded up. I fought the urge to run and instead turned around. I refused to end up as one of those corpses found with knife wounds in the back.

The street was narrow, the shadows deep. The figure moved toward me with a slightly unsteady gait. The man was alone, and unless I was mistaken, had been drinking too much wine. It's the poet Catullus after all, I thought, the man whom Clodius told me not to fear.

Unless, of course, it was Marcus Caelius, drunk and coming after me with a knife. Or some nameless henchman of King Ptolemy. Or a garlic-eating gladiator sent by Pompey. Or someone else with a reason to kill me, thinking I knew something I didn't.

He stopped several paces away. I still couldn't make out his face, but it obviously wasn't the Ethiop; the man wasn't big enough. He appeared to be of medium height, with a slender build. When he spoke, I recognized Catullus's voice.

"So she's gotten tired of picking apples off the tree the moment they're ripe. Now she's poking around in the mulch heap." He sounded only slightly drunk, sarcastic but not particularly threatening.

"I'm afraid I don't follow you," I said.

"Aren't you awfully old to be warming a spot in her bed?"

"Whose bed? I don't know what you're talking about."

He came a few steps closer. "We should find a patch of light so I can watch your face while you lie to me. You know whose bed."

"Maybe. But you're mistaken."

"Am I? The damned gallus carries messages back and forth between you, takes you to her horti. You go riding around in her litter with the curtains closed, and stay at her house until the middle of the night. You must be her new lover."

"Don't be absurd."

He backed off a bit and began to circle around me. I suddenly realized that he might be more frightened of me than I was of him. He was the one who had turned to flee on the Ramp.

"At least she's finished with Caelius, though I can't see why she'd throw him over for the likes of you."

"You insult me," I said. "Shall I go on insisting on the truth — that I'm not Clodia's lover — and let the slur against my manhood stand? Or shall I tell a lie to refute the insult, say that Clodia *is* my lover and tells me nightly that I'm twice the man Caelius is, and four times the man that you are, Gaius Valerius Catullus."

I thought I might have pushed him too far, but my instinct was true: he came to a stop and barked out a laugh. "You must be a nit-picking orator, like Caelius. One of those word-murdering, truth-twisting advocates from the Forum. Why haven't I heard of you before, old man?"

"Because I'm not an orator. I'm a Finder, Catullus."

"Well, you found out my name. What's yours?"

"Gordianus."

He nodded. I saw him more clearly now. He still had the scraggly beard on his jaw, despite his trip to the baths. The tragic look had returned to his eyes, even when he smiled.

"Are you thirsty, Gordianus?"

"Not particularly."

"I am. Come with me."

"Where?"

"It's time we talked. About her."

"I didn't say *why*. I said *where*."

"Where else, at this time of night?"

Take a winding pathway to the foot of the Palatine, to a spot just behind the Temple of Castor and Pollux. Turn left. Proceed down the narrow alley (stinking of urine, and black as pitch at night) that runs behind the buildings on the north side of the Forum. As the slope of the Palatine curves away on the left-hand side, letting the alley open a bit, you will come to a cluttered area of little workshops and warehouses south of the Forum, east of the cattle markets and the river. Look for the little pillars which name the shops and businesses. As you draw near to the ninth signpost you will see the pool of light cast by the lamp

303

hung outside, welcoming those who cannot or will not sleep, and who cannot or will not stop drinking, whoring and gambling. This is the place which Catullus called the Salacious Tavern.

Actually, the place has no name, or none to be read on the signpost outside. Atop the little pillar, instead of an inscription, is an upright marble phallus. The lamp which casts such a lurid glow is carved in a similarly suggestive shape. Perhaps inspired by these fine examples of craftsmanship, less skilled artists have drawn crude graffiti on the wall outside, graphically depicting various uses to which such phalli might be put.

Catullus rapped on the door. A little trap opened. A bloodshot eye peered at us. The door swung open.

"They know me here," said Catullus. "And I know them. The wine is wretched, the whores are lice-ridden, and the patrons are the lowest of the low. I should know. I've come here every night since I got back."

We stepped into a long narrow room partitioned here and there by folding screens. The room was packed with patrons who stood in groups or sat on chairs and benches around little tables. The lamps were fueled by an inferior oil that created as much smoke as light, filling the room with an amber haze that made my eyes water. I heard laughter and cursing and the clatter of dice followed by hoots of triumph and groans of despair. The crowd was made up almost entirely of men. The few women were obviously there to ply their trade.

One of them suddenly emerged from the haze and wrapped herself around Catullus like a clinging vine. I blinked my watery eyes and the vine resolved into a supple redhead with a heart-shaped face.

"Gaius," she purred. "One of the girls told me you were back. And with a beard! Here, let me kiss it."

Catullus stiffened and drew back with a pained expression. "Not tonight, Ipsithilla."

"Why not? It's been a whole year since I've made a meal of you. I'm famished."

Catullus managed to smile. "Not tonight."

She drew back, lowering her eyes. "Still pining for your Lesbia?"

He winced and took my arm, leading me to a bench that had just been vacated. A slave brought us wine. Catullus was right; the quality was wretched, especially after the honeyed wine that Clodius had given me. But Catullus drank without hesitation.

Next to us, clustered around a little table, a group of rough-looking young men were playing with dice of the old-fashioned kind, made from the rectangular anklebones of a sheep, with numbers — I, III, IV, VI — painted on each of the four long sides. Each man in turn would scoop the four dice up in a cup, rattle them, cry out the name of a deity or his mistress, and cast them on the table. A referee figured out the combination and shouted the name of the throw, which would be followed by cries of gloating or derision.

"When I was young, the laws against gambling

were more strictly enforced," I said, "except of course during the Saturnalia."

"It's always Saturnalia inside the Salacious Tavern," quipped Catullus.

"Hercules!" shouted one of the gamblers. The box rattled, the bones clattered. "A Taurus Throw!" declared the referee — three ones and a six.

The next gambler cried a woman's name and tossed the dice. "Dogs!" cried the referee. "Four ones — nothing lower!" The player groaned at such bad fortune, and cursed the mistress whose name he had called out for luck.

Catullus stared blearily at the crowd. The haze was so thick I could hardly make out faces, let alone recognize anyone. "You wanted to talk," I said.

"I've lost my tongue for it. I want more wine."

"Then I'll talk. Was it you who followed me up the Ramp two nights ago?"

"Yes."

"Who sent you?"

"No one."

"Then why follow me?"

"I was following you before that. Perhaps you're not as sharp as you think. I was outside her house when you came calling that afternoon with Trygonion. I'd just gotten back into town."

"You'd just arrived and you went straight to Clodia's house?"

He put a finger to his lips. "In this place, call her Lesbia."

"Why?"

"It's my secret name for her. In the poems.

In places like this."

"Why 'Lesbia'?"

"Lesbos was the island of Sappho, who understood love better than any poet before or since. And Homer called the women of Lesbos 'the most beautiful women in the world.' "

"Wasn't Homer blind?"

He gave me a sour look. "Agamemnon speaks the line."

"Very well: Lesbia. When you went to Lesbia's house that day, didn't they tell you she'd gone out?"

"No. I didn't knock on the door. I was waiting. Watching. I wasn't ready to see her again, not face to face."

"Waiting and watching from where? It's a dead-end street."

"There are doorways deep enough to hide in. Then you came along with your bodyguard and the little gallus. I was close enough to overhear the word 'horti,' so when you headed off, I followed. What did the two of you get up to, alone inside her tent?"

"I don't think that's any of your business."

"More to the point, what did the three of you do after Lesbius showed up, naked and dripping from the river?"

"Lesbius?"

"You know whom I mean."

"You saw him come into the tent?"

"I hid among the trees and bushes on the riverbank." He grinned bleakly. "You must think I'm an utter fool."

"Did you follow me when I left?"

"All the way to your house, then over to that other house in the Subura, then back. You never knew until the Ramp, did you? You set a trap for me at the top, you and your bodyguard, so I made like a rabbit. If you're like most of the low-lifes she takes for lovers, I figured you might be pretty dangerous."

"I told you, I'm not her lover. Just her 'hireling,' as Clodius calls me."

"Lesbius!" he insisted. The cheap wine was beginning to take effect. "Anyway, you could be her lover and her hireling both. She's far above the likes of you, but she's been known to bend over for love."

"The Venus Throw!" shouted the referee, setting off an uproar next to us. Someone slammed his fist on the table, making the dice jump, and shouted an accusation of cheating. The others closed ranks to calm him down.

"The Venus Throw," said Catullus. "When all four dice come up different. Not the highest total, just the luckiest. Why do you suppose that is?"

"Because Venus craves variety?"

"Like Lesbia. Except when she craves her own flesh:

Lesbius is Pulcher — Pulcher meaning beautiful —
and he must be, because Lesbia loves him
far better than Catullus and all his clan,
whom Lesbius would sell down the river
to pay three upright men willing to let him blow
   them . . . a kiss!"

I smiled and nodded. "Clodius said you made better poems than Milo's men. And nastier."

"*Lesbius,*" insisted Catullus, "demeans me with such praise."

"You seem to be talkative after all."

"But as thirsty as ever. Where is that serving slave?" He banged his cup against the bench, but the noise was lost in the hubbub.

"I suppose you'll see her again, eventually," I said.

He stared bleakly into the amber haze. "I already have."

"I mean face to face. To speak to her."

"I spoke to her today. I spent the afternoon with her."

"What?"

"This morning I finally knocked on her door. The old slave told me she'd gone out early, taking her daughter to visit some cousin. So I wandered around and ended up at the Senian baths. It was only coincidence that I happened to see you there, and that ridiculous chase after Caelius's friend. What was it all about?"

"I'll tell you later. Go on, about . . . Lesbia."

"I finally left the baths and headed back to her house. On the way I recognized her litter outside the house of one of the Metelli. She was just leaving, with her daughter. The two of them were stepping out the door. Before I could turn, she saw me. It was hard to read her face. It always has been. A face unlike any other, except one. Do you suppose that Lesbia and Lesbius can read each other at a glance? Like looking in a mirror? The rest of us study their faces for hours and still can't be sure what's behind them. Something about her eyes — like a poem in a foreign tongue. But more perfect than any poem. More painful.

"She invited me into her litter. 'To go where?' I said. 'Home. I'm expecting a man to bring me some news,' she said. I suppose she meant you? 'I don't want to go there if there'll be someone else,' I told her. She paused for a long time, looking at me. Finally she said, 'Metella can stay here with her cousins a while longer. You and I will go to the horti.'

"That was a mistake, of course. On a warm day like this, with all the naked toads jumping about in the water and leering at her while Lesbia leered back at them. Did she flirt with them merely to hurt me? Or do I flatter myself? At least Chrysis wasn't there to fetch the comeliest toad into her tent, which is their usual game. She invited me to her upcoming party. She was very polite. 'You must have some new poems you can read for us, something inspired by your travels.' As if I was an acquaintance she could call on to entertain her admirers. But do you know what?" He smiled grimly. "It so happens that I *do* have a new poem, and I *will* be reading it at her party. Something to fit the theme of the Great Mother festival. I suppose you'll be there."

"Me? I haven't been invited. Strange, isn't it, considering that I'm her new lover and all."

"Don't needle me, Finder. I've been pricked

310

enough for one day. At sundown she decided it was time to leave the horti, just when I'd made up my mind to say what I needed to say to her. She had to pick up Metella, she said, and she was expecting her brother tonight. 'You're welcome to come along,' she said — as if I could stomach being with both of them at once. I told her I'd walk back into town by myself."

"But you ended up outside her door again."

"Like a moth to a flame, except that this flame freezes instead of burns."

The serving slave suddenly appeared and at Catullus's insistence poured fresh wine into our cups. I sampled it and was tempted to spit it out, but Catullus drank without complaint.

"So, what exactly happened at the baths today?" he said. "At the horti, when I told Lesbia I'd been at the Senian baths, she was suddenly all ears, pressing me for everything I'd seen of that ridiculous chase. She knew what it was about, didn't she? But she was as tight-lipped as you."

No wonder Clodia hadn't bothered to wake me when she came in, I thought. From Catullus and then from Barnabas she had probably heard more than enough details about the botched capture of Licinius and the pyxis. Or had she been too eager to be with her brother to bother with the hireling's report?

"You know about charges pending against Marcus Caelius?" I said.

"It's all I've heard about since I got back to Rome. They say he's up to his neck in it this time."

"Your Lesbia and Lesbius have a hand in the prosecution. Not officially, but they're eager to gather evidence against him on a particular charge of attempted murder."

"So I've heard. Is that what she's hired you for?"

"Yes."

"Then it's come to that, between her and Caelius. I've loved them both. The glittering Venus of Roman society, the petulant Adonis. Who could be surprised when the two of them decided to love each other and turn the country bumpkin from Verona out of their beds? Those two together, without me — that was more than I could stand." The wine was beginning to slur his speech. "It was better when her husband was still alive. Good old Quintus Metellus Celer, the stodgy goat. She was faithful to me then! But after Celer died, she became her own woman, and everyone else's woman as well. Even that was better than having her choose a favorite and shut me out altogether. But then she picked Caelius and I became just another of her multitude of used-up lovers. This tavern is full of the wretches. I could point out a dozen men who've had her. I thought a year away would dull the pain. But the wound still bleeds, and I still crave the knife that cut me."

"She doesn't love Caelius anymore," I said. "He rejected her, as far as I can tell. She's bitter. She's determined to see him destroyed, obsessed with it, if that's any comfort to you."

"Comfort? To know that another man truly got

inside her, made her care enough to feel pain when he turned away, made her ache enough to want to destroy him? Me she dismissed with a flick of her wrist — no more scraps for the dog! Caelius deserts her and she goes crazy. Where's the comfort in that?"

"The desire for destruction is mutual, at least according to Lesbia. That's what the incident at the baths was about. Caelius's friend Licinius was there to deliver poison to some of her slaves, because Caelius thought he could bribe them to murder their mistress."

"Murder Clodia?" Catullus was startled enough, or drunk enough, to forget the pseudonym. "No, Caelius would never do that. I don't believe it."

"She claims he tested the poison on a slave first, and watched the man die before his eyes."

"I can believe that. Caelius could kill a slave without a twinge of guilt. But I can't believe that he would use the same poison on her."

"Not even out of desperation? The charges against him are serious. He'll be ruined for life if he's found guilty. Humiliated, forgotten, exiled from Rome."

"Exiled from Rome — I know that loneliness." Catullus stared into his cup.

"To save himself, don't you believe that Caelius would destroy your Lesbia?"

"Destroy Lesbia? No, not her. Never."

"Perhaps he never loved her quite as you did."

"None of them ever loved her as I did." Catullus stared bleakly into the crowd, then stiffened.

"Hades!" he whispered. "Look who just came in."

I squinted through the haze at three newcomers who stood near the entrance, searching the room for a place to sit. "Marcus Caelius himself," I said. "Accompanied, if I'm not mistaken, by his friends Asicius and Licinius."

Caelius saw Catullus. His face registered simple surprise, followed by a lightning flash of emotion. Then a mask fell into place, which lifted for only an instant to show his confusion when he saw me. He hesitated, then gestured for his companions to follow as he approached us.

"Catullus!" he said, flashing a sardonic grin. "How long have you been back?"

"A few days."

"And you haven't come to call on me? My feelings are hurt."

"Actually, I did drop by your place," said Catullus. "Your *old* place. The neighbors said Clodius had kicked you out and put the building up for sale. They said I'd find you back at your father's hovel on the Quirinal Hill."

"You should drop by." Caelius's smile never wavered.

"The Quirinal is a little out of my usual orbit. Besides, I shouldn't think that your father's house would be a suitable place for entertaining guests in your accustomed style."

"I don't know what you mean."

"The wine, the singing, the whores, the inventive sleeping arrangements. I can't see your papa approving."

"All that's behind me now," said Caelius.

"At least until after your trial. Then you may have to leave everything behind whether you want to or not."

The mask almost cracked. "I mean to say that I've seen fit to put aside some of the more boisterous habits of my youth, and to sever some of my more questionable associations. Perhaps you were right not to come calling on me after all, Catullus. One does have to hold to certain standards when inviting a guest into the house of one's father. It was thoughtful of you to spare me the embarrassment of shutting the door in your face."

There was a long pause, during which Catullus swirled the dregs in his cup and watched them spin, pursing his lips thoughtfully. "I think," he finally said, in a hard, low voice that made me hold my breath, "that for you to insult me in that way, Marcus Caelius — "

Caelius stiffened, as did his friends.

"For you to have insulted me in that fashion," Catullus went on, "by which I mean building an argument out of complicated sentences by logical steps — well, what I think about that, Marcus Caelius, is that you haven't drunk enough wine tonight!"

Caelius's face went blank, then he laughed. "Not nearly enough. And for you to do such a sloppy job of insulting me, Gaius Catullus, I think you must have already had far too much to drink!"

"I can't argue with that," said Catullus, grinning and swallowing the dregs.

"No matter," said Caelius. "The night's still young. Plenty of time for me to get stinking drunk, and for you to sober up."

"I take it that you know my friend here, Gratidianus," said Catullus.

"Gordianus," I corrected him. "Yes, Marcus Caelius and I are acquainted. We used to be neighbors."

"And a few times our paths have crossed in the courts," added Caelius. "Though never quite as they are crossing now."

I shrugged. "I'm not sure I — "

"But isn't it true, Gordianus, that a certain lady has hired you, and not for the purpose that she usually hires men?"

"You aren't worthy of kissing her middle finger," said Catullus, no longer friendly. "You certainly aren't worthy of insulting her."

Licinius, who had been peering at me, suddenly spoke up. "Wait, now I remember where I've seen this man before. He was there today, at the baths, when I — "

"Shut up, Licinius," growled Caelius.

"It isn't true, is it, Caelius?" Catullus leaned forward earnestly, his mood having shifted in the blink of an eye. "It isn't true, what Gratidianus tells me — you wouldn't actually do her harm, would you? Not to her. Not for any reason. And certainly not by — "

"Shut up, Catullus," I said, clenching my teeth.

"Say, I recognize him, too!" Asicius stepped closer, peering at me. "He's the one who was hiding in the shadows across the street from your old apartment on the Palatine, Caelius, on the night that we took care of the old — "

"Shut up, Asicius!" cried Caelius, loudly enough to startle the gamblers next to us. One of them scratched his throw, sending the dice flying onto the floor — a bad omen which caused some of the players to vacate the table at once, whereupon those who remained began to shout accusations of bad faith at the quitters.

Catullus stood, a little unsteadily. "Are you looking for a place to sit, Caelius? Here, take my seat. The Salacious Tavern just became a little too salacious for even my tastes. Are you coming, Gratidianus?"

"Gordianus," I said under my breath, getting to my feet. Asicius and Licinius shoved past me and sat on the bench. As I stepped by him, Caelius seized my arm and put his mouth to my ear. "You're mistaken, you know. I didn't kill Dio, I swear."

"That's only one of the charges against you, Marcus Caelius."

He gripped my arm painfully hard and kept his voice low. "But you're only concerned with Dio, aren't you? You want to put his spirit to rest, because you knew him in Alexandria back in the old days." His handsome face was no longer nonchalant. *A reckless, desperate man*, Clodius had called him. I looked into his eyes and saw fear.

"How do you know these things, Marcus Caelius? How do you know about Dio and me,

317

and about Clodia hiring me?"

"Never mind. What matters is that you're mistaken. It wasn't me. I didn't kill the old Egyptian. I swear to you by the shades of my ancestors!"

"And your friend Asicius?"

"He didn't kill Dio, either."

"Who did?"

"I don't know. But it wasn't me."

"And the night of the murder — where had you been with Asicius, before I saw you? What were the two of you up to? Tell me that, and swear by your ancestors."

"That's more than I can tell you."

"But still not enough."

Caelius squeezed my arm. "Gordianus — "

"Gratidianus!" said Catullus, seizing my other arm. Caelius released me and I found myself being pulled toward the entrance, my head reeling from the stench of oil smoke and cheap wine.

Behind me I heard a stranger cry out, "By Venus! I wager everything and put my trust in the goddess of love!" Then a clatter of dice, and then the same voice, exultant amid groans of defeat: "The Venus Throw! The Venus Throw! It conquers all!"

Out in the street I breathed the fresh air and looked up at a clear sky spangled with stars. "Why such a rush to get me out of that place?"

"I couldn't leave you behind to tell them everything I'd just told you . . . about her."

"I wouldn't have done that. And please, stop

calling me Gratidianus. My name — "

"I know what you call yourself. But for me you'll always have another name, the one I give you. Just as she has another name. In case I should write a poem about you."

"I can't imagine what sort of poem that would be."

"No?

Gratidianus thinks he's clever, and he must be, because Lesbia loves him, far better than Catullus and all his clan — "

"Stop, Catullus. You're too drunk to know what you're saying."

"A man is never too drunk to make a poem."

"Just too drunk to make sense. I think I'd better find my way home." I looked up the alley. Beyond the lurid glow cast by the phallic lamp above the door, the way was swallowed up by an unreassuring darkness.

"I'll walk you home," offered Catullus.

A drunken poet for a bodyguard! What would happen if Caelius and his friends decided to come after us? "Quickly then. Do you know another route? Where no one would think to follow?"

"I know every path leading to and from the Salacious Tavern. Follow me."

He led me on a circuitous route, slipping between warehouses set so close that I had to walk sideways to get through, picking a way around trash heaps where rats scurried and squeaked, and finally ascending a steep footpath up the western slope of the Palatine. It seemed a good route for avoiding assassins, but rather treacherous for a man who had been drinking as much as Catullus. I expected him to fall and break his neck at any moment, taking me with him, but he attacked the climb with only an occasional misstep. The climb seemed to sober him. His lungs were certainly strong enough. While I labored for breath, he had plenty left over to give vent to his thoughts.

"If only we could all become eunuchs!" he declared. "What man wouldn't be happier?"

"I suppose we could become eunuchs, if we wanted."

"Ha! The act is harder than you might think. I know, I've seen it with my own eyes. While I was in Bithynia, I took a journey to the ruins of old Troy, to find the place where my brother's buried. So far from home! On the way back a stranger asked me if I'd like to see the initiation rites of the galli. He wanted money, of course. Took me to a temple on the slopes of Mount Ida. The priests wanted money, too. I felt quite the gawking tourist, dropping coins into all those eager hands, just another crass, thrill-seeking Roman looking for a taste of the 'real' East. They took me to a room so smoky with incense I could hardly see, and so loud with flutes and tambourines I thought I'd go deaf. The rite was under way. The galli chanted and whirled in a weird dance, like fingers of the goddess keeping time. The young initiate had worked himself into a frenzy, naked, covered with sweat, undulating with the music. Someone put a shard of broken pottery into his hand — 'Samian pottery,' the guide whispered in my ear, 'the only kind sure to avoid a putrid wound.' While I watched, the fellow turned himself into a gallus before my eyes. All by himself — no one helped him. It was quite a thing to see. Afterward, when the blood was running down his legs and he couldn't stand any longer, the others swarmed around him, swaying, chanting, shrieking. The guide sniggered and poked me in the ribs and made a show of covering his balls. I ran out of the place in a panic."

Catullus fell silent for a while. We reached the top of the path and entered the maze of dark, silent streets.

"Imagine the freedom," Catullus whispered. "To leave the appetites of the flesh behind."

"The galli have appetites," I said. "They eat like men."

"Yes, but a man eats and is done with it. The craving I'm talking about feeds on itself. The more it's fed, the hungrier it grows."

"A Roman controls his appetites, not vice versa."

"Then perhaps we aren't Romans any longer. Show me a man in Rome who's larger than his appetites."

I thought about this while we made our way through the winding, deep-shadowed streets.

"But even castration can't guarantee an end to passion," Catullus resumed. "Look at Trygonion!"

"What about him?"

"Don't you know where his name comes from? The famous epitaph by Philodemus?"

"Should I recognize that name?"

"Barbarian! Philodemus of Gadera. Probably the greatest living poet of the Greek tongue."

"Oh, *that* Philodemus. An epitaph, you say?"

"Written years and years ago for a dead gallus called Trygonion. Can you follow the Greek?"

"I'll translate in my head."

"Very well:

Here lies that tender creature of ladylike limbs,
Trygonion, prince of the sex-numb emasculates,
Beloved of the Great Mother, Cybele,
He alone of the galli was seduced by a woman.
Holy earth, give to this headstone a pillow
Of budding white violets.

"That old poem is how *our* Trygonion got his name. I don't remember what he was called before, something Phrygian and unpronounceable. One time, teasing him about his weakness for Lesbia, I called him our little Trygonion, the gallus who fell for a woman. The name stuck to Trygonion the way Trygonion sticks to Lesbia. I think of him whenever I consider castrating myself. It might do no good, you see. A useless gesture. Sometimes passion is stronger than flesh. Love can last beyond death, and in some rare instances a man's weakness for beauty can even outlive his testicles."

"Trygonion is that devoted to Lesbia?"

"He suffers as I suffer, but with one great difference."

"Which is?"

"Trygonion suffers without hope."

"And you?"

"While a man still has his balls, he has hope!" Catullus laughed his peculiar, barking laugh. "Even slaves have hope, as long as they have their balls. But a gallus in love with a beautiful woman — "

"So much in love that he would do anything for her?"

"Any at all, without question."

"So much in love that he might be blinded by jealousy?"

"Driven mad by it!"

"He could be dangerous. Unpredictable . . ."

"Not nearly as dangerous as Lesbia." Catullus was suddenly giddy, trotting ahead of me and circling back, leaping up to swing at lamps hung from upper-story windows along the street. "Damned bitch! The Medea of the Palatine!"

"Medea was a witch, as I recall, and rather wicked."

"Only because she was 'sick at heart, wounded by cruel love,' as the playwright says. A witch, yes, and wounded — only it's me she's bewitched, and Caelius who wounded her. Medea of the Palatine! Clytemnestra-for-a-quadrans!"

"A quadrans? As cheap as that?"

"Why not? The price of admission to the Senian baths."

"But Clytemnestra murdered her husband."

"Agamemnon deserved it!" He whirled like a frenzied gallus. "Medea of the Palatine! Clytemnestra-for-a-quadrans!" he chanted.

"Who calls her such things?"

"I do!" said Catullus. He abruptly stopped his whirling and staggered ahead of me, gasping for breath. "I just made them up, out of my head. What do you think? I'll need some fresh invectives if I'm to get her attention again."

"You're a strange suitor, Catullus."

"I love a strange woman. Do you want to know a secret about her? Something that no else in all the world knows, not even Lesbius? I wouldn't know myself if I hadn't spied on her one night. Do you know that giant monstrosity of a Venus in her garden?"

"I happened to notice it, yes."

"The pedestal appears to be solid, but it's not. There's a block that slides out, opening a secret compartment. It's where she keeps her trophies."

"Trophies?"

"Mementos. Keepsakes. One night in bed with her, happily dozing after hours of making love, I felt a tickling at my groin. I opened one eye to see her clipping away a bit of my pubic hair! She stole out of the room with it. I followed her to the garden. From the shadows I watched her open the pedestal and put what she had taken from me inside. Later I went back and figured out how to open the compartment, and I saw what she kept there. Poems I had sent her. Letters from her other lovers. Bits of jewelry, clippings of hair, childish gifts her brother must have given her when they were little. Her love trophies!"

He suddenly staggered against a wall and clutched his face. "I wanted to destroy it all," he whispered hoarsely. "I wanted to scoop up all her treasures and throw them on the brazier and watch them burst into flame. But I couldn't. I felt the eyes of the goddess on me. I stepped back from the pedestal and looked up at her face. I left her mementos alone. If I destroyed them, I knew she would never forgive me."

"Who would never forgive you — Venus or Lesbia?"

He looked at me with tragic eyes. "Is there any difference?"

CHAPTER EIGHTEEN

The wrath of Achilles would pale beside the wrath of Bethesda.

Her anger runs cold, not hot. It freezes rather than scalds. It is invisible, secretive, insidious. It makes itself felt not by blustering action, but by cold, calculated inaction, by words unspoken, glances unreturned, pleas for mercy unheeded. I think Bethesda shows her anger in this passive way because she was born a slave, and remained a slave for much of her life, until I manumitted and married her to bear our daughter in freedom. Her way is the way of slaves (and the hero of Homer's *Iliad*): she sulks, and broods, and bides her time.

It was bad enough that I had sent Belbo home alone from Clodia's house, leaving myself without a bodyguard to cross the Palatine by night. Bad enough, too, that I eventually came home smelling of cheap wine and the rancid smoke of tavern lamps. But to have spent the night with *that* woman!

This was ridiculous, of course, and I said so, especially as I hadn't even seen Clodia all night.

How then did I explain the lingering smell of perfume on me?

A smarter man (or even myself, less worn out

and sleepy) would have thought twice before explaining that the perfume came from a blanket that the lady in question must have put over him when he unwittingly dozed off in her garden —

That was that. I spent what little remained of the night trying to find a comfortable position on a cramped dining couch in my study. I'm used to sleeping with a warm body next to me.

I'm also used to sleeping until at least daybreak, especially after having stayed up half the night. This was not to be. It wasn't that Bethesda woke me; she simply made it impossible for me to go on sleeping. Was it really necessary to send the scrub maid to clean my study before dawn?

Once I was awake, Bethesda didn't refuse to feed me. But the millet porridge was lumpy and cold, and there was no conversation to warm it up.

After breakfast, I shooed the scrub maid from my study and shut the door. It was a good morning, I decided, to write a letter.

To my beloved son Meto, serving under the command of Gaius Julius Caesar in Gaul, from his loving father in Rome, may Fortune be with you.

I write this letter only three days after my last; Martius is gone and the Kalends of Aprilis is upon us. Much has happened in the meantime, all revolving about the murder of Dio.

Our neighbor Marcus Caelius (now our former neighbor; Clodius evicted him) has been accused of the murder of Dio, and related crimes having to do with the harassment of the Egyptian envoys, as well as a previous attempt (by poison) on Dio's life. I have been hired by friends of the prosecution to help find evidence against Caelius. My only interest is to determine who killed Dio, so that I can put this nagging affair to rest, for my own peace of mind if not for justice's sake.

I will attempt to explain the details later. (Perhaps after the trial, which begins the day after tomorrow.) What is foremost in my mind now, what I would long to discuss if you were here with me, is something else.

What is this madness which poets call love?

What power compels a man to thrust himself against the lacerating indifference of a woman who no longer loves him? What drives a woman to seek the absolute destruction of a man who rejects her? What cruel appetite makes a man of rational intellect crave the debasement of his helpless partners in sex? How does a eunuch, supposedly impervious to love, become enamored of a beautiful woman? Is it natural for a brother and sister to share a bed, as we are told the gods and goddesses of Egypt sometimes do? Why do the worshipers of the Great Mother emasculate themselves in religious ecstasy? Why would a woman steal a lock of her lover's pubic hair to cherish as a keepsake?

You must wonder if I'm mad to pose such questions. But in fact they may have as much to do with the murder of Dio and the upcoming trial of Caelius as do the intrigues of Egyptian politics, and I find myself baffled. I fear I have become too old for this kind of work, which requires a mind in empathy with the world around it. I like to think I am wiser than I used to be, but what use is wisdom in making sense of a world that follows the dictates of mad passion? I feel like a sober man on a ship of drunkards.

We say it is the hand of Venus that compels these strange behaviors, as if that put the matter to rest, when in fact we say "the hand of Venus" precisely because we do *not* understand these passions and cannot explain them, only suffer them when we must and watch, perplexed, the suffering of others . . .

There was a rapping at the door. I steeled myself for a chill wind and called, "Come in." But it was not Bethesda who entered. It was Diana.

She closed the door behind her and sat in the chair across from my writing table. There was a shadow on her face. Something was troubling her.

"Mother is angry at you," she said.

"Is she? I hadn't noticed."

"What are you doing?"

"Writing a letter to Meto."

"Didn't you write to him just a few days ago?"

"Yes."

"What does the letter say?"

"This and that."

"Is it about your work?"

"In a way. Yes, it's about my work."

"You're writing to Meto because you've sent Eco on a trip, and you need someone to talk to. Isn't that it?"

"You're very perceptive, Diana."

She lifted her hand and pushed back a strand of hair that had fallen over her cheek. What remarkably lustrous hair she had, like her mother's before the strands of gray began to dull it. It fell past her shoulders almost to her breasts, framing her face and throat. In the soft morning light her skin shone like dusky rose petals.

"Why don't you share your troubles with me, Papa? Mother does. She tells me everything."

"I suppose that's the way of the world. Mothers and daughters, fathers and sons."

She looked at me steadily. I tried to look back at her, but found myself looking away. "The boys are older than you, Diana. They've shared my work, my travels." I smiled. "Half the time when I begin a sentence, Eco finishes it."

"And Meto?"

"Meto is different. You're old enough to remember some of what happened while we were on the farm — Catilina, the trouble between Meto and me, Meto's decision to become a soldier. That was a great test of the bond between us. He's his own man now and I don't always understand him. Even so, I can always tell him what I think."

"But Eco and Meto aren't even your flesh. You adopted them. I carry your blood, Papa."

"Yes, Diana, I know." Why then are you so mysterious, I thought, and why is there such a gulf between us? And why do I keep these thoughts to myself instead of speaking them aloud?

"Can I read the letter, Papa?"

This took me aback. I looked down at the parchment, scrutinizing the words. "I m not sure you'd understand, Diana."

"Then you could explain."

"I'm not sure I'd want to. If you were older, perhaps."

"I'm not a child anymore, Papa."

I shook my head.

"Mother says I'm a woman now."

I cleared my throat. "Yes, well, then I suppose you have every right to read your mother's personal letters."

"That's cruel, Papa. You know that Mother can't read or write, which is hardly her fault. If she had been raised as a Roman girl . . . ."

Instead of an Egyptian slave, I thought. Was that what was disturbing Diana, her mother's origins, the fact that she was the child of a woman born in slavery? Diana and I had never really talked about this, but I assumed that Bethesda had discussed it with her, in some way. They certainly spent enough time talking to each other in private. Did Diana bear some resentment against me, for

331

having bought her mother in an Alexandrian slave market? But I was also the man who had freed Bethesda. It all seemed terribly complicated, suddenly.

"Even most Roman women don't learn to read, Diana."

"The woman you're working for can read, I imagine."

"I'm sure she can."

"And you made sure I was taught to read."

"Yes, I did."

"But what good is the skill, if you forbid me to use it?" She looked at the letter in front of me.

It was uncanny, the way she used her mother's stratagems to get what she wanted — circular logic, stubborn persistence, the uncovering of guilts I hadn't known I felt. They say the gods can put on the guise of someone we know and move among us without anyone guessing. For a brief, strange moment a veil seemed to drop, and I sensed that it was Bethesda herself in the room with me, disguised to confound me. Who was this creature Diana, after all, and where had she come from?

I handed her the letter and watched her read it. She read slowly, moving her lips slightly. She had not been taught as well as Meto.

I expected her to ask the identity of the people I referred to, or perhaps for a clearer explanation of the passions I described, but when she put down the letter she said, "Why do you want so badly to find the person who killed Dio, Papa?"

"What is it I say in the letter? 'For my own peace of mind.' "

"But why should your mind be unsettled?"

"Diana, if someone who was close to you had been hurt, wouldn't you want to avenge that person, to redress the wrong done to them, if you could?"

She thought about this. "But Dio wasn't close to you."

"That's presumptuous of you, Diana."

"You hardly knew him."

"In a way, that's true. But in another way — "

She picked up the letter. "Is he the one you mean, when you speak of the 'man of rational intellect'?"

"Yes, as a matter of fact."

"Wasn't he a cruel man, then?"

"I don't really know."

"But in the letter, you say — "

"Yes, I know what I say." I cringed at the idea of hearing her read it aloud.

"How do you know such a thing about him?" She peered at me intently.

I sighed. "From certain things I was told by the men who played host to him. Dio apparently took liberties with some of their slave girls. He may have been rather abusive. But I don't really know. People don't like to talk about that sort of thing."

"He wasn't that way when you knew him in Alexandria?"

"If he was, I knew nothing about it. I saw a

very different side of him."

She looked at me thoughtfully for a long moment. It was not a look she had learned from Bethesda. It was a keen, pensive look, very deep and entirely her own — or perhaps she had picked it up from me, I thought, flattering myself. How foolish and remote it suddenly seemed, that strange, disoriented moment when I had imagined she was her mother in disguise.

She stood and nodded gravely. "Thank you for letting me read the letter, Papa. Thank you for talking to me." Then she left the room.

I picked up the letter and read it through again. I winced at the catalogue I had made of other people's passions, and especially at what I had said of Dio: *What cruel appetite makes a man of rational intellect crave the debasement of his helpless partners in sex?*

What had I been thinking, to put such thoughts in a letter?

I would wait until after the trial to write to Meto, when I had something of substance to relate. I called on one of the slaves to light a taper from the fire in the kitchen and bring it to me. When she returned I took the taper from her, put the parchment into the empty brazier and burned it to ashes.

I spent the day snooping.

If Caelius had indeed plotted to poison both Dio and Clodia, where had he obtained the poison?

Poisonings have become lamentably common in

Rome, and in recent years I have become more familiar with deadly potions and powders than I would have dreamed possible. From time to time considerable quantities of various kinds of poison pass through my own hands, and I have a strong-box especially for storing them; clients, having seized a quantity of poison as evidence, prefer to safeguard the stuff with me rather than in their own homes, especially if they suspect a family member or a slave of wanting to do them in.

For a price, anyone can obtain poison in Rome, but the reliable, discreet sources — the sort to which I imagined Caelius would go — are relatively few. Over the years my work has acquainted me with most of them to one degree or another. Interviewing these creatures was a job I would rather have left to Eco, but since Eco was away I set out to do it myself, with a purse full of coins for bribes and Belbo for protection. It was a miserable task, rather like hunting for snakes under rocks. Since I happened to know which stones the snakes preferred, I simply went from one to the next, lifting them up and bracing myself for a succession of unpleasant encounters.

The search took me to a number of disreputable shops on the outskirts of the Forum; over to the old, run-down baths near the Circus Flaminius; to the waterfront shipyards and warehouses of the Navalia; and finally, following the advice of an informant, back to the place that Catullus had called the Salacious Tavern. By the light of day it had an air more decrepit than salacious; the gamblers were gone and the whores looked ten years older. The only patrons were a few unshaven drunkards who looked incapable of getting up from their benches; some, whom I recognized from the previous night, had apparently never left.

I had been told to seek out a man who called himself Salax ("The tavern is named after him," my source had joked). He was easy enough to spot, since in place of a real nose he wore a leather one. ("Whatever you do, don't ask him how he lost his nose!" I had been warned.) He admitted readily enough to knowing Marcus Caelius — a frequent visitor to the tavern — but about poisons he declared himself completely ignorant, and became no more knowledgeable even when I rattled my coin purse. Instead he pointed toward the idle whores and suggested another way to lighten my purse.

I had looked under all the rocks I knew. The snakes had all bared their fangs and hissed, but for better or worse not one of them had produced any poison.

It was possible, even likely, that Caelius had obtained poison not on his own but from the same source which had hired or compelled him to harass the Alexandrian envoys — directly from King Ptolemy, or perhaps from the king's friend Pompey. In that case I could expect no luck at all in tracking the poison. The network of spies and lackeys who worked for Pompey and the king would reveal nothing to an outsider.

If Caelius killed Dio at the bidding of Dio's

enemies, why had he done so? Because he was in debt to Pompey? That seemed distinctly possible. If so, I might be able to find someone who at least knew of the debt. I returned to the Forum and sought out a different set of sources, more conversant with politics than poison. It was easy enough to find men willing to talk, but impossible to find hard facts. It was as Clodius had said: plenty of people professed to 'know' the 'truth' (Caelius tried to poison Dio and failed, then Caelius and Asicius together stabbed Dio), but no one seemed to have any real evidence.

I found men who had attended the trial of Asicius and talked with them at length. The common knowledge was that Asicius was guilty and everyone knew it, but among the judges the weak-minded had been dazzled by Cicero's defense and the weak-willed bribed by King Ptolemy's gold — together, a safe majority. Yet, when I questioned these men about the trial itself, about the speeches and the witnesses who had given evidence, it seemed to me that the prosecution had been able to come up with little more than I had — hearsay and innuendo. Perhaps the judges had simply acquitted Asicius for lack of proof.

It was a frustrating day.

The sun was beginning to set as Belbo and I trudged up the Ramp. I suddenly realized that I had seen nothing of Catullus all day. Perhaps I had finally convinced him that I was not his rival in love. The absurdity of the notion made me smile.

But my smile stiffened when we reached the top of the Ramp and I saw what was in front of my house.

"Belbo, I must be seeing things. I hope so."

"What do you mean, Master?"

"Do you see a group of idle bodyguards lounging outside my front door?"

"Yes, Master."

"And do their faces look familiar?"

"They do, Master. An ugly lot."

"And is that not a litter in their midst, set against the wall while the bearers relax in the street?"

"It is, Master."

"And does the litter not have red and white striped curtains, drawn back so that we can see that the box is empty?"

"That is so, Master."

"Do you know what this means, Belbo?"

He quailed at the realization. "I think so, Master . . ."

"Cybele, spare my manhood! Clodia is in my house — and so is Bethesda."

One of Clodia's bodyguards had the temerity to challenge me outside my own front door. Fortunately the man's captain recognized me. He berated his underling and then actually had the manners to apologize to me. Not all of Clodius's gangsters were completely uncivilized, but every one of them looked capable of killing a man without blinking. Seeing them gathered outside my house set my teeth on edge.

Once inside, I drew aside a slave girl who was passing through the foyer. "Is your mistress here?"

"Yes, Master. In the garden."

"Shhh. Keep your voice down. Do I have a visitor?"

"There is a visitor, Master, yes."

"Tell me that your mistress is napping in the garden, and that my visitor is quietly secluded in my study."

The slave looked at me, perplexed. "No, Master. The mistress is entertaining the visitor in the little garden at the back of the house."

"Oh, dear. Has the visitor been here long?"

"Quite some time, Master. Long enough to have finished the first ewer of wine and sent for another."

"Have you heard . . . shouting?"

"No, Master."

"Harsh words?"

She frowned. "Please, Master, I never eavesdrop."

"But you'd notice if your mistress had, say, strangled the other woman, or vice versa?"

The girl looked at me strangely, then managed an uneasy laugh. "Oh, you're making a joke, aren't you, Master?"

"Am I?"

"Shall I go tell the mistress that you're home?"

"No! Just go on about your business, as if I'd never come in."

I quietly made my way to the back of the house.

It was possible, from a little passageway off my bedroom, to look through a screen of ivy into the small private garden where Bethesda and Clodia were sitting. They were not alone. Chrysis sat on a pillow at her mistress's feet. Diana was seated next to her mother, holding her hand. Their voices were low, hardly more than a murmur. Their tone was somber. They seemed to be deep in serious discussion. That was the last thing I had expected. What on earth could these women have in common?

I reached out with my forefinger and pushed aside an ivy leaf to get a better look at Clodia. Even in an unassuming stola of soft gray wool she was stunningly beautiful. At least she'd had the sense to put on decent clothing before she came calling at my house. I looked at Bethesda, expecting to see jealousy on her face. Instead her expression was pensive and melancholy, mirroring that of the other women.

Clodia's voice was so low that I had to strain to hear.

"With me, it was an uncle, not blood-kin, but one of my stepmother's brothers. Like you, I kept it a secret. I was fifteen, a bit older than your Diana. My father had just betrothed me to my cousin Quintus, but with Father away from Rome the wedding had to wait. That was quite all right by me. I wasn't eager for marriage, like some girls. But of course, if I *had* been married, then perhaps . . ." She took a breath and went on. "Uncle Marcus had always looked at me in a certain way.

You know what I mean." The other women nodded sympathetically. "Perhaps it was the betrothal that set him off, thinking that once Quintus took me he would never have the chance again. One day, at the family horti, he caught me alone." She took a deep breath. "Afterward, one wonders how the gods could allow such a thing to happen."

"You never told your stepmother?" said Bethesda.

"I hated her then. I hated her even more after what Uncle Marcus did. He was her brother, after all. I didn't trust her. I thought she might take his side."

"What about your own brothers?" said Diana.

"I should have told them. I did tell Publius, but not until many years later, after Uncle Marcus was dead."

"But your sisters — surely you told them," said Bethesda.

"My half sisters were closer to their mother than to me. I couldn't trust them not to tell her. No, the only person I told was an old slave woman who had been with my father since long before I was born, and I told her only when I began to realize that Uncle Marcus had planted a baby in me. She showed me what to do, but she warned me that if I aborted the child I might never be able to have sons."

"A Roman superstition!" Bethesda clucked her tongue.

"Still, it proved to be true. That was another reason I never told my husband about what Uncle

Marcus did to me, and what followed; Quintus would have blamed me for giving him a daughter instead of a son. He would probably have blamed me for tempting Uncle Marcus. It's the way men think. Quintus knew he wasn't the first, but he never knew about Uncle Marcus. He died, never knowing."

I listened, disturbed, and then astonished by what Clodia did next: she leaned forward and took Bethesda's hand, the one Diana was not already holding, and pressed it between her palms. "But you said that it was the same with you, Bethesda — that you kept it a secret."

Bethesda lowered her eyes. "Who could I have told? A free Roman girl might have recourse to law or family — but an Egyptian slave girl in Alexandria? The man had done the thing often to my mother while she lived; she told me that the master's abuse would kill her in the end, and it finally did. After she died, he turned to me. I was much younger than you were, Clodia, not even old enough to bear a child. He did the thing to me only once, or tried to. I suppose he thought I would be docile, like my mother, but after the things she had told me I knew what to expect and I decided I would die before I let him have his way with me. He tied my wrists with a rope, the way he had tied her so many times. He liked to hang her on a hook on the wall. I had seen her like that, seen what he did to her, and when he tried to do the same things to me a kind of madness came into me, the madness the gods put

342

into men and women to give them strength beyond their bodies. I was more limber than he realized. I wriggled free. It turned into a battle. I bit him as hard as I could. He threw me against the wall, so hard I thought I'd been crushed like a beetle. I couldn't breathe. My heart stopped beating. He could have had his way with me then. He could have killed me. He was a powerful, respected man. No one would have thought the less of him for the death of a slave. No one questioned the death of my mother. No one would have questioned my death."

"Oh, Mother!" Diana drew closer to her. Clodia bit her lip. Chrysis bowed her head. Bethesda's eyes glittered, but her cheeks remained dry. "I lay on the floor, stunned. I couldn't move, not even a finger. I waited for the sky to fall. But do you know what he did? He turned as white as a cloud, mumbled a curse and left the room. I think the shade of my mother must have spoken in his ear, shaming him. Instead of having me killed, he simply got rid of me. He sent me to the slave market. I was not a very satisfactory slave, apparently." She managed a brittle smile. "Men would buy me and return me before the day was done. I was sent back to be resold so many times that the man at the slave market made a joke of it. I was still young. I suppose I was beautiful — almost as beautiful as you, Diana. But word spread among the buyers that I was poison, and no one would bid on me. Finally, of course, the right man came for me. I think it must have been a whim of the goddess the Romans call Venus that sent him to the slave market that day, with barely enough coins in his purse. I was the cheapest slave on the block, and still he could barely afford me!"

The other women laughed at that, even as they wiped their eyes.

"And your husband knows nothing of what happened to you before you met? Of what the man did to you, and your mother?" said Clodia.

"Nothing. I never told him, and I think I never will. I told my daughter, because I thought she should know what befell her grandmother. And now I have told you."

I was appalled, bewildered, dumbfounded — not only at what Bethesda had said, and the fact that she had kept such a secret from me, but at the unaccountable intimacy between the women in my garden. What strange alchemy had transpired to make them so unguarded with one another? Where were the normal barriers of slavery and status that should have separated them? The world seemed to tremble beneath my feet, just as my fingers trembled as I closed my spy-hole in the ivy and silently fled to my study.

CHAPTER NINETEEN

At length, I sent a slave girl to inform Bethesda that I had returned and was in my study. Clodia appeared soon after, along with Chrysis. They were both smiling, as if they had just shared a good laugh. The visit with Bethesda and Diana had apparently ended on a happy note, which confused me all the more — how could they speak of such dreadful things and then part laughing?

"I dropped by to see if you had anything to report, and you weren't here," said Clodia, feigning petulance. "I trust you've been busy on my behalf, out scraping up something useful about Caelius — perhaps some fresh news about those slaves he bribed to poison Dio?"

"Nothing as useful as that, I'm afraid. Have you been here long?"

"A while."

"I hope you weren't bored."

"Not at all. Your wife made me feel very welcome."

"Did she?"

"Yes."

"Good."

That was the gist of the interview, and Clodia and Chrysis soon departed.

Darkness fell. Dinner was served. I was uneasy, unable to look at Bethesda or at Diana in quite the usual way. I asked Bethesda what she had thought of our visitor. "An interesting woman" was all she said.

"I take it she put your mind to rest, concerning my whereabouts last night."

"Yes." Bethesda did not elaborate.

"Well, good. All's back to normal, then?"

"I was never aware of any disruption to our routine," said Bethesda.

I bit into a crust of bread. This saved me from biting my tongue.

It was a quiet meal. As the last course of savory onions with wine was served, Bethesda cleared her throat. "Our visitor invited us to a party."

"A party?"

"The day after tomorrow. Clodia says she has a party every year, to mark the beginning of the Great Mother festival."

"And she invited *you?*"

Bethesda bristled at my skepticism. "She invited both of us."

"I don't think the sort of parties Clodia throws are likely to be — "

"I shall be hard pressed to find a suitable stola for the occasion." She peered thoughtfully into the middle distance, contemplating her wardrobe.

I sighed. For Bethesda, a personal invitation from a patrician like Clodia must have seemed almost too good to be true, an opportunity not to be missed, an acceptance into Palatine society. I was surprised myself, though I was beginning to learn not to be surprised by anything Clodia did.

Later that night, in bed, Bethesda pressed herself against me and asked me to hold her. As I took her in my arms, I longed to tell her that I knew her secret, that I understood her silence, that it made no difference. But the words did not come. Instead, I used my hands and lips and tongue to show her what I felt. Afterward, contented, she fell into a deep sleep. But I remained awake long into the night, staring into the darkness above, wondering how a man can ever think he knows the whole truth of anything.

The next morning I sent a messenger to Eco's house, to see if he had returned. The messenger came back with the news I expected: Eco was not yet back. He would come to me as soon as he arrived, I thought, no matter what the hour.

If he didn't arrive soon, anything he discovered would be of no use. The trial would begin the next morning.

I decided to spend the day in my study rather than to go down to the Forum again to search for evidence concerning Caelius and poison. I had spoken in enough ears; word of what I was seeking would continue to spread without me. Perhaps a limb that was barren yesterday would bear fruit today. If so, it would be wise to stay where any messenger could be sure to find me. And of course, Eco might arrive at any moment.

I began another letter to Meto, and ended by burning it, as I had the last. The thing on my mind was not something I could share with him in a letter. Bethesda and Diana spent the day sewing in the garden. They seemed to be in good spirits, talking to one another in low voices and laughing. I watched in silence, content merely to observe, like a guardian keeping watch on the living.

It was not an informer, but Trygonion who finally came knocking at my door that afternoon, so frantically that Belbo made no effort at all to restrain the little gallus from rushing into my study.

"Come!" he cried, trembling and gasping for breath. "Come at once!"

"What now, Trygonion?" I sighed.

"He's done it! He's actually done it! Despite all her precautions. Oh, Cybele, damn his eyes!" He clutched his face and stamped his feet.

"Trygonion! What's happened?"

"He's poisoned her. She's dying! Oh, please, come at once!"

It was no wonder that Trygonion was out of breath; he had run all the way from Clodia's house, and expected me to run all the way back with him. We arrived in the little dead-end street like gasping runners after a marathon. The door to Clodia's house was not even shut, but stood open as Trygonion had left it.

"Hurry!" He grabbed my hand and pulled me

after him. He was surprisingly strong for one who looked so delicate. I tried to keep up, but he was faster, and ended up dragging me through the foyer and the atrium, across the central garden, under the portico and down a long hallway. Outside a doorway hung with a heavy curtain a group of slaves were gathered, murmuring among themselves. They parted for Trygonion, who pulled me past the curtain into the room beyond.

Outside was bright sunshine, but inside the room it might have been midnight. The windows, like the door, were covered with heavy curtains. The only illumination came from a few lamps, which burned very low.

As my eyes adjusted to the darkness, I saw Clodia reclining on a sleeping couch with ornately carved ivory legs and plush pillows. She was covered with a woolen blanket. Her face and hands looked pale and waxen in the dim light. "Trygonion?" she whispered.

"Mistress!" he cried, addressing her as if he were her slave. He ran to her side and took her hand. "I came back as quickly as I could."

"Is Gordianus with you?"

"Yes. Save your breath, please."

"Why? Do you think I have so little left?" She laughed weakly. The gallus contorted his face. "Trygonion thinks I'm going to die," she said, turning her glittering eyes to me.

"What happened, Clodia?"

"I think it must have been something I ate." She made an arch expression, then winced.

"Have you summoned a physician?"

"My brother owns a very skilled healer who happens to know a great deal about poisons. Publius has reason to be concerned about poison, as you can imagine. The physician came while Trygonion was gone. He's outside the door now, I imagine; I couldn't stand having him in the room with me."

"What did he say?" asked Trygonion frantically.

"He said, 'I think it must have been something you ate.'" She smiled wanly. "He wanted to know how much of the powder I swallowed, and when. Early this morning, I told him, but I felt no ill effects until almost midday. He says I'm very lucky to have eaten so little of it. As it is — "

"What powder?" I said.

"Didn't Trygonion explain?"

"No time. We ran all the way," the gallus said.

"The powder that I came across in the kitchen," she said. "Imagine that! How many mornings have I ventured into the kitchen before my breakfast is ready? Never. But today, for some reason, I was awake early, and hungry, and when I called for Chrysis she didn't come, so I went to the kitchen myself. You should have seen how Chrysis jumped when I stepped into the room. She stood by a little table, and on the table was a bowl of honeyed millet. 'Is that for me?' I said. Chrysis said nothing. I walked to the bowl and saw the little box beside it, and the crumbly yellow powder inside the box. 'Some sort of spice?' I said. I suspected nothing, you see."

"A crumbly yellow powder?"

"Yes, not like any spice I know of. I touched my finger to my tongue, dabbed it in the powder and touched my tongue again. I did it without thinking. The powder didn't taste at all bad, really, only a bit earthy. Then I saw the look on Chrysis's face. All at once I knew."

I heard a strange whimpering behind me. I turned my head. The whimpering seemed to come from the opposite corner of the room, from near the floor. I thought it might be a dog. Then my eyes caught a slight movement, higher up. I peered into the deep-shadowed gloom, confused, then suddenly perceived the shape of a body suspended upside down from the roof. It was a nude woman hanging from a rope tied around her ankles, twisting very slightly. She whimpered again.

"Silence!" shouted Clodia. She sat upright, then fell back against her pillows. Trygonion fretted over her until she slapped his fawning hands away. "I sent for Trygonion at once. He came running from the House of the Galli. He was the one who thought of sending for Publius's physician. I waited and waited for the man to come; it turned out he was down at the herb market and no one knew where he had gone. At first I wasn't worried. I felt fine. Then at midday the discomfort began, and the physician still hadn't arrived. I took to my bed, and Trygonion kept fretting over me until I thought to send him for you, Gordianus."

"Why me?"

"You must know more than most men about

351

poisons. I thought you might be able to tell me something about the yellow powder. Fetch it, Trygonion."

He tore himself from her side and went to a little table crowded with tiny boxes and bottles. A burnished mirror was hung on the wall above the table, reflecting the somber light of the lamps and affording a startling glimpse of Chrysis hanging from the ceiling across the room. Trygonion returned with a little pyxis. I stepped to the nearest lamp and studied the contents.

"Is it too dark to see?" said Clodia. "I can't have the lamps any brighter. The light hurts my eyes."

"I can see well enough. I may be wrong, but I suspect this is a substance called gorgon's hair. It comes from the root of a plant that grows wild on the shores of Mauretania. It used to be quite rare in Rome, but one sees it more and more nowadays. It's very potent, acts fairly quickly, and has almost no flavor, so that it can be mixed with almost any kind of food."

Clodia closed her eyes and nodded. "You see, Trygonion, I told you that Gordianus would know. The physician said the same thing."

"Did he explain the effects?"

"He hardly needed to. I've discovered them for myself."

"Dizziness, nausea, a sensation of coldness, a painful sensitivity to light?"

She nodded, keeping her eyes shut.

"How much did you swallow?"

"Only that single small taste. Once I saw the look on Chrysis's face I knew what I'd done."

Again, I heard the whimpering from the corner of the room. "Silence!" cried Clodia.

"If you swallowed no more than that — "

"Then I'll survive, yes? That's what the physician said."

It would be a stupid physician who told a powerful, dangerous woman that she was going to die, if there was even the slightest possibility that she might survive. The powerful do not appreciate being given bad news, especially if it turns out to be false. Better for the physician to assure his master's sister that she would live; if she didn't, she would be in no position to vent her disappointment on him. But the physician was probably right. I knew something of gorgon's hair and its effects, and such a small dose seemed unlikely to kill her.

"If the physician said you'll be better, then I'm sure — "

"Don't you have your own opinion?" Her voice was sharp. "You recognized the poison. You must know how it works."

"I know many poisons by sight, but it's others who use them, not me."

"Of course you're not going to die!" Trygonion insisted. Clodia allowed him to fuss with her blanket and caress her hands.

"I thought you'd forestalled the poison plot against you," I said.

"So did I. But that farce at the Senian baths

must have been only a diversion staged by Caelius. He wanted me to think I had got the better of him, when all the time his viper was already at my breast. The slave I trusted more than any other!"

Over in the corner, Chrysis whimpered and twisted in space. My eyes had grown used to the darkness and I was able to see her more clearly. Her smooth, naked flesh was scored with mottled stripes.

"The little spy weeps because I had her beaten," said Clodia in a low voice. "Her punishment has only begun."

"She confessed to you?"

"Not yet. But Caelius must have spies in my house, just as I have spies in his. Who better than Chrysis? And I caught her in the act of poisoning my food! If I hadn't happened to step into the kitchen at that moment — "

"Why do you think this poison came from Caelius?"

Clodia gave me such a withering look that I sucked in my breath. Had Catullus ever known that look? Then she shuddered and winced and shut her eyes. "Who else?" she demanded in a weak voice. "We know he already had the poison. What I didn't know was the slave he would use to get the stuff into my house. Chrysis, not Barnabas!"

"You think this is the same poison that he tested on his own slave?"

"Of course."

"It's not."

She bit her lips and shifted beneath the blanket. "What do you mean?"

"The poison Caelius administered to his slave acted very quickly. You told me so yourself, and I assume that your spies gave you an accurate report. The slave died in agony, you said, while Caelius watched. 'It took only moments,' you said. This can't be the same poison. The Mauretanians say that gorgon's hair is like 'a coiled snake in the belly.' Once ingested, it bides its time before striking. The victim feels no ill effects for a while, then the symptoms come on suddenly. You told me that you tasted the powder in the morning but felt no effects until midday. That hardly sounds like Caelius's 'quick-acting' poison."

"So? He decided to use a different poison."

"Perhaps. If you'd let me, I'd like to take what's left of this poison with me. If I remember correctly, I happen to have a bit of gorgon's hair at my house, locked in a box where I keep such things." My son Eco had been given the stuff months ago, by a man whose wife was trying to poison him. Eco passed it on for safekeeping to me; he won't have poison in his house because of the twins. I'd almost forgotten about it. "I should like to compare this powder with the bit I have at home — "

Clodia hesitated. "Be sure to return it," she whispered, closing her eyes. "It's evidence against Caelius."

The interview seemed to be over. Clodia turned uncomfortably on the bed. Chrysis twisted from the ropes. Then Trygonion bent close to Clodia's ear and said in a low voice, "The other box."

She frowned.

"Mistress, the other box," he said again.

The grimace she made came from something other than physical discomfort. "Yes, show him. Let him see for himself."

Trygonion took the box of poison from me. He went to the little cosmetics table and came back holding a different pyxis in the palm of his hand, with his nose wrinkled and his arm extended, as if to keep the thing as far from himself as possible. I recognized it at once.

"It's the same pyxis Licinius was carrying at the Senian baths," I said.

"Are you sure?" whispered Clodia.

"Bronze, with raised knobs and inlays of ivory. Exactly the same."

"The brute! The monster!" said Trygonion, thrusting the box at me. "Go on, look inside."

"It arrived this morning," said Clodia. "Left by a messenger on the front doorstep. What was he thinking? To torture me with this obscene joke while I lay dying? Is he laughing even now?" She sucked in a shuddering breath and began to sob.

I took the tiny box from Trygonion and opened the lid. Within was a pearly, opalescent liquid, perhaps a kind of lotion or cream, I thought. I touched my finger to it and gave such a start that I dropped the box, spilling its contents on the floor. Trygonion stared at the globules of congealed semen with fascinated revulsion.

"Damn him!" Clodia thrashed on the bed. Trygonion rushed to her. I backed away and bumped into the cosmetics table. I turned and stared blindly at the unguents and philters. Among them I noticed a little clay figurine of Attis, Cybele's eunuch consort, exactly like the ones I had seen in the room of Lucius Lucceius's wife. The dim lamplight caught his red cap and lit up his serenely smiling face.

Clodia continued to moan and curse. Trygonion hovered over her. The dropped pyxis lay on the floor, its spattered contents glistening in the lamplight.

I backed away again. One of the lamps began to gutter and the room grew darker. I bumped into something solid but yielding. The rope made a cracking noise above and behind me. A low whimpering rose from below. With a start I turned and realized I had collided with the suspended body of Chrysis. Seen upside down in the flickering light, her staring eyes and nostrils were so grotesque that her face became inhuman, unreadable. Her lips moved. I bent my head, straining to hear, but her whisper was drowned by Clodia's sobbing cry behind me.

"Punish her! Punish her again!"

Beyond the heavy curtain that blocked the door I heard a murmur and a rustling among the slaves gathered in the hall. I stared at Chrysis's soundlessly moving lips, hardly knowing what I was seeing, then finally came to my senses. I stepped toward the door and pushed my way past the curtain.

The slaves in the hallway scattered and regrouped like brooding hens. As I made my way down the hall a figure approached and passed me, taking long, quick steps toward Clodia's room. It was the slave Barnabas, clutching a leather whip between his fists. He stared straight ahead, his jaw tightly clenched. His face was drained of all emotion except for his eyes, in which I glimpsed a strange mixture of determination and dread.

At home, I found Bethesda going through her wardrobe, trying to find something suitable to wear for Clodia's party. "What do you think, the blue stola or the green one? And for a necklace — the carnelian beads, or the lapis lazuli ones you gave me last year?"

"I'm afraid it's rather unlikely that there'll be a party after all."

"But why not?"

"Clodia is ill." To explain what had just transpired at Clodia's house was beyond my energy.

"Perhaps she'll feel better in the morning," said Bethesda, frowning.

"Perhaps. We'll see whether she shows up at the trial tomorrow morning."

"Yes, the trial! She won't miss that. She'll have to feel better, and then she'll have the party after all. She's put so much planning into it."

"Into the trial?"

"Into the party, silly."

I nodded. "No word from Eco?"

"None."

I suddenly realized that I had forgotten the box of gorgon's hair which I had intended to borrow from Clodia, to compare with the poison stored in my own strongbox. I had no desire to go back for it. For the moment, I forgot about it.

CHAPTER TWENTY

Bethesda was prescient. In the morning, when we went down to the Forum to watch the trial, Clodia was already there in the great square in front of the Rostra, seated behind the prosecutors in the midst of a great many of her retainers. She was pale and her eyes were listless, but the crisis had apparently passed. She looked in our direction and smiled wanly — not at me, I realized, but at Bethesda, who nodded and smiled in return. For me Clodia had no smile, only a raised eyebrow, as if to ask if I had any last bit of information to give her. I pursed my lips and shook my head. Eco had still not returned, and none of my nets had snagged a fish.

It was the day before the beginning of the Great Mother festival. For six days Rome would celebrate with games and competitions, religious processions and plays, private parties and public ceremonies. After the festival, members of the Senate would briefly reconvene before taking their traditional Aprilis holiday at their country estates. Rome would shut down, like a great gristmill grinding to a halt. On the eve of all this, the mood in the Forum was a combination of rush and relaxation — hectic hurry to take care of final business together with the delicious anticipation of the coming days of indolence and pleasure.

This giddy mood was heightened even more by the raucous atmosphere which always attends a major trial, especially a trial as rich with the promise of scandal as this one. With no other courts in session, every advocate in Rome was in attendance, and with so much recent debate over the Egyptian situation and Dio's death, most of the Senate had come to watch. Those wise enough to plan ahead had sent slaves to the Forum at dawn to put down folding chairs and hold places for them. I had sent Belbo to do just that for Bethesda and myself. I scanned the cluttered rows and spotted him waving to us from an excellent place near the front, just behind the benches where the seventy-odd judges would sit. We made our way to our seats. Before Belbo withdrew to the great crowd of gawkers and idlers that continued to gather at the periphery, I told him to keep an eye out for Eco, who might still show up at the last moment.

Before us, beyond the judges' benches, was the open square, from which the advocates would deliver their speeches. To the left sat the prosecutors with their assistants and witnesses. This was where Clodia sat. Barnabas sat next to her, and nearby I recognized "Busy Fingers" Vibennius and several others who had taken part in the fruitless chase at the Senian baths.

Directly opposite the prosecutors, to our right, were the benches of the defendant, accompanied by his advocates, family, supporters and character witnesses. The parents of Marcus Caelius were dressed all in black, as if in mourning. His mother's eyes were puffy and red and her cheeks were wet with tears; his father had white stubble on his jaw and unkempt hair, giving him the look of a man half crazy with worry. The parents of every accused man show up in court looking just the same. If Caelius had children, they would have been standing in rags, weeping. Such traditional means of evoking pity in the judges began so long ago that no advocate would consider allowing his client's family to show up looking less than wretched.

Seated beside Caelius were his two advocates. Cicero was looking leaner and sharper than when I had seen him last; a year of bitter exile had trimmed his belly, taken in his jowls and polished his eyes to a fine glitter. Gone was the fat complacency that had settled on him after his year as consul and his triumph over Catilina. In its place was a look at once haunted and eager — haunted because he had learned that Rome could turn viciously against him, eager because he had successfully lashed back at his enemies and was again in the ascendant. The eagerness in his eyes recalled the headstrong young advocate I had first met many years ago, but the hard set of his jaw and the bitter line of his lips belonged to a much older man. As an advocate Cicero had been ambitious, unscrupulous and brilliant from the very beginning — a dangerous man to take on in a court of law.

Now he looked more formidable than ever.

As for Marcus Crassus, the richest man in Rome seemed to have stopped aging in recent years. He was a few years older than I, but looked closer to forty than sixty. Some joked that Crassus had made a deal with the gods to let him grow richer with passing time instead of older. If so, even that deal was not sweet enough to satisfy him; he looked as stern and discontented as ever. Crassus was a man who could never succeed enough for his own satisfaction. This restlessness drove him from triumph to triumph in the arenas of finance and politics, setting a pace that his less gifted colleagues could not hope to match and bitterly resented.

Beside these two old foxes, Marcus Caelius looked strikingly young and fresh, almost boyish. A good night's sleep or some other tonic had erased the slack dissolution I had seen on his face at the Salacious Tavern. Caelius had always been a mime of sorts, able to put on roles and shrug them off to suit the moment, and for this occasion he mimed the bright-eyed innocence of youth with uncanny precision. His cleverness had gotten him into trouble before; in recent years he had strayed from his mentors Crassus and Cicero, perhaps even betrayed them in the pursuit of his own fortunes. They might reasonably have turned their backs on him now, but all differences had apparently been reconciled. They were three foxes sitting in a row.

I turned my eyes from the defense to the prosecution. Leading them was young Lucius Sempronius Atratinus. If Caelius looked fresh beside his weathered advocates, Atratinus looked positively childlike. He was only seventeen, barely a man in the eyes of the law. But youthful passion can count for much with Roman judges, who have sat through too many speeches to be much impressed by false indignation or tired blustering, no matter how experienced the advocate. Young Atratinus's interest in prosecuting Caelius was the extension of a family feud; it was Atratinus's father, Bestia, against whom Caelius made his notorious pun about the "finger of guilt." Atratinus's pursuit of Caelius's destruction was a virtuous act in the eyes of a Roman court, where loyalty to fathers counts for so much.

Flanking Atratinus were his fellow prosecutors. I knew little about them. Lucius Herennius Balbus was a friend of Bestia's and more familiar to me by sight than by ear; I had never heard him argue a case, but the sight of his well-fed body scurrying back and forth in the Forum (like a giant egg wearing a toga, Eco had once said) was impressed on my memory. Publius Clodius was the third prosecutor — not Clodia's brother, but one of his freedmen, who accordingly bore the same name; thus the Clodii were represented among the prosecutors in an indirect way, as they no doubt preferred, by name but not by blood.

Gnaeus Domitius, the presiding magistrate, mounted his tribunal. The judges were sworn in. The trial commenced with the reading of the formal charges.

There were five charges in all. The first four dealt with incidents of violence against foreign dignitaries, whose persons were sacrosanct; violence against them was technically violence against their protector, the Roman state, and so qualified for prosecution under the law against political terror. The charges were grave: that Marcus Caelius masterminded attacks at Neapolis to intimidate the newly arrived Alexandrian delegation; that he instigated a riot against the delegation at Puteoli; that he perpetrated arson against the delegation during their stay at the property of Palla, on their way to Rome; that he attempted to poison the head of the delegation, Dio, and subsequently took part in Dio's murder.

To these was added another, new allegation: that Caelius had attempted to poison Clodia. There were reactions of surprise among many in the crowd, including Bethesda.

"What are they talking about?" she whispered.

I shrugged and tried to look ignorant.

"You told me she was ill, not poisoned!"

I put a finger to my lips and nodded toward the defendant's bench, where Crassus had risen to make a statement. "It should be noted by our presiding magistrate Gnaeus Domitius and by the judges that this final charge is a new one, appended by the prosecution only yesterday, in fact. The defense has hardly been given the customary amount of time to prepare an argument in response to so serious an accusation. Thus we would be within our rights to protest the inclusion of this charge, indeed, to insist that it be thrown out and argued in a separate trial, or, if it is to be included, to demand a postponement of this trial. Further, given that this is a court convened solely to try cases of political violence, it hardly seems suitable to include a charge of attempted poisoning against a private citizen. However, as the prosecution seems to believe that this charge is in fact related to the others, and as my esteemed friend and colleague Marcus Cicero assures me that he is fully prepared to defend our client against it, we make no objection to its inclusion in this trial."

Crassus nodded gravely to the presiding magistrate and the judges and sat. On Cicero's face I saw the quiver of a smirk, barely repressed. It was a look I knew well; the great orator was feeling smug about something. Could it be that he was secretly pleased to have the charge of the attempted poisoning of Clodia included among the rest? What conjurer's trick was he planning this time?

Formalities concluded, the trial could begin. The three prosecutors would speak first, then Caelius and his advocates would respond. After the orations, witnesses for both sides would deliver their statements. Given the number of speakers and the numerous charges to be discussed, the trial would surely last for more than one day.

A Roman trial is only ostensibly about establishing guilt or innocence. At Rome, all trials are to some extent political, and a trial for political violence is overtly so. Roman judges are not merely citizens seeking the truth about a specific act; they are a committee of the state, and their purpose is to make a political as well as a moral judgment. A trial typically deals with the whole life of the accused — his reputation, family connections, political affiliations, sexual practices, virtues, vices. Judgment is rendered not merely on whether the accused did or did not commit a specific crime, but on the entire character of the accused, and for the good of the body politic as a whole. Cicero himself put it plainly at a trial held the year before his own exile: "When rendering their verdict, judges must consider the good of the community and the needs of the state."

Moreover, everyone knows that judges are more influenced by the orations of the advocates than by the testimony of the witnesses who follow. "Arguments count for more than witnesses," as Cicero has often said. The deductions a good orator draws from the internal evidence of a case (asserting, "Because of this, it stands to reason that . . .") are more persuasive than the bald statements of any given witness, no matter that the witness testifies under oath (or in the case of slaves, under torture).

Atratinus rose to deliver the first speech. His clear young voice carried exceedingly well, and his oratorical delivery, if not polished to a dazzling shine, had the ring of sincerity.

Atratinus dwelled exclusively on Caelius's character — his well-known dissipation, his extravagance, the disreputable haunts he was known to frequent. Atratinus's righteous indignation would have sounded forced and false coming from many older advocates, but Atratinus was young and unsullied enough to be credible when he frowned on Caelius's excesses.

Caelius was untrustworthy, said Atratinus. No wise man would turn his back on Caelius, or else Caelius was likely to slander and mock him, as he had slandered and mocked his own mentors behind their backs, *those who were at this very moment closest to him;* his notorious lack of respect for these men was sadly evident to everyone else in the court except themselves, apparently. Now that he had finally gotten himself into more trouble than he could handle, the crass opportunist was only too happy to make use of the elders he had betrayed, not only his mentors, but his own father, whom he had abandoned to go live by himself in a Palatine apartment where he could indulge all his vices away from paternal eyes, and make fun of the humble house on the Quirinal Hill from which he had fled, and to which he had now unwillingly returned in his distress. There were more sincere ways to show respect to one's father, Atratinus insisted, pausing with a meaningful smile so that no one would miss the example he himself presented.

Nor would it be wise for any woman to turn her back on Caelius, he said, for the fellow was capable of far worse than mockery and slander — as we would see when the charge of the attempted poisoning of Clodia was dealt with by another speaker.

Atratinus played on these themes of dissipation and disreputable conduct, turning them over and over as a man turns a jewel in his hand, to see the various ways it catches the light. By turns he sought to outrage the judges, to appeal to sentiment, to make them laugh.

Politically, he said, Caelius had flirted with the cause of the depraved revolutionary Catilina. Sexually, he had assaulted the wives of Roman citizens; witnesses would be called to verify these charges. Witnesses would also be called to attest to Caelius's violent nature; there was the case of a senator named Fufius whom Caelius had beaten up at the pontifical elections in front of a crowd of horrified onlookers. And if these indications of Caelius's character were not damning enough, consider the way he swaggered and strutted and spat out his speeches when playing the prosecutor at other men's trials, or debating in the Senate. And the appalling color of the stripe on his senatorial toga! Where everyone else's was traditionally somber, almost black, his was a garishly bright, bold purple. At the reminder of this impropriety, I saw quite a few judges nod their gray heads.

Worst of all — because it was this vice which most seriously threatened to destroy the republic — was Caelius's extravagance with money. In this Caelius represented the very worst aspect of his generation, which was set so firmly apart from wiser, more senior men such as the judges, as well as from less experienced but more virtuous young men of Atratinus's age, who looked on the spendthrift habits of men like Caelius with dread and dismay. What would become of the Republic if such men were not stopped? They squandered fortunes on licentious behavior and spent huge sums on electoral bribery, corrupting everyone and everything they touched. Then, finding themselves bankrupt, as they inevitably must, and stripped by their own debauchery of all moral sense, such men resorted without hesitation to the most fiendish crimes to replenish their coffers. To get his hands on Egyptian gold, Caelius had covered his hands with Egyptian blood. In so doing he had cast a bloody stain on the dignity and honor of the Roman state.

"If ever there was a case which proved the sad necessity for courts such as this one, this is that case. If ever there was a man who fully deserved the condemnation of this court, Marcus Caelius is that man." So Atratinus concluded.

I turned to Bethesda and asked what she thought. "Rather too young for my taste," she said. "But a pleasant voice."

The freedman Publius Clodius spoke next. His speech dealt with the first three charges against Caelius. Where Atratinus had shown a kind of prim distaste at having to pollute himself with cataloguing Caelius's crimes, Clodius attacked with the relish of a man wielding a red-hot poker. He did not hesitate to make crude jabs and thrusts, but he also pulled back from time to time, confident

370

in his weapon's power to inflict damage even from a distance. Paroxysms of disgust were punctuated with abrupt full stops, during which, standing stock-still and emotionless, Clodius would deliver some of his most acid comments, eliciting gasps and laughter from the crowd. It was a technically dazzling speech.

The virtues or vices of Caelius's character might ultimately be matters of opinion, he conceded, especially in a time when so many Romans had become sadly confused about such things, but the outrages committed against the Alexandrian envoys were simple matters of fact. A hundred of the most respected men in Egypt had come to Rome to petition the Senate. As ambassadors, they carried the protection of the gods and the state. Yet they had been met with unremitting violence, intimidation, fire and ultimately murder. Word of this scandal had spread from the Pillars of Hercules to the borders of Parthia, undermining Rome's prestige with her subjects and allies and inflaming her already precarious relations with the volatile kingdom of Egypt.

The places and dates of these attacks were well documented. The prosecution would produce witnesses who would swear that in each instance — at Neapolis, at Puteoli, and at Palla's estate — Marcus Caelius had been seen in the vicinity shortly before the attack, in the company of known assassins. Further, as other witnesses would attest, Caelius had been heard shamelessly bragging in public about his part in the massacres. What sort of man was so imprudent as to boast of engineering such atrocities? Clearly, a man with the depraved character of Marcus Caelius.

Clodius proceeded to give a vivid account of each attack, piling on gory details, painting tableaus of pity and terror, invoking the shades of the un-avenged dead.

Why, he asked, had Marcus Caelius perpetrated such violence? The reason was obvious: for finan-cial gain. A man like Marcus Caelius, from a hum-ble but respectable family, could hardly engage in the high living he was famous for without in-curring massive debts. Witnesses would be called to document his reckless spending habits. If Caelius wished to dispute these witnesses, and if he had nothing to hide, let him open his private account books for the court. Was he willing to do that? If not, why not? Because, Clodius alleged, those account books would reveal the payments Caelius had received to mount his campaign of terror against the Alexandrian envoys. To finance his own disgusting pleasures, Caelius had sold out the good name of the whole Roman people. Clodius's indignation came to an appropriately thunderous climax that had the crowd stamping their feet with appreciation. He returned to the bench mopping sweat from his forehead like a boxer.

I turned to Bethesda and raised an eyebrow. "Well?"

"Everybody knows that freedmen try harder," she said. "But all that blustering and waving of arms only makes me nervous."

"I noticed you fidgeting. Afraid for your precious Marcus Caelius?"

" 'Oratory is all very well when there are no facts to go on,' " she said. I looked at her amazed, as I always am when she unexpectedly quotes some old Roman proverb. It's natural of course that she should pick up such things from me and from going to trials, but there's something jarring about hearing them repeated with an Egyptian accent. "And so far," she said, "they've said nothing about the death of Dio, nor about any attempt to poison Clodia."

"I suspect that will come next."

Lucius Herennius Balbus mounted the Rostra to conclude for the prosecution. If Atratinus had played outraged youth, Herennius was the stern, admonishing uncle, castigating Caelius's character from an older, wiser, but no less scandalized perspective. He began and ended his speech by reciting the litany of Caelius's vices. In between, he dealt with the death of Dio and the "bare escape" of a certain Roman lady who had the misfortune to know more about Caelius's crimes than was healthy for her.

That lady, he said, would testify about a loan which she had made to Caelius, ostensibly to put on games in his hometown for the sake of his political career — when in fact no such games had taken place. The money she lent him had been used to bribe slaves in the house of Lucius Lucceius, in an attempt to murder Dio by poison, and thus put an end once and for all to the decimated

Alexandrian delegation by destroying its leader. That particular plot had failed, but Dio, alerted to the danger, had fled to another house, and it was there that he eventually met his end. By whose hand, everyone in the court must know: the assassin Publius Asicius. Never mind that Asicius had been acquitted at his own trial; it was common knowledge that the prosecution and defense had conspired together to throw the case in Asicius's favor. Caelius and Asicius, partners in so many other vices, had been partners in this outrage as well — witnesses would be called who would place the two very close to the house where Dio was staying on the night of his murder. Like a tree with many branches, the Alexandrian delegation had been ruthlessly hacked away, limb by limb, until only the trunk remained. Caelius had not been satisfied until that, too, was destroyed.

Here Herennius delivered an encomium to Dio, reciting his many honors and achievements, naming the men who had bravely given him shelter in his days of despair, mourning the loss of so brilliant a philosopher, lamenting the shame that had been visited upon Rome by his murder.

What of the final charge against Caelius, that of ruthlessly seeking the death by poison of a great Roman lady, the descendant of one of the city's oldest and proudest families, the widow of one of her most distinguished citizens? The lady was present and would, strength permitting, testify herself to the outrage plotted against her.

At one point, Caelius had aligned himself with

the lady's brother — just one more of his fickle, never-to-be-trusted alliances — and this brought him into the lady's acquaintance. Sad day for her! Young and good-looking, Caelius was quite a charmer, to be sure — proof of that was the fact that he'd talked two men he'd stabbed in the back into representing him today! Using all his skills he had charmed the lady out of a rather large loan. Later, she had cause to regret her trust in the scoundrel, not only because the loan was never repaid — typical, predictable! — but because with mounting horror she realized the use to which Caelius had put the money. His Egyptian coffers had run dry, but his mission was not yet finished, so he used her gold to bribe another man's slaves to poison Dio. The realization shocked the lady to her senses. Disgusted with Caelius's indecency and his murderous bent, outraged that she had been duped into financing his crimes, she decided to do something about it; she agreed to appear as a witness at this trial. A brave act, to make herself the enemy of a murderer — and almost fatal, as it turned out. To silence her, Caelius decided to poison her.

"Those of us who have attended all too many trials for murder know the sad pattern," said Herennius, lowering his voice to a confidential tone. "Let a man once descend to using poison on another human being and, sooner or later, he will try the same thing again. Poisoning becomes a habit, a secret vice, like certain other things men do in the dark. Until he is stopped, by the law or by the gods, a poisoner will repeat his vile crime over and over again."

Thus, having fallen into this vice with his attempt on Dio — if indeed it was his first poisoning! — Caelius not surprisingly resorted to poison to rid himself of the troublesome lady. He tested the stuff first on one of his own slaves. (Not on one of his old, trusted slaves, to be sure; Caelius had purchased a slave specifically to test his poison, as one might buy a cheap garment intending to use it as a rag and then throw it away. If he cared to deny the fact, let Caelius produce that slave in court alive and well.) Then Caelius approached some of the lady's slaves (like a typical poisoner, repeating the same mode of operation) and tried to bribe them to administer the poison. But the loyal slaves betrayed the plot to their mistress, and she cleverly sought to trap Caelius's agent in the act of handing over the deadly stuff.

Herennius proceeded to give a completely straight-faced account of the disaster at the Senian baths, which provoked some snickering among the spectators; the story had made the rounds. To verify the incident, he said, the slaves whom Caelius had thought to suborn would testify. So that they would not have to suffer the indignities of torture, and to reward them for their loyalty, these slaves had been manumitted and would testify as freedmen.

Herennius sighed with exasperation. "Caelius's attempt to poison Dio failed. So did his first attempt on the lady. But still Caelius did not give up! Only hours ago, the lady came very close to death, thanks to Caelius's relentless, insidious efforts to do her in. Look at her now, at her pale face and languid eyes, at her helpless trembling! One need only see her to know that something truly terrible has transpired. 'What awful thing was done to her?' you ask. But no, I shall refrain from relating the sordid details of this latest, almost successful attempt to murder her. Since the gods have seen fit to spare her from Caelius's murderous plots, let her tell the story. Let the tale of her hairbreadth escape emerge from her own shocking testimony. I only pray to the gods that she will continue to recover and be strong enough to testify!"

Regarding this latest outrage, the judges would also hear the written confession of the wretched slave girl Caelius had seduced into betraying her mistress. Her testimony was even now being extracted under torture, as the law required.

There would also be a third, surprise witness to corroborate. Herennius cast a chilly smile at the bench opposite. "That man's testimony should be of special interest to the defense, I imagine. The esteemed Marcus Cicero himself has declared this witness to be 'the most honest man in Rome.' Wait until you hear what that fellow has to tell us about the attempts to poison this lady, Cicero! I wonder what you'll have to say then about the depraved murderer sitting beside you!"

This struck me as a clever but dangerous ploy on the part of Herennius, to leave a damaging revelation to his witnesses so that it could emerge as a surprise at the very end of the trial, rather than to include it in his oration, where he could shape and deliver the accusation himself. The advantage was the sympathy to be stirred by a poison survivor telling her own story; the defense would be hard-pressed to anticipate and neutralize ahead of time any surprises that might emerge from such testimony. Who, I wondered, was this alleged "most honest man in Rome"? I looked at Cicero to catch his reaction and found him, oddly enough, staring straight at me.

CHAPTER TWENTY-ONE

"I don't believe for a moment that he poisoned her," said Bethesda, "any more than I believe that he killed the Egyptian."

After three long orations, the court had adjourned early so that the defense advocates could present their responses in succession on the following day. Bethesda and I immediately headed home, where she proceeded to get ready for Clodia's party, even though nightfall was still hours away.

"But Clodia insists that he did."

"She's mistaken," Bethesda frowned at the burnished mirror she held in her hand. "This necklace will never do. Hand me the silver one."

"It can't be both ways," I said. "One of them is lying. What a pity that you have to choose between Clodia and Caelius. What a choice for anyone to have to make!"

"Right now, I am trying to choose a necklace," she said. "The silver one, please."

I searched her dresser for a silver necklace and found myself lost amid the clay jars of unguents and little glass vials of perfume. My eye caught a flash of bright red. "What's this?"

"What?"

I picked up the little clay figure of Attis, identical

to the ones I had seen in the room of Lucceius's wife and on Clodia's dresser. The smiling eunuch stood with his hands on his fat belly, with a bright red Phrygian cap on his head. Bethesda glimpsed its reflection and put down her mirror. "You shouldn't touch that."

"Where did it come from?"

"It came while we were at the trial today."

"I asked *where* it came from, not when."

"It's a gift."

"Who sent it?"

"Who do you think?" Bethesda took the statue from me. She put it back on the dresser, then scooped up a long silver necklace and reached for her mirror. "You're hopeless. Go away and tell Diana to come help me dress."

We arrived at Clodia's door at the last moment of twilight, when the hard edges of the world begin to soften and grow hazy like the mind of a man ready for sleep. But while the world might be drowsy, the party-goers at Clodia's house were wide awake. The brightly lit dining room off her garden was alive with music and conversation. Slaves were just beginning to show the guests to their places at the dining couches when we arrived. It was an odd mixture of impeccably dressed patricians and scruffy-looking young poets, of radical politicians and aging courtesans, of exotic-looking foreigners and even a few galli. The air was heavy with the world-weary sophistication that passes for style in Rome these days.

Bethesda clutched my arm. On her face was a look so unlike her that it took me a moment to figure out what it was: panic. "What are we doing here?" she whispered.

"Attending what appears to be a very fashionable party, with very fashionable people."

"Why?"

"I think it was you who insisted that we come," I said dryly.

"I must have been out of my mind. Take me home at once."

"But we haven't eaten yet." The smells wafting from the kitchen made my mouth water. "We haven't even said hello to our hostess."

"That is exactly why we should go this instant. It will be as if we never came."

"Bethesda — "

"This is absurd. Look at me."

I stepped back and did just that. "Yes? I see a beautiful woman, immaculately dressed and made up. She looks like no one else here."

"Exactly! Anyone can tell I don't belong."

"Why not?"

"I'm not even Roman."

"Of course you are. You're my wife."

"We're not rich."

"No one could tell from the jewelry you're wearing."

"My accent!"

"It gives you an air of mystery."

"I'm the oldest woman here."

"You're the most beautiful woman here."

"He's absolutely right, you know." I turned to see Catullus at my elbow, holding a cup of wine and wearing a slack grin. "Gratidianus, I didn't expect to see you here."

"Clodia invited us," said Bethesda, a little too insistently.

"She invited me, too, do you believe it?" said Catullus. "Against her better judgment, I'm sure, or against her brother's judgment, anyway. But he's not here — busy with tomorrow's festivities — and I am, so to Hades with him! Let nothing spoil my triumphant return to Palatine society! What a bunch of leeches, lechers and losers." Catullus surveyed the crowd, his grin dripping with acid. "What a bizarre menagerie Clodia's put together: the worst poets and the crookedest politicians in Rome; bankrupt nobles and obscenely wealthy ex-slaves; beautiful boys and homely prostitutes. Did I say homely? Ugly enough to turn a man to stone — no obscene pun intended. And here before me, the most honest man in Rome, accompanied by — " He paused and his expression sobered a bit. "Just as you put it, Gordianus: the most beautiful woman here."

"My wife," I said. "And this, Bethesda, is Gaius Valerius Catullus, just back from a year of government service in Bithynia."

Bethesda nodded knowingly. "The poet," she said.

He raised an eyebrow. "Am I that famous? Or have you been talking about me behind my back, Gordianus?"

"Not me," I said, trying to make something of the cryptic smile on Bethesda's face and wondering what else Clodia confided to her about Catullus at their first and only meeting. At least Bethesda seemed to be getting her bearings, for which I was glad.

A serving slave arrived to show us to our places. Couches were gathered in U-shaped groups around serving tables. The seating was two to a couch, allowing plenty of room to sit up or recline. As it turned out, Catullus was put at the couch next to ours, at my right. For the moment there was no one else to share his couch. Had Clodia placed us together on purpose, or simply because we were the last guests to be invited? Our group of couches was situated in a corner of the room, the farthest away from the hostess's. That suited me; it would allow Bethesda to feel less conspicuous. But Catullus was not pleased. "Banished back to Bithynia," I heard him grumble.

A senator named Fufius was shown to the couch at Bethesda's left. He was the man whom Atratinus had accused Caelius of assaulting during an election, and would be testifying as a prosecution witness. Fufius was accompanied by a very young courtesan. Bethesda raised an eyebrow, and I could read her mind: the girl was hardly older than Diana. But Bethesda seemed somewhat mollified when the senator gave her an appraising look and an appreciative smile.

Clodia had not yet appeared and her couch was unoccupied. Catullus scanned the faces of those who still stood and milled about. "Who will take the place of honor beside our hostess tonight? Let me see: husband Quintus is down in Hades, brother Publius is off making last-moment arrangements for tomorrow's festival, and lover Caelius — ah, he's on trial for murder, isn't he? Poison, wasn't it? Well, I suppose we wouldn't want a poisoner at our dinner party, no matter how superior his stud service. Still, someone will have to share the couch with our queen. Not one of her other brothers, I think; Publius would go crazy with jealousy. Perhaps that ranting freedman who spoke at the trial today. He has Publius's name, if not his looks, and we've seen that he can fill in for his ex-master, in public speaking anyway. But it's rather hard to imagine the likes of him lying with his head on her lap while she dabbles sautéed sparrow brains into his mouth, isn't it? Ah, there she is, our Lesbia. Almighty Venus! Where on earth did she get that dress?"

"You can see right through it," murmured Bethesda.

"I happen to know that the fabric comes from Cos," I said, showing off. "Something new from a famous silkmaker there."

"I thought you weren't her lover," growled Catullus. Was he teasing me again, or truly angry? Suddenly he let out a barking laugh, so loud that several heads turned to look. "Oh no, not Egnatius!" he whispered. "I thought she was done with him."

Clodia took her place at her couch. Joining her

was a tall, muscular young man with a full black beard and a dazzling smile. I recognized his face from the Salacious Tavern.

"Very handsome," said Bethesda.

"If a stud horse could stand upright and grin he'd look like Egnatius, and women would call him handsome, I suppose." Catullus curled his upper lip. "The foul-mouthed Spaniard with the sparkling smile. But then, don't Spaniards always have the whitest teeth? You know how they get such white teeth, don't you?"

Bethesda inclined her head inquiringly.

"If Egnatius is the lord of the feast, all I can say is: check your wine cup before you take a swig."

"What do you mean?" asked Bethesda.

Catullus cleared his throat and began:

"Egnatius is forever smiling to show off that dazzling grin.
  Go to a trial — "

He started to laugh and covered his mouth until he could stop. The senator and his courtesan leaned closer to listen. "No, wait, let me start over. I'll change it up a bit, especially for tonight. Let me think . . ." He clapped his hands. "Yes:

Egnatius is forever smiling to show off that dazzling grin.
  In court tomorrow, Cicero will have everyone weeping:

'Pitiful poisoner, er, prisoner!' — except for Eg-
    natius, who'll grin.
And when Caelius is run out of town, his mother
    mourning,
'Only son! Good as dead!' — for her sake, Eg-
    natius will grin.
It's a sickness, that grin: everywhere, every-
    when.
Social grace? Social disease, I'd call it!
Look Egnatius, listen up: Had you been born
    Roman,
Or Sabine, or Tiburtine, obese Etruscan or Um-
    brian slob,
Or a swarthy Lanuvian with teeth just as perfect,
Or a Transpadane from my own dear, sweet Ve-
    rona,
Or any man who cleans his teeth in the regular
    way,
Still I'd curse that grin. It's inane. It offends!
Ah, but you come from Spain — and Spaniards
    every morning,
As we know, scrub their teeth white and rub
    their gums rosy
With the stuff that squirts out of their bladders.
    Yellow cleanser!
So flash that perfect grin — it only goes to show
    how much
You've been guzzling from your own chamber-
    pot.
I'd rather my own teeth should rot!"

The old senator clapped. His courtesan giggled.

Bethesda grudged a crooked smile and whispered in my ear: "Are all his poems so vulgar?"

"All the bits I've heard."

"Surely his love poems are different," she sighed, looking puzzled. Clodia's attraction to Marcus Caelius made perfect sense to her, but Catullus's appeal eluded her.

At that moment, Catullus's couch partner arrived. I should have known who it would be; his presence added the final measure of perverse imbalance to our little dining group. "Have I just arrived at the *end* of one of your poems?" quipped Trygonion, sliding onto the couch. "What fortunate timing."

Catullus scowled and snorted, but only to hide a deeper reaction. His jaw stiffened and quivered. He blinked uncontrollably. Not only had Clodia banished him back to Bithynia; she had seated him side by side with her emasculated pet. No one but me seemed to notice that Catullus was barely managing to fight back tears.

When everyone was seated, Clodia welcomed her guests with a very brief speech and the promise that she would strive to greet everyone more personally as the evening progressed; this evoked a low, suggestive whistle from a young man with a scraggly beard and a very bad haircut at a table nearby. His companions made a playful show of slapping him down for his presumptuousness. I saw Catullus wince.

The evening commenced with the arrival of the

first course, a goose-liver paste fit for the gods of Olympus. An exquisite Falernian wine washed away all cares. Soon Bethesda was charming Senator Fufius with stories of her native Alexandria, while his neglected young courtesan played with her food and pouted. The senator seemed genuinely fascinated by everything Bethesda had to say. "I've never been to Egypt myself," he wheezed, "but of course with all this debate and controversy of late, one has to wonder what all the fuss is about." Even Trygonion and Catullus began to converse in fits and starts, if only because neither of them could keep his mouth shut for long. They traded barbs and competed at casting aspersions on various people in the room. They kept silent about those within earshot — the chief advantage of sitting next to them, I decided.

At length the dinner ended, or at least the first dinner of the evening; there would be more food and wine later. The time for entertainment had arrived. The guests moved to the garden, where folding chairs and couches had been placed in front of the little stage. I was happy to take my leave of Catullus and Trygonion, but the senator stayed close to Bethesda, with his courtesan following behind. Slaves continued to move among the guests, offering tidbits and delicacies to those with bottomless stomachs and making sure that no cup stayed empty for long.

The entertainment began with a mime show, one of those performances with a single unmasked actor speaking all the roles. The performer was new to Rome ("Just arrived in town," announced Clodia, "after spreading laughter from Cyprus to Sicily"), but the little playlets he performed were the old standards, raunchy skits about a slave talking back to his master, and a matchmaker trying to convince a husband he needs a second wife, and a doctor accidently treating the wrong patient with a series of hilariously painful cures. The actor suggested costume changes in an instant with the barest theatrical devices — a scarf transformed him into a bashful young maiden, a hideously exaggerated bracelet made him a rich lady, a child's wooden play-sword turned him into a swaggering general.

The crowd tittered at every obscenity, groaned at the terrible puns, and roared with laughter at the climax of each skit. The actor was quite extraordinary; Clodia knew how to choose an entertainer. In the gaps between skits, Bethesda informed the old senator that mimes had originated in the streets and squares of Alexandria, where wandering actors would set down their boxes of props and put on impromptu shows for whatever coins the crowd might toss their way. That was still the only real way to see a mime, Bethesda insisted, though she supposed that the man Clodia had found was clever enough for a Roman audience.

The actor concluded his final skit to great applause. Clodia stepped onto the stage.

"And now, something very special," she said. "An old friend has returned from his wanderings in the East — ”

"Like Odysseus?" said someone. I looked around and saw that it was the young man with the bad haircut.

"If Catullus is Odysseus, does that mean Clodia is Penelope?" said one of his friends.

"I hope not," said another. "You know what Odysseus did to Penelope's suitors — he crashed a party and killed them all!"

"As I was saying," said Clodia, raising her voice above the laughter, "an old friend is back. Wiser, one presumes; certainly older, if only by a year; and with new poems to share with us. I mean our dear friend from Verona, Gaius Valerius Catullus, whose words have touched us all."

"And wounded a few of us!" yelled someone.

"While he was in the East, Catullus tells me, he took a journey to look at the ruins of ancient Troy. He climbed pine-covered Mount Ida, where Jupiter sat to watch the Greeks and Trojans do battle on the plain below. He saw the place where his beloved brother is buried, and performed a funeral rite. And while he was there, he saw something that few men have ever seen. He was invited to witness the secret rites at the Temple of Cybele, including the ceremony by which a man becomes a gallus in the service of the Great Mother."

I expected to hear more lewd comments at this point, but instead a hush fell over the crowd.

"This experience, Catullus tells me, moved him to compose a poem in honor of Attis, the consort of Cybele, the lover who gave up his sex in her worship, the inspiration of all the galli since. On the eve of the Great Mother festival, what could be more appropriate than the first public recitation of this poem?"

She left the platform. Catullus took her place. His lids looked heavy, his eyes bleary and he seemed to barely avoid falling as he stepped onto the stage. I held my breath, wondering how he could possibly perform before an audience. He was too drunk, too bitter, too unsure of himself, too weak. He seemed to be thinking the same thing. For a long time he stood completely still, his shoulders slumped, staring first at his feet, then at something above the heads of the audience. Was he bemused by the giant Venus behind us, or simply gazing into space?

But when he finally opened his mouth to speak, the voice that emerged was unlike anything I had ever heard before. It was light and airy yet strangely powerful, like a glittering net thrown over the audience, like a whisper in a dream.

I have heard countless orators in the Forum, listened to many actors on the stage. Their voices are their tools, skilled at shaping utterances suitable to the occasion; words emerge at their decree like slaves suited to a particular task. But with Catullus, everything seemed reversed. The words were in control; the poem ruled the poet, and used not just his voice but his whole body for its delivery, shaping his face, gesturing with his hands, causing his feet to pace the stage all to the poem's purpose. The poem would have existed with or without the poet. His presence was merely a convenience, since he happened to have a tongue which the poem could use to deliver itself to the ears of Clodia's guests on that warm spring night in her garden on the Palatine:

"Attis sailed his swift vessel through the deep
    waves
And set his eager feet upon the Phrygian shore.
He entered the sunless forest, where his mind
    became
As dark as the dense woods around him.
Moved by madness, he picked up a sharp stone.
He sliced off his manhood. He rose up trans-
    figured:
A woman, the blood dripping from between her
    legs
Giving life to the dank, pungent earth.
Attis snatched up a drum and beat it, making
    music
To the Great Mother and her mysteries,
Singing rapturous falsetto to the servants of Cy-
    bele:
'Come galli, all together, to the groves on the
    mountain.
Sea salt stings the wound — turn away from the
    sea.
Turn away from Venus. Rid yourselves of man-
    hood.
Leave that loathsome sort of love behind you,
Embrace the ecstasies of unsexed passion . . . ' "

It was a long, strange poem. At times it became a chant, and the poet a dancer, moved to sway and stamp his feet by the poem that possessed him. The audience watched and listened, spellbound.

It was the story of Attis, and the madness of Attis, which moved him on a dark night, in a dense forest, far from home, to castrate himself and consecrate his existence to the Great Mother, Cybele. Still bleeding from his wound, he summoned the followers of the goddess and led them in a wild, ecstatic procession up the slopes of Mount Ida to her temple. They sang shrill chants, beat on drums, clanged cymbals, whirled about in frenzied, delirious dances with Attis leading them, until at last they fell exhausted into a deep, dreamless sleep.

When Attis woke, his madness had passed. He saw what he had done. He was horrified. He ran to the seashore and gazed at the horizon, sorry that he had ever left his homeland. As a boy he had been a champion of the games, a decorated athlete, a wrestler. With his beard he became a man of the city, known, respected, called upon. What was he now? A shipwrecked soul unable ever to return to his home, neither man nor woman, a fragment of his former self, sterile, miserable, terribly alone. His fanatic devotion had cut him off from all that mattered to him, had cost him everything, even his humanity.

Up on Mount Ida, Cybele heard his wretched lament. She looked down to see Attis weeping on the beach. Did Cybele take mercy on Attis, or was she only being practical when she sent her lion down to the beach, not just to fetch Attis back, but to rend Attis's mind and make him mad once and for all? Attis in his sanity was too miserable for a life of worshiping Cybele, but in his unsexed state what other life was he fit for? So the roaring lion went crashing down the mountainside and drove Attis back into the forest, back into the madness and raving ecstasy, back into a life of loyal, unsexed slavery to the Great Mother.

Catullus shivered, as if the poem were slowly releasing him from its grip. His voice began to fade, until the final lines were barely audible:

"Goddess, Great Mother Cybele, guardian of
   Ida,
Madden other men — not me! Give others your
   raving dream.
Avert your furies from my house. Draw others
   into your scheme!"

Catullus was transformed. Mounting the stage, he had looked like a man stupefied by wine and self-pity, all soft and uncertain. Now his face was haggard and his eyes glowed, like a man emerging from a terrible ordeal, winnowed to his essential core. He stumbled a bit leaving the stage, not like a drunken man but like a man drained of all energy.

The garden was silent. Around me I saw raised eyebrows, uncertain frowns, thoughtful nods, grimaces of distaste. Sitting close by the stage, Clodia stared unblinking at the spot Catullus had vacated.

Her face was blank. Did she consider the poem a tribute to her, or the opposite, an insult? Or could she not see herself in a young man's poem about inescapable obsession, the obliteration of dignity and freedom by overwhelming passion, and the unequal, disastrous union of a mere mortal with an aloof, uncaring goddess?

Behind me I heard a stifled sob, like the sound of a woman weeping, so soft that except for the utter quiet I would never have noticed. I turned my head. Away from the other guests, on the steps leading down into the garden, a figure sat by the pedestal of the monstrous Venus, concealed in its shadow. He hugged his ankles as if to keep from shivering and hid his face against his knees, but by his dress I knew it was Trygonion.

CHAPTER TWENTY-TWO

After Catullus's performance, the party never regained quite the same air of levity, despite the relentless parade of entertainments that followed. This included several other poets, better known than Catullus, who had been placed at the beginning of the evening as a sort of warm-up for those who followed. But no other poet who recited that evening left any lasting impression, at least not on my ears.

There were also dancers and jugglers and a concluding set of excruciatingly crude but very funny skits by the mime. During a break in all this entertainment our hostess found her way to our corner. She greeted Bethesda with outstretched arms and a kiss. "Did you receive the gift?"

"Yes, thank you. It arrived at the house while we were down at the Forum." Bethesda gave me a sidelong glance.

Clodia nodded. "Good. Now you're one of us. Yes, I saw you both at the trial. What do you think, Gordianus? How did it go for us today?"

"I suppose Bethesda said it best: 'Oratory is all very well when there are no facts to go on.' "

Clodia gave me a quizzical smile. "Was it Bethesda who said that? I thought it was my ancestor Appius Claudius, the one who . . . well, never mind. May I talk to you privately? Senator, amuse this lady for a moment while I take her husband away on business."

She led me out of the garden, into a private chamber. The walls were painted a rich red, decorated with rustic scenes of satyrs and nymphs.

"You're looking much better today," I said.

"Am I? I thought I looked rather horrible when I saw myself in the mirror this morning. I considered calling off the party, but it would have been the first time I ever missed giving a party on the eve of the Great Mother festival. Even when Quintus and I were up in Cisalpine Gaul — "

"Did you have Chrysis tortured today?"

She looked at me blankly for a moment. Even by the lamplight reflected off the red walls her face looked pale. "Actually, I took you aside to talk about more important matters. But since you ask, Gordianus — yes, Chrysis was tortured today. Not by me, of course. By officials of the court. Surely you know that a slave can't give a statement in a trial without being tortured? Otherwise she might simply say whatever her mistress told her to say."

"So the logic goes."

"The bitch was about to poison me. I caught her in the act."

"Did she confess?"

"Yes."

"Did she implicate Caelius?"

"Of course. You can hear her statement read

tomorrow, just before my own testimony."

"The statement which she gave under torture."

"You seem to have an unwholesome fixation on torture tonight, Gordianus. I should think you'd had enough of torture listening to that awful poem of Catullus's! Really, when he told me that he had an ideal poem for the Great Mother festival . . ." She gave a little shudder, then brightened. "But I won't have to use torture to get you to testify tomorrow, I hope."

"Me?"

"Of course. Who else could Herennius have meant when he said the man Cicero called 'the most honest man in Rome' would be testifying against Caelius? You need only tell what you witnessed with your own eyes at the Senian baths, and here in my house yesterday, when you saw what was done to me."

"What if I decline to testify?"

She seemed surprised. "No one can compel you. But I thought you wanted to see Caelius punished."

"I wanted to discover Dio's killer."

"It's the same thing, Gordianus. Everyone else in Rome has figured that out, so why haven't you? Oh, yes, I know, you're a man who demands proof. Well then, you should have come up with those slaves of Lucceius's, the ones involved in the poison plot. You were going to track them down and buy them for me, you said. Did anything ever come of that?"

"No."

"Too bad. They would have made superb

witnesses. I gave you silver to buy them, didn't I?"

"I'll return the silver."

"The trial's not over yet. There's no hurry."

"I'll have to wait until my son Eco gets back to Rome — "

"Forget about the silver, Gordianus. There's no need to return it. Do you understand?"

"I'm not sure."

"Consider it part of your fee. Now, of course you'll testify tomorrow. You must."

"Must I?"

"If you care about justice at all. If you want to put Dio's shade to rest."

"If only it was clear to me exactly how Dio died."

She sighed, exasperated. "Asicius and Caelius broke into Coponius's house and stabbed the poor wretch."

I ignored her, counting days in my head. "There's still a chance that Eco might arrive tonight, or tomorrow — "

"Good. If he does, and if he brings word of those slaves, then perhaps we can add their testimony. But I told you, forget about the silver."

We were speaking at such cross-purposes that I hardly heard her. "There was something else," I said. "Something I'd forgotten. When I left your house yesterday, I intended to take with me that bit of gorgon's hair, to compare it to some of the same poison in my strongbox at home. I forgot it, somehow . . ." I shuddered, remembering the ugliness of Chrysis's degradation and my flight from Clodia's bedchamber. "Could I take the gorgon's hair home with me tonight?"

Clodia hesitated. "I'm afraid not. Herennius has it. He said he might want to produce it as evidence tomorrow, when I give my testimony. Though I don't suppose showing the judges a lump of poison is likely to be as shocking as showing them a bloody dagger or whatever. Is it important?"

"No, I suppose not. I only wanted to make sure that I knew what the stuff was, for my own satisfaction."

"If it would help convince you to testify, then I wish I still had it. I suppose I could somehow arrange to get the stuff back from Herennius, though it's rather late. In the morning there'll hardly be time — "

I shook my head. "Don't bother."

"No? Good!" She laughed weakly. "I don't think I could stand to deal with one more troublesome detail tonight. I really am awfully tired. Clodius's physician says that I shouldn't expect to feel completely well for quite some time. To tell you the truth, I feel quite awful. I couldn't eat a bite of anything that was put in front of me tonight. I'll simply have to trust that the cook was up to his usual standard. Now, Gordianus, assure me that you *will* testify tomorrow. Don't make me go to bed fretting about it. As I said, you need only tell the court what you've seen with your own eyes."

I looked at her for a long moment, at her huge

green eyes made all the more lustrous by illness, at the smooth white flesh of her throat curving down to her breasts and the sleek lines of her body wrapped in the transparent silk. I breathed in her perfume. What if Caelius had succeeded in poisoning her? She would be dead now, already beginning to rot. The idea was appalling, intolerable: the glittering eyes shut forever, the perfect body eaten by worms, the perfume overpowered by the stench of putrefaction

"Yes, I'll testify. I don't see why not."

She smiled and kissed me, full on the mouth, and pressed her body against me as if she had read my thoughts and wanted to show me that she was still very much alive and warm to the touch. From the garden I heard the sound of a poet declaiming, punctuated by laughter and applause.

Clodia broke the kiss and stepped back. "I'd better take you back to Bethesda before she comes looking for you. Egyptian women are uncommonly jealous, I'm told."

The party had no formal ending, or at least none that I stayed for. After the mime's encore, another meal commenced with the guests seated in new combinations. Eventually, those who had eaten and conversed and laughed and drunk enough began to wend their ways to the front door. Bethesda and I were among the first to leave. Catullus and Trygonion seemed to have disappeared.

"You look very thoughtful," said Bethesda on the way home.

"And you look rather smug. Did you enjoy yourself that much?"

"Enjoyment was not really the point," she said, suddenly haughty.

"What did Clodia mean by what she said to you?"

"When?"

"She asked if you had gotten the little statue of Attis. You said yes, and then she said, 'Good, now you're one of us.' "

"Did she say that?"

"Bethesda, I'm in no mood to be teased."

"She only meant that I had been accepted by the other women here on the Palatine. The women who matter, anyway. Thanks to Clodia."

"Is that all she meant?"

"What do you mean, is that all? Think of it, of where I come from, who I am. I dreaded it when we moved from the farm back to Rome, into such a house, such a neighborhood. I never let you see how I felt, of course, but it was just as I feared. They treated me very badly at first."

"Treated you badly?"

"Ignored me, shut me out. But after tonight, things will change. The others will treat me differently. As if I were one of them."

This struck me as highly unlikely, but I shrugged. "Why not? Almost anything seems to be possible in Rome these days."

For some reason Bethesda took offense at this comment and didn't say another word to me all the way home.

Diana had stayed up for us. She demanded that her mother tell her everything about the party. While they settled in Diana's room, talking of what the women had worn and how they had dressed their hair, I escaped to our bedroom.

I stripped off my toga and put on a shabby tunic. I kept a lamp burning so that Bethesda could find her way around the room. I lay down on the sleeping couch and shut my eyes against the flickering light, but I couldn't sleep. I had drunk too much, eaten too much, heard too much poetry. From down the hall I could hear Diana's and Bethesda's muffled laughter. The sound reminded me of the sound of distant laughter in the garden, when Clodia had kissed me . . .

I had asked her for something, hadn't I? The poison, that was it! The gorgon's hair, so that I could compare it to the same stuff that Eco had given me to safeguard. Again, I had come home without it. Of course, I didn't really need Clodia's sample to make the comparison; I remembered clearly enough what the stuff had looked like. I had held it up to the lamplight, while Chrysis twisted in the corner and sobbed . . .

I shifted on the sleeping couch, determined to fall asleep, but the laughter from Diana's room kept me up, and my thoughts kept twisting endlessly in space, like Chrysis suspended upside down from the ceiling. Finally I got up and reached for the lamp.

There was a little storage room down the hallway from our bedroom, cluttered with rolled rugs and folded chairs and wooden boxes. After a brief search I found the strongbox amid the jumble. I tried to remember where I had hidden the key, and then realized I didn't need it. The little lock on the strongbox had been broken.

I took the box into the bedroom and set down the lamp so that it would light the inside.

There wasn't much inside the box — a blood-encrusted dagger that had been important at another trial, a few letters and some other mementos that I didn't want anyone else to touch. Among them was the little pyxis of poison that Eco had asked me to keep for him, not wanting to have it in his own house with the twins.

I picked up the pyxis by the rim of the lid, which came open. I gave a jerk, thinking I had clumsily spilled the contents, then realized there were no contents to be spilled.

The pyxis was empty. Only a few traces of poison remained, compacted against the inside corners of the box, identical to the crumbly yellow powder that Clodia had shown me.

What did it mean?

I set the pyxis aside and looked in the strongbox again, thinking the poison must have spilled inside. I saw no yellow powder, but I did see something else, a small object easily overlooked: an earring. It was a simple design, a little silver crook with a green glass bead for ornament. I recognized it at once; it was one of Bethesda's old earrings.

The crook of the earring was bent. I looked again at the broken lock of the strongbox. The metal facing was scored with tiny scratches. The aperture was small; the crook of the earring would have been ideal for poking inside.

What had happened was obvious: the earring had been used to force the lock.

I sat and stared dumbly at the earring, the strongbox and the empty pyxis, at first puzzled, then stunned, then furious.

Diana and her mother gave a start when I pushed aside the curtain and stepped into the room. I held the empty pyxis in my outstretched hand.

"Can you explain this?" I said, trying to keep my voice steady.

They both looked at me as if they hardly knew me. Would I have known myself in a mirror at that moment?

Neither of them spoke. "I asked if you could explain this." I said. They stared at me dumbly.

"Very well. It needs no explaining." I held up the earring. "You must have been in a considerable hurry, Bethesda, to have left this behind. That was careless, very careless. Didn't you realize I'd find it eventually?"

She stared blankly at the earring. "Please, Bethesda, don't pretend that you don't recognize it. Even I recognized it, and you claim I never notice jewelry! It's one of a pair that you've had for years." I sighed, suddenly more sad than angry. "Did gaining her favor mean so much to you? Did you not know how she would use the poison — not just to fool the court, but to make a fool of me!" I snapped the pyxis shut and threw the earring on the floor. Diana gave a start and drew against her mother, frightened. For a moment I felt ashamed, but then my anger returned. I paced the floor.

"She's made a fool of you as well, can't you see that? Inviting you to her party, giving you that abominable statue, making you think you could belong to her circle. Sharing shameful secrets with you, whispering behind my back in the garden! She made up whatever you wanted to hear, I imagine. She's had a lot of practice at that. It's what she does with her lovers, so why not with you? Did you really think she wanted to be your friend, a woman who talks about her ancestors as if they were gods, stooping to share gossip with a woman who was born a slave?"

I stopped my pacing, trying to quiet my rage, but I only grew angrier. I clutched the pyxis so hard that the corners cut the palm of my hand. "Wife, you have taken part in deceiving me! Do you deny it?"

Bethesda made no answer.

"You have deliberately deceived me! Do you deny it?"

"Mother — " said Diana, clutching at Bethesda's arm. Bethesda covered the girl's face and pulled Diana against her breast to quiet her.

"Do you deny it?" I shouted.

Bethesda looked steadily into my eyes, shrewd and unflappable to the last. "No, husband. I do not deny it."

"You took part in deceiving me?"

"Yes."

We stared at each other for a long moment. Bethesda never blinked. I threw the pyxis on the floor and left the room in a rage. My shouting had roused Belbo, who rushed after me as I raced out the door and up the night-dark street.

The polite manner of knocking on a door is with the foot, but that night I used my fist to bang on Clodia's door. The banging reverberated in the still night air, loud enough to wake neighbors, I thought, but the slaves took a long time to answer. Did the noise frighten them, or did they simply think me rude? At last a slotted peephole slid open and two eyes peered out. Even in the darkness I recognized them by the single brow above them.

"I want to see your mistress, Barnabas."

"It's late. You can see her tomorrow at the trial."

"No, I must see her tonight."

The eyes studied me dispassionately. I realized how I must look, wearing my sleeping tunic, my hair mussed. The peephole closed. I paced back and forth on the narrow doorstep while Belbo stood in the street behind me, yawning and blinking.

At last the door opened. I slipped inside, but Barnabas closed the door in Belbo's face.

He led me through the foyer, down the steps and across the garden. By the light of a few low-burning lamps I was able to see that the garden was not entirely deserted. Coupled figures moved and whispered in the shadows. Suddenly, like a fawn in the forest, a naked girl went running across our path, taking great bounding strides. It was the girl who had dined with Senator Fufius. She turned her head and gave a startled laugh as she passed, then vanished. A moment later Fufius, naked and drunk, went chasing after her.

Barnabas led me into the red-paneled room off the garden. He set a lamp on a small table and left. I had plenty of time to study the nymphs and satyrs on the walls before Clodia appeared in the doorway. Her hair was unpinned and hung down past her shoulders. She wore a transparent white robe belted only at the waist, so that it was open between her breasts. The naked patch of flesh shimmered in the red light reflected off the walls. She smiled wearily.

"If you wanted to stay, Gordianus, why did you leave? Ah yes, to take Bethesda home. But now you're back. Did someone at the party catch your eye?" She moved sinuously toward me, her eyes heavy-lidded, a faint smile on her lips.

"You had a slave tortured today for no reason."

The lids became heavier. The smile stiffened. "That again? Please, Gordianus, surely a man of your age has accustomed himself to the ways of the world."

"Some things a man never gets used to. Lies, deceptions, conspiracy."

"What are you talking about?"

"And bribery, of course. That's what the silver

was for, wasn't it? Not for purchasing slaves to testify, but an outright bribe, nothing more or less — so that when the time came I would do whatever you wanted. The man whose honesty was boasted of by Cicero himself — that's why you wanted me in the first place, thinking I'd come in handy somehow or other. Ah, yes: we'll throw the fellow in Cicero's face on the last day of the trial. Let Cicero spin out his oration, then have this fellow who Cicero says is honesty personified take the stand and make Cicero look like an idiot. Did you think you could buy me with silver? Or have you never met a man whom silver, or that smile of yours, couldn't purchase?"

"Really, Gordianus, it's awfully late in the evening — "

"— and late in the trial for me to be upsetting your scheme. The supposed delivery of the poison at the Senian baths — were you behind that as well?"

"Don't be absurd!"

"Perhaps it was a part of your scheme, perhaps it wasn't. But whatever your intention, something went wrong. The evidence against Caelius that you hoped to capture, or manufacture, never came together. You realized that the mere allegation that Caelius wanted to poison you was too thin to impress the judges. So you came up with this further scheme. How did you know there would be poison in my house? Or did Bethesda just happen to volunteer the knowledge, and you instantly saw how to make use of it?"

"I don't know what you're talking about. I told you, Gordianus, it's late — "

"Did you merely fake the symptoms? Your brother's physician could have told you how to do that, once you showed him what kind of poison you'd come up with. Or did you actually swallow a bit of the stuff, letting him advise you on the dose — not enough to kill you, certainly, but just enough to make you sick, to make your performance perfect, to be sure that you fooled me and everyone else. Yes, I think that would be more like you, to exercise your dramatic flair to the limit, to court a bit of danger, to play for the highest possible stakes. But to hand that poor slave girl over to the torturers for the sake of authenticity — that was really going too far, Clodia, even for you. Of course, you could be sure that she'd tell them the story exactly as you wanted, since they'll only hand her back to you once they're finished, and if she hasn't done her job properly you can make things even worse for her. This absurdity of torturing slaves to get at the truth — "

"You've gone completely mad, Gordianus. You're raving."

"Then why do I suddenly feel so perfectly lucid, for the first time since I met you, really. It's just as they say: you cast a spell. I thought I'd be immune, but only a fool could think that, and that's what you've played me for. But now my eyes are open, and I have to wonder just how deeply you've dug yourself into this campaign of destruction against Marcus Caelius. If the poison charges are a fake, then what about the murder charges? What about Dio — 'that poor wretch,' as you call him? Might *you* have had some hand in murdering him — for no better reason than to incriminate Marcus Caelius?"

"Ridiculous! When Dio died, Caelius and I were still — "

"Then perhaps Caelius did take part in the murder. But who's to say that your brother isn't ultimately behind it all, if he and Caelius were still allies then, just as you and Caelius were still lovers? And this money you loaned to Caelius, that you claim he used in his poison plot against Dio — perhaps you knew all along what the money was for; perhaps the plot was your idea to begin with, and Caelius just another of your puppets. My eyes are open, Clodia, yet everything becomes more and more obscure to me. In light of my growing confusion, I think I should decline to testify at the trial tomorrow, don't you? Not for the prosecution, anyway. Perhaps I might testify for the defense — yes, let Cicero call the most honest man in Rome to talk about how Clodia set him up to make Marcus Caelius look like a would-be poisoner."

"You wouldn't dare!"

"Wouldn't I? Then I suggest that you drop everything to do with this fake poisoning. Tear up the deposition that Chrysis gave under torture. Don't whisper a word about the gorgon's hair poisoning when you testify. Do you understand? Because if you do, I'll give testimony myself and refute everything you say. How will your case against Caelius look then, with your own scheme exposed? So much for the shocking revelations that Herennius promised as a climax to the trial!"

Clodia's eyes flashed. Her lips trembled. Fury flared on her face and then dimmed as she struggled to contain it. Once again I was struck by her wan and haggard look — was she really mad enough to have poisoned herself deliberately? Was she so totally, relentlessly consumed with destroying Caelius? What was such a love like, to end in such hatred and degradation? And most puzzling of all, at least to me: at that moment — her body ravaged by self-induced poisoning, her duplicity exposed, her scheme to use me in tatters — how could Clodia still look so breathtakingly beautiful to my eyes? So beautiful that I couldn't stand to look at her, but had to turn my back and look elsewhere, at the rutting nymphs and satyrs who cavorted with mindless, guiltless, sterile passion on the walls.

"Outrageous," she finally muttered. "What you say is utterly outrageous. Where do I begin? It's absurd. It's mad. Has Caelius somehow gotten to you? Or Cicero? Why have you turned against me, Gordianus?"

"I told you in the beginning, my only interest was to find Dio's killer. I won't be used as a tool to help satisfy your spite against an ex-lover. I suppose you're accustomed to using men and having them enjoy it, but I have no appetite for that sort of thing, Clodia."

"Yes, I could tell that from the beginning." Her voice was low and weary. Though my back was turned, I sensed her approach. I felt her warm breath against the back of my neck. "That's why I never tried to use that sort of persuasion with you. You'd only have seen through it, resented it. You're an unusual man, Gordianus. I'm not used to such strength, such integrity — yes, just as Cicero said. Lucky Bethesda! So I never considered seducing you, Gordianus. I rejected the thought, knowing it would only offend you. Even though I was tempted, more than once . . ."

I took a deep breath and turned to face her. The expression on her face was dejected, poignant, utterly convincing. "Clodia. You are a remarkable woman. You never give up, do you?"

I expected a flash of anger or the hint of a smirk, but her expression only became more perplexed, more pained. "Remarkable!" I whispered.

I stepped past her, suddenly anxious to leave, thinking that I might yet do something I would later regret. But the doorway was filled by a tall, imposingly muscular young man who stood with his arms crossed, wearing only a tiny loincloth. Catullus's lampoon was uncannily, unerringly accurate. Even as he made a point of blocking my exit, Egnatius the Spaniard had a grin on his face.

"Who is this worm?" he said. "Should I smash his face in?"

"Shut up, you fool," growled Clodia. "Get out of his way."

Egnatius stepped aside. As I passed I wrinkled my nose. It was stale wine I smelled, but I pretended otherwise. "Is that urine on your breath?" The Spaniard's grin finally cracked.

CHAPTER TWENTY-THREE

Belbo was waiting for me outside the front door. Without a word I started walking down the street, then realized I had no idea where to go. Going home to Bethesda was out of the question.

I might have imposed on Menenia, but what would my daughter-in-law have thought if I came begging for a place to sleep in the middle of the night? If only Eco would come back . . .

Suddenly Belbo grunted and pulled me aside. His alarm was caused by a figure who stood concealed in the shadows of a doorway. Poor Belbo thought the man might be a thief or killer. I knew better.

I shook my head, partly in disgust, partly in relief. "Catullus! Don't you have any better place to be at this time of night?"

"No. And neither do you, apparently." He stepped from the doorway to show a face that looked as haggard and pained as my final glimpse of Clodia's face. We stared at each other in the moonlight. "I hope I don't look as wretched as you do," said Catullus.

"I was about to say the same thing to you."

He managed a crooked smile. "What shall we do?"

"Wait for the sun to come up, I suppose."

"And until then? Where shall we go?"

"Where else?"

The Salacious Tavern was doing great business on the eve of the festival. We were lucky to find places to sit.

"I don't like the look of this place, Master," said Belbo.

"Ah, but some of the girls seem to like the looks of you, big fellow," said Catullus. Belbo looked around uncertainly.

"I don't suppose we'll run into Marcus Caelius and his friends again." I surveyed the crowd through the amber haze of lamplight and smoke.

"Here? In the middle of his trial?" Catullus barked a laugh. "Not likely. Don't you imagine he's home with papa and mama, humming funeral dirges and looking through his wardrobe for something suitably shabby to wear tomorrow? 'Oh, Papa, I know I'm supposed to look down-trodden, but can I help it if I look stunning in everything?' "

Even Belbo cracked a smile. Wine was brought. Catullus drank greedily and wiped his mouth. "What were you doing in her house tonight, wearing nothing but an old sleeping tunic?"

"Catullus, please! No more of this nonsense about her . . . and me."

"Then why?"

"There was some unfinished business between us."

"In the middle of the night?"

"It couldn't wait."

He snorted, then called to the serving slave for more to drink.

I swirled the untouched wine in my cup. "If Caelius is guilty of all those crimes against the Alexandrian envoys, isn't that enough? Why would she feel compelled to manufacture new charges against him? You know her better than I do. Would she actually poison herself in order to make others think that Caelius had poisoned her?"

"You're distracting me with riddles," grumbled Catullus.

"It's Clodia who's driven us both to distraction."

"Lesbia!" he insisted.

I stared at my wine and felt queasy. "If I'm going to drink any of this, I'll need to cut it with plenty of water."

"Well, then, we'll have the man fetch you some fresh water from the Appian aqueduct!"

"You mean the one that *her* ancestor built for us?" I said.

"Exactly!" Catullus smirked. "Then we can head out on one of the roads her ancestors so thoughtfully laid down for us — "

"And pour a libation to a god in one of the temples they erected for us."

Catullus laughed. "I see she's given you the grand speech about the feats of her ancestors and their incomparable largesse. Rome would still be a pigsty beside the Tiber if it hadn't been for all those Appius Claudii at the dawn of history."

"So Clodia — Lesbia — seems to think."

"But I'll wager she didn't tell you about the Appius Claudius who tried to rape Verginia."

"No. A scandal?"

"Well, it's not one of those edifying ancestor legends the Clodii like to repeat to every stranger they meet. But the story's just as true, and it tells more about Lesbia than all that crowing about aqueducts and roads."

"Tell me."

Catullus paused to hold out his cup to the serving slave, but provided such a wobbly target that the wine spilled all over the floor.

"Perhaps you've had enough," I said.

"Perhaps you're right."

"What I need is a bed under my back."

Catullus burped and nodded. "Me, too."

"Where are you staying in the city?"

"I keep some rooms in a place up on the Palatine. Just a bed and some books. Do you want to go there?"

"You'd share your bed with me?"

"You wouldn't be the first!" Catullus laughed. "Bring along your slave to play watchdog. He can sleep on the floor in the anteroom and start barking if he hears you cry 'rape!' "

Catullus's place on the Palatine was as sparsely furnished as he had said. Against one wall was a large sleeping couch. Against the other was a pigeonhole bookcase filled with scrolls.

He saw me squinting at the little tags in the dim lamplight. "Greek poetry, mostly," he explained, taking off his toga. "Books and bed. All a man needs. Anything more would only distract from the experience."

"Of reading the books?"

"Or using the bed." He slipped into a tunic and fell back onto the sleeping couch. "Come on, there's room enough for two. Though I warn you, I'm drunk enough that I might attack you."

"I'm an old man with stiff joints and a grizzled beard."

"Yes, but you smell irresistible."

"What?"

"You smell of her perfume."

"And you stink of wine, Catullus. Better than urine, I suppose."

"What?"

I told him briefly of my encounter with Egnatius, thinking it would amuse him that I had been able to use something from his poem for my own parting shot, not realizing until I was well into the story that telling it was a mistake.

"Then he's with her right now," he said, gritting his teeth. "Egnatius and Lesbia. Damn them both!"

"You started telling me a story at the tavern," I said, thinking to distract him.

"A story?"

"A scandal about one of her ancestors. An Appius Claudius. Not the builder of the temple, or the aqueduct — "

"Oh yes, the one who tried to rape Verginia. The only ancestor they *don't* like to talk about. Yet he exemplifies the current generation better than any of those virtuous paragons on their pedestals. You asked me if she would do something as mad as poisoning herself, just to spite a lover. Of course she would. It's in her blood."

"Her blood?"

"Here, I'll tell you the story. This was long ago, in the first days of the republic, after the kings had been thrown down but before the patricians and plebeians found a way to live together in peace. The chronology's rather vague to me — I'm a poet, not a historian! — but at some point a group of ten strongmen managed to seize control of the state. They called themselves decemvirs and set off a reign of terror. For the good of Rome, of course — to solve the current crisis, in response to the growing emergency, et cetera, et cetera."

"And Appius Claudius was one of these decemvirs?"

"Yes. Now there was also in Rome at this time a beautiful young girl named Verginia, the daughter of Verginius. She was a virgin, betrothed to a rising young politician. But one day Appius Claudius happened to see her on her way to the girls' school in the Forum and fell head over heel in lust for her. He followed her everywhere, in the streets and markets, trying to lure her away from the watchful eyes of her nurse, determined to seduce her. But Verginia was a virtuous girl and wanted nothing to do with the lecher. She spurned him outright, but the more she rejected him, the more determined he was to have her.

"Finally he hatched a scheme to get his hands on her, if only for long enough to give her a poke. He waited until her father was away on military duty, then gave instructions to one of his lackeys, a man named Marcus. One morning, when Verginia was entering the Forum with her nurse to attend the girls' school, Marcus and some of his men seized her. The people around were shocked and wanted to know what was happening. Marcus said that the girl was his slave and he was reclaiming her. People knew perfectly well that Verginia was the daughter of Verginius, but they also knew that Marcus was Appius Claudius's lackey, and they were afraid of him, so when he made such a show of blustering about justice and the law and his rights they allowed him to take Verginia off to the tribunal to decide the matter legally.

"Of course the sole presiding judge was none other than the decemvir Appius Claudius. His lackey Marcus recited a preposterous story: that Verginia was not Verginius's daughter at all — she was actually the daughter of one of his own slaves and had been stolen from his house as an infant and palmed off on Verginius as his own flesh and blood. Marcus claimed he could produce the evidence for all this later. The point was that the girl was actually a slave, his slave, and he was reclaiming her as was his legal right.

"Up on the tribunal, Appius Claudius pretended

to consider all this as if he'd just heard it for the first time, when of course he was the author of the plot. You can imagine him moving his lips along with Marcus as the man recited the lines Appius had written for him! Finally he declared that only a formal hearing could determine the girl's status. Verginia's friends explained that her father was away on military duty, but could be back in Rome the next day. Appius Claudius agreed to hear the case then. In the meantime, he ruled, the girl would remain in the custody of Marcus. Verginia shrieked! The crowd shouted in protest and the girl's nurse fainted dead away, but Appius Claudius pointed out that according to the law Marcus couldn't be made to hand the girl over to the custody of anyone but her father, and since Verginius was not present, she would therefore have to remain in Marcus's custody until such time as her father arrived to claim her. Verginia would be in Marcus's hands — in Appius Claudius's power — for the whole night to come. Can't you see the fox licking his chops up on the tribunal, playing with himself beneath his toga?

"The ruling was crazy, and there was plenty of muttering and indignation, but nobody ventured to speak openly against it. That's how cowed the people were under the rule of the decemvirs. Marcus started to leave the court, hustling the weeping Verginia along with him.

"At this point Verginia's betrothed young lover, the rising politician, arrived on the scene, and delivered an outraged speech about how Appius

Claudius was using the law to make slaves of everyone in Rome just for the purpose of satisfying his own lust. He would die himself, the young man vowed, before he would let his betrothed spend a night away from her father's house. The girl was a virgin, and it was a virgin he intended to marry.

"He stirred the crowd to a frenzy. Appius Claudius called for armed lictors to keep order, and threatened to have the young orator arrested for starting a riot. But to keep the situation from getting completely out of hand, Appius Claudius agreed to let the girl go home with her uncle for the night and made the man post a huge bond in silver to make sure Verginia would show up for her hearing.

"At dawn the next morning the city woke in a fever of excitement. Verginius, back from his military duty, appeared in the Forum leading his daughter by the hand — he in mourning, she in rags, followed by all the women of the family making lamentations. There was a trial, or something resembling a trial, with each of the sides presenting arguments and Appius Claudius presiding as sole judge. Evidence and common sense counted for nothing. The verdict was decided before the trial began. As soon as the arguments were finished, Appius Claudius announced that Verginia was the slave of Marcus, not the daughter of Verginius. Marcus was free to claim his property.

"The crowd was stupefied. Nobody uttered a word. Marcus began pushing his way through the crowd, heading for Verginia. The women around her burst into tears. Verginius shook his fist at Appius and cried out, 'I meant my daughter for a bridal bed, not for your brothel! No man who owns a sword will put up with this sort of outrage!'

"Appius Claudius was prepared for this. He'd received alarming reports of an uprising being planned against the decemvirs, he claimed, and so just happened to have a troop of armed lictors on hand to keep order. He called them out and told them to draw their swords and clear the way so that Marcus could claim his property. Anyone who obstructed this act of justice would be killed on the spot as a disturber of the peace. Marcus strode forward through the cordon of steel and laid his hands on Verginia.

"Verginius finally seemed to lose heart. With tears in his eyes he called to Appius Claudius: 'Perhaps I *have* been terribly mistaken all these years. Yes, perhaps you're right and the girl isn't really my daughter after all. Let me take the child and her nurse aside for just one moment so that I can talk to them both privately. If I can reconcile myself to this mistake, I can give her up without violence.' Appius granted this request, though in retrospect one has to wonder why. Perhaps he wanted to savor the actual moment of acquiring the girl, of seeing her fall into Marcus's clutches, and didn't mind an excuse for stretching out the ordeal just a bit longer.

"Verginius took his daughter to a little street

off the Forum. He ran into a butcher's shop, grabbed a knife, and ran back to Verginia. Before anyone could stop him, he stabbed her in the heart. She died in his arms, convulsing and spitting blood, while he stroked her hair and whispered to her over and over, 'It was the only way to set you free, my child, the only way.' He staggered back into the Forum carrying her body. The crowd parted for him, stunned into silence, so that Verginius's cries echoed through the Forum. 'This blood is on your hands, Appius Claudius! The curse of my virgin daughter's blood is on your head!' "

Catullus fell silent. I stared into the darkness above us. "Quite a story," I finally said. "What happened next?"

"Verginius and the young man who was to have been his son-in-law led an uprising. The decemvirs were brought down. Appius Claudius was arrested."

"Was he punished?"

"He killed himself in prison, awaiting trial."

"No wonder the Clodii don't brag about him. But I don't see how the story relates to your Lesbia."

"Don't you? You see, there's this particular strain of madness in their blood. Yes, the Clodii have a heritage of building, creating, rising to glory and triumph. But there's also this other aspect, this unwholesome tendency to obsess, this inability to see beyond a thing they desire but cannot have. If they come to want a thing, they'll do anything

425

to get it. Anything! And if their skewed judgment takes them down the wrong path, don't expect them to realize the error and turn back. Oh no, once set upon it, they'll run the course, even straight into disaster. And all in the name of love! They'll wager everything on the slim chance that when the dice are cast they'll score the Venus Throw."

"Are you sure you're speaking of Clodia? Or could it be yourself you're describing, Catullus?"

He was silent for a long moment. "I suppose I wouldn't love her as I do if we weren't alike in certain ways."

He was quiet then for so long that I thought he must have fallen asleep, until he murmured, "Cicero speaks tomorrow."

"What?"

"At the trial."

"Yes."

"She should have known better than to take him on. Cicero is a dangerous man."

"I know. I saw what he did to Catilina when he made up his mind to destroy him. All it took were words."

"Clodia thinks everything comes down to bodies, and sex. She doesn't understand the power of words. It's why she thinks my poetry is weak." He was quiet, then said, "Cicero was in love with her once. Did you know that?"

"I once heard a very vague rumor of some such thing, but it sounded like nonsense to me. Cicero, in love with anyone but himself?"

"Infatuated, anyway. He was great friends with her husband, Quintus. Always visiting their house, back when Quintus was alive and the place was . . . well, respectable enough for a man like Cicero to feel at home. Clodia was a lot more restrained back then; more discreet, anyway. I think she rather liked having to carry on her affairs behind someone else's back — the secret meetings, the danger of getting caught, the wicked thrill of cuckolding her husband. And of course, a married woman can simply turn her back on a lover the moment she tires of him . . ."

"But Cicero? Preposterous. He despises people like her."

"Are there other people like Clodia?"

"You know what I mean."

"Perhaps he despises her now, but back then . . . this was during the worst part of Clodia's marriage, the last few years before Quintus died, when the two of them fought all the time, even in front of company. Especially in front of company. They fought about everything — Clodia's affairs, her brother's career, money, politics. I've always thought that's what intrigued Cicero — seeing her at her most argumentative. He could ignore the fact that she was beautiful, but she was also clever and sharp-tongued. A voluptuous beauty who could argue a man like Quintus into the ground — well, Cicero developed quite a fascination for her. That happens to men like him sometimes, who keep their natural appetites all bottled up. Suddenly they find themselves madly in love with the most inappropriate person. I suspect Clodia was a bit intrigued by him — the perverse attraction of opposites. I'm not sure whether they ever did anything about it. She told me they did, but I figured she was just lying to hurt me. This was years ago, but it makes him all the more dangerous to her now."

"Dangerous?" I said, not quite sure what he meant. I was getting very sleepy.

"Men like Cicero don't like to dwell on that sort of memory. They see it as weakness. They prefer to stamp it out."

I tried to imagine Cicero as a lover — prim, dyspeptic Cicero — but I was too sleepy to make the mental effort, or too afraid it would give me bad dreams.

"Tomorrow — oh, no, light's coming through the shutters. The sky's beginning to lighten already," Catullus groaned. "Not tomorrow, then: today. Today the Great Mother festival begins, and down in the Forum, someone will be destroyed."

"How can you be certain?"

He tapped his earlobe. "The gods whisper in a poet's ear. Today, someone will be publicly annihilated. Humiliated. Ruined forever."

"You mean Marcus Caelius."

"Do I?"

"Who else?"

He stretched his body in a paroxysm of yawning. "Things could go one way or the other. Even the gods will have to wait and see."

"What do you mean?" I murmured. Then I must have fallen asleep, or else Catullus did, because I never heard him answer.

PART FOUR

NEXUS

CHAPTER TWENTY-FOUR

After a fitful hour or two of sleep I opened my eyes. Morning light was creeping in around the shuttered windows, but I think it was Catullus's snoring that woke me.

I crept to the anteroom, kicked Belbo awake, and told him to run home as fast as he could and fetch my best toga. He was back before I had finished washing my face.

"I suppose someone was minding the door," I said, while he helped me dress.

"Yes, Master."

"Was there any word of Eco?"

"No, Master."

"Nothing at all?"

"Nothing, Master."

"Was your mistress up?"

"Yes, Master."

"What did she have to say? Any message for me?"

"No, Master. She didn't say a word. But she looked — "

"Yes, Belbo?"

"She looked more displeased than usual, Master."

"Did she? Come, Belbo, we'll need to hurry to

catch the start of the trial. I'm sure we can find something to eat on the way. There'll be plenty of vendors out for the festival." As we were leaving, Catullus appeared from the bedroom, looking haggard and bleary-eyed. He assured me he would be down at the Forum before the trial started, but he looked to me as if he would have to be raised from the dead first.

Belbo and I arrived just as the defense was beginning its arguments. With no slaves sent ahead to hold a chair for me, I found myself near the back of the crowd, which was even larger than the day before. I had to stand on tiptoes to see, but I had no trouble hearing. The well-trained orator's voice of Marcus Caelius rang through the square.

As Atratinus, the youngest of the prosecutors, had begun their case the day before, so young Caelius began his own defense; as Atratinus had dwelled on the defendant's character, so did Caelius. Was this the morally depraved, sensation-seeking, too-handsome young murderer that the prosecution had portrayed? One would never have known it from Caelius's appearance and manner. He was dressed in a toga so old and faded that even a poor man might have thrown it out. It must have come from a musty chest in his father's storage room.

His manner was as humble as his clothes were shabby. The fiery young orator famous for his rapid delivery and biting invectives spoke on this day in a calm, measured, thoughtful cadence, oozing with respect for the judges. He declared himself innocent of all charges; these horrible, spurious accusations had been lodged against him by people who had once been his friends but were now his enemies, and their only goal was to destroy him for their personal satisfaction. A man could hardly be blamed for the treachery of false friends; still, Caelius regretted his poor judgment in ever having associated with such people, for he could see the pain and suffering it had caused his father and mother, who were with him again today, dressed in mourning and barely controlling their tears. He regretted, too, the burden that the trial had placed on his loyal friends, beloved mentors and trusted advocates, Marcus Crassus and Marcus Cicero, two truly great Romans whose example he had admittedly failed to live up to, but to whom he would turn again for renewed inspiration when this ordeal had passed, provided the judges in their wisdom saw fit to give him that chance.

Caelius was deferential but not servile; modest but not cringing; adamant about his innocence, but not self-righteous; saddened by the wickedness of his enemies but not vindictive. He was the model of an upstanding citizen falsely accused and confidently looking to the revered institutions of the law to give him justice.

I felt a tap on my shoulder and turned to see the bloodshot eyes of Catullus. "I don't suppose I've missed much blood and gore yet," he said.

"Milk and honey is more like it," quipped a man nearby. "This fellow Caelius wouldn't harm

435

a fly!" There was a ripple of laughter, then a round of shushing from those who wanted to hear every word of the speech.

"Milk can curdle," Catullus whispered in my ear, "and sometimes you find a bee drowned in the honey, with its stinger intact."

"What do you mean?"

"Caelius fights better with a sword than with a shield. Wait and listen."

Sure enough, the tone of Caelius's speech began to change, as if, having gotten the necessary business of humbling himself out of the way, it was time for him to go on the offensive. The shift was so gradual, the insinuations of sarcasm so subtle, that it was impossible to say exactly when the speech was transformed from a meek protestation of innocence into a biting invective against his accusers. He attacked the speeches that had been made against him, pointing out their reliance on hearsay and circumstantial evidence, their lapses of logic, their obvious intent to besmirch his character. The prosecutors were made to look not just vindictive, but petty as well, and slightly absurd, not least because Caelius himself managed to maintain an aura of impeccable dignity while he insulted their logic and motives and assaulted them with vicious puns.

"Stingers in the honey," whispered Catullus.

"How did you know?"

He shrugged. "You forgot how well I know Caelius. I could lay out the entire course of his speech for you. For example, he'll be turning to *her* next." He looked toward the bench where Clodia sat, and the sardonic smile on his lips faded until he looked as grim as she did.

Sure enough, Caelius proceeded to make a veiled attack on Clodia, though not by name. Behind the prosecution and its sham arguments, he said, there was a certain person intent on doing him harm — not the other way around, as she had charged. The judges would know whom he meant — "Clytemnestra-for-a-quadrans." The crude joke, implying that Clodia was both a husband-killer and a cheap whore, elicited a wave of raucous laughter. Where had I heard it before?

"I make no claim to being ignorant of the lady," said Caelius. "Yes, I know her — or knew her — quite well. To my discredit, alas, and to my dismay. But little to my profit; sometimes Cos in the dining room turns out to be Nola in the bedroom." This elicited more laughter and even some appreciative applause. The pun was multiple and all the more stinging for its wicked intricacy. Cos suggested the island from which Clodia's transparent silks had come, and therefore the open, vulgar allure of sex; Nola was famous for its impregnable fortress, which had resisted not just Hannibal but a siege by Clodia's own father. Cos also punned with *coitus,* sex, and Nola with *nolo,* or no sex. In other words, what the lady lewdly promised at dinner was later frigidly withheld in the bedroom. With a single turn of phrase, and without saying anything explicit, Caelius had managed to suggest that Clodia was not just a temptress but a tease (likely to give poor value even for a quadrans!), to suggest that he had never actually slept with her, and to remind the court of one of her father's military defeats, the siege of Nola. After a moment's pause there was another smattering of applause, as more listeners realized just what a gem of compression Caelius had delivered.

Catullus didn't laugh or applaud, I noticed. "Wickedly clever," I said, wondering if he had missed the pun.

"Thank you," he muttered, apparently not listening. His eyes were on Clodia, who looked distinctly uncomfortable. Catullus smiled sadly.

Caelius expanded on the metaphor. Just as a man could be in the vicinity of Nola without breaching her walls (more laughter from those finally getting the joke), so one could be in the vicinity of Neapolis or Puteoli without being guilty of staging an attack on foreign visitors; or take an innocent stroll across the Palatine at night without dropping in to murder an ambassador. "Has it come to this?" said Caelius. "Not guilt by association, but guilt by geographical proximity? Shall a man's enemies follow his footsteps, note any crimes which happen to take place in the immediate area, and then accuse him so that he has no alibi? It seems hardly credible that even the most inept of advocates could expect a panel of Roman judges to take this kind of 'evidence' seriously. Assumptions should be based on what is seen, not unseen; known, not merely 'suspected.' "

He pulled a small object from the folds of his

toga. A few spectators in the front rows laughed out loud when they saw what it was. "For instance," he went on, holding up the object so that it glinted in the sunlight, "when one sees a simple little pyxis such as this, what does one assume that it contains? A medicinal unguent of some sort, or a cosmetic powder, or a perfume infused into wax, perhaps — the sort of thing that anybody might take along to the baths. Or so a reasonable person might assume. A person of a more morbid state of mind might guess that something else was in the box — poison, perhaps. Especially if that person was herself well acquainted with using poison." From my distant vantage, there was no way I could be sure of what the pyxis looked like. It must have been only my imagination that perceived it to be made of bronze, with little raised knobs and inlays of ivory that caught the sunlight — identical to the pyxis that Caelius's confederate Licinius had brought to the Senian baths, and that had been left, filled with something unspeakable, on Clodia's doorstep as she lay poisoned in her house.

More laughter spread through the crowd. I looked at Clodia. Her eyes were aflame and her jaw like granite.

"An imagination of a particularly lewd bent might imagine something even more outrageous in such an innocent little pyxis — a token of spent desire, perhaps, deposited by a frustrated lover weary of trying to shimmy up Nola's walls." At this there were outright hoots of laughter. Somehow the story of the pyxis and its obscene contents must already have spread through the city. Who had repeated such a scandalous story — a slave in Clodia's household? Or the man who had sent her the box? It was clear from the look on Clodia's face that Caelius's brazen allusion to the indecent gift had taken her completely by surprise, and the callous amusement of the spectators appalled her even more. Caelius, never once looking at her, put the pyxis away and smiled blandly.

"Master!" Belbo tugged at my toga.

"Belbo, I'm trying to listen."

"But Master, he's here!"

I turned about, prepared to snap at him, then felt a surge of joy. Not far away, at the edge of the crowd, Eco stood on his toes peering into the sea of heads.

"Belbo, you sharp-eyed lookout! Come, he'll never spot us in this crowd. We'll go to him."

"You're not leaving, are you?" said Catullus.

"I'll be back."

"But the best is yet to come."

"Memorize the jokes for me," I said.

We came upon Eco just as he was beginning to push his way into the throng. His tunic was dirty and his brow pasted with sweat, as might be expected of a man who had just finished a hard ride up from Puteoli. His face was haggard but when he saw us his eyes lit up and he managed a weary smile.

"Papa! No, don't hug me, please. I'm filthy. And sore! I rode all night, knowing the trial must have already started. It's not over, is it?"

"Not yet. Another full day of speeches — "

"Good. Perhaps there's still time, then."

"Time for what?"

"To save Marcus Caelius."

"If he needs saving," I said, thinking Caelius was doing a pretty good job of defending himself. "If he deserves to be saved."

"I only know that he doesn't deserve to be punished for Dio's murder."

"What are you saying?"

"Caelius didn't kill Dio."

"You're certain?"

"Yes. I found the slave girl, Zotica, the one who was with Dio the night he died . . ."

"If it wasn't Caelius and Asicius, then who?"

"I brought the girl back with me . . ." Eco suddenly looked very tired.

"The girl killed Dio?" I frowned. We had considered and rejected that possibility already.

"No."

"But she knows who did?"

"Not exactly." Why would Eco not look me in the eye? "All I can say is that your intuition was right, Papa. The girl was the key."

"Well? What did you find out?"

"I think you'd better talk to her yourself, Papa."

The crowd behind us laughed at something, then laughed again, louder. I looked over my shoulder. "Caelius is just getting to the heart of his speech. Then Crassus will speak, then Cicero — "

"Still, I think you'd better come, Papa. Quickly, before the trial gets any further along."

"Can't you just tell me what the girl told you?"

His face darkened. "I don't think that would be wise, Papa. It wouldn't be fair."

"To whom, the slave girl?"

"Please, Papa! Come with me." The look on his face convinced me. What terrible secret had so unnerved my son, who had seen all the corruption and duplicity that Rome had to offer?

He had left the girl at his house in the Subura. We walked there as quickly as we could, threading our way through streets crowded with food vendors, acrobats and merry-makers.

"Where did you find her?" I asked, stepping out of the way of a drunken band of gladiators coming up the street. They snarled at Belbo as they passed.

"In one of the hill towns of the far side of Vesuvius, miles from Puteoli. It took some looking. First I had to find the brothel-keeper who'd bought the allotment of slaves that included Zotica. Do you have any idea how many establishments like that there are down on the bay? One after another told me he'd never seen Zotica, and they all wanted a bribe just to tell me that much, and even then they all seemed to be lying just to spite me. Finally I found the man who'd purchased her. But she'd been useless to him, he said. 'Worse than useless — nobody wants a girl with scars on her,' he told me, 'not even the mean ones.' Besides that, she'd turned wild."

"Wild?"

"That's what he calls it. I suppose a man like that tends to see slaves in conditions that most of us don't, or not very often. Her mind isn't quite right. Maybe she was always a little addled; I don't know. I think she must have been treated well enough in Coponius's house at the beginning, though the other slaves tended to pick on her. Then Dio came along. The girl was innocent, naive, maybe even a virgin. She had no idea of the kinds of things that Dio had in mind for her. She couldn't understand why he wanted to punish her when she'd done nothing wrong. She kept quiet about it at first, too afraid of Dio to resist him, too ashamed to tell anyone. When she finally did complain to the other slaves, some of them tried to intercede for her, but Coponius couldn't be bothered. Then, after Dio was killed, Coponius couldn't get rid of the girl fast enough. Since then she's been traded from hand to hand, abused, ill treated, unwanted. It must have seemed like a nightmare from which she couldn't wake up. It's done something to her mind. She can be perfectly lucid sometimes, but then . . . you'll see. It's made her unfit to be any kind of slave. When I finally found her she was living in the fields outside a farmer's house. He'd bought her for a kitchen slave and found her useless even for that. 'The girl's a scratcher and a biter,' he told me. 'Scratches and bites for no reason, like an Egyptian cat. Even beating won't do any good.' No one around would

443

buy her, so the farmer turned her loose, like people do to old or crippled slaves, making them fend
for themselves. I didn't even have to pay for her.
I just had to find her, and then make her come
with me. I thought I'd gained her trust, but even
so she tried to run away twice, first outside of
Puteoli and then again as we got close to Rome
this morning. You see why it's taken me so long
to get home. And I thought you were sending me
on an easy job, Papa!"

"If the girl told you what we needed to know,
maybe you should have let her go."

Darkness shadowed his face again. "No, Papa.
I couldn't just repeat her story to you. I had to
bring her back to Rome, so you could hear her
for yourself."

Menenia was waiting for us at the door, with
folded arms and an uncharacteristically sour look
on her face. I thought the look must be for Eco,
for having brusquely rushed off to find me after
dropping off the slave girl — young wives expect
a bit more attention from husbands arriving home
after a trip. But then I realized that the look was
aimed at me. What had I done, except quarrel
with my wife and not come home last night?
Menenia couldn't possibly know about that already
— or could she? Sometimes I think that the ground
beneath the city must be honeycombed with tunnels where messengers constantly run back and
forth carrying secret communications between the
women of Rome.

Eco had locked the girl in a small storage room

off the kitchen. At the sight of us, she jumped up from the wooden chest where she'd been sitting and cowered against the wall.

"I imagine she's frightened of Belbo," said Eco.

I nodded and sent him out of the room. The girl relaxed, but only a little.

"There's nothing to be afraid of. I already explained that to you, didn't I?" said Eco, in a voice more exasperated than comforting.

Under better circumstances, the slave girl Zotica might have been at least passably pretty. She was far too young for my taste, as flat and bony as a boy, but one could see the delicate beginnings of a woman's face in her high cheekbones and dark eyebrows. But now, with her unwashed hair all sweaty and tangled and dark circles beneath her eyes, it was hard to imagine her as the object of anyone's desire. She certainly had no place in a brothel. She looked more like one of those furtive, abandoned children who haunt the city's streets looking for scraps of food and run in packs like wild beasts.

Eco sighed. "Did you eat anything, Zotica? I told my wife to see that you were fed."

The girl shook her head. "I'm too tired to eat. I want to sleep."

"So do I. You can sleep soon. But now I want you to talk to someone."

The girl looked at me warily.

"This is my father," Eco went on, though I wondered what the word could mean to the child, who had probably never known a father. "I want you to tell him what you told me. About the man who came to stay at your master's house here in Rome."

The very mention of Dio caused her to shiver. "About how he died, you mean?"

"Not only that. I want you to tell him everything."

The girl stared forlornly into space. "I'm so tired. My stomach hurts."

"Zotica, I brought you here so that you could tell my father about Dio."

"I never called him that. I never even knew his name until you told me."

"He came to your master's house and stayed there for a time."

"Until he died," she said dully.

"He abused you."

"Why did the master let him? I didn't think the master knew, but he did. He just didn't care. Then I was spoiled and he had to get rid of me. Now no one has any use for me."

"Look at her wrists, Papa. The rope cut them so badly that you can still see the scars."

"It's because I pulled at them," the girl murmured, rubbing at her wrists. "He tied them so tight, then put me over the hook."

"The hook?" I said.

"There were metal hooks in the walls in his room. He'd tie my wrists and lift up my arms and trap me on the hook, so my toes barely touched the floor. My wrists would bleed. The rope would twist up even tighter when he'd turn me around.

He would use me from the front, then the back. Beat and pinch and prod. Stuff things in my mouth to keep me quiet."

"You should see the scars, Papa, but I'd be ashamed to make her lift up her dress to show you. You realize she's talking about Dio." Eco looked at me accusingly, as if I were responsible for the secret vices of a man I'd admired for so many years. My face turned hot.

"A hook," I whispered.

"What?"

"A *hook*."

"Yes, Papa, imagine it!"

"No, Eco, it's something else . . ."

"Yes, there's more. Go on, Zotica. Tell him about that final night."

"No."

"You have to. After that, we'll leave you alone, I promise. You can sleep for as long as you want."

The girl shuddered. "He came in dressed . . ." She made a miserable face and shrugged. "Like a woman, I suppose. He looked awful. He made me come to his room. He made me take off my gown. 'Use it for a rag,' he said. 'Wipe off this silly makeup.' He sat in a chair while I cleaned his face. He kept stopping me, fondling me, sliding his hand between my legs, making me bend over — acting just like always." The girl shook her head and hugged herself.

"But then he pushed me away. He made a face and grabbed his stomach. He crawled onto his bed and made me lie next to him. Because he was cold,

447

he said. But he felt hot to me. He pressed himself against me naked and I felt like I was being burned wherever he touched me. Then he started shivering, so much that his teeth chattered, and he made me fetch him more blankets. He told me to lower the lamp because the light hurt his eyes. He tried to get up from the bed but he was too dizzy. I asked him if I should go for help, but he told me not to. He was afraid. More afraid than I'd ever seen anybody, even a slave about to be whipped. So afraid I almost stopped hating him. He covered himself with the blankets and rocked back and forth on the bed, clutching himself, biting his hands. I stood across the room as far away as I could, hugging myself because I was naked and it was cold. Then he turned on his side and vomited on the floor. It was awful. He closed his eyes and wheezed and gasped for air. Then he was quiet. After a while I shook him, but he wouldn't wake up. I just sat there on the bed, looking at him for a long time, afraid to move. Then it was over."

"What do you mean, over?"

She looked me in the eye for the first time. "He died. I saw him die."

"How could you be sure?"

"His whole body suddenly shook with a terrible fit. He opened his eyes and his mouth gaped open, like he was going to scream, but nothing came out except a horrible rattle. I jumped up from the bed and stood against the wall. He seemed to have turned to stone just like that, with his eyes and mouth wide open. After a while I walked over to him and put my ear to his chest. There was no heartbeat. If you'd seen his eyes — anyone would know they were the eyes of a dead man."

"But the stab wounds," I said. "The window broken open, and the room a shambles — "

"Let her finish, Papa." Eco nodded to the girl.

"I didn't know what to do." Her jaw quivered and she wiped her eyes. "All I could think was that the master would blame me, and punish me. He would think that I killed the old man somehow. So I cleaned up the vomit — I used my gown, the one he'd already made me use for a rag to clean his face. Then I crept out of the room."

"Where the door slave Philo saw you in the hallway," I said. "Naked and weeping, clutching your gown. He thought Dio had finished with you early. But Dio was already dead. Did you tell your master?"

She shivered and shook her head.

"But why not?"

"All that night I lay awake in the slave quarters, thinking about what had happened. The master would think I had poisoned the old man. I didn't! But the master would think I did, and what would he do to me? I cried and cried, while the other slaves hissed at me to be quiet and go to sleep. But how could I sleep? Then there was an awful commotion from the old man's room. The whole house came awake. They'd broken into the room and found him. Now they'll come to me, I thought. They'll kill me, right here and now! My heart pounded in my chest so hard I thought I'd die."

She let out a sob, then twisted her lips into a crooked smile. "But something amazing had happened. They didn't blame me at all. They thought the old man had been stabbed to death. Killers had broken into his room after I left him, they said, and cut him up with knives. I didn't know what to think. But the master never blamed me, so I never told anybody what had happened. With the old man dead, I thought everything would be like it was before." The smile vanished. "But instead everything changed. The master sold me. Everything just got more and more awful . . ."

"You're safe now," said Eco gently.

The girl sagged against the wall and closed her eyes. "Please don't make me talk anymore. If only I could sleep . . ."

"No more talk," Eco agreed. "Stay here for now. One of the slaves will come to show you where you can sleep."

We left her weeping softly and muttering to herself, her face pressed against the wall as if she could somehow melt into it.

I followed Eco into the garden. "What does it mean?"

"It means that Dio was poisoned, Papa."

"But the stabbing — "

"He was stabbed *after* he was already dead. You remarked yourself how little blood there seems to have been for so many wounds, how the wounds were all close together in his chest and there was no sign that he put up a struggle.

Because he was already dead."

"But someone broke into the room that night and scattered everything about. Someone stabbed him. Why?"

"Perhaps it was Titus Coponius himself, because he didn't want it to get out that Dio was poisoned under his roof, and he wanted to make the death look like the work of assassins. But that's not really the point, is it?"

"What do you mean, Eco?"

"The important thing is that Dio was poisoned."

"But how? Where? By whom? We know that he would touch no food in Coponius's house. And only a short time before, he left my house with a full stomach! As cautious as he was, he wouldn't have eaten anything else that night."

"Exactly, Papa."

"Eco, say what you mean!"

"You needn't shout, Papa. You must be thinking the same thing."

I stopped pacing. We stared at each other. "Perhaps."

"The symptoms the girl described: if it was poison, what do you think — "

"Gorgon's hair," I said.

"Yes, I thought the same thing. Some time ago I gave you some gorgon's hair for safekeeping. I didn't want the stuff in my house with the twins. Do you remember?"

"Oh yes," I said. My mouth was dry.

"Do you still have it? Is it still where you put it?"

My silence gave him the answer. Eco nodded slowly. "The last meal Dio ate was at your house, Papa."

"Yes."

"That's where he must have been poisoned."

"No!"

"Did someone use the gorgon's hair I gave you? Do you still have it or not?"

"Clodia!" I whispered. "She wasn't pretending to be poisoned, then. The gorgon's hair she showed me could have come from Caelius, after all. Certainly not from Bethesda — not if the gorgon's hair in my house had already been used . . ."

"What are you whispering, Papa?"

"But Caelius couldn't have killed Dio, not if he was poisoned first. You're right, he's innocent, of that crime at least . . ."

"I can't hear you, Papa." Eco shook his head, tired and exasperated. "The only thing I can't figure out is why anyone in your household would have wanted to poison Dio in the first place. Who knew the man, much less had any reason to want him dead?"

I thought of my old Egyptian mentor, who secretly liked to tie up young slave girls and abuse them, and particularly liked to bind their wrists and hang them on hooks. I remembered the women in my garden, exchanging secrets about men who had raped them when they were young. I thought of Bethesda when she had been a slave in Alexandria, and the powerful, respected master who had used her so cruelly that he killed

452

her, and would have done the same to Bethesda if she hadn't fought back and found herself carted off to the slave market instead, where a poor young Roman smitten by her beauty emptied his purse to pay for her, never dreaming he would take her back to Rome and make her his wife, obliging her to serve dinner to his guests and to give the first heaping portion to an esteemed visitor such as Dio of Alexandria . . .

I had said to her, *You have deliberately deceived me! Do you deny it?*

And she had answered, *No, husband, I do not deny it.*

"And I thought I understood!"

"Papa, speak up — "

"Cybele help us!" I shook my head. "I think I know the answer, Eco."

CHAPTER TWENTY-FIVE

Eco pressed me for an explanation, but I only shook my head. We made our way back to the Forum in silence through the hot, crowded streets of the Subura. The sky was cloudless and the sun directly overhead, casting a harsh, glaring light onto a world without shadows. Lit so brightly, objects became perversely indistinct. Edges ran together and views of the distance had no depth. The throngs of people going about their holiday business seemed faceless. I stared at them, not quite able to make them out. Old or young, male or female, smiling or frowning, standing quietly or shoving their way through the street, all seemed blurred together and equally strange. The city itself was unreal, dreamlike and slightly absurd. This feeling only intensified as we entered the Forum and rejoined the immense crowd attending the trial of Marcus Caelius.

Catullus was where I had left him. "You missed Caelius's climax!" he said. "He did it into that little pyxis, to show everyone how. No, I'm only joking! But it was a good climax for all concerned. One thing about Caelius, he always strives to satisfy whoever he's with, not just himself. No judges or spectators left hankering and unfulfilled at

454

Nola's walls, so to speak."

I stared at him blankly, unable to make sense of what he was saying. He went on, nonetheless. "Then you missed Crassus's whole speech. Just as well, actually. Nobody had a climax there! Seems Crassus was trying to get Caelius off the hook for all those killings on the way up from Neapolis, but if you ask me, Crassus never did learn how to give a decent speech. Plodding, plodding! Words, words, words, and not a memorable pun among them. He should stick to what he knows, making piles of money, and simply bribe the judges instead of boring them to death with bad rhetoric. He made Caelius look as guilty as Caelius managed to make himself look innocent! It's all up to Cicero now. Who's this?"

"My son," I said absently, and introduced Eco.

"Well, good, you're both here for the *real* speech. Cicero's about to begin. Come, let's see if we can't move up a bit . . ."

We managed to move considerably closer, so that I was able to see quite clearly the figure now stepping before the judges. Slender and frail when I first met him long ago, Cicero had become plump and thick-jowled in the years of his prosperity. The political triumph of his consulship had been followed by near-ruin, when his enemies managed to banish him; counterlegislation passed by Cicero's allies eventually welcomed him back, but not before the great man passed eighteen months in exile, during which time much of his property was destroyed by the mob. In his months away from Rome, Cicero had grown lean with worry, or so it was said. From the way his toga clung to his frame as he swaggered before the court, it looked to me that he had made short work of regaining both his girth and his stature.

Clodius had once been Cicero's political ally, then his nemesis. Even now Clodius was attempting to keep Cicero from rebuilding his ruined house on the Palatine, claiming that the property had been legally seized by the state and sanctified for religious use, and so could not be recovered by Cicero. The two enemies waged war against one another in every arena they could find — on the floor of the Senate, in courts of law, in the reading of omens by priests and augurs. Between them burned the kind of hatred that can be extinguished only by death.

That was reason enough for Cicero to hate Clodia, perhaps, since she was her brother's staunchest supporter and a party to his schemes. But what of the vague rumor which Catullus had repeated, about a stunted love affair between Clodia and Cicero, back when her brother and Cicero were allies? Perhaps he hated Clodia for reasons that had nothing to do with politics, or with Clodius. That would help to account for what he did to her that day. Or perhaps, like a good advocate, he simply did whatever was necessary to make sure Marcus Caelius was acquitted of the charges against him.

As I watched Cicero deliver the final oration of the trial — one of the finest of his career, some would later say — I felt as if I were watching a play. Like a play, the action seemed distant from me, the dialogue out of my control; I was a spectator, powerless to stop or alter the course of unfolding events. But a playwright strives to elucidate some truth, whether mundane and comic or grand and tragic. Where was the truth in this strange play? Who was the villain, and who the tragic figure? It seemed to me that I was witnessing the sort of play where the action becomes increasingly tangled and absurd, until there is no way out of the mess except to bring on a god or a messenger to deliver a speech that makes sense of everything. But the messenger from offstage had already arrived: Eco, bringing the slave girl up from the south. Now I knew the truth about Dio's death, but no one on the stage seemed to know — not Cicero, nor Caelius, nor Clodia. For me to reveal what I knew, to play the part of the god from the machine, was impossible. How could I incriminate my own wife?

I could only watch, helpless and mute, as the battle between Clodia and Caelius reached its climax. Poison, deception and false accusation had already been deployed to attack and counterattack. Now Cicero, like a hoary old general, was brought out to deliver the final assault. Words would be his weapon. *She doesn't understand the power of words*, Catullus had said of Clodia. She was about to learn, in front of all Rome.

"Judges," Cicero began, bowing his head respectfully and surveying the long rows of the jurymen, looking from face to face. "If there should be anyone present here today unfamiliar with our law courts and their customs, he must wonder at the terrible urgency of this particular case, seeing that all other public business has been suspended for the holiday and this is the one and only trial being held in the midst of public festivities and games. Such an observer would undoubtedly conclude that the defendant must be quite a dangerous fellow, a hardened renegade guilty of some crime so terrible that the whole state will collapse unless his transgressions are dealt with at once!

"One would explain to such an observer that we have a special law which deals with criminal behavior against the state. When traitorous Roman citizens take up arms to obstruct the Senate, or to attack magistrates, or to try to destroy the government itself, we are obliged to proceed with trying such men regardless of holidays. Our observer would surely not object to such a law, dedicated to the preservation of the state itself. But he would want to know exactly what sort of charges were involved in the present case. Just imagine his reaction at being informed that no real crime or outrage was before the court at all. Instead, a talented, vigorous, well-liked young fellow is being prosecuted by the son of a man against whom the defendant recently brought charges. Furthermore, the whole prosecution has been organized and financed by a whore."

The crowd collectively sucked in a breath. There were a few outbursts of laughter which rang all the louder in the general silence. Caelius had made fancy allusions to Clytemnestra, and convoluted puns about Cos and Nola. He had even held up a pyxis and alluded to the story of the semen-filled box. But Cicero, in the first moments of his speech, had called Clodia an outright prostitute. It was an announcement and a warning: nothing would be held back. I tried to see Clodia's reaction, but the crowd had shifted and my view was blocked.

"What would our hypothetical observer think of all this?" Cicero continued. "No doubt he would conclude that the chief prosecutor should be excused for bringing such a flimsy case — Atratinus is very young and inexperienced, and his devotion to his father is understandable. Our observer would further conclude that the malicious tantrums of the woman in question ought to be better controlled, or at least confined to her bedroom. Also, good judges, our observer would conclude that you are being sorely overworked, since everyone but you has the day off!"

This brought a round of appreciative laughter from the front rows and a lessening of tension, except from the prosecutor's section, where I caught a glimpse of Clodia. Her face looked so rigid she seemed to be wearing a mask.

Cicero continued with a defense of Caelius's character. He dismissed whatever political differences might have put a distance between himself and his young protégé. That was all over now. If Caelius had made mistakes, he was entitled to do so, as was every young man so long as he conducted himself with integrity and honesty.

"Ah, but the prosecutors have accused Caelius of being in debt, and thus, presumably, vulnerable to bad influences and a life of crime. They have demanded that he hand over his account books for inspection. My reply to this is simple. There are no account books! A young man like Caelius, still subject to his father's authority, doesn't keep his own account books. The prosecution says that Caelius has borrowed heavily, but they will be unable to show any proof of this. Ah, but he must have been living beyond his means, they say, because of that luxurious apartment he kept on the Palatine, which he rented from Clodius for the amazing sum (so they tell us) of thirty thousand sesterces a year. The figure is absurd! Ten thousand sesterces is more like it. Well, you can see what's going on here when you realize that Clodius recently put the building up for sale and is asking a lot more than it's worth. The prosecution is doing Clodius a favor by inflating his rent receipts, so that he can swindle some fool into paying him three times what that rat-infested eyesore is really worth!"

The crowd laughed. Cicero shook his head in mock dismay, but seemed barely able to keep from smiling at his own cleverness. A serious trial about the assassination of foreign dignitaries had suddenly become an inquiry into malicious female revenge and shady real estate dealings. Was Caelius on trial for murder, or the Clodii for their vices? The crowd seemed happy to follow Cicero's lead so long as he amused them.

"You reproach Marcus Caelius for moving out of his father's house into that apartment on the Palatine, as if it showed him to be a bad son, when in fact he took the place with his father's blessing. You imply that he moved there so that he could throw wild parties, when in fact he moved there because he was beginning his political career and needed a place closer to the Forum. But you're absolutely right when you say that it was a mistake for Caelius to take that apartment on the Palatine. What a source of grief the place turned out to be! That was when all his troubles began — or more precisely, when all this malicious gossip began — when our young Jason went a-journeying and found himself in the neighborhood of that Medea of the Palatine."

"Medea of the Palatine" — I had heard the phrase before, just as I had heard someone call Clodia "Clytemnestra-for-a-quadrans" before Caelius did so. It was Catullus, on the night he first took me to the Salacious Tavern. *Who calls her such things?* I had asked him. *I do! I just made them up, out of my head. What do you think? I'll need some fresh invectives if I'm to get her attention again . . .*

I turned and stared at Catullus, who kept his gaze straight ahead.

"I shall come back to this Medea and her part in this affair in due course," said Cicero, with a hint of menace. "Right now I should like to spare a few words for the so-called witnesses and the various fictions which have apparently been con-

461

cocted to support the prosecution's case. One of these tales refers to a certain Senator Fufius. The old fellow will supposedly testify that during the election of pontiffs Caelius physically assaulted him. If the senator decides to go ahead and testify, I shall ask him why he did not press charges shortly after the alleged assault took place, instead of waiting so long. Does he come forward now on his own initiative, or at the behest of those behind the prosecution? If it's the latter, as I think we all know it must be, then what a sad reflection on the producers of this tawdry drama, that they can coerce only one member of the Senate into putting on an actor's mask and speaking the lines they've scripted!

"Nor am I impressed by the witnesses who will supposedly tell us how their virtuous wives were molested by Caelius on their way home from a dinner party one night. What high principles these outraged nighthawks must have, to wait until now to bring these charges. At the time, they didn't even ask to meet informally with Caelius to resolve any grievances they may have had.

"Supposedly there will be yet more witnesses, with shocking revelations. But I don't think we should count on hearing anything the least bit believable, or expect to see anyone even remotely credible on the witness stand. You know as well as I do, judges, the sort of riffraff that can be found loitering around the Forum on any given day, men with nothing better to do who are willing to come forward and testify to almost anything under oath, so long as someone pays them to do so. If the prosecution insists on bringing hired actors into these proceedings, I have faith, gentlemen, that your experienced judgment and common sense will see through their testimony to the greed that underlies it."

Was it my imagination, or was Cicero looking directly at me? So much for the surprise witness whom Herennius had promised to bring forth, the man whose honesty had awed even Cicero! With a single preemptive remark I was dismissed as a bribed perjurer. The attack was wasted, of course. I had already refused to appear as Clodia's surprise witness. But that was when I had cause to think that her poisoning was a sham, that she had borrowed the gorgon's hair from Bethesda to deceive me. Now it seemed that she truly had been poisoned. I glanced at her face and saw how listless she still seemed. Had she really come so close to death?

"For my part," Cicero continued, "I have no intention of troubling you with any witnesses. The facts of the case are solid and unshakable. The truth doesn't hinge on what a given witness may or may not say. What value is 'evidence' that can be distorted and manipulated or purchased outright? I prefer to use the rational method, rebutting error with proof, answering falsehoods with facts, laying everything open to the harsh scrutiny of reason.

"You've just heard my colleague Marcus Crassus do exactly that. He took on the charges about

Caelius's role in the disturbances at Neapolis and Puteoli with such clear elucidation that I wish he had also dealt with the question of Dio's murder. But really, what more is there to be said about that matter? We all know the ultimate perpetrator of the crime. We also know that he fears no retribution and doesn't even bother to deny what he's done. The man's a king, after all, and not subject to Roman justice. Furthermore, the fellow who was accused of being that king's agent — Publius Asicius — has already stood trial. He was found innocent. Some say the trial was tainted, but I say that's nonsense — and I should know, as I defended Asicius myself. Now the prosecutors are trying to make us think that Caelius was another of the king's agents, that he was Asicius's confederate in that terrible murder. Where have the prosecutors been for the last few months? Could it be that they never got the news that Asicius was acquitted? What a waste of their time, and yours, judges, for them to try to link Caelius with Asicius, since Asicius was found innocent!" Cicero threw up his hands in exasperation.

"Let us move on to the heart of the matter. The prosecution has said a great deal about character. I agree absolutely that character is the central issue here, though not necessarily the character of Marcus Caelius. Yesterday, judges, I saw how closely you followed the arguments of my friend Lucius Herennius. He said a great deal about financial irresponsibility, unbridled lust, immorality, and other youthful vices. Herennius is usually a mild-mannered fellow, tolerant, urbane, very temperate and modern in his outlook. But here in court yesterday he seemed to turn into one of those frowning, moralizing, upright old tutors who made us quiver with dread when we were boys. He called Marcus Caelius to task in terms harsh enough to make even the sternest father blanch. He went on and on about the evils of wild living until even I began to quail a bit. Was it proper, he demanded to know, that I should defend a man who has sometimes accepted dinner invitations, who has gone for walks in fashionable gardens along the Tiber, who has on one or two occasions in his life splashed on scent from a bottle, who has even gone wading in mixed company down at the beaches at Baiae? Such appalling behavior is unforgivable!

"Or is it? Come, Herennius, I think we all know of men who have indulged in a bit of high living in their youth, who have then turned around and made themselves into perfectly respectable citizens. Everyone agrees that young men must be allowed a certain amount of recklessness. Nature has given them strong sexual appetites, and as long as they indulge those appetites without wrecking someone else's home, the wise thing is to let nature run its course. Understandably, those of an older generation like myself are concerned over the troubles that can arise from the excesses of youth. But it seems to me unfair, Herennius, that you should exploit our reasonable concern to stir up suspicion and prejudice against a particular young man. You recite a whole catalogue of vices to incite our moral abhorrence, but your posturing distracts us from the actual person of Marcus Caelius. He is no more guilty of such excesses than most young men. He deserves our indulgence no less. He should not be condemned for the failings of his entire generation!

"Let us move on to something more specific, namely this business about gold and poison. Both of these alleged transactions revolve around the same person: supposedly, the gold was taken from Clodia and the poison was given to her. Now here at least we have some genuine accusations! All the other charges in this case amount to innuendos and insults, better suited to a shouting match than to a sober court of law. Saying that Caelius seduces other men's wives, that he brawls and takes bribes and so on and so forth — these are slanders, not accusations, groundless slurs of the sort uttered by prosecutors who tend to let their blustering get out of control. But about these last two charges, concerning the gold and the poison, there's something a bit more tangible. Yes, I sense that there must be something to these accusations — or rather, someone behind them, a certain individual with a very deliberate goal.

"Here's the first story: Caelius needed gold and got it from Clodia — with no witnesses about, mind you. Proof, anyone would think, of considerable friendship between them. The second story: Caelius decided to murder Clodia, got hold of some poison, bribed collaborators, fixed a time and place to convey the poison to those who would administer it. Evidence this time of overpowering hatred!

"Judges, this entire case revolves around Clodia, a woman of high birth — and low reputation. I'm not here to rake up scandal, and I get no enjoyment from impugning the virtue of a Roman lady. However, since the whole case against my client originates from this woman, and since it's my duty to defend my client, I have no choice but to deal with the accusations as forthrightly as I can. Still, in talking about this woman I will strive to say no more than is absolutely necessary to refute the charges. Indeed, I feel obliged to watch what I say very carefully, since everyone knows of the unfortunate enmity that exists between myself and this woman's husband."

There was a burst of laughter. Cicero pretended to look confused. "Oh, did I say *husband?* I meant to say her *brother*, of course; I can't imagine why I'm always making that mistake." He shrugged and smiled. "Well then, my apologies, judges, for having to drag a lady's name into these proceedings. Really, I never imagined I should find myself in a court of law fighting with a woman — especially this woman, who is said to be the friend of every man she meets."

He waited for the laughter to die down. The crowd had shifted and I was able to see Clodia again. Her face was stiff but even from a distance I could see the alarm in her eyes. She had begun to realize the full magnitude of the mistake she had made in taking her grievances against Caelius into a public arena.

Cicero cleared his throat. "Let me begin by asking the lady this: shall I lecture her in the stern manner of our forefathers, or in a milder, more moderate fashion? If it's the former, then I should call on the dead to do the lecturing, one of those stern-looking, full-bearded fellows who gaze down on us from old statues. Why not one of the lady's own ancestors? Appius Claudius the Blind would be appropriate, since he won't have to suffer the pain of looking at her."

There was laughter, then a murmur of anticipation as Cicero slipped into the role of the blind ancestor, narrowing his eyes, holding up his arms, removing all traces of the comic from his voice. "Woman! What sort of legitimate interest could you possibly have in a fellow like Caelius, so much younger than yourself? How did you ever come to feel so close to him that you lent him gold, or to feel such hatred that you came to fear poison? Have you no pride, no sense of decorum? Are you totally ignorant of your family and its achievements? Don't you know that your father, and uncle, and grandfather, and great-grandfather, and great-great-grandfather, and his father all served as consuls? Or that you yourself were the wife, *while he lived,* of Quintus Metellus Celer, a man whose virtues surpassed those of all other men? Having come from so great a household, and having married into another great house, what was your business with this youth, Marcus Caelius? Was he a cousin, an in-law, a close friend of your

468

husband? No, none of these things. What reason did you have to insinuate yourself so intimately into his life, except a wanton desire to exercise your own voracious appetite for young flesh?"

Still playing blind Claudius, Cicero shook his head and went on. "If the example set by the men of your lineage fails to shame you, then perhaps the women can do so. What of Claudia Quinta, who proved her purity when she saved the ship that brought to Rome the Great Mother, whose festival we celebrate today? Consider the renown that her virtue added to your house. Or the famous Vestal Virgin, Claudia, who shielded her father against an angry mob with her own pure body? Why do you share your brother's vices instead of your ancestors' virtues? We famous Claudii of old, did we refuse the peace offered by Pyrrhus and tear up his bargain, only so that you could drive your daily sexual bargains? Did we build the first aqueduct to bring water to Rome, only so that you could use it to wash yourself after your incestuous copulations? Did we build our great road, only so that you could parade up and down it in the company of other women's husbands?"

The harshness of Cicero's voice kept anyone from laughing. He lowered his arms and looked straight at Clodia, who returned his stare with a look of pure malice. "I drop the role. I speak to you directly now. If you intend to go on with your testimony, then you will also have to explain how such intrigues could have come about in the first place. The prosecutors, at your behest, have dinned a list of suggestive phrases into our ears: adulterous orgies, wild beach parties, all-night revels, dancing at dawn, unending drunken debaucheries. Did you think you could accuse Caelius of debauchery without exposing your own debauchery to the scrutiny of the court? It was madness to think so. I see by your face that you would like to avoid such an unpleasant spectacle. Too late to stop now!"

For a long moment Cicero and Clodia stared at one another in silence while the spectators looked on. Then he stepped back and softened his posture. He smiled sweetly. "But I see you don't care for the stern-lecture approach. Well, then, forget those rustic old ancestors and their upright morals. I'll borrow a more modern voice to try to talk some sense into you — why, I'll pretend to be your own beloved little brother. That should be appropriate. No one is more worldly, that's for sure. And no one has ever loved you better, ever since you were children. Does he still have those nightmares that make him wet the bed, so that he has to come sleep in yours? Pity he's in charge of the festivities today and can't be here beside you. But I can imagine what he might say."

Cicero put on a simpering expression and waved his arms in a spastic manner while the crowd shrieked with laughter. "Sister, sister, what a mess you've gotten yourself into! What's this craziness all about? Have you lost your mind? Yes, I know, I know, it was that boy down the street who caught your attention — tall, good-looking, pretty eyes.

It set your old, tired blood racing. You wanted to see more of him — every inch of him! Getting your hands on him would be easy enough, you thought. Young men are always short of money, and you love to flaunt our inheritance.

"But sister, sister, it didn't work out the way you wanted, did it? Some young men don't care for the company of a grasping, older woman, no matter how much money she's got. Well then, get over it! You've got your horti on the Tiber, where you go to watch the young swimmers and size them up. What's the place for, except to provide you with a new lover every day? Why keep pestering this particular young fellow, who obviously doesn't want you?"

Cicero dropped the simpering role of Clodius and turned his back on Clodia. He strode across the open space toward the defendant's benches. "And now it's your turn to receive a lecture, Marcus Caelius." He wagged his finger. Caelius put on the face of an attentive schoolboy, all raised eyebrows and bland innocence. "I'll need a father's voice to deal with you, young man — but what sort of father? One of those old men with hearts of iron, who would blame you for everything and say, 'Why on earth did you settle so close to that whore in the first place? Why didn't you have the sense to run away the first moment you saw her!' To such a gloomy old man Caelius might well defend himself by saying that nothing improper ever occurred, whatever gossips may say to the contrary. How can a young man in a city so full of malicious rumors possibly avoid being tarnished by loose talk? Living so close to that woman and being seen in her company, it's no wonder people assumed the worst. Even the lady's own brother can't visit her without wriggling his tongue — I mean, setting tongues wagging.

"Now, as regards the woman, at the moment it's not my object to criticize her. My point is to lecture Marcus Caelius. So for the sake of argument, let us imagine a purely hypothetical woman; any resemblance to Clodia will be purely coincidental, I assure you. Imagine a woman who shamelessly offers herself to every man she meets, who has to mark a calendar to keep her lovers straight, who opens the doors of her houses at Rome and Baiae to every sort of lecherous degenerate, who lavishes expensive gifts on her stable of kept young studs. Imagine a wealthy, lascivious widow carrying on like a common whore, without the least regard for what anyone thinks. Now I ask you, if a young man should happen to be a bit free in his relationship with such a woman, can any man here really hold him accountable for his misconduct?

"Imagine a woman so deeply sunk in depravity that she no longer bothers to seek privacy and darkness to practice her vices. Quite the opposite — she builds a stage in her garden so that she can show off her special skills before an audience lined up to enjoy them! Bear in mind, I'm speaking hypothetically, simply to make a point — don't laugh! Now with this woman, this hypothetical woman, everything about her is an invitation to sex: the way she walks, the see-through gowns she wears, the obscenely pouting way she holds her mouth, her smoldering gaze, the foul language she uses, the easy way she embraces everyone at her parties, pressing herself against them and kissing them with her open mouth. She's not simply a whore, but a particularly lewd and depraved old whore. Now, really, if a young man should find himself in the clutches of such a woman, can anyone be genuinely outraged if he should follow the course of nature? Is that young man guilty of vice — or of simply seeking relief?

"The woman is a whore, after all — the hypothetical woman, I mean — and even the sternest moralist looks the other way when a young man goes off to relieve himself with a prostitute. That is the way of the world, and not just in our present permissive age. Even our virtuous ancestors allowed for the use of prostitutes. The practice has never been frowned upon or forbidden in any time or place that I know of.

"Now someone will object, and say, 'Is this the sort of standard to which Cicero would hold a young man, especially a young man who was given into his charge to be educated in rhetoric? Loose morals, easy virtue, a nod and a wink?' Of course not. But judges, honestly, was there ever a man on earth so high-minded and strong-willed that he could reject all temptation and devote himself exclusively to the pursuit of virtue? A man without the least interest in leisure or lovemaking or simply having fun? Show me such a man and I will declare him superhuman! Such men exist in our history books, fine moral examples from the days of Rome's rise to greatness, but you will look for them in vain in the streets of the city today. These days, even among the Greek philosophers, who once set so high a moral standard in their writings (unmatched by their actions, unfortunately), you will find little to encourage adherence to pure virtue; quite the opposite, in fact. The Epicureans tell us that a wise man does everything for pleasure. The Academics, by twisting words, claim that virtue and pleasure can be one and the same. Alas, the old-fashioned Stoics, who cling to the straight and narrow path of virtue, find themselves stranded all alone in their lecture halls.

"Nature herself has endless tricks to lull a man's virtue to sleep while waking up his appetite for pleasure. She tempts the young down all sorts of dangerously slippery paths, but to compensate she lavishes on them great stamina and exquisite sensitivity. Show me a young man who despises the sight of beauty, who derives no pleasure from scent or touch or taste, who plugs his ears to keep out sweet music; I and a few others might argue that a youth of such purity has been blessed, but I think most of you would say he was cursed by the gods!

"Enough, then, of absolute standards! Let youth be permitted its pleasures. Let immaturity be allowed to flirt with foolishness. If he has a strong character, a young man will not be diminished by these experiences but will eventually outgrow them and be ready to take his place as a man of affairs in the Forum. Who can doubt that Marcus Caelius has already done so? You've watched him match wits with me here in the Forum. You've seen how eloquently he defended himself here today. What a superb orator! Let me tell you, from my own experience, cultivating that degree of skill requires enormous dedication and discipline. Marcus Caelius has reached a stage in his career where he no longer has the time or inclination to follow frivolous pursuits.

"Now then, we have navigated our way through the rocky shoals and treacherous reefs. From here on, clear sailing! Let us get back to those two charges against Caelius. The gold: Caelius is said to have gotten it from Clodia in order to bribe the slaves of Lucius Lucceius to kill Dio. Grave charges, to be sure, asserting that a man plotted to murder a diplomatic envoy, and instigated slaves to kill their master's guest — heinous crimes!

"But I have to wonder: would Clodia have given this gold to Caelius without asking why he wanted it? Surely not! If he told her it was to murder Dio, then she was in on the plot. Is that why you came here today, woman, to make a confession? To tell us how you raided your secret treasure chest, denuded that statue of Venus in your garden adorned with all those pretty trophies from your lovers, so that you could hand over the booty to Caelius for criminal use? Did you make Venus herself an accomplice in crime?"

I glanced at Catullus, for it seemed to me that from the corner of my eye I had seen his lips moving, as if he was reciting Cicero's speech along with him. He noticed my scrutiny, flashed something between a smile and a wince, and turned away. I looked at Clodia and caught a glimpse of her pale, rigid face before the crowd blocked my view.

Cicero went on. "If Caelius was as intimate with Clodia as the prosecutors maintain, then surely he shared with her the purpose to which he intended to put the gold. On the other hand, if the two of them were *not* on such intimate terms, then surely she never gave him the gold at all! Which is it, Clodia? Did you lend a man money to commit an unspeakable crime, making a criminal of yourself? Or is the truth that you never lent him the money at all?

"The accusation simply will not stand up, and not just because the character of Marcus Caelius is wholly at odds with such a loathsome, skulking plot. He's too smart, for one thing. No man with any sense would entrust a crime of such magnitude to the slaves of another man! On purely practical grounds, I have to ask: how is Caelius supposed to have made contact with these slaves of Lucius Lucceius? Did he meet with them directly — very rash — or through an intermediary? May we have the name of this go-between? No, because no such person exists. I could go on and on with such questions. How many must I ask to show how totally implausible the whole charge is, and how utterly without proof?

"To put the matter to rest, let us hear from Lucius Lucceius himself, who has provided a sworn deposition on the matter. I remind you that he was not only Dio's good friend and dutiful host, but a man who pays scrupulous attention to detail, as anyone familiar with his historical writings can attest. Surely if Lucceius had discovered that slaves belonging to him were plotting with an outsider to murder his guest, if he ever had even the least suspicion of such a thing, Lucceius would have gotten to the bottom of it. What citizen could do less, with his own honor at stake? Listen, then, to what he has to tell us."

A clerk came forward to read the deposition. Cicero walked to the defendant's bench, where his secretary, Tiro, handed him a cup of water. I thought back to my interview with Lucceius, how adamantly he had refused to acknowledge the slightest possibility that something had been amiss in his house, how his wife had known better, how the kitchen slaves who must have known something had been sent off to the mines and would never tell anyone what they knew.

The clerk cleared his throat, "I, Lucius Lucceius, under solemn oath, make this statement on the Kalends of Aprilis: That for a period in the month of Januarius, Dio of Alexandria, my esteemed friend, was a guest under my roof; that while he was my guest, nothing occurred to endanger his safety; that any rumors to the contrary, particularly rumors asserting a breach of loyalty among my household slaves, are completely scurrilous; that Dio left my house of his own choice and in good health; that I myself know nothing which might shed light on the circumstances of his death."

Cicero stepped before the judges. "There you have it: a wild, wholly unfounded accusation that emanates from a household of wanton debauchery and wickedness; and a ievel-headed, sober response, from a household of impeccable standards. On one hand, we have the word of a foul-tempered, raving, sex-crazed woman; on the other, the sworn affidavit of one of the most respectable men in Rome. Need we hesitate about choosing whom to believe?

"On then to the accusation that Caelius plotted to poison Clodia. I confess, I can't make heads or tails of this story. Why should Caelius want to do such a thing? To avoid paying back the alleged loan? But did Clodia ever ask to be repaid? To keep Clodia from telling what she knew about the attempt on Dio's life? But there was no such attempt, as we have just established. Indeed, I would suggest that this nonsense about gold and a plot against Dio was fabricated precisely to provide a motive for this other fabrication, that Caelius tried to poison Clodia. One fabrication is invented to provide a motive for another fabrication! Lie builds upon lie, slander upon slander.

"The prosecution alleges that Caelius once again attempted to commit murder by bribing someone else's slaves — this time, Clodia's slaves, to do in their mistress. And this, after having failed to pull off the same kind of plot with Lucceius's slaves! What kind of man puts his whole fate into the hands of another person's slaves, not once but twice? At least credit my client with having a brain!

"And just what sort of slaves are we talking about? In the case of Clodia's household, this is an important point. As Caelius must have known if he ever visited her house, the relationship between Clodia and her slaves can scarcely be described as normal. In a household like that, headed by a woman who behaves like a prostitute, where abnormal lusts and unheard-of vices are practiced on a daily basis, where slaves are invited to share an inordinate amount of intimacy with their superiors — well, those slaves are slaves no longer. They share *everything* with their mistress, including her secrets. They become her companions in loose living. In a household like that, the people on the bottom are sometimes quite literally on top."

I caught sight of Clodia, who seemed to physically shrink from the gales of laughter that roared through the Forum. Cicero held up his hand to quiet the crowd. "Keeping slaves in that fashion has one virtue, at least: such corrupted, pampered slaves must be almost impossible to bribe. Caelius must have known that, if he was as intimate with Clodia as we've been led to believe. If he knew the situation, surely he would have known better than to try to insinuate himself between such a woman and her slaves — a tight spot for any man to wriggle into! If he didn't realize the situation, then how could he have been so intimate with the slaves that he would consider bribing them? The allegation contradicts itself.

"Now, about the alleged poison — where it came from, how it was to be handed over, and so on. The prosecutors tell us that Caelius had it in his house. He wanted to test it, so he bought a slave for just that purpose. The poison was effective. The slave died very quickly. The poison . . ."

Cicero's voice was suddenly choked by a sob. He clenched his fists and rolled his eyes upward. "Oh, immortal gods! When a mortal commits a terrible crime, why do you close your eyes to it? Why do you allow the villain to go unpunished?" He gasped and shivered, as if struggling to hold back tears. The rollicking speech came to an abrupt halt. The crowd was jolted into uneasy silence.

Cicero stood absolutely still, like a man paralyzed by emotion and fighting to regain control. "Forgive me," he finally said, in a hoarse, trembling voice. "But the very mention of poison . . .

"Let me explain myself, judges. It was the bitterest day of life, that day when I saw my friend Quintus die before my eyes. Quintus Metellus Celer, I mean, the man whose death made that woman a widow and freed her to do as she pleased. Such a fine man he was, dedicated to serving Rome and full of the strength to do it! I remember the last time I saw him here in the Forum, going about his business, in excellent health and high spirits, full of plans for the future. Two days later I was called to his deathbed, where I found him racked with pain, barely able to breathe. His mind had begun to fail, but at the very end he became lucid again. His last thoughts were not of himself, but of Rome. He fixed his gaze on me as I wept, and in broken words he tried to warn me of the storm that hung over my head, the tempest that was brewing for the whole state. 'Cicero, Cicero, how will you hold out against them without me to hold them in check?' He wept then, not for himself, but for the future of the city he loved, and for the friends who would no longer have his protection. I often wonder how differently things might have turned out had he lived. Would his cousin Clodius have succeeded with a tenth of his mad schemes if Quintus Metellus Celer had been alive to oppose him? Would his wife Clodia have fallen into the downward spiral of disrepute that has ultimately brought us here today?

"And now that woman has the audacity to speak of fast-acting poisons! How much does she know about the subject? Enough, apparently! If she goes ahead with her testimony, perhaps she will tell us *exactly* how much she knows about poison, and how she came to know it. When I think that she still lives in the house where Celer died, when I think of what she has since turned that house into, I wonder that the walls themselves had not rebelled in disgust and come toppling down around her!"

Cicero bowed his head for a long moment, seemingly overcome with emotion. As for Clodia, one would never have known what a famous beauty she was, from the way she looked at that moment. The bones of her face seemed ready to break through the skin. Her eyes smoldered like coals. Her mouth was a hard, straight line showing a glint of teeth between bloodless lips.

"Excuse me, judges," said Cicero, recovering himself. "My memories of a noble and valiant friend have greatly upset me, I fear. And some of you, too, as I can see. But let us persevere with this distasteful, petty business, and be done with it.

"Very well: the story goes that after testing the poison on a hapless slave, Caelius handed it over to a friend of his, Publius Licinius. You see him here today, sitting proudly among Caelius's supporters, not the least bit ashamed to show his face despite the slander against him. Licinius, they say, was to give the poison to some of Clodia's slaves at the Senian baths, in a little pyxis. Ah, but the slaves had betrayed the plot to their mistress, so she sent some friends to lurk on the premises and seize Licinius in the act of handing over the poison. So goes the story, anyway.

"I am eagerly waiting to discover the identities of the upstanding witnesses who are supposed to have seen, with their own eyes, the poison in Licinius's hands. So far, their names have not been mentioned, but they must be very reputable fellows indeed. In the first place, they are intimates of such a lady. In the second, they agreed to lurk about the baths in the middle of the day, a job suitable only to the most respectable of men."

I felt the skin prickle on the back of my neck. Cicero was talking about me, among others. Even without hearing my name mentioned, I felt cut by his scorn, exposed and flustered. What then was Clodia feeling at this moment?

"But don't take my word for the worthiness of these witnesses, these midday bathhouse skulkers," Cicero continued. "Their actions speak for them. We are told, 'They hid out of sight and watched everything.' I'm sure they did. That type loves to watch! 'They bolted out of hiding accidentally.' Oh dear, premature ejaculators — what a deplorable lack of manly self-control! The story goes that Licinius made his entrance and was just about to hand over the incriminating pyxis but had not quite done so, when these superb, anonymous witnesses burst forth — whereupon Licinius drew back the pyxis and took to his heels in flight!"

Cicero shook his head and made a face of disgust. "Sometimes, no matter how badly a tale is told, a shred of truth shines through. Take this shabby little drama, for instance, authored by a lady with so many other tawdry tales to her credit. How devoid of plot, how sorely lacking for an ending! How could all these fellows have let Licinius slip from their grasp, when they were posted and ready, and he suspected nothing? What was the point of capturing him as he handed over the poison, anyway? Once it passed out of his hands he could claim he had never seen it before. Why not seize him the moment he entered the baths, hold him down and force a confession from him with all those bystanders for witnesses? Instead, off Licinius goes, with the lady's gang in hot pursuit, bumbling and tripping all over each other. In the end, we are left with no pyxis, no poison, not a single shred of evidence. Really, what we have here is the finale of a mime show, not a proper play but the sort of silly farce that sputters to an unsatisfying end — no climax, just a bunch of clowns bumbling off the stage.

"If they come forward to testify, I look forward to seeing the cast of this little mime show. This trial could use some comic relief! Let's have a look at these young dandies who enjoy play-acting as warriors under their mistress's command, scouting the familiar terrain at the Senian baths, laying an ambush, crowding into a bathtub and pretending it's the Trojan Horse. I know the type: all glib and witty at dinner parties, and the more they drink the wittier they become. But idling on soft couches and chattering by lamplight is one thing; telling the truth beneath the hot sun in a court of hard wooden benches is something else again. If they can't even find their way around the baths, how will they find the witness stand? I give these so-called witnesses fair warning: if they decide to come forward, I will turn them upside down and shake the foolishness out of them, so that we can all see what's left. I suggest they keep their mouths shut and find other ways to curry their lady's favor. Let them cling to her, do tricks and compete to grovel at her feet — but let them spare the life and career of an innocent man!

"And what of that slave to whom the poison was to be handed over, who is also to appear as a witness?" I searched the faces of those on the prosecutors' benches — a glum lot of faces, at the moment — and spotted Clodia's man Barnabas, looking as if he had swallowed something unpleasant. "I am told that he has just been freed by his mistress, made a citizen by her hand — or by her brother's hand, since a woman cannot legally manumit a slave on her own. What was behind this act of liberation? Was it a reward for loyalty and services beyond the normal call of duty? Or was there a more practical consideration? For, now that he's a citizen, the fellow cannot be subjected to the normal means of obtaining evidence from a testifying slave. Torture tends to bring out the truth; no amount of rehearsal can prepare even the best comic actor to recite falsehoods to a hot poker.

"Incidentally, we should hardly be surprised that all this bother about a pyxis has given rise to an extremely indecent story concerning another pyxis and its contents. You know the story I mean, judges. Everyone's talking about it. Everyone seems to think it's true. Why not, since it fits so well with the lady's indecent reputation? And everyone finds the story hilarious, despite the obscenity of it. The gift could hardly be called inappropriate, when one considers the receptive nature of the butt of the joke. There, you see, you're all laughing even now! Well, true or not, obscene or not, funny or not, don't blame Marcus Caelius. The joke must have been pulled by some young wanker with a clever hand and a wayward bent."

Again, from the corner of my eye I thought I saw Catullus's lips moving. When I turned to stare at him he looked at me darkly and moved away, losing himself in the crowd.

Clodia's face was a study in misery. Cicero accepted another sip of water from Tiro and waited for the laughter to die down. "I have now stated my case, judges. My task is done. The task is now yours, to decide the fate of an innocent young man."

He proceeded to his summation: a brief recapitulation of Caelius's career, a recitation of his virtues, an appeal to be merciful to his distraught father, a final, scornful dismissal of the spurious charges against him. I heard these words only vaguely. I couldn't take my eyes off Clodia. I saw a woman utterly unnerved, pale, defeated, confused, resentful. She looked as if she had been poisoned again, and polluted as well: Medea had become Medusa, to judge by the shifty-eyed friends who squirmed on the benches around her. They looked nervously here and there but turned their faces from Clodia, as if the merest glance from those haunted eyes might turn a man to stone.

CHAPTER TWENTY-SIX

Cicero's speech was followed by a recess, after which, the magistrate declared, the testimony of witnesses would commence. The common sentiment in the crowd was that the trial would probably carry over for at least another day, given the number of witnesses expected to testify. But when the court reassembled, the prosecutors were embarrassed to reveal that most, indeed virtually all, of their scheduled witnesses had declined to appear. The coterie of young men who had filled the benches around Clodia had vanished. So had Clodia herself.

The supporters of Caelius could hardly contain their triumph. Even Caelius's father, dressed in his ragged funeral garments, looked smug.

A handful of witnesses dared to appear — some of the outraged husbands whose wives had been insulted by Caelius, Senator Fufius, and even a couple of the "bathhouse skulkers." The prosecutors, who had clearly lost heart, perfunctorily interviewed them. Cicero cross-examined them with effortless panache, restraining his wit lest it appear wasted on such minor opponents. The spectators began to disperse. The drama had reached its climax with Cicero's oration, and only the most inveterate believers in surprise endings held out to see what the verdict would be.

The judges tallied their votes and announced their decision. Marcus Caelius was not guilty.

I felt relieved of a great burden. What if they had declared him guilty of all the charges against him, including Dio's murder? How could I have remained silent? But they had not declared him guilty; the crisis was averted. Still, what of the poison plot against Clodia? Cicero had argued that it was all a fiction concocted by Clodia herself, just another part of her scheme to take vengeance on Caelius, and the judges had agreed. But what if Caelius *had* tried to poison her? Had I no obligation to speak up?

The moment had passed, and there was no undoing it. I told myself that my sole intention from the outset was to discover the truth about Dio's death. As for Caelius and Clodia, whatever the truth of their intrigues against each other, surely I owed nothing to either of them.

After the verdict was announced, Caelius's supporters broke into cheering and gathered in a ring around him. The prosecutors and their assistants glumly dispersed. Some of the judges went to congratulate Caelius and pay compliments to Cicero and Crassus for their orations. Spectators headed off to see what activities connected with the Great Mother festival were still going on elsewhere in the city. Slaves gathered up folding chairs and carried them off.

"Where shall we go now?" said Eco.

"I think I want to be alone for a while," I said. "Take Belbo with you. I don't need a bodyguard anymore. The trial's over and I'm no danger to anybody."

"Still, Papa, it's a holiday. People get rowdy — "

"Please, Eco, take Belbo with you. Or better yet, send him home to Bethesda. I'll feel better knowing he's there while I'm not."

"Where are you going?"

"I'm not sure."

"Why don't you go home yourself?"

I shook my head. "Not yet."

"Papa, what's going on?" He lowered his voice. "If Dio was poisoned in your house, who did it? And why? You know, don't you?"

I shook my head. "We'll talk about it later."

"But Papa — "

"I'll spend the night at your house, if that's all right. Have the slaves fix up a couch for me to sleep on."

"Of course, Papa. Are you sure you don't want me to come with you? We could talk."

"Talk is not what I need. I need to think, and I can think more clearly if I'm by myself."

This last turned out to be untrue. I wandered the city in a daze, paying no attention to where I was going, my thoughts turning in sluggish circles.

Why had Bethesda deceived me? Had it been left to her, would she ever have told me the truth? Of course, I knew why she had remained silent.

How does a woman tell her husband that she's poisoned his respected old mentor under his roof, right under his very nose? Still, she had reason. Did she think I wouldn't understand? Why had she never told me of her mother's death and about the terrible thing that had happened to her before I found her? Did she trust me so little, even after all our years together?

My own feelings confused me no less. Was I angry, or hurt? Did I want to punish Bethesda, or beg for her forgiveness? I felt as if I had done something wrong, but I couldn't say what it was. I knew I had been made a fool of; Bethesda had known the truth all along and yet had let me plod down the wrong path in darkness. Was she amused at my folly? Did she fear my reaction if I should discover the truth? Or did she simply think that she could get away with never telling me, and considered that easiest for everybody? She knew the truth was precious to me, and she had withheld it from me. I resented her for that. Under my roof, before my eyes, she had murdered a man she hated. I understood her reason, but still I was appalled and shaken by the enormity of it. Perhaps she was right not to trust me with the truth after all.

I passed revelers and vendors in the street, heard the roar of a large crowd from the Circus Maximus, went by a square where a stage was being put up for a performance the next day, heard tambourines and looked up to see a group of galli dancing on a rooftop. Now and again I heard snatches of conversation which must have been about the trial: *So the young man got off completely . . . clever Cicero . . . had no idea the woman was such a wanton . . . the Clodii will think twice before trying a stunt like that again . . . everybody laughed — you should have seen the bitch's face . . . who gives a damn about those Egyptians anyway? . . . they stone women like that in other countries . . .* 'Did I say husband? I mean brother, of course — I'm always making that mistake!' . . . 'Not just a whore, but a particularly lewd and depraved old whore' . . . *from what's said about her, someone probably should go ahead and poison the monster. . .*

I kept walking. Hours passed. The sky grew dark. The streets became empty. Still I walked. I never knew where I was headed until I got there.

The phallic lamp above the entrance burned bright, promising warmth and light within. I rapped on the door of the Salacious Tavern and the doorman let me inside.

As a rule I drink no more than other men, and less than most. That night, I felt like getting drunk. The slave who brought wine was glad to help me in the pursuit.

The room was so noisy that I could hear only snatches of conversation, much of which was about the trial. Cicero's jokes were repeated and obscenely embellished. The story of the pyxis and its contents was told in numerous variations, and arguments broke out over which version was correct. Wine prompted crude bursts of insight: "Caelius may have screwed the bitch before, but

491

it was Cicero who screwed her today!" The consensus seemed to be that Caelius had escaped by the skin of his teeth, and that Clodia had been ruined for good, and it was all for the best. I sat and drank, making no particular effort either to listen or not listen, letting the words of strangers enter my ears as they might. When my cup was empty, I called for the server to fill it again.

It was quite late in the evening when the door opened and a large party came stamping in. They were mostly young, too well groomed and poshly dressed for the place. They had obviously come from some other, more respectable venue. There were shouts of greeting and then a general cheer as the patrons recognized Marcus Caelius. He acknowledged the show of support with a smile and a wave, then made a tipsy bow that turned into a stumble. His friends Licinius and Asicius each grabbed an arm to pull him upright. I was surprised, but only a little, to see Catullus in the group, looking even drunker than Caelius.

Caelius and his friends took over a corner of the room. He ordered a round of the tavern's best wine for everyone, which earned him another cheer. The drowsy midnight mood of the place was dispelled and the room was suddenly loud and festive again. I stared glumly at the dregs in my cup and wondered if I dared to have it filled again. The glow of the wine had begun to pall and I was beginning to feel slightly queasy. When the server passed me I covered my cup with my hand and shook my head.

"What's wrong?" a voice shouted. "Gordianus won't drink the wine I offer? I'll wager it's better than whatever cheap slop you've been guzzling."

I turned and saw Caelius watching me from across the room, his lips pushed out in a mock pout.

"No insult intended," I muttered.

"What's that? Can't hear you!" Caelius cupped his ear and grinned. "You'll have to come closer."

I shook my head.

Caelius snapped his fingers, and a moment later a couple of brawny bodyguards were on either side of me, lifting me up by my elbows and carrying me across the room. They sat me down on a bench across from Caelius, who laughed and clapped his hands like a child watching a magic trick.

"You're in an awfully good mood tonight," I said.

"Why not? If things had gone badly today I'd be on a boat heading for Massilia right now." He made a face. "Instead, here I am surrounded by my friends, in the heart of the most wonderful city in the world." Licinius and Asicius sat on one side of him, Catullus on the other. The rest of his party had gathered around a nearby table to throw dice. "I'm free!"

"Free? I thought Cicero had you in his snare again. You owe him quite a favor now. Does he know you're out carousing tonight, making a liar of him?"

"Cicero?" Caelius made a rude noise with his lips. "Don't worry, I can handle him. I've been doing it for years."

"The student controls the teacher?"

"Something like that."

"You're a spoiled brat, Marcus Caelius."

"And people love me for it! Except maybe you. Why won't you drink the wine I offer?"

"I've had enough tonight. You look like you've already had rather a lot yourself. You, too, Catullus."

Catullus looked back at me blearily and blinked a few times. He seemed to be at a level of inebriation that made him neither giddy nor maudlin, but simply numb.

"So you think we've had too much to drink?" said Caelius. "We've only started! Server! Bring out more of your best wine, for everyone!"

"Are you sure you can afford such extravagance?" I said.

Caelius smiled. "All my debts are paid off."

"I thought you had no debts."

"Didn't you pay attention to Cicero in court today? I don't even keep ledger books, Gordianus! All my finances are in Papa's name."

"I see. Technically, you have no debts."

"That's how it works nowadays. But like I said, all the debts are paid off."

"Even the ones you owed to Pompey?"

He hesitated for only a moment. "Even those."

"But not repaid with coin?"

"No. With services rendered."

Next to him, Licinius and Asicius stiffened. "Caelius!" said Asicius.

Caelius laughed. "Don't worry, the trials are over. Your trial, Asicius, and my trial, and we are both as innocent as lambs."

"You should learn how to shut up, Caelius!" snapped Licinius.

"Shut up about what?" I said.

"Oh, my friends think I talk too much. But where's the danger now? I'm free!"

"Then perhaps you could set my mind at rest about a few things," I said.

Licinius and Asicius fidgeted, but Caelius smiled blandly at me. "Why not?" Next to him Catullus stared obliviously into space and moved his lips, composing a poem in his head, perhaps.

"Do you remember when I last saw you, Caelius, here at the tavern? You swore to me by the shades of your ancestors that you didn't murder Dio."

"Yes, I remember. I told you the truth."

"And you swore that it wasn't Asicius, either."

"Also true."

"But when I asked where you were and what you were up to on the night Dio died, you refused to tell me."

"How could I tell you, with the trial still pending — "

"Caelius, shut up!" snapped Asicius.

"I believe you," I said, "when you swear that you didn't kill Dio. It's my belief that he died of poison. And yet, someone broke into Coponius's house that night, and Dio was found with stab wounds in his chest. Can you explain that, Caelius?"

"Now you bring up a very interesting point," Caelius said, raising one eyebrow, "and as a matter of fact — "

"Caelius, you fool, shut up!"

"Relax, Asicius. The trial is over, and Gordianus can be trusted with the truth. Can't you, Gordianus? Swear to me by the shade of your father that you'll keep secret what I'm about to tell you."

I hesitated only a moment. "I swear."

"Caelius, you're an idiot!" Asicius stamped his foot and angrily left the room. Licinius stayed behind, looking around warily for eavesdroppers. Catullus stared blankly into his cup.

"Asicius! What an ass. He always was death to a good conversation." Caelius smiled. "Where were we?"

"The night Dio died — "

"Ah, yes. Well, it was the oddest thing. You see, I was *supposed* to kill Dio. It's exactly as you had it figured, I'm sure. King Ptolemy wanted to get rid of Dio, and so did Pompey. I owed Pompey a pile of gold which I couldn't possibly repay. So it was up to me to do old Dio in."

"Just as you arranged the attack on the Alexandrian envoys when they arrived in Neapolis."

Caelius nodded. "And kept up the attacks in Puteoli and on the way up to Rome. The Egyptians were almost too easy to frighten. They're about as courageous as pigeons. But pigeons scatter when they're attacked, and there were so damned many of them!"

"And the last one left was Dio."

"Exactly. And that pigeon made a nasty mess."

Licinius rolled his eyes. "Caelius, you're crazy to be telling him this."

"Shut up, Licinius. Has my judgment ever steered me wrong? Gordianus is like a dog with a bone. He'll never let go of this thing until he's got the truth. Now that it can't hurt us, better to simply tell him so that he can go find another bone to chew. He's sworn himself to secrecy! Now where was I?"

"All the Egyptians gone but Dio."

"Ah, yes. Well, I tried to get the kitchen slaves to poison him at Lucius Lucceius's house, of course. Having met that idiot Lucceius once at a party, I figured I could get away with just about anything under his roof. But the slaves bungled it and killed Dio's taster instead, and off Dio went to Coponius's house. A good thing Lucceius is the type to see no evil, or he could have forced his slaves to testify against me and ruined everything.

"So it was on to Titus Coponius's house. Titus is no fool, and his slaves are as loyal as slaves come. Added to that, Dio was more wary than ever, and Pompey was really beginning to press me. Well, there was nothing to do but sharpen the daggers and go on a midnight raid. I needed help for that, so I called on Asicius. He's the one who actually staged the raids on the envoys down south for me. He's been one of King Ptolemy's agents for years. Knows a lot more about daggers and blood and that sort of thing than I do."

"Thank the gods he's not here to hear you!" groaned Licinius, covering his face. Catullus was busy poking at something in the bottom of his wine cup.

I nodded. "Then you and Asicius — "

"Oh yes, we went out that night with every intention of killing old Dio. Sorry. I know he was your old teacher and all that. But Egyptian politics is a nasty business."

"You had no confederates inside Coponius's house?"

"Not a single one. Too dangerous. His slaves are too loyal, as I said."

"But you knew the room where Dio was staying."

Caelius shrugged. "Not too hard to figure out. I'd stayed in the house as a guest myself."

"So the two of you climbed over the wall, broke in the window, burst into Dio's room — "

"And found him lying on his couch as dead as King Numa. I'll never forget the sight of him — mouth gaping open, eyes staring. Oh yes, most definitely dead."

"Then what?"

"What else could we do? Pompey had sent us to kill Dio, and he knew we intended to use daggers. I didn't want Pompey to think that Dio had died of natural causes, or that someone else had murdered him. I wanted my debt discharged! So we went ahead and stabbed him, enough times to kill him if he'd still been living — "

498

"More than enough, from what I heard."

Caelius shrugged. "Then we made a bit of a mess in the room, as if there might have been a struggle, and then we got out of there as quickly as we could. The next day everyone was saying that Dio had been stabbed to death in his bed. Pompey was satisfied, my debts were discharged, and I figured that was the end of it. But Asicius was never secretive about his links to King Ptolemy. His enemies decided to put him on trial for murdering Dio. Ptolemy hired Cicero to handle the defense, and Cicero got Asicius off. The prosecution never really had enough evidence against him."

"Nor against you, it seems."

"Especially not with Cicero on my side." Caelius grinned.

"Yes, that explains it," I said. "Stabbed after he was already dead. No one in Coponius's house noticed the discrepancies — hardly enough blood spattered about for so many wounds, and the wounds all neatly close together, not spread around. No struggle. And the slave girl, too afraid to tell what she knew . . ."

"What's that?" said Caelius. "You're muttering to yourself, Gordianus."

"Was I? A bad habit. Yes, you've put my mind to rest about Dio. The old dog can stop gnawing that bone. But I have another bone with some marrow still left in it."

"Do you? Server, more wine!"

"The violence against Dio and the Alexandrian

envoys weren't the only charges against you."

"No — and a good thing, too!"

"What do you mean?"

"Why, Clodia adding that poisoning charge at the last minute. Crassus said we should disallow it. He said it was technically too late for the prosecutors to include it and that we didn't have time to prepare a defense. Cicero told him he was mad, that it was a gift from the gods. 'Don't you see? They've given us exactly what we need! Now we have every reason to drag Clodia into the case, and that will be the end of the prosecution.' And he was right, of course. If Clodia had kept out of sight, I'd have been in much worse trouble. But with Clodia right there, showing her face, bringing her own accusation against me, Cicero was able to turn the trial on its head. Not 'Did Caelius murder the Egyptians?' but 'Why is that wicked woman trumping up charges against the poor boy?' And it worked, brilliantly! The prosecution was totally discredited. Accusing me of trying to poison Clodia actually *weakened* all the other charges."

"Yes, Caelius," I said quietly, "but what about the accusation itself?"

Catullus suddenly looked up from his wine cup and showed signs of life. Caelius gave me a supercilious grin. "Gordianus, a Roman court has declared me to be an innocent man, wrongfully accused. What more do you need to know?"

"The truth," I said. I reached for his arm. The force I used caught him by surprise.

He dropped his cup. Wine splashed on the floor. Caelius's bodyguards lurched forward. He kept them back with a shake of his head and spoke to me through gritted teeth.

"Gordianus, you're hurting my wrist. Let go, or I shall tell them to cut your hand off."

"The truth, Caelius. It goes no further than me. I swear by the shade of my father."

"The truth? Licinius here very nearly got caught with a pyxis full of poison at the Senian baths. He managed to empty the stuff into one of the tubs on his way out — a waste of good poison! But I put the pyxis to good use later."

"Caelius, shut up!" Licinius clenched his fists.

"And the second attempt?" I said. Catullus stared at Caelius.

"The truth?"

"Tell me!"

He jerked his arm free and rubbed his wrist. "The second attempt almost succeeded. I'm glad now that it didn't. Cicero was right. Dead, Clodia would have been truly dangerous to me, an object of sympathy. Alive, she was an object of scorn, an asset to me in spite of herself. So it worked out for the best. Clodia got off with a bit of indigestion, and I got the sympathy of the judges."

"The poison you used for the second attempt — "

"Different from the first time. I'd wanted to use something very quick to act; I didn't want her to suffer. But Licinius threw that batch away, so I ended up trying something called — what is it called, Licinius?"

"Gorgon's hair."

"Yes, that's it. It would have taken a bit longer, I'm told, but been just as effective. I am sorry that Chrysis got caught, poor thing. She's so delicate, and now Clodia will take it all out on her."

Catullus spoke in a slurred voice. "Caelius, you told me — "

"What you wanted to hear, Catullus, and you never want to hear the truth, do you? So what if I tried to poison her? What do you care? She despises you even more than she does me."

"Caelius, you lying bastard!" Catullus lurched toward him.

Caelius drew back and lifted his hands, a signal for his bodyguards to rescue him. It happened so quickly that I experienced the journey from the bench to the street outside as a blurred moment of levitation, followed by a hard landing on my posterior. When my head stopped spinning I saw that Catullus was sitting on the paving stones beside me. After a moment, he rolled forward onto his hands and knees, crawled to the gutter and was violently ill.

A little later he crawled back to me. "You should try that," he said, wiping his chin. "You'd feel better."

"I don't want to feel better."

"Self-pitying bastard. You sound like me. What have you got to be sad about?"

"Woman trouble."

"At your age?"

"Live long enough, whelp, and you'll see. It never ends."

"Then how do men stand it?" The brief relief of vomiting gave way to his usual misery. "So Caelius really did try to poison her?"

"Not once, but twice. He told you otherwise?"

"He lied to my face."

"Imagine that! What were you doing in his company tonight, anyway?"

Catullus looked even more miserable.

"Don't tell me," I said. "Let me guess. You were sharing in the celebration, since you helped him write his speech. You helped Cicero write his speech as well."

"How did you know?"

"The look on your face at the trial today. You couldn't help but enjoy hearing your phrases spoken aloud. That business about 'Clytemnestra for-a-quadrans' and 'Medea of the Palatine' — it had to come from you. Likewise the reference to those lovers' trophies Clodia keeps in her secret treasure box under her statue of Venus. You told me no one knew about that but you, and you only found out by accident. I saw her face when Cicero mentioned it. So did you. That was the last straw for her, the moment she broke. He stripped her naked, and you helped. You knew the jokes that would hurt her the most. The cruelest puns, the nastiest metaphors. Are you the poet of love, Catullus, or the poet of hate?"

" 'I hate and I love. If you ask me how, I do not know — ' "

"Stop quoting yourself! Why did you do it?"

"Don't you know?"

"I thought you loved Clodia. I thought you hated Caelius."

"Which is precisely why I had to help him destroy her."

"You baffle me, Catullus!"

"She had to be destroyed. It was the only way. Now I can reclaim her."

"What are you talking about, Catullus?"

He clutched my arm. "Don't you see? As long as she had this burning passion for Caelius, I could never get her back. She'd put up with anything from him, any abuse. But now he's gone too far. Now she can't possibly love him anymore, not after what they did to her at the trial today. Caelius and his advocates have made her the laughingstock of Rome! Yes, I helped. I went to Caelius the morning after we ran into him here at the tavern. I told him I had some ideas for his speech. Cicero was quite excited to have me along. The three of us had quite a time, going through the orations, adding jokes, wondering just how far we should go. That pun about the pyxis — "

"Don't make me hear it all again!"

"It's not that I'm proud. But it had to be done. She had to be brought down. She'd become too full of herself, too proud, too arrogant, ever since Celer died and she started running her own household. Now she's been broken, in the only way it could be done. We took everything that made her strong — her beauty, her pride, her love of pleasure — and turned it against her. Her own ancestors were turned against her, the ones she's always gloating about! She'll never be able to brag about the family monuments again without everyone snickering behind her back. She can't even turn to Clodius, not in public. It's me she'll turn to."

I shook my head. "Catullus, you are surely the most deluded man I ever met."

"You think so? Come with me right now, to her house. You'll see."

"No, thank you. Clodia's house is the *last* place on earth I'd care to be at this moment. No, that's not quite true. The last place I'd want to be is in my own house. But then, it's also the only place I want to be."

"Now who's not making sense?" Catullus staggered to his feet. "Are you coming with me or not?"

I shook my head, which seemed to go on spinning after I stood up.

"Farewell then, Gordianus."

"Farewell, Catullus. And — " He turned and looked back at me blearily. "— good luck."

He nodded and stumbled off into the darkness. I waited for my head to stop spinning and tried to figure out the direction to Eco's house. The Subura seemed a long way off.

CHAPTER TWENTY-SEVEN

I woke late the next morning. My head felt as if a whole toga had been stuffed inside it; I could taste scratchy wool on my tongue.

Dunking my head in cold water helped. So did eating a bit of food. I stepped shakily into the garden at the heart of Eco's house and found a place to sit in the sun. After a while Menenia walked by, beneath the portico. She acknowledged my presence with a nod but did not smile. A little while later Eco sauntered out to join me.

"You came in awfully late last night, Papa."

"Who's the son here, and who's the father?"

"Can we talk now?"

"I suppose so."

"About Dio, and how he died. You never told me yesterday what you think."

I sighed. "You were right, about the poison in my house being used to kill him."

"But who did it?"

I took a deep breath, then another. It was hard to say it aloud. "Bethesda."

Eco looked at me steadily, less surprised than I expected him to be. "Why?"

I told him about the conversation I had overheard in my house, between Clodia and Bethesda.

"It must have been Dio she was talking about. Dio was the powerful, respected man who owned her mother. She never said anything about it to me. Never! Not a single word! But she must have recognized Dio the moment she saw him."

"Did he recognize her?"

"He looked at her strangely, I remember. But she was hardly more than a child when he last saw her, and he had a great many things on his mind. No, I don't think he knew who she was. But she surely recognized him. I think back now and realize how oddly she behaved that night. I thought it was because I was going away! What I find so appalling is how quickly she must have made the decision to kill him — no deliberation, no hesitation. She got the poison, fixed the dinner, made a special portion for the guest and then watched him eat it, right in front of me!"

"You have to talk to her, Papa."

"I'm not ready. I don't know what to say."

"Tell her you know what she did. Go on from there."

"Go on, as if it makes no difference that my wife is a murderer? That she compromised the honor of my house by killing a guest? She should have come to me."

"Before or after she poisoned Dio?"

"If not before, then certainly after! There, you see how angry it makes me to talk about it? No, I'm not ready to go home to her yet. I wonder if I ever will be."

"Don't talk that way, Papa. You must understand why she did it. Look, I wasn't taken entirely by surprise by what you've just told me. I had a lot of time to think on the ride up from Puteoli, wondering how Dio could have been poisoned in your house and by whom. Bethesda does the cooking, Alexandria was a common thread — I figured she might somehow be responsible. So I've had more time to think about this than you have, and to make up my mind that it makes no difference. I was with Zotica all that time, seeing what the brute did to her. I can't be sorry that someone killed him. If it was Bethesda, and if she had as much reason to hate the man as Zotica did, then what is there to forgive?"

"But it was murder, Eco! Cold-blooded, calculated, committed in secret. Does my name and my household stand for nothing? We are not murderers!" I stood and began to pace around the garden. "Talking does no good. I need to be alone again. I need to think."

"Not another walk?"

"Why not?"

"You'll wear out the streets, Papa. Where will you go?"

A completely unrelated thought entered my head. "I'll take care of my last bit of business with Clodia. The money I gave you for your trip south — you must have a lot left over."

"Quite a bit."

"It's Clodia's money. It was meant to bribe me so that I'd testify for her, or else it was meant to pay for the slaves of Lucceius. Who knows what she really had in mind? Either way, she didn't get what she paid for, did she? Never say I'm like Caelius, that I took money from Clodia and didn't return it. Go fetch it, will you? I'll take it back to her right now. At least I can wash my hands of that affair and put it behind me for good."

Eco went into the house and returned with a purse full of coins.

"By the way, how is Zotica doing?" I said. "Now that she's rested, is she any calmer?"

Eco lowered his eyes.

"Is something wrong?"

"After we talked to her yesterday, Menenia showed her to a place where she could sleep, and left her alone. It was a mistake to let her out of the locked pantry. When I came home from the Forum . . ."

"Oh, no!"

"She ran away, Papa. I can't say I'm surprised. I told you, she's turned wild, like an animal. I doubt that we'll ever see her again."

Heading to Clodia's house by the shortest way would have taken me by my own front door, so I took a roundabout route. The day was hot and the way was steep. I arrived sweaty and winded.

I rapped on the door. After a long pause I rapped again. Finally the peephole opened. A dispassionate eye observed me. "My name's Gordianus," I said. "I have business with your mistress."

The peephole was shut. After a long wait it opened again. The eye that now perused me was penciled with makeup. From the other side of the door I heard a familiar but unexpected voice. "It's all right, I know him. We can let him in."

The door swung open to reveal the gallus Trygonion. After I stepped inside he motioned to the slave to shut the door behind us. "What business could you possibly have with Clodia?" he said tersely. He walked at a hurried clip toward the garden and I followed. "Did she forget to pay you?"

"As a matter of fact, she overpaid me; gave me money for expenses I didn't incur." I jiggled the bag of coins. "I'm here to return it."

Trygonion looked at me as if I were mad, then nodded and sighed. "I understand. You wanted an excuse to see her again."

"Don't be ridiculous!"

"No, really, I do understand. But I'm afraid you can't see her."

"Why not?"

"She's gone."

"Where?"

He hesitated. "Down to her villa at Solonium. She left early this morning, before dawn. She wanted to slip out of the city without being seen." We arrived at the steps leading down to the garden and stopped beneath the giant Venus. I found my eyes wandering to the pedestal, where Catullus had said she kept her trophies in a secret compartment. Trygonion noticed.

"She emptied it before she left. She burned everything that could be burned. You can see the ashes in that brazier over there. The things that wouldn't burn — jewels and necklaces and such — she took with her. To throw into the sea, she said."

"But why?"

He shrugged. "How can a eunuch understand these things?" He walked to the fountain. Suddenly the sound of chanting echoed through the garden, coming from the House of the Galli.

"Why aren't you with them?" I said.

"I'll join them soon enough. She sent a messenger for me in the middle of the night, saying she needed my help. 'I have to leave,' she said. 'I can't stand it here.' She always goes south for a month right after the Great Mother festival, like a lot of rich people do. Down to Baiae, usually. But she wasn't waiting for the festival to be over, and she wasn't going to Baiae. 'Solonium,' she said. 'It's closer, and nobody ever goes there. I never want to see anybody again.' " He smiled ruefully. "I thought she intended for me to go with her."

The chanting grew louder and faster. Trygonion closed his eyes and moved his lips with the words, then blinked and gazed at the sunlight reflected in the fountain. "But she didn't want me to go with her. 'I need someone to close up the house for me,' she said. 'I'd ask Clodius, but he mustn't come near this place, not for a while. You'll do it for me, won't you, Trygonion? Make sure the windows are all shuttered and locked, put the good wine away so the slaves can't get to it, dispatch some last-minute letters for me, that sort of thing.' I said, 'Yes, of course. Have a good trip.' "

Together we studied the broken sunlight on the water. "Right before she left, as she was going out the door, she turned back. She called my name. I ran to her. She said, 'Oh, and don't tell anyone where I've gone.' I said, 'Of course I won't.' But I suppose it's all right to tell you, Gordianus. You can keep a secret. You *are* the most honest man in Rome, aren't you?" His lips curled into a sardonic smile.

"Did a visitor come, late last night?"

Trygonion gave me a blank look, then smiled wanly. "Oh, you mean the poet, the one who recited that awful thing about Attis at the party. Yes, one of the slaves told me he came beating on the door in the middle of the night, drunk and demanding. Bad timing; Clodia was in no mood to be harassed. She sent Barnabas and some of the burlier freedmen to run him off. I think he got away with nothing worse than a broken nose."

I thought of poor Catullus, lying alone in his dreary little room with his books, hung over with a bloody nose. "And a broken heart. She's a cold woman."

Trygonion looked at me sharply. "You're like all the rest. You think she feels nothing. Of course she feels everything. How could she not, being who she is? She feels *everything*. It amazes me that she can bear it."

The chanting became dreamlike, magical. The bits of sunlight on the water were dazzling. "And you, Trygonion? Are you the same? Everyone thinks you feel nothing, but in reality — "

He looked at me steadily, his eyes swimming with tears, daring me to go on, but I left the rest of the thought unspoken.

I took the same circuitous route back to Eco's house.

"Perhaps you should write a letter to Meto," Eco suggested. "Doesn't that often help to clear your head?"

"I don't think it would be wise to put incriminating information about my wife in a letter."

"You can always burn it afterward. Don't you often do that, anyway?"

I sometimes think my sons know me too well. I asked Eco to show me where he kept his writing tools.

I sat in his little study and stared at the blank parchment for a long time, then finally wrote:

To my beloved son Meto, serving under the command of Gaius Julius Caesar in Gaul, from his loving father in Rome, may Fortune be with you.

I write this letter on the Nones of Aprilis, the second day of the Great Mother festival . . .

I put down the stylus and stared again at the parchment. There was a sound from the doorway. I looked up and saw Meto looking back at me.

The gods delight in catching us off our guard. The threads of our lives weave back and forth across one another, intersecting in a pattern no mortal can discern: my thoughts had turned to Meto and now he stood before me in the flesh, as if my desire had conjured him up.

"By Hercules!" I whispered. "What are you doing here?"

His older brother suddenly appeared behind him. They both burst out laughing.

"You knew, Eco!" I said. "He was already here when you suggested I write the letter!"

"Of course! I couldn't resist the joke. Meto arrived right after you left for Clodia's house. When we heard you coming back, I made him go and hide. You should see the look on your face!"

"Playing tricks on your father is despicable."

"Yes, but at least you're smiling," said Eco.

I pushed the parchment away from me. "A good thing you're here, Meto. Writing it all down would have been impossible!"

He smiled and sat down beside me. "I'm lucky to be here in one piece."

I put my hand over his and drew in a breath. I was always worried for him, knowing the dangers he faced in Gaul. But that wasn't what he meant.

"The riot, over near the Forum," he explained. "Surely it's still going on. Didn't you see it on your way back from the Palatine?"

"I took a roundabout route . . ."

"There's a play being put on for the festival," Eco interjected. "Apparently some of Clodius's hooligans commandeered the stage and set off a riot. Instant revenge for the nasty things that were said about him at the trial yesterday."

"Put a man like Clodius in charge of a festival and he'll use it for his own petty ends," said Meto in disgust. "Politicians are all the same. But what's this business about a trial?"

I tried to explain as succinctly as I could, but after a moment Meto held up his hand. "It's all too complicated. Give me military strategy any day!"

I laughed. "But what are you doing in Rome? Is Caesar here?"

"He's up in Ravenna, actually, but you never heard me say that. Having a secret meeting with Crassus. Then he's going to Luca to meet with Pompey. Caesar wants to appoint more generals and raise four legions; he'll need the help of those two to get the Senate to approve the expenditures and to quash complaints that he's becoming too powerful. If you ask me, the three of them are going to resurrect the Triumvirate, and make it work this time. It's inevitable. Sooner or later, the Senate will become entirely defunct. The Senate can't rule itself, much less an empire! It's nothing more than a hindrance now, another obstacle in Caesar's way. A rotten limb that needs to be pruned. All this judicial haggling, politicians constantly dragging each other into court — this nonsense has to stop sooner or later. From what you've said, this trial of Caelius is just one more example of how far the standard has fallen."

"But what's the alternative?" said Eco.

Meto looked at his brother blandly. "Caesar, of course."

"You're talking about a dictator, like Sulla," I said, shaking my head.

"Or worse," said Eco, "an outright king, like Ptolemy."

"I'm talking about a man who can lead. I've seen with my own eyes what Caesar can do. All this petty squabbling in Rome seems quite absurd when you're up in Gaul, watching Romans conquer the world."

"Pompey and Crassus are hardly petty," I said.

"That's why a triumvirate is the answer," said Meto. "Temporarily, anyway. But you never heard me say that."

"What about men like Clodius and Milo?" said Eco. "Or Cicero, for that matter? Or Caelius?"

Meto made an expression to show that such men were beneath contempt. What had his service to Caesar done to my son?

I had only a moment to ponder the question, for the twins suddenly rushed into the room in a burst of laughter and golden hair. Meto might know a thing or two about military strategy, but he was no match for his niece and nephew. Titania advanced from the left, Titus from the right. Each grabbed hold of an arm and climbed onto him.

"When did they get so big? And so strong!" Meto laughed.

"They intend to wrestle you, I think," said Eco, chagrined.

"Or at least immobilize you," I said.

"They've succeeded." Meto grunted. The twins squealed with triumph.

"You'd better give up now, while you can," I suggested. "Gaul-fighting Uncle Meto can take a lot rougher treatment than their delicate old grandpa, and they know it."

"I give up!" gasped Meto. The twins released him at once and then turned to mount a skirmish against me. Their attack turned out to be an assault of harmless hugs and kisses, to which I submitted without a struggle.

"But what's this?" I said.

"What?" said Titania.

"This piece of jewelry pinned on your tunic?"

"A gorgon's eye!" cried Titus. "It gives her magical powers, and I have to get it away from her, even if I have to chop her head off!"

"But where did it come from?" My mouth was suddenly dry. It was an earring of simple design, a silver crook with a green glass bead — the twin of the earring which had been used to force the lock of my strongbox, and which had been carelessly dropped inside when the poison was taken.

"It came from the land of Libya, where the Gorgons live," said Titania. "It can make you invisible. That's what Titus says."

"Yes, but how did you come to have it?" From the tone of my voice she knew I wanted a serious answer.

"She *gave* it to me," said Titania. "She told me

she'd lost the other one and she didn't want it anymore."

"Who gave it to you?"

Titania told me. My heart sped up.

"And will it really make me invisible?" she said.

"No." My voice shook. "I mean, yes. Why not? The other earring made her invisible. To my eyes, anyway. It made me think I saw the truth, when I couldn't begin to see it. Oh, Cybele!"

Eco furrowed his brow. "Papa, what are you talking about?"

"I have to go home now. I think I may have been very, very wrong about something."

Belbo answered the front door. At the sight of me he broke into a grin. "Master! Thank the gods you're here!"

"Is something wrong?"

"No, nothing at all . . . now that you're back."

"Has her mood been that terrible?"

Belbo rolled his eyes in answer, then jumped at the voice from behind him.

"Whose mood?" Bethesda's voice was like frost in the springtime.

I nodded to dismiss Belbo, who quickly disappeared. Bethesda and I looked at each other in silence for a long moment. "Where have you been?" she finally said.

"I spent the night at Eco's house."

"And the night before that?"

"I was in bed with a drunken poet, actually."

She snorted. "Did you see the trial yesterday?"

"Yes."

"Quite a spectacle, wasn't it?"

"You were there?"

"Of course. Belbo held me a place at the very front. I never saw you, though."

"I was standing at the back. I never saw you either."

"Strange, isn't it, that we could be so close and yet not see each other." Her gaze softened a bit. "Caelius was acquitted. I was glad."

"So was I, I suppose."

"But what they did to Clodia was horrible."

"Yes, it was appalling."

"I wanted to stop them. I would have stopped them, if I could have."

"I felt the same."

"Now she's left the city," said Bethesda.

"How did you know that?"

Bethesda saw the look on my face and scowled. "Don't be so suspicious. Do you imagine there's some sort of secret conspiracy of women? A slave brought a note from Clodia this morning. I was supposed to visit her tomorrow, and she wanted to let me know that she wouldn't be home. She didn't say where she was going, only that she was leaving Rome at once."

She crossed her arms and walked into the garden. I followed. She kept her back to me. "I apologize for deceiving you, husband. You know the truth, don't you?"

"I think I do."

"I should explain. That man — Dio — I can hardly say his name. Back in Alexandria, before you bought me — "

"I know."

"How could you?"

"I overheard you talking to Clodia the other day, in the garden at the back of the house."

She looked over her shoulder. Her eyes lit up as she comprehended, then became clouded. "But I never said his name! I made a point of not saying his name to Clodia."

"Even so . . ."

She nodded and turned her face away.

"You should have told me, Bethesda. You should have told me long ago." I stepped closer and put my hand on the back of her neck.

She reached up and touched my fingers. "Then you understand?"

"I can't be sorry that Dio's dead. When I think of what he did to you and your mother, and to who knows how many others . . ."

"Then say you forgive me."

"Forgive me first, Bethesda, for having had less faith in you than I should have."

"I forgive you, husband."

"And I forgive you, wife, for deceiving me."

"And for poisoning a guest in your house?"

"You confess?"

She took a deep breath. "Yes."

I shook my head. "No. I can't forgive you for poisoning Dio."

She stiffened.

"But I will forgive you for continuing to deceive me with a false confession."

She turned. From the way she looked up at me, searching my face for signs of what I knew, I was satisfied that I had found the truth at last.

A little while later I was sitting in my library, looking out the open windows onto the garden. The vines and flowers were in bloom. Bees and butterflies flitted in the bright sunshine.

Diana appeared in the doorway. "You wanted to see me, Papa?"

"Yes."

She looked grave for a moment, then brightened. "Mother says that Meto is back."

"Yes, for a short visit. He's at Eco's house. They'll all be coming over for dinner soon."

"I can't wait to see him."

I nodded and found myself unable to look at her. I watched the bees and butterflies instead. "Did your mother tell you what I wanted to talk to you about?"

"Yes, Papa." She suddenly hardened her voice, the way her mother always did at the beginning of an argument to show that she would not be shaken.

"When did your mother first tell you about Dio? About what he did to her?"

"Years ago, Papa. As soon as I was old enough to understand."

"And yet she never told me!"

"It was between her and me, Papa. A thing for

a mother to tell a daughter. Men have secrets they never share with women."

"I suppose we do. So, when Dio came to the house that day — "

"When you introduced him, I had no idea who he was. Mother had never told me the man's name, only how wicked he was. But when I told Mother the visitor's name and where he was from, I saw from her face that something was terribly wrong. All at once I knew. 'It's him, isn't it?' I said. She couldn't be sure, so we went to have a look."

"Yes, I remember the way you both looked at him, and the way he looked at you. No wonder he was startled by the sight of you, especially when the two of you stood side by side! How much you look like her, when she was young. I saw every look that passed between the three of you, and yet I understood nothing — like a dog watching orators debate. And to think, I was the one who suggested that the two of you fix something for Dio to eat! Was it your mother who told you to get the poison?"

"No, Papa. I thought of it myself. I knew where the poison was — "

"Of course you did, because I made such a point of warning you about it when I got it from Eco. So dangerous, I thought, to have poison in a house with a child. Dangerous in a way I never considered! But your mother must have known when you mixed it into Dio's portion?"

"No. I did it while her back was turned, then

made sure that I did the serving."

"You did it all on your own! In the blink of an eye you made up your mind to kill a man, then fetched the poison, slipped it into his food, and . . ."

Diana lowered her eyes.

"All on your own!"

She nodded. I shook my head. "When did Bethesda give you those old green-glass earrings of hers?"

Diana sighed. "Ages ago, Papa. She tired of them, and there were scratches in the glass, so she let me have them. I wore them from time to time."

"And I never noticed. Of course, Bethesda wears her hair up, showing her ears. You still wear your hair down, like a girl . . ."

"It's funny. I can't remember wearing them that day. I can't even remember using one of them to pry open the lock on the strongbox to get at the poison, but I suppose I must have. It's like it all happened underwater. I didn't realize until days later that I'd lost the earring. I looked everywhere for it. Everywhere but inside your strongbox. Finally I gave up on finding it. I gave the widowed earring to Titania."

"Yes, Titania told me." I shook my head. "You left the lock just as it was, broken. You never even tried to replace the poison you'd taken, if only with something that looked similar." I winced. "That fact alone should have told me that Bethesda wasn't responsible. She would have covered her tracks! You behaved like a child, Diana, thinking you could leave such clues and not be found out. When did you tell your mother?"

"Not until just the other day, after Clodia's visit."

"Why did you wait so long? I'm not surprised that you didn't tell me, but I thought you had no secrets from your mother?"

"I meant to tell her right after Dio left the house. I wanted to. But I was suddenly afraid. Then I was confused. The next day, after you were gone, we heard that Dio had died. I could see that Mother was pleased, though she never spoke a word. But everyone said that Dio had been stabbed to death, and if that was so, how could I have poisoned him? Maybe the stuff was harmless, I thought, not poison at all, just a yellow spice. Maybe I had only imagined doing it. It all seemed so strange. I didn't know what to do. I just wanted to forget and be done with it."

I nodded. "So Bethesda didn't know the truth until after Clodia's visit. All her protests that Caelius was innocent were only statements of opinion! She was also sure that Caelius could never have poisoned Clodia. Well, she was wrong on both counts — Caelius tried his best to kill Dio and Clodia both. So much for Bethesda as a judge of character. So much for me, admiring Dio! What prompted you to finally tell her?"

"It was hearing her tell Clodia what happened to her and her mother when she was a girl. I was amazed to hear her talk about it to anyone but me. It made me cry. That was when I finally made up my mind to tell her I poisoned Dio, not because I was proud of what I did, but because I didn't want to have any secrets from her. So that night, after Clodia left, I told her. She said that we mustn't tell anyone. 'Not even Papa?' I said. 'Especially not him!'

"But a couple of days later, after the two of you came back from Clodia's house, Mother came into my room to tell me about the party, and then you burst in, shouting at her. You'd gone looking for the poison and found the broken lock and the empty pyxis. You threw the earring on the floor — and suddenly I realized where I had lost it. But what you said made no sense. You seemed to think that for some reason Mother had stolen the poison for Clodia . . ."

I groaned and shook my head. "I accused her of deceiving me, and she admitted it — but we were talking about different things! I thought she had given the poison to Clodia behind my back, but the deception was something else — she knew you had poisoned Dio and kept it from me."

Diana nodded. "After you went storming out of the house, Mother told me, 'If he does figure out the truth, keep your mouth shut. Let me take the blame.' But you found me out, didn't you, Papa?" She spoke without recrimination, but rather with a hint of pride — of Bethesda for shielding her, of me for finding her out.

I looked at her face in the soft light from the garden and saw a girl-child with lustrous black hair and the beginnings of a woman's beauty. "I don't know what to make of you, Diana. You're a mystery, like your mother. Why did you do it? What gave you the strength to go through with it?"

"How can you not understand, Papa? Do you remember when we were in this room the other day and I wanted to see the letter you were writing to Meto? It was a letter about the work you were doing, looking into Dio's death. I asked you why it was so important for you to know who killed Dio. You talked about peace of mind. You said to me, 'If someone who was close to you had been hurt, wouldn't you want to avenge that person, to redress the wrong that was done to them, if you could?' Of course, Papa! That's exactly what I did. I did it for Mother. I did it for the grandmother I'll never know. Would you have me undo it, if I could? If you could turn back time, would you have me do nothing, instead?"

I studied her face, confused, and tried to remember what I believed about murder and justice, right and wrong.

"Wouldn't you have done the same thing yourself, Papa?"

For an instant the veil of mystery dissolved. The eyes that looked back at me were as familiar and empty of secrets as my own eyes in a mirror. Flesh of my flesh, blood of my blood. I put my hands on her shoulders and kissed her brow. From the garden came the noise of the family arriving for dinner — Eco, Menenia, Meto, the all-conquering twins. I drew back and looked into Diana's eyes again, and saw with a shiver of regret that the veil had returned. She was a mystery again, distinct and wholly of herself, another mortal adrift in the cosmos: out of my control, beyond my comprehension. The moment of recognition was fleeting, as such moments always are, like music which fills the void to overflowing and then vanishes in the twinkling of an eye.

AUTHOR'S NOTE

Within thirteen years, many of the players in the trial of Marcus Caelius would be, in the historian T. P Wiseman's phrase, "spectacularly dead" — Clodius murdered during a skirmish with Milo's gang (an angry mob burned the Senate House the next day); Crassus massacred along with twenty-thousand troops in his ill-fated campaign for military glory against the Parthians; Pompey a casualty of the tumultuous Civil War; Cicero a casualty of the peace. Republican judicial restraints on "political violence" clearly failed, as did the second attempt by Crassus, Caesar and Pompey to form a stabilizing triumvirate; at the end of the road stood Augustus.

King Ptolemy would also be dead, leaving his children (including the famous Cleopatra) to fight over Egypt and to fend off Roman domination for a little while longer.

As for Marcus Caelius, he shifted allegiance once too often, and against the wrong man. Unable to convince a garrison of soldiers to revolt against Caesar in the middle of the Civil War, his ambitions ended in a violent death. His colorful correspondence with Cicero survived to make him the darling of historians like Gaston Boissier ("In the history we are studying, there is perhaps no more curious figure than Caelius") and W. Warde Fowler (who called Caelius "the most interesting figure in the life of his age"). Early on, the first-century commentator Quintilian delivered the judgment of posterity: Marcus Caelius "deserved a cooler head and a longer life."

Catullus died the soonest of any, in 54 B.C., of unknown causes. He was probably about thirty years old.

What of Clodia? After the trial, she vanishes from the scene (though I suspect that Gordianus may not have seen quite the last of her). We get a glimpse of her again nine years later in some of Cicero's letters to his friend Atticus, who appears to have been on good terms with Clodia. Looking to buy property where he can enjoy his retirement ("A place to grow old in," Atticus assumes, to which Cicero bluntly replies, "A place where I can be buried"), Cicero asks his friend to check out various horti that might be for sale around Rome. This is Cicero, in Shackleton Bailey's translation: "Clodia's gardens I like, but I don't think they are for sale." And a few days later: "But you say something or other about Clodia. Where is she then or when is she coming? I prefer her grounds to anyone's except Otho's. But I don't think she will sell: she likes the place and has plenty of money: and how difficult the other thing is, you are well aware. But pray let us make an effort to think out some way of getting what I want."

So far as I can tell, the very last we hear of her

is in a letter of April 15, 44 B.C., in which Cicero writes to Atticus: *Clodia quid egerit, scribas ad me velim* ("I should like you to tell me what Clodia has done"). Was Cicero seeking clarification of a bit of gossip he had heard? Was he inquiring about Clodia out of the blue? We do not know.

I should like to acknowledge some of the books I encountered in my research. Foremost among them is T. P. Wiseman's superbly annotated *Catullus and His World: A Reappraisal* (Cambridge University Press, 1985), which ranges far and wide to render a vivid picture of Catullus and his circle of history, fiction, and academic myth.

Studies of Catullus abound, from Tenney Frank's venerable *Catullus and Horace* (Henry Holt and Company, 1928) to Charles Martin's insightful and thoroughly modern *Catullus* (Yale University Press, 1992). There are numerous translations of his poems. The Penguin edition by Peter Whigham is accessible (in every sense); Horace Gregory's 1956 translation may be harder to find, but rewards the search. Readers with some Latin will find *The Poems of Catullus: A Teaching Text* by Phyllis Young Forsyth (University Press of America, 1986) frank and useful.

The famous oration in defense of Marcus Caelius can be found in Michael Grant's translation of *Selected Political Speeches* by Cicero (Penguin, 1969). R. G. Austin's commentary on the Latin text (Oxford, 1933; third edition 1960) is delightfully sharp.

Some odds and ends: *Cybele and Attis: The Myth and the Cult* by Maarten J. Vermaseren (Thames and Hudson, London, 1977) is a treasure trove of information about the Great Mother and her eunuch priests. *Back From Exile: Six Speeches Upon His Return,* translated with notes by D. R. Shackleton Bailey (American Philological Association, 1991), gives a lucid picture of Cicero's ongoing feud with Clodius. The melodramatic tale of Appius Claudius the decemvir and the hapless Verginia is found in Book Three of Livy's *History of Rome.* An explication of the Nola pun in Caelius's speech (of which we have only a few secondhand quotations) can be found in T. W. Hillard's "*In triclinio Coam, in cubiculo Nolam:* Lesbia and the Other Clodia" *(Liverpool Classical Monthly,* June 1981).

Much of my research was conducted at Doe Library at the University of California at Berkeley and at the Perry-Casteñeda Library at the University of Texas at Austin.

Special thanks to Brad Craft, who helped get me in the mood to take on Clodia and company with a copy of Forberg's 1844 *Manual of Classical Erotology (De figuris Veneris);* to Penni Kimmel, for her comments on the manuscript; to Terri Odom, for reading the galleys; to Barbara Saylor Rogers, who showed me that the world is full of the most unexpected interconnections; and to my Austin friends, Gary Coody and Anne and Deborah Odom, who gave the author places to retreat from his labors.

NORTHERN
CELESTIAL
HEMISPHERE

PISCES

Ecliptic

CETUS

TRIANGULUM   ARIES

ROMEDA

PERSEUS

CASSIOPEIA

TAURUS   Aldebaran

CAMELOPARDALIS

ORION

Capella   AURIGA

olaris

Betelgeuse

MONOCEROS

GEMINI

LYNX

Castor

Pollux

CANIS
MINOR

URSA
MAJOR

Procyon

CANCER

LEO
MINOR

LEO   HYDRA

Regulus

EYEWITNESS ● HANDBOOKS

STARS
—AND—
PLANETS

EYEWITNESS ◉ HANDBOOKS

STARS
AND
PLANETS

IAN RIDPATH

Editorial Consultant
AMIE GALLAGHER
American Museum of Natural History, Hayden Planetarium

Star charts by
ROYAL GREENWICH OBSERVATORY

DK PUBLISHING, INC.
www.dk.com

DK

A DK PUBLISHING BOOK

Important Notice
Observing the Sun through any kind of optical instrument can cause blindness.
The author and publishers cannot accept any responsibility for readers who
ignore this advice.

Project Editor Peter Frances
Project Designer Helen Taylor
DTP Designer Rob Campbell
US Editors Jill Hamilton, Ray Rogers, Mary Sutherland
Picture Research Angela Anderson, Robin Scagell
Production Controllers Michelle Thomas, Alison Jones
Managing Editor Jonathan Metcalf
Managing Art Editors Peter Cross, Steve Knowlden

First American Edition, 1998

4 6 8 10 9 7 5 3

Published in the United States by DK Publishing, Inc.,
95 Madison Avenue, New York, New York 10016

Visit us on the World Wide Web at http://www.dk.com

Library of Congress Cataloging-in-Publication Data
Ridpath, Ian.
Stars and planets / Ian Ridpath. – 1st American ed.
p. cm. – (Eyewitness handbooks)
Includes index.
ISBN 0-7894-3560-8 hardcover
ISBN 0-7894-3521-7 flexibinding

1. Astronomy – Observers' manuals. 2. Stars – Observers'
manuals. 3. Planets – Observers' manuals. I. Title. II. Series.

QB63.R527 1998   98–11961
520–dc21   CIP

Text film output by The Right Type, Great Britain
Reproduced by Colourscan, Singapore
Printed and bound by Kyodo Printing Co., Singapore

CONTENTS

AUTHOR'S INTRODUCTION

As the Sun sets and the sky darkens, the marvels of the night sky come into view: planets in our Solar System; stars, star clusters, and nebulae in our Galaxy; and other galaxies, unimaginably distant. Examples of all these objects can be seen with the naked eye, while binoculars or a small telescope reveal many more. This book shows you where and how to find them.

ASTRONOMY IS USUALLY regarded as the oldest of the sciences – yet, with the continuing development of orbiting telescopes and space probes to the planets, it is also among the most modern.

ANCIENT ASTRONOMY

Serious study of the sky began thousands of years ago in the Middle East and, at least in the ancient world, reached a pinnacle with the Greeks 2,000 years ago. At that time, the stars and planets were still mysterious lights in the sky, and the Earth was thought to be at the center of the Universe. This view was not seriously challenged until the 16th century, when Nicolaus Copernicus, a Polish astronomer, proposed that the Earth is simply a planet and that all planets orbit the Sun. His revolutionary view was confirmed in the following century by the Italian Galileo Galilei, using the newly invented telescope. Johannes Kepler, a German mathematician, worked out that planets orbit on elliptical paths, and the Englishman Isaac Newton explained the gravitational forces governing all orbital motions.

THE FARNESE ATLAS
The celestial globe held here by Atlas shows the constellations known to the ancient Greeks.

MODERN ASTRONOMY

From Newton's time in the 17th century onward, it was recognized that the stars are other suns, but only in the 20th century, with the work of the American astronomer Edwin Hubble, did it become clear that our Galaxy of stars is only one among countless others and that the Universe as a whole is expanding, as though from a massive explosion billions of years ago. And only with the development of nuclear physics has it become clear how the stars generate the energy that makes them shine.

SKYWATCHING

For all its modern advances, astronomy remains a branch of science where amateurs can make a real contribution, often with modest equipment – for example, monitoring changes in the brightness of variable stars, logging meteor showers, following storms in the atmospheres of Mars, Jupiter, and Saturn – and, if you're lucky, discovering an exploding star (a nova) or a comet. Perhaps one of the readers of this book will go on to make such a discovery.

HOW THIS BOOK WORKS

T HIS BOOK IS divided into four parts: a general introduction to astronomy; a detailed guide to the Solar System; an alphabetical catalog of the constellations; and a month-by-

month companion to the night sky. Sample pages from the three main sections (excluding the Introduction) are shown below. Further explanation appears at the start of each section.

THE SOLAR SYSTEM, PP.25–62

This section contains descriptions of the nine planets, the Sun and Moon, and the more significant smaller bodies. It also includes advice on how and where to find them.

THE CONSTELLATIONS, PP.63–141

Entries on the 88 constellations are arranged alphabetically by name. Collectively, the charts in this section form a complete atlas of the sky. The text describes the origins of the constellations and selected features of interest.

MONTHLY SKY GUIDE, PP.142–215

An introduction to each month, with easy-to-use charts and descriptions of what to look out for, is followed by more detailed charts of the night sky as seen from northern and southern latitudes.

INTRODUCTION TO THE MONTH

KEY TO SYMBOLS

GREEK ALPHABET
Greek letters form part of the names of certain stars and appear on some of the charts in this book.

α alpha	ι iota	ρ rho
β beta	κ kappa	σ sigma
γ gamma	λ lambda	τ tau
δ delta	μ mu	υ upsilon
ε epsilon	ν nu	φ phi
ζ zeta	ξ xi	χ chi
η eta	ο omicron	ψ psi
θ theta	π pi	ω omega

DEEP-SKY OBJECTS
These symbols appear in red on the constellation and whole-sky charts.

🝔 Galaxy

⊕ Globular cluster

⁙ Open cluster

☐ Diffuse nebula

◎ Planetary nebula

△ X-ray and radio sources

OBSERVATION SYMBOLS
These symbols indicate the type of instrument needed to observe features described in the Constellations section.

◉ Naked eye

♠ Binoculars

↗ Telescope

♣ Not observable with amateur equipment

THE UNIVERSE

THE UNIVERSE is everything that exists – all matter, space, and time. It extends as far as the largest telescopes can see, at least 10 billion light-years in all directions around us. The Universe is thought to have formed in a gigantic explosion, called the Big Bang, about 10 to 20 billion years ago and is still expanding. Within the Universe, matter is held together by gravity in structures of varying size.

OUR GALAXY

Most of the visible matter in the Universe is grouped in huge aggregations of stars, gas, and dust called galaxies. Our nearest star, the Sun, is an insignificant star in a galaxy of at least 100 billion others (usually known as "the Galaxy"). Although it is difficult to tell from our position inside it, the Galaxy is thought to be spiral in shape. There is some evidence indicating that there is a bar of material across the center. The Galaxy is about 100,000 light-years in diameter, and we are located about two-thirds of the way from the center to the rim, in one of its spiral arms. The stars that we see in the sky are all part of the Galaxy. Those nearest to us appear in all directions in the sky, and form the constellations (see p.18). Since the Galaxy is flattened in shape, more distant stars mass into a hazy band known as the Milky Way.

△ THE MILKY WAY
The Milky Way, a pale band that can be seen arching across the sky on dark nights, consists of innumerable distant stars within our Galaxy. In this view of the Milky Way, looking toward the center of the Galaxy, apparent gaps are caused by clouds of dark dust that lie in the spiral arms, obscuring the light from stars behind.

stars orbit the center of the Galaxy

outer stars take longer to orbit the center than inner stars

Perseus Arm

bright nucleus

outer arm

Solar System is located in Orion (Local) Arm

Sagittarius Arm

OVERHEAD VIEW OF OUR GALAXY

halo contains oldest stars

spiral arms contain mainly younger stars

from the side, spiral arms look like a flat disk

nucleus

100,000 light-years

SIDE VIEW OF OUR GALAXY

OTHER GALAXIES

The Universe contains countless galaxies, some of which we can see from the Earth. Galaxies are divided into spirals, barred spirals, ellipticals, and irregulars. Spirals have arms that consist of relatively young stars, gas clouds, and dust, and that curve out from a central bulge of old stars. In barred spirals, the arms extend from the ends of a central bar. Elliptical galaxies, consisting of old stars, have no arms and very little gas or dust. Irregular galaxies have no regular shape or structure. The largest galaxies are ellipticals, with more than ten times the mass of our Galaxy; some giant ellipticals may have formed by the merger of smaller galaxies. Far off in the Universe are objects called quasars that emit as much energy as a galaxy from an area not much larger than the Solar System. Quasars, and their less luminous relatives, known as Seyfert galaxies and BL Lacertae objects, are thought to be galaxies with massive black holes at their centers.

SPIRAL GALAXY
This galaxy, M83, appears "face-on" to us, so that we see its nucleus and curving arms.

BARRED SPIRAL GALAXY
In a barred spiral, such as NGC 1365, a bar of stars and gas lies across the nucleus.

ELLIPTICAL GALAXY
Elliptical galaxies range from dwarfs to giants. M87 is an example of a giant elliptical.

GROUPS OF GALAXIES

Galaxies usually occur in groups known as clusters. Our Galaxy is the second largest in a small family of about 30 galaxies called the Local Group, about 3 million light-years across. The Group's largest member is the Andromeda Galaxy, a spiral galaxy more than 2 million light-years away and the most distant object visible to the naked eye. Some clusters have thousands of members, as does the Virgo Cluster, the nearest large cluster to us, about 50 million light-years away. Its brightest members can be seen with the size of telescope used by amateur astronomers.

THE LOCAL GROUP

IC 10 (dwarf irregular galaxy)

Leo A (dwarf irregular galaxy)

Andromeda Galaxy

M33

Milky Way

Large Magellanic Cloud

Small Magellanic Cloud

WHAT IS A STAR?

STARS ARE BALLS of gas that release energy produced by nuclear reactions within their cores. Most stars are similar to the Sun, our nearest star, but because they are so far away they appear to us as mere points of light. Throughout the Galaxy, stars are forming, evolving, and being destroyed. By studying a range of stars, astronomers have been able to build a picture of how stars change over time and hence understand more about the past and probable future of the Sun.

STAR FORMATION

Stars form in huge clouds of gas and dust in space called nebulae, in a process that is continuing today. The nebula shrinks under the inward pull of its own gravity, forming an embryonic star known as a protostar. Eventually, the density and temperature of the gas at the protostar's center become high enough for nuclear reactions to begin. The object "switches on" to become a true star, generating its own heat and light. The star is then said to be on the main sequence. How long it stays like this and what happens next depend on the star's mass.

STAR FORMATION

dense area in nebula begins to contract •

contraction causes temperature of protostar to rise to about 15 million °C (27 million °F) •

star emits heat and light produced by nuclear fusion •

125 TRILLION MILES
NEBULA

60 MILLION MILES
PROTOSTAR

600,000 MILES
MAIN-SEQUENCE STAR

NEBULAE

Nebulae are clouds of gas and dust within galaxies. Bright diffuse nebulae are areas of hydrogen gas where new stars are being formed. Two types of nebula are linked with the late stages of star development: planetary nebulae are shells of gas thrown off by red giant stars, while supernova remnants are the twisted wreckage of exploded massive stars. Some nebulae are dark because they contain no stars to illuminate them and are visible only when silhouetted against a brighter background.

GREAT ORION NEBULA
(BRIGHT DIFFUSE NEBULA)

VELA SUPERNOVA REMNANT
(SUPERNOVA REMNANT)

CAT'S EYE NEBULA
(PLANETARY NEBULA)

MASSIVE STARS

A main-sequence star with a mass of more than about 10 Suns experiences a spectacular end. It swells into a red supergiant with cooling, expanding outer layers. Eventually its core collapses, causing a huge explosion known as a supernova. For a few weeks, the supernova shines as brightly as an entire galaxy. While the outer layers of the star are scattered in space, the fate of the core again depends on its mass. A core of relatively low mass will be crushed into a tiny, superdense neutron star. If the core has a mass of more than about two Suns, its own gravity will squash it further, into a black hole.

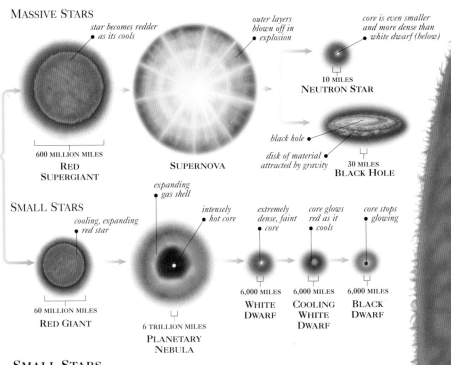

MASSIVE STARS

star becomes redder as its cools

outer layers blown off in explosion

core is even smaller and more dense than white dwarf (below)

10 MILES
NEUTRON STAR

600 MILLION MILES
RED SUPERGIANT

SUPERNOVA

black hole

disk of material attracted by gravity

30 MILES
BLACK HOLE

SMALL STARS

cooling, expanding red star

expanding gas shell

intensely hot core

extremely dense, faint core

core glows red as it cools

core stops glowing

6,000 MILES
WHITE DWARF

6,000 MILES
COOLING WHITE DWARF

6,000 MILES
BLACK DWARF

60 MILLION MILES
RED GIANT

6 TRILLION MILES
PLANETARY NEBULA

SMALL STARS

A star of similar mass to the Sun undergoes a quieter end than a massive star. It swells into a red giant, eventually losing its outer layers, which form a gas shell known as a planetary nebula (because of its resemblance to the disk of a distant planet). The core is exposed as a hot white dwarf that cools and fades over billions of years. On ceasing to emit light, it will become a black dwarf. The least massive stars, red dwarfs with only about one-tenth the Sun's mass, can last for 100 billion years or more, whereas the most massive stars burn out after only about a million years. The Sun, which formed about 5 billion years ago, is about halfway through its life cycle.

STAR SIZES

Stars vary greatly in size. A red giant may have a diameter of up to 100 million miles (150 million km). The Sun (a main-sequence star) is 865,000 miles (1.39 million km) in diameter, while a white dwarf, the size of which is exaggerated on this diagram, is typically only 6,000 miles (10,000 km) across.

white dwarf

main sequence star

red giant

STAR FAMILIES AND VARIABLE STARS

STARS ARE not always the simple, unchanging points of light that they may at first appear to be. Many of them occur in families of two or three, or sometimes in much larger groupings.

Others vary in brightness in cycles that last days, months, or years. Examples of double and multiple stars, star clusters, and variable stars can be seen with small instruments or even the naked eye.

DOUBLE AND MULTIPLE STARS

When seen with binoculars or a telescope, many stars turn out to have one or more companions. Sometimes the companion stars are unrelated objects in the foreground or background, in which case the pair form what is called an optical double. But in most cases, the stars lie close together in space, forming a pairing known as a binary. Linked by gravity, the members of a binary orbit around each other, although it usually takes many years to detect any motion, and in the case of multiple stars the orbital motions can be very complex. Separating the components of double stars is a popular activity among amateur astronomers. The closer together the stars are as seen from Earth, the larger the aperture of telescope needed to divide

ALBIREO
A color contrast of orange and blue makes this a particularly attractive double star for users of small telescopes.

(or "split") them. When the stars are very unequal in brightness, the fainter star (the secondary) can be difficult to see because of the glare from the brighter one (the primary). Some doubles, called spectroscopic binaries, have components that are too close together to be separated through an optical telescope. Only by studying the spectra of light from these stars are professional astronomers able to establish that they are double.

OPTICAL DOUBLE STARS
Two stars that lie in the same line of sight but are at different distances from us are known as an optical double. Double stars of this type are less common than genuine binaries. In fact, more than three-quarters of all stars are linked to one or more companions by gravity.

STARS LINKED BY GRAVITY

EQUAL MASS
In a binary star with members of equal mass, the stars orbit around a center of mass midway between them.

UNEQUAL MASS
When one member of a binary is more massive than the other, the center of mass lies closer to the heavier star.

A MULTIPLE STAR
Here, four stars of equal mass form two pairs orbiting a center of mass. Multiple star orbits are usually highly elliptical.

STAR CLUSTERS

Rather than originating singly, most stars form as part of a group or cluster, of which there are two distinct types. Open clusters, the more common type, have no specific shape, being scattered collections of dozens to hundreds of relatively young stars lying in the spiral arms of our Galaxy. Globular clusters, which lie in a halo around our Galaxy, are spherical or slightly elliptical in shape and contain large numbers of very old stars.

OMEGA CENTAURI ▷
(GLOBULAR CLUSTER)

△ THE PLEIADES
(OPEN CLUSTER)

VARIABLE STARS

A variable star is one that varies in brightness over time. Nearly 20 percent of such stars are eclipsing binaries – very close pairs in which one star periodically passes in front of the other, causing a drop in the total amount of light reaching the Earth. The most famous eclipsing binary is a star called Algol (in the constellation Perseus). But most stars that vary in brightness do so because they pulsate in size. The most common of these are red giants and supergiants called Mira stars, after their prototype, Mira (in Cetus). Such stars vary by up to 25,000 times in cycles lasting 3 months to 3 years. Many other red giants and supergiants also pulsate, but with less regularity and smaller changes in output than Mira stars. Relatively rare, but important, are Cepheid variables, named after Delta Cephei (in Cepheus). The pulsation period of these yellow supergiant stars is directly related to their luminosity, so by timing a star's variations astronomers can work out its actual brightness. Since the brightness of a star in our sky depends on its distance from us, such stars act as valuable "standard candles" for measuring distances in space.

BRIGHTNESS OF ALGOL AND DELTA CEPHEI

These graphs show how the apparent brightness (or magnitude) of these two stars varies over time. While the curve for Delta Cephei is relatively smooth, the brightness of Algol falls dramatically when the primary is eclipsed by its fainter partner.

DELTA CEPHEI

ALGOL

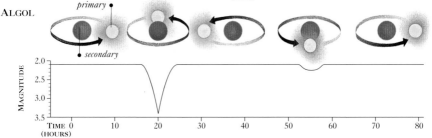

THE SOLAR SYSTEM

T HE HUB of the Solar System is the Sun. Around it orbit nine planets and their moons, along with a swarm of asteroids (also known as minor planets) and smaller pieces of debris. The Sun contains about 99.9 percent of the Solar System's total mass, and all the objects in the system are held in place by its gravity. At the edge of the Solar System is a cloud of comets that extends roughly halfway to the nearest star, a distance of about 2 light-years.

THE SUN AND PLANETS

The Solar System is orbiting the center of the Galaxy. At the same time, the planets are in orbit around the Sun, all moving counterclockwise as viewed from over the Sun's north pole. Each planet also spins on its own axis of rotation. The four innermost planets – Mercury, Venus, Earth, and Mars – are small, rocky bodies, sometimes known as the terrestrial planets. Beyond Mars is the asteroid belt and then the gas giants: Jupiter, Saturn, Uranus, and Neptune, so called because they are much larger than the Earth and consist mostly of hydrogen and helium. All four have ring systems and numerous moons. Pluto is a small, frozen oddity, which for part of its orbit is closer to the Sun than Neptune is. The planets are thought to have formed from a disk of gas and dust around the newly formed Sun about 4.6 billion years ago. Astronomers have found evidence that planets exist around other stars, too.

ORBITS OF THE INNER PLANETS ▷
The Earth is the largest of the four rocky inner planets. Mercury and Venus, which orbit between the Sun and Earth, are known as inferior planets.

Mars Sun Mercury

Venus Earth

Pluto

Uranus

THE PLANETS IN SCALE

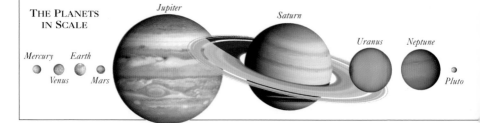

Mercury Earth Jupiter Saturn Uranus Neptune

Venus Mars Pluto

OBSERVING THE PLANETS

The orbits of the Earth and other planets are in much the same plane. As a result, the planets stay close to an imaginary line called the ecliptic (see p.16) that represents the Sun's apparent path across the sky over the course of a year. Inferior planets (Mercury and Venus) are always close to the Sun in the sky, appearing before dawn or after sunset, but never in a truly dark sky. Five planets – Mercury, Venus, Mars, Jupiter, and Saturn – are bright enough to be seen with the naked eye. They can be identified by watching their movement from night to night against the backdrop of seemingly fixed stars, noting how they disturb the shapes of the constellations. The outermost planets are harder to see: Uranus and Neptune can be found with binoculars, but Pluto can be seen only with a telescope.

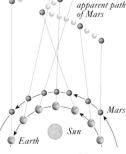

apparent path of Mars

Mars

Sun

Earth

RETROGRADE MARS

RETROGRADE MOTION
Relative to the stars, the planets seem to move across the Earth's sky from west to east. But when the Earth, which is traveling more quickly on its inside track around the Sun, overtakes a superior planet, the planet seems to execute a backward loop in the sky. Known as retrograde motion, this effect is most obvious in the motion of Mars.

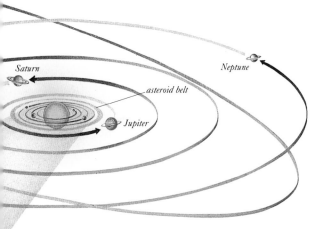

Saturn

Neptune

asteroid belt

Jupiter

△ ORBITS OF THE OUTER PLANETS
The six planets beyond the Earth are referred to as superior planets. Like all planets, their orbits take longer to complete the farther they are from the Sun.

OPPOSITION AND CONJUNCTION

The ease with which most planets can be seen depends on their position in relation to the Sun and Earth. The angle between the Sun and a planet, as seen from the Earth, is known as elongation. At their greatest eastern and western elongations, inferior planets lie in the evening and morning skies respectively. At conjunction (when elongation is zero), a planet is lost in the Sun's glare. A superior planet can lie opposite the Sun in the sky, a position called opposition; at this time, it looks largest, is visible all night, and at midnight lies due south from northern latitudes and due north from southern latitudes.

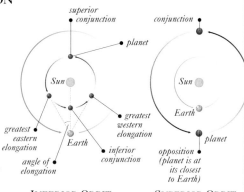

superior conjunction

conjunction

planet

Sun

Sun

Earth

greatest western elongation

greatest eastern elongation

Earth

inferior conjunction

angle of elongation

planet

opposition (planet is at its closest to Earth)

INFERIOR ORBIT

SUPERIOR ORBIT

THE CELESTIAL SPHERE

ALL CELESTIAL OBJECTS appear to be attached to an invisible sphere of infinite size centered on the Earth. Known as the celestial sphere, this seems to spin around the Earth once a day, although it is actually the Earth that is rotating. The portion of the celestial sphere seen from the Earth depends on the observer's latitude, the time of night, and the time of year.

THE CELESTIAL SPHERE

There are various important points and lines on the celestial sphere, similar to those on the Earth's globe. Directly over the Earth's poles lie the celestial poles, around which the sphere appears to turn each day. The celestial equator is a circle on the celestial sphere above the Earth's equator. Another circle, known as the ecliptic, represents the Sun's apparent path around the sphere each year. Of course, the Sun's motion is actually due to the Earth orbiting the Sun; hence the ecliptic is really the plane of the Earth's orbit projected on to the celestial sphere. Because the Earth's axis is tilted at 23.5 degrees, the celestial equator is tilted at the same angle to the ecliptic.

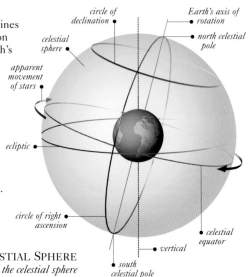

THE CELESTIAL SPHERE
Viewed from the Earth's north pole, the celestial sphere appears to turn anti-clockwise, with the stars and other objects moving parallel to the celestial equator.

LATITUDE

How much of the celestial sphere we can see depends on our latitude. From either pole, only half the sky can ever be seen; on any night, objects circle the celestial pole but do not rise or set (they are circumpolar). At the equator, the whole celestial sphere can be seen in a year; the celestial poles lie on the horizons to the north and south, and all objects rise and set. At midlatitudes, all of one celestial hemisphere is visible over a year, plus part of the other one. Only some objects are circumpolar.

APPARENT MOTION
Seen from various locations on the surface of the globe, celestial objects appear to move differently.

NORTH POLE (90°N)
All objects move without rising or setting.

MIDLATITUDE (45°N)
Some objects rise and set; others are circumpolar.

EQUATOR (0°)
All celestial objects rise and set.

TIME OF NIGHT AND TIME OF YEAR

As the Earth spins, the stars seem to move across the sky; hence our view of the sky changes as the night progresses. The celestial sphere turns once in the time it takes the Earth to spin on its axis relative to the stars – 23 hours 56 minutes. But the time between successive noons (a meantime day) is longer, 24 hours, since the Earth is also orbiting the Sun. This means a star will rise four minutes earlier each night, as measured in mean time. The Earth's orbit of the Sun also means that a star near the celestial equator that is in the night sky (and hence visible) at one time of year will be in the daytime sky (and hence invisible) six months later.

TIME OF NIGHT ▷
In this picture, taken with a long exposure, the images of the stars have been drawn into curving lines around the north celestial pole by the Earth's rotation.

constellations of the zodiac • • *ecliptic*

Sun

Earth

THE ZODIAC

During one year, the Sun passes in front of a band of constellations (see p.18) along the ecliptic. Collectively known as the zodiac, they form an area in which the planets are always to be seen. The dates when the Sun is in each constellation no longer accord with the dates attached to the astrological house of the same name.

THE ECLIPTIC AND THE ZODIAC
As the Earth moves around the Sun, the Sun appears to move against the background of stars.

CELESTIAL COORDINATES

Positions of objects on the celestial sphere are measured in coordinates called right ascension (RA) and declination (dec.). Right ascension is the equivalent of longitude on the Earth. It is measured in hours, counter-clockwise around the celestial equator, starting at the point where the Sun moves northward across the equator each year (the vernal equinox). Declination, the equivalent of latitude on the Earth, is measured from 0 degrees at the celestial equator to 90 degrees at the celestial poles.

$90°$

$60°$

star's position is 2h +45°

$30°$

one hour of right ascension equals 15 degrees of rotation • 12^h

declination is measured in degrees

6^h

declination of star is +45°

right ascension of star is 2 hours

18^h

celestial equator •

0^h

vernal equinox

STAR NAMES AND CONVENTIONS

THE SKY is divided into 88 interlocking areas known as constellations, whose boundaries were defined by the International Astronomical Union in 1930. Within these areas, astronomers use an agreed system of names, letters, and numbers to identify celestial objects.

THE CONSTELLATIONS

In his book *The Almagest* (*c.* AD 150), the Greek astronomer Ptolemy listed 48 constellations, many of them depicting characters or creatures from Greek myth. Others were added later, making the modern total of 88. Many of the more recent constellations lie in the far southern sky that was below the horizon of the Greeks and depict scientific or technical instruments or exotic animals. On star charts, some of the stars in a constellation may be joined by lines to form a pattern that symbolizes the object after which the constellation is named. However, the resemblance to the real object is usually slight, and the way the linking lines are arranged varies between charts. Constellations are often referred to by a set of standard three-letter abbreviations – for example, Sagittarius is abbreviated to Sgr, Ursa Major to UMa.

star forming part of constellation pattern

linking line

CEN

LUP

CRU

NOR CIR

MUS

ARA

TrA

APS CHA

VOL

TEL

south celestial pole MEN

PAV OCT

HYI

IND

TUC

constellation boundary

abbreviated constellation name

CONSTELLATIONS AROUND THE SOUTH CELESTIAL POLE

MAGNITUDE

The brightness of an object in the night sky is called its apparent magnitude and depends on both its actual luminosity and its distance from the Earth. Astronomers use a numerical scale to describe the magnitude of celestial objects. Bright stars are given low or negative numbers, while faint objects are given high numbers. Under good conditions, it is possible to see stars down to about magnitude 6 with the naked eye, while binoculars or a telescope are needed to see objects with higher values. The scale is logarithmic, so a star of magnitude 1 is 100 times brighter than a star of magnitude 6.

APPARENT MAGNITUDE

Betelgeuse is nearly 10,000 times brighter than the Sun, yet it looks fainter than Sirius (which is only 20 times brighter than the Sun), because it is 50 times farther away.

Sun

Sirius (8.6 light-years from the Sun)

Betelgeuse (430 light-years from the Sun)

DISTANCE IN LIGHT-YEARS

0 1 2 3 4 5 6 7 8 9 10   100 200 300 400 500

STAR NAMES

There is no single system used to assign names to stars. Instead, several different systems are used to name the various stars in a constellation. A large number of stars are referred to by letters or numbers, linked to the (Latin) genitive case of the name of the constellation; the brightest stars are given Greek letters, called Bayer letters, which are assigned alphabetically in roughly the order of brightness – hence the brightest star in Cygnus is named Alpha (α) Cygni. Most naked-eye stars have Flamsteed numbers (e.g. 61 Cygni), which run in order of right ascension. Some stars not in the Flamsteed catalog are identified by upper- and lower-case letters, especially in southern constellations. A separate lettering system, starting with the capital letter R, is used for certain variable stars (e.g. T Cygni). Some bright stars also have common names derived from Latin, Greek, or Arabic – e.g. Deneb (Arabic). Deep-sky objects (such as nebulae, clusters, and galaxies) are given numbers preceded by the letters M, NGC, or IC , taken from the Messier, New General, or Index catalogs.

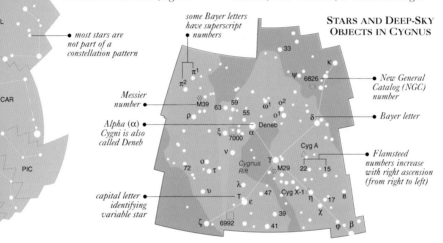

STARS AND DEEP-SKY OBJECTS IN CYGNUS

some Bayer letters have superscript numbers

most stars are not part of a constellation pattern

Messier number

Alpha (α) Cygni is also called Deneb

capital letter identifying variable star

New General Catalog (NGC) number

Bayer letter

Flamsteed numbers increase with right ascension (from right to left)

DISTANCE

Astronomers measure distances to stars in the same way that a surveyor would: by taking bearings from two different places – in this case, from opposite sides of the Earth's orbit, six months apart. Even then, the shift in position, or parallax, is only tiny. If the shift is too small to detect, astronomers estimate how far away a star is by calculating how much light it emits and comparing this with how bright it appears in the sky.

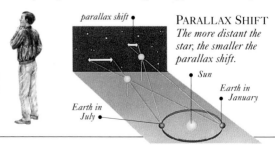

PATTERNS IN THREE DIMENSIONS

The stars in the constellation patterns usually lie at various distances from the Earth and have no real connection with each other. For example, the stars in the Great Square of Pegasus range from 97 to 330 light-years away.

parallax shift

PARALLAX SHIFT

The more distant the star, the smaller the parallax shift.

Sun

Earth in January

Earth in July

OBSERVING THE STARS

IDENTIFYING objects in the night sky for the first time can be a daunting experience. A good way to start is by learning to gauge distance and finding a few bright stars and key constellations.

Once these reference points have been identified, imaginary lines can be drawn outward from them to find other stars and patterns, which in turn act as useful stepping-stones to the rest of the sky.

SCALE IN THE SKY

It can be difficult to judge how large a feature will appear in the sky by looking at a map. Fortunately, a hand held at arm's length acts as a convenient measuring scale. For example, an index finger easily covers the Moon or Sun, both of which are only half a degree across. The back of a hand is about 10 degrees across, the width of the bowl of the Big Dipper (Plough). To cover the Great Square of Pegasus (16 degrees across), the fingers must be splayed.

▽ USING HANDSPANS
A hand held at arm's length can be used as a measuring device by both adults and children.

full Moon

the Big Dipper in Ursa Major

the Great Square of Pegasus

ONE FINGER   **CLOSED HAND**   **OPEN HAND**

NORTHERN SKIES

The Big Dipper, or Plough, which is high in Northern-Hemisphere skies in spring, is a key pattern in the northern sky. Two stars in the bowl of the Dipper, Alpha and Beta Ursae Majoris, point to the north pole star, Polaris. On the other side of the celestial pole is the W-shaped constellation Cassiopeia. The Dipper's bowl can also be used to locate the bright star Vega, prominent in northern skies in summer. A line extended from the curving handle of the Dipper leads first to Arcturus, a beacon of spring skies, and then to Spica, the brightest star in Virgo. Also to the south of the bowl of the Dipper are Leo and the stars Castor and Pollux in Gemini.

NORTHERN SIGNPOSTS

Vega • LYRA

CASSIOPEIA

URSA MINOR   *North celestial pole*
◂ Polaris

BOÖTES

Alpha

Big Dipper   Beta

URSA MAJOR

Arcturus

Castor
Pollux

LEO   GEMINI

VIRGO

Regulus

Spica

SCALE

MIDLATITUDE SKIES

Orion is a prominent constellation in the evening skies of northern winter and southern summer. The line of three stars that forms Orion's Belt points to the brightest star in the sky, Sirius (in Canis Major). Sirius marks one corner of a huge triangle (known in the Northern Hemisphere as the Winter Triangle). The other corners are marked by the bright stars Betelgeuse (in Orion) and Procyon (in Canis Minor). Another prominent star in Orion is Rigel. A line from Rigel through Betelgeuse points to Castor and Pollux in the neighboring constellation of Gemini. On the other side of Orion is Aldebaran, the brightest star in Taurus; beyond Aldebaran, in the same direction, is the Pleiades open cluster. Almost directly to the north of Orion lies Capella, the brightest star in Auriga, which is overhead on January evenings from midnorthern latitudes.

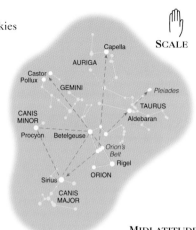

SCALE

MIDLATITUDE
SIGNPOSTS

SOUTHERN SKIES

Two bright stars in Centaurus and the familiar shape of Crux, the Southern Cross – all of which are at their highest on April and May evenings – are the starting points for finding a way around southern skies. A line from Alpha through nearby Beta Centauri points to Crux, the smallest constellation in the sky but also one of the most distinctive. The Southern Cross is not to be confused with the slightly larger False Cross, which is closer to the bright star Canopus. Unlike in the Northern Hemisphere, there is no bright star near the south celestial pole, but the longer axis of Crux points toward the pole, as does a line at right angles to the one linking Alpha and Beta Centauri (see also p.87). Canopus and Achernar form a large triangle with the south celestial pole.

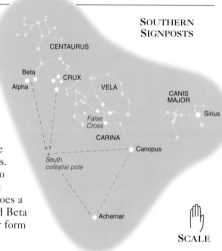

SOUTHERN
SIGNPOSTS

SCALE

SKYWATCHING TIPS

- Always wear warm clothing – even summer evenings can be cool.
- Allow at least 10 minutes for your eyes to adapt to the dark before beginning serious observations.
- If needed, use only a dim red flashlight, so that your eyes remain adapted to the dark.

PLASTIC-COVERED FLASHLIGHT

- Observe objects when they are well clear of the horizon wherever possible.
- To see faint objects more easily, look slightly to one side of them; their light will then fall on the more sensitive outer part of your eye. This technique is called averted vision.
- Keep a log of your observations, always noting the date and time.

BINOCULARS AND TELESCOPES

ASTRONOMERS use binoculars and telescopes to make objects appear brighter and larger. These instruments collect more light than the human eye, which means that much fainter objects can be seen than with the eye alone. They also magnify objects, so that small details can be distinguished. Binoculars are usually recommended for beginners; more serious study requires a telescope.

BINOCULARS OR A TELESCOPE?

For simple stargazing, binoculars are ideal, being portable and relatively cheap. They show many more stars than the naked eye, and their wide field of view makes them especially useful for looking at large areas of sky or objects such as comets. They also produce upright images. Telescopes have larger apertures and higher magnifications than binoculars, and show inverted images. The aperture of a telescope is fixed, but the magnification can be altered by changing the eyepiece. When assessing a telescope's performance the aperture is more important than the magnification (see below). Another critical requirement is a steady mounting, to prevent images from shaking. Most amateur astronomers use a telescope of "small" to "moderate" aperture – where small is less than 4 in (100 mm) and moderate is 4–10 in (100–250 mm); anything greater than this is considered large.

finder scope
eyepiece
cradle
equatorial mount
stand
◁ REFLECTING TELESCOPE

▽ BINOCULARS
Binoculars have apertures up to 2 in (50 mm) and magnify up to about 10 times. High magnification makes objects look larger, but with magnification greater than 10 times it is not easy to hold binoculars steady enough to see objects clearly.

focusing knob
eyepiece lens
prism
prism
pivot bar
objective lens

APERTURE AND MAGNIFICATION

Although magnification makes objects appear larger and closer, there are limits to the magnification that can be used. An image looks fainter as it gets bigger. As a guide, expect a maximum magnification of about 50 times the telescope aperture in inches (twice the aperture in millimeters). No matter how large the aperture, as the magnification increases, the unsteadiness of the atmosphere, caused by air currents, becomes more noticeable, which limits the powers that can be used.

MAGNIFICATION
High powers of magnification are useful when viewing the Moon (shown here), planets, or close double stars. Low powers are better for diffuse objects such as comets, nebulae, and galaxies.

NAKED EYE

BINOCULARS

TELESCOPE

REFRACTING TELESCOPES

Refractors have a main lens, called the object glass or objective lens, which collects and focuses light. The image is magnified by an eyepiece at the opposite end of the tube. In some small refractors, a prism is used to bend the light so that the eyepiece is more conveniently positioned for observation, as in the photograph here. Most small refractors have a simple type of mounting known as an altazimuth, which allows the telescope to tilt up and down and swivel from side to side.

REFRACTOR
This small refracting telescope is on an altazimuth mounting.

finder scope (for aiming at objects)

eyepiece

objective lens housing

altazimuth mount

tripod

objective lens

incident light

refracted light

eyepiece

HOW A REFRACTOR WORKS

REFLECTING TELESCOPES

Most reflectors used by amateur observers are of the Newtonian type, in which light is collected by a concave primary mirror and deflected into an eyepiece at the side of the tube by a flat secondary mirror. They often have an equatorial mounting, which allows them to track objects across the sky simply by turning one axis, called the polar axis, which points to the celestial pole; a motor drive can accomplish this automatically. However, a Dobsonian mounting, which is a form of altazimuth mounting, is also now popular.

REFLECTOR
This reflecting telescope of Newtonian design is on a Dobsonian mounting.

eyepiece

lightweight tube

Formica ring

Teflon pad

primary mirror

incident light

eyepiece

reflected light

secondary mirror

HOW A NEWTONIAN REFLECTOR WORKS

CASSEGRAIN TELESCOPES

Another type of reflector, called the Cassegrain, uses a secondary mirror with a convex surface to reflect light back through a hole in the center of the main mirror, where the eyepiece is inserted. Because the light path is folded back on itself within the tube, this design is more compact than the Newtonian. A modified form, called a Schmidt–Cassegrain, is popular among amateurs. This has a thin lens, known as a corrector plate, across the front of the tube to increase the field of view.

CASSEGRAIN
This Schmidt–Cassegrain telescope is supported on an equatorial fork mounting.

finder scope

reflected light

secondary mirror

primary mirror

eyepiece

motor-driven equatorial mount

incident light

eyepiece

HOW A CASSEGRAIN WORKS

ASTROPHOTOGRAPHY

A SINGLE-LENS REFLEX camera can be used to take attractive pictures of the night sky, from snapshots of bright stars and planets to long, guided exposures that show objects that are far too faint for the naked eye. For close-ups, a telescope can be used to replace the camera lens. More advanced astro-photographers use electronic detectors called CCDs in place of film.

CONVENTIONAL PHOTOGRAPHY

A time exposure with a fixed camera will record star trails like those shown on p.17. Fast film (such as ISO 400) should be used and the camera lens set to its widest aperture. Exposures should be tailored to the sky conditions – in cities, light pollution (p.37) will start to fog the film after only a few minutes. To produce sharp images of stars, the camera must track the stars as the Earth rotates. This can be done by attaching the camera to a motor-driven mounting or to the tube of a telescope that has such a mounting. For detailed views, the camera lens can be removed and the telescope itself used as a telephoto lens. In this case, the telescope must be guided very accurately on the target, particularly during exposures lasting more than a few seconds.

camera attached to tube on mounting bracket

cable shutter-release

eyepiece can be used to align camera

motor-driven mounting to track movement of stars

adaptor

CAMERA TO EYEPIECE ▷
The lens of the camera is removed and the body attached to the telescope in place of the eyepiece.

camera body

cable shutter-release

telescope

△ CAMERA ON TELESOPE
The telescope drive is used to keep the camera pointed at its target, allowing long exposures without star trailing.

CCD CAMERAS

Charge-coupled devices (CCDs) are light-sensitive silicon chips that can be used in place of a conventional camera and film. They are much more sensitive than normal photographic film, so that an exposure of only a few minutes can show as much as an hour-long exposure would on film. CCD images can be stored in a computer and viewed on its screen.

MOUNTING A CCD CAMERA

CCD camera replaces eyepiece

cable connecting CCD camera to computer

CCD MICROCHIP
A CCD chip is much smaller than a frame of 35 mm film, which can be a drawback.

THE SOLAR SYSTEM

HOW THIS SECTION WORKS

THIS SECTION is about the Sun and the bodies in orbit around it. There are entries on the nine planets (including the Earth), each consisting of an illustrated description of the planet, advice on observation, and charts and diagrams that show where it can be located. Other entries cover the Sun itself, the Moon, and smaller bodies such as comets and meteors.

locator strip shows planet's position in relation to the Sun and Earth

planet's size compared with that of the Earth

diagram illustrating planet's tilt, rotation, and orbit

observation section contains tips on finding and studying the planet

structure of planet's interior

vertical section through atmosphere

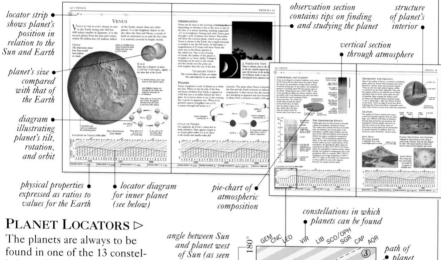

physical properties expressed as ratios to values for the Earth

locator diagram for inner planet (see below)

pie-chart of atmospheric composition

PLANET LOCATORS ▷

The planets are always to be found in one of the 13 constellations of the zodiac (see p.17). The constellation in which the planets Mercury, Venus, Mars, Jupiter, and Saturn can be found at a particular time is shown on a strip diagram.

angle between Sun and planet west of Sun (as seen from Earth)

angle between Sun and planet east of Sun (as seen from Earth).

constellations in which planets can be found

path of planet

planet disappears in Sun's glare when path line is within this band

horizontal scale shows month and year

△ THE OUTER PLANETS

Uranus, Neptune, and Pluto seem to move relatively slowly. Their location in the night sky is therefore shown on more conventional charts.

△ HOW TO USE THE STRIP DIAGRAM

1. Find the date on the horizontal scale. For example, to find Venus in January 2004 on the segment above, first locate January at the bottom of the diagram.
2. Read upwards to the curved path line.
3. Read diagonally up along the tinted band to identify the constellation in which the planet appears. In January 2004, Venus is in Aquarius. Use one of the charts in the Monthly Sky Guides to find Aquarius.

THE SUN

THE SUN is our local star. It is a ball of incandescent gas of average size, temperature, and brightness compared with other stars. The Sun dominates the Solar System: it is the source of heat and light for all the planets, and its great mass exerts a gravitational pull that keeps them in orbit around it.

WARNING: Never look directly at the Sun through binoculars or a telescope.

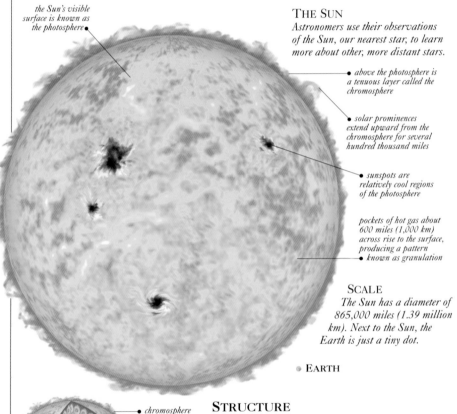

the Sun's visible surface is known as the photosphere

THE SUN
Astronomers use their observations of the Sun, our nearest star, to learn more about other, more distant stars.

above the photosphere is a tenuous layer called the chromosphere

solar prominences extend upward from the chromosphere for several hundred thousand miles

sunspots are relatively cool regions of the photosphere

pockets of hot gas about 600 miles (1,000 km) across rise to the surface, producing a pattern known as granulation

SCALE
The Sun has a diameter of 865,000 miles (1.39 million km). Next to the Sun, the Earth is just a tiny dot.

⚬ EARTH

chromosphere

photosphere

core

radiative zone

convective zone

INTERNAL STRUCTURE

STRUCTURE
The Sun's energy is generated at its core, where temperatures are estimated to reach 27 million°F (15 million°C). Under these extreme conditions, hydrogen is converted to helium by nuclear fusion. Energy from these reactions travels outward, first by radiation and then by convection, eventually reaching the photosphere. Above the photosphere is a less dense layer of gas, the chromosphere, from which bright clouds called prominences extend into the rarefied outermost region, the corona.

Diameter (Earth = 1) 109	Mass (Earth = 1) 333,000	Volume (Earth = 1) 1,300,000

SUNSPOTS

Sunspots, dark patches on the Sun's surface, are actually areas of cooler gas. They can last from a few days to several months and range in size from a few hundred miles across to complex groups extending for 60,000 miles (100,000 km). Occasional eruptions near sunspots, called flares, shoot out atomic particles that reach the Earth and can cause glows in the atmosphere termed aurorae.

SUNSPOT CYCLES

Sunspot numbers rise and fall in a cycle lasting about 11 years. At the start of the cycle, spots are few in number and appear away from the equator. Approaching solar maximum, the spots become more numerous (with up to 100 visible at one time) and appear closer to the equator.

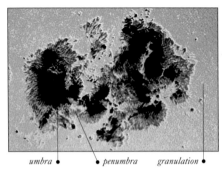

umbra •   • penumbra   granulation •

△ SUNSPOT GROUP
The center of a sunspot, known as the umbra, is its darkest, coolest part, at about 8,100°F (4,500°C). The umbra is surrounded by a lighter, warmer area called the penumbra.

first spots of new cycle •   *last spots of old cycle* •   *spots appear nearer the equator* •   *number of spots falls* •   *last spots of old cycle* •   *first spots of new cycle* •

| YEAR 1 | YEAR 3 | YEAR 5 | YEAR 7 | YEAR 9 | YEAR 11 |
| SOLAR MINIMUM | | SOLAR MAXIMUM | | SOLAR MINIMUM | |

OBSERVING SUNSPOTS

Looking at the Sun with binoculars or a telescope can cause blindness. The only safe way to observe the Sun is to project its image on to a white surface, as shown below. The rim of the Sun appears darker than its center, an effect known as limb darkening. Sunspots appear as small, dark marks that change position daily as the Sun rotates.

sunspot •

1. For safety, place a cap over the finder scope. If you are using a refractor, also cap the main lens.

2. Aim the telescope at the Sun by minimizing the size of the shadow cast by the telescope or the finder.

3. Remove the lens cap (if using a refractor) and focus the Sun's image onto a piece of white cardboard.

| Density (water = 1) 1.41 | Gravity (Earth = 1) 27.94 | Surface temperature 9,900°F (5,500°C) | Magnitude −26.7 |

ECLIPSES OF THE SUN

Occasionally, the Moon passes in front of the Sun, briefly blocking its light to cause a solar eclipse. At least two solar eclipses occur each year, but not everyone will see them. During a solar eclipse, the Moon's shadow falls on the Earth. Anyone within the dark inner part of the shadow (the umbra) will see a total eclipse. From the lighter, outer shadow (the penumbra), a partial eclipse is seen. Because the umbra is quite narrow, total solar eclipses are rare at any one place on the Earth.

When the Sun's disk is entirely covered, its faint outer halo of gas, the corona, becomes visible. Scientists travel the world for the rare glimpses of the corona that an eclipse affords. A total eclipse can last for up to 7½ minutes, but 2 to 3 minutes is more usual; a partial eclipse can last for up to 3 to 4 hours. As with all solar observations, an eclipse is best viewed by projecting the Sun's image, but when the Sun is totally eclipsed the corona can safely be viewed with binoculars.

SEQUENCE OF A TOTAL SOLAR ECLIPSE

1. A partial eclipse – the Moon moves across the face of the Sun.

2. Just before totality, a shape similar to a diamond ring is seen.

3. At totality, the Sun's faint but extensive corona is visible.

4. The Moon moves away again and the eclipse ends.

HOW A SOLAR ECLIPSE OCCURS

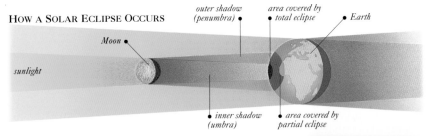

outer shadow (penumbra) • • area covered by total eclipse • Earth

Moon •

sunlight

• inner shadow (umbra) • area covered by partial eclipse

ANNULAR ECLIPSE

When the Moon is at its farthest from the Earth, it does not appear quite big enough to cover the Sun completely. This gives rise to an annular eclipse, so named because a ring, or annulus, of light remains visible at mid-eclipse.

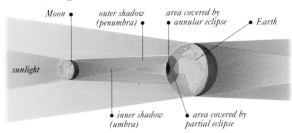

Moon • outer shadow (penumbra) • area covered by annular eclipse • Earth

sunlight

• inner shadow (umbra) • area covered by partial eclipse

HOW AN ANNULAR ECLIPSE OCCURS

RING OF SUNLIGHT

An annulus of light is seen around the eclipsing Moon. The photosphere (rather than the corona) is visible here.

| Diameter (Earth = 1) 109 | Mass (Earth = 1) 333,000 | Volume (Earth = 1) 1,300,000 |

MERCURY

MERCURY is the closest planet to the Sun and is difficult to see because it is always low in the sky in the evening or morning twilight. It is a small, rocky planet, less than half the diameter of the Earth, and it resembles our own Moon in appearance, being covered with craters. Mercury has no air or water. During the day its surface is scorched by intense sunlight, while at night its temperature plummets far below freezing.

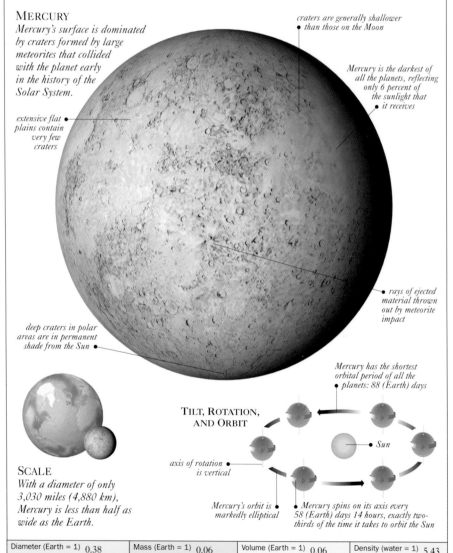

MERCURY
Mercury's surface is dominated by craters formed by large meteorites that collided with the planet early in the history of the Solar System.

craters are generally shallower than those on the Moon

Mercury is the darkest of all the planets, reflecting only 6 percent of the sunlight that it receives

extensive flat plains contain very few craters

rays of ejected material thrown out by meteorite impact

deep craters in polar areas are in permanent shade from the Sun

Mercury has the shortest orbital period of all the planets: 88 (Earth) days

TILT, ROTATION, AND ORBIT

Sun

axis of rotation is vertical

SCALE
With a diameter of only 3,030 miles (4,880 km), Mercury is less than half as wide as the Earth.

Mercury's orbit is markedly elliptical

Mercury spins on its axis every 58 (Earth) days 14 hours, exactly two-thirds of the time it takes to orbit the Sun

| Diameter (Earth = 1) | 0.38 | Mass (Earth = 1) | 0.06 | Volume (Earth = 1) | 0.06 | Density (water = 1) | 5.43 |

OBSERVATION

Of the five planets visible to the naked eye, Mercury is the most difficult to spot because it is always close to the Sun. Binoculars are usually needed to locate it. The best time to observe Mercury is around greatest elongation (see p.15), when it is farthest from the Sun. At that time, at a magnification of 250 times Mercury will appear as large as the full Moon looks to the naked eye. Like Venus and the Moon, Mercury's disk shows phases, which can be seen through a small telescope. Moderate to large apertures show dark, smudgy surface markings.

TRANSITS

Occasionally, Mercury can be seen crossing the Sun's disk, an event known as a transit. In this photograph, taken at the transit of 1993, Mercury appears as a small, round dot. Future transits will occur on November 15, 1999, May 7, 2003, and November 8, 2006.

MERCURY IN THE EVENING SKY

At optimal viewing times, Mercury resembles a first-magnitude star. In this picture, it can be seen near the horizon, above and to the right of the large tree.

ATMOSPHERE AND CLIMATE

Mercury is airless and waterless. The barren, rocky surface is blasted by solar radiation, which raises its temperature to above 840°F (450°C) at noon on the equator when the planet is nearest the Sun. However, some shaded areas in craters near the poles are probably permanently below freezing, and it is thought possible that ice exists there. At night the surface temperature plummets to below –290°F (–180°C).

LOCATION OF MERCURY 1998–2009

| Diameter (Earth = 1) 0.38 | Mass (Earth = 1) 0.06 | Volume (Earth = 1) 0.06 | Density (water = 1) 5.43 |

GEOGRAPHY AND GEOLOGY

Mercury looks much like our own Moon, since the rocky surfaces of both bodies have been extensively cratered by impacts from meteorites, and Mercury's diameter is only 40 percent greater than that of the Moon. One distinct difference is that Mercury has cliffs up to 2 miles (3 km) high running for several hundreds of miles, probably caused by shrinking and wrinkling of the planet as it cooled. Mercury is thought to have a large iron core that occupies three-quarters of its diameter.

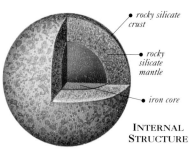

rocky silicate crust

rocky silicate mantle

iron core

INTERNAL STRUCTURE

CRATERS

As on the Moon, the youngest craters on Mercury are bright and surrounded by rays of material ejected by the force of the meteorite impact. Between Mercury's main craters are older, smoother areas called intercrater plains, dotted with small craters. Secondary craters, caused by debris from the main impact, lie closer to the main craters than on the Moon because of Mercury's stronger gravity. Mercury has one large lowland plain, the Caloris Basin, which resembles the mare areas of the Moon. There are no known volcanic craters on Mercury.

△ **THE CALORIS BASIN**
Part of this basin, 800 miles (1,300 km) across, can be seen on the left of this picture. It was formed by a meteorite impact and later flooded with lava.

DEGAS AND BRONTË ▷
These two ray craters (at the center left in this photograph) are each about 37 miles (60 km) across.

| Gravity (Earth = 1) 0.38 | Number of moons 0 | Average temperature 333°F (167°C) | Maximum magnitude −1.5 |

VENUS

VENUS IS THE PLANET closest in size to the Earth, being only 400 miles (650 km) smaller in diameter. It is the second planet from the Sun and comes within 25 million miles (40 million km) of the Earth, nearer than any other planet. It is the brightest object in the sky after the Sun and Moon, a result of both its closeness to us and the fact that it is entirely covered in bright clouds.

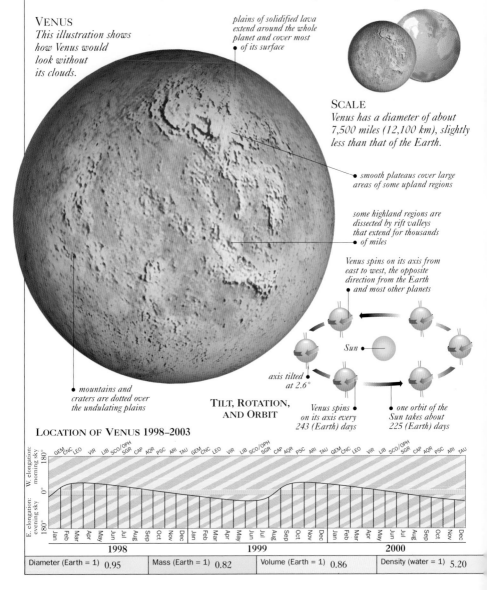

VENUS
This illustration shows how Venus would look without its clouds.

plains of solidified lava extend around the whole planet and cover most • of its surface

SCALE
Venus has a diameter of about 7,500 miles (12,100 km), slightly less than that of the Earth.

• smooth plateaus cover large areas of some upland regions

some highland regions are dissected by rift valleys that extend for thousands • of miles

Venus spins on its axis from east to west, the opposite direction from the Earth • and most other planets

Sun •—

axis tilted • at 2.6°

TILT, ROTATION, AND ORBIT

• mountains and craters are dotted over the undulating plains

Venus spins • on its axis every 243 (Earth) days

• one orbit of the Sun takes about 225 (Earth) days

LOCATION OF VENUS 1998–2003

| Diameter (Earth = 1) 0.95 | Mass (Earth = 1) 0.82 | Volume (Earth = 1) 0.86 | Density (water = 1) 5.20 |

OBSERVATION

Venus can be seen in the morning or evening sky, depending on whether it lies to the west or east of the Sun. It is always dazzling, reaching magnitude –4.7 at its brightest. During each orbit, Venus goes through a cycle of phases (see below). Binoculars will show the crescent phase, which occurs when Venus is closest to the Earth, but a small telescope is needed to see the full series. At half phase, a magnification of 75 times will show Venus the same size as the Moon appears to the naked eye. Due to its covering of clouds, the surface of the planet is invisible to us. Some dusky, V-shaped markings can be seen in the clouds, and the clouds over the poles can look brighter than the rest of the disk.

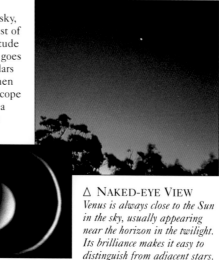

TELESCOPE VIEW ▷
Two crescent phases of Venus are shown here superimposed on one another.

△ NAKED-EYE VIEW
Venus is always close to the Sun in the sky, usually appearing near the horizon in the twilight. Its brilliance makes it easy to distinguish from adjacent stars.

PHASES

Venus completes a cycle of phases as it orbits the Sun. When on the far side of the Sun, and hence farthest from Earth, it appears as a full disk but is invisible behind the Sun's glare. As it moves closer to us, in the evening sky, it grows in apparent size. When at its greatest eastern elongation (see p.15), it passes through half phase to a crescent. The point when Venus is between the Sun and the Earth is known as inferior conjunction. It then moves into the morning sky, shrinking in apparent size but increasing in phase from a crescent via half to full again.

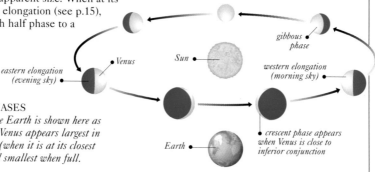

gibbous phase

eastern elongation (evening sky) •

• Venus

Sun •

western elongation (morning sky) •

CYCLE OF PHASES
For simplicity, the Earth is shown here as being stationary. Venus appears largest in its crescent phase (when it is at its closest to the Earth) and smallest when full.

Earth •

• crescent phase appears when Venus is close to inferior conjunction

Gravity (Earth = 1) 0.91	Number of moons 0	Average temperature 867°F (464°C)	Maximum magnitude –4.7

ATMOSPHERE AND CLIMATE

Venus is enveloped in clouds of sulfuric acid that lie 30–45 miles (50–70 km) above its surface. Below the clouds, the atmosphere consists almost entirely of carbon-dioxide gas. At the surface, the atmospheric pressure is crushing, about 90 times greater than on the Earth. Temperatures soar to 867°F (464°C) due to the greenhouse effect (see below). Surface winds are gentle, only a few miles per hour, but above the clouds they reach hundreds of miles per hour. As a result, the clouds whip around the planet in four Earth days, far faster than the planet rotates on its axis, which takes 243 days. Like the planet itself, the clouds rotate from east to west.

ATMOSPHERIC STRUCTURE

upper clouds of sulfuric acid •

thin sulfuric acid haze •

dense clouds • producing rain of sulfuric acid

lower haze of • dust and very small sulfuric acid droplets

lower • atmosphere almost entirely carbon dioxide

THERMOSPHERE

TROPOSPHERE

ATMOSPHERIC COMPOSITION

• nitrogen (3.5%) and trace gases

• carbon dioxide (96.5%)

RADIATION BALANCE

• sunlight

• most of the sunlight Venus receives is reflected back by its clouds

• clouds

• less than half of the infrared radiation from the surface is released back into space

• surface emits infrared radiation

THE GREENHOUSE EFFECT

Visible light from the Sun streams in through a planet's atmosphere, heating its surface. The surface then releases the heat as invisible infrared radiation, but certain gases in the atmosphere, notably carbon dioxide, prevent some of the infrared radiation from escaping directly into space, causing the temperature to increase. This is termed the greenhouse effect. In the case of the Earth, where carbon dioxide makes up only a small fraction of the atmosphere, the greenhouse effect raises the temperature by about 63°F (35°C). On Venus, where the atmosphere is almost entirely carbon dioxide, the increase in temperature due to the greenhouse effect is a massive 900°F (500°C), resulting in an average temperature of 867°F (464°C). Unlike on the Earth, the temperature on Venus differs by only a few degrees between the equator and the poles.

LOCATION OF VENUS 2004–2009

| Diameter (Earth = 1) 0.95 | Mass (Earth = 1) 0.82 | Volume (Earth = 1) 0.86 | Density (water = 1) 5.20 |

GEOGRAPHY AND GEOLOGY

Most of the surface of Venus is covered by undulating plains that are dotted with mountains and craters formed by volcanic action and meteorite impacts. There are also two main upland regions, similar to continents on the Earth: Aphrodite Terra near the equator, which is over half the area of Africa, and Ishtar Terra in the far north, about the size of Australia. Ishtar contains the highest point on Venus, the Maxwell Montes mountain range, 7 miles (11 km) high – taller than Mount Everest on the Earth. There are signs of recent lava flows, indicating that Venus may still be volcanically active today. Since Venus is so hot, all its water has evaporated.

silicate crust

rocky mantle

iron and nickel core

INTERNAL STRUCTURE

CRATERS

The surface of Venus is dotted with craters caused by meteorite impacts. Most are quite large, up to 185 miles (300 km) in diameter, because large meteorites can penetrate the atmosphere whereas smaller ones burn up. Like the craters on the Moon, many on Venus have central peaks and are surrounded by ejected material. In addition, there are numerous craters formed by volcanic action.

volcanic peak • *flat, rocky plain* • *impact crater* • *lava flow*

MAAT MONS

This volcanic mountain in Aphrodite Terra is the second highest peak on Venus.

summit is 5.2 miles (8.5 km) high

PLAINS, MOUNTAINS, AND CRATERS

Although its clouds prevent us from seeing its surface with a telescope, Venus has been mapped by radar. This image (and the two below) are based on data from the Magellan space probe.

SAPAS MONS

This volcano has two central peaks surrounded by an expanse of solidified lava.

	2007		2008		2009

Gravity (Earth = 1) 0.91	Number of moons 0	Average temperature 867°F (464°C)	Maximum magnitude −4.7

THE EARTH

THE EARTH, our home world, is the third planet from the Sun and the largest of the four rocky inner planets. Among the planets of the Solar System, the Earth is unique in having abundant surface water and an atmosphere rich in nitrogen and oxygen. It is also the only planet known with certainty to harbor life, supporting a complex population of plants and animals.

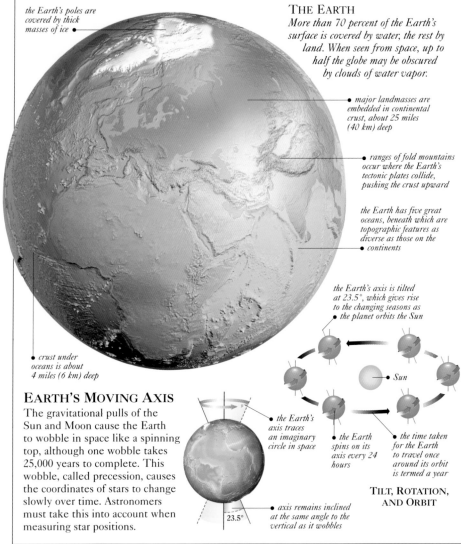

the Earth's poles are covered by thick masses of ice

THE EARTH
More than 70 percent of the Earth's surface is covered by water, the rest by land. When seen from space, up to half the globe may be obscured by clouds of water vapor.

major landmasses are embedded in continental crust, about 25 miles (40 km) deep

ranges of fold mountains occur where the Earth's tectonic plates collide, pushing the crust upward

the Earth has five great oceans, beneath which are topographic features as diverse as those on the continents

the Earth's axis is tilted at 23.5°, which gives rise to the changing seasons as the planet orbits the Sun

crust under oceans is about 4 miles (6 km) deep

Sun

EARTH'S MOVING AXIS
The gravitational pulls of the Sun and Moon cause the Earth to wobble in space like a spinning top, although one wobble takes 25,000 years to complete. This wobble, called precession, causes the coordinates of stars to change slowly over time. Astronomers must take this into account when measuring star positions.

the Earth's axis traces an imaginary circle in space

the Earth spins on its axis every 24 hours

the time taken for the Earth to travel once around its orbit is termed a year

TILT, ROTATION, AND ORBIT

axis remains inclined at the same angle to the vertical as it wobbles

23.5°

| Diameter 7,926 miles (12,756 km) | Mass 6.59×10^{21} tons | Volume 2.6×10^{11} mile^3 (1.08×10^{12} km^3) |

ATMOSPHERE AND CLIMATE

The layer of gases that surrounds the Earth plays an important part in protecting and sustaining life. Not only does it shield the surface from excessive solar radiation and meteorite impacts, but its density, combined with Earth's favorable distance from the Sun, provides the right temperature for water to exist as a liquid. Water and carbon dioxide are used as food by plants, which in turn release the oxygen that is essential for animal life. Circulation in the atmosphere is also an important mechanism by which heat energy is redistributed poleward from the equator.

ATMOSPHERIC STRUCTURE

water vapor (1%) and trace gases

meteoroids burn up in the upper atmosphere

nitrogen (78.1%)

oxygen (20.9%)

ATMOSPHERIC COMPOSITION

ozone layer absorbs ultra-violet radiation

clouds of water vapor

THERMOSPHERE

MESOSPHERE

STRATOSPHERE

TROPOSPHERE

GEOGRAPHY AND GEOLOGY

The Earth's crust is made up of sections, called plates, that float on the surface of the viscous mantle and slowly move apart or slip beneath one another. Mountain ranges, volcanoes, and earthquakes occur along the margins of the plates. The Earth has a core of iron and nickel, the outer part of which is liquid. Motions in the liquid outer core give rise to the Earth's magnetic field, which extends into space, creating a magnetic cocoon around our planet termed the magnetosphere.

thin, brittle crust

dense, partially molten mantle

molten metal outer core

solid metal inner core

INTERNAL STRUCTURE

LIGHT POLLUTION

Light pollution is caused by artificial lights shining into the sky. The problem is greatest in urban areas and is so extensive that in some developed countries there are now few places with truly dark skies. As well as being a waste of energy, light pollution is a growing nuisance to astronomers, as relatively faint celestial objects become lost in the glare from surface lighting.

THE EARTH AT NIGHT

At the top left of this picture are the lights of industrialized Europe, and at the top right is Japan. The yellow areas, such as those around the Middle East, represent gas burned off in oil fields, while the red specks in equatorial Africa are due to agricultural burning. The line of light in North Africa is the Nile Valley.

| Density (water = 1) 5.52 | Gravity 1 | Number of moons 1 | Average temperature 59°F (15°C) |

THE MOON

THE MOON is the Earth's only natural satellite. It is so close to the Earth – at an average distance of only 238,900 miles (384,400 km) – that even binoculars will reveal features on its surface in fascinating detail. The Moon has no air or liquid water, and hence no weather; it is also lifeless and without geological activity. Its main landforms have all resulted from meteorite impact.

THE NEAR SIDE OF THE MOON

The Moon's distinctive lowland plains, the maria, are labeled here; other features are cross-referred to the panel on the facing page.

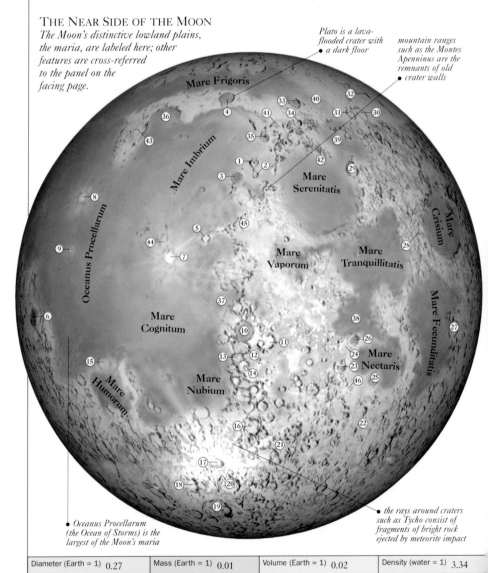

Plato is a lava-flooded crater with a dark floor

mountain ranges such as the Montes Apenninus are the remnants of old crater walls

Mare Frigoris

Mare Imbrium

Oceanus Procellarum

Mare Serenitatis

Mare Crisium

Mare Vaporum

Mare Tranquillitatis

Mare Fecunditatis

Mare Cognitum

Mare Nectaris

Mare Humorum

Mare Nubium

Oceanus Procellarum (the Ocean of Storms) is the largest of the Moon's maria

the rays around craters such as Tycho consist of fragments of bright rock ejected by meteorite impact

| Diameter (Earth = 1) 0.27 | Mass (Earth = 1) 0.01 | Volume (Earth = 1) 0.02 | Density (water = 1) 3.34 |

SCALE
The Moon's diameter is 2,160 miles (3,476 km), just over a quarter of that of the Earth.

one orbit of the Earth takes 27 (Earth) days 7 hours

the Moon's axis is tilted at 6.7° from the vertical

Earth

the Moon takes exactly the same amount of time to spin on its axis as it takes to orbit the Earth

TILT,
ROTATION,
AND ORBIT

OBSERVING THE MOON

Since the Moon spins on its axis exactly once in the time it takes to orbit the Earth, the same hemisphere, termed the near side, is always turned toward Earth. Hence, we only ever see about half of the lunar surface. The main features can be seen with the naked eye. Dark lowland plains, known as maria, contrast with the bright highlands. Binoculars or a small telescope reveal innumerable craters and mountain ranges. Surface relief is most conspicuous near the border between lit and unlit areas, called the terminator, where shadows are longest. When the surface is illuminated at high angles near full Moon, it appears washed out, and even large craters can vanish. However, some features need high contrast to be seen and are at their most prominent near full Moon; these include the dark maria and the bright rays around some craters.

imaginary point always faces the Earth

Day 14

Day 7

Moon

Day 21

Earth

Day 1

△ CAPTURED ROTATION
The Earth's gravitational influence has slowed the Moon's rotation so that it is exactly synchronized with its orbit.

◁ THE FAR SIDE
The Moon's far side, invisible from the Earth, has been photographed from space.

KEY TO LUNAR FEATURES

CRATERS			LOWLAND FEATURES
1. Aristillus	13. Alpetragius	25. Fracastorius	36. Sinus Iridum
2. Autolycus	14. Arzachel	26. Theophilus	37. Sinus Medii
3. Archimedes	15. Gassendi	27. Langrenus	38. Sinus Asperitatis
4. Plato	16. Walter	28. Proclus	39. Lacus Somniorum
5. Eratosthenes	17. Tycho	29. Posidonius	40. Lacus Mortis
6. Grimaldi	18. Longomontanus	30. Atlas	UPLAND FEATURES
7. Copernicus	19. Clavius	31. Hercules	41. Montes Alpes
8. Aristarchus	20. Maginus	32. Endymion	42. Montes Caucasus
9. Marius	21. Stöfler	33. Aristoteles	43. Montes Jura
10. Ptolemaeus	22. Piccolomini	34. Eudoxus	44. Montes Carpatus
11. Albategnius	23. Catharina	35. Cassini	45. Montes Apenninus
12. Alphonsus	24. Cyrillus		46. Rupes Altai

| Gravity (Earth = 1) 0.17 | Average temperature 0°F (–18°C) | Maximum magnitude –12.7 |

PHASES OF THE MOON

The Moon's phases arise because we see differing amounts of its sunlit side as it orbits the Earth. At new Moon, the near side of the Moon is in complete shadow. As it orbits the Earth, the visible area grows, or waxes, from a crescent via a gibbous phase to full, when the disk is fully illuminated. The phases then occur in reverse, as the visible area shrinks, or wanes. When the Moon is a thin crescent, the unlit part can be seen faintly illuminated by light reflected from the Earth, an effect known as earthshine.

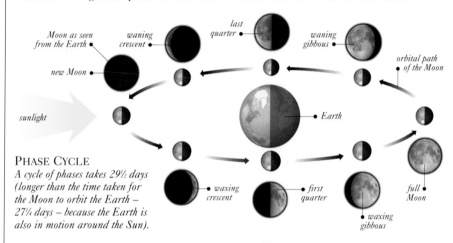

Moon as seen from the Earth

waning crescent

last quarter

waning gibbous

orbital path of the Moon

new Moon

sunlight

Earth

PHASE CYCLE

A cycle of phases takes 29½ days (longer than the time taken for the Moon to orbit the Earth – 27¼ days – because the Earth is also in motion around the Sun).

waxing crescent

first quarter

full Moon

waxing gibbous

ECLIPSES OF THE MOON

Occasionally, the full Moon moves into the Earth's shadow and is eclipsed. From the Moon's first entry into the shadow until it has completely reemerged can take up to four hours, and the period during which the eclipse is total can be well over an hour. Up to three lunar eclipses may occur in a year, although in some years there are none. Lunar eclipses are widely visible on the Earth's surface from wherever the Moon is above the horizon.

SEQUENCE OF A LUNAR ECLIPSE

Sunlight bent into the Earth's shadow by its own atmosphere often prevents the eclipsed Moon disappearing completely and makes it appear red.

inner shadow (umbra)

outer shadow (penumbra)

sunlight

Earth

the light outer shadow may produce only slight darkening of the Moon

HOW A LUNAR ECLIPSE OCCURS

Diameter (Earth = 1) 0.27	Mass (Earth = 1) 0.01	Volume (Earth = 1) 0.02	Density (water = 1) 3.34

HISTORY AND GEOLOGY

The Moon is thought to have formed about 4.5 billion years ago when a body the size of Mars struck the Earth, which itself was still less than 100 million years old. Debris from the collision was thrown into orbit and coalesced to form the Moon. The young Moon was bombarded by meteorites until about 3.9 billion years ago, when the storm of impacts subsided. Molten lava then oozed out from the interior, creating the maria, a process that continued for more than 2 billion years. Maria are scarce on the far side because the crust is thicker there, and so less lava reached the surface.

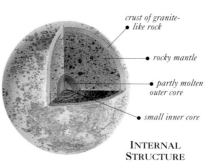

crust of granite-like rock

rocky mantle

partly molten outer core

small inner core

INTERNAL STRUCTURE

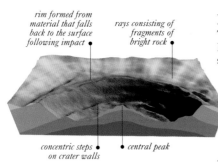

rim formed from material that falls back to the surface following impact

rays consisting of fragments of bright rock

concentric steps on crater walls

central peak

METEORITE IMPACT CRATER
Large craters often have a flat floor with one or more mountains at their center. Since there is no erosion on the Moon, craters are well preserved from the time of impact.

LANDFORMS

The Moon's lowland maria bear few large craters. In contrast, the highlands, which are older, are saturated with craters of all sizes, from tiny pits to huge walled plains over 125 miles (200 km) across. With the exception of a few small volcanic craters, they were all formed by meteorite impacts. Large craters often have central peaks, caused by rebounding of the crater floor during impact, and stepped walls caused by subsequent slumping. Young craters are bright and surrounded by rays of pulverized rock thrown out by the impact. The Moon also has valleys, termed rilles, of which there are two main types: those caused by faulting, which can be straight or curved; and sinuous rilles, which look like rivers but are actually lava channels.

◁ **CRATERS AND RILLES**
Aristarchus (on the left) is a young ray crater. A long rille leads away from the adjacent crater Herodotus.

▽ **OVERLAPPING CRATERS**
The crater Theophilus (on the right) has a central peak and terraced wall.

Gravity (Earth = 1) 0.17	Average temperature 0°F (–18°C)	Maximum magnitude –12.7

MARS

MARS IS A small, rocky planet that in some ways is similar to the Earth. It has a 24-hour day, a pattern of seasons that resembles our own, and polar ice-caps. However, there are important differences: temperatures on Mars rarely rise above freezing, and the atmosphere is thin and contains almost no oxygen. Mars is often called the Red Planet because it is covered by red deserts.

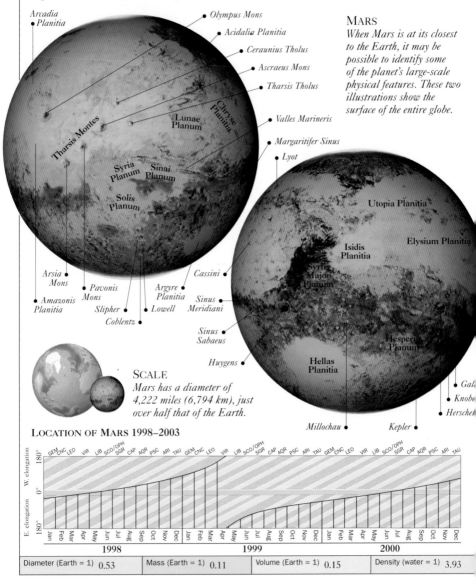

MARS
When Mars is at its closest to the Earth, it may be possible to identify some of the planet's large-scale physical features. These two illustrations show the surface of the entire globe.

Arcadia Planitia
Olympus Mons
Acidalia Planitia
Ceraunius Tholus
Ascraeus Mons
Tharsis Tholus
Chryse Planitia
Lunae Planum
Valles Marineris
Margaritifer Sinus
Lyot
Tharsis Montes
Syria Planum
Sinai Planum
Solis Planum
Utopia Planitia
Isidis Planitia
Elysium Planitia
Syrtis Major Planum
Arsia Mons
Pavonis Mons
Cassini
Argyre Planitia
Amazonis Planitia
Slipher
Lowell
Sinus Meridiani
Coblentz
Hesperia Planum
Sinus Sabaeus
Galle
Knobel
Herschel
Huygens
Hellas Planitia
Millochau
Kepler

SCALE
Mars has a diameter of 4,222 miles (6,794 km), just over half that of the Earth.

LOCATION OF MARS 1998–2003

| Diameter (Earth = 1) 0.53 | Mass (Earth = 1) 0.11 | Volume (Earth = 1) 0.15 | Density (water = 1) 3.93 |

OBSERVATION

Mars is easy to spot with the naked eye at or near times of opposition (see below), when it resembles a bright and distinctly orange-colored star. Binoculars show only a tiny disk, but with a small telescope the planet's polar caps and the largest of its dark surface markings may be seen. For serious observing, a telescope with an aperture of 8 in (200 mm) or more is recommended. At its average opposition distance, a magnification of about 100 times makes Mars appear as large as the full Moon does to the naked eye.

◁ **NAKED EYE**
Mars is the orange dot above the right-hand side of the spire.

△ **BINOCULARS**
Mars is the disk below center in this picture.

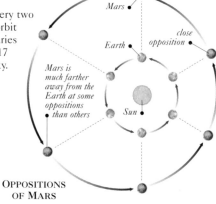

◁ **TELESCOPE**
Large-scale surface features appear as light and dark markings.

TILT, ROTATION, AND ORBIT

one orbit of the Sun takes 687 (Earth) days

Sun

axis tilted at 25.2°

Mars spins on its axis every 24 (Earth) hours 37 minutes

OPPOSITIONS

Mars comes to opposition (see p.15) roughly every two years and two months, but its highly elliptical orbit means that its distance from us at opposition varies appreciably. At close oppositions – every 15 or 17 years – it appears largest and brightest in the sky.

DATES OF OPPOSITIONS

DATE	WHERE MARS APPEARS	MAGNITUDE	DISTANCE from Earth (million mi)
April 24, 1999	Virgo	−1.5	54
June 13, 2001	Ophiuchus	−2.1	42
August 28, 2003	Aquarius	−2.7	35
November 7, 2005	Aries	−2.1	43
December 24, 2007	Gemini–Taurus	−1.4	55
January 29, 2010	Cancer	−1.1	62

Mars

close opposition

Earth

Mars is much farther away from the Earth at some oppositions than others

Sun

OPPOSITIONS OF MARS

| Gravity (Earth = 1) | 0.38 | Number of moons | 2 | Average temperature | −81°F (−63°C) | Maximum magnitude | −2.8 |

ATMOSPHERE AND CLIMATE

Mars has an atmosphere that consists mostly of carbon dioxide. It is so thin that the pressure at the surface is less than 1 percent of that on Earth, and the temperature is usually well below freezing. In winter, the atmosphere freezes at the poles, adding a layer of carbon-dioxide frost to the permanent polar caps of frozen water. Morning mists and high-altitude clouds, particularly in polar areas, can be seen from the Earth. Localized dust storms occur throughout the Martian year. However, when Mars is at its closest to the Sun – and temperature and wind speed are at their maximum – storms can cover the whole planet, enveloping it in dust.

ATMOSPHERIC STRUCTURE

THERMOSPHERE

STRATOSPHERE

TROPOSPHERE

thin clouds of frozen carbon dioxide •

isolated clouds and fog of icy water vapor •

iron-rich red dust •

oxygen and carbon monoxide (0.2%), • and trace gases

argon • (1.6%)

ATMOSPHERIC COMPOSITION

nitrogen (2.7%) •

carbon dioxide (95.3%) •

MOONS

Mars has two small moons called Phobos and Deimos, with average diameters of about 14 miles (22 km) and 7 miles (12 km). Both moons are irregularly shaped and are thought to be asteroids that have been pulled into orbit around Mars by the planet's gravity. Phobos orbits Mars more quickly than Mars rotates on its axis, so from the planet's surface it appears to rise in the west and set in the east. Phobos and Deimos are too faint to be seen without a large telescope. Close-up photographs from space probes have shown that both are heavily cratered.

Stickney •

PHOBOS
The largest crater on Phobos, called Stickney, is about 6 miles (10 km) in diameter.

DEIMOS
The smaller of the two moons, Deimos has no large craters.

• Phobos

Deimos •

MOON ORBITS
Phobos and Deimos are shown here orbiting Mars (not to scale).

1 2 3 4 5 6 7 8 *Scale in radiuses of Mars*

LOCATION OF MARS 2004–2009

| | | | Diameter (Earth = 1) 0.53 | Mass (Earth = 1) 0.11 | Volume (Earth = 1) 0.15 | Density (water = 1) 3.93 |

GEOGRAPHY AND GEOLOGY

Mars is a planet of two halves: the Southern Hemisphere is mainly upland, heavily cratered by meteorites; the Northern Hemisphere is smoother and on average a few miles lower in altitude. There are several huge volcanoes, the most impressive being Olympus Mons, a mountain 400 miles (600 km) wide and 17 miles (27 km) high, and often covered by white clouds that can be seen with a telescope on Earth. Another spectacular feature is a system of canyons, Valles Marineris, more than 2,500 miles (4,000 km) long, one-fifth of the planet's circumference and visible through a telescope as a dark streak. The surface of Mars resembles a rock-strewn desert, colored a rusty red by iron oxide and frozen to a depth of several miles. There are signs that water has flowed over the surface in the past, when the climate was warmer.

- rock crust
- mantle of silicate rock
- small, probably solid core

INTERNAL STRUCTURE

◁ SYRTIS MAJOR
Once thought to be an area of vegetation, this elongated dark marking actually consists of darker rock and dust.

THE THARSIS BULGE ▷
There are three volcanoes in this upland region, forming a chain 1,250 miles (2,000 km) long. The edge of the Valles Marineris is at the right of the picture.

CHIMP ROCK ▷
This boulder seems to have been scoured by wind-blown dust. Winds on Mars can reach 125 miles (200 km) an hour.

PATHFINDER ON MARS ▷
In 1997, the Pathfinder lander sent back pictures of a frozen, rocky desert.

| Gravity (Earth = 1) | 0.38 | Number of moons | 2 | Average temperature | −81°F (−63°C) | Maximum magnitude | −2.8 |

JUPITER

JUPITER IS THE largest planet in the Solar System, weighing more than twice as much as all the other planets put together. It spins on its axis faster than any other planet – one rotation takes less than 10 hours. The visible surface of Jupiter consists of swirling, distinctively banded clouds. Beneath them, the planet is composed mostly of liquid hydrogen and helium.

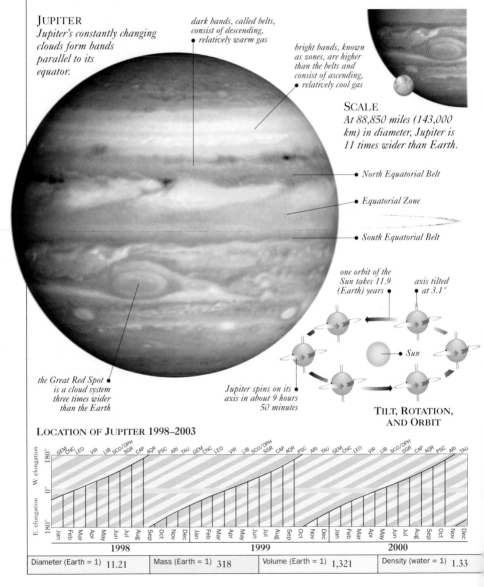

JUPITER
Jupiter's constantly changing clouds form bands parallel to its equator.

dark bands, called belts, consist of descending, relatively warm gas

bright bands, known as zones, are higher than the belts and consist of ascending, relatively cool gas

SCALE
At 88,850 miles (143,000 km) in diameter, Jupiter is 11 times wider than Earth.

North Equatorial Belt

Equatorial Zone

South Equatorial Belt

one orbit of the Sun takes 11.9 (Earth) years

axis tilted at 3.1°

Sun

the Great Red Spot is a cloud system three times wider than the Earth

Jupiter spins on its axis in about 9 hours 50 minutes

TILT, ROTATION, AND ORBIT

LOCATION OF JUPITER 1998–2003

| Diameter (Earth = 1) 11.21 | Mass (Earth = 1) 318 | Volume (Earth = 1) 1,321 | Density (water = 1) 1.33 |

OBSERVATION

Jupiter is one of the most interesting planets for the amateur observer. It is usually the brightest planet after Venus (although at times Mars can become slightly brighter), and it is so large that even binoculars show it as a rounded disk. A small telescope reveals the most prominent cloud bands, which are usually the dark North and South Equatorial Belts, either side of the bright Equatorial Zone. An aperture of 3 in (75 mm) reveals some of the larger features within the clouds.

Over a period of about 10 minutes, these features can be seen to be moving. A small telescope also shows Jupiter's disk to be elliptical – the planet's equatorial diameter is over 5,600 miles (9,000 km) greater than its polar diameter, due to its rapid rotation. Jupiter looks biggest and brightest when it is at opposition (see p.15), which occurs every 13 months. At that time, at a magnification of only 40 times it will appear as large as the full Moon looks to the naked eye.

OBSERVING JUPITER
Through binoculars, Jupiter can be distinguished from stars because it appears as a disk rather than a point of light. Telescopes and CCD cameras show the surface of the disk in greater detail.

BINOCULARS

TELESCOPE   **CCD**

OBSERVING THE GALILEAN MOONS

Jupiter's four largest moons – Io, Europa, Ganymede, and Callisto – were first seen in 1610 by the Italian scientist Galileo Galilei and are now known as the Galilean moons. Through a small telescope or binoculars, they appear like faint stars lined up on either side of the planet's equator, changing position as they orbit the planet. Sometimes one or more may be missing, either passing in front of or behind Jupiter or lost in its shadow.

DAY 1

DAY 2

DAY 3

DAY 4

TRACKING THE MOONS
The moons' positions are shown here over four nights. The moons are shown as colored disks but appear through binoculars or a telescope as small points of light.

KEY
🔵 Callisto (C)
⚪ Europa (E)
🔵 Ganymede (G)
🔵 Io (I)

| Gravity (Earth = 1) 2.36 | Number of moons 16 | Average temperature −227°F (−144°C) | Maximum magnitude −2.9 |

STRUCTURE AND ATMOSPHERE

Jupiter is enveloped in a cloudy atmosphere about 600 miles (1,000 km) deep. Clouds of different composition form at various levels depending on the temperature and pressure, which both increase with depth. Beneath the clouds there is no solid surface. Instead, hydrogen and helium are compressed into liquids by Jupiter's great gravitational pull. Deep in the interior, where liquid hydrogen acts like molten metal, convection produces a strong magnetic field that extends for millions of miles into space. There is thought to be a rocky core at Jupiter's center.

ATMOSPHERIC STRUCTURE

STRATOSPHERE

TROPOSPHERE

white clouds of ammonia crystals ●

dark orange clouds of ammonium hydrosulfide ●

bluish clouds of water ice and water droplets ●

INTERNAL STRUCTURE

● *atmosphere*

liquid hydrogen and helium

● *liquid metallic hydrogen*

● *rocky core about twice the size and ten times the mass of Earth*

ATMOSPHERIC COMPOSITION

● *helium (10.2%) and trace gases*

● *hydrogen (89.8%)*

CLOUD BELTS AND STORMS

Jupiter's rapid rotation draws its clouds into light and dark bands. In the lighter areas, termed zones, gas rises from the warm interior and condenses to form high-altitude clouds. The darker clouds, called belts, occur at lower altitudes, where gas descends. The colors of the belts range from red and brown to blue, depending on the compounds that they contain. Individual cloud features seldom last more than a few weeks, but some white oval clouds have lasted for over half a century. The most prominent feature is the Great Red Spot on the southern edge of the South Equatorial Belt. This swirling, high-altitude storm cloud rotates counterclockwise once a week or so. It has been tracked since 1831, although a similar feature was seen in the 17th century.

THE GREAT RED SPOT

This image was taken from the Galileo space probe. The coloring of the spot may be due to elemental red phosphorus or perhaps carbon compounds.

LOCATION OF JUPITER 2004–2009

| Diameter (Earth = 1) 11.21 | Mass (Earth = 1) 318 | Volume (Earth = 1) 1,321 | Density (water = 1) 1.33 |

RINGS AND MOONS

Jupiter's 16 known satellites fall into three groups: the inner eight, including the four Galilean moons, which have circular orbits in the planet's equatorial plane; the middle four, which have elliptical orbits inclined at about 25 to 30 degrees to Jupiter's equator; and the outer four, which have elliptical and retrograde (east-to-west) orbits. The last two groups are probably captured asteroids. Apart from the Galilean moons, the satellites are small and faint – a large telescope is needed to see them. Jupiter has a faint ring of dust over 60,000 miles (100,000 km) wide.

RINGS AND INNERMOST MOONS

Scale in radiuses of Jupiter

OUTERMOST MOONS

Sinope | Pasiphae | Carme | Ananke | Elara | Lysithea | Leda | Himalia | Callisto | Ganymede | Io | Europa | Jupiter

THE GALILEAN MOONS

Io, the innermost Galilean satellite, is similar in size to our Moon, having a diameter of 2,260 miles (3,630 km). It is covered with yellow-orange sulfur, erupted by volcanoes that are still active. Its interior is kept molten by Jupiter's gravitational forces. Europa, 1,950 miles (3,140 km) in diameter, is the smallest of the four. Its smooth, icy surface resembles a cracked eggshell. Ganymede – diameter 3,270 miles (5,260 km) – is the largest moon in the Solar System, bigger than Mercury. Its complex, partly cratered surface has dark patches and lighter grooves. Outermost of the four moons is Callisto – diameter 2,980 miles (4,800 km) – the dark surface of which is covered with impact craters.

IO

EUROPA GANYMEDE

CALLISTO

2007	2008	2009

| Gravity (Earth = 1) | 2.36 | Number of moons | 16 | Average temperature | −227°F (−144°C) | Maximum magnitude | −2.9 |

SATURN

SATURN, THE MOST DISTANT planet known to ancient astronomers, is in fact the second largest in the Solar System and the easiest one to recognize through a telescope because of the broad, bright rings that encircle its equator. Like Jupiter, it has a cloudy atmosphere that overlies an interior of liquid hydrogen and helium. Saturn has 18 moons, more than any other planet.

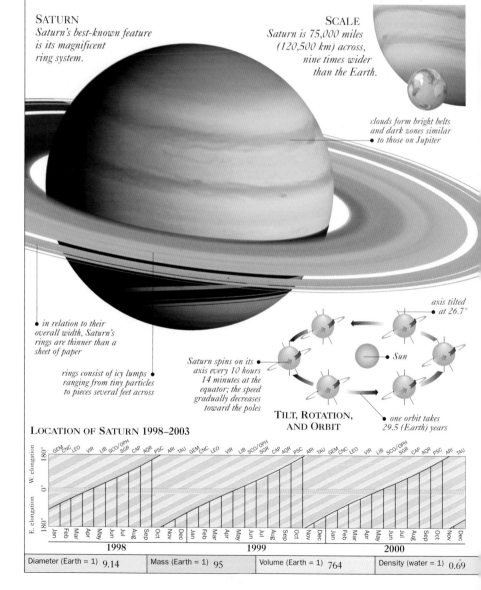

SATURN
Saturn's best-known feature is its magnificent ring system.

SCALE
Saturn is 75,000 miles (120,500 km) across, nine times wider than the Earth.

clouds form bright belts and dark zones similar to those on Jupiter

axis tilted at 26.7°

• in relation to their overall width, Saturn's rings are thinner than a sheet of paper

rings consist of icy lumps ranging from tiny particles to pieces several feet across

Saturn spins on its axis every 10 hours 14 minutes at the equator; the speed gradually decreases toward the poles

• *Sun*

TILT, ROTATION, AND ORBIT

• one orbit takes 29.5 (Earth) years

LOCATION OF SATURN 1998–2003

| Diameter (Earth = 1) | 9.14 | Mass (Earth = 1) | 95 | Volume (Earth = 1) | 764 | Density (water = 1) | 0.69 |

OBSERVATION

To the naked eye, Saturn looks like a bright, yellowish star. Binoculars just reveal a small disk, with a hint of elongation caused by its rings. With a small telescope, the rings, which are over twice as wide as the planet itself, can be seen clearly. Of the five planets visible to the naked eye, Saturn is the slowest moving, its oppositions (see p.15) occurring a year and two weeks apart. When Saturn is viewed at a magnification of 100 times at opposition, its globe looks the same size as the full Moon seen with the naked eye. Saturn's disk is crossed by cloud belts, but these are not as prominent as those of Jupiter, nor is there an equivalent of the Great Red Spot. However, white spots appear in the equatorial zone about every 30 years, during summer in the planet's Northern Hemisphere.

NAKED-EYE VIEW △
Saturn is the bright, starlike object at the center of this picture.

CCD VIEW
With a CCD camera, it is possible to see the major divisions of the rings.

◁ TELESCOPE VIEW
A small telescope shows the outline of Saturn's rings.

VIEWING SATURN'S RINGS

As Saturn orbits the Sun, we see its rings from various angles because of the combined effect of Saturn's axial tilt and the inclination of its orbit to our own. At most, the rings are tipped toward us at about 27 degrees. Twice in each orbit of Saturn around the Sun the rings appear to us edge-on, when they disappear from view because they are so thin. The next time this will happen will be in September 2009.

THE EARTH AND SATURN IN SPACE

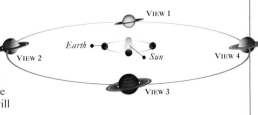

VIEW 1

VIEW 2   Earth   Sun   VIEW 4

VIEW 3

APPEARANCE OF RINGS AS VIEWED FROM THE EARTH

VIEW 1   VIEW 2   VIEW 3   VIEW 4

| Gravity (Earth = 1) 0.92 | Number of moons 18 | Average temperature −285°F (−176°C) | Maximum magnitude −0.3 |

STRUCTURE AND ATMOSPHERE

Saturn's cloudy atmosphere is similar to that of Jupiter, only colder. Near the equator, wind speeds reach 1,100 miles (1,800 km) per hour, faster than on any other planet. Beneath the clouds is an interior of liquid hydrogen and helium, plus a rocky core. Saturn's average density is only about 70 percent that of water, the lowest of any planet. This low density, combined with its rapid rotation, gives it a highly elliptical shape, its equatorial diameter being nearly 7,500 miles (12,000 km) greater than its polar diameter.

- atmosphere
- liquid hydrogen and helium
- liquid metallic hydrogen and helium
- massive core of rock and ice

INTERNAL STRUCTURE

ATMOSPHERIC STRUCTURE

- haze of ammonia crystals
- white clouds of ammonia crystals
- dark orange clouds of ammonium hydro-sulfide crystals
- blue clouds of water ice and water vapor

STRATOSPHERE

TROPOSPHERE

hydrogen (96.3%)

helium (3.3%) and trace gases

ATMOSPHERIC COMPOSITION

RINGS AND MOONS

Saturn's rings consist of an orbiting swarm of icy chunks, each no more than several feet across. The orbits of the innermost moons lie among the rings. Pan orbits in a gap called the Encke Division in the outer part of Saturn's A ring. The next moon, Atlas, orbits at the edge of ring A, while Prometheus and Pandora orbit either side of ring F. Some moons actually share the same orbits.

Helene
Dione
Telesto
Calypso
Tethys
Enceladus
Mimas
Epimetheus
Janus
Prometheus
Pandora
Atlas
Pan
Saturn

INNER RINGS AND MOONS

ring E
ring G
ring A
ring B
ring C
ring D
ring F

7   6   5   4   3   2   1
Scale in radiuses of Saturn

220   210   200   70   60   50   40   30   20   10

OUTER MOONS

Phoebe

Iapetus

Hyperion

Rhea
Titan
Dione
Saturn
Helene

LOCATION OF SATURN 2004–2009

Diameter (Earth = 1)	Mass (Earth = 1)	Volume (Earth = 1)	Density (water = 1)
9.14	95	764	0.69

INNER RINGS

The outermost part of Saturn's ring system visible from the Earth is ring A, which is nearly 170,000 miles (275,000 km) across. This is separated from the brightest and widest part, ring B, by the Cassini Division, a gap of 2,800 miles (4,500 km), visible with a 3 in (75 mm) telescope. Next is the partly transparent ring C (or crepe ring). Fainter rings, called D and F, lie inside and outside the visible rings. Two other very faint rings, known as G and E, lie beyond ring F but are not shown here.

Saturn's cloud top •

ring D •

ring C •
(crepe ring)

ring B •

Cassini •
Division

ring F •

**INNER RINGS AND
DIVISIONS**

Encke •
Division

ring A •

VOYAGER'S VIEW OF SATURN'S RINGS
This enhanced image of ring C and part of ring B (taken by the probe Voyager 2 in 1981) shows that each of the main rings consists of thousands of tiny ringlets. Saturn's rings are 260,000 miles (420,000 km) wide but have a thickness of just about a mile.

MOONS

Saturn has 18 known moons. The largest is Titan, 3,200 miles (5,150 km) in diameter. It is the second largest moon in the Solar System (after Jupiter's Ganymede) and the only one with a substantial atmosphere. At magnitude 8, it can be seen with a small telescope as it orbits the planet every 16 days. An aperture of 6 in (150 mm) should show several other moons – notably Rhea, Tethys, Dione, Iapetus, Enceladus, and perhaps Mimas. Iapetus is unusual in being over four times fainter when on one side of Saturn than on the other, because it has one bright and one dark hemisphere.

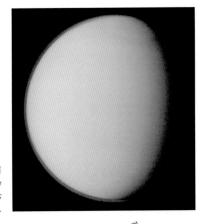

TITAN
Titan's surface is obscured by orange hazes suspended in its nitrogen-rich atmosphere.

| Gravity (Earth = 1) 0.92 | Number of moons 18 | Average temperature −285°F (−176°C) | Maximum magnitude −0.3 |

URANUS

A COLD GAS GIANT, Uranus is the third largest planet in the Solar System. Its most unusual characteristic is that its axis of rotation lies almost in the plane of its orbit, and so it seems to orbit the Sun on its side. Although it can be seen with the naked eye when at its brightest, Uranus was not discovered until 1781, when it was found by a British astronomer, William Herschel.

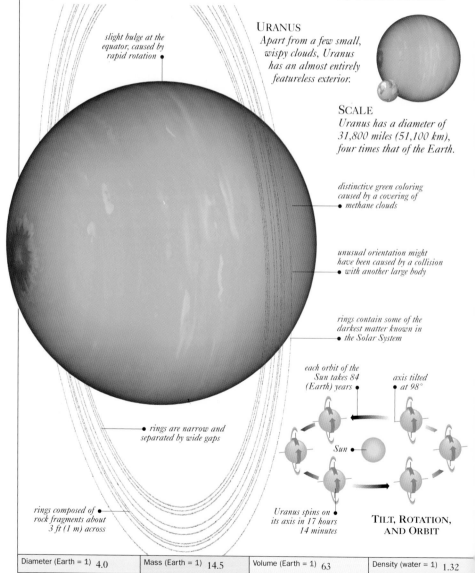

slight bulge at the equator, caused by rapid rotation

URANUS
Apart from a few small, wispy clouds, Uranus has an almost entirely featureless exterior.

SCALE
Uranus has a diameter of 31,800 miles (51,100 km), four times that of the Earth.

distinctive green coloring caused by a covering of methane clouds

unusual orientation might have been caused by a collision with another large body

rings contain some of the darkest matter known in the Solar System

each orbit of the Sun takes 84 (Earth) years

axis tilted at 98°

Sun

rings are narrow and separated by wide gaps

rings composed of rock fragments about 3 ft (1 m) across

Uranus spins on its axis in 17 hours 14 minutes

TILT, ROTATION, AND ORBIT

| Diameter (Earth = 1) 4.0 | Mass (Earth = 1) 14.5 | Volume (Earth = 1) 63 | Density (water = 1) 1.32 |

ATMOSPHERE AND CLIMATE

Uranus is covered in methane clouds that absorb red light, giving the planet a greenish appearance. Its disk is nearly featureless, but some bright clouds were seen by the Voyager 2 space probe in 1986 and later by the Hubble Space Telescope. The planet's extreme axial tilt means that in the course of each orbit the Sun appears overhead at the equator and both poles; each pole experiences 42 years of daylight followed by 42 years of darkness. The interior is probably significantly different from those of Jupiter and Saturn, consisting mostly of water, methane, ammonia, and rock, rather than liquid hydrogen.

atmosphere of hydrogen, helium, and methane gases

dense interior of water ice, methane, and ammonia

core of silicate rock

INTERNAL STRUCTURE

methane (2.3%) and trace gases

helium (15.2%)

hydrogen (82.5%)

ATMOSPHERIC COMPOSITION

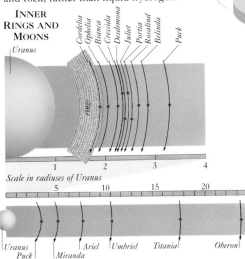

INNER RINGS AND MOONS

Uranus

Cordelia, Ophelia, Bianca, Cressida, Desdemona, Juliet, Portia, Rosalind, Belinda, Puck

Scale in radiuses of Uranus

1   2   3   4
5   10   15   20

Uranus, Puck, Miranda, Ariel, Umbriel, Titania, Oberon

OUTER MOONS

RINGS AND MOONS

Uranus has 11 thin rings and 17 known moons (two only recently identified), all in the plane of its highly inclined equator. The rings are too faint to be seen with the size of telescope used by amateur observers. The outermost ring, called the Epsilon ring, is 60 miles (100 km) wide and has "shepherd" moons, Cordelia and Ophelia, one on each side. The moons, too, are faint; even the biggest and brightest, Titania, is of only 14th magnitude and hence cannot be seen without a large telescope.

OBSERVATION

Under good conditions, and when its position is known, Uranus can be located with the naked eye, resembling a star of 6th magnitude. It is easy to find with binoculars, even from urban areas. Its identity can be confirmed by watching its movements from night to night. At oppositions, which occur a year and four days apart, a magnification of 500 times will show Uranus about the same size as the full Moon.

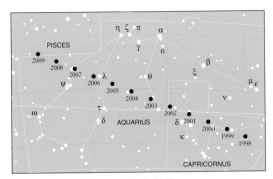

LOCATION OF URANUS 1998–2009

| Gravity (Earth = 1) 0.89 | Number of moons 17 | Average temperature −355°F (−215°C) | Maximum magnitude 5.5 |

NEPTUNE

NEPTUNE IS THE outermost of the gas giants. Like Uranus, it has an atmosphere rich in hydrogen, helium, and methane, and a faint ring system. Neptune was discovered in 1846, after its position had been predicted based on disturbances to the motion of Uranus caused by its gravitational pull. The planet remained poorly known until the space probe Voyager 2 flew past in 1989.

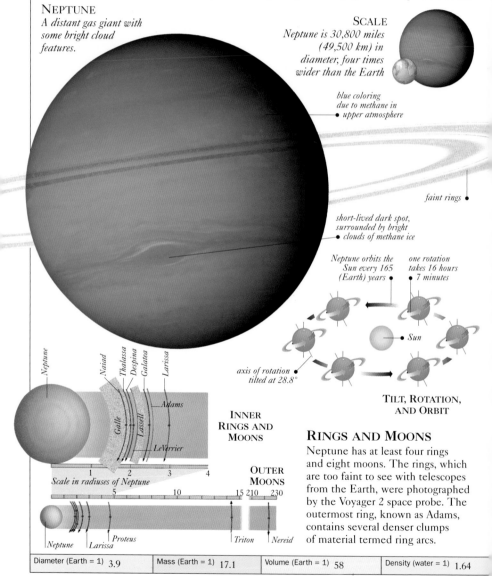

NEPTUNE
A distant gas giant with some bright cloud features.

SCALE
Neptune is 30,800 miles (49,500 km) in diameter, four times wider than the Earth

blue coloring due to methane in upper atmosphere

faint rings

short-lived dark spot, surrounded by bright clouds of methane ice

Neptune orbits the Sun every 165 (Earth) years

one rotation takes 16 hours 7 minutes

Sun

axis of rotation tilted at 28.8°

TILT, ROTATION, AND ORBIT

Neptune
Naiad
Thalassa
Despina
Galatea
Larissa
Galle
Lassell
Adams
LeVerrier

INNER RINGS AND MOONS

1 2 3 4
Scale in radiuses of Neptune
5
10
15 210 230

OUTER MOONS

Neptune Larissa Proteus Triton Nereid

RINGS AND MOONS

Neptune has at least four rings and eight moons. The rings, which are too faint to see with telescopes from the Earth, were photographed by the Voyager 2 space probe. The outermost ring, known as Adams, contains several denser clumps of material termed ring arcs.

Diameter (Earth = 1)	Mass (Earth = 1)	Volume (Earth = 1)	Density (water = 1)
3.9	17.1	58	1.64

ATMOSPHERE AND CLIMATE

The atmospheres of Neptune and Uranus are similar, although Neptune's is stormier and appears blue (rather than blue-green) because there is more methane in its upper levels. In 1989 Voyager 2 photographed a large dark spot, reminiscent of Jupiter's Great Red Spot, in the Southern Hemisphere. Five years later, when the Hubble Space Telescope observed Neptune, the spot had vanished but another dark spot, this time in the Northern Hemisphere, appeared late in 1994. Bright streaks of methane cirrus clouds were recorded by both Voyager and Hubble. The composition of the main cloud deck is not known with certainty, but hydrogen sulfide and ammonia are probably present. Neptune's interior is thought to resemble that of Uranus, consisting of water, ammonia, and methane above a rocky core.

INTERNAL STRUCTURE

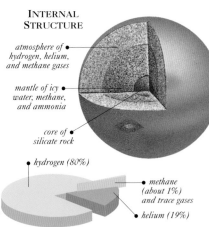

atmosphere of hydrogen, helium, and methane gases

mantle of icy water, methane, and ammonia

core of silicate rock

hydrogen (80%)

methane (about 1%) and trace gases

helium (19%)

ATMOSPHERIC COMPOSITION

MOONS

Of Neptune's eight known moons, Triton is the only one of any significance. It is also the largest, having a diameter of 1,680 miles (2,700 km). The surface is covered with nitrogen and methane frost and, at −391°F (−235°C), is the coldest known place in the Solar System. Liquid nitrogen bursts through the surface to create geysers that leave dark streaks. Triton has a retrograde orbit (it moves in the opposite direction to Neptune) and is thought to have been a separate body, like Pluto, that was captured by Neptune's gravity. Triton is actually larger than Pluto, and the two may be physically similar.

TRITON'S SOUTH POLE
The nitrogen and methane ice at Triton's poles has a slight but distinctive pink coloring.

OBSERVATION

Neptune never becomes brighter than 8th magnitude and so is invisible to the naked eye, but it can be located with binoculars, through which it resembles a faint star. Sightings of Neptune can be confirmed by observing its gradual movement against the background of stars over several nights. Through a telescope, the planet appears as a featureless bluish disk about two-thirds the apparent size of Uranus. Neptune comes to opposition (see p.15) only two and a half days later each year.

LOCATION OF NEPTUNE 1998–2009

| Gravity (Earth = 1) | 1.12 | Number of moons | 8 | Average temperature | −355°F (−215°C) | Maximum magnitude | 7.6 |

PLUTO

A TINY WORLD of rock and ice, Pluto is the smallest of all the planets, only two-thirds the size of our Moon. It is usually the outermost planet, but it has a highly elliptical orbit that for short periods takes it closer to the Sun than Neptune. Pluto was discovered in 1930 by Clyde Tombaugh, an American astronomer, who used photographs to search for a planet beyond Neptune.

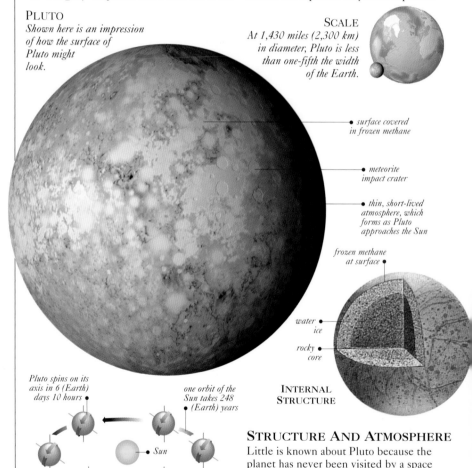

PLUTO
Shown here is an impression of how the surface of Pluto might look.

SCALE
At 1,430 miles (2,300 km) in diameter, Pluto is less than one-fifth the width of the Earth.

surface covered in frozen methane

meteorite impact crater

thin, short-lived atmosphere, which forms as Pluto approaches the Sun

frozen methane at surface

water ice

rocky core

INTERNAL STRUCTURE

Pluto spins on its axis in 6 (Earth) days 10 hours

one orbit of the Sun takes 248 (Earth) years

Sun

axis tilted at about 123°

TILT, ROTATION, AND ORBIT
Pluto's axis is so steeply tilted that its north pole lies below the plane of its orbit

STRUCTURE AND ATMOSPHERE
Little is known about Pluto because the planet has never been visited by a space probe. Its surface is thought to be covered with methane ice, some of which evaporates to form a thin temporary atmosphere for a few decades when Pluto is at its closest to the Sun. Below the methane ice is thought to be a layer of frozen water and a large rocky core.

| Diameter (Earth = 1) 0.18 | Mass (Earth = 1) 0.002 | Volume (Earth = 1) 0.006 | Density (water = 1) 2.0 |

CHARON

Pluto's only moon, Charon, was discovered in 1978. It has more than half the diameter and about one-fifth the mass of Pluto, making it the largest moon in relation to its parent in the Solar System. In effect, the two bodies form a double planet. Charon orbits about 11,400 miles (18,400 km) above Pluto's surface every 6.4 days. Pluto and Charon each spin on their axes in 6.4 days as well, so each body always presents the same face to the other.

CHARON'S SURFACE

Charon is thought to be covered in frozen water (as shown here), unlike Pluto, which is coated with methane ice.

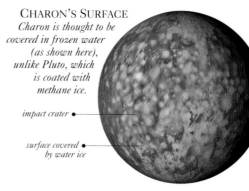

impact crater •

surface covered • by water ice

a spot drawn on Pluto's surface faces a spot on Charon

as Pluto and Charon rotate, the two spots still face each other

Charon is never • visible from this side of Pluto

△ SYNCHRONIZED ORBITS
From one hemisphere of Pluto, Charon is always visible and remains motionless in the sky. It can never be seen from the other hemisphere.

PLUTO AND CHARON ▷
It is very difficult to separate Pluto and Charon using a telescope on Earth. This image, taken by the Hubble Space Telescope, is the best picture that has so far been taken of Pluto and its moon.

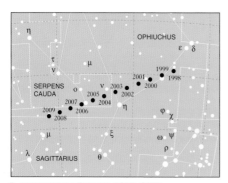

LOCATION OF PLUTO 1998–2009

OBSERVATION

Pluto is of only 14th magnitude. This means that a telescope with an aperture of 8 in (200 mm) is needed just to see it. Even through a large telescope, Pluto appears as a mere starlike point of light. No detail can be detected on its surface. The easiest way to identify Pluto is to study its motion against the stars on a series of photographs – this is similar to the technique used by Clyde Tombaugh in his search for the planet. Pluto's orbit is tilted at 17 degrees to that of the Earth, and so it strays farther from the ecliptic (see p.15) than any other planet.

| Gravity (Earth = 1) 0.07 | Number of moons 1 | Average temperature −369°F (−223°C) | Maximum magnitude 14 |

COMETS AND METEORS

COMETS, consisting of frozen gas and dust, exist in a swarm at the edge of the Solar System. Sometimes they approach the Sun on highly elongated orbits, warming up and releasing gas and dust before receding back into the darkness. Dust particles from comets can enter the Earth's atmosphere, where they burn up to create bright streaks in the sky called meteors or shooting stars.

COMETS

Comets are icy remnants from the formation of the outer planets. They usually orbit unseen in the so-called Oort Cloud, which extends to one light-year or more from the Sun. Sometimes the gravity of a passing star nudges a comet from the cloud into the inner Solar System, so that it becomes visible from Earth. About 1,000 comets are known, but the Oort Cloud and its inner region, called the Kuiper Belt, are thought to contain billions of them.

THE SOURCES OF COMETS
Comets of long orbital period are thought to come from the Oort Cloud (at the edge of this picture); those of shorter period come from the Kuiper Belt (the lighter blue area).

NUCLEI AND TAILS

The only solid part of a comet is its nucleus, which is typically less than a mile across. As it approaches the Sun, the nucleus warms up, emitting gas and dust to form a glowing head, termed the coma, up to 60,000 miles (100,000 km) across. In some comets, gas and dust from the coma form tails.

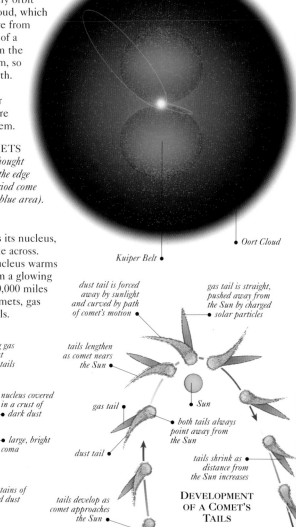

Oort Cloud

Kuiper Belt

escaping gas
and dust
form tails

nucleus covered
in a crust of
dark dust

large, bright
coma

fountains of
gas and dust

**FEATURES OF
A COMET**

dust tail is forced
away by sunlight
and curved by path
of comet's motion

gas tail is straight,
pushed away from
the Sun by charged
solar particles

tails lengthen
as comet nears
the Sun

gas tail

Sun

dust tail

both tails always
point away from
the Sun

tails shrink as
distance from
the Sun increases

tails develop as
comet approaches
the Sun

**DEVELOPMENT
OF A COMET'S
TAILS**

COMET OBSERVATION

About two dozen comets can be seen each year with a large telescope, but only rarely is one bright enough to be visible to the naked eye. There are two main classes: periodic comets orbit the Sun in under 200 years, while long-period comets may take hundreds of thousands of years to return. Large, bright comets develop tails, of which there are two types: one consists of gas and looks bluish; the other consists of dust and appears yellowish. Gas tails are usually narrow and straight, while dust tails are often broad and curved. Both are visible through binoculars.

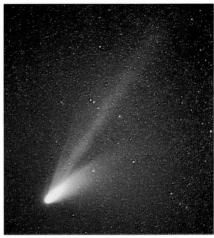

COMET HALE–BOPP
This bright comet was easily visible to the naked eye in 1997. It will not return for 2,400 years.

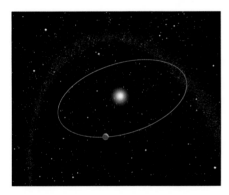

THE ORIGIN OF A METEOR SHOWER
Individual meteor showers occur at the same time each year as the Earth's orbit passes through the trail of dust left along a comet's orbit.

METEORS

On a clear night, bright streaks can be seen in the sky from time to time. They appear suddenly and last for less than a second. These are meteors, or shooting stars, caused by specks of comet dust burning up in the atmosphere at a height of about 60 miles (100 km). A handful of so-called sporadic (random) meteors can usually be seen in an hour, but several times each year the Earth passes through a trail of dust left by a comet, resulting in a meteor shower. Meteors in a shower appear to diverge from a single point called the radiant, and the shower is named after the constellation in which the radiant is found – hence, the Leonids appear to come from Leo. Meteors are easy to see with the naked eye, and useful data have been derived from the records kept by amateur observers.

SHOWER	DATE	CONSTELLATION	HOURLY RATE
Quadrantids	January 3–4	Boötes	100
Lyrids	April 21	Lyra	10
Eta Aquarids	May 5	Aquarius	35
Delta Aquarids (S)	July 29	Aquarius	25
Delta Aquarids (N)	August 6	Aquarius	10
Perseids	August 12	Perseus	80
Orionids	October 20–22	Orion	25
Taurids	November 5	Taurus	10
Leonids	November 17	Leo	10
Geminids	December 13	Gemini	100
Ursids	December 23	Ursa Minor	10

BRIGHT METEOR SHOWERS
This table shows the main meteor showers that the Earth encounters each year. The hourly rate is the maximum number visible under ideal conditions. The date given indicates the time of maximum activity – smaller numbers of meteors can usually be seen for some days either side of this date.

ASTEROIDS AND METEORITES

ASTEROIDS – or minor planets – are small bodies of iron and rock left over from the formation of the Solar System. Most asteroids orbit the Sun in a belt between Mars and Jupiter, but some stray from this group to cross the paths of the inner planets. Meteorites are small fragments, usually from asteroids, that have entered the Earth's atmosphere and fallen to the surface.

ASTEROIDS

Over a million asteroids are thought to exist, although only about 10,000 have so far been discovered. Most asteroids orbit in the belt between Mars and Jupiter, but there is a group, known as the Trojan asteroids, that moves along Jupiter's orbit. Members of another group, named the Apollo asteroids, cross the Earth's orbit and may therefore collide with our planet. The largest asteroid, known as Ceres, is 580 miles (940 km) in diameter. The brightest is Vesta, 360 miles (580 km) across, which can be as bright as 5th magnitude, making it easily visible with binoculars.

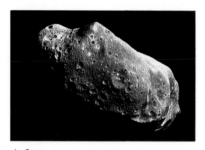

△ IDA
This asteroid, 34 miles (55 km) in length, is orbited by a small satellite known as Dactyl.

△ ASTEROID ORBITS
The asteroid belt lies between about 200 and 305 million miles (320 and 490 million km) from the Sun. The Trojans orbit either side of Jupiter.

- Trojan asteroids
- asteroid belt
- orbit of an Apollo asteroid

Sun, Earth, Venus, Mars, Mercury, Jupiter, Trojan asteroids

METEORITES

Every day about 10 meteorites fall to Earth, although most land in remote areas or the oceans and go unnoticed. Over 10,000 meteorites have been found, many long after their fall. Meteorites are composed of rock or iron, or a mixture of both. Large meteorites are usually moving fast enough to dig a crater when they hit the Earth, but smaller ones are slowed by the atmosphere and drop harmlessly to the surface.

METEOR CRATER ▷
This crater, 0.75 mile (1.2 km) wide, was formed in the desert of Arizona by the impact of an iron meteorite about 50,000 years ago.

STONY-IRON METEORITE

THE CONSTELLATIONS

HOW THIS SECTION WORKS

THIS SECTION contains entries on the 88 constellations, arranged alphabetically by their internationally accepted names. The charts are the most detailed in the book, showing all stars above the approximate threshold of naked-eye visibility. The text covers the origin of the constellations and a selection of the stars and deep-sky objects that they contain.

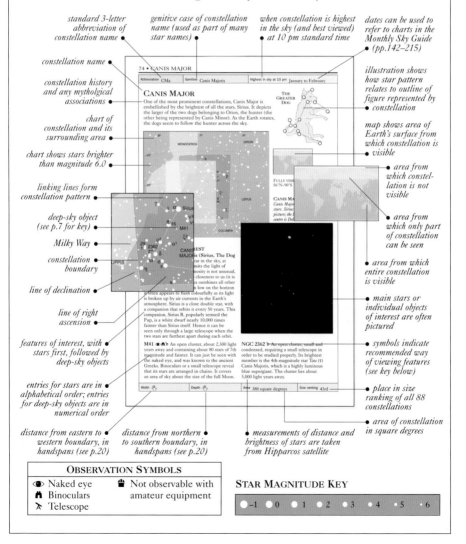

standard 3-letter abbreviation of constellation name

genitive case of constellation name (used as part of many star names)

when constellation is highest in the sky (and best viewed) at 10 pm standard time

dates can be used to refer to charts in the Monthly Sky Guide (pp.142–215)

constellation name

constellation history and any mythological associations

chart of constellation and its surrounding area

chart shows stars brighter than magnitude 6.0

linking lines form constellation pattern

deep-sky object (see p.7 for key)

Milky Way

constellation boundary

line of declination

line of right ascension

features of interest, with stars first, followed by deep-sky objects

entries for stars are in alphabetical order; entries for deep-sky objects are in numerical order

distance from eastern to western boundary, in handspans (see p.20)

distance from northern to southern boundary, in handspans (see p.20)

measurements of distance and brightness of stars are taken from Hipparcos satellite

illustration shows how star pattern relates to outline of figure represented by constellation

map shows area of Earth's surface from which constellation is visible

area from which constellation is not visible

area from which only part of constellation can be seen

area from which entire constellation is visible

main stars or individual objects of interest are often pictured

symbols indicate recommended way of viewing features (see key below)

place in size ranking of all 88 constellations

area of constellation in square degrees

OBSERVATION SYMBOLS

- ◉ Naked eye
- ♠ Binoculars
- ✷ Telescope
- ♣ Not observable with amateur equipment

STAR MAGNITUDE KEY

| -1 | 0 | 1 | 2 | 3 | 4 | 5 | 6 |

Abbreviation And	Genitive Andromedae	Highest in sky at 10 pm October to November

ANDROMEDA

One of the most famous constellations, Andromeda depicts the princess in Greek myth who was chained to a rock as a sacrifice to a sea monster but was saved by the hero Perseus. The constellation contains the nearest major galaxy to us, M31, the Andromeda Galaxy, which is the most distant object visible to the naked eye.

ANDROMEDA

FULLY VISIBLE 90°N–37°S

M31 (THE ANDROMEDA GALAXY)
This spiral galaxy looks elliptical because it is tilted at an angle to us.

AROUND M31
M31 is at the top of this picture. The bright star at the bottom left is Beta (β) Andromedae.

FEATURES OF INTEREST

Gamma (γ) Andromedae ☀ One of the most attractive double stars in the sky. It appears to the naked eye as single star of magnitude 2.1, but even a small telescope will reveal an orange-colored primary, which is a giant star, and a blue companion of 5th magnitude.

M31 (The Andromeda Galaxy) 👁 ♟ ☀
A spiral galaxy, similar to the Milky Way but larger. On a clear, dark night, it can be seen by the naked eye as an elongated smudge. With binoculars or a small telescope, it looks much

larger, extending for several Moon diameters. Even so, this is only the central part of the galaxy, and a larger telescope is needed to see any trace of its spiral arms. Lying about 2.4 million light-years away, M31 is the largest galaxy in the Local Group. It has two small elliptical companion galaxies (the equivalent of our Magellanic Clouds), M32 and NGC 205 (or M110), which can be seen with a telescope with an aperture of 4 in (100 mm) or more.

NGC 752 ♟ An open cluster, visible through binoculars, consisting of faint stars spread over an area of sky wider than the full Moon. It lies about 1,300 light-years away.

NGC 7662 ☀ A planetary nebula, about 4,000 light-years away. It looks small but prominent through a telescope, like a blue-green star of 9th magnitude; high magnification reveals a rounded outline, like an out-of-focus star.

Width 🖐🖐	Height 🖐🖐	Area 722 square degrees	Size ranking 19th

Abbreviation Ant	Genitive Antliae	Highest in sky at 10 pm March to April

ANTLIA

Antlia is a faint constellation, considerably overshadowed by its glorious southern neighbors Centaurus and Vela. Antlia was invented in the 18th century by the French astronomer Nicolas Louis de Lacaille and represents a mechanical air pump. Its brightest star is Alpha (α) Antliae, magnitude 4.3.

THE
AIR PUMP

FULLY VISIBLE
49°N–90°S

FEATURES OF INTEREST

Zeta (ζ) Antliae 🔭 A multiple star that appears as a wide 6th-magnitude double when viewed through binoculars. When a small telescope is turned on it, the brighter star of the pair is seen also to be double. All three stars lie 370 light-years away.

Width	Height	Area 239 square degrees	Size ranking 62nd

Abbreviation Aps	Genitive Apodis	Highest in sky at 10 pm May to July

APUS

Apus lies near the south celestial pole, to the south of Centaurus. It is not easy to identify and contains few objects of note. It is one of the constellations invented at the end of the 16th century by the Dutch navigators Pieter Dirkszoon Keyser and Frederick de Houtman, and represents a New Guinea bird of paradise. Its brightest star is Alpha (α) Apodis, magnitude 3.8.

THE BIRD
OF PARADISE

FULLY VISIBLE
7°N–90°S

FEATURES OF INTEREST

Delta (δ) Apodis 🔭 A wide double star, easily divided with binoculars. The two stars are of magnitudes 4.7 and 5.3. They are both red giants but are estimated to lie at different distances from us, 760 and 660 light-years respectively, so they probably form an optical double rather than a genuine binary.

Width	Height	Area 206 square degrees	Size ranking 67th

Abbreviation Aqr	Genitive Aquarii	Highest in sky at 10 pm August to October

AQUARIUS

This well-known constellation represents a youth pouring water from a jar. The "Water-jar" is represented by a Y-shaped group of four stars, Gamma (γ), Zeta (ζ), Eta (η), and Pi (π) Aquarii. The stream of water flows into the mouth of a large fish, represented by the constellation of Piscis Austrinus to the south. Aquarius is a constellation of the zodiac, the Sun passing through it from February 16 to March 11.

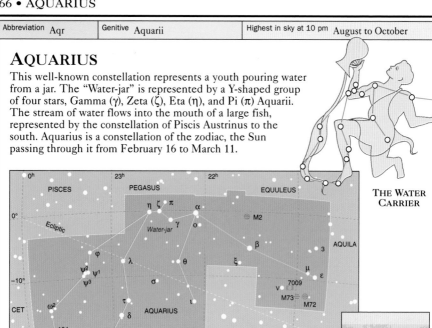

THE WATER CARRIER

FULLY VISIBLE
65°N–86°S

FEATURES OF INTEREST

Zeta (ζ) Aquarii ☌ A close binary, consisting of two white, 4th-magnitude stars that orbit each other every 850 years or so. Using high magnification, a telescope with an aperture of 3 in (75 mm) or more should separate them.

M2 ♊☌ A globular cluster, just too faint to be seen with the naked eye in all but the best conditions, but easy to see with binoculars or a small telescope. It resembles a fuzzy star.

NGC 7009 (The Saturn Nebula) ☌
A planetary nebula. When seen through a telescope with an aperture of 8 in (200 mm) or more, it appears to have appendages that resemble the rings of Saturn, hence its popular name. A smaller telescope will show it as an 8th-magnitude disk of similar apparent size to the globe of Saturn.

NGC 7293 (The Helix Nebula) ♊☌
Possibly the closest planetary nebula to Earth (only about 300 light-years away), and one of the largest in apparent size, at over a third

the diameter of the full Moon. Being so large, its light is spread over a wide area, making it difficult to spot. Under clear, dark skies, it can be seen through binoculars or a wide-field telescope as a pale gray patch.

NGC 7293 (THE HELIX NEBULA)
On color photographs, the Helix Nebula resembles an exotic flower. The shell of gas has been discarded from the faint star at the center of the nebula.

Width 🖐🖐🖐	Height 🖐🖐	Area 980 square degrees	Size ranking 10th

Abbreviation Aql	Genitive Aquilae	Highest in sky at 10 pm July to August

AQUILA

Aquila lies on the celestial equator and represents the eagle that carried the thunderbolts of the Greek god Zeus. The Milky Way passes through the constellation, and there are dense star fields toward the border with Scutum; the brightest part is an area known as the Scutum Star Cloud.

THE
EAGLE

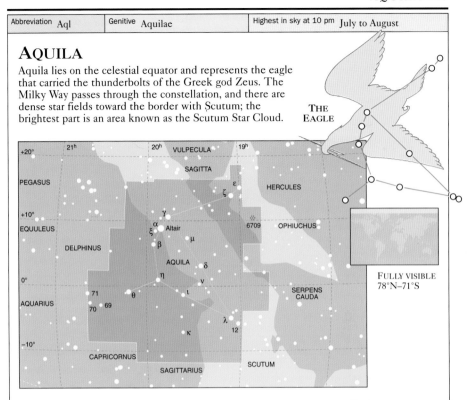

FULLY VISIBLE
78°N–71°S

FEATURES OF INTEREST

Alpha (α) Aquilae (Altair) ◉ Among the 20 brightest stars in the sky, at magnitude 0.8, and also one of the closest first-magnitude stars to us, only 17 light-years away. It marks the neck of the eagle and forms one corner of the Summer Triangle, completed by Deneb (in Cygnus) and Vega (in Lyra). Altair is flanked by two stars, the 4th-magnitude Beta (β) Aquilae (also known as Alshain) and 3rd-magnitude Gamma (γ) Aquilae (or Tarazed).

Eta (η) Aquilae ◉ ⋔ A Cepheid variable star, one of the brightest in this important class. Its magnitude varies from 3.6 to 4.5 in a cycle lasting 7 days 4 hours, and the changes can be followed with the naked eye or through binoculars. It is a supergiant star, estimated to lie about 1,200 light-years away.

THE BORDER
BETWEEN AQUILA
AND SCUTUM
This distinctive hook-shaped group of stars is in the southern part of Aquila. The brightest star in the group (center left) is Lambda (λ) Aquilae, magnitude 3.4.

THE MAIN STARS IN AQUILA
Altair is the bright star at the top left of this picture, flanked on its left and right by Beta (β) and Gamma (γ) Aquilae, also known as Alshain and Tarazed.

Width 🖐✋	Height 🖐✋	Area 652 square degrees	Size ranking 22nd

Abbreviation Ara	Genitive Arae	Highest in sky at 10 pm June to July

ARA

Ara lies in the Milky Way, south of Scorpius. It is well to the south of the celestial equator but was known to the ancient Greeks, who visualized it as the altar on which their gods swore an oath of allegiance before challenging the Titans for control of the Universe. It is also depicted as the altar on which Centaurus is about to sacrifice Lupus, the wolf.

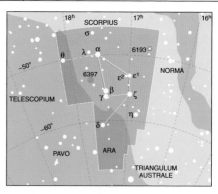

THE ALTAR

FULLY VISIBLE 22°N–90°S

FEATURES OF INTEREST

NGC 6193 ♙ An open cluster, consisting of a handful of stars scattered over an area half the apparent size of the full Moon. Its brightest star is of 6th magnitude, and the whole cluster is best seen with binoculars.

NGC 6397 ♙ ⊁ A large globular cluster, about two-thirds the apparent size of the full Moon and one of the closest to us, at slightly over 7,000 light-years away. It is just visible to the naked eye and easy to find with binoculars. The stars, less densely packed than in many globulars, form chains in the outer regions that can be seen with a moderate-sized telescope.

Width ✋	Height ✋	Area 237 square degrees	Size ranking 63rd

Abbreviation Ari	Genitive Arietis	Highest in sky at 10 pm November to December

ARIES   THE RAM

Aries depicts the ram with the golden fleece, famous from Greek mythology. Its only noticeable feature is a line of three stars: Alpha (α), Beta (β), and Gamma (γ) Arietis. It is a constellation of the zodiac, the Sun passing through it from April 18 to May 14. Aries lies between Pisces and Taurus.

THE CENTRAL PART OF ARIES
Alpha (α), Beta (β), and Gamma (γ) Arietis are to the right in this picture.

FEATURES OF INTEREST

Gamma (γ) Arietis ⊁ A wide double star, easily divided with a small telescope. The two stars are nearly identical, both being blue-white and of magnitude 4.6. Found by the English scientist Robert Hooke in 1664, when telescopes were still quite crude, this was one of the first double stars to be discovered.

FULLY VISIBLE 90°N–58°S

Width ✋	Height ✋	Area 441 square degrees	Size ranking 39th

Abbreviation Aur	Genitive Aurigae	Highest in sky at 10 pm December to February

AURIGA

THE CHARIOTEER

Auriga represents the driver of a horse-drawn chariot. According to one myth, he is Erichthonius, a legendary king of Athens. However, there is no explanation in mythology for his depiction in the sky with a goat and its kids on his left arm. The goat is marked by the constellation's brightest star, Capella (a Latin name, meaning "she-goat"), while the kids (also known as the Haedi, another Latin name) are depicted by Zeta (ζ) and Eta (η) Aurigae. In Greek and Roman times, the figure's right foot was represented by a star now assigned to Taurus, Beta (β) Tauri.

FULLY VISIBLE
90°N–34°S

THE MAIN STARS IN AURIGA
Capella is at the top of this picture.
M36, M37, and M38 are just visible.

FEATURES OF INTEREST

Alpha (α) Aurigae (Capella) ◉ The sixth brightest star in the sky, at magnitude 0.1. To the naked eye, it appears yellowish. It is, in fact, a spectroscopic binary, consisting of two yellow-colored giants that orbit each other every 104 days. It lies 42 light-years away.

Epsilon (ε) Aurigae ◉ One of the most extraordinary variable stars in the sky. It is an eclipsing binary, consisting of a brilliant white supergiant orbited by an odd dark companion that passes in front of it every 27 years, the longest known period between eclipses of any variable star. The star's brightness is more than halved by the eclipse, from magnitude 2.9 to 3.8, and it remains dimmed for over a year. After observing the last eclipse, which ended in 1984, astronomers think that the mystery partner might be a close binary, surrounded by an elongated cloud of dark dust and gas. The next eclipse is due to start at the end of 2009.

Zeta (ζ) Aurigae ◉ An eclipsing binary, consisting of an orange giant orbited every 2.7 years by a smaller blue star. During an eclipse, which lasts 40 days, the star's brightness drops from magnitude 3.7 to 4.0.

M36, M37, and M38 ♠ ⚹ Just visible with the naked eye and easy to see with binoculars, these three open clusters lie 4,000–4,500 light-years away. In a binocular field of 6 degrees or more, all three can be seen as misty patches. The smallest of the trio, M36, is the easiest to spot, a small telescope resolving its brightest stars. M37, the largest of the clusters at about two-thirds the width of the full Moon, contains more stars but they are fainter. M38 is the most scattered cluster; a small telescope reveals that many of its stars form chains.

Width ✋✋	Height ✋🖐	Area 657 square degrees	Size ranking 21st

Abbreviation Boo	Genitive Boötis	Highest in sky at 10 pm May to June

BOÖTES

THE HERDSMAN

Boötes is an elongated constellation depicting a man herding a bear, represented by Ursa Major. The name of its brightest star, Arcturus, is Greek for "bear guard." The northern part of Boötes contains the faint stars that formed the now-defunct constellation of Quadrans Muralis, the mural (or wall) quadrant, which gave its name to the Quadrantid meteor shower that radiates from this area every January.

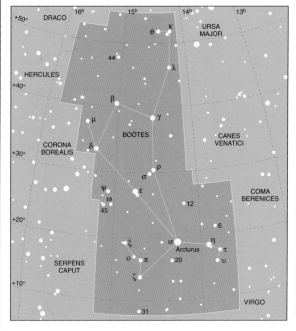

FULLY VISIBLE 90°N–35°S

THE MAIN STARS IN BOÖTES
The bright star at the bottom of this picture is Arcturus.

FEATURES OF INTEREST

Alpha (α) Boötis (Arcturus) ◉ The brightest star north of the celestial equator, and, at magnitude –0.1, the fourth brightest overall. It is a red giant, 100 times more luminous than the Sun but with a cooler (and hence redder) surface. To the naked eye, it has a noticeably warm tint, which becomes stronger when it is viewed with binoculars.

Epsilon (ε) Boötis ⚹ A beautiful double star but a difficult one to divide. To the naked eye, it appears of magnitude 2.4. A telescope of aperture 3 in (75 mm) or more shows a red-giant primary and a close, blue-green partner of 5th magnitude. High magnification and a steady night are needed to separate the stars.

Kappa (κ) Boötis ⚹ A double star, easily divided with a small telescope into a pair of white stars of 5th and 7th magnitudes.

Mu (μ) Boötis ♊⚹ A multiple star. Binoculars show a wide double, with stars of magnitudes 4.3 and 6.5. The fainter star is itself double, with 7th- and 8th-magnitude components that orbit each other every 260 years. They should be divisible in moderate apertures, but are just too close to be split with a small telescope.

Xi (ξ) Boötis ⚹ A double star, divisible with a small telescope. The stars, of magnitudes 4.7 and 7.0, are both yellow-orange, one slightly deeper in tone than the other. They form a true binary with an orbital period of 152 years.

Width 🖐🤏🤏	Height 🖐🖐🤏🖐	Area 907 square degrees	Size ranking 13th

Abbreviation Cae	Genitive Caeli	Highest in sky at 10 pm December to January

CAELUM

THE CHISEL

Caelum is a small, faint constellation in an inconspicuous area of the Southern-Hemisphere sky. It represents a stonemason's chisel and was introduced into the sky in the 18th century by the French astronomer Nicolas Louis de Lacaille. Its brightest star, Alpha (α) Caeli, is of magnitude 4.4.

FULLY VISIBLE
41°N–90°S

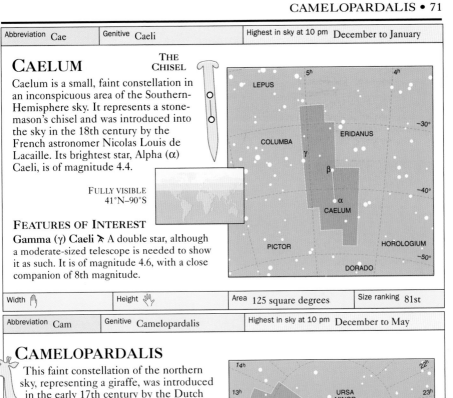

FEATURES OF INTEREST

Gamma (γ) Caeli ⋟ A double star, although a moderate-sized telescope is needed to show it as such. It is of magnitude 4.6, with a close companion of 8th magnitude.

Width 🖐	Height 🖐	Area 125 square degrees	Size ranking 81st

Abbreviation Cam	Genitive Camelopardalis	Highest in sky at 10 pm December to May

CAMELOPARDALIS

This faint constellation of the northern sky, representing a giraffe, was introduced in the early 17th century by the Dutch astronomer Petrus Plancius. An obsolete variant of its name is Camelopardus.

THE GIRAFFE

FULLY VISIBLE
90°N–3°S

FEATURES OF INTEREST

Beta (β) Camelopardalis ♠ ⋟ A wide double star. The brighter component is the brightest star in the constellation, at magnitude 4.0. It has a companion of magnitude 7.4 that is easy to see with a small telescope, or even a pair of powerful binoculars. In the same binocular field, an even wider pairing can be seen; the two stars, 11 and 12 Camelopardalis, are of magnitudes 5.2 and 6.1.

NGC 1502 ♠ ⋟ An open cluster, visible with binoculars or a small telescope. Although small, its stars are moderately bright, and include a noticeable 7th-magnitude double.

Width 🖐🖐	Height 🖐🖐	Area 757 square degrees	Size ranking 18th

Abbreviation Cnc	Genitive Cancri	Highest in sky at 10 pm February to March

CANCER

Cancer represents the crab that, in Greek mythology, was crushed underfoot by Hercules during his battle with the multiheaded Hydra. It lies between Gemini and Leo and is the faintest constellation of the zodiac; its brightest star, Beta (β) Cancri, is of magnitude 3.5. The Sun is within Cancer's boundaries from July 20 until August 10.

THE CRAB

FULLY VISIBLE
90°N–57°S

M44 (PRAESEPE)
M44 is too large to fit in the field of view of most telescopes. This picture shows the cluster as it looks through binoculars. The two stars known as the aselli that are useful in locating the cluster are just out of view.

FEATURES OF INTEREST

Zeta (ζ) Cancri ✴ A multiple star. Through a small telescope, it is seen to consist of two stars, of magnitudes 5.1 and 6.2. A telescope with an aperture larger than about 6 in (150 mm) will show that the brighter component has a much closer companion, of magnitude 6.1, which orbits it every 60 years.

Iota (ι) Cancri ✴ A wide double star, with components of magnitudes 4.2 and 6.6 that are easy to divide with a small telescope.

M44 (Praesepe) ♠ An open cluster, also known as the Beehive Cluster or the Manger. (Praesepe is Latin, meaning both "manger" and "hive.") It appears as a cloudy patch at the limit of naked-eye visibility – its brightest stars are of 6th magnitude, and it was known to the ancient Greeks – but binoculars show it as a field of stars more than three times the apparent width of the full Moon. It lies about 520 light-years away. To the north and south of the cluster are the stars Gamma (γ) Cancri

(magnitude 4.7) and Delta (δ) Cancri (magnitude 3.9). In ancient times, these were visualized as donkeys feeding at the manger, hence they are known as the aselli, or asses.

M67 ♠✴ An open cluster. It contains more stars than M44 (Praesepe), but it is farther away from us (about 2,600 light-years) and so appears fainter and smaller.

Width 🖐	Height 🖐🖐	Area 506 square degrees	Size ranking 31st

Abbreviation CVn	Genitive Canum Venaticorum	Highest in sky at 10 pm April to May

CANES VENATICI

Canes Venatici represents two hunting dogs, held on a leash by the herdsman Boötes. The constellation was formed in 1687 by Johannes Hevelius from stars that had formerly been part of Ursa Major.

THE
HUNTING DOGS

FULLY VISIBLE
90°N–37°S

M51 (THE WHIRLPOOL GALAXY)
This spiral galaxy is interacting with a smaller companion galaxy, NGC 5195. M51 appears to us face-on, with NGC 5195 at the end of one of its spiral arms.

FEATURES OF INTEREST

Alpha (α) Canum Venaticorum (Cor Caroli) ☆ A double star. A small telescope will easily separate the two components of magnitudes 2.9 and 5.6. Although both should appear white, some observers have reported delicate color tints. This is possibly because the brighter star has an unusual composition, as revealed by spectroscopic studies. The name Cor Caroli means "Charles's heart," and commemorates King Charles I of England.

M3 ♠☆ A globular cluster on the verge of naked-eye visibility. It is easy to find with binoculars or a small telescope, in which it appears about half the size of the full Moon. A telescope with an aperture of about 4 in (100 mm) or more is needed to see the cluster's individual stars.

M51 (The Whirlpool Galaxy) ♠☆ A spiral galaxy, seen almost face-on. This is one of the most famous galaxies in the sky and one of the easiest in which to see spiral structure. The galaxy can be located using binoculars. A small telescope reveals its bright nucleus,

as well as the nucleus of a smaller, irregularly shaped galaxy, NGC 5195, which is passing close by. Using a telescope of moderate to large aperture – 8 in (200 mm) or more – it should be possible to trace the outline of M51's arms. M51 and NGC 5195 are both about 25 million light-years away.

Width 🖐🤏	Height 🖐	Area 465 square degrees	Size ranking 38th

Abbreviation CMa	Genitive Canis Majoris	Highest in sky at 10 pm January to February

CANIS MAJOR

One of the most prominent constellations, Canis Major is embellished by the brightest of all the stars, Sirius. It depicts the larger of the two dogs belonging to Orion, the hunter (the other being represented by Canis Minor). As the Earth rotates, the dogs seem to follow the hunter across the sky.

FULLY VISIBLE
56°N–90°S

CANIS MAJOR
Canis Major contains several bright stars. Sirius is near the top of this picture; the bright star nearest the center is Delta (δ) Canis Majoris.

FEATURES OF INTEREST

Alpha (α) Canis Majoris (Sirius, The Dog Star) ◉ The brightest star in the sky, at magnitude –1.44. Sirius emits the light of about 20 Suns. This luminosity is not unusual, but because of its relative closeness to us (it is 8.6 light-years away), Sirius outshines all other stars. It is white, but when low on the horizon it often appears to flash colorfully as its light is broken up by air currents in the Earth's atmosphere. Sirius is a close double star, with a companion that orbits it every 50 years. This companion, Sirius B, popularly termed the Pup, is a white dwarf nearly 10,000 times fainter than Sirius itself. Hence it can be seen only through a large telescope when the two stars are farthest apart during each orbit.

M41 ◉ ♠ ⊁ An open cluster, containing about 80 stars of 7th magnitude and fainter, about 2,300 light-years away. It can just be seen with the naked eye, and was known to the ancient Greeks. Binoculars or a small telescope reveal that its stars are arranged in chains. It covers an area of sky about the size of the full Moon.

NGC 2362 ⊁ An open cluster, small and condensed, requiring a small telescope in order to be studied properly. Its brightest member is the 4th-magnitude star Tau (τ) Canis Majoris, which is a highly luminous blue supergiant. The cluster lies about 5,000 light-years away.

Width 🖐	Height 🖐	Area 380 square degrees	Size ranking 43rd

Abbreviation CMi	Genitive Canis Minoris	Highest in sky at 10 pm February

CANIS MINOR

THE
LESSER DOG

Canis Minor represents the smaller of the two dogs of Orion, the hunter. Both Orion and Canis Major, which depicts the larger dog, lie nearby. Apart from its two brightest stars, Canis Minor contains little of note.

FULLY VISIBLE
89°N–77°S

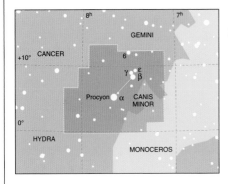

FEATURES OF INTEREST

Alpha (α) Canis Minoris (Procyon)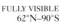
The eighth brightest star in the sky, at magnitude 0.4. The name Procyon is of Greek origin, meaning "before the dog," from the fact that it rises before the other dog star, Sirius. It is a white star, slightly less luminous than Sirius, and slightly farther away, at 11.4 light-years. Like Sirius, it is unusual in having a white-dwarf partner, Procyon B; this is over 10,000 times fainter than Procyon and orbits it every 41 years. The two appear so close that only large telescopes, of the type used by professional astronomers, can separate them.

Width 🖐	Height 🖐	Area 380 square degrees	Size ranking 71st

Abbreviation Cap	Genitive Capricorni	Highest in sky at 10 pm August to September

CAPRICORNUS

THE
SEA GOAT

The smallest constellation of the zodiac, lying between Sagittarius and Aquarius, Capricornus depicts a fish-tailed goat. The constellation originated among the Babylonian and Sumerian peoples of the Middle East, but in Greek myth it is linked with the goatlike god Pan, who turned his lower half into a fish to escape the sea monster Typhon. Capricornus is not prominent: its brightest star, Delta (δ) Capricorni (Deneb Algedi), is of magnitude 2.9. The Sun passes through it from January 19 to February 16.

FULLY VISIBLE
62°N–90°S

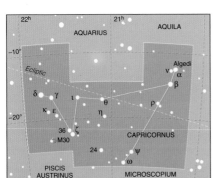

FEATURES OF INTEREST

Alpha (α) Capricorni (Algedi, Giedi)
A wide double star. Ordinary binoculars, or good eyesight, reveal two stars, of magnitudes 3.6 and 4.3. Both are yellowish in color, but they are unrelated. The brighter star is a giant, 110 light-years away, while the fainter one is a supergiant, over six times more distant.

Beta (β) Capricorni A wide double star. The primary is a yellow giant, magnitude 3.1, visible to the naked eye. Binoculars or a small telescope show the second star, of magnitude 6.0. Both stars lie about 300 light-years away.

Width 🖐	Height 🖐	Area 414 square degrees	Size ranking 40th

Abbreviation Car	Genitive Carinae	Highest in sky at 10 pm January to April

CARINA

Carina is an impressive constellation, containing the second brightest star of all, Canopus, and lying in a rich part of the Milky Way. In Greek times, it formed part of a much larger constellation, Argo Navis, representing the ship of the Argonauts, but was made separate in the 18th century by the Frenchman Nicolas Louis de Lacaille. It represents the ship's keel, with Canopus marking the rudder. The other parts of the ship – Vela (the sails) and Puppis (the stern) – lie to the north of Carina.

THE KEEL

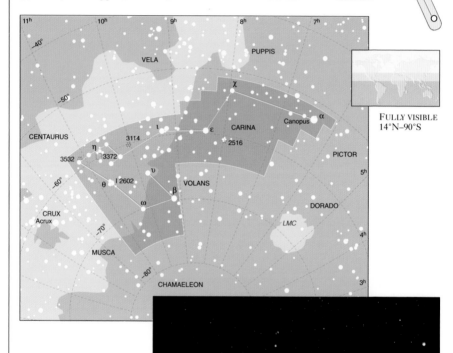

FULLY VISIBLE
14°N–90°S

STAR CLUSTERS AND
NEBULAS IN CARINA
*This picture shows the whole
of this magnificent southern
constellation, with the bright star
Canopus at the top right.
The Eta Carinae Nebula
(NGC 3372) lies on the far left,
with the open cluster IC 2602
(also known as the Southern
Pleiades) below and to its right.
NGC 2516, another prominent
cluster, is to the right of center.*

Width	Height	Area 494 square degrees	Size ranking 34th

FEATURES OF INTEREST

Alpha (α) Carinae (Canopus) ◉

The second brightest star in the sky, at magnitude –0.6. It is a white supergiant, 14,000 times more luminous than the Sun, lying 310 light-years away.

Eta (η) Carinae ♏ ☉

A remarkable variable star. Currently it is of 6th magnitude, but it has been much brighter in the past, most noticeably in the 19th century, when it flared up to nearly –1. Eta Carinae is thought to be either a supergiant with a mass of 100 Suns, one of the most massive stars known, or possibly a massive binary. Through a telescope, it appears as a hazy orange ellipse, because of matter thrown off in its last outburst. Its distance is estimated at over 8,000 light-years, and it lies within the extensive nebula NGC 3372 (see below).

NGC 2516 ◉ ♏

An open cluster, visible to the naked eye. Using binoculars, it is possible to pick out its individual stars, the brightest being a 5th-magnitude red giant, scattered over an area of sky the size of the full Moon. It is about 1,300 light-years away.

NGC 3114 ◉ ♏

An open cluster, visible to the naked eye and appearing about the same

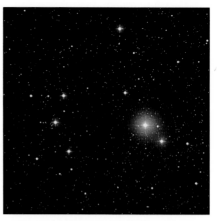

IC 2602 (THE SOUTHERN PLEIADES)
This large, bright open cluster contains several stars visible to the naked eye. The bright star at the right of the picture is Theta (θ) Carinae.

size as the disk of the full Moon. Its individual stars can be seen through binoculars. It lies nearly 3,000 light-years away.

NGC 3372 (The Eta Carinae Nebula)

◉ ♏ ☉ A large, bright diffuse nebula, four times the apparent width of the full Moon, surrounding the star Eta (η) Carinae (see above). The nebula is visible to the naked eye against the Milky Way and is best seen with binoculars. A V-shaped lane of dark dust runs through it. Near Eta Carinae itself, telescopes show a dark and bulbous cloud of dust called the Keyhole Nebula.

NGC 3532 ◉ ♏

A bright and dense open cluster, elliptical in shape. It is visible to the naked eye and is a glorious sight through binoculars, being nearly twice the apparent diameter of the full Moon at its widest. It is 1,300 light-years away.

IC 2602 (The Southern Pleiades) ◉ ♏

A large and prominent open cluster, containing eight stars brighter than magnitude 6. The brightest member is Theta (θ) Carinae, a blue-white star of magnitude 2.7. The cluster appears twice the size of the full Moon and lies about 500 light-years away.

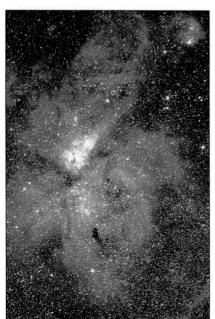

NGC 3372 (THE ETA CARINAE NEBULA)
This magnificent nebula surrounds the peculiar variable star Eta (η) Carinae. It is dissected by dark lanes of dust. Eta Carinae itself is in the brightest part of the nebula, just above center in this photograph.

Abbreviation Cas	Genitive Cassiopeiae	Highest in sky at 10 pm October to December

CASSIOPEIA

This attractive constellation represents the mythical Queen Cassiopeia. Her husband and daughter are represented by the adjacent constellations Cepheus and Andromeda. Cassiopeia was notoriously vain and is depicted sitting on a throne, fussing with her hair. Cassiopeia's brightest stars form a distinctive W-shape. Epsilon (ε) Cassiopeiae, at one end of the W, marks the queen's ankle while Beta (β), at the other end, lies in her shoulder.

CASSIOPEIA

FULLY VISIBLE
90°N–12°S

THE MAIN STARS IN CASSIOPEIA
The distinctive W-shape formed by Cassiopeia's brightest stars makes the constellation easy to recognize.

FEATURES OF INTEREST

Gamma (γ) Cassiopeiae ◉ A variable star, currently about magnitude 2.2. Its rapid spin causes rings of gas to be thrown off its equator, changing its brightness temporarily.

Eta (η) Cassiopeiae ➤ A double star. It consists of a yellow star of magnitude 3.5 and an orange companion of magnitude 7.2 that can be seen with a small telescope. The two stars lie 19 light-years away, forming a genuine binary pair with an orbital period of 480 years.

Rho (ρ) Cassiopeiae ◉ ♠ A highly luminous yellow supergiant. As a result of pulsations in its size, it varies between about 4th and 5th magnitudes in a cycle that lasts just under a year.

M52 ♠ ➤ An open cluster. It is visible with binoculars, covering an area about one-third

the apparent size of the full Moon, although a telescope is needed to show its individual stars. It lies 5,200 light-years away. A 5th-magnitude star that appears to be a member of the cluster actually lies much closer to us.

NGC 457 ♠ ➤ An elongated open cluster, about one-third the apparent size of the full Moon and visible through binoculars or a small telescope. The cluster's appearance has been compared to an owl, with its two brightest stars marking the owl's eyes. The brightest star is the 5th-magnitude Phi (φ) Cassiopeiae, a luminous supergiant.

Width 🤚🤏	Height 🤚🤏	Area 598 square degrees	Size ranking 25th

Abbreviation Cen	Genitive Centauri	Highest in sky at 10 pm April to June

CENTAURUS

This large constellation in the southern Milky Way depicts a centaur, the mythical beast with the legs of a horse and the upper body of a man. In Greek mythology, this centaur is identified as Chiron, tutor to the offspring of the gods. Its brightest star, Alpha (α) Centauri, is the third brightest in the sky. A line drawn between Alpha (α) and Beta (β) Centauri points to the Southern Cross, Crux.

THE CENTAUR

FULLY VISIBLE 25°N–90°S

NGC 5139 (OMEGA CENTAURI)
When seen through a telescope, this bright globular cluster often appears elliptical rather than circular.

FEATURES OF INTEREST

Alpha (α) Centauri (Rigil Kentaurus) ◉ ♙
A nearby multiple star. To the naked eye, it appears at magnitude –0.3, the third brightest star in the sky. A small telescope shows it to be a glorious binary, consisting of two yellow and orange stars of magnitudes 0.0 and 1.4. They orbit each other every 80 years, so one complete orbit can just be followed in a human lifetime. Lying 2 degrees away from this pair is a much fainter third star, an 11th-magnitude red dwarf called Proxima Centauri. This is the closest star to the Sun, 4.2 light-years away, about 0.2 light-years closer to us than the two brighter members of the Alpha Centauri system.

Beta (β) Centauri ◉
A blue-white giant star, magnitude 0.6 and 11th brightest in the sky, about 525 light-years away.

NGC 5139 (Omega (ω) Centauri) ◉ ♙ ✻
The largest and brightest globular cluster in the sky, about 17,000 light-years away. Seen with the naked eye or binoculars, it appears as a hazy 4th-magnitude patch larger than the full Moon. A small telescope shows its main stars.

NGC 3918 (The Blue Planetary) ✻
A planetary nebula, visible through a small telescope as a rounded blue disk.

NGC 5128 (Centaurus A) ✻
An unusual galaxy. With a small telescope, it looks like an elliptical galaxy, but larger apertures and long-exposure photographs show that it is bisected by a dark dust lane, evidently due to a merger with another galaxy. It is a strong radio source, referred to as Centaurus A.

Width 〰〰	Height 〰	Area 1,060 square degrees	Size ranking 9th

Abbreviation Cep	Genitive Cephei	Highest in sky at 10 pm September to October

CEPHEUS

This far-northern constellation, adjoining Cassiopeia and extending almost to the north celestial pole, represents the mythical King Cepheus, the husband of the vain Queen Cassiopeia and father of Andromeda. Its brightest star is Alpha (α) Cephei, of magnitude 2.5.

CEPHEUS

FULLY VISIBLE
90°N–1°S

DELTA AND MU CEPHEI

The following stars are useful for gauging the magnitude of Delta (δ) and Mu (μ) Cephei: Zeta (ζ), magnitude 3.4, Epsilon (ε), magnitude 4.2, and Lambda (λ), magnitude 5.1.

FEATURES OF INTEREST

Beta (β) Cephei ⚹ A double and variable star. The brighter component is a blue giant of magnitude 3.2, about 600 light-years away. It is a pulsating variable star (the prototype of a group called Beta Cephei stars), although its variations are so small that they are barely perceptible to the eye. A small telescope shows a companion of magnitude 7.9.

Delta (δ) Cephei ◉ ♇ ⚹ A double star and a famous variable. The brighter star, a yellow supergiant, is the prototype of the so-called Cepheid variables, which astronomers use for finding distances in space. Such stars change in brightness as they pulsate in size. Delta Cephei itself varies between magnitudes 3.5 and 4.4 every 5 days 9 hours. It lies about 1,000 light-years away. A small telescope shows a wide companion of magnitude 6.3.

KEY

◯	–1
◯	0
◯	1
◯	2
◯	3
◯	4
◯	5
·	6
·	7

Mu (μ) Cephei (The Garnet Star) ◉ ♇ ⚹ A variable star with a strong red color, hence its popular name, which is noticeable through binoculars or a small telescope. It is a red supergiant that pulsates in size, varying from magnitude 3.4 to 5.1 about every 2 years.

Width 🖐	Height 🖐	Area 588 square degrees	Size ranking 27th

| Abbreviation Cet | Genitive Ceti | Highest in sky at 10 pm October to December |

CETUS

Cetus, which straddles the celestial equator south of Pisces and Aries, is a large constellation representing the mythical sea monster from whose jaws Andromeda was rescued by the hero Perseus. The brightest star in the constellation is Beta (β) Ceti, magnitude 2.0.

THE SEA MONSTER
OR WHALE

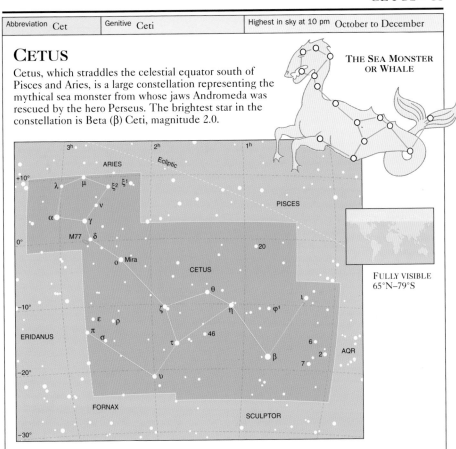

FULLY VISIBLE
65°N–79°S

FEATURES OF INTEREST

Omicron (o) Ceti (Mira) 👁 🔭 A famous variable star. Mira is a red giant star, about 300 times larger than the Sun, that varies widely in brightness as it swells and contracts in size in a cycle that lasts approximately 11 months.

OMICRON (o)
CETI (MIRA)
The variable star Mira (below center in picture) is seen here at its maximum brightness.

At its brightest, it can reach 3rd or even 2nd magnitude, but it drops to 10th magnitude at its minimum. Mira, which was first identified as being variable in 1596, is the prototype of a class of long-period variables; referred to as Mira stars, they form the largest group of variable stars. Mira is Latin for "wonderful."

Tau (τ) Ceti 👁 A nearby, Sunlike star. It is similar to the Sun in temperature and luminosity, and at a distance of 11.9 light-years it is among the 20 closest stars to Earth. It appears of magnitude 3.5.

M77 🔭 A spiral galaxy, seen face-on from Earth. A telescope shows it as a small, round patch. It is the brightest of a class of galaxies known as Seyfert galaxies, which have particularly bright centers.

| Width 🖐🖐🖐 | Height 🖐🖐 | Area 1,231 square degrees | Size ranking 4th |

Abbreviation Cha	Genitive Chamaeleontis	Highest in sky at 10 pm February to May

CHAMAELEON

Chamaeleon is a small, faint constellation near the south celestial pole. Introduced at the end of the 16th century by the Dutch navigators Pieter Dirkszoon Keyser and Frederick de Houtman, it depicts a chameleon, the lizard that changes its skin color to camouflage itself. Its brightest stars are of 4th magnitude.

THE CHAMELEON

FULLY VISIBLE
7°N–90°S

FEATURES OF INTEREST

Delta (δ) Chamaeleontis 🌢 A wide double star. With binoculars, it is easy to see the two components, of magnitudes 4.4 and 5.5. Both stars lie about 360 light-years away.

NGC 3195 🔭 A faint planetary nebula of similar apparent size to the disk of Jupiter, visible with a moderate-sized telescope.

Width 🖐	Height 🖐	Area 132 square degrees	Size ranking 79th

Abbreviation Cir	Genitive Circini	Highest in sky at 10 pm May to June

CIRCINUS

This small constellation next to Centaurus was introduced in the 18th century by the French astronomer Nicolas Louis de Lacaille. It represents a pair of dividing compasses, of the type used by surveyors and chart makers, and is suitably placed in the sky next to Norma, the level. Despite its insignificance, Circinus is easy to find, since it lies next to Alpha (α) Centauri in Centaurus. Although it is in the Milky Way, it contains no notable star clusters.

THE COMPASSES

FULLY VISIBLE
19°N–90°S

FEATURES OF INTEREST

Alpha (α) Circini 🔭 A double star. The primary, of magnitude 3.2, is the brightest star in the constellation. It lies 54 light-years away. Its companion, of magnitude 8.6, is visible through a small telescope.

Width 🖐	Height 🖐	Area 93 square degrees	Size ranking 85th

Abbreviation Col	Genitive Columbae	Highest in sky at 10 pm January

COLUMBA

THE DOVE

Columba was introduced in the late 16th century by the Dutch astronomer Petrus Plancius, who created it from stars near Canis Major. It represents Noah's dove.

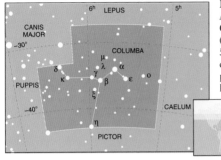

FEATURES OF INTEREST

Alpha (α) Columbae 👁
A blue-white star, 270 light-years away, of magnitude 2.6.

Mu (μ) Columbae 👁 📷
A so-called runaway star, moving through our Galaxy at unusually high speed, about 60 miles (100 km) per second. At least two fainter stars, 53 Arietis and AE Aurigae (not shown on the chart), seem to be diverging from the same point, south of Orion's belt. They might once have been part of a multiple star system that was disrupted when one of the stars exploded as a super-nova, 2–3 million years ago.

FULLY VISIBLE 46°N–90°S

Width	Height	Area 270 square degrees	Size ranking 54th

Abbreviation Com	Genitive Comae Berenices	Highest in sky at 10 pm April to May

COMA BERENICES

This constellation represents the hair of Queen Berenice of Egypt. According to legend, she cut off her locks to thank the gods for the safe return of her husband, King Ptolemy, from battle. It was formed in the 16th century by Gerardus Mercator, the Dutch cartographer, from a group of faint stars that the Greeks regarded as the tail of Leo. The galaxies in its southern region belong to the Virgo Cluster.

BERENICE'S HAIR

NGC 4565
A telescope of moderate size reveals the shape of this spiral galaxy, seen edge-on. A lane of dark dust runs across it.

FULLY VISIBLE
90°N–55°S

FEATURES OF INTEREST

M64 (The Black Eye Galaxy) 🔭 A spiral galaxy, visible through a small telescope as an elliptical haze. Larger apertures show a dark cloud of dust silhouetted against the galaxy's center, which gives rise to its popular name.

The Coma Star Cluster (Melotte 111) 👁 📷
An open cluster, consisting of a scattered group of stars stretching southward in a fan shape from Gamma (γ) Comae Berenices, its brightest member at magnitude 4.4. The cluster lies 260 light-years away.

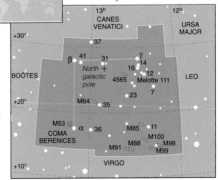

Width	Height	Area 386 square degrees	Size ranking 42nd

Abbreviation CrA	Genitive Coronae Australis	Highest in sky at 10 pm July to August

CORONA AUSTRALIS

The ancient Greeks visualized this small but pretty constellation as a wreath lying at the forefeet of Sagittarius. Its main feature is an arc of stars, distinctive even though the brightest is of only 4th magnitude.

THE SOUTHERN CROWN

FEATURES OF INTEREST

Gamma (γ) Coronae Australis ⚹ A close binary, divisible through a telescope with a moderate-sized aperture. The stars, both of 5th magnitude, orbit each other every 120 years. They lie 58 light-years away.

Kappa (κ) Coronae Australis ⚹ A double star, with components of magnitudes 5.7 and 6.3, easily divided with a small telescope.

NGC 6541 ♆⚹ A globular cluster, visible with a small telescope, or even binoculars. It covers an area about one-third the apparent size of the full Moon.

FULLY VISIBLE 44°N–90°S

Width 🖐	Height ✋	Area 128 square degrees	Size ranking 80th

Abbreviation CrB	Genitive Coronae Borealis	Highest in sky at 10 pm June

CORONA BOREALIS

Corona Borealis is a semicircular pattern lying between Boötes and Hercules. It depicts the crown worn by the mythical Princess Ariadne of Crete when she married the god Dionysius, who threw it into the sky, where its jewels turned into stars. Appropriately, its brightest star, Alpha (α) Coronae Borealis, magnitude 2.2, is named Gemma, Latin for "jewel."

THE NORTHERN CROWN

ARC OF CORONA BOREALIS
Seven stars form the Northern Crown.

FEATURES OF INTEREST

Zeta (ζ) Coronae Borealis ⚹ A double star, with components of magnitudes 5.0 and 6.0, divisible with a small telescope.

Nu (ν) Coronae Borealis ♆ A double star. Binoculars show the two stars, both red giants, of magnitudes 5.2 and 5.4; they lie about 550 light-years away but do not orbit each other.

R Coronae Borealis ♆⚹ An unusual variable star, usually of around 6th magnitude. It is a highly luminous yellow supergiant about 7,000 light-years away. Occasionally and unpredictably, it can fade within a few weeks to as faint as 15th magnitude, remaining there for some months before increasing in brightness again.

FULLY VISIBLE 90°N–50°S

Width 🖐	Height ✋	Area 179 square degrees	Size ranking 73rd

Abbreviation Crv	Genitive Corvi	Highest in sky at 10 pm April to May

CORVUS

This small constellation south of Virgo represents a crow perched on the coils of Hydra, the water-snake. In Greek mythology, the crow was sent by Apollo to fetch water in a cup (represented by the adjoining constellation of Crater), but greedily stopped to eat figs instead. On its return, the crow blamed the water-snake for delaying it. But Apollo, who was not fooled by the lie, condemned the crow to a life of thirst, just out of reach of the cup in the heavens. Its brightest star, Gamma (γ) Corvi, is of magnitude 2.6.

THE
CROW

FULLY VISIBLE
65°N–90°S

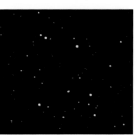

THE MAIN STARS IN CORVUS
Four bright stars in Corvus form a distinctive shape called a keystone. Beta (β) Corvi is at the bottom left.

FEATURES OF INTEREST

Delta (δ) Corvi ✯ A double star, with components of widely differing brightness. The brighter star, of magnitude 3.0, has a 9th-magnitude partner, which is visible through a small telescope.

NGC 4038 and 4039 (The Antennae) ✯
A famous pair of interacting galaxies. They are small and of 11th magnitude, so a telescope of moderate to large aperture is needed to see them. Long-exposure photographs show two streamers of stars and gas that extend from the colliding galaxies like the feelers of an insect, giving rise to the popular name.

Width 🖐	Height 🖐	Area 184 square degrees	Size ranking 70th

Abbreviation Crt	Genitive Crateris	Highest in sky at 10 pm April

CRATER

This undistinguished constellation represents a cup or chalice. In Greek myth, it is linked with its neighboring constellations, Corvus, the crow, and Hydra, the water-snake. Crater's brightest star is Delta (δ) Crateris, magnitude 3.6, but it contains no objects of interest for observers using small telescopes.

THE
CUP

FULLY VISIBLE
65°N–90°S

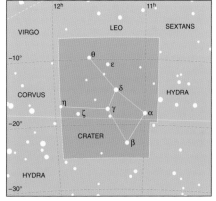

Width 🖐	Height 🖐	Area 282 square degrees	Size ranking 53rd

Abbreviation Cru	Genitive Crucis	Highest in sky at 10 pm April to May

CRUX

The smallest constellation in the sky, Crux covers a mere 5 percent of the area of the largest constellation, Hydra. Nevertheless, it is one of the most famous and easily recognized star patterns of all. To the ancient Greeks, its stars formed part of the hind legs of Centaurus, the centaur. Crux became a recognized constellation in its own right in the late 16th century as Europeans explored the southern oceans, although no one is credited with its invention. It lies in a brilliant region of the Milky Way. Its longer axis points to the south celestial pole.

THE SOUTHERN CROSS

FULLY VISIBLE
25°N–90°S

FEATURES OF INTEREST

Alpha (α) Crucis (Acrux) ◉ ♙ ⚹ A double star, appearing to the naked eye as a single object of magnitude 0.8, the 13th brightest star in the sky. A small telescope divides it into a glittering blue-white pair, of magnitudes 1.3 and 1.7. Both stars are 320 light-years away and probably form a true binary, although the orbital period is unknown. There is a much wider 5th-magnitude star, visible through binoculars, which is not related.

Beta (β) Crucis ◉ A blue-white giant, lying 350 light-years away. At magnitude 1.3, it is among the 20 brightest stars in the sky. It pulsates in size five times a day, varying by under a tenth of a magnitude as it does so, not enough to be noticeable to the naked eye.

THE SOUTHERN CROSS
The four brightest stars of Crux form a distinctive shape known as the Southern Cross. A fifth bright star, Epsilon (ε) Crucis, lies close to the center of the cross.

Width ᔐ	Height ᔐ	Area 68 square degrees	Size ranking 88th

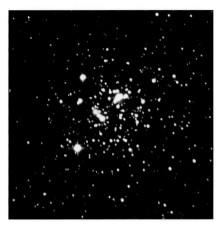

THE COALSACK
This dark cloud of dust, seen below and to the left of the cross-shape of Crux, is easy to see with the naked eye. The stars that are visible in this area lie between us and the nebula.

NGC 4755 (THE JEWEL BOX)
This sparkling open cluster was given its name in the 19th century by the English astronomer John Herschel, who described it as resembling a "casket of variously colored precious stones."

Gamma (γ) Crucis ◉ ♓ A wide optical double star. The brighter star is a red giant of magnitude 1.6, 88 light-years away. Binoculars show an unrelated 6th-magnitude companion, which is over three times more distant.

Iota (ι) Crucis ⚲ A wide double star, with components of magnitudes 4.7 and 9.5 that can be separated with a small telescope.

Mu (μ) Crucis ◉ ⚲ A wide optical double. A small telescope, or powerful binoculars, shows the two stars, of magnitudes 4.0 and 5.1. The fainter component is a rapidly rotating star that throws off rings of gas, causing occasional small variations in its brightness.

NGC 4755 (The Jewel Box, The Kappa (κ) Crucis cluster) ◉ ♓ ⚲ A magnificent open cluster, visible to the naked eye as a bright knot in the Milky Way between Beta (β) Crucis and the Coalsack. It is, in fact, far more distant than either of them, lying 7,600 light-years away. Binoculars or a small telescope show its individual stars, of 6th magnitude and fainter, covering an area of sky about one-third the apparent size of the full Moon. Most of its stars are blue-white super-giants, although near its center there is a prominent red supergiant of 8th magnitude. The star near the center of the cluster that is

actually designated Kappa (κ) Crucis is a blue-white supergiant of magnitude 5.9.

The Coalsack ◉ ♓ A prominent dark nebula, a wedge-shaped cloud of dust and gas about 600 light-years away that blots out the light from the stars in the Milky Way behind it. The Coalsack is large enough for 13 full Moons to be lined up across it. It has no NGC or other catalog number. Although the Coalsack lies mainly in Crux, it spills over the borders of Crux into Centaurus and Musca.

USING CRUX TO LOCATE THE
SOUTH CELESTIAL POLE
The south celestial pole lies roughly at the intersection of two imaginary lines. One is formed by extending the line between Alpha (α) and Gamma (γ) Crucis (top of picture); the other lies at right angles to a line joining Alpha (α) and Beta (β) Centauri (bottom).

Abbreviation Cyg	Genitive Cygni	Highest in sky at 10 pm August to September

CYGNUS

This large constellation depicts the swan into which, according
to Greek myth, the god Zeus transformed himself for one of his
illicit love trysts. One story says that the object of his desire was
Queen Leda of Sparta, and that their union produced either one
or two eggs, from which hatched the twins Castor and Pollux,
as well as Helen of Troy. The swan's beak is marked by Beta
(β) Cygni and its tail by Alpha (α) Cygni, named Deneb
(from an Arabic word meaning "tail"). Deneb forms one
corner of the Summer Triangle, with Vega (in Lyra) and
Altair (in Aquila) marking the other two. Since it is also
identifiable by its cross-shape, Cygnus is sometimes called
the Northern Cross. It lies in a rich part of the Milky Way.

THE
SWAN

FULLY VISIBLE
90°N–28°S

FEATURES OF INTEREST

Alpha (α) Cygni (Deneb) ◉ The brightest
star in Cygnus, at magnitude 1.3. It is a
luminous blue-white supergiant lying more
than 3,000 light-years away, which makes it
the most distant of all first-magnitude stars.

Beta (β) Cygni (Albireo) ♁ ⚹ A beautiful
double star. The two stars, magnitudes 3.1 and
5.1, can be divided with powerful binoculars.
They are easy to separate with a telescope,
through which they present a striking contrast
of orange and blue-green. Both stars lie about
380 light-years away, but it is not known
whether they form a true binary.

CYGNUS (INSET: ALBIREO)
*Cygnus, the swan, forms a large cross-shape in the
northern Milky Way. The star marking the head of the
swan (or the foot of the cross) is Albireo, a beautiful
double star, divisible with a small telescope.*

Width ✋✋	Height ✋✋	Area 804 square degrees	Size ranking 16th

NGC 7000 (THE NORTH AMERICA NEBULA)
This large nebula can be found between Deneb and Xi (ξ) Cygni. Its resemblance to the outline of the North American continent is evident in this photograph; a dark inlet similar in shape to the Gulf of Mexico can be made out at the bottom of the picture. The nebula is a bright cloud of gas, which is thought to be lit up by a partially obscured star within it.

Omicron-1 (o¹) Cygni (31 Cygni) ♠ ⟁ An orange-colored giant, magnitude 3.8, which has a wide 5th-magnitude, bluish companion (30 Cygni), ideal for binocular observation. A closer bluish star of 7th magnitude is also visible with binoculars or a small telescope.

Chi (χ) Cygni ◉ ♠ A pulsating red giant, one of the Mira class of variable stars, that ranges in brightness between 3rd and 14th magnitudes every 13 months or so.

61 Cygni ⟁ An attractive double star. The two components, of magnitudes 5.2 and 6.1, can be seen separately through a small telescope or even powerful binoculars. Both are orange dwarfs, smaller and fainter than the Sun, and are easily visible only because they are relatively close to us, 11.4 light-years away. They orbit each other every 650 years.

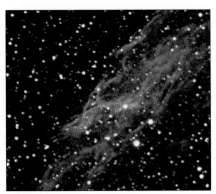

NGC 6992 (THE VEIL NEBULA)
The Veil Nebula, in the southern part of Cygnus, is the wispy remnant of an exploded star.

M39 ♠ ⟁ An open cluster, just visible to the naked eye under good conditions. Binoculars or a small telescope show its brightest stars. It covers the same area of sky as the full Moon, and lies nearly 900 light-years away.

NGC 6826 (The Blinking Planetary) ⟁ A planetary nebula visible with a small telescope as a bluish disk of similar size to the disk of Jupiter. Looking alternately at it and to one side gives the impression that it is blinking on and off, which explains its popular name.

NGC 6992 (The Veil Nebula) ♠ ⟁ Part of a large, complex nebula called the Cygnus Loop which is the remains of a star that exploded as a supernova perhaps 50,000 years ago. In clear skies, the Veil Nebula section can be seen with binoculars or a small telescope, but the whole nebula is best seen on photographs.

NGC 7000 (The North America Nebula) ♠ ⟁ A large nebula, visible under dark skies with binoculars or a wide-field telescope, extending for up to four Moon diameters. It is best seen on long-exposure photographs, where it takes the shape of the continent of North America, hence its popular name.

Cygnus A ♻ A peculiar galaxy, thought to be two distant galaxies in collision. A large telescope is needed to see it, as it is of 15th magnitude. It is also a strong radio source.

Cygnus X-1 ♻ A possible black hole, and one of the strongest X-ray sources in the sky. It appears optically as a 9th-magnitude blue supergiant, about 8,000 light-years away. The X rays come from an invisible companion, which orbits the supergiant every 5.6 days. This companion is the supposed black hole.

Abbreviation Del	Genitive Delphini	Highest in sky at 10 pm August to September

DELPHINUS

This small but distinctive constellation is tucked in
between Aquila and Pegasus. Delphinus is associated
with two different Greek myths. According to one
account, it represents the dolphin sent by Poseidon,
the sea god, to fetch Amphitrite, a sea nymph, to be his bride.
It has also been identified as the dolphin that saved Arion, a
poet and musician, when he was attacked on board a ship by
a gang of robbers. The constellation's two brightest stars are
Alpha (α) and Beta (β) Delphini, magnitudes 3.8 and 3.6
respectively. These stars bear the unusual names Sualocin
and Rotanev. When written backward, the names spell
Nicolaus Venator. This is the Latinized version of Niccolò
Cacciatore, an astronomer at Palermo Observatory, Italy,
who named the stars after himself in the early 19th century.

THE
DOLPHIN

THE MAIN STARS IN DELPHINUS
*The attractive shape of Delphinus
represents a leaping dolphin. Four
stars at the top left of this picture
form the shape called Job's Coffin.*

FULLY VISIBLE
90°N–69°S

FEATURES OF INTEREST

Job's Coffin 👁 ♙ A name given to the box
shape formed by the four stars Alpha (α), Beta
(β), Gamma (γ), and Delta (δ) Delphini, all of
which are of 4th magnitude.

Gamma (γ) Delphini ≯ A double star.
A small telescope will separate the two
components, which appear yellow and white,
of magnitudes 4.3 and 5.2. Both stars lie
approximately 100 light-years away. A fainter
and closer pair of 8th-magnitude stars, known
as Struve 2725 (about 125 light-years away),
should be visible in the same field of view.

NOVA DELPHINI
*This nova is now very faint, but in 1967 (when this
photograph was taken) it flared to naked-eye visibility.*

Width 🖐	Height 🖐	Area 189 square degrees	Size ranking 69th

Abbreviation Dor	Genitive Doradus	Highest in sky at 10 pm December to January

DORADO

Dorado, one of several southern constellations representing exotic creatures, was introduced in the late 16th century by the Dutch navigators Pieter Dirkszoon Keyser and Frederick de Houtman. It represents not the goldfish found in ornamental ponds but the dolphinfish of tropical seas, a member of the family Coryphaenidae. It has also been depicted as a swordfish. For astronomers, Dorado is significant because it contains the bulk of the Large Magellanic Cloud, our nearest neighboring galaxy. Its brightest star is Alpha (α) Doradus, magnitude 3.3.

THE "GOLDFISH" OR SWORDFISH

FULLY VISIBLE 20°N–90°S

NGC 2070 (THE TARANTULA NEBULA)
Loops of glowing gas extending from the Tarantula Nebula give it the appearance of a large spider.

FEATURES OF INTEREST

Beta (β) Doradus 👁 A bright Cepheid variable, ranging between magnitudes 3.5 and 4.1 every 9.8 days. It is a yellow-white super-giant and lies about 1,000 light-years away.

NGC 2070 (The Tarantula Nebula)
👁 A bright nebula in the Large Magellanic Cloud (see below), visible to the naked eye. It appears about the the same size as the full Moon, but its true diameter is about 800 light-years, making it far larger than the Orion Nebula. The nebula is a star-forming region, and binoculars or a small telescope reveal a star cluster, 30 Doradus, at its center.

Supernova 1987A ✤ The brightest super-nova visible from Earth since 1604. In 1987 it flared up in the Large Magellanic Cloud, near the Tarantula Nebula, reaching magnitude 2.8 at its brightest. It remained visible to the naked eye for 10 months.

The Large Magellanic Cloud (LMC)
👁 A small galaxy, a satellite of our own, lying 170,000 light-years away. It resembles a detached part of the Milky Way, somewhat elongated in shape. It has about one-tenth the mass of our Galaxy and a true diameter of 20,000 light-years. It is usually classified as an irregular galaxy, but there are traces of a barred spiral structure. Scanning across it with binoculars or a small telescope brings numerous star clusters and glowing nebulae into view. The largest and brightest nebula is NGC 2070, also known as the Tarantula Nebula (see above).

Width 🖐	Height 🖐	Area 179 square degrees	Size ranking 72nd

Abbreviation Dra	Genitive Draconis	Highest in sky at 10 pm March to September

DRACO

This extensive constellation of the far-northern sky winds around Ursa Minor. It represents the dragon that in Greek mythology guarded the golden apples of the Hesperides, the daughters of Atlas, and which was slain by Hercules as one of his labors. In the sky, Hercules is represented with one foot on the dragon's head. Despite its considerable size, Draco contains no really prominent stars, the brightest being Gamma (γ) Draconis, magnitude 2.2, a red giant about 150 light-years away. With the stars Beta (β), Nu (ν), and Xi (ξ) Draconis, it forms a lozenge shape that marks the head of the dragon. The constellation is noted chiefly for its double stars.

THE
DRAGON

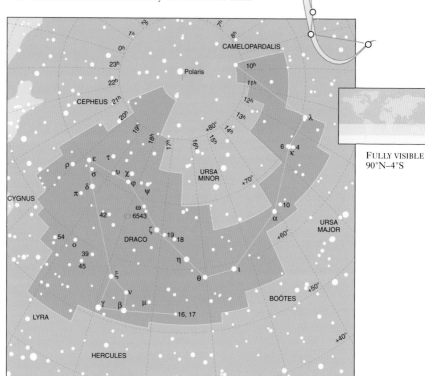

FULLY VISIBLE
90°N–4°S

FEATURES OF INTEREST

Mu (μ) Draconis ⚹ A double star with components that are too close be separated with a small telescope. An aperture of at least 3 in (75 mm), with high magnification, will usually be needed to see the two 6th-magnitude stars. They are 88 light-years away and orbit each other every 480 years.

Nu (ν) Draconis ♍⚹ A wide double star with twin white 5th-magnitude components that are virtually identical in color and brightness. The pair form an excellent sight through binoculars and are easy to see with the smallest telescopes. Both stars lie 100 light-years away.

Width	Height	Area 1,083 square degrees	Size ranking 8th

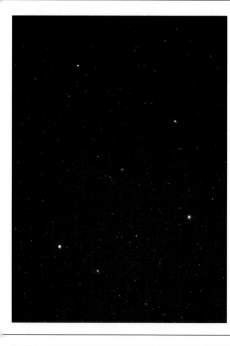

Psi (ψ) Draconis ♊ ✶ A double star, easy to divide through a small telescope. The two components of magnitudes 4.6 and 5.8 may even be divided with powerful binoculars.

16 and 17 Draconis ♊ ✶ A multiple star. Binoculars show a wide double with 5th- and 6th-magnitude components. A telescope with high magnification reveals that the brighter star, 17 Draconis, is itself a close double.

39 Draconis ♊ ✶ A multiple star. Through a small telescope, or even binoculars, it appears as a wide pair of 5th- and 8th-magnitude stars. Examination of the brighter star under high magnification will show a much closer star, also of 8th magnitude.

NGC 6543 ✶ A planetary nebula visible with a small telescope. It appears as a bluish disk of similar size to the globe of Saturn.

THE HEAD OF DRACO
A group of four stars represents the head of Draco. The brightest of them, at the lower left in this photograph, is Gamma (γ) Draconis.

Abbreviation Equ	Genitive Equulei	Highest in sky at 10 pm September

EQUULEUS

The second smallest constellation in the sky, Equuleus represents a small horse that lies next to Pegasus, the well-known flying horse. It first appeared among the 48 constellations described by the Greek astronomer Ptolemy, but there appear to be no legends about it. Its brightest star is Alpha (α) Equulei, magnitude 3.9.

THE
LITTLE HORSE
OR FOAL

FULLY VISIBLE
90°N–77°S

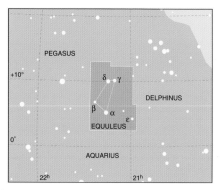

FEATURES OF INTEREST

Gamma (γ) Equulei ♊ An optical double star, divisible with binoculars. It consists of a star of magnitude 4.7 with a very wide companion, 6 Equulei, of magnitude 6.1.

Epsilon (ε) Equulei ✶ A multiple star. A small telescope shows it as a double with components of magnitudes 5.2 and 7.4. The brighter star is, in fact, a binary with an orbital period of 100 years, but the stars are too close together to be separated with a small aperture.

Width ⬠	Height ⬠	Area 72 square degrees	Size ranking 87th

Abbreviation Eri	Genitive Eridani	Highest in sky at 10 pm November to January

ERIDANUS

This long, straggling constellation represents a river in Greek mythology. The River Eridanus features in the story of Phaethon, who fell into it after a disastrous attempt to drive the chariot of his father, the sun-god Helios. The constellation extends for nearly 60 degrees from north to south, the greatest range in declination of any constellation.

THE RIVER

FULLY VISIBLE
32°N–89°S

OMICRON-2 (o²) ERIDANI

All three components of this multiple star are visible in this telescopic view. The primary is in the center with the two dwarf stars, overlapping each other, to its right.

FEATURES OF INTEREST

Alpha (α) Eridani (Achernar) ◉ A blue-white star of magnitude 0.5, the brightest star in Eridanus and the ninth brightest in the sky. It lies 140 light-years away. Its name, Achernar, is of Arabic origin, meaning "river's end," and the star marks the constellation's southernmost tip. Nearby is p Eridani, a wide pair of 6th-magnitude stars visible with a small telescope.

Width ⛏⛏	Height ⛏⛏⛏	Area 1,138 square degrees	Size ranking 6th

Epsilon (ε) Eridani One of the closest naked-eye stars to the Sun. It is 10.5 light-years distant and appears of magnitude 3.7. Although somewhat cooler and fainter than the Sun, it is otherwise similar.

Theta (θ) Eridani An attractive double star. The two components, twin white stars of magnitudes 3.2 and 4.3, can be separated with a small telescope.

Omicron-2 (o²) Eridani (40 Eridani) A multiple star with three components, including a red dwarf and a white dwarf together. The brightest of the trio, magnitude 4.4, is similar to the Sun. A small telescope shows that this star has a 10th-magnitude companion, which is the white dwarf; this is the easiest white dwarf to see with small instruments. It forms a binary with an 11th-magnitude red dwarf, although a larger aperture may be needed to spot this. This remarkable trio lies 16.5 light-years away.

32 Eridani A double star with components of contrasting colors. A small telescope reveals a red giant of magnitude 4.8 and a blue-white companion of magnitude 6.1.

THE SOUTHERN TIP OF ERIDANUS
A small part of this large constellation can be seen here. Achernar is just above the horizon, while Chi (χ) and Phi (φ) Eridani are below and just to the left of center.

Abbreviation For	Genitive Fornacis	Highest in sky at 10 pm November to December

FORNAX

Fornax is an undistinguished constellation in an unremarkable area of sky. It lies on the shores of the celestial river Eridanus and the southern border of Cetus. Invented in the 18th century by the French astronomer Nicolas Louis de Lacaille, it represents a chemical furnace.

THE
FURNACE

FULLY VISIBLE
50°N–90°S

FEATURES OF INTEREST

Alpha (α) Fornacis The brightest star in the constellation, appearing to the naked eye as a single star of magnitude 3.8. A small telescope shows that it has a 7th-magnitude companion. The two stars form a true binary, orbiting each other every 300 years or so. They lie 46 light-years away from the Earth.

The Fornax Cluster A cluster of galaxies about 75 million light-years away, the brightest of which, notably NGC 1316 and NGC 1365, can be seen with a small telescope. NGC 1316 is a peculiar spiral, also known as radio source Fornax A. NGC 1365 is a barred spiral.

Width	Height	Area 398 square degrees	Size ranking 41st

Abbreviation Gem	Genitive Geminorum	Highest in sky at 10 pm January to February

GEMINI

A constellation of the zodiac, Gemini depicts the mythological twins Castor and Pollux, after whom its two brightest stars are named. The twins sailed with the Argonauts in search of the golden fleece, and they were later regarded by the ancient Greeks as patrons of seafarers. The two stars themselves are not related, though, lying at different distances from us. Gemini sits between Taurus and Cancer, and the Sun passes through it from June 21 to July 20.

THE
TWINS

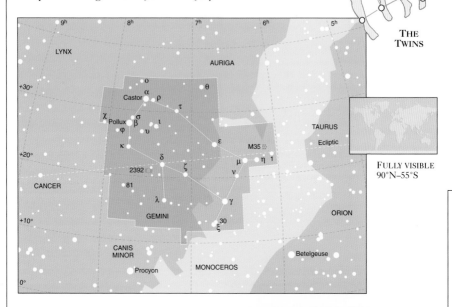

FULLY VISIBLE
90°N–55°S

FEATURES OF INTEREST

Alpha (α) Geminorum (Castor) 👁 ✴

A remarkable multiple star. To the naked eye, it appears as a single star of magnitude 1.6. A small telescope divides it into a blue-white pair of stars of magnitudes 1.9 and 2.9. These form a genuine binary with an orbital period of about 470 years. Both of these stars are spectroscopic binaries. A wider companion of 9th magnitude can also be seen with a small telescope. This is, in fact, a close pair of red dwarfs, forming an eclipsing binary. The whole six-star family is just over 50 light-years away.

CASTOR AND POLLUX
The two brightest stars in Gemini are Castor (top right) and Pollux (bottom left). Although it has been assigned the letter Beta (β), Pollux is actually the brighter star.

Width 🖐🤏🤏	Height 🖐🤏🤏	Area 514 square degrees	Size ranking 30th

Beta (β) Geminorum (Pollux) ◉ ♪ The brightest star in the constellation and among the 20 brightest in the sky, at magnitude 1.2. It is an orange-colored giant, 34 light-years away. The coloration is more noticeable when the star is viewed through binoculars.

Zeta (ζ) Geminorum ◉ ♪ A Cepheid variable star, ranging between magnitudes 3.6 and 4.2 in a cycle lasting just over 10 days. It is a yellow supergiant, about 1,200 light-years away. Binoculars show a wide 8th-magnitude companion, which is unrelated.

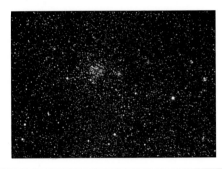

Eta (η) Geminorum ◉ ♪ A variable red giant about 350 light-years away. It pulsates in size in a cycle lasting about 8 months, varying between magnitudes 3.2 and 3.9 as it does so.

M35 ♪ ✶ A rich open cluster, just visible to the naked eye and easy to see with binoculars. It appears almost as large as the full Moon. Binoculars or a small telescope resolve its individual stars of 8th magnitude and fainter. The cluster lies nearly 3,000 light-years away.

NGC 2392 (The Clown-Face Nebula, The Eskimo Nebula) ✶ A planetary nebula. Its bluish disk, similar in size to the globe of Saturn, is visible through a small telescope, but large apertures are needed to detect the surrounding features that lend it the appearance of a face and give rise to its popular names.

M35
The open cluster M35, discernible at the center of this photograph with Iota (ι) Geminorum to its lower right, contains about 200 stars. Inspection with a telescope reveals that the stars are arranged in curved lines.

Abbreviation Gru	Genitive Gruis	Highest in sky at 10 pm September to October

GRUS

Grus is one of the dozen southern constellations introduced at the end of the 16th century by the Dutch navigators Pieter Dirkszoon Keyser and Frederick de Houtman. It represents the long-necked wading bird of the family Gruidae. Its brightest star is Alpha (α) Gruis, known as Al Na'ir, magnitude 1.7.

THE CRANE

FULLY VISIBLE
33°N–90°S

FEATURES OF INTEREST

Beta (β) Gruis ◉ A variable red giant, 170 light-years away, that fluctuates from magnitude 2.0 to 2.3 with no set period.

Delta (δ) Gruis ◉ A double star with components that can be separated with the naked eye. Both stars lie about 300 light-years away. Delta-1 is a yellow giant of magnitude 4.0; Delta-2 is a red giant of magnitude 4.1.

Mu (μ) Gruis ◉ ♪ A wide naked-eye double. Both stars are yellow giants: Mu-1 (μ^1), 260 light-years distant, is of magnitude 4.8; Mu-2 (μ^2), 240 light-years away, is of magnitude 5.1.

Width	Height	Area 366 square degrees	Size ranking 45th

Abbreviation Her	Genitive Herculis	Highest in sky at 10 pm June to August

HERCULES

A large but not prominent constellation depicting the hero of Greek myth, Hercules lies between the bright stars Arcturus and Vega. The body of Hercules is inverted in the sky, the head being marked by Alpha (α) Herculis, in the south, and the feet by the stars to the north. Hercules was ordered by King Eurystheus of Mycenae to perform 12 labors, one of which was to slay a dragon (marked by adjacent Draco). Hercules is depicted resting on his right knee, with his left foot on the dragon's head. The constellation features the brightest globular cluster in northern skies, M13, and some notable double stars. Its brightest star is Beta (β) Herculis, magnitude 2.8.

HERCULES

FULLY VISIBLE
90°N–38°S

FEATURES OF INTEREST

Alpha (α) Herculis (Rasalgethi) 👁 ⚹
A red giant of variable brightness. It ranges between 3rd and 4th magnitudes, with no set period, as a result of fluctuations in its size. A small telescope shows a companion of magnitude 5.4. Hercules is depicted kneeling, and the name Rasalgethi is derived from an Arabic term meaning "the kneeler's head."

Rho (ρ) Herculis ⚹ An optical double star. The two components of magnitudes 4.6 and 5.4 can be separated using a small telescope with high magnification.

95 Herculis ⚹ A silver and gold pair of stars of magnitudes 5.0 and 5.2, divisible through a small telescope.

100 Herculis ⚹ A pair of almost identical white stars, both of magnitude 5.8, that can be separated with a small telescope. The two stars do not form a true binary.

Width 🖐🖐	Height 🖐🖐🖐	Area 1,225 square degrees	Size ranking 5th

M13 ◉ ♁ ✹ The brightest globular cluster in the northern sky. Under dark skies, it appears to the naked eye like a hazy star. Binoculars show it clearly, about half the apparent width of the full Moon, and a small telescope shows its brightest stars. It is 23,500 light-years away.

M92 ♁ ✹ A globular cluster, fainter and smaller than M13 but still worthy of attention. Binoculars are needed to find it, and a telescope of moderate aperture will show its stars.

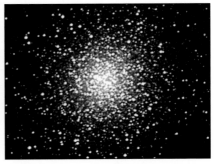

HERCULES, INCLUDING THE KEYSTONE
Pi (π), Eta (η), Zeta (ζ), and Epsilon (ε) Herculis (at the center of this picture) form a four-sided figure called the Keystone that marks the pelvis of Hercules.

M13
This spectacular cluster lies on one side of the Keystone, a third of the way between Eta (η) and Zeta (ζ) Herculis. It contains hundreds of thousands of stars.

Abbreviation Hor	Genitive Horologii	Highest in sky at 10 pm November to December

HOROLOGIUM

This unrenowned southern constellation, invented in the 18th century by the French astronomer Nicolas Louis de Lacaille, lies between the bright stars Achernar and Canopus. It represents a pendulum clock, with its brightest star, Alpha (α) Horologii (magnitude 3.9), marking the pendulum weight.

THE PENDULUM CLOCK

FEATURES OF INTEREST

R Horologii ♁ ✹ A variable red giant of the type known as a Mira star. It ranges between 5th and 14th magnitudes every 13 months or so.

TW Horologii ♁ A variable red giant. Over a period of approximately five or six months, it ranges between about 5th and 6th magnitudes.

FULLY VISIBLE
23°N–90°S

Width 〽	Height 〽	Area 249 square degrees	Size ranking 58th

Abbreviation Hya	Genitive Hydrae	Highest in sky at 10 pm February to June

HYDRA

Despite being the largest of all the 88 constellations, Hydra is far from prominent. Its head, formed by a loop of six stars of 3rd and 4th magnitudes, lies just north of the celestial equator under Cancer, while the tip of its tail is 90 degrees away between Libra and Centaurus. In Greek mythology, Hydra was a multiheaded monster slain by Hercules as one of his 12 labors. During the fight, Hercules was attacked by a crab, represented by the constellation Cancer. Hydra is also linked with a moral tale involving a crow sent to fetch a cup of water; the crow and cup are depicted by the constellations Corvus and Crater, which are represented lying on Hydra's back.

THE WATER-SNAKE

FULLY VISIBLE
54°N–83°S

M83
The bright core and spiral arms of this galaxy, seen face-on from Earth, are visible on photographs and digital images such as this one taken using a CCD camera.

FEATURES OF INTEREST

Alpha (α) Hydrae (Alphard) 👁 An orange-colored giant about 175 light-years away. The name Alphard comes from an Arabic term that means "the solitary one." It is an apt name because, at magnitude 2.0, Alphard is the only star in Hydra brighter than 3rd magnitude.

Epsilon (ε) Hydrae 🔭 A double star. A telescope of moderate aperture is needed to split the two close components of magnitudes 3.4 and 6.5, which orbit each other every 900 years or so. They lie 135 light-years away.

R Hydrae 👁🖐🔭 A variable red giant of the Mira type that ranges between 3rd and 11th magnitudes every 13 months or so.

U Hydrae 🖐 A variable red giant that fluctuates between 4th and 6th magnitudes

with little regularity as the star changes in size. It lies about 530 light-years away.

M48 🖐🔭 An open cluster, just visible to the naked eye under good conditions but best seen with binoculars or a wide-field telescope. It is larger in apparent size than the full Moon and lies nearly 2,000 light-years away.

M83 🔭 A spiral galaxy that appears face-on to us, so that its arms are clearly visible through a large-aperture telescope and on photographs. When viewed through a small telescope, it appears as a rounded patch.

NGC 3242 (The Ghost of Jupiter) 🔭
A planetary nebula, visible through a small telescope as a bluish, planetlike disk, hence its popular name.

Width 🖐🖐🖐🖐	Height 🖐🖐	Area 1,303 square degrees	Size ranking 1st

Abbreviation Hyi	Genitive Hydri	Highest in sky at 10 pm October to December

HYDRUS

This constellation of the far-southern skies was invented in the late 16th century by the Dutch navigators Pieter Dirkszoon Keyser and Frederick de Houtman. Lying between the bright star Achernar and the south celestial pole, it depicts a small water-snake. It should not be confused with the large water-snake, Hydra, known since the time of the ancient Greeks. The constellation's brightest star is Beta (β) Hydri, magnitude 2.8.

FULLY VISIBLE
8°N–90°S

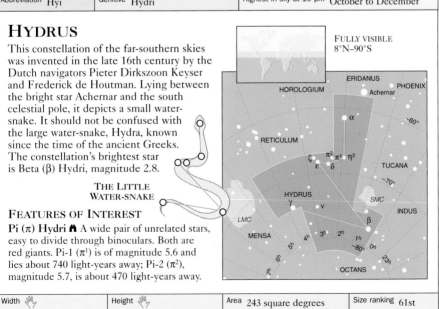

THE LITTLE WATER-SNAKE

FEATURES OF INTEREST

Pi (π) Hydri 🄼 A wide pair of unrelated stars, easy to divide through binoculars. Both are red giants. Pi-1 (π¹) is of magnitude 5.6 and lies about 740 light-years away; Pi-2 (π²), magnitude 5.7, is about 470 light-years away.

Width 🖐	Height 🖐	Area 243 square degrees	Size ranking 61st

Abbreviation Ind	Genitive Indi	Highest in sky at 10 pm August to October

INDUS

THE INDIAN

This southern constellation, lying between Pavo and Tucana, was introduced in the late 16th century by the Dutch navigators Pieter Dirkszoon Keyser and Frederick de Houtman. It depicts a native Indian, although from exactly where remains unclear; on old maps, the figure is shown holding arrows and a spear. Indus's brightest star, Alpha (α) Indi, is of magnitude 3.1.

FEATURES OF INTEREST

Epsilon (ε) Indi 👁 Among the nearest stars to us, Epsilon Indi is only 11.8 light-years away and has a magnitude of 4.7. It is a somewhat smaller and cooler star than the Sun.

Theta (θ) Indi ➤ A double star consisting of components of magnitudes 4.5 and 6.9 that are visible through a small telescope.

FULLY VISIBLE
15°N–90°S

Width 〰	Height 〰🖐	Area 294 square degrees	Size ranking 49th

Abbreviation Lac	Genitive Lacertae	Highest in sky at 10 pm September to October

LACERTA

THE LIZARD

Lacerta is a small and insignificant constellation of the northern sky on the edge of the Milky Way, sandwiched between Cygnus and Andromeda. It was introduced in the 17th century by the Polish astronomer Johannes Hevelius. Its brightest star is Alpha (α) Lacertae, magnitude 3.8. Three naked-eye novas have erupted within its boundaries during the 20th century.

FULLY VISIBLE
90°N–33°S

FEATURES OF INTEREST

BL Lacertae ♟ The nucleus of a distant elliptical galaxy, originally classified as a variable star, hence its designation. It has given its name to a class of similar objects, the BL Lacertae (or BL Lac) objects, which are thought to be galaxies with powerful energy sources, perhaps massive black holes, at their centers. BL Lacertae varies between about 12th and 16th magnitudes.

Width 🖐	Height 〰	Area 201 square degrees	Size ranking 68th

| Abbreviation Leo | Genitive Leonis | Highest in sky at 10 pm March to April |

LEO

This large, impressive constellation depicts a crouching lion. In Greek myth, this was the lion that Hercules killed as one of his 12 labors. Leo is a constellation of the zodiac, lying between Cancer and Virgo. The Sun passes through it from August 10 to September 16.

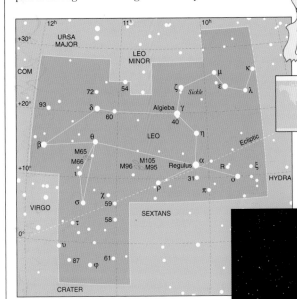

THE LION

FULLY VISIBLE
82°N–57°S

THE MAIN STARS IN LEO
Leo's main stars form a shape that closely resembles the outline of a crouching lion. Regulus and the Sickle are at the right of the picture.

FEATURES OF INTEREST

The Sickle ◉ An easily recognizable pattern of six stars, shaped like a reversed question mark or a hook, which forms the head and chest of the lion. It consists of the stars Epsilon (ε), Mu (μ), Zeta (ζ), Gamma (γ), Eta (η), and Alpha (α) Leonis.

Alpha (α) Leonis (Regulus) ◉ ♙ ☇ The faintest of the first-magnitude stars, magnitude 1.4. It is a blue-white star about 77 light-years away. Binoculars or a small telescope show that it has a wide companion of 8th magnitude.

Gamma (γ) Leonis (Algieba) ☇ A glorious double star consisting of two golden orange giants of magnitudes 2.4 and 3.5, which make an excellent sight through a small telescope. They are a genuine binary pair, orbiting each other every 600 years or so. Binoculars (or even sharp eyesight) show a much wider 5th-magnitude star, 40 Leonis, which is unrelated.

Zeta (ζ) Leonis ♙ A wide triple formed by unrelated stars. Zeta itself is of magnitude 3.4. Binoculars show a 6th-magnitude star, 35 Leonis, to its north. Farther south is 39 Leonis, also of 6th magnitude.

R Leonis ♙ ☇ A red-giant Mira variable ranging in brightness between about 4th and 11th magnitudes every 10 months or so.

M65 and M66 ☇ Two 9th-magnitude spiral galaxies visible with a small telescope. Being tilted at an angle to us, they appear elliptical.

M95 and M96 ☇ A pair of spiral galaxies visible through a small telescope as elongated smudges. They lie at similar distances to M65 and M66, namely 20–25 million light-years.

| Width 〰〰 | Height 〰〰 | Area 947 square degrees | Size ranking 12th |

Abbreviation LMi	Genitive Leonis Minoris	Highest in sky at 10 pm March to April

LEO MINOR

This faint constellation, representing a lion cub, is squeezed between Leo and Ursa Major. It was invented in the 17th century by Johannes Hevelius. Its brightest star is 46 Leonis Minoris, magnitude 3.8, but it contains little to interest owners of small instruments.

THE LESSER LION

FULLY VISIBLE 90°N–48°S

FEATURES OF INTEREST

Beta (β) Leonis Minoris ♟ A close double star. It appears to the naked eye as a single star of magnitude 4.2, and its components can be separated only through a telescope of very large aperture. The two stars, which are 145 light-years away, have an orbital period of 37 years. This is the only star in the constellation to have been assigned a Greek letter.

Width 🖐	Height 🖐	Area 232 square degrees	Size ranking 64th

Abbreviation Lep	Genitive Leporis	Highest in sky at 10 pm January

LEPUS

THE HARE

Lepus lies under the feet of Orion, the hunter, and is pursued across the sky by his dog Canis Major. The constellation was known to the ancient Greeks. Its brightest star is Alpha (α) Leporis, magnitude 2.6, whose name, Arneb, comes from an Arabic term meaning "the hare."

FULLY VISIBLE 62°N–90°S

FEATURES OF INTEREST

Gamma (γ) Leporis ♟ A double star with components of magnitudes 3.6 and 6.2 that are visible through binoculars. Both stars are at a similar distance from us, about 30 light-years.

R Leporis ♟✸ A Mira variable noted for its deep red color. It ranges from about 6th to 12th magnitude every 14 months or so.

M79 ✸ A small globular cluster of 8th magnitude, visible with a small telescope. It lies about 40,000 light-years away. In the same field of view is a triple star called h3752 (the h stands for John Herschel, who first cataloged it). This consists of a close pair

of stars of 5th and 7th magnitudes, with a wider companion of 9th magnitude.

NGC 2017 ✸ A small star cluster, the main members of which are cataloged as the multiple star h3780. A small telescope reveals a 6th-magnitude star with four companions of 8th to 10th magnitude. A larger aperture will separate two of the components into close doubles, and there is also a fainter 12th-magnitude star that completes the group.

Width 🖐	Height 🖐	Area 290 square degrees	Size ranking 51st

Abbreviation Lib	Genitive Librae	Highest in sky at 10 pm May to June

LIBRA

A constellation of the zodiac, Libra lies just south of the celestial equator, between Virgo and Scorpius. Originally it was seen to represent the claws of Scorpius, the scorpion, which is why its brightest stars have names that mean the northern and southern claw. Libra was first visualized as a balance by the Romans over 2,000 years ago, and it is now usually depicted as the scales held by the adjacent figure of Virgo, who is seen as the goddess of justice. The Sun passes through Libra from October 31 to November 23.

THE
SCALES

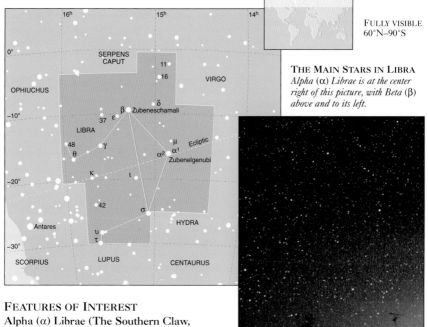

FULLY VISIBLE
60°N–90°S

THE MAIN STARS IN LIBRA
Alpha (α) Librae is at the center right of this picture, with Beta (β) above and to its left.

FEATURES OF INTEREST

Alpha (α) Librae (The Southern Claw, Zubenelgenubi) ◉ � A wide double star. The two components of magnitudes 2.8 and 5.2 can be separated with binoculars or even good eyesight.

Beta (β) Librae (The Northern Claw, Zubeneschamali) ♓ The constellation's brightest star, at magnitude 2.6. It is said by some observers to have a greenish tinge, which is highly unusual. Binoculars or a small telescope should reveal its color.

Delta (δ) Librae ♓ An eclipsing binary of the same type as Algol (in Perseus). Its variations in magnitude, from 4.9 to 5.9 over 2 days 8 hours, are easy to follow through binoculars.

Iota (ι) Librae ♓ A complex multiple star appearing to the naked eye as a single star of magnitude 4.5. Binoculars show a wide 6th-magnitude companion, 25 Librae. A telescope with an aperture of 3 in (75 mm) or more shows that the primary has a 9th-magnitude partner. High magnification should reveal that this fainter companion is itself a close pair.

Mu (μ) Librae ♓ A double star with components of magnitudes 5.7 and 6.7. A telescope with an aperture of about 3 in (75 mm) is needed to separate them.

Width 🖐️🤚	Height 🖐️🤚	Area 538 square degrees	Size ranking 29th

Abbreviation Lup	Genitive Lupi	Highest in sky at 10 pm May to June

LUPUS

Lupus lies in the Milky Way to the south of Libra. It represents a wolf that in Greek and Roman times was visualized as being held on a pole by a centaur, depicted by the adjacent Centaurus. It seems, however, that there are no myths specifically about the wolf. Lupus's brightest star is Alpha (α) Lupi, magnitude 2.3.

THE
WOLF

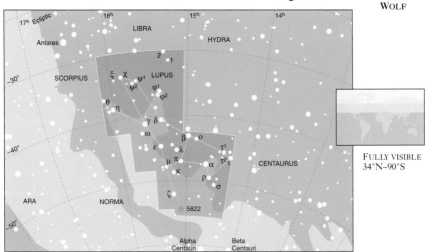

FULLY VISIBLE
34°N–90°S

FEATURES OF INTEREST

Kappa (κ) Lupi ✷ A double star. The unrelated components of magnitudes 3.9 and 5.7 are easy to divide with a small telescope.

Mu (μ) Lupi ✷ A multiple star. With a small telescope, it appears as a wide double star with components of magnitudes 4.3 and 6.9. An aperture of 4 in (100 mm) or more with high magnification shows that the primary is, in fact, a close pair of 5th-magnitude stars.

Xi (ξ) Lupi ✷ A double star. Its components of magnitudes 5.1 and 5.6 can be separated with a small telescope.

Pi (π) Lupi ✷ A matching pair of 5th-magnitude blue-white stars. A telescope with an aperture of 3 in (75 mm) or more is needed to see them separately.

NGC 5822 ♠✷ A rich open cluster of similar apparent size to the full Moon. Visible with binoculars or a small telescope, it contains over 100 faint stars and lies 1,800 light-years away.

NGC 5822
This large open cluster is shown here as it would look through a small telescope.

Width 🖐	Height 🖐🖐	Area 334 square degrees	Size ranking 46th

| Abbreviation Lyn | Genitive Lyncis | Highest in sky at 10 pm January to March |

LYNX

The Polish astronomer Johannes Hevelius, who invented this faint constellation in the 17th century, named it the Lynx because, he said, only the lynx-eyed would be able to spot it. It lies in the northern sky between Ursa Major and Auriga, and is surprisingly large – greater in area than Gemini, for example. Except in good dark-sky conditions, naked-eye observers will see little more than its brightest star, Alpha (α) Lyncis, magnitude 3.1. There are, however, numerous double stars to attract telescope users.

THE
LYNX

FULLY VISIBLE
90°N–28°S

FEATURES OF INTEREST

12 Lyncis ☆ A multiple star. Through a small telescope it appears double, with components of magnitudes 4.9 and 7.3. An aperture of 3 in (75 mm) or more reveals that the brighter star is a close pair of 5th- and 6th-magnitude stars that orbit each other every 700 years.

19 Lyncis ☆ An easily divided multiple star. A small telescope separates it into a double with components of magnitudes 5.8 and 6.9. Farther away, a third star of 8th magnitude should also be visible.

38 Lyncis ☆ A tight double star requiring a telescope of 3 in (75 mm) aperture to split it into components of magnitudes 3.9 and 6.3.

NGC 2419 ♣ A globular cluster notable for its remoteness. At 300,000 light-years away, it is more distant than the Magellanic Clouds and so appears small and of only 10th magnitude.

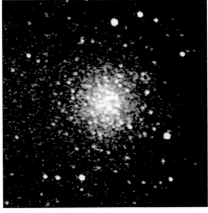

NGC 2419
It is thought likely that this cluster, seen here in a CCD image, lies outside our Galaxy in intergalactic space.

| Width ✋🤚 | Height ✋🤚 | Area 545 square degrees | Size ranking 28th |

Abbreviation Lyr	Genitive Lyrae	Highest in sky at 10 pm July to August

LYRA

This prominent constellation of the northern sky lies between Cygnus and Hercules. It represents the lyre played by Orpheus, the great musician of Greek mythology. Arab astronomers, though, visualized the pattern as an eagle, and the name of its brightest star, Vega, comes from their term meaning "swooping eagle." Vega forms one corner of a large triangle of stars known to northern observers as the Summer Triangle, completed by Deneb (in Cygnus) and Altair (in Aquila).

THE LYRE

FULLY VISIBLE
90°N–42°S

Delta (δ) Lyrae ♈ A wide pair of unrelated stars, divisible with binoculars or the naked eye. One is a red giant that varies slightly between about magnitudes 4.2 and 4.3, and the other is a blue-white star of magnitude 5.6.

Epsilon (ε) Lyrae (The Double Double) ♈ ⚹ A striking quadruple star. When viewed with binoculars, or even sharp eyesight, it appears as a pair of 5th-magnitude stars. A telescope with an aperture of 2½–3 in (60–75 mm), with high magnification, will divide both stars into closer binaries. The slightly wider pair, of magnitudes 5.0 and 6.1, has a calculated orbital period of over 1,000 years. The other pair, of magnitudes 5.2 and 5.5, has an orbital period of about 600 years. All four stars lie about 130 light-years away.

Zeta (ζ) Lyrae ♈ ⚹ A double star. The two components, magnitudes 4.3 and 5.7, are easy to divide with binoculars or a small telescope.

FEATURES OF INTEREST

Alpha (α) Lyrae (Vega) 👁 The fifth brightest star in the sky, at magnitude 0.0. It is a blue-white star, 25 light-years away.

Beta (β) Lyrae ⚹ A double star, the brighter component of which is variable. Beta Lyrae itself is an eclipsing binary that varies between magnitudes 3.3 and 4.4 in a cycle that lasts 12 days 22 hours. A small telescope shows that it has a wide companion of magnitude 7.2.

M57 (The Ring Nebula) ⚹ A planetary nebula, visible through a small telescope as an elliptical disk. Larger apertures show it as a ring, which is how it appears on photographs.

EPSILON (ε) LYRAE AND VEGA
The famous Double Double, Epsilon (ε) Lyrae, is at the top left in this picture, with the bright star Vega to its right.

M57 (THE RING NEBULA)
A small telescope shows this planetary nebula as an elliptical disk.

Width 🖐	Height 🖐	Area 286 square degrees	Size ranking 52nd

| Abbreviation Men | Genitive Mensae | Highest in sky at 10 pm December to February |

MENSA

This small and faint constellation near the south celestial pole was introduced in the 18th century by the French astronomer Nicolas Louis de Lacaille. He named it after Table Mountain, near the modern Cape Town in South Africa, from where he charted the southern sky. Mensa's only notable feature is part of the Large Magellanic Cloud, which extends into it from neighboring Dorado.

THE TABLE MOUNTAIN

FULLY VISIBLE
5°N–90°S

FEATURES OF INTEREST

Alpha (α) Mensae ◉ ♠ A yellow star 30 light-years away and similar in nature to the Sun. At magnitude 5.1, it is the brightest star in the constellation.

| Width 🖐 | Height 🖐 | Area 153 square degrees | Size ranking 75th |

| Abbreviation Mic | Genitive Microscopii | Highest in sky at 10 pm August to September |

MICROSCOPIUM

Microscopium is a faint constellation to the south of Capricornus. It was introduced in the 18th century by the French astronomer Nicolas Louis de Lacaille and represents a microscope. The constellation's brightest stars, Gamma (γ) and Epsilon (ε) Microscopii, are both of magnitude 4.7.

THE MICROSCOPE

FULLY VISIBLE
45°N–90°S

FEATURES OF INTEREST

Alpha (α) Microscopii ⟐ An orange giant star of magnitude 4.9. A telescope shows a companion of 10th magnitude.

| Width 🖐 | Height 🖐 | Area 210 square degrees | Size ranking 66th |

Abbreviation Mon	Genitive Monocerotis	Highest in sky at 10 pm January to February

MONOCEROS

THE
UNICORN

Monoceros straddles the celestial equator between Orion and Canis Minor. Introduced in the early 17th century by the Dutchman Petrus Plancius, it represents the mythical unicorn. Its brightest star is Alpha (α) Monocerotis, magnitude 3.9. Monoceros is often overlooked in favor of its glittering neighboring constellations, but it lies in the Milky Way and contains much of interest for owners of any size of instrument.

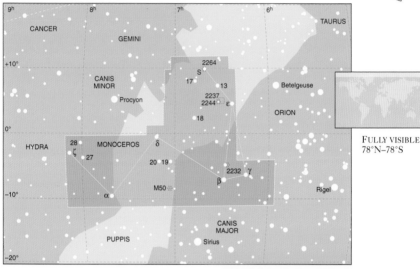

FULLY VISIBLE
78°N–78°S

FEATURES OF INTEREST

Beta (β) Monocerotis ⚹ A triple star, divisible with a small telescope. The three stars, magnitudes 4.6, 5.0, and 5.4, form an arc.

Epsilon (ε) Monocerotis (8 Monocerotis) ⚹ A double star with components of magnitudes 4.4 and 6.7 that are easy to divide through a small telescope.

S Monocerotis (15 Monocerotis) ⚹ A highly luminous blue-white star, magnitude 4.7 (but slightly variable), in the cluster NGC 2264 (see next page). It has a companion of 8th magnitude, visible with a small telescope.

M50 ♑⚹ An open cluster about half the apparent size of the full Moon and visible with binoculars. A small telescope reveals its individual stars of 8th magnitude and fainter. It lies 3,000 light-years away.

NGC 2244 AND THE ROSETTE NEBULA
The stars of the open cluster NGC 2244 (at the center of this picture) are enveloped in the Rosette Nebula.

Width 🤚🤚	Height 🤚	Area 482 square degrees	Size ranking 35th

NGC 2232 ♦ A scattered open cluster. The same apparent size as the full Moon, it is just visible to the naked eye. Its brightest star is 5th-magnitude 10 Monocerotis, and several other individual member stars are visible with binoculars. It lies 1,300 light-years away.

NGC 2244 ♦ An open cluster at the heart of the much larger Rosette Nebula. The cluster is easily visible through binoculars as an elongated group about two-thirds the apparent width of the full Moon. However, excellent skies are needed to trace the outline of the surrounding Rosette Nebula, which is three to four times larger and shows up well only on photographs. The cluster and nebula lie 5,500 light-years away.

NGC 2264 ♦ An open cluster. It is visible with binoculars; when viewed through a small telescope it appears triangular in shape. Its brightest member is S Monocerotis (see previous page). Long-exposure photographs show a surrounding area of faint nebulosity, which includes a dark lane known as the Cone Nebula. The cluster and associated nebula are about 2,500 light-years away.

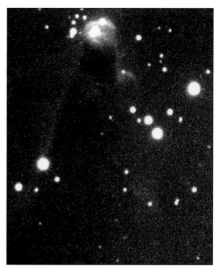

THE CONE NEBULA
The Cone Nebula is a tapering column of dark dust in the southern part of the faint area of nebulosity that surrounds the star cluster NGC 2264.

Abbreviation Mus	Genitive Muscae	Highest in sky at 10 pm April to May

MUSCA

Musca lies in the Milky Way, to the south of Centaurus and Crux. It depicts a fly and is one of the dozen southern constellations invented in the late 16th century by the Dutch navigators Pieter Dirkszoon Keyser and Frederick de Houtman. Its brightest star is Alpha (α) Muscae, magnitude 2.7.

THE
FLY

FULLY VISIBLE
14°N–90°S

FEATURES OF INTEREST

Beta (β) Muscae ⚹ A close binary that appears through a small telescope as a single star of magnitude 3.0. An aperture of around 4 in (100 mm) will divide it into two stars of magnitudes 3.6 and 4.1 that orbit each other every 400 years or so.

Theta (θ) Muscae ⚹ A double star. The two components of magnitudes 5.6 and 7.6 are divisible with a small telescope. The brighter star is a luminous blue supergiant, while its companion is an example of a Wolf–Rayet star, a hot star that has lost its outer layers.

Width 🖐	Height ✋	Area 138 square degrees	Size ranking 77th

Abbreviation Nor	Genitive Normae	Highest in sky at 10 pm June

NORMA

Norma lies in the Milky Way between Ara and Lupus. Introduced in the 18th century by the French astronomer Nicolas Louis de Lacaille, it depicts a draftsman's level or try square. It adjoins another Lacaille invention, Circinus, the compasses.
There are no stars labeled Alpha (α) or Beta (β) Normae due to boundary changes since Lacaille's time.

THE LEVEL

FULLY VISIBLE
29°N–90°S

FEATURES OF INTEREST

Gamma (γ) Normae 👁 A double star, consisting of unrelated components that can be separated with the naked eye. The primary, Gamma-2 (γ²), is the brightest star in the constellation; it is an orange giant star of magnitude 4.0, 130 light years away. Gamma-1 (γ¹), magnitude 5.0, is an immensely luminous yellow supergiant more than 100 times farther away.

Epsilon (ε) Normae ⚹ A double star, with components of magnitudes 4.5 and 6.7 that can be separated with a small telescope.

Iota-1 (ι¹) Normae ⚹ A double star. The components, of magnitudes 4.6 and 8.1, can be divided with a small telescope. Iota-2 (ι²) is an unrelated 6th-magnitude star that lies some distance away.

Width	Height	Area 165 square degrees	Size ranking 74th

Abbreviation Oct	Genitive Octantis	Highest in sky at 10 pm October

OCTANS

Octans contains the south celestial pole. The constellation, which represents a navigator's octant, a predecessor of the sextant, was introduced in the 18th century by the French astronomer Nicolas Louis de Lacaille. Its brightest star is Nu (ν) Octantis, an orange giant of magnitude 3.7. Other than its location at the south celestial pole, there is little notable about Octans.

FULLY VISIBLE
0°–90°S

THE
OCTANT

FEATURES OF INTEREST

Sigma (σ) Octantis 👁 This is the nearest naked-eye star to the south celestial pole (lying about 1 degree away), although at magnitude 5.5 it is hardly prominent. It is a yellow-white giant star, 270 light-years away.

Lambda (λ) Octantis ⚹ A close double star divisible with a small telescope. The two components are of magnitudes 5.5 and 7.2.

Width	Height	Area 291 square degrees	Size ranking 50th

Abbreviation Oph	Genitive Ophiuchi	Highest in sky at 10 pm June to July

OPHIUCHUS

THE SERPENT HOLDER

This large constellation extends from Hercules in the north, across the celestial equator, to Scorpius in the south. It represents the Greek god of medicine, Asclepius, who is depicted holding a serpent (the constellation Serpens), a traditional symbol for healing. The constellation contains several globular clusters. Its brightest star is Alpha (α) Ophiuchi, magnitude 2.1, also known as Rasalhague, derived from an Arabic term meaning "head of the serpent collector."

FULLY VISIBLE
59°N–75°S

M10
This is the most impressive of several globular clusters in Ophiuchus.

FEATURES OF INTEREST

Rho (ρ) Ophiuchi ♙≽ A multiple star. Binoculars show it as a star of magnitude 4.6 with two wide companions of magnitudes 6.8 and 7.3. A small telescope with high magnification reveals that the brightest star has a closer companion of magnitude 5.7.

36 Ophiuchi ≽ A pair of near-identical orange dwarf stars of 5th magnitude, divisible with a small telescope. They lie 20 light-years away and orbit each other every 500 years or so.

70 Ophiuchi ≽ A binary star consisting of yellow and orange dwarfs, magnitudes 4.2 and 6.1, that lie 17 light-years away and orbit each other every 88 years. They are slowly moving apart as seen from Earth, and should currently be divisible with all but the smallest apertures.

Barnard's Star ≽ The second closest star to the Sun, 5.9 light-years away. It is a cool and faint red dwarf of magnitude 9.5 and is hence far too faint to be seen with the naked eye.

M10 and M12 ♙≽ Two globular clusters about 3 degrees apart. Both are visible through binoculars, appearing about half the size of the full Moon, although a telescope of moderate aperture is needed to resolve individual stars. M10 is the closer cluster at 14,000 light-years, compared with 18,000 light-years for M12.

NGC 6633 ♙ An open cluster of similar apparent size to the full Moon, visible through binoculars.

IC 4665 ♙ A large and scattered open cluster visible with binoculars.

Width 🖐🖐	Height 🖐🖐	Area 948 square degrees	Size ranking 11th

Abbreviation Ori	Genitive Orionis	Highest in sky at 10 pm December to January

ORION

Orion is the most magnificent of all the constellations. Being positioned on the celestial equator, it is visible from most places on Earth. It represents a hunter with his dogs (marked by Canis Major and Canis Minor) at his heels. In Greek mythology, Orion was the son of Poseidon, the sea god. He was supposedly killed by the sting of a scorpion, and his position in the sky is such that he sets as the scorpion (the constellation Scorpius) rises. According to another story, Orion became enamored of a group of nymphs called the Pleiades, depicted by a star cluster in the adjoining constellation of Taurus. As the Earth turns, Orion seems to chase the Pleiades across the sky. The constellation contains several bright stars, but its most celebrated feature is the huge nebula (M42) that lies within the hunter's sword, south of the line of three stars marking his belt.

ORION

FULLY VISIBLE
79°N–67°S

ORION
The magnificent constellation of Orion, with Betelgeuse at the top left, Rigel at the bottom right, and the Orion Nebula and the stars of the belt in the center.

FEATURES OF INTEREST

Alpha (α) Orionis (Betelgeuse) 👁 A red supergiant star of variable brightness ranging from about magnitude 0 to 1.3 every 6 years or so. It lies 430 light-years away. The name Betelgeuse is derived from an Arabic term that incorporates a reference to a hand, although the star actually lies on the hunter's shoulder.

Beta (β) Orionis (Rigel) 👁 A blue super-giant star of magnitude 0.2, the brightest star in the constellation and the seventh brightest in the sky. It is 770 light-years away. The name Rigel is derived from an Arabic word meaning "foot," which is the part of the hunter's body that the star represents.

Width 🖐🤏	Height 🖐🤏	Area 594 square degrees	Size ranking 26th

MAGNITUDE KEY

1
2
3
4
5
6
7

DETAIL OF THE M42 (ORION NEBULA) REGION

M42 (ORION NEBULA) WITH THE TRAPEZIUM INSET
M42 is a mass of glowing gas where stars are forming. At its heart is the multiple star Theta-1 (θ¹) Orionis.

Theta-1 (θ¹) Orionis (The Trapezium) ⍟
A multiple star, located at the heart of the Orion Nebula (see below). A small telescope shows it as a quadruple star with components of magnitudes 5.1, 6.7, 6.7, and 8.0 arranged in a trapezium shape. A larger aperture reveals two other 11th-magnitude stars in the group.

Theta-2 (θ²) Orionis ♠ A double star. The two stars, magnitudes 5.0 and 6.4, are divisible through binoculars. Theta-2 also forms a wide, bright binocular double with Theta-1 Orionis.

Iota (ι) Orionis ♠⍟ A double star. The two components of magnitudes 2.8 and 7.0 can be split with a small telescope. Binoculars show another double nearby: called Struve 747, it consists of stars of magnitudes 4.8 and 5.7.

Sigma (σ) Orionis ⍟ A remarkable multiple star. The main star of magnitude 3.8 has two 7th-magnitude companions to one side and a 9th-magnitude companion on the other. A faint triple star, called Struve 761, should be visible in the same telescopic field of view.

M42 (The Orion Nebula) ⊕♠⍟ One of the most spectacular objects in the sky. It is a cloud of glowing gas with an apparent diameter over twice that of the full Moon. Visible to the naked eye, it becomes larger and more complex when viewed with binoculars and telescopes of increasing aperture. It is 1,500 light-years away and is lit up by the stars of the Trapezium (see Theta-1 (θ¹) Orionis,

above) that lie within it. A northern extension of the nebula is known as M43.

NGC 1981 ♠ A large, scattered open cluster visible with binoculars, its brightest stars being of 6th magnitude. The cluster appears to the north of the Orion Nebula and lies at about the same distance from us, 1,400 light-years.

The Horsehead Nebula ♟ A dark nebula shaped like a chess knight, seen silhouetted against a strip of brighter nebulosity that extends south from Zeta (ζ) Orionis. However, it is too faint to be viewed without a large telescope, and its shape is most easily seen on a long-exposure photograph.

THE HORSEHEAD NEBULA
This distinctively shaped cloud of gas is visible against a background of brighter hydrogen gas.

Abbreviation Pav	Genitive Pavonis	Highest in sky at 10 pm July to September

PAVO

Pavo, which represents a peacock, is one of the 12 southern constellations invented in the late 16th century by the Dutch navigators Pieter Dirkszoon Keyser and Frederick de Houtman. The constellation's brightest star, Alpha (α) Pavonis, magnitude 1.9, is also named Peacock. Being a modern constellation, there are no myths associated with it.

THE PEACOCK

FULLY VISIBLE
15°N–90°S

FEATURES OF INTEREST

Kappa (κ) Pavonis ◉ A Cepheid variable star. It is a yellow-white supergiant that ranges between magnitudes 3.9 and 4.8 every 9 days 2 hours. It lies about 540 light-years away.

Xi (ξ) Pavonis ⋆ A close double star with components of unequal brightness. It consists of a red giant of magnitude 4.4 and an 8th-magnitude companion, both about 420 light-years away. With a telescope of small aperture, it may be difficult to pick out the fainter star in the glare around the brighter component.

NGC 6752 ♠⋆ A globular cluster, just visible to the naked eye and easy to see through binoculars or a small telescope. A telescope with an aperture of 3 in (75 mm) will resolve individual stars. The cluster has an apparent size about half that of the full Moon and lies 14,000 light-years away.

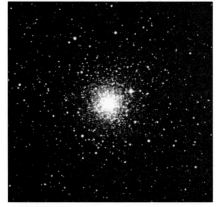

NGC 6752
This large globular cluster, one of the brightest in the sky, has many outlying stars.

Width	Height	Area 378 square degrees	Size ranking 44th

Abbreviation Peg	Genitive Pegasi	Highest in sky at 10 pm September to October

PEGASUS

THE WINGED HORSE

This large constellation north of Aquarius and Pisces adjoins Andromeda. It represents the upper body of the winged horse that, in Greek mythology, sprang from the body of Medusa when she was beheaded by Perseus. The most distinctive feature in Pegasus is the Great Square formed by Alpha (α), Beta (β), and Gamma (γ) Pegasi, and Alpha (α) Andromedae. The area inside the square is relatively barren, containing no stars brighter than 4th magnitude.

FULLY VISIBLE
90°N–53°S

M15
This is one of the finest globular clusters in northern skies, appearing through binoculars like a hazy star.

FEATURES OF INTEREST

Beta (β) Pegasi ◉ A variable red giant that forms one corner of the Great Square. It varies unpredictably from magnitude 2.3 to 2.7.

Epsilon (ε) Pegasi (Enif) ♠ ↗ A wide double star, which consists of a yellow supergiant of magnitude 2.4 and an 8th-magnitude partner that can be seen with a small telescope or even good binoculars. This star represents Pegasus's muzzle; its popular name is derived from the Arabic word for "nose."

M15 ♠ ↗ A globular cluster clearly visible with binoculars or a small telescope and about one-third the apparent width of the full Moon. It lies about 30,000 light-years away.

Width 🖐🖐	Height 🖐🖐	Area 1,121 square degrees	Size ranking 7th

Abbreviation Per	Genitive Persei	Highest in sky at 10 pm November to December

PERSEUS

Perseus represents the mythological Greek hero who decapitated the fearsome Medusa, whose gaze could turn men to stone. On his way back from this exploit, Perseus rescued Andromeda from the jaws of a sea monster. In the sky, Perseus lies next to Andromeda and her mother, Cassiopeia, forming part of a great tableau depicting this most famous of Greek myths. Perseus is represented brandishing his sword in his right hand, marked by the twin star clusters NGC 869 and NGC 884, while in his left hand he holds the head of Medusa, marked by the star Beta (β) Persei, better known as Algol. A rich part of the Milky Way runs through Perseus, making it an attractive constellation for binocular users.

PERSEUS

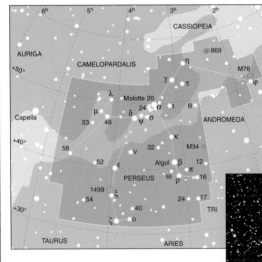

FULLY VISIBLE
90°N–31°S

**NGC 869 AND NGC 884
(THE DOUBLE CLUSTER)**
These twin star clusters both lie about 7,300 light-years away in the Perseus spiral arm of the Galaxy. NGC 869 is the richer of the two.

FEATURES OF INTEREST

Alpha (α) Persei A yellow-white supergiant of magnitude 1.8, the brightest star in the constellation. It is the most prominent member of a large and loose cluster of stars known as Melotte 20, visible with binoculars, which lies 550 light-years away.

Beta (β) Persei (Algol) A famous eclipsing binary star consisting of a close pair of stars in orbit around each other. When the brighter star is eclipsed by the fainter one, every 2 days 21 hours, the magnitude drops from 2.1 to 3.4 for about 10 hours.

Rho (ρ) Persei A variable red giant. Due to changes in size, it varies from magnitude 3.3 to 4.0 in a cycle lasting about 7 weeks.

M34 An open cluster about 1,400 light-years away. It is visible with binoculars or a small telescope and appears about the same size as the full Moon. The cluster's brightest stars are of 7th magnitude.

NGC 869 and NGC 884 (η and χ Persei, The Double Cluster) Two open clusters just visible to the naked eye; an excellent sight through binoculars or a small telescope. Each cluster covers about the same area of sky as the full Moon.

Width	Height	Area 615 square degrees	Size ranking 24th

| Abbreviation Phe | Genitive Phoenicis | Highest in sky at 10 pm October to November |

PHOENIX

Phoenix lies near the southern end of Eridanus, close to the bright star Achernar. It is the largest of the 12 constellations invented at the end of the 16th century by the Dutch navigators Pieter Dirkszoon Keyser and Frederick de Houtman and represents the mythical bird that was supposedly reborn from the dead body of its predecessor. Its brightest star is Alpha (α) Phoenicis, magnitude 2.4.

THE
PHOENIX

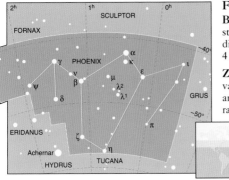

FEATURES OF INTEREST

Beta (β) Phoenicis ⚹ A double star. The two stars of magnitudes 4.0 and 4.2 are not easy to divide: a telescope with an aperture of at least 4 in (100 mm) is needed to separate them.

Zeta (ζ) Phoenicis ◐ ♠ ⚹ A star that is both variable and double. The brighter component, an eclipsing binary of the same type as Algol, ranges between magnitudes 3.9 and 4.4 every 1 day 16 hours. The fainter star of 8th magnitude can be seen with a small telescope.

FULLY VISIBLE
32°N–90°S

| Width 🤚🖐 | Height 🤚 | Area 469 square degrees | Size ranking 37th |

| Abbreviation Pic | Genitive Pictoris | Highest in sky at 10 pm December to February |

PICTOR

Pictor is one of the constellations representing instruments of science and the arts that were introduced in the 18th century by Nicolas Louis de Lacaille. It depicts an easel, and lies due south of Columba between the bright star Canopus in Carina and the Large Magellanic Cloud. Its brightest star is Alpha (α) Pictoris, magnitude 3.2.

FULLY VISIBLE
26°N–90°S

THE
PAINTER'S EASEL

FEATURES OF INTEREST

Beta (β) Pictoris ♒ A blue-white star of magnitude 3.9, lying 63 light-years away. Astronomers have found that it is surrounded by a disk of dust, thought to be a planetary system in the early stages of formation.

Iota (ι) Pictoris ⚹ A double star. The two components of magnitudes 5.6 and 6.4 are easy to separate with a small telescope.

| Width 🤚 | Height 🖐 | Area 247 square degrees | Size ranking 59th |

Abbreviation Psc	Genitive Piscium	Highest in sky at 10 pm October to November

PISCES

This constellation of the zodiac, lying between Aquarius and Aries, depicts two fishes whose tails are each tied with cord. The star Alpha (α) Piscium marks a knot that joins the two cords. The constellation originated among the Babylonians of the Middle East, from whom it was inherited by the ancient Greeks. In one Greek myth, the fish represent Aphrodite and her son Eros, who plunged into the Euphrates to escape Typhon, a multiheaded monster. The Sun lies in Pisces from March 12 to April 18 and hence is in the constellation at the March equinox.

THE FISHES

FULLY VISIBLE
83°N–56°S

M74
The structure of this spiral galaxy, which appears face-on to us, can be seen through a large telescope.

FEATURES OF INTEREST

The Circlet ◑ A ring of seven stars of 4th and 5th magnitudes, south of the Great Square of Pegasus, that represents the head of the southernmost of the two fish. It consists of Gamma (γ), Kappa (κ), Lambda (λ), TX (or 19), Iota (ι), Theta (θ), and 7 Piscium.

Alpha (α) Piscium ⚹ A binary star. A telescope with an aperture of 3 in (75 mm) or more is needed to separate the close blue-white components of magnitudes 4.2 and 5.2. The two stars, which lie 140 light-years away, have an orbital period of nearly 1,000 years and are currently moving closer together as seen from Earth.

Zeta (ζ) Piscium ⚹ A wide double star. The unrelated components of magnitudes 5.2 and 6.4 lie 150 and 195 light-years away. They can be divided with a small telescope.

Psi-1 (ψ¹) Piscium ⚹ A wide double star with components of magnitudes 5.3 and 5.5 that can be separated with a small telescope. Both stars lie about 230 light-years away.

TX Piscium (19 Piscium) ◑ ♙ A variable red giant that ranges from about magnitude 4.8 to 5.2 with no set period.

M74 ⚹ A spiral galaxy visible through a small telescope as a rounded, misty patch.

Width 🖐🖐✌🖐	Height 🖐✌🖐	Area 889 square degrees	Size ranking 14th

Abbreviation PsA	Genitive Piscis Austrini	Highest in sky at 10 pm September to October

PISCIS AUSTRINUS

Piscis Austrinus is a small constellation of the southern sky that was known to the ancient Greeks. It depicts a fish into whose mouth Aquarius, represented by the constellation to the north, pours water from his urn. In Greek mythology, this fish was also the parent of the two fish represented by Pisces. The name of the constellation is sometimes given as Piscis Australis.

THE SOUTHERN FISH

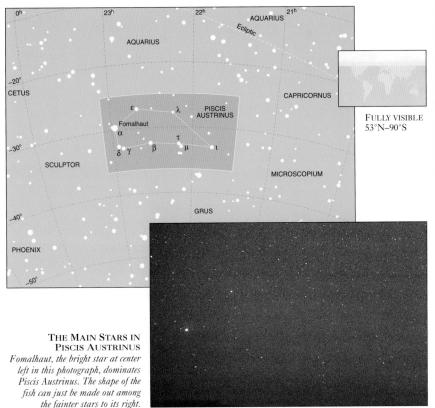

FULLY VISIBLE
53°N–90°S

THE MAIN STARS IN PISCIS AUSTRINUS
Fomalhaut, the bright star at center left in this photograph, dominates Piscis Austrinus. The shape of the fish can just be made out among the fainter stars to its right.

FEATURES OF INTEREST

Alpha (α) Piscis Austrini (Fomalhaut) ☞
A blue-white star that lies 25 light-years away. At magnitude 1.2, it is not only the brightest star in the constellation but also ranks among the 20 brightest stars in the sky. The name Fomalhaut is derived from an Arabic term that means "fish's mouth," which describes the place the star occupies in the celestial pattern.

Beta (β) Piscis Austrini ☆ A wide double star divisible with a small telescope. Its two components are of magnitudes 4.3 and 7.7.

Gamma (γ) Piscis Austrini ☆ A double star. With a small telescope it is difficult to separate the stars, as the 5th-magnitude primary greatly outshines its close 8th-magnitude neighbor.

Width 🖐	Height 🖐🖐	Area 245 square degrees	Size ranking 60th

Abbreviation Pup	Genitive Puppis	Highest in sky at 10 pm January to February

PUPPIS

THE STERN

This rich constellation lies in the Milky Way next to Canis Major. It represents the stern of the ship of the Argonauts. Ancient Greek astronomers represented the whole ship as one constellation, Argo Navis. This was later divided into three parts, with Puppis being the largest section. Because it is only part of a once-larger constellation, Puppis has no stars labeled Alpha (α), Beta (β), Gamma (γ), Delta (δ), or Epsilon (ε).

FULLY VISIBLE 39°N–90°S

NGC 2451

This scattered open cluster covers a larger area of sky than the full Moon. The star at the center of the photograph is c Puppis.

FEATURES OF INTEREST

Zeta (ζ) Puppis (Naos) ◉ The brightest star in the constellation, at magnitude 2.2. It is a hot and luminous blue-white supergiant, lying about 1,400 light-years away. Its name is derived from a Greek word meaning "ship."

k Puppis ⟩ A double star. A small telescope reveals two similar blue-white stars of almost equal brightness at magnitudes 4.5 and 4.6.

L Puppis ◉ ♙ A wide pair of unrelated stars, each visible to the naked eye. L¹ Puppis is a blue-white star of magnitude 4.9, while L² is a red giant that varies between about 3rd and 6th magnitudes every 5 months or so.

V Puppis ◉ ♙ An eclipsing binary that varies between magnitudes 4.4 and 4.9 every 1 day 11 hours.

M46 ♙⟩ An open cluster just visible to the naked eye and appearing the same size as the full Moon. A small telescope resolves its stars. It lies over 5,000 light-years away.

M47 ♙ A scattered open cluster visible to the naked eye and slightly larger than M46 but much closer, about 1,500 light-years away. Its brightest stars are of 6th magnitude.

NGC 2451 ◉ ♙ An open cluster visible to the naked eye and through binoculars. It lies 850 light-years away. Its brightest member is an orange giant, c Puppis, of magnitude 3.6.

NGC 2477 ♙⟩ An open cluster 4,200 light-years away. It is so rich that it resembles a globular cluster when seen through binoculars. A telescope will resolve individual stars.

Width	Height	Area 673 square degrees	Size ranking 20th

Abbreviation Pyx	Genitive Pyxidis	Highest in sky at 10 pm February to March

PYXIS

FULLY VISIBLE
52°N–90°S

This southern constellation lies on the edge of the Milky Way between Hydra and Puppis. Invented by Nicolas Louis de Lacaille in the 18th century, it represents a magnetic compass of the type used by mariners.

FEATURES OF INTEREST

T Pyxidis ♫ A nova that has flared to 6th or 7th magnitude on five known occasions since 1890, the last in 1966.

THE COMPASS

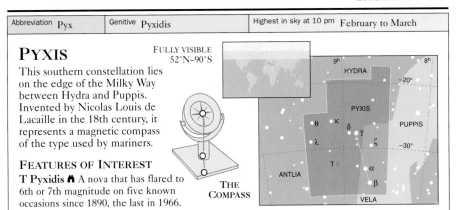

Width ⤷	Height ⤷	Area 221 square degrees	Size ranking 65th

Abbreviation Ret	Genitive Reticuli	Highest in sky at 10 pm December

RETICULUM

FULLY VISIBLE
23°N–90°S

This small southern constellation near the Large Magellanic Cloud dates from the 18th century. It depicts a device called a reticle, or grid, that was used in telescope eyepieces for recording star positions. The brightest star in the constellation is Alpha (α) Reticuli, magnitude 3.3.

THE NET

FEATURES OF INTEREST

Zeta (ζ) Reticuli ⊙ ♫ A double star divisible with the naked eye. The two 5th-magnitude yellow stars, similar to the Sun, lie 39 light-years away.

Width ⤷	Height ⤷	Area 114 square degrees	Size ranking 82nd

Abbreviation Sge	Genitive Sagittae	Highest in sky at 10 pm August

SAGITTA

THE ARROW   FULLY VISIBLE
90°N–69°S

Although it lies in the Milky Way, with Vulpecula and Cygnus to the north and Aquila to the south, Sagitta contains little that is of interest. The third smallest constellation, it has been visualized since ancient Greek times as an arrow, with its brightest star, Gamma (γ) Sagittae, magnitude 3.5, marking the arrowhead.

FEATURES OF INTEREST

M71 ♫ ⋏ A small globular cluster visible with binoculars or a small telescope.

Width ⤷	Height ⤷	Area 80 square degrees	Size ranking 86th

Abbreviation Sgr	Genitive Sagittarii	Highest in sky at 10 pm July to August

SAGITTARIUS

This constellation of the zodiac lies between Scorpius and Capricornus. It depicts Crotus, the son of the Greek god Pan and the inventor of archery, aiming his bow at a scorpion, represented by the neighboring constellation of Scorpius. The center of our Galaxy lies in the same direction as Sagittarius, and binoculars show that the star fields in this part of the Milky Way are particularly dense. The Sun passes through Sagittarius from December 18 to January 19, a period that includes the December solstice. The constellation's brightest star is Epsilon (ε) Sagittarii, magnitude 1.8.

THE ARCHER

FULLY VISIBLE 44°N–90°S

FEATURES OF INTEREST

The Teapot ◉ A group of eight stars: Gamma (γ), Epsilon (ε), Delta (δ), Lambda (λ), Phi (φ), Zeta (ζ), Sigma (σ), and Tau (τ) Sagittarii. Together, they form the outline of a teapot, with a pointed lid and a large spout. The stars Lambda (λ), Phi (φ), Zeta (ζ), Sigma (σ), and Tau (τ) Sagittarii also form a shape known as the Milk Dipper, so named because it lies in a rich area of the Milky Way.

Beta (β) Sagittarii ◉ ♏ A multiple star, although all the components lie at different distances and are unrelated. The naked eye shows it as a wide double with components of magnitudes 4.0 and 4.3. The brighter star, Beta-1 (β¹), has a 7th-magnitude companion that can be seen through a small telescope.

THE MAIN STARS IN SAGITTARIUS
The Teapot is at the center in this picture. Also visible are M7 (an open cluster in Scorpius) at center right, and the arc of Corona Australis below the Teapot.

Width 🖐️🖐️	Height 🖐️🖐️	Area 867 square degrees	Size ranking 14th

M8 (THE LAGOON NEBULA)
This bright nebula lies in the Milky Way in the eastern part of Sagittarius. The curving lane of dust after which the nebula is named is at the center of the photograph. Immediately to the left of the dust lane is a sprinkling of stars that belong to the cluster NGC 6530, while the star enveloped in nebulosity to its right is 9 Sagittarii.

M8 (The Lagoon Nebula) 👁 ♏ ⚲ A bright nebula visible to the naked eye and a good target for binoculars. Elongated in shape, it is almost three times the apparent width of the full Moon. A dark lane of dust bisects it: one half contains the cluster NGC 6530 with stars of 7th magnitude and fainter, while the most prominent object in the other half is the 6th-magnitude star 9 Sagittarii. The nebula, and the stars within it, are 5,200 light-years away.

M17 (The Omega Nebula) ♏ ⚲ A cloud of glowing gas of similar apparent size to the full Moon. It can be seen through binoculars, although a telescope is needed to see its true shape. A small telescope shows a star cluster, NGC 6618, within the cloud. The nebula and cluster both lie about 4,900 light-years away.

M20 (The Trifid Nebula) ⚲ A nebula with a faint double star at its center, both visible with a small telescope. Larger apertures and photographs show dust lanes trisecting the nebula.

M22 ♏ ⚲ The third brightest globular cluster in the sky, 10,000 light-years away. It is just visible to the naked eye under good conditions and easy to find with binoculars, which show it as a rounded patch about two-thirds the apparent size of the full Moon. A telescope of moderate aperture resolves its brightest stars.

M23 ♏ ⚲ A rich open cluster, elongated in shape and almost the same apparent width as the full Moon. It can be seen with binoculars, while a small telescope will resolve its stars. It lies 2,100 light-years away.

M24 👁 ♏ ⚲ A large and bright field of stars in the Milky Way, visible to the naked eye and an excellent sight through binoculars. A small telescope reveals a small open cluster, NGC 6603, at its center.

M25 ♏ ⚲ An open cluster just visible to the naked eye and a good object for observation with binoculars or a small telescope. Its stars, of 7th magnitude and fainter, are scattered over an area of sky the same apparent size as the full Moon. It lies 1,900 light-years away.

M17 (THE OMEGA NEBULA)
When viewed with a telescope, this nebula resembles the capital letter Omega (Ω) in the Greek alphabet.

M20 (THE TRIFID NEBULA)
A telescope reveals the three main lanes of dust that cross this nebula and give rise to its popular name.

Abbreviation Sco	Genitive Scorpii	Highest in sky at 10 pm June to July

SCORPIUS

A constellation of the zodiac, Scorpius lies between Libra and Sagittarius. It depicts the scorpion that, in Greek mythology, killed Orion with its sting – fittingly, Orion sets as Scorpius rises. The constellation lies in a rich region of the Milky Way, in the same direction as the center of our Galaxy. The Sun passes through it briefly from November 23 to 29. The old version of its name, Scorpio, is used only in astrology.

THE SCORPION

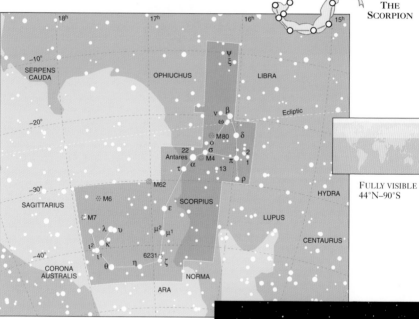

FULLY VISIBLE 44°N–90°S

FEATURES OF INTEREST

Alpha (α) Scorpii (Antares) 👁 ♏ A red supergiant of variable brightness ranging between magnitudes 0.9 and 1.2 in a cycle lasting approximately 4–5 years. It has a close blue-white companion of 5th magnitude that orbits it every 900 years or so and can be seen with a telescope of moderate aperture. The name Antares is usually translated as "rival of Mars," referring to its reddish color, although it can also mean "like Mars."

Beta (β) Scorpii ♐ A double star with components of magnitudes 2.6 and 4.9 that are easy to separate with a small telescope. The two stars are unrelated, lying at distances of 530 and 1,100 light-years.

THE MAIN STARS IN SCORPIUS
The stars representing the scorpion's head are at the top right here. Orange Antares marks the heart, and the stars in the body and tail curve down and to the left.

Width 🖐🤏	Height 🖐🤏	Area 497 square degrees	Size ranking 33rd

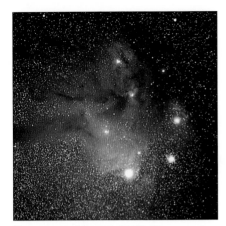

NEBULOSITY AROUND ANTARES
A faint area of nebulosity, visible only on long-exposure photographs, extends northward from Antares (below center in this picture) to Rho (ρ) Ophiuchi (top center).

Zeta (ζ) Scorpii ◉ ♙ A wide pair of unrelated stars divisible with the naked eye by those with good eyesight. Zeta-1 (ζ¹) is a blue-white supergiant of magnitude 4.7, the brightest star in the cluster NGC 6231 (see below). Zeta-2 (ζ²), a red giant of magnitude 3.6, is much closer at 150 light-years away.

Mu (μ) Scorpii ◉ ♙ A double star that can be divided with the naked eye. The brighter component is an eclipsing binary that varies between magnitudes 2.9 and 3.2 every 1 day 10 hours. Its companion is of magnitude 3.6.

Nu (ν) Scorpii ⋇ A multiple star. A small telescope, or good binoculars, will reveal an optical double with components of magnitudes

4.0 and 6.3. The fainter star of the pair has an 8th-magnitude companion that can be seen through a telescope with an aperture of 3 in (75 mm). Larger apertures – 4 in (100 mm) or more – show that the brighter star has an even closer companion of 5th magnitude. Hence Nu Scorpii is an apparent quadruple.

Xi (ξ) Scorpii ⋇ A multiple star. Like Nu (ν) Scorpii, this is a quadruple. A small telescope reveals a pair of 5th- and 7th-magnitude stars; in the same field of view, a wider pair of 7th- and 8th-magnitude stars can also be seen.

Omega (ω) Scorpii ◉ ♙ A naked-eye double star with components of magnitudes 3.9 and 4.3, 420 and 260 light-years away.

M4 ♙ ⋇ One of the closest globular clusters to us, under 7,000 light-years away. It is visible with binoculars or a small telescope, but a dark sky is needed as its light is spread over a large area two-thirds the apparent size of the Moon.

M6 ◉ ♙ ⋇ An open cluster, 2,000 light-years away. It is visible to the naked eye, and its individual stars can be seen with binoculars. Its brightest star is BM Scorpii, an orange giant that varies between 5th and 7th magnitudes.

M7 ◉ ♙ A large, glorious open cluster, visible with the naked eye and binoculars and more than twice the apparent width of the full Moon. Its brightest stars, of 6th magnitude, are seen against a bright Milky Way background. The cluster is 780 light-years away.

NGC 6231 ♙ ⋇ A prominent open cluster, 5,900 light-years away. Its individual stars are easy to see with binoculars or a small telescope. The 5th-magnitude star Zeta-1 (ζ¹) Scorpii (see above) is its brightest member.

M4
This globular cluster, between Antares and Sigma (σ) Scorpii, is large but faint and hence difficult to see.

M6 AND M7
M6 is at center right in this picture, with M7 to its left in front of the bright band of the Milky Way.

Abbreviation Scl	Genitive Sculptoris	Highest in sky at 10 pm October to November

SCULPTOR

This faint constellation is to the south of Aquarius and Cetus. It was invented in the 18th century by the French astronomer Nicolas Louis de Lacaille, who visualized it as a sculptor's studio, although its name has since been changed. Its brightest star, Alpha (α) Sculptoris, is of only magnitude 4.3. Sculptor contains the south pole of our Galaxy – the point 90 degrees south of the plane of the Milky Way. In this region, our view into the Universe is uninterrupted by intervening gas and dust in our Galaxy, so many faint and distant galaxies are visible. The north galactic pole lies in Coma Berenices.

SCULPTOR

FULLY VISIBLE
50°N–90°S

FEATURES OF INTEREST

Epsilon (ε) Sculptoris ✶ A double star that can be divided with a small telescope. The 5th- and 9th-magnitude components are a true binary pair that orbit each other every 1,200 years or so. They are 89 light-years away.

R Sculptoris ♙ A variable red giant that ranges between 6th and 8th magnitudes in a cycle lasting about a year.

NGC 55 ✶ A spiral galaxy, tilted nearly edge-on to us, so that it appears cigar-shaped when viewed with a small telescope.

NGC 253 ♙✶ A spiral galaxy. Like NGC 55, it appears to us edge-on, but it is brighter and hence visible with binoculars. A telescope of moderate to large aperture shows traces of dark dust clouds silhouetted against its stars.

NGC 253 AND NGC 288
These two objects are in the northern part of Sculptor. NGC 288 (on the left in this picture) is a globular cluster that can be seen through a telescope. The spiral galaxy NGC 253 is on the right.

Width 〰〰〰	Height 〰〰	Area 475 square degrees	Size ranking 36th

| Abbreviation Sct | Genitive Scuti | Highest in sky at 10 pm July to August |

SCUTUM

Scutum is a small constellation that lies just south of the celestial equator in a rich area of the Milky Way between Aquila and Sagittarius. It was introduced in the late 17th century by the Polish astronomer Johannes Hevelius, who originally termed it Sobieski's Shield in honor of his patron, King John Sobieski. Its brightest star is Alpha (α) Scuti, magnitude 3.9.

THE
SHIELD

FULLY VISIBLE
74°N–90°S

M11 (THE WILD DUCK CLUSTER)

The open cluster M11 lies in a bright section of the Milky Way near the border between Aquila and Scutum. On this photograph, taken through a telescope, it is just possible to see the V-shape, with the apex at the top right of the cluster.

FEATURES OF INTEREST

Delta (δ) Scuti ◐ ♏ A pulsating giant, the prototype of a class of variable stars that show very small fluctuations in brightness (a few tenths of a magnitude or less) over short periods of time (no more than a few hours). Delta Scuti itself varies between magnitudes 4.6 and 4.8 over a period of less than 5 hours. It lies 190 light-years away.

R Scuti ♏ A pulsating orange supergiant that varies between magnitudes 4.2 and 8.6 in a 20-week cycle.

M11 (The Wild Duck Cluster) ♏ ⚹ A rich open cluster consisting of hundreds of stars, visible in binoculars as a fuzzy ball nearly half the apparent size of the full Moon. In a small telescope it appears V-shaped like a flight of ducks, hence its popular name. Near the apex of the V is the cluster's brightest star, of 8th

magnitude. M11 is 5,600 light-years away and lies on the northern edge of a particularly bright section of the Milky Way known as the Scutum Star Cloud.

| Width 🖐 | Height 🖐 | Area 475 square degrees | Size ranking 84th |

Abbreviation Ser	Genitive Serpentis	Highest in sky at 10pm June to August	

SERPENS

Uniquely, Serpens consists of two separate areas that, taken together, are regarded as one constellation. It depicts a serpent coiled around Ophiuchus, who holds the head (Serpens Caput) in his left hand and the tail (Serpens Cauda) in his right. The constellation's brightest star, Alpha (α) Serpentis, magnitude 2.6, is also known as Unukalhai, a name derived from an Arabic term that means "the serpent's neck."

THE SERPENT

FULLY VISIBLE
74°N–64°S

FEATURES OF INTEREST

Delta (δ) Serpentis ✶ A binary star. The 4th-magnitude primary and its 5th-magnitude partner can be divided with a small telescope and high magnification. Their orbital period is estimated to be several thousand years.

Theta (θ) Serpentis ✶ A wide double star. The components of magnitudes 4.6 and 5.0 can be separated through a small telescope.

Nu (ν) Serpentis ♠✶ A wide double with 4th- and 8th-magnitude components that are divisible with binoculars or a small telescope.

Tau-1 (τ¹) Serpentis ♠ The brightest and easternmost member of a triangular field of stars that fans out toward Iota (ι) and Kappa (κ) Serpentis.

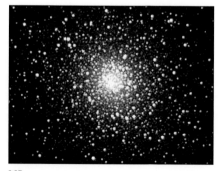

M5
This globular cluster in the southern part of Serpens Caput is visible through binoculars. It is one of the finest objects of its type in northern skies.

Width 🖐🖐🖐	Height 🖐🖐	Area 637 square degrees	Size ranking 23rd

M5 ♙ ⋟ A globular cluster about 25,000 light-years away. It can be seen through binoculars, appearing about half the size of the full Moon. A telescope of moderate aperture resolves its brightest stars; it also reveals a condensed center and chains of stars in the outer regions.

M16 ♙ ⋟ An open cluster visible through binoculars or a small telescope. It appears hazy, since the stars are embedded in the Eagle Nebula, which shows up well only with larger apertures and on photographs. Cluster and nebula are over 8,000 light-years away.

◁ THE EAGLE NEBULA
This nebula can be seen through a telescope of large aperture or on a long-exposure photograph.

▽ DARK COLUMNS IN THE EAGLE NEBULA
This close-up, taken by the Hubble Space Telescope, shows dark fingers of dust against areas of brighter gas.

Abbreviation Sex	Genitive Sextantis	Highest in sky at 10 pm March to April

SEXTANS

This faint constellation is on the celestial equator, south of Leo. It was invented in the late 17th century by the Polish astronomer Johannes Hevelius and represents the sextant with which he measured star positions. Its brightest star is Alpha (α) Sextantis, magnitude 4.5.

THE SEXTANT

FULLY VISIBLE
78°N–83°S

FEATURES OF INTEREST

17 and 18 Sextantis ◉ ♙ A wide pair of unrelated stars detectable with the naked eye by those with good eyesight and easy to divide with binoculars. They are of magnitudes 5.9 and 5.6, and lie 530 and 470 light-years away.

NGC 3115 (The Spindle Galaxy) ⋟
An elliptical galaxy visible through a telescope of small to moderate aperture. Its elongated shape gives rise to its popular name.

Width 🖐	Height 🖐	Area 314 square degrees	Size ranking 47th

Abbreviation Tau	Genitive Tauri	Highest in sky at 10 pm December to January

TAURUS

THE BULL

This imposing constellation of the zodiac lies between Aries and Gemini. It represents the bull into which the Greek god Zeus transformed himself to abduct Princess Europa of Phoenicia. Zeus then swam to Crete with the princess on his back. The constellation represents the front half of the bull's body – the part visible above the Mediterranean waves. It contains two major star clusters, the Pleiades and Hyades. In mythology, the Pleiades were the seven daughters of Atlas and Pleione, and the cluster is also known as the Seven Sisters; the Hyades were the daughters of Atlas and Aethra. In the sky, the Hyades cluster marks the bull's face, while the red giant star Aldebaran forms the creature's bloodshot eye. The tips of the bull's horns are marked by Beta (β) and Zeta (ζ) Tauri, magnitudes 1.7 and 3.0. The Sun passes through Taurus from May 14 to June 21.

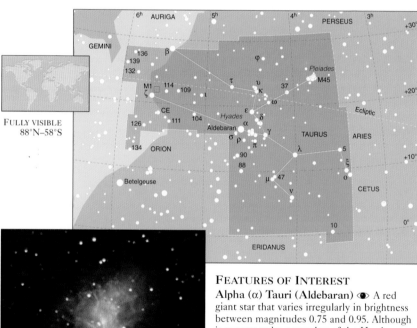

FULLY VISIBLE
88°N–58°S

M1 (THE CRAB NEBULA)
This remarkable object is the remains of a massive star that exploded as a supernova.

FEATURES OF INTEREST

Alpha (α) Tauri (Aldebaran) 👁 A red giant star that varies irregularly in brightness between magnitudes 0.75 and 0.95. Although it appears to be a member of the Hyades cluster, it is actually much closer to us, being 65 light-years away.

Theta (θ) Tauri 👁 ♙ A wide double star in the Hyades cluster. Observers with good eyesight can divide the two stars with the naked eye. Theta-1 (θ^1) is a yellow giant, magnitude 3.8; Theta-2 (θ^2) is a white giant of magnitude 3.4, the brightest member of the Hyades.

Width	Height	Area 797 square degrees	Size ranking 17th

△ THE PLEIADES

△ THE HYADES AND
PLEIADES
*These two outstanding open clusters
lie close together in the sky.*

◁ THE HYADES

△ MAGNITUDE KEY

Lambda (λ) Tauri ◉ An eclipsing binary
star of the same type as Algol. It ranges
between magnitudes 3.4 and 3.9 in a cycle
lasting just under 4 days.

M1 (The Crab Nebula) ♛ ⚹ The remains
of a supernova that was seen from Earth in
AD 1054. Under excellent conditions it can be
found with binoculars or a small telescope, but
a moderate aperture is needed to see it well.
It is elliptical in shape, appearing midway in
size between the disk of a planet and the full
Moon. It lies about 6,500 light-years away.

M45 (The Pleiades) ◉ ♛ ⚹ A large, bright
open star cluster, easy to see with the naked
eye and a superb sight through binoculars,

appearing almost four times wider than the
full Moon. Its brightest star is Eta (η) Tauri
(Alcyone), a blue-white giant of magnitude
2.9. Those with normal eyesight can see about
six stars, but dozens are visible with binoculars
or a small telescope. The cluster is just over
400 light-years away. Long-exposure photographs show nebulosity around the stars, but
a large telescope is needed to see this directly.

The Hyades ◉ ♛ ⚹ A large, loose, V-shaped
star cluster easily visible to the naked eye.
It is best viewed with binoculars because of its
considerable size, being scattered across the
apparent width of 10 full Moons. The cluster
lies about 150 light-years away.

Abbreviation Tel	Genitive Telescopii	Highest in sky at 10 pm July to August

TELESCOPIUM

This unremarkable constellation
south of Sagittarius was introduced
by the French astronomer Nicolas
Louis de Lacaille. In its original form,
it represented a large telescope supported
by a winch, but it is a poor tribute to such
an important instrument. Its brightest star
is Alpha (α) Telescopii, magnitude 3.5.

FULLY VISIBLE
33°N–90°S

THE
TELESCOPE

FEATURES OF INTEREST

Delta (δ) Telescopii ◉ ♛ An optical double
star divisible without optical aid by those with
good eyesight and easy to see with binoculars.
Delta-1 (δ¹), magnitude 4.9, is about 800 light-
years away; Delta-2 (δ²) is of magnitude 5.1
and lies more than 1,100 light-years away.

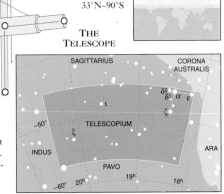

Width 🖐	Height 🖐	Area 252 square degrees	Size ranking 57th

Abbreviation Tri	Genitive Trianguli	Highest in sky at 10 pm November to December

TRIANGULUM

This small constellation can be found between Andromeda and Aries. It was known to the ancient Greeks, many of whom visualized it as the Nile delta, while for others it represented the island of Sicily. Its brightest star is Beta (β) Trianguli, magnitude 3.0.

THE
TRIANGLE

FULLY VISIBLE
90°N–52°S

FEATURES OF INTEREST

6 Trianguli ⚹ A binary star. A small telescope is needed to divide the 5th-magnitude primary from its close 7th-magnitude companion.

M33 ♙ ⚹ A spiral galaxy about 2.6 million light-years away and the third largest member of the Local Group of galaxies. It covers about the same area of sky as the full Moon. Because its light is so spread out, a clear, dark sky is needed to see it. Under good conditions, this galaxy can be detected through binoculars or a small telescope.

Width 🖐	Height ✋	Area 132 square degrees	Size ranking 78th

Abbreviation TrA	Genitive Trianguli Australis	Highest in sky at 10 pm June to July

TRIANGULUM AUSTRALE

Lying in the Milky Way near Alpha (α) and Beta (β) Centauri is the southern counterpart of the northern triangle, Triangulum. Although smaller than Triangulum, it is more prominent because its main stars are brighter. It is the smallest of the 12 constellations introduced at the end of the 16th century by the Dutch navigators Pieter Dirkszoon Keyser and Frederick de Houtman. Its brightest star is Alpha (α) Trianguli Australis, magnitude 1.9.

THE
SOUTHERN
TRIANGLE

TRIANGULUM AUSTRALE
The three corners of the triangle stand out among the fainter stars in the surrounding Milky Way.

FULLY VISIBLE
19°N–90°S

FEATURES OF INTEREST

NGC 6025 ♙ ⚹ An open cluster in the Milky Way, about one-third the apparent width of the full Moon and easy to see with binoculars or a small telescope, its brightest star being of 7th magnitude. It lies 2,700 light-years away.

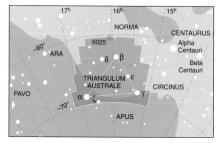

Width ✋	Height ✋	Area 110 square degrees	Size ranking 83rd

| Abbreviation Tuc | Genitive Tucanae | Highest in sky at 10 pm September to November |

TUCANA

This southern constellation, representing a toucan, the large-beaked bird of South and Central America, lies close to the bright star Achernar and south of two other celestial birds, Grus and Phoenix. It was invented in the late 16th century by the Dutch navigators Pieter Dirkszoon Keyser and Frederick de Houtman. Its brightest star is Alpha (α) Tucanae, magnitude 2.9, but its most notable naked-eye object is the Small Magellanic Cloud.

THE
TOUCAN

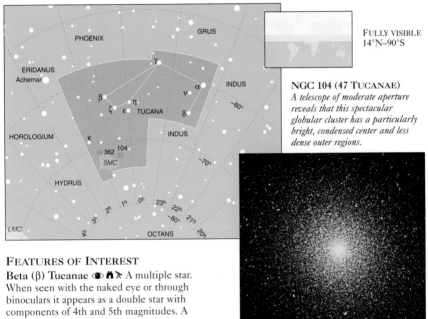

FULLY VISIBLE
14°N–90°S

NGC 104 (47 TUCANAE)
A telescope of moderate aperture reveals that this spectacular globular cluster has a particularly bright, condensed center and less dense outer regions.

FEATURES OF INTEREST

Beta (β) Tucanae ◉ ♁ ⊁ A multiple star. When seen with the naked eye or through binoculars it appears as a double star with components of 4th and 5th magnitudes. A small telescope further divides the primary into components of magnitudes 4.4 and 4.5.

Kappa (κ) Tucanae ⊁ A double star with components of 5th and 8th magnitudes that can be separated through a small telescope.

NGC 104 (47 Tucanae) ◉ ♁ ⊁ A globular cluster, rated the second best of its type in the whole sky. To the naked eye it appears similar to a hazy star of 4th magnitude. Binoculars or a small telescope show it covering the same area of sky as the full Moon, although an aperture of 4 in (100 mm) is needed to resolve its stars. The cluster lies 15,000 light-years away.

NGC 362 ♁ ⊁ A globular cluster visible with binoculars or a small telescope. It appears to

lie near the Small Magellanic Cloud (see below) but is, in fact, only 29,000 light-years away and hence is in our own Galaxy.

The Small Magellanic Cloud (SMC)
◉ ♁ ⊁ The smaller of the Milky Way's two satellite galaxies. It appears to the naked eye as an elongated patch of light seven times wider than the full Moon, while binoculars or a small telescope resolve individual clusters and nebulae within it. This galaxy is much smaller than our own, having only a few percent our Galaxy's mass and less than 10 percent of its diameter. It is about 190,000 light-years away.

| Width 🖐🤏 | Height 🖐 | Area 295 square degrees | Size ranking 48th |

Abbreviation UMa	Genitive Ursae Majoris	Highest in sky at 10 pm February to May

URSA MAJOR

Ursa Major is among the most famous constellations. It is the third largest in the sky, occupying a much wider area than that covered by the group of seven stars that form the asterism of the Big Dipper (Plough). Ursa Major represents Callisto, a mortal in Greek myth and a hunting partner of Artemis, who was seduced by Zeus. In different versions of the story, she was turned into a bear either by Zeus's jealous wife, Hera, or by the angry Artemis. Its brightest stars are Alpha (α) and Epsilon (ε) Ursae Majoris, both magnitude 1.8. A line drawn from Beta (β) through Alpha (α) Ursae Majoris points toward Polaris, the north Pole Star, in adjacent Ursa Minor.

THE GREAT BEAR

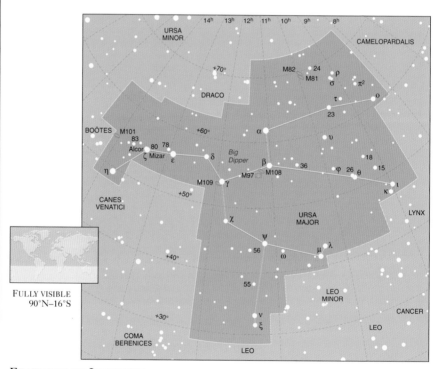

FULLY VISIBLE
90°N–16°S

FEATURES OF INTEREST

The Big Dipper (The Plough) 👁 One of the best-known patterns in the sky, consisting of the naked-eye stars Alpha (α), Beta (β), Gamma (γ), Delta (δ), Epsilon (ε), Zeta (ζ), and Eta (η) Ursae Majoris. The outline that they form is visualized in various cultures as that of a plow, a ladle, a saucepan, and even a wagon. All the stars in the Big Dipper, with the exception of the outermost two (Alpha and Eta), are traveling in the same direction through space and form what is known as a moving cluster.

Zeta (ζ) Ursae Majoris (Mizar) 👁 ♙ ⚹
A multiple star. Observers with good eyesight or using binoculars will see that this star of

Width 🖐🖐✋	Height 🖐✋	Area 1,280 square degrees	Size ranking 3rd

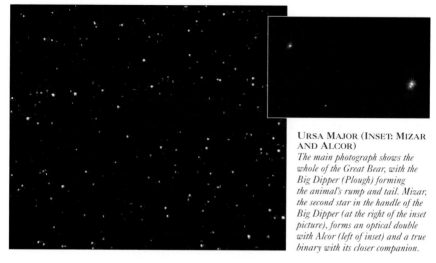

URSA MAJOR (INSET: MIZAR AND ALCOR)
The main photograph shows the whole of the Great Bear, with the Big Dipper (Plough) forming the animal's rump and tail. Mizar, the second star in the handle of the Big Dipper (at the right of the inset picture), forms an optical double with Alcor (left of inset) and a true binary with its closer companion.

magnitude 2.2 has a partner of magnitude 4.0, known as Alcor or 80 Ursae Majoris. Mizar and Alcor are 78 and 81 light-years away, so they are not a true binary pair. However, a small telescope reveals that Mizar has a closer 4th-magnitude companion. This pair forms a true binary with a very long orbital period.

Xi (ξ) Ursae Majoris ⋆ A binary star with close components of magnitudes 4.3 and 4.8 that can be separated through a telescope of 3 in (75 mm) aperture. The yellowish stars, similar to the Sun, are 26 light-years away and have an orbital period of 60 years.

M81 and M82 ♋⋆ Two contrasting galaxies about 10 million light-years away. M81 is a beautiful spiral, visible with binoculars or a small telescope. One Moon diameter to the north is the smaller and fainter M82, a galaxy of peculiar appearance, which is now thought to be a spiral seen edge-on that is passing through a dust cloud.

M101 ♋⋆ A spiral galaxy that appears face-on to us. It covers almost as much sky as the full Moon but is quite faint, and good conditions are required if it is to be seen with binoculars or a small telescope.

M81
This beautiful spiral galaxy is one of the easiest examples of its type to see with a small telescope.

M101
The arms of this spiral galaxy can be seen with a large telescope or on a long-exposure photograph.

Abbreviation UMi	Genitive Ursae Minoris	Highest in sky at 10 pm May to June

URSA MINOR

Ursa Minor contains the north celestial pole. By chance, there is a moderately bright star, known as Polaris (or the north Pole Star), about 1 degree from the pole. Navigators have long recognized that when looking at Polaris one is facing almost due north. Ursa Minor's main stars form a shape known as the Little Dipper, while the stars Beta (β) and Gamma (γ) Ursae Minoris (Kochab and Pherkad), in the dipper's bowl, are known as the Guardians of the Pole. Ursa Minor is named after a nymph who nursed the infant Zeus, although it is not clear why she is depicted as a bear.

THE LESSER
BEAR

FULLY VISIBLE
90°N–0°

THE MAIN STARS IN URSA
MINOR (INSET: POLARIS)
Polaris (at the top of the main photograph and inset) marks the tip of the lesser bear's tail.

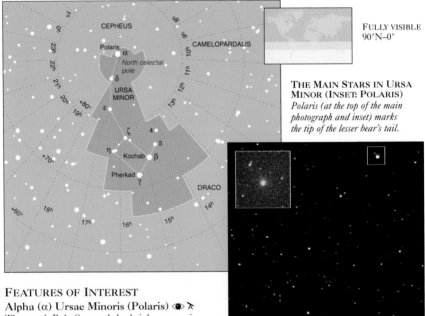

FEATURES OF INTEREST

Alpha (α) Ursae Minoris (Polaris) ◉ ✹
The north Pole Star and the brightest star in the constellation, a yellow-white supergiant of magnitude 2.0. It is in fact a Cepheid variable, although its fluctuations in magnitude are so slight that they cannot be detected with the naked eye. A small telescope shows an unrelated 8th-magnitude companion.

Gamma (γ) Ursae Minoris (Pherkad) ◉ ♠
An optical double star with components that are divisible with the naked eye or binoculars. Gamma itself is a blue-white giant star of magnitude 3.0, 480 light-years away. Its partner, 11 Ursae Minoris, is an orange giant, of magnitude 5.0, 390 light-years away.

Eta (η) Ursae Minoris ◉ ♠ An optical double star. It is a white star of magnitude 5.0 lying 97 light-years away. The naked eye and binoculars show a wide companion, 19 Ursae Minoris, of magnitude 5.5, which is almost seven times farther away than the primary.

Width 🖐	Height 🖐🖐	Area 256 square degrees	Size ranking 56th

Abbreviation Vel	Genitive Velorum	Highest in sky at 10 pm February to April

VELA

This is one of the three parts into which the ancient
Greek constellation of Argo Navis (the ship of the
argonauts) was divided by Nicolas Louis de Lacaille.
It represents the sails of the ship. Vela lies in the Milky
Way with Carina and Puppis, the other two portions of
the ship, on one side, and Centaurus on the other.
Since it is only a part of the once-larger constellation,
Vela contains no stars labeled Alpha (α) or Beta (β).

THE
SAILS

FULLY VISIBLE
32°N–90°S

NGC 3132 (THE EIGHT-BURST NEBULA)
*Long-exposure photographs such
as this one reveal the loops of gas,
intertwined like figure eights, after
which this nebula is named.*

FEATURES OF INTEREST

Gamma (γ) Velorum �}{ ⊁ A multiple star.
Through a small telescope or even good
binoculars, it appears as a wide double star.
The primary, Gamma-2 (γ^2), is the brightest
star in the constellation, at magnitude 1.8. It
is a spectroscopic binary, one component of
which is a Wolf–Rayet star, a rare type of ultra-
hot star that has lost its outer hydrogen layers.
The primary's visible partner, Gamma-1 (γ^1),
is an ordinary blue-white star of magnitude
4.3. There are also two wider companions
of 8th and 9th magnitudes, which are visible
through a small telescope.

NGC 2547 ♁ ⊁ An open cluster visible with
binoculars or a small telescope. It is more than
half the apparent size of the full Moon and lies
1,300 light-years away.

NGC 3132 (The Eight-Burst Nebula) ⊁
A planetary nebula. Its rounded disk is visible

with a small telescope, which may also reveal
the 10th-magnitude star at its center. Photographs show complex loops within the nebula.

IC 2391 ◉ ♁ ⊁ A large open cluster, visible
to the naked eye and an ideal object for
binocular observation, covering a greater area
of sky than the full Moon. Its brightest star
is Omicron (o) Velorum, magnitude 3.6. The
cluster lies nearly 600 light-years away.

Width ✋🤚	Height ✋	Area 500 square degrees	Size ranking 32nd

| Abbreviation Vir | Genitive Virginis | Highest in sky at 10 pm April to June |

VIRGO

This is the largest constellation of the zodiac and the second largest of all the constellations. It lies on the celestial equator between Leo and Libra. The constellation is usually identified as Dike, the Greek goddess of justice, or sometimes as Demeter, the corn goddess. Virgo is of particular interest because it contains the nearest large cluster of galaxies, the Virgo Cluster. The Sun passes through the constellation from September 16 to October 31.

THE
VIRGIN

FULLY VISIBLE
67°N–75°S

FEATURES OF INTEREST

Alpha (α) Virginis (Spica) ◉ The brightest star in Virgo and, at magnitude 1.0, among the 20 brightest in the sky. It is a blue-white star, 260 light-years away. Spica is Latin for "ear of wheat," an object Virgo holds in her left hand.

Gamma (γ) Virginis ⋟ A binary star. To the naked eye it looks like one star of magnitude 2.7. In fact, there are two yellow-white stars (both of magnitude 3.5) orbiting a common center of mass every 169 years. This motion affects the stars' appearance: in the 1990s they can be split with a moderate aperture; around 2005, when they will be closest to each other as seen from Earth, a 10 in (250 mm) aperture will be needed to divide them. They will then move rapidly apart and will be divisible with a small aperture for the rest of the century.

M87 ⋟ A famous giant elliptical galaxy near the center of the Virgo Cluster (see below).

It is probably the easiest member of the cluster to see through a small telescope.

M104 (The Sombrero Galaxy) ⋟ A spiral galaxy that appears almost edge-on to us and looks elongated when seen with a small telescope. Larger apertures show a dark lane of dust in the spiral arms, crossing the central nucleus of stars. The galaxy is not part of the Virgo Cluster but lies somewhat closer to us.

The Virgo Cluster (The Virgo–Coma Cluster) ⋟ A cluster of 2,000 or more galaxies about 50 million light-years away that extends from Virgo into Coma Berenices. Its brightest members, notably the elliptical galaxies M49, M60, M84, M86, and M87, are visible with the size of telescope used by amateur observers.

M104 (THE
SOMBRERO
GALAXY)
*This spiral
galaxy owes
its name to
its flattened
appearance.*

| Width 🖐🖐🖐 | Height 🖐🖐 | Area 1,294 square degrees | Size ranking 2nd |

Abbreviation Vol	Genitive Volantis	Highest in sky at 10 pm January to March

VOLANS

THE FLYING FISH

This faint southern constellation adjoins Carina. Invented at the end of the 16th century by the Dutch navigators Pieter Dirkszoon Keyser and Frederick de Houtman, it represents the fish of tropical waters that can glide above the waves on its outstretched fins.

FULLY VISIBLE
14°N–90°S

FEATURES OF INTEREST

Gamma (γ) Volantis ⚹ An attractive double star. A small telescope reveals its orange and yellow components of magnitudes 3.8 and 5.7.

Epsilon (ε) Volantis ⚹ A double star with 4th- and 7th-magnitude components that can be divided with a small telescope.

Width 🖐	Height 🖐	Area 141 square degrees	Size ranking 76th

Abbreviation Vul	Genitive Vulpeculae	Highest in sky at 10 pm August to September

VULPECULA

Vulpecula is in the Milky Way, to the south of Cygnus. When it was introduced in the late 17th century by the Polish astronomer Johannes Hevelius, it was named Vulpecula cum Anser (the Fox and Goose). Its brightest star is Alpha (α) Vulpeculae, magnitude 4.4.

THE FOX

FULLY VISIBLE
90°N–61°S

FEATURES OF INTEREST

M27 (The Dumbbell Nebula) 🔭⚹ A large planetary nebula appearing through binoculars as a rounded patch about a quarter the size of the full Moon. Its twin-lobed shape, which explains its popular name, can be seen with a telescope of moderate to large aperture or on a photograph. It is about 1,000 light-years away.

Brocchi's Cluster (Collinder 399, The Coathanger) 🔭 An unusual open cluster that is easy to find with binoculars. It consists of a line of six stars of 6th and 7th magnitudes, from the center of which extends a "hook" formed by four other stars, giving it the appearance of a coathanger.

BROCCHI'S CLUSTER
This open cluster lies in the southern part of Vulpecula within the division in the Milky Way known as the Cygnus Rift.

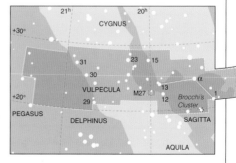

Width 🖐🖐	Height 🖐	Area 268 square degrees	Size ranking 55th

MONTHLY SKY GUIDES

HOW THIS SECTION WORKS

THIS SECTION INCLUDES detailed sky charts for every month of the year, with a separate chart for each hemisphere. Each month is introduced by a double-page feature, which looks at interesting celestial phenomena and uses simplified charts to assist in identifying prominent stars and constellations.

USING THE CHARTS

Both the introductory charts (see below) and the whole-sky charts (see opposite) show the night sky as it appears from latitudes 60–20°N (northern hemisphere) and 0–40°S (southern hemisphere). Use the world map (right) to identify your own latitude and associated color code, then decide which hemisphere map is best for you. You can then use the color-coded lines and crosses on all charts to identify the viewing horizon and zenith (point overhead) for your latitude. Compared with the whole-sky charts, the introductory charts show a simplified and less detailed view of the night sky.

	80°N
	60°N
	40°N
	20°N
	0
	20°S
	40°S
	60°S

△ FINDING YOUR COLOUR CODE
Use this map to identify the color of the latitude line nearest to your geographical location. Bear in mind that 10 degrees difference in latitude will have little effect on the stars you can actually see.

clocks indicate times at which charts apply (see panel opposite)

text draws attention to bright stars and prominent constellations visible in the month

charts show all stars brighter than magnitude 3.0 and a selection of constellation patterns

color-coded lines define view from zenith to eastern and western horizons

compass direction

colour-coded horizon lines

times of sunrise and sunset in midmonth

photograph of easily recognizable star pattern or bright deep-sky object

key to star magnitudes

panel refers to objects shown on whole-sky charts on following pages

descriptions of stars and deep-sky objects

cross-references to well-placed features described under other months

description of bright meteor showers (not shown on charts)

ecliptic

△ INTRODUCTION TO THE MONTH
A variety of features on these pages introduce whatever is of interest in the month. The maps are to be held vertically, and show the view ahead and to the sides, facing north or south.

HOW TO USE THE WHOLE-SKY CHARTS

To view the sky to the south, hold the book flat with the SOUTH label (at the edge of the chart) nearest your body. Your color-coded line (around the near edge of the chart) indicates the horizon in front of you; the cross near the chart center represents the zenith (the point directly overhead). The area of the chart beyond your zenith represents the sky to the north; to view this, turn the book around.

when looking south, hold right-hand edge of book nearest to you

WHOLE-SKY CHART ▷

chart shows all stars brighter than magnitude 5.0 •

all 88 constellation • patterns are plotted on the charts

symbol for deep-sky object •

color-coded • crosses indicate zeniths from various latitudes

compass direction •

color-coded horizon lines for use when facing north

key to star • magnitudes

STAR-MOTION DIAGRAMS

NORTHERN HEMISPHERE

SOUTHERN HEMISPHERE

Next to each whole-sky chart is a diagram showing the direction in which the stars appear to move as the night progresses. The arrows show a general motion from east to west, due to the Earth's rotation, but circumpolar stars (at one end of each chart, as shown by the diagram) rotate around one of the celestial poles without setting.

• star-motion diagram (see above)

• color-coded horizon lines for use when facing south

• ecliptic (useful for locating planets)

• Milky Way

• center of chart shows sky directly overhead

• sides of chart show stars visible to east and west

• table shows times when chart is applicable (see panel below)

• key to deep-sky objects

TIME

The charts for a particular month show the sky as it appears at 10 PM in mid-month – that is, at 10 PM standard (Std) time for a given time zone. When daylight savings time (DST or summer time) is in use, they show the sky as it appears one hour later. The sky will look the same at 11 PM at the start of the month and at 9 PM at the end of the month as it does at 10 PM in mid-month. If you wish to look at the sky at a different time, you will need to use charts shown under a different month: for every two hours of time before or after 10 PM, go one month backward or forward. So, if you want to look at the sky at midnight on January 15, turn to the chart for February.

JANUARY

J ANUARY EVENING SKIES are the most magnificent of the year, with Orion surrounded by a host of bright stars, including Sirius, the brightest of all. From southern latitudes, Canopus, the second-brightest star, and the nearby small galaxy known as the Large Magellanic Cloud add to the richness of the scene.

SUNRISE AND SUNSET ON JANUARY 15

Latitude	Sunrise	Sunset
60°N	08:50	15:30
40°N	07:20	17:00
20°N	06:40	17:40
0°	06:10	18:10
20°S	05:30	18:50
40°S	04:50	19:30

January 1 Std time ◷ DST ◷ | January 15 Std time ◷ DST ◷ | January 30 Std time ◷ DST ◷

NORTHERN LATITUDES

• **LOOKING NORTH** The saucepan shape of the Big Dipper (Plough) stands on its handle to the right of Polaris, the Pole Star. The W-shape of Cassiopeia is to Polaris's left, with Cepheus beneath it. Capella is almost overhead. Leo rises in the northeast, while the Great Square of Pegasus sets in the northwest.

• **LOOKING SOUTH** Magnificent Orion commands center stage, to the right of his dogs, marked by Sirius (in Canis Major) and Procyon (in Canis Minor). Aldebaran glints above and to the right of Orion, with the Pleiades cluster (see p.147) higher and farther to the right. Nearly overhead are Castor and Pollux, along with Capella.

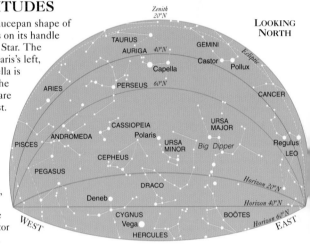

LOOKING NORTH

SOUTHERN LATITUDES

• **LOOKING NORTH** Orion stands high, with Capella and the other stars of Auriga closer to the northern horizon. Brilliant Sirius and Procyon are visible to Orion's right. Aldebaran and the stars of Taurus are to the lower left of Orion, with Castor and Pollux to Orion's lower right, in the northeast. Perseus sets in the northwest.

• **LOOKING SOUTH** Canopus is high in the south, with Sirius above it, almost overhead. Lower down, to the southwest, Achernar marks the end of the celestial river, Eridanus. Just below Canopus is the Large Magellanic Cloud (LMC); the Small Magellanic Cloud (SMC) is to its lower right (see p.149).

LOOKING NORTH

ORION'S BELT
The three stars at the center of this picture form a distinctive line that marks the belt of Orion, the hunter (pp.114–15). They are (from left to right): Delta (δ) Orionis (also known as Mintaka), Epsilon (ε) Orionis (Alnilam), and Zeta (ζ) Orionis (Alnitak).

Star magnitudes	−1	0	1	2	3

WHOLE-SKY CHARTS

JANUARY FEATURES

☐ **M42 (ORION).** This diffuse nebula forms part of the sword that hangs from Orion's belt. It is one of the most celebrated objects in the entire sky and the most prominent of all nebulae, being visible to the naked eye under good conditions as a hazy, milky white or greenish patch, although it is better seen with binoculars. A huge cloud of dust and gas, M42 consists mainly of hydrogen gas, which shows as a reddish color on photographs. It glows by the light of a star that formed within it, Theta-1 (θ¹) Orionis, also called the Trapezium since it in fact consists of four stars, visible through a small telescope. See also pp.114–15.

ALSO VISIBLE
● Castor (p.151)
✲ M36, M37, and M38 (p.211)
✲ M41 (p.151)
✲ M44 (p.157)
☐ NGC 2244 (p.151)
● The Hyades and Pleiades (p.211)

LOOKING SOUTH

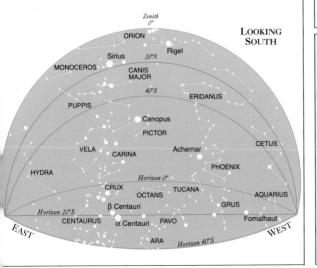

LOOKING SOUTH

JANUARY METEORS

THE QUADRANTIDS. This shower, visible to Northern-Hemisphere observers only, appears in the first week of January, radiating from northern Boötes, near the Big Dipper's handle. This area was once known as the constellation of Quadrans, hence the shower's name. Activity reaches about 100 meteors an hour on January 3 and 4, but the peak is short-lived, the meteors are usually faint, and the radiant does not rise very high until after midnight.

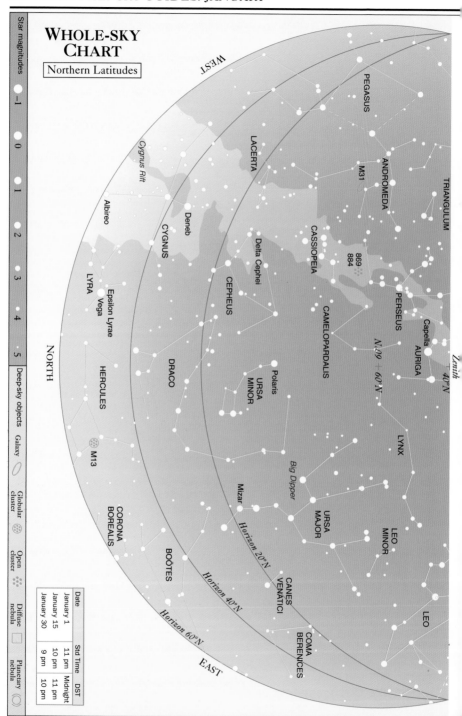

WHOLE-SKY CHART

Northern Latitudes

Star magnitudes

-1
0
1
2
3
4
5

Deep-sky objects

Galaxy
Globular cluster
Open cluster
Diffuse nebula
Planetary nebula

WEST

PEGASUS

LACERTA

ANDROMEDA

M31

TRIANGULUM

Cygnus Rift

CASSIOPEIA

869
884

Albireo

Deneb

CYGNUS

Delta Cephei

CEPHEUS

PERSEUS

Capella

AURIGA

N 60°

Zenith
40°N

LYRA

Epsilon Lyrae
Vega

CAMELOPARDALIS

N 60° + 60°N

HERCULES

DRACO

Polaris

URSA
MINOR

LYNX

NORTH

M13

Mizar

Big Dipper

URSA
MAJOR

LEO
MINOR

CORONA
BOREALIS

BOÖTES

Horizon 20°N

CANES
VENATICI

LEO

Horizon 40°N

COMA
BERENICES

Horizon 60°N

EAST

Date	Std Time	DST
January 1	11 pm	Midnight
January 15	10 pm	11 pm
January 30	9 pm	10 pm

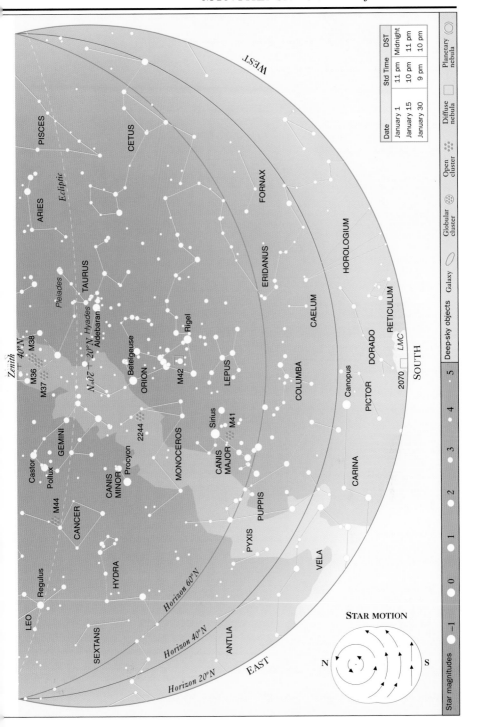

Date	Std Time	DST
January 1	11 pm	Midnight
January 15	10 pm	11 pm
January 30	9 pm	10 pm

WEST

PISCES

CETUS

ARIES

Ecliptic

FORNAX

ERIDANUS

HOROLOGIUM

Pleiades

TAURUS

CAELUM

Zenith

40°N

M38

M36

M37

20°N Hyades

Aldebaran

Rigel

RETICULUM

Plantary nebula

Betelgeuse

M42

LEPUS

COLUMBA

DORADO

LMC

ORION

2070

SOUTH

GEMINI

Castor

Pollux

Sirius

M41

Canopus

PICTOR

Castor

M44

2244

CANIS MAJOR

MONOCEROS

CANIS MINOR

Procyon

CANCER

CARINA

VELA

PUPPIS

PYXIS

Regulus

LEO

HYDRA

Horizon 60°N

SEXTANS

Horizon 40°N

ANTLIA

Horizon 20°N

EAST

Star magnitudes

−1 0 1 2 3 4 5

Deep-sky objects

Galaxy Globular cluster Open cluster Diffuse nebula Planetary nebula

STAR MOTION

N S

WHOLE-SKY CHART

Southern Latitudes

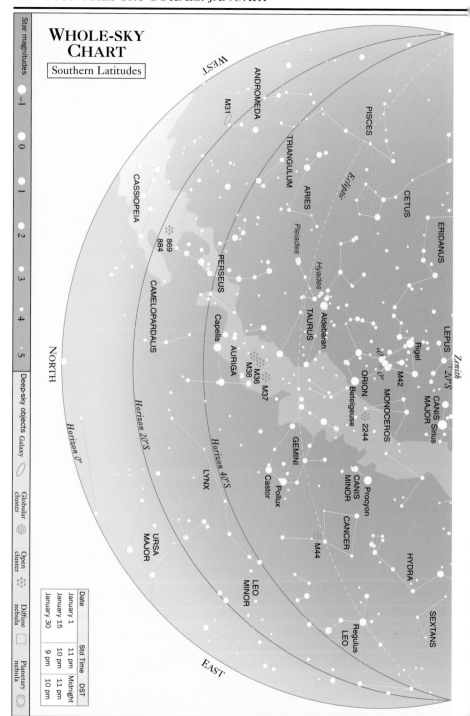

Star magnitudes
- −1
- 0
- 1
- 2
- 3
- 4
- 5

Deep-sky objects
Galaxy
Globular cluster
Open cluster
Diffuse nebula
Planetary nebula

Date	Std Time	DST
January 1	11 pm	Midnight
January 15	10 pm	11 pm
January 30	9 pm	10 pm

WEST

NORTH

EAST

Zenith

ANDROMEDA

M31

PISCES

TRIANGULUM

CASSIOPEIA

ARIES

CETUS

ERIDANUS

869
884

Pleiades

PERSEUS

Hyades

LEPUS

CAMELOPARDALIS

Capella

TAURUS

Aldebaran

Rigel

M42

ORION

Betelgeuse

M44

20°S

CANIS MAJOR

Sirius

AURIGA

M36
M38

M37

Ecliptic

MONOCEROS

2244

GEMINI

Castor

Pollux

CANIS MINOR

Procyon

LYNX

CANCER

HYDRA

URSA MAJOR

LEO MINOR

M44

LEO

Regulus

SEXTANS

Horizon 0°

Horizon 20°S

Horizon 40°S

20°S

0°

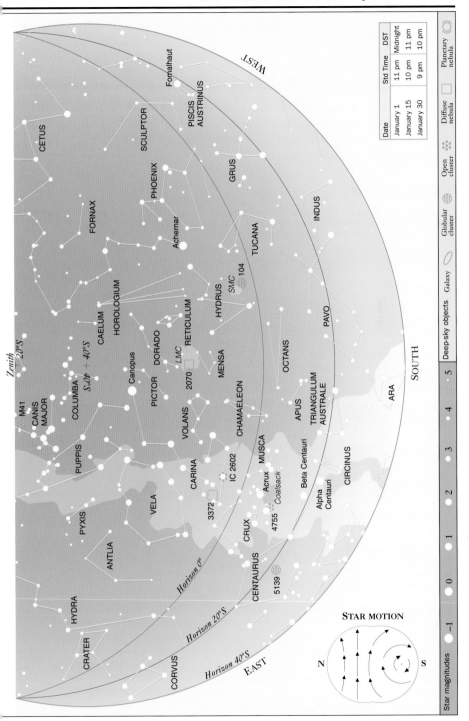

Date	Std Time	DST
		Midnight
January 1	11 pm	11 pm
January 15	10 pm	11 pm
January 30	9 pm	10 pm

WEST

SOUTH

EAST

Zenith
20°S

CETUS

Fomalhaut

PISCIS
AUSTRINUS

SCULPTOR

GRUS

PHOENIX

FORNAX

Achernar

TUCANA

INDUS

SMC
104

HYDRUS

HOROLOGIUM

CAELUM

RETICULUM

DORADO

MENSA

PAVO

LMC
2070

OCTANS

COLUMBA

S₂0° + 40°S

Canopus

PICTOR

CHAMAELEON

APUS

TRIANGULUM
AUSTRALE

ARA

M41

CANIS
MAJOR

PUPPIS

VOLANS

MUSCA

CIRCINUS

PYXIS

VELA

CARINA

IC 2602

Acrux
Coalsack

Beta Centauri

Alpha
Centauri

3372

4755

ANTLIA

CRUX

CENTAURUS

5139

HYDRA

CRATER

CORVUS

Horizon 0°

Horizon 20°S

Horizon 40°S

STAR MOTION

N   S

| Star magnitudes | −1 | 0 | 1 | 2 | 3 | 4 | 5 | Deep-sky objects | Galaxy | Globular cluster | Open cluster | Diffuse nebula | Planetary nebula |

FEBRUARY

S IRIUS, the brightest star, is visible in the evening sky at all latitudes, while observers in the south can also see Canopus, the second-brightest star. High in southern skies are the three constellations – Carina, Puppis, and Vela – that the ancient Greeks regarded as one: Argo Navis, the ship of Jason and the Argonauts.

SUNRISE AND SUNSET ON FEBRUARY 15

Latitude	Sunrise	Sunset
60°N	07:40	16:50
40°N	06:50	17:40
20°N	06:30	18:00
0°	06:10	18:20
20°S	05:50	18:40
40°S	05:30	19:00

February 1 Std time 🕐 DST 🕐 | February 15 Std time 🕐 DST 🕐 | March 1 Std time 🕐 DST 🕐

NORTHERN LATITUDES

• **LOOKING NORTH** Perseus and Cassiopeia are easy to find in the northwest, with the bright star Capella in Auriga above them. The familiar seven-star outline of the Big Dipper (Plough) is the main feature in the northeast. Due north, the faint constellations Cepheus and Draco skim the horizon.
• **LOOKING SOUTH** Orion and Taurus are prominent in the southwest. Sirius, the brightest star in the sky, lies almost due south, with Procyon above and slightly to its left. Castor and Pollux, the two brightest stars in Gemini, are overhead, with Cancer to their left. In the southeast, the distinctive shape of Leo is becoming well placed.

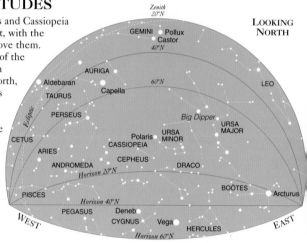

SOUTHERN LATITUDES

• **LOOKING NORTH** Castor and Pollux in Gemini lie due north, with Procyon in Canis Minor above them. Sirius shines near the zenith. The stars of Orion and Taurus are prominently placed in the northwest, while Leo follows Cancer into the northeastern sky.
• **LOOKING SOUTH** The three parts of Argo Navis, the ship of the Argonauts, are easily seen: Carina, the keel (with its brightest star Canopus); Puppis, the stern; and Vela, the sails, in between them. Achernar, in Eridanus, lies in the southwest with the Magellanic Clouds close by (see p.155). In the southeast, Centaurus and Crux (the Southern Cross) are rising.

THE WINTER TRIANGLE
Three brilliant stars in separate constellations form an equilateral triangle in the skies of northern winter and southern summer. Sirius in Canis Major forms the southern apex, while Betelgeuse (top right) in Orion and Procyon (top left) in Canis Minor complete the figure. The Winter Triangle straddles the celestial equator and is clearly visible from all latitudes.

WHOLE-SKY CHARTS

FEBRUARY FEATURES

● **CASTOR (GEMINI).** This star, also known as Alpha (α) Geminorum, can be seen as a close double through a telescope with magnification of about 100 times. The two stars orbit each other about every 470 years. There are other stars connected to Castor by gravity, too, completing a family of six stars in all, including a pair of faint red dwarfs. All six stars formed from the same cloud of gas. See also p.96.

❖ **M41 (CANIS MAJOR).** Observers in high northern latitudes often overlook this open cluster four degrees south of Sirius because from their locations it lies close to the horizon. However, it is easy to see with binoculars and can be detected with the naked eye under favorable conditions. See also p.74.

❖ **NGC 2244 (MONOCEROS).** The brightest members of this large open cluster are easily visible through binoculars. The stars are arranged in a rectangle, but the brightest of them, 6th-magnitude 12 Monocerotis, is a foreground object. The cluster lies at the center of the Rosette Nebula (NGC 2237), a flowerlike loop of gas that shows up well only on photographs. See also pp.110–11.

Star magnitudes	–1	0	1	2	3

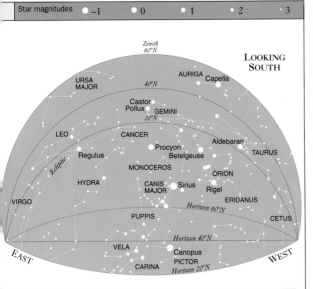

LOOKING SOUTH

Zenith 60°N

URSA MAJOR
AURIGA Capella
40°N
Castor Pollux GEMINI
20°N
LEO
CANCER
Regulus
Procyon
Betelgeuse
Aldebaran
TAURUS
Ecliptic
MONOCEROS
ORION
HYDRA
CANIS MAJOR
Sirius
Rigel
ERIDANUS
VIRGO
Horizon 60°N
PUPPIS
CETUS
Horizon 40°N
VELA
Canopus
PICTOR
EAST
CARINA
Horizon 20°N
WEST

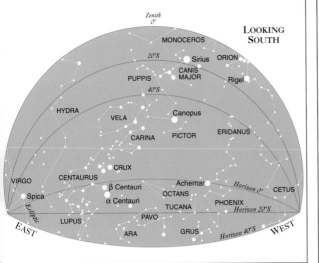

LOOKING SOUTH

Zenith 0°

MONOCEROS
20°S
Sirius ORION
CANIS MAJOR
PUPPIS
Rigel
40°S
HYDRA
VELA
Canopus
CARINA
PICTOR
ERIDANUS
CRUX
CENTAURUS
VIRGO
Achernar
Horizon 0°
CETUS
Spica
β Centauri
OCTANS
α Centauri
TUCANA
PHOENIX
Horizon 20°S
Ecliptic
PAVO
LUPUS
EAST
ARA
GRUS
Horizon 40°S
WEST

ALSO VISIBLE
❖ M36, M37, and M38 (p.211)
☐ M42 (p.145)
❖ M44 (p.211)
☐ NGC 3372 (p.157)
❖ IC 2602 (p.157)
● The Hyades and Pleiades (p.211)

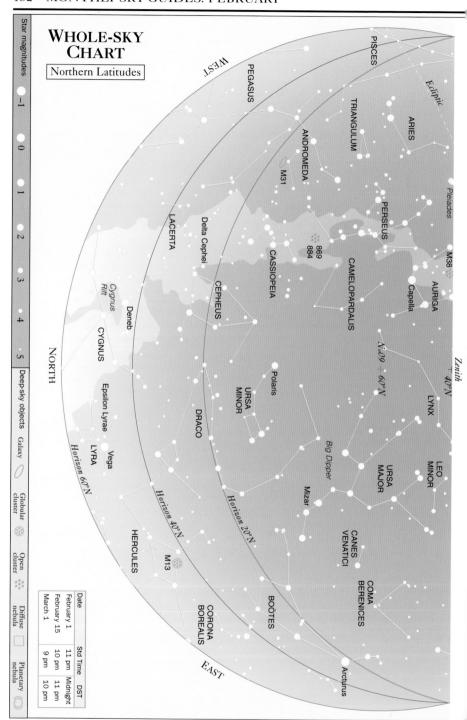

WHOLE-SKY CHART

Northern Latitudes

Star magnitudes

● −1
● 0
● 1
● 2
● 3
● 4
· 5

Deep-sky objects

Galaxy ◯
Globular cluster
Open cluster
Diffuse nebula
Planetary nebula ◎

WEST

PISCES
PEGASUS
TRIANGULUM
ARIES
ANDROMEDA
M31
PERSEUS
Ecliptic
Pleiades
M38
Capella
AURIGA
CAMELOPARDALIS
869 884
CASSIOPEIA
LACERTA
Delta Cephei
CEPHEUS
Cygnus Rift
Deneb
CYGNUS
Epsilon Lyrae
Vega
LYRA
Horizon 60°N
Horizon 40°N
Horizon 20°N
DRACO
URSA MINOR
Polaris
Zenith 40°N
Nadir 60°N
LYNX
LEO MINOR
URSA MAJOR
Big Dipper
Mizar
CANES VENATICI
COMA BERENICES
NORTH
HERCULES
M13
CORONA BOREALIS
BOÖTES
Arcturus
EAST

Date	Std Time	DST
February 1	11 pm	Midnight
February 15	10 pm	11 pm
March 1	9 pm	10 pm

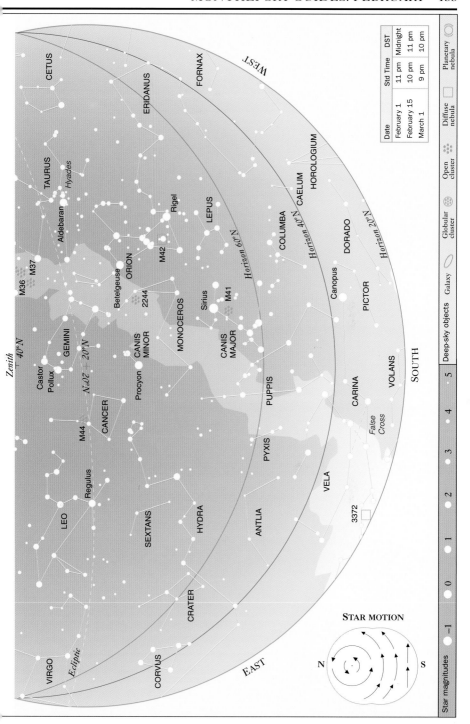

Date	Std Time	DST
February 1	11 pm	Midnight
February 15	10 pm	11 pm
March 1	9 pm	10 pm

Deep-sky objects

Galaxy | Globular cluster | Open cluster | Diffuse nebula | Planetary nebula

Star magnitudes

−1 0 1 2 3 4 5

STAR MOTION

N   S

WEST

SOUTH

EAST

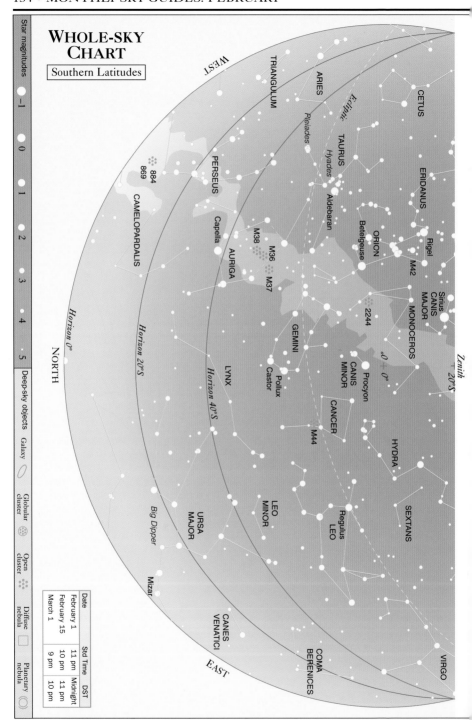

WHOLE-SKY CHART

Southern Latitudes

Star magnitudes

−1 0 1 2 3 4 5

Deep-sky objects

Galaxy

Globular cluster

Open cluster

Diffuse nebula

Planetary nebula

NORTH

WEST

EAST

Zenith 20°S

Horizon 0°

Horizon 20°S

Horizon 40°S

TRIANGULUM
ARIES
CETUS
ERIDANUS
Rigel
ORION
Betelgeuse
M42
Aldebaran
Hyades
TAURUS
Pleiades
Ecliptic
PERSEUS
Capella
AURIGA
M38
M36
M37
CAMELOPARDALIS
884
869
Sirius
CANIS MAJOR
MONOCEROS
2244
GEMINI
Castor
Pollux
CANIS MINOR
Procyon
+0° 0°
CANCER
M44
HYDRA
LYNX
LEO MINOR
CANCER
Regulus
LEO
SEXTANS
URSA MAJOR
Big Dipper
Mizar
CANES VENATICI
COMA BERENICES
VIRGO

Date	Std Time	DST
February 1	11 pm	Midnight
February 15	10 pm	11 pm
March 1	9 pm	10 pm

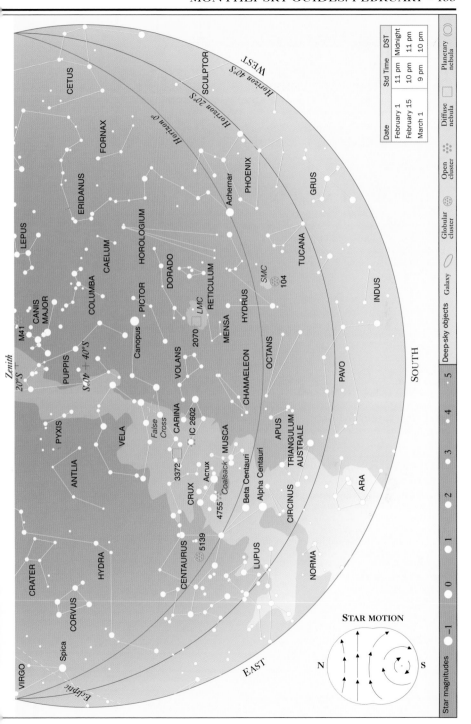

Date	Std Time	DST
February 1	11 pm	Midnight
February 15	10 pm	11 pm
March 1	9 pm	10 pm

Deep-sky objects

| Galaxy | Globular cluster | Open cluster | Diffuse nebula | Planetary nebula |

Star magnitudes

| −1 | 0 | 1 | 2 | 3 | 4 | 5 |

STAR MOTION

MARCH

D AY AND NIGHT are nearly equal in length all over the world as the equinox approaches, around March 21, the start of northern spring and southern fall. Orion and the bright stars around it are in the west, while from southern latitudes rich fields of stars, from Carina to Centaurus, lie south and southeast.

SUNRISE AND SUNSET ON MARCH 15

Latitude	Sunrise	Sunset
60°N	06:20	18:00
40°N	06:10	18:10
20°N	06:10	18:10
0°	06:10	18:10
20°S	06:00	18:20
40°S	06:00	18:20

March 1 Std time 🕐 DST 🕐 | March 15 Std time 🕐 DST 🕐 | March 30 Std time 🕐 DST 🕐

NORTHERN LATITUDES

• **LOOKING NORTH** The Big Dipper (Plough) stands high in the northeast. Its bowl opens downward, toward Polaris, while its handle points east to Arcturus, whose rising signals the arrival of spring. Capella is the most prominent star in the northwest, with Perseus and Cassiopeia now sinking low toward the western horizon.

• **LOOKING SOUTH** Leo, shaped like a crouching lion, lies due south, with the fainter stars of Cancer to its right. Virgo, with its brightest star Spica, is rising in the southeast, while Orion and the other stars of winter depart in the south-west. Sirius appears to twinkle above the southwestern horizon.

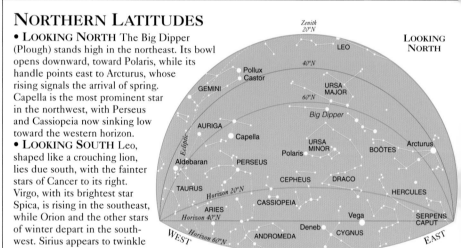

SOUTHERN LATITUDES

• **LOOKING NORTH** The zodiacal constellations of Gemini, Cancer, and Leo follow each other across the sky from northwest to northeast. The faint stars around the head of Hydra are high in the north. Arcturus can just be seen above the northeastern horizon, heralding the change of season.

• **LOOKING SOUTH** Carina and Vela, which lie almost due south, are densely packed with stars. Sirius, Canopus, and the Large Magellanic Cloud (see p.161) lie to the southwest. In the southeast, Centaurus and Crux (the Southern Cross) are rising. Orion is sinking in the west, while Virgo and the other stars of winter enter from the east.

THE FALSE CROSS
Four stars in the adjacent constellations Carina and Vela form the False Cross, sometimes mistaken for the smaller but brighter true Southern Cross. The stars are Kappa (κ) and Delta (δ) Velorum (top left and right) and Iota (ι) and Epsilon (ε) Carinae (bottom left and right).

WHOLE-SKY CHARTS

MARCH FEATURES

✢ **M44 (CANCER).** Cancer, the faintest constellation of the zodiac, contains a major attraction: the open cluster M44, popularly known as Praesepe or the Beehive. Binoculars show it as a rounded patch of faint stars, resembling a swarm of bees. It can be detected with the naked eye in rural skies. The stars Gamma (γ) and Delta (δ) Cancri, to the north and south of the cluster, were visualized in ancient times as donkeys feeding at a manger. See also p.72.

☐ **NGC 3372 (CARINA).** This diffuse nebula, which contains the 6th-magnitude star Eta (η) Carinae, is commonly known as the Eta Carinae Nebula. On dark nights it can be seen with the naked eye, appearing as a particularly bright patch in the Milky Way. Its large size makes it ideal for observation through binoculars. A dark, V-shaped lane of dust runs through it. See also pp.76–77.

✢ **IC 2602 (CARINA).** This bright open star cluster, popularly termed the Southern Pleiades, consists of a handful of naked-eye stars, the brightest of which is Theta (θ) Carinae, magnitude 2.7. Binoculars show about two dozen stars. See also pp.76–77.

| Star magnitudes | –1 | 0 | 1 | 2 | 3 |

LOOKING SOUTH

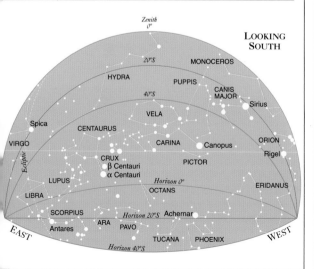

LOOKING SOUTH

ALSO VISIBLE

● Acrux (p.163)
● Castor (p.151)
✢ M36, M37, and M38 (p.211)
✢ M41 (p.151)
☐ M42 (p.145)
☐ NGC 2244 (p.151)
✢ NGC 4755 (p.163)

WHOLE-SKY CHART

Northern Latitudes

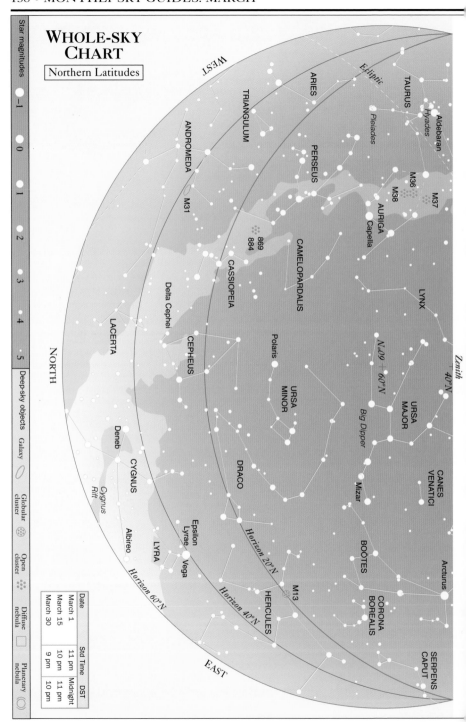

WEST

Ecliptic

ARIES

TAURUS

Aldebaran

Hyades

Pleiades

TRIANGULUM

PERSEUS

M36

M38

M37

ANDROMEDA

AURIGA

Capella

M31

CAMELOPARDALIS

LYNX

869
884

CASSIOPEIA

Delta Cephei

LACERTA

CEPHEUS

Polaris

URSA
MINOR

N°09 ⊹ 60°N

URSA
MAJOR

Zenith
40°N

CANES
VENATICI

Big Dipper

NORTH

Deneb

CYGNUS

DRACO

Mizar

Cygnus
Rift

Albireo

Epsilon
Lyrae

Vega

LYRA

BOÖTES

Horizon 20° N

Horizon 60° N

M13

HERCULES

Horizon 40° N

CORONA
BOREALIS

Arcturus

SERPENS
CAPUT

EAST

Star magnitudes

● −1	● 0	● 1	● 2	● 3	• 4	· 5

Deep-sky objects

Galaxy	Globular cluster	Open cluster	Diffuse nebula	Planetary nebula
⬭	⊛	⁙	▫	◎

Date	Std Time	DST
March 1	11 pm	Midnight
March 15	10 pm	11 pm
March 30	9 pm	10 pm

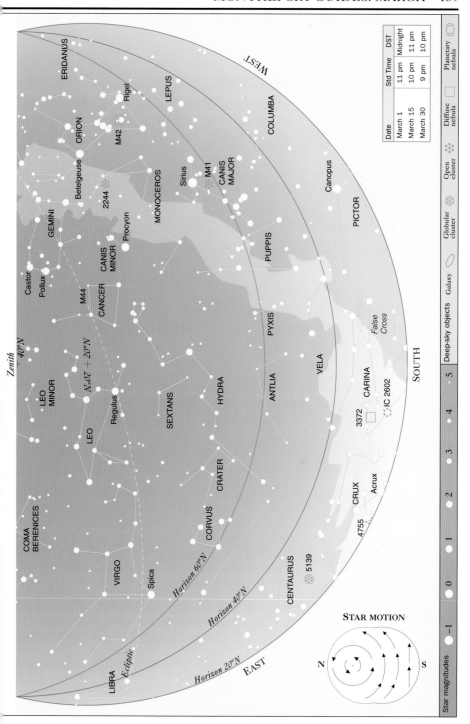

Date	Std Time	DST
March 1	11 pm	Midnight
March 15	10 pm	11 pm
March 30	9 pm	10 pm

STAR MOTION

Deep-sky objects

Galaxy · Globular cluster · Open cluster · Diffuse nebula · Planetary nebula

Star magnitudes: −1 0 1 2 3 4 5

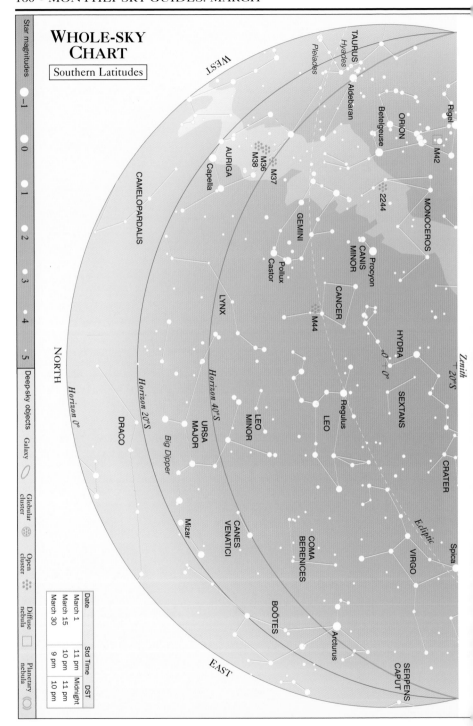

WHOLE-SKY CHART

Southern Latitudes

Date	Std Time	DST
March 1	11 pm	Midnight
March 15	10 pm	11 pm
March 30	9 pm	10 pm

Star magnitudes

- −1
- 0
- 1
- 2
- 3
- 4
- 5

Deep-sky objects

Galaxy
Globular cluster
Open cluster
Diffuse nebula
Planetary nebula

NORTH

WEST

EAST

TAURUS
Hyades
Pleiades
Aldebaran
Betelgeuse
ORION
Rigel
M42
MONOCEROS
2244
AURIGA
Capella
M36
M38
M37
GEMINI
CANIS MINOR
Procyon
Pollux
Castor
CANCER
M44
HYDRA
SEXTANS
CAMELOPARDALIS
LYNX
LEO MINOR
LEO
Regulus
URSA MAJOR
Big Dipper
Mizar
DRACO
CANES VENATICI
COMA BERENICES
CRATER
VIRGO
Spica
BOÖTES
Arcturus
SERPENS CAPUT
Zenith
20°S
Ecliptic
0°
Horizon 0°
Horizon 20°S
Horizon 40°S

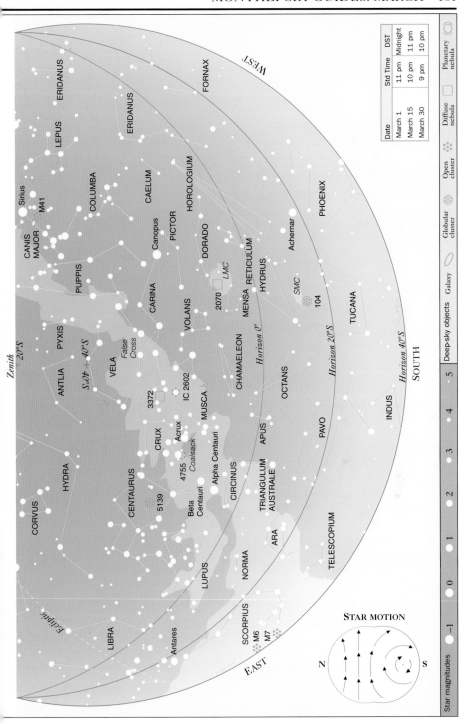

Date	Std Time	DST
March 1	11 pm	Midnight
March 15	10 pm	11 pm
March 30	9 pm	10 pm

Deep-sky objects

Galaxy · Globular cluster · Open cluster · Diffuse nebula · Planetary nebula

Star magnitudes: −1 · 0 · 1 · 2 · 3 · 4 · 5

STAR MOTION

N · S

APRIL

D AYLIGHT SAVINGS TIME is in use in most northern latitudes, while darkness now arrives earlier in the south. The Big Dipper (Plough) is high in the northern sky, Leo is prominent from all latitudes, and the Milky Way, containing a wealth of bright stars, is well placed for those in the Southern Hemisphere.

SUNRISE AND SUNSET ON APRIL 15

Latitude	Sunrise	Sunset
60°N	04:40	19:20
40°N	05:20	18:40
20°N	05:40	18:20
0°	06:00	18:00
20°S	06:10	17:50
40°S	06:30	17:30

April 1 Std time 🕐 DST 🕐   April 15 Std time 🕐 DST 🕐   April 30 Std time 🕐 DST 🕐

NORTHERN LATITUDES

• **LOOKING NORTH** The familiar shape of the Big Dipper (Plough) is almost overhead, the stars in its bowl pointing downward to Polaris. Capella is in the northwest, while to its right the constellations Perseus and Cassiopeia sink low. In the east, Vega and Deneb lead the stars of summer into view.

• **LOOKING SOUTH** Leo is high in the south. Beneath it is the relatively blank area of sky around Hydra. Left of Leo, in the southeast, the bright star Arcturus is prominently placed, with Spica in Virgo closer to the horizon. Above the western horizon, Castor and Pollux, in Gemini, are still visible, with Procyon just beneath them.

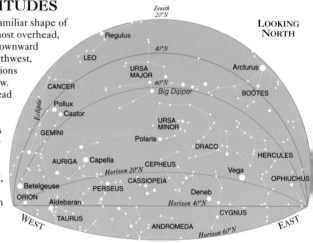

SOUTHERN LATITUDES

• **LOOKING NORTH** Due north, Leo resembles a lion lying on its back, while Arcturus is prominent in the east, with Spica high above. Procyon remains on view in the northwest, as Castor and Pollux, in Gemini, set beneath it. The large but faint constellation of Hydra arches overhead from northwest to northeast.

• **LOOKING SOUTH** Crux (the Southern Cross) is high in the south with Vela and Carina to its right and Alpha (α) and Beta (β) Centauri to its left. Canopus is in the southwest, the Large Magellanic Cloud (LMC) to its lower left (see p.167). Sirius is almost due west, while Scorpius lies southeast.

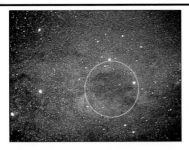

THE COALSACK (CRUX)
What appears to be a hole in the Milky Way next to Crux (the Southern Cross) is in fact a huge cloud of dust that blots out light from the stars behind it. This dark nebula, known as the Coalsack, is about 60 light-years in diameter, and is thought to lie about 600 light-years from us.

WHOLE-SKY CHARTS

APRIL FEATURES

● ACRUX (CRUX). The brightest star in the Southern Cross, known as Acrux or Alpha (α) Crucis, is in fact a close double star. A small telescope will divide it into two sparkling points. A fainter star, which is not related to the main pair, can be seen through binoculars. See also pp.86–87.

✤ NGC 4755 (CRUX). This open cluster, popularly known as the Jewel Box, is visible to the naked eye as a hazy star, and is best viewed through binoculars or a small telescope. The English astronomer Sir John Herschel described it in the 1830s as resembling "a casket of variously colored precious stones." Although it appears to lie next to the Coalsack (see photograph, above), it is in fact over 12 times more distant. See also pp.86–87.

ALSO VISIBLE
● Alpha (α) Centauri (p.169)
● Mizar (p.169)
✤ M44 (p.157)
✤ NGC 2244 (p.151)
☐ NGC 3372 (p.157)
✤ NGC 5139 (p.169)
✤ IC 2602 (p.157)

Star magnitudes –1 0 1 2 3

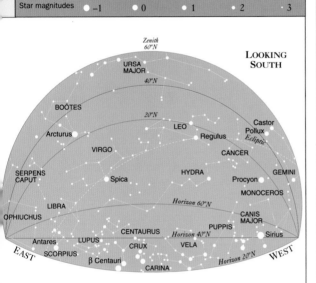

Zenith
60°N

LOOKING SOUTH

URSA MAJOR
40°N
BOÖTES
20°N
LEO
Castor
Pollux
Arcturus
Regulus
Ecliptic
VIRGO
CANCER
SERPENS CAPUT
HYDRA
GEMINI
Spica
Procyon
MONOCEROS
Horizon 60°N
LIBRA
OPHIUCHUS
CANIS MAJOR
CENTAURUS
PUPPIS
Horizon 40°N
Antares
LUPUS
CRUX
VELA
Sirius
EAST
SCORPIUS
β Centauri
Horizon 20°N
WEST
CARINA

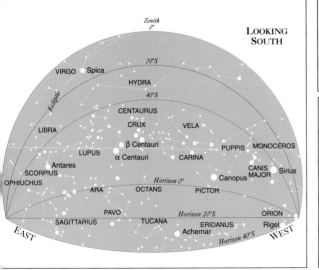

Zenith
0°

LOOKING SOUTH

20°S
VIRGO
Spica
HYDRA
40°S
Ecliptic
CENTAURUS
CRUX
VELA
LIBRA
β Centauri
PUPPIS
MONOCEROS
LUPUS
α Centauri
CARINA
Antares
CANIS MAJOR
Sirius
SCORPIUS
Canopus
OPHIUCHUS
Horizon 0°
ARA
OCTANS
PICTOR
PAVO
ORION
SAGITTARIUS
TUCANA
ERIDANUS
Rigel
EAST
Achernar
Horizon 20°S
WEST
Horizon 40°S

APRIL METEORS

THE LYRIDS. The Lyrid meteor shower, most easily seen from northern latitudes, reaches its peak around April 21. It is one of the poorer showers, with a maximum rate of only about 10 meteors an hour, but the meteors are fast, bright, and often leave trains. The radiant is in the constellation Lyra, close to the bright star Vega.

WHOLE-SKY CHART

Northern Latitudes

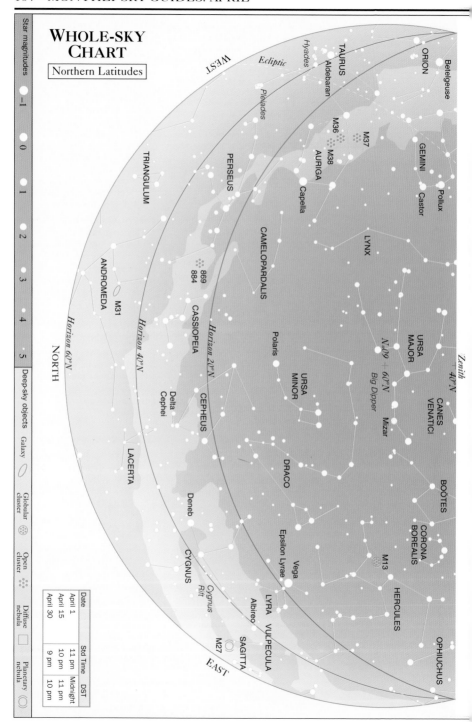

Star magnitudes: −1 0 1 2 3 4 5

Deep-sky objects

Galaxy

Globular cluster

Open cluster

Diffuse nebula

Planetary nebula

NORTH

WEST

EAST

Zenith 40°N

Ecliptic

Hyades

TAURUS

Aldebaran

Pleiades

ORION

Betelgeuse

GEMINI

Pollux

Castor

M36

M37

M38

AURIGA

Capella

PERSEUS

TRIANGULUM

CAMELOPARDALIS

LYNX

ANDROMEDA

M31

869

884

CASSIOPEIA

Polaris

URSA MAJOR

Big Dipper

Mizar

N 69 + 60°N

CANES VENATICI

BOÖTES

Delta Cephei

CEPHEUS

URSA MINOR

DRACO

CORONA BOREALIS

M13

HERCULES

LACERTA

Deneb

Epsilon Lyrae

Vega

LYRA

VULPECULA

OPHIUCHUS

CYGNUS

Cygnus Rift

Albireo

SAGITTA

M27

Horizon 60°N

Horizon 40°N

Horizon 20°N

Date	Std Time	DST
April 1	11 pm	Midnight
April 15	10 pm	11 pm
April 30	9 pm	10 pm

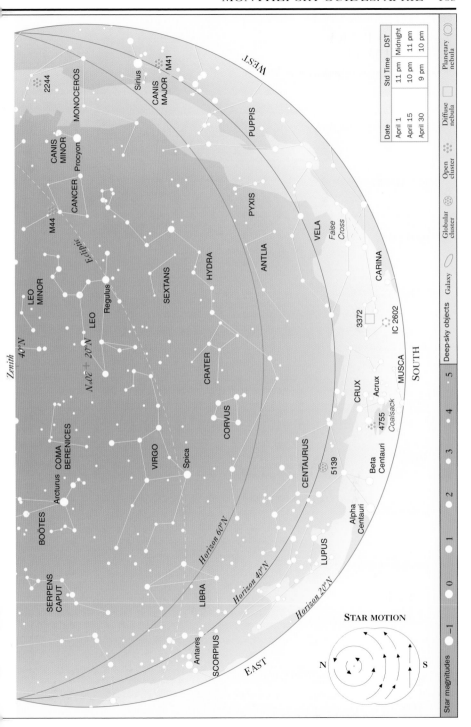

Date	Std Time	DST
April 1	11 pm	Midnight
April 15	10 pm	11 pm
April 30	9 pm	10 pm

STAR MOTION

Star magnitudes: −1 0 1 2 3 4 5

Deep-sky objects: Galaxy Globular cluster Open cluster Diffuse nebula Planetary nebula

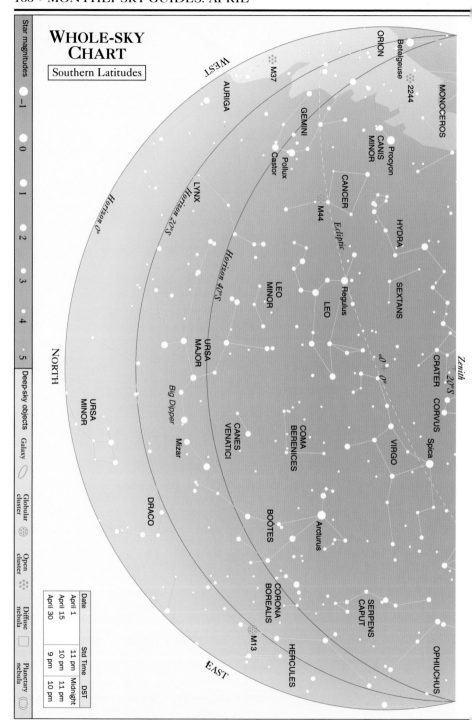

WHOLE-SKY
CHART

Southern Latitudes

Star magnitudes

−1　0　1　2　3　4　5

Deep-sky objects

Galaxy　Globular cluster　Open cluster　Diffuse nebula　Planetary nebula

Date	Std Time	DST
April 1	11 pm	Midnight
April 15	10 pm	11 pm
April 30	9 pm	10 pm

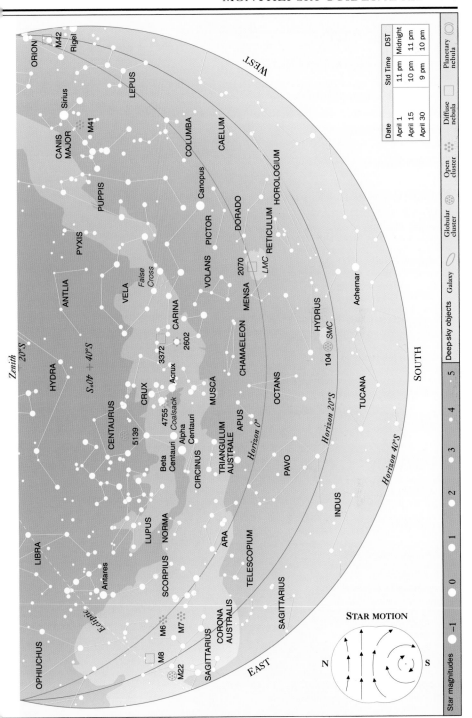

Date	Std Time	DST
April 1	11 pm	Midnight
April 15	10 pm	11 pm
April 30	9 pm	10 pm

STAR MOTION

Star magnitudes −1 0 1 2 3 4 5

Deep-sky objects Galaxy Globular cluster Open cluster Diffuse nebula Planetary nebula

MAY

L ENGTHENING TWILIGHT can make early evening observing more difficult in northern latitudes, where the sparkling stars of winter are being replaced by those of summer. In the Southern Hemisphere, this is the best time of year to see Crux (the Southern Cross) and its "pointers," Alpha and Beta Centauri.

SUNRISE AND SUNSET ON MAY 15

Latitude	Sunrise	Sunset
60°N	03:20	20:30
40°N	04:40	19:10
20°N	05:20	18:30
0°	05:50	18:00
20°S	06:20	17:30
40°S	07:00	17:00

May 1 Std time 🕐 DST 🕐	May 15 Std time 🕐 DST 🕐	May 30 Std time 🕐 DST 🕐

NORTHERN LATITUDES

• **LOOKING NORTH** The Big Dipper (Plough) stands almost overhead, while Cygnus and the bright star Vega climb higher in the northeast as a foretaste of summer. The faint constellation of Cepheus is between Polaris and the northern horizon. Gemini is the last of the winter constellations to sink below the northwestern horizon.
• **LOOKING SOUTH** The bright stars Arcturus in Boötes and Spica in Virgo are high in the south. Ophiuchus and both halves of Serpens occupy much of the southeastern sky, with Hercules above them. Leo dominates the southwest, with the largely blank area of sky occupied by Hydra beneath it.

SOUTHERN LATITUDES

• **LOOKING NORTH** Arcturus, in Boötes, glitters in the north, with Spica, in Virgo, nearly overhead. Hercules is close to the northeastern horizon, to the lower right of Arcturus, while Ophiuchus and the two halves of Serpens cover much of the eastern sky. Leo is prominent in the northwest.
• **LOOKING SOUTH** Centaurus and its adjoining constellations dominate the southern sky, with Alpha (α) and Beta (β) Centauri pointing toward Crux (the Southern Cross). While Canopus sets in the southwest, the well-stocked constellations Sagittarius and Scorpius are rising in the southeast, a sign that winter is on its way.

THE BIG DIPPER
The familiar shape of the Big Dipper (Plough), formed by seven stars in Ursa Major (pp.136–37), is a prominent sight in northern skies in spring. The second star in the handle, called Mizar, has a fainter partner, visible to observers with normal eyesight (see panel, right).

Star magnitudes   –1   0   1   2   3

LOOKING SOUTH

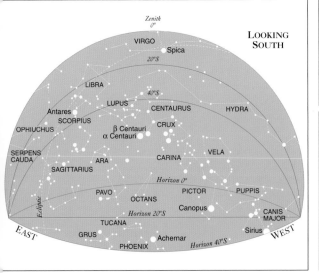

LOOKING SOUTH

WHOLE-SKY CHARTS

MAY FEATURES

● **ALPHA (α) CENTAURI.**
A mere 4.3 light-years away, this is the closest star to the Earth after the Sun. A small telescope reveals two yellow stars, the brighter of which is similar in temperature and brightness to the Sun. A third member of the family, Proxima Centauri, is much fainter. See also p.79.

● **MIZAR (URSA MAJOR).**
The second star in the handle of the Big Dipper, known as Mizar or Zeta (ζ) Ursae Majoris, is a wide double. Its companion, Alcor, is visible to the naked eye, while a small telescope shows another star, closer to Mizar. See also pp.136–37.

⊛ **NGC 5139
(CENTAURUS).** The largest and brightest globular cluster in the sky, also called Omega (ω) Centauri, is visible to the naked eye as a hazy star. It is clearer through binoculars, and a small telescope shows the brightest of its 100,000 or more stars. See also p.79.

ALSO VISIBLE
● Acrux (p.163)
✶ M6 and M7 (p.175)
⊛ M13 (p.175)
✶ M44 (p.157)
✶ NGC 4755 (p.163)

MAY METEORS

THE ETA AQUARIDS.
These fast-moving, bright meteors, caused by dust from Halley's Comet, radiate from a point near the "water jar" in Aquarius, and are best seen from southern latitudes. Activity begins in late April, peaks at about 35 meteors an hour in the first week of May, and ends in late May.

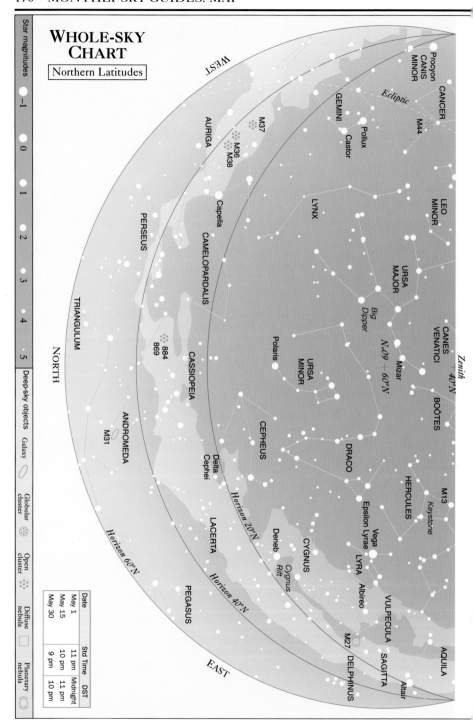

WHOLE-SKY CHART

Northern Latitudes

Date	Std Time	DST
May 1	11 pm	Midnight
May 15	10 pm	11 pm
May 30	9 pm	10 pm

Star magnitudes

−1 0 1 2 3 4 5

Deep-sky objects

Galaxy

Globular cluster

Open cluster

Diffuse nebula

Planetary nebula

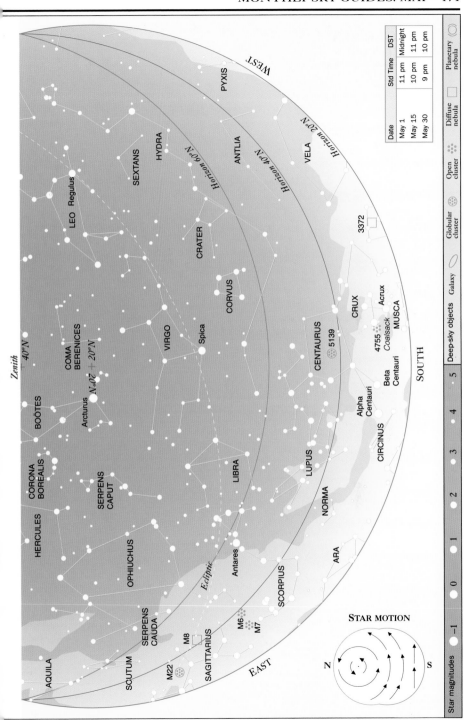

Date	Std Time	DST
May 1	11 pm	Midnight
May 15	10 pm	11 pm
May 30	9 pm	10 pm

STAR MOTION

Star magnitudes: −1 0 1 2 3 4 5

Deep-sky objects: Galaxy · Globular cluster · Open cluster · Diffuse nebula · Planetary nebula

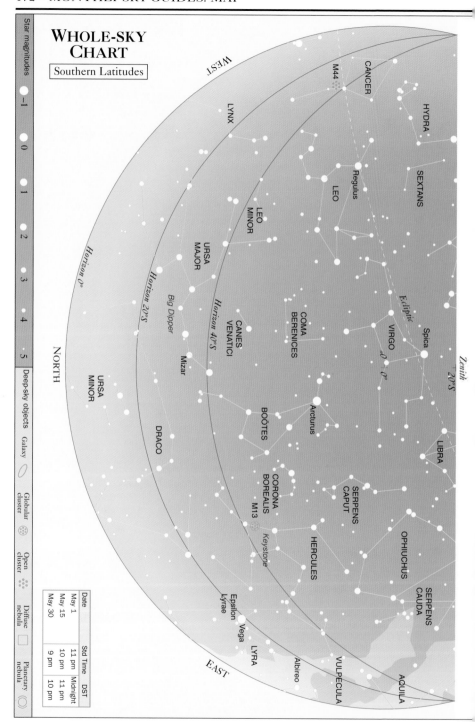

WHOLE-SKY CHART

Southern Latitudes

Star magnitudes

●	−1
●	0
●	1
●	2
●	3
●	4
·	5

Deep-sky objects

Galaxy

Globular cluster

Open cluster

Diffuse nebula

Planetary nebula

WEST

NORTH

Zenith

EAST

Horizon 0°

Horizon 20°S

Horizon 40°S

Ecliptic

CANCER

M44

HYDRA

LYNX

SEXTANS

Regulus

LEO

LEO MINOR

URSA MAJOR

Big Dipper

CANES VENATICI

COMA BERENICES

VIRGO

Spica

Mizar

URSA MINOR

DRACO

BOÖTES

Arcturus

CORONA BOREALIS

M13

Keystone

SERPENS CAPUT

HERCULES

OPHIUCHUS

SERPENS CAUDA

LIBRA

VULPECULA

AQUILA

Epsilon Lyrae

Vega

LYRA

Albireo

Date	Std Time	DST
May 1	11 pm	Midnight
May 15	10 pm	11 pm
May 30	9 pm	10 pm

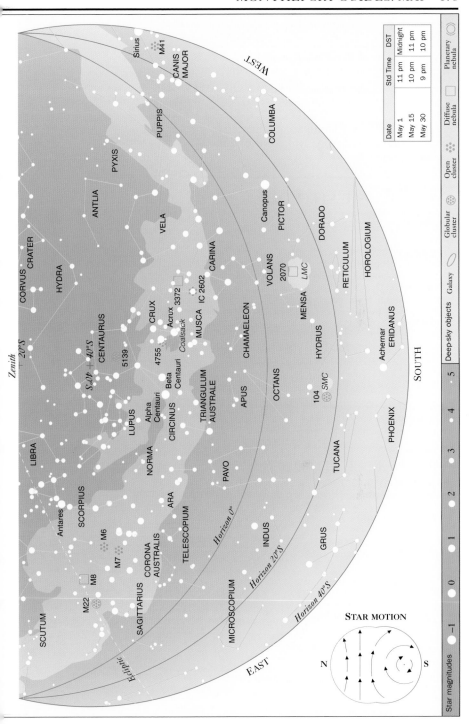

Date	Std Time	DST
May 1	11 pm	Midnight
May 15	10 pm	11 pm
May 30	9 pm	10 pm

Deep-sky objects

Galaxy

Globular cluster

Open cluster

Diffuse nebula

Planetary nebula

Star magnitudes   −1   0   1   2   3   4   5

STAR MOTION

WEST

SOUTH

EAST

Zenith

20°S

S. at 40°S

40°S

Horizon 0°

Horizon 20°S

Horizon 40°S

Ecliptic

N   S

Constellations and objects labeled:
Sirius, M41, CANIS MAJOR, PUPPIS, PYXIS, ANTLIA, VELA, CANOPUS, PICTOR, COLUMBA, DORADO, RETICULUM, HOROLOGIUM, Achernar, ERIDANUS, PHOENIX, TUCANA, 104, SMC, HYDRUS, MENSA, LMC, 2070, VOLANS, CHAMAELEON, OCTANS, APUS, CARINA, IC 2602, MUSCA, Coalsack, 3372, Acrux, CRUX, 4755, 5139, CENTAURUS, HYDRA, CRATER, CORVUS, Beta Centauri, Alpha Centauri, CIRCINUS, TRIANGULUM AUSTRALE, PAVO, INDUS, GRUS, MICROSCOPIUM, NORMA, LUPUS, ARA, TELESCOPIUM, CORONA AUSTRALIS, SCORPIUS, Antares, M6, M7, M8, M22, SAGITTARIUS, SCUTUM, LIBRA

JUNE

N IGHTS ARE AT THEIR SHORTEST and days at their longest in northern latitudes in June, and vice versa in the Southern Hemisphere. In the far north, twilight is now permanent throughout the night, while the winter skies of the south are dominated by a band of prominent constellations lying in the Milky Way.

SUNRISE AND SUNSET ON JUNE 15		
Latitude	Sunrise	Sunset
60°N	02:40	21:20
40°N	04:30	19:30
20°N	05:20	18:40
0°	06:00	18:00
20°S	06:30	17:30
40°S	07:20	16:40

June 1 Std time 🕐 DST 🕐 | June 15 Std time 🕐 DST 🕐 | June 30 Std time 🕐 DST 🕐

NORTHERN LATITUDES

• **LOOKING NORTH** Ursa Minor (the Little Bear) stands on its tail, and Draco arches above the north celestial pole, marked by Polaris. The Big Dipper (Plough) is high in the northwest. Toward the east, the stars that form the Summer Triangle are in view: Vega, Deneb in Cygnus, and Altair in Aquila (far left of Looking South map).
• **LOOKING SOUTH** Hercules is high in the southeast, with Vega to its left and Arcturus, in Boötes, to its right. Ophiuchus, Virgo, and both halves of Serpens are below them. Antares, in Scorpius, glints red above the southern horizon, the faint stars of Libra to its right. Leo is setting in the west.

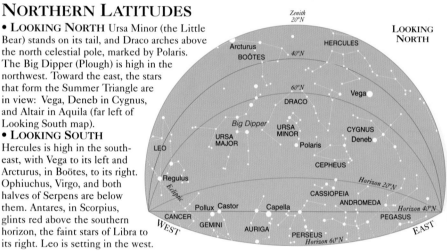

SOUTHERN LATITUDES

• **LOOKING NORTH** Boötes and Hercules are prominently placed almost due north, with Virgo, Ophiuchus, and both parts of Serpens above them. Antares (in Scorpius) is overhead. Altair (in Aquila) and Vega are the most prominent stars in the northeast. Leo is setting in the northwest.
• **LOOKING SOUTH** The constellations Sagittarius, Ara, Scorpius, Lupus, Centaurus, Crux (the Southern Cross), Carina, and Vela form a bright band, from southeast to southwest, against dense star fields in the Milky Way. The brightest stars along this band are Antares, Alpha (α) and Beta (β) Centauri, and Acrux (see also p.179).

THE KEYSTONE (HERCULES)

Four stars form a shape known as the Keystone that represents the pelvis of Hercules (pp.98–99). Clockwise from top left, they are Pi (π), Eta (η), Zeta (ζ), and Epsilon (ε) Herculis. The star cluster M13 (see panel, right) lies between Eta and Zeta.

Star magnitudes	–1	0	1	2	3

LOOKING SOUTH

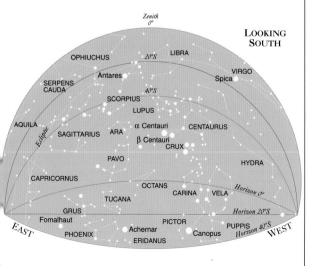

LOOKING SOUTH

WHOLE-SKY CHARTS

JUNE FEATURES

✶ **M6 (SCORPIUS).** This open cluster and the nearby M7 lie near the "sting" in the tail of Scorpius, the scorpion. M6 can be seen with the naked eye and is an impressive sight through binoculars. It is sometimes called the Butterfly Cluster because its stars are arranged in the shape of a butterfly with open wings. See also pp.126–27.

✶ **M7 (SCORPIUS).** This open cluster appears to the naked eye as a bright patch in front of dense fields of stars in the Milky Way, and is a superb sight when seen through binoculars. It is larger and brighter than its neighbor M6, being less than half the distance from us (800 light-years, compared with 2,000 light-years for M6). See also pp.126–27.

⊕ **M13 (HERCULES).** This is the most prominent globular cluster in northern skies; even so, it is barely visible to the naked eye, and from urban areas it can be seen only with the aid of binoculars, through which it resembles a glowing ball with a bright center. It lies on one side of the Keystone of Hercules (see photograph, above), one-third the way between Eta (η) and Zeta (ζ) Herculis. See also pp.98–99.

ALSO VISIBLE

- Albireo (p.187)
- Alpha (α) Centauri (p.169)
- Antares (p.181)
- Epsilon (ε) Lyrae (p.181)
- Mizar (p.169)
- ☐ M8 (p.181)
- ⊕ M22 (p.181)
- ◯ M27 (p.193)
- ⊕ NGC 5139 (p.169)

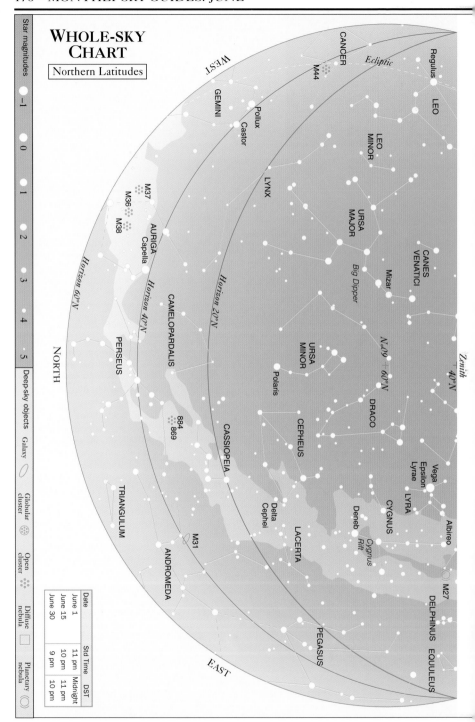

WHOLE-SKY CHART

Northern Latitudes

Star magnitudes

● −1
● 0
● 1
● 2
● 3
• 4
· 5

NORTH

Deep-sky objects

◯ Galaxy

◉ Globular cluster

⁙ Open cluster

▢ Diffuse nebula

◎ Planetary nebula

Date	Std Time	DST
June 1	11 pm	Midnight
June 15	10 pm	11 pm
June 30	9 pm	10 pm

WEST

CANCER
M44
Ecliptic
Regulus
LEO
GEMINI
Pollux
Castor
LEO MINOR
LYNX
URSA MAJOR
Big Dipper
Mizar
CANES VENATICI
M37
M36
M38
AURIGA
Capella
Horizon 60°N
Horizon 40°N
Horizon 20°N
CAMELOPARDALIS
PERSEUS
URSA MINOR
Polaris
DRACO
Horizon 60°N
60°N
CEPHEUS
884
869
CASSIOPEIA
Vega
Epsilon Lyrae
LYRA
Zenith 40°N
Deneb
CYGNUS
Cygnus Rift
Albireo
M27
DELPHINUS
EQUULEUS
Delta Cephei
LACERTA
TRIANGULUM
M31
ANDROMEDA
PEGASUS
EAST

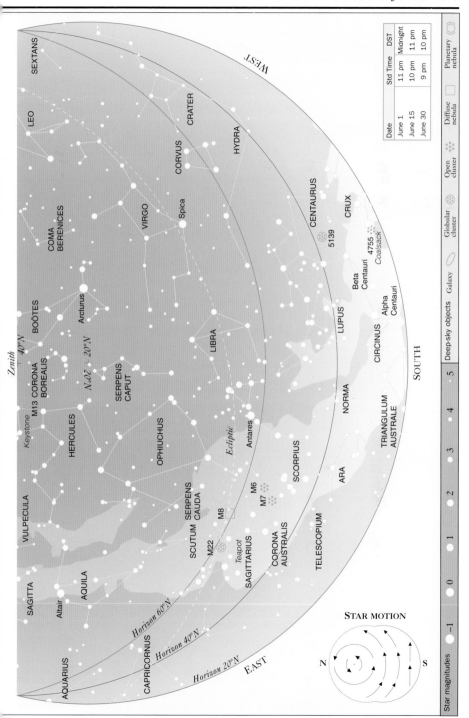

Date	Std Time	DST
June 1	11 pm	Midnight
June 15	10 pm	11 pm
June 30	9 pm	10 pm

SEXTANS

LEO

WEST

CRATER

CORVUS

HYDRA

VIRGO

Spica

COMA BERENICES

CENTAURUS

CRUX

5139

Beta Centauri

4755
Coalsack

Arcturus

BOÖTES

40°N

20°N

Alpha Centauri

Zenith

CORONA BOREALIS

M13

LIBRA

LUPUS

HERCULES

SERPENS CAPUT

CIRCINUS

Keystone

SOUTH

OPHIUCHUS

Ecliptic

NORMA

Antares

TRIANGULUM AUSTRALE

SERPENS CAUDA

SCUTUM

SCORPIUS

ARA

M6

VULPECULA

M7

M8

TELESCOPIUM

M22

Teapot

CORONA AUSTRALIS

SAGITTA

AQUILA

SAGITTARIUS

Altair

Horizon 60°N

Horizon 40°N

CAPRICORNUS

Horizon 20°N

EAST

AQUARIUS

STAR MOTION

N   S

Star magnitudes   −1   0   1   2   3   4   5   Deep-sky objects   Galaxy   Globular cluster   Open cluster   Diffuse nebula   Planetary nebula

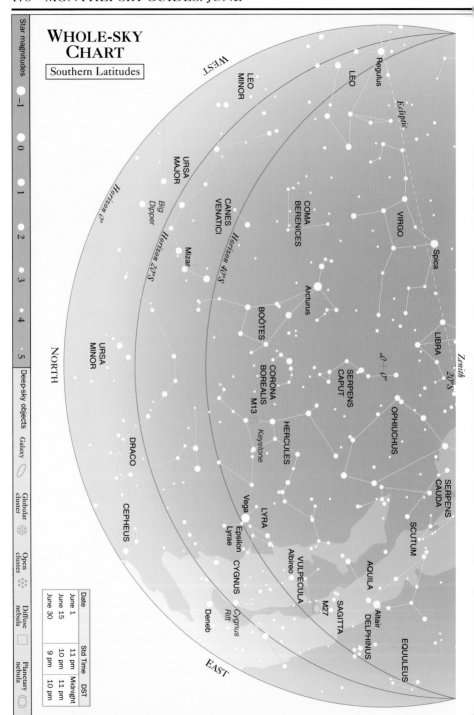

WHOLE-SKY CHART

Southern Latitudes

Star magnitudes:

- −1
- 0
- 1
- 2
- 3
- 4
- 5

Deep-sky objects

Galaxy

Globular cluster

Open cluster

Diffuse nebula

Planetary nebula

Date	Std Time	DST
June 1	11 pm	Midnight
June 15	10 pm	11 pm
June 30	9 pm	10 pm

NORTH

WEST

EAST

Zenith

LEO MINOR

LEO

Regulus

Ecliptic

URSA MAJOR

Big Dipper

CANES VENATICI

Mizar

VIRGO

COMA BERENICES

Spica

Arcturus

BOÖTES

LIBRA

URSA MINOR

CORONA BOREALIS

M13

Keystone

SERPENS CAPUT

HERCULES

OPHIUCHUS

DRACO

Vega

LYRA

SERPENS CAUDA

SCUTUM

CEPHEUS

Epsilon Lyrae

CYGNUS

Albireo

VULPECULA

AQUILA

Deneb

Cygnus Rift

M27

SAGITTA

DELPHINUS

Altair

EQUULEUS

Horizon 0°

Horizon 20°S

Horizon 40°S

20°S

0°+0°

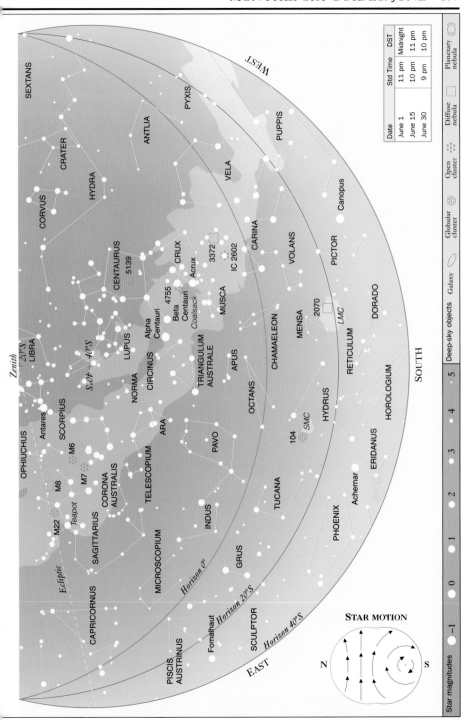

Date	Std Time	DST
June 1	11 pm	Midnight
June 15	10 pm	11 pm
June 30	9 pm	10 pm

STAR MOTION

N   S

Star magnitudes

−1   0   1   2   3   4   5

Deep-sky objects

Galaxy   Globular cluster   Open cluster   Diffuse nebula   Planetary nebula

SOUTH

WEST

EAST

JULY

T HIS IS THE BEST TIME for northern observers to see the rich southern constellations Sagittarius and Scorpius. The center of our Galaxy is in Sagittarius, so the Milky Way star fields are particularly dense in this region. For southern observers, these constellations are almost overhead and dominate the scene.

SUNRISE AND SUNSET ON JULY 15		
Latitude	Sunrise	Sunset
60°N	03:00	21:10
40°N	04:40	19:30
20°N	05:30	18:40
0°	06:00	18:10
20°S	06:40	17:40
40°S	07:20	16:50

July 1 Std time 🕐 DST 🕐 | July 15 Std time 🕐 DST 🕐 | July 30 Std time 🕐 DST 🕐

NORTHERN LATITUDES

• **LOOKING NORTH** Ursa Minor (the Little Bear) remains well placed, with Draco coiled around it. The Big Dipper (Plough) is in the northwest, with Cassiopeia and Cepheus in the northeast. The Great Square of Pegasus is rising in the east, while Arcturus, in Boötes, remains high in the west.
• **LOOKING SOUTH** Due south, Ophiuchus is entwined by both halves of Serpens with Hercules above it. In the east, the Summer Triangle of Vega, Deneb, and Altair is well placed. Antares in Scorpius is near the southern horizon, with Sagittarius visible to its left for observers in southerly locations. Virgo is setting in the far west.

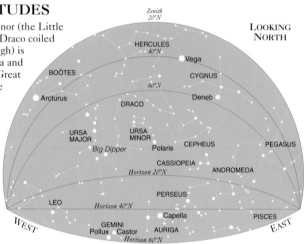

SOUTHERN LATITUDES

• **LOOKING NORTH** Ophiuchus and both parts of Serpens are centrally placed, with Aquila to their right. Hercules is closer to the northern horizon, midway between reddish Arcturus in the northwest and blue-white Vega in the north. To the right of Vega, Cygnus is rising.
• **LOOKING SOUTH** Scorpius, shaped like a fish hook, and Sagittarius are almost overhead, containing dense fields of stars near the center of our Galaxy. To the southwest, along the star trail of the Milky Way (see pp.184–85), are Centaurus and Crux (the Southern Cross); Virgo is setting farther west. In the east, Capricornus, Aquarius, and the star Fomalhaut are rising.

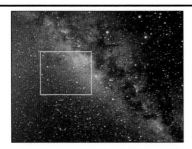

THE GALACTIC CENTER (SAGITTARIUS)
From southern latitudes on July evenings, the center of our Galaxy lies overhead, among dense Milky Way star fields in Sagittarius. Eight stars in Sagittarius (enclosed here in a rectangle) form a shape known as the Teapot (see pp.124–25).

Star magnitudes   ● –1   ● 0   ● 1   • 2   · 3

LOOKING SOUTH

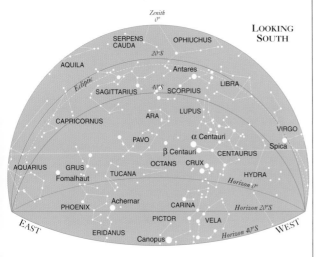

LOOKING SOUTH

WHOLE-SKY CHARTS

JULY FEATURES

● **ANTARES (SCORPIUS).**
Also known as Alpha (α) Scorpii, this is one of the largest stars visible to the naked eye. It is a red super-giant, around 500 times larger than the Sun. If it were placed where our Sun is, it would engulf the orbit of Mars. See also pp.126–27.

● **EPSILON (ε) LYRAE.**
Near the bright star Vega lies this remarkable multiple star. Binoculars, or even sharp eyesight, show that it is double. Through a telescope, each of these stars is itself seen to be a close double, hence this star's popular name, the Double Double. See also p.108.

□ **M8 (SAGITTARIUS).**
This diffuse nebula is visible to the naked eye in rural skies and is easy to find with binoculars. It is elongated in shape and is also called the Lagoon Nebula, the lagoon being a dark lane of dust that crosses its center. M8 contains NGC 6530, a cluster visible through binoculars. See also pp.124–25.

⊕ **M22 (SAGITTARIUS).**
This globular cluster, which lies near the lid of the Teapot in Sagittarius, is rated the third best of its kind in the sky, after Omega (ω) Centauri and 47 Tucanae. It can be seen as a hazy star with the naked eye, and is easy to find with binoculars. See also pp.124–25.

ALSO VISIBLE
● **Albireo** (p.187)
❖ **M6 and M7** (p.175)
⊕ **M13** (p.175)
⊕ **M27** (p.193)
● **The Cygnus Rift** (p.187)

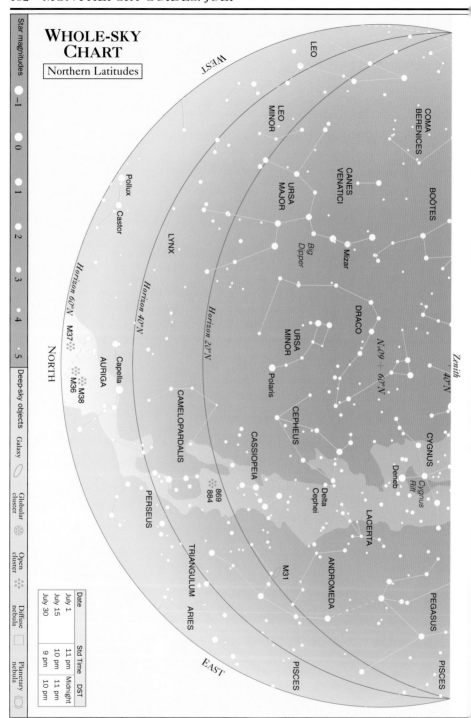

WHOLE-SKY CHART

Northern Latitudes

Star magnitudes: −1 0 1 2 3 4 ·5

NORTH

Deep-sky objects

Galaxy

Globular cluster

Open cluster

Diffuse nebula

Planetary nebula

WEST

LEO

COMA BERENICES

BOÖTES

LEO MINOR

CANES VENATICI

URSA MAJOR

Pollux

Castor

LYNX

Big Dipper

Mizar

DRACO

Horizon 60°N

Horizon 40°N

Horizon 20°N

M37

M36

M38

Capella

AURIGA

CAMELOPARDALIS

URSA MINOR

Polaris

N°09 + 60°N

Zenith 40°N

CYGNUS

Cygnus Rift

CEPHEUS

Deneb

CASSIOPEIA

869 884

Delta Cephei

LACERTA

ANDROMEDA

M31

PEGASUS

PERSEUS

TRIANGULUM

ARIES

PISCES

PISCES

EAST

Date	Std Time	DST
July 1	11 pm	Midnight
July 15	10 pm	11 pm
July 30	9 pm	10 pm

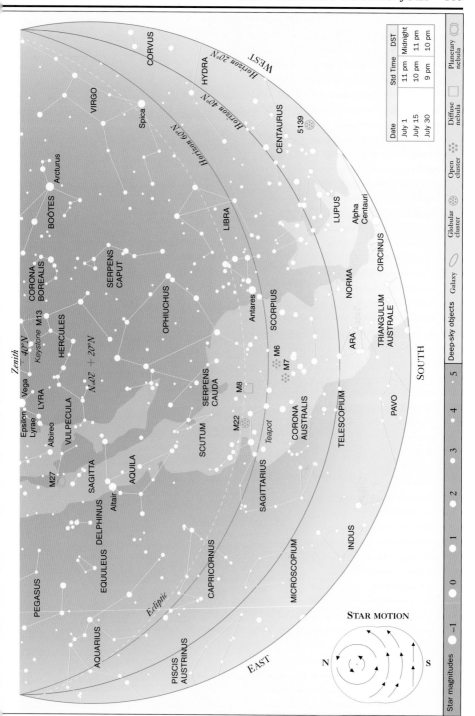

Date	Std Time	DST
July 1	11 pm	Midnight
July 15	10 pm	11 pm
July 30	9 pm	10 pm

Star magnitudes: −1   0   1   2   3   4   5

Deep-sky objects: Galaxy   Globular cluster   Open cluster   Diffuse nebula   Planetary nebula

STAR MOTION

N   S

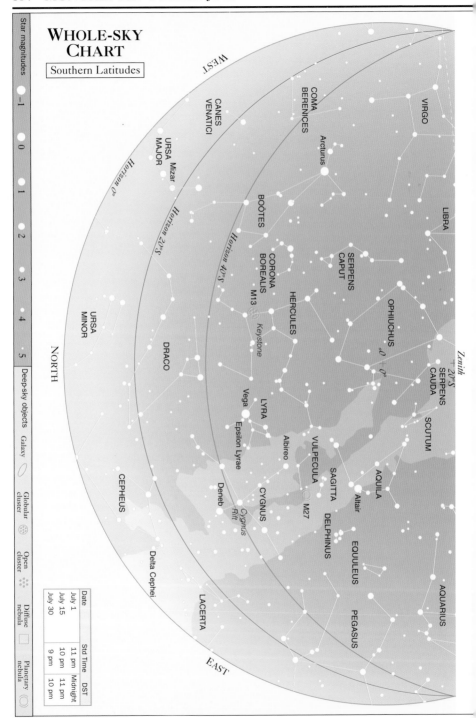

WHOLE-SKY CHART

Southern Latitudes

Star magnitudes

-1   0   1   2   3   4   5

NORTH

Deep-sky objects

Galaxy

Globular cluster

Open cluster

Diffuse nebula

Planetary nebula

Date	Std Time	DST
July 1	11 pm	Midnight
July 15	10 pm	11 pm
July 30	9 pm	10 pm

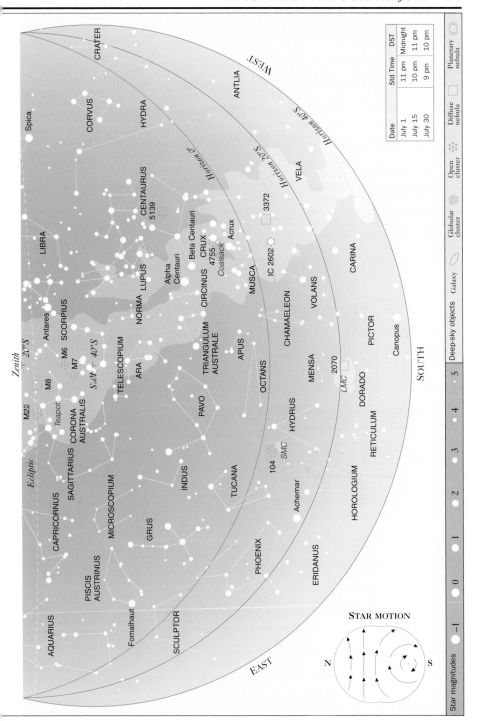

Date	Std Time	DST
July 1	11 pm	Midnight
July 15	10 pm	11 pm
July 30	9 pm	10 pm

Deep-sky objects

Galaxy

Globular cluster

Open cluster

Diffuse nebula

Planetary nebula

STAR MOTION

Star magnitudes

−1 0 1 2 3 4 5

AUGUST

T HE BRIGHT STARS Altair, Deneb, and Vega form a prominent triangle that is well seen on August evenings from all but the most southerly latitudes. In the Northern Hemisphere, it is known as the Summer Triangle. Another major sight for northern observers is the Perseid meteor shower, visible in mid-month.

SUNRISE AND SUNSET ON AUGUST 15

Latitude	Sunrise	Sunset
60°N	04:10	19:50
40°N	05:10	17:00
20°N	05:40	18:30
0°	06:00	18:10
20°S	06:20	17:50
40°S	06:50	17:20

August 1 Std time 🕐 DST 🕐 | August 15 Std time 🕐 DST 🕐 | August 30 Std time 🕐 DST 🕐

NORTHERN LATITUDES

• **LOOKING NORTH** The Big Dipper (Plough) is in the northwest with Arcturus to its left. The bowl of the Little Dipper (in Ursa Minor) is to the left of Polaris, while to the right Cassiopeia appears like a back-to-front letter E. Perseus is rising lower down, with Pegasus and Andromeda farther east.
• **LOOKING SOUTH** The stars of the Summer Triangle – Vega, Deneb, and Altair – are overhead. The Milky Way (see pp.188–89) runs southwest to northeast, and seems to divide in two in Cygnus. Ophiuchus and both parts of Serpens are in the west, with Sagittarius and Scorpius beneath them. Aquarius and Capricornus are in the southeast.

SOUTHERN LATITUDES

• **LOOKING NORTH** The bright stars Vega, Altair (in Aquila), and Deneb (in Cygnus) form a large triangle due north. The Milky Way (see pp.190–91), running northeastward from near the zenith, seems to split in Cygnus. Ophiuchus and both parts of Serpens dominate the western sky, with Hercules just beneath them. In the northeast, the Great Square of Pegasus is rising.
• **LOOKING SOUTH** In the southeast, Achernar is rising, with Fomalhaut above it and slightly to the left. Higher up are Capricornus and Aquarius. Sagittarius is near the zenith, with Scorpius to its lower right. Centaurus and Crux (the Southern Cross) are setting in the southwest.

THE SUMMER TRIANGLE
Three stars in three separate constellations form a large isosceles triangle, which is a familiar feature in skies of northern summer and fall, and southern winter and spring. The brightest of the three is Vega (top right) in Lyra, followed by Altair (bottom) in Aquila, and Deneb (top left) in Cygnus. The Cygnus Rift (see panel, right) runs through the triangle.

WHOLE-SKY CHARTS

AUGUST FEATURES

● **ALBIREO (CYGNUS).** This star, also known as Beta (β) Cygni, is one of the most celebrated doubles in the sky, on account of the coloration of its component stars and the ease with which they may be separated. The smallest of telescopes will show the stars; they appear amber and greenish, like two lamps in a celestial traffic light. See also p.88.

● **THE CYGNUS RIFT (CYGNUS).** This dark nebula, also known as the Northern Coalsack, divides the Milky Way into two. It can be traced with the naked eye from Cygnus, through Aquila, and into Ophiuchus, where it broadens out. See also p.88.

Star magnitudes	● −1	● 0	● 1	● 2	● 3

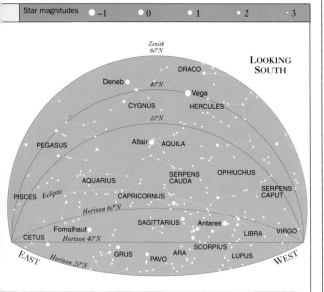

Zenith 60°N

LOOKING SOUTH

DRACO · Deneb · 40°N · Vega · CYGNUS · HERCULES · 20°N · PEGASUS · Altair · AQUILA · AQUARIUS · SERPENS CAUDA · OPHIUCHUS · SERPENS CAPUT · PISCES · *Ecliptic* · CAPRICORNUS · *Horizon 60°N* · SAGITTARIUS · Antares · LIBRA · VIRGO · Fomalhaut · *Horizon 40°N* · SCORPIUS · CETUS · GRUS · ARA · LUPUS · PAVO · *EAST* · *Horizon 20°N* · *WEST*

ALSO VISIBLE

● Antares (p.181)
● Delta (δ) Cephei (p.193)
● Epsilon (ε) Lyrae (p.181)
☐ M8 (p.181)
✸ M13 (p.175)
✸ M22 (p.181)
◯ M27 (p.193)
✸ NGC 104 (p.193)

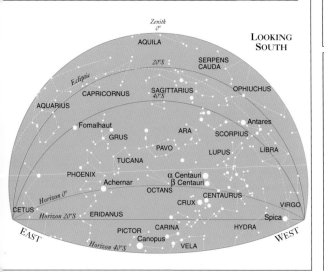

Zenith 0°

LOOKING SOUTH

AQUILA · 20°S · SERPENS CAUDA · *Ecliptic* · CAPRICORNUS · SAGITTARIUS 40°S · OPHIUCHUS · AQUARIUS · Fomalhaut · ARA · Antares · GRUS · SCORPIUS · PAVO · LUPUS · LIBRA · TUCANA · PHOENIX · α Centauri · β Centauri · Achernar · OCTANS · CENTAURUS · CRUX · VIRGO · CETUS · *Horizon 0°* · ERIDANUS · Spica · *Horizon 20°S* · PICTOR · CARINA · HYDRA · *EAST* · Canopus · VELA · *WEST* · *Horizon 40°S*

AUGUST METEORS

THE PERSEIDS. Observers in the Northern Hemisphere have an opportunity this month to see the finest meteor shower of the year, the Perseids, which radiate from near the Double Cluster (NGC 869 and 884) in Perseus (see p.118). The meteors are bright, can flare up, and often leave trains. A peak of 75 or more meteors an hour is reached around August 12, and activity can be seen for at least a week either side of this date.

WHOLE-SKY CHART

Northern Latitudes

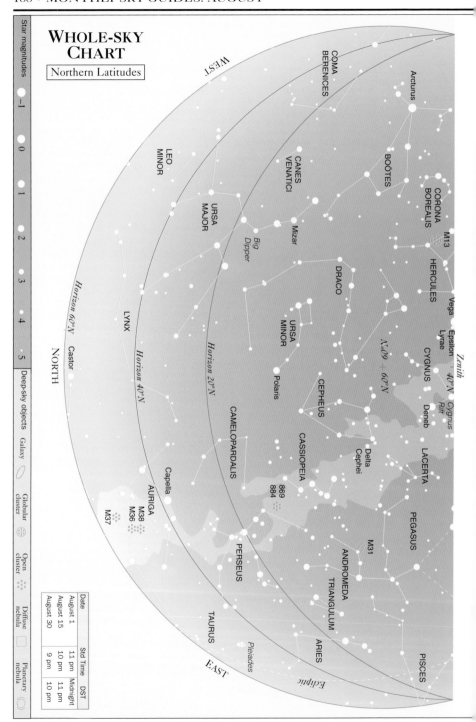

Star magnitudes

-1
0
1
2
3
4
5

NORTH

Deep-sky objects

Galaxy
Globular cluster
Open cluster
Diffuse nebula
Planetary nebula

Date	Std Time	DST
August 1	11 pm	Midnight
August 15	10 pm	11 pm
August 30	9 pm	10 pm

WEST

Zenith

40°N

Cygnus Rift

Horizon 60°N

Horizon 40°N

Horizon 20°N

Horizon 40°N

EAST

Ecliptic

COMA BERENICES
Arcturus
LEO MINOR
BOÖTES
CORONA BOREALIS
CANES VENATICI
M13
HERCULES
Vega
Epsilon Lyrae
CYGNUS
Deneb
LACERTA
URSA MAJOR
Mizar
Big Dipper
DRACO
URSA MINOR
Polaris
CEPHEUS
Delta Cephei
PEGASUS
LYNX
Castor
CAMELOPARDALIS
CASSIOPEIA
869
884
M31
ANDROMEDA
Capella
AURIGA
M38
M36
M37
PERSEUS
TRIANGULUM
ARIES
PISCES
TAURUS
Pleiades

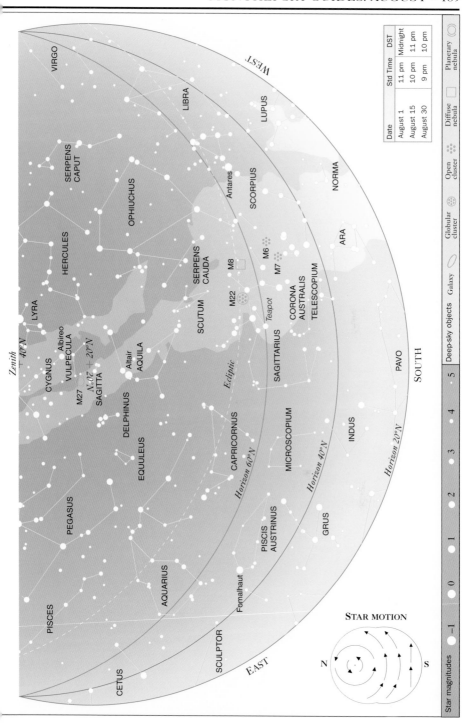

Date	Std Time	DST
August 1	11 pm	Midnight
August 15	10 pm	11 pm
August 30	9 pm	10 pm

Deep-sky objects

Galaxy · Globular cluster · Open cluster · Diffuse nebula · Planetary nebula

Star magnitudes

−1 · 0 · 1 · 2 · 3 · 4 · 5

STAR MOTION

N · S

SOUTH
WEST
EAST

Zenith
40°N

Horizon 60°N
Horizon 40°N
Horizon 20°N

Ecliptic

VIRGO
SERPENS CAPUT
OPHIUCHUS
HERCULES
LYRA
CYGNUS
Albireo
VULPECULA
SAGITTA
M27
DELPHINUS
EQUULEUS
PEGASUS
PISCES
AQUARIUS
CETUS
SCULPTOR
PISCIS AUSTRINUS
Fomalhaut
GRUS
INDUS
MICROSCOPIUM
CAPRICORNUS
Altair
AQUILA
SCUTUM
SERPENS CAUDA
M22
M8
SAGITTARIUS
Teapot
CORONA AUSTRALIS
TELESCOPIUM
PAVO
ARA
NORMA
LUPUS
LIBRA
SCORPIUS
Antares
M6
M7

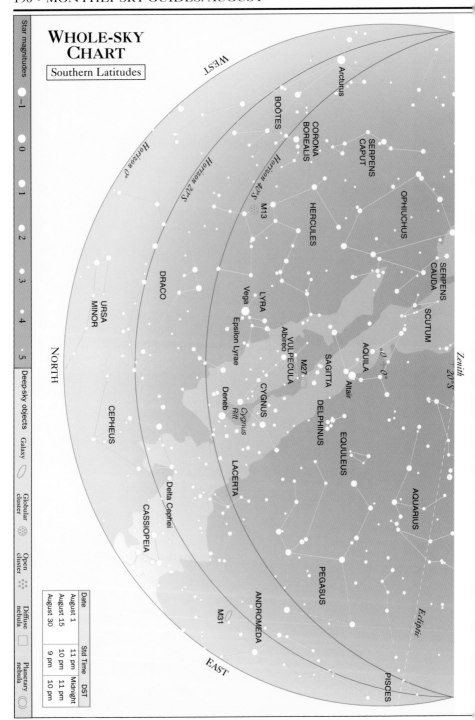

WHOLE-SKY CHART

Southern Latitudes

Star magnitudes

●−1 ●0 ●1 ●2 ●3 ●4 ●5

Deep-sky objects

Galaxy ⬭   Globular cluster ◉   Open cluster ⁙   Diffuse nebula ▢   Planetary nebula ◎

NORTH

WEST

EAST

Zenith
20°S

Horizon 0°
Horizon 20°S
Horizon 40°S

Arcturus
BOÖTES
CORONA BOREALIS
SERPENS CAPUT
OPHIUCHUS
M13
HERCULES
SERPENS CAUDA
SCUTUM
DRACO
Vega
LYRA
Epsilon Lyrae
Albireo
VULPECULA
M27
SAGITTA
AQUILA
Altair
0° + 0°
URSA MINOR
CYGNUS
Deneb
Cygnus Rift
DELPHINUS
EQUULEUS
CEPHEUS
LACERTA
AQUARIUS
Delta Cephei
CASSIOPEIA
M31
PEGASUS
ANDROMEDA
PISCES
Ecliptic

Date	Std Time	DST
August 1	11 pm	Midnight
August 15	10 pm	11 pm
August 30	9 pm	10 pm

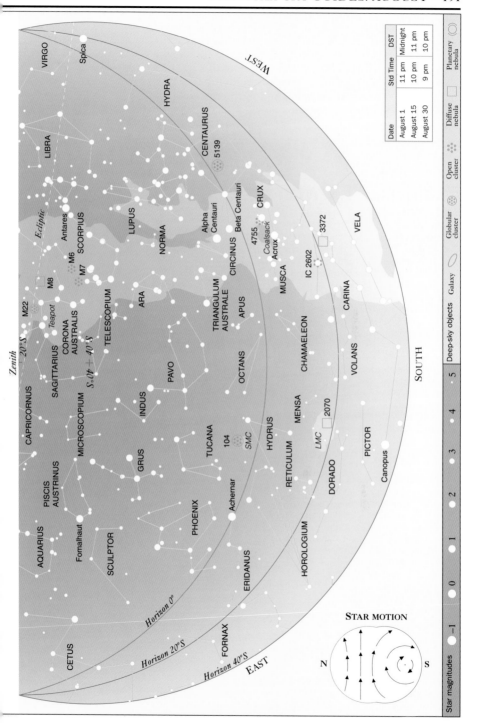

Date	Std Time	DST
August 1	11 pm	Midnight
August 15	10 pm	11 pm
August 30	9 pm	10 pm

Deep-sky objects

Galaxy · Globular cluster · Open cluster · Diffuse nebula · Planetary nebula

Star magnitudes

−1 · 0 · 1 · 2 · 3 · 4 · 5

STAR MOTION

SEPTEMBER

D AYS AND NIGHTS BECOME EQUAL in length as the equinox approaches, around September 23, marking the start of northern fall and southern spring. The Great Square of Pegasus is well placed for observers in northern latitudes, while in the Southern Hemisphere the brightest stars are in the western sky.

SUNRISE AND SUNSET ON SEPTEMBER 15		
Latitude	Sunrise	Sunset
60°N	05:30	18:20
40°N	05:40	18:10
20°N	05:50	18:00
0°	05:50	18:00
20°S	06:00	18:00
40°S	06:00	17:50

September 1 Std time 🕐 DST 🕐 | September 15 Std time 🕐 DST 🕐 | September 30 Std time 🕐 DST 🕐

NORTHERN LATITUDES

• **LOOKING NORTH** The view to the north contains relatively few bright stars this month. Cepheus is due north, with Cassiopeia to its right. Andromeda and Pegasus are high in the eastern sky, while Perseus is rising in the northeast, followed by Auriga. Draco and Hercules are in the northwestern sky.

• **LOOKING SOUTH** Aquarius and Capricornus are centrally placed, with Fomalhaut below them. The Great Square of Pegasus, with Pisces to its lower left, dominates the view to the southeast. The Summer Triangle of Altair, Deneb, and Vega is almost overhead in the southwest, while Ophiuchus and Serpens Cauda set farther west.

SOUTHERN LATITUDES

• **LOOKING NORTH** The large triangle formed by the bright stars Altair, Deneb, and Vega is prominent in the northwest. The Great Square of Pegasus dominates the northeastern sky, with Andromeda closer to the horizon and Pisces farther east. Capricornus and Aquarius are almost overhead. Ophiuchus and Serpens Cauda are setting in the west.

• **LOOKING SOUTH** Achernar in Eridanus is prominent in the southeast, an otherwise fairly blank area of sky, with the Small Magellanic Cloud (SMC, see p.197) to its right. Fomalhaut is almost overhead. Scorpius is in the south-west, with Sagittarius above it.

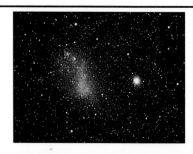

THE SMALL MAGELLANIC CLOUD (TUCANA)
This is the smaller, fainter, and more distant of two irregularly shaped small galaxies accompanying our own. To the naked eye, it looks like a cut-off part of the Milky Way. The cluster to its right is NGC 104 (see panel, right).

Star magnitudes ● −1 ● 0 ● 1 ● 2 ● 3

LOOKING SOUTH

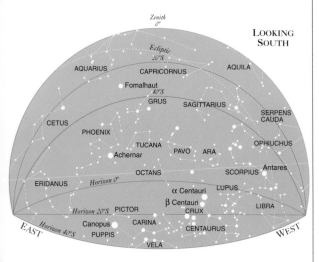

LOOKING SOUTH

WHOLE-SKY CHARTS

SEPTEMBER FEATURES

● **DELTA (δ) CEPHEI.**
This is the prototype of the Cepheid variable stars that are used for finding distances in space. The brightness of Delta Cephei rises and falls every 5 days as it pulsates in size; at its peak, the star is more than twice as bright as when at its faintest. Changes in its brightness can be followed with the naked eye by comparing it with nearby stars of known magnitude. Delta Cephei is also an attractive double star, having a fainter companion that is visible with the smallest telescopes. See also p.80.

(○) **M27 (VULPECULA).**
The easiest planetary nebula to see with binoculars lies in the often-overlooked constellation of Vulpecula, midway between the bright stars Deneb and Altair. Its popular name, the Dumb-bell Nebula, comes from its structure – more like a bow tie than a dumbbell – but this is visible only through a telescope. See also p.141.

(⊛) **NGC 104 (TUCANA).**
Also known as 47 Tucanae, this is the second most prominent globular cluster in the entire sky – only Omega (ω) Centauri is brighter. To the naked eye, it resembles a hazy star. It appears in the sky near the Small Magellanic Cloud (SMC) but is actually within our own Galaxy. See also p.135.

ALSO VISIBLE

● **Albireo** (p.187)
● **Epsilon (ε) Lyrae** (p.181)
◖ **M31** (p.199)
∴ **NGC 869 and NGC 884** (p.199)
● **The Cygnus Rift** (p.187)

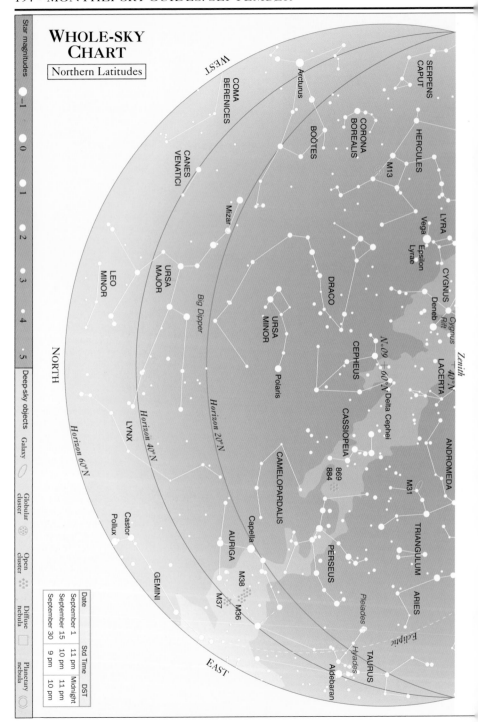

WHOLE-SKY CHART

Northern Latitudes

Star magnitudes

-1 0 1 2 3 4 5

NORTH

Deep-sky objects

Galaxy

Globular cluster

Open cluster

Diffuse nebula

Planetary nebula

WEST

SERPENS CAPUT

COMA BERENICES

Arcturus

CORONA BOREALIS

BOÖTES

HERCULES

M13

CANES VENATICI

Mizar

Vega
Epsilon
Lyrae

LYRA

CYGNUS

Deneb

Cygnus
Rift

Zenith

40°N

LEO MINOR

URSA MAJOR

Big Dipper

DRACO

URSA MINOR

Polaris

CEPHEUS

60°N

N. 09

Delta Cephei

LACERTA

ANDROMEDA

Horizon 20°N

CASSIOPEIA

869
884

M31

TRIANGULUM

Horizon 40°N

LYNX

CAMELOPARDALIS

Horizon 60°N

Castor
Pollux

Capella

AURIGA

PERSEUS

ARIES

Pleiades

GEMINI

M38
M36
M37

TAURUS

Hyades

Aldebaran

Ecliptic

EAST

Date	Std Time	DST
September 1	11 pm	Midnight
September 15	10 pm	11 pm
September 30	9 pm	10 pm

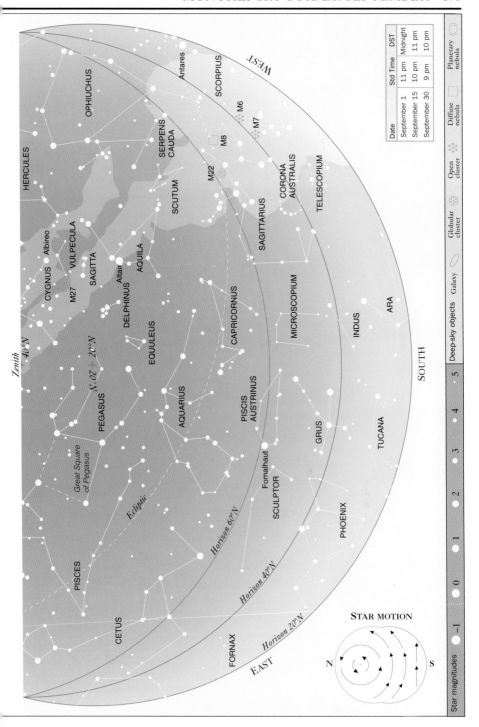

Date	Std Time	DST
September 1	11 pm	Midnight
September 15	10 pm	11 pm
September 30	9 pm	10 pm

STAR MOTION

Star magnitudes: −1 0 1 2 3 4 5

Deep-sky objects: Galaxy · Globular cluster · Open cluster · Diffuse nebula · Planetary nebula

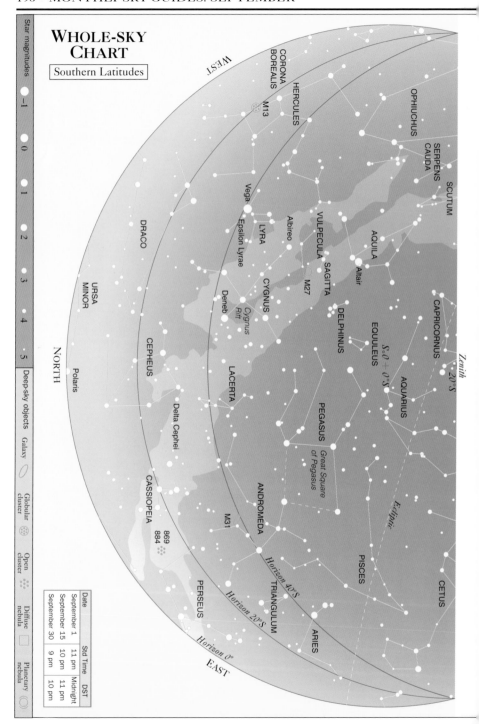

WHOLE-SKY CHART

Southern Latitudes

Star magnitudes

- −1
- 0
- 1
- 2
- 3
- 4
- 5

NORTH

Deep-sky objects

Galaxy

Globular cluster

Open cluster

Diffuse nebula

Planetary nebula

Date	Std Time	DST
September 1	11 pm	Midnight
September 15	10 pm	11 pm
September 30	9 pm	10 pm

WEST

CORONA BOREALIS

M13

HERCULES

OPHIUCHUS

SERPENS CAUDA

SCUTUM

Vega

DRACO

LYRA

Epsilon Lyrae

Albireo

VULPECULA

SAGITTA

M27

AQUILA

Altair

AQUARIUS

CAPRICORNUS

URSA MINOR

Deneb

CYGNUS

Cygnus Rift

DELPHINUS

EQUULEUS

$S_0 0 + 0°S$

20°S

Zenith

CEPHEUS

Polaris

LACERTA

PEGASUS

Great Square of Pegasus

Ecliptic

AQUARIUS

Delta Cephei

ANDROMEDA

PISCES

CASSIOPEIA

M31

TRIANGULUM

869 884

ARIES

CETUS

PERSEUS

Horizon 40°S

Horizon 20°S

Horizon 0°

EAST

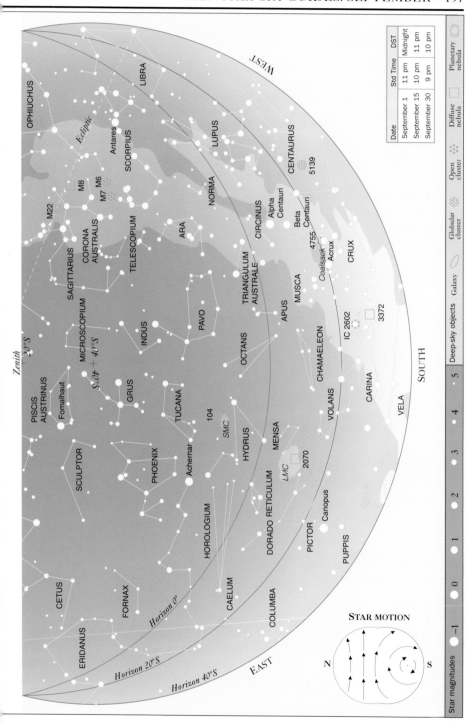

Date	Std Time	DST
September 1	11 pm	Midnight
September 15	10 pm	11 pm
September 30	9 pm	10 pm

Deep-sky objects

| Galaxy | Globular cluster | Open cluster | Diffuse nebula | Planetary nebula |

Star magnitudes

−1 · 0 · 1 · 2 · 3 · 4 · 5

STAR MOTION

N S

OCTOBER

T HE ANDROMEDA GALAXY, M31, is almost overhead for observers in northern latitudes, although for those in the Southern Hemisphere it remains disappointingly low. There are few bright stars on display at this time of year, but the Great Square of Pegasus is easy to see from both hemispheres.

SUNRISE AND SUNSET ON OCTOBER 15

Latitude	Sunrise	Sunset
60°N	06:40	16:50
40°N	06:10	17:20
20°N	05:50	17:40
0°	05:40	17:50
20°S	05:30	18:00
40°S	05:10	18:20

October 1 Std time ⏰ DST ⏰ | October 15 Std time ⏰ DST ⏰ | October 30 Std time ⏰ DST ⏰

NORTHERN LATITUDES

• **LOOKING NORTH** The Milky Way arches overhead from west to east (see pp.200–201). Cassiopeia is high up, above and to the left of Perseus. Capella and the other stars of Auriga are rising in the northeast along with Taurus, a foretaste of winter. The Summer Triangle can still be seen in the west, with Altair lying in the southwestern sky (far right of Looking South map).

• **LOOKING SOUTH** High in the south, the Great Square of Pegasus is well placed, with Andromeda above and to its left, almost overhead. Pisces lies to the left of Pegasus, and Aquarius is to its lower right. Low in the south is Fomalhaut, with Cetus in the southeastern sky.

SOUTHERN LATITUDES

• **LOOKING NORTH** The Great Square of Pegasus is centrally placed, with Andromeda to its lower right. Pisces is above and to the right of Pegasus, with Aquarius above left, nearly overhead. Altair, Vega, and Deneb are setting in the northwest. Aldebaran and the other stars of Taurus are just starting to appear above the northeastern horizon.

• **LOOKING SOUTH** Achernar is high in the south-east with Canopus rising below it. The only other objects of note in this relatively blank area are the Large and Small Magellanic Clouds (LMC and SMC, see p.203). Low in the southwestern sky, Sagittarius is following Scorpius below the horizon.

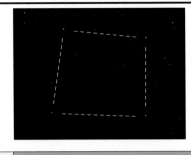

THE GREAT SQUARE OF PEGASUS
The corners of this huge square are marked by three stars in Pegasus and one in Andromeda (top left). Despite the figure's considerable size (about 15 degrees to a side, large enough to enclose 900 full Moons), it contains few naked-eye stars.

WHOLE-SKY CHARTS

OCTOBER FEATURES

M31 (ANDROMEDA).
The most distant object visible to the naked eye is a spiral galaxy similar to our home galaxy. Also called the Andromeda Galaxy, it can be seen with the naked eye in rural skies, but its full extent is better appreciated through binoculars. M31 is more than 2 million light-years away, so the light by which we now see it left when mankind's ancestors still roamed the plains of Africa. See also p.64.

NGC 869 AND NGC 884 (PERSEUS).
Two open clusters, known as the Double Cluster, mark the hand of Perseus. When seen with the naked eye, the pair resembles a knot that appears brighter than the surrounding Milky Way. They are easy to see through binoculars. See also p.118.

Star magnitudes	● −1	● 0	● 1	• 2	· 3

Zenith 60°N

LOOKING SOUTH

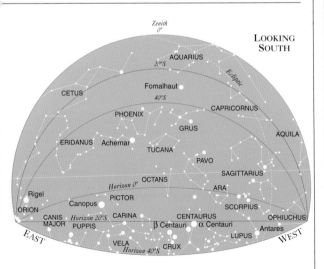

Zenith 0°

LOOKING SOUTH

ALSO VISIBLE
● **Albireo** (p.187)
● **Delta (δ) Cephei** (p.193)
○ **M27** (p.193)
⊕ **NGC 104** (p.193)
□ **NGC 2070** (p.205)
● **The Cygnus Rift** (p.187)
● **The Hyades and Pleiades** (p.211)

OCTOBER METEORS

THE ORIONIDS. Radiating from northern Orion, near the border with Gemini, the Orionids reach a peak of about 25 meteors an hour around October 21. Since this area of sky does not rise until late, the shower is best viewed after midnight. The Orionids are fast moving but faint. Like the Eta Aquarids of May, they are caused by dust from Halley's Comet.

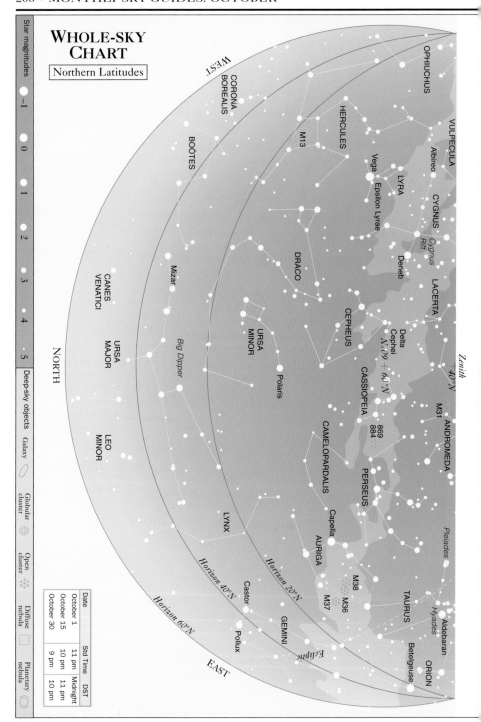

WHOLE-SKY CHART

Northern Latitudes

Star magnitudes

- −1
- 0
- 1
- 2
- 3
- 4
- 5

Deep-sky objects

Galaxy

Globular cluster

Open cluster

Diffuse nebula

Planetary nebula

Date	Std Time	DST
October 1	11 pm	Midnight
October 15	10 pm	11 pm
October 30	9 pm	10 pm

WEST

NORTH

EAST

Zenith
40°N

60°N

Horizon 20°N

Horizon 40°N

Horizon 60°N

OPHIUCHUS
VULPECULA
CORONA BOREALIS
CYGNUS
Albireo
HERCULES
M13
LYRA
Vega
Epsilon Lyrae
BOÖTES
LACERTA
Cygnus Rift
Deneb
DRACO
CEPHEUS
Delta Cephei
CASSIOPEIA
ANDROMEDA
M31
CANES VENATICI
Mizar
URSA MINOR
Polaris
Big Dipper
869
884
CAMELOPARDALIS
PERSEUS
Pleiades
URSA MAJOR
LEO MINOR
Capella
AURIGA
Hyades
Aldebaran
LYNX
M38
M36
M37
TAURUS
GEMINI
Castor
Pollux
Betelgeuse
ORION
Ecliptic

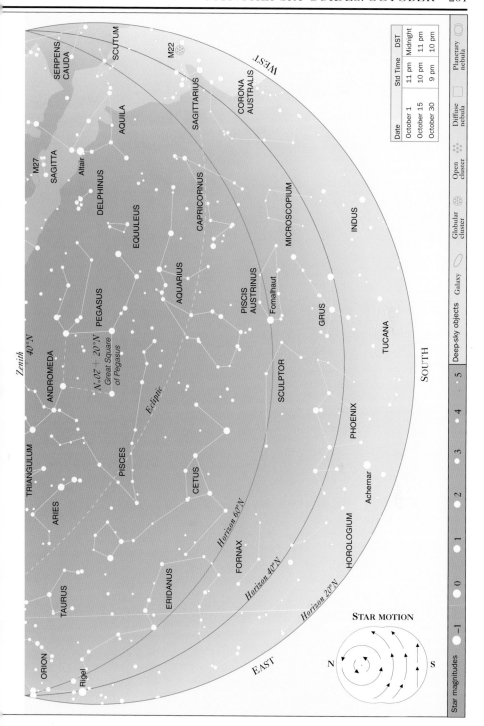

Date	Std Time	DST
October 1	11 pm	Midnight
October 15	10 pm	11 pm
October 30	9 pm	10 pm

Deep-sky objects

Galaxy — Globular cluster — Open cluster — Diffuse nebula — Planetary nebula

Star magnitudes: −1 0 1 2 3 4 5

STAR MOTION

N S

EAST WEST SOUTH

Zenith 40°N

Great Square of Pegasus

Ecliptic

Horizon 60°N
Horizon 40°N
Horizon 20°N

ORION TAURUS ERIDANUS Rigel ARIES TRIANGULUM ANDROMEDA PISCES CETUS FORNAX HOROLOGIUM Achernar PHOENIX SCULPTOR TUCANA GRUS PISCIS AUSTRINUS Fomalhaut AQUARIUS EQUULEUS PEGASUS DELPHINUS Altair SAGITTA M27 AQUILA SERPENS CAUDA SCUTUM M22 SAGITTARIUS CAPRICORNUS MICROSCOPIUM INDUS CORONA AUSTRALIS

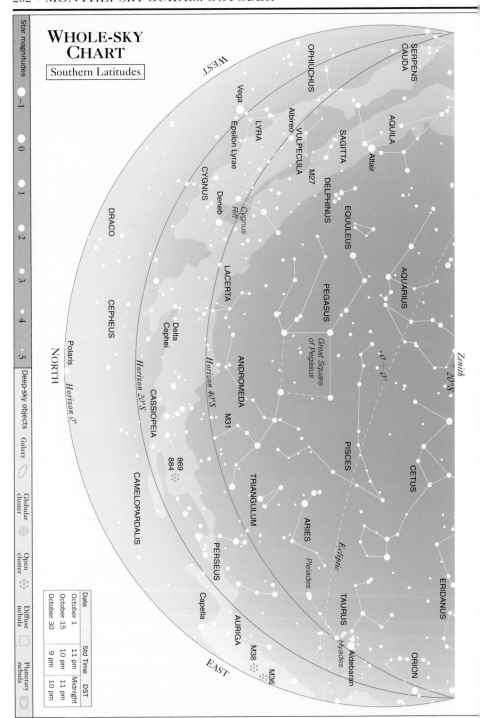

WHOLE-SKY CHART

Southern Latitudes

Star magnitudes

- −1
- 0
- 1
- 2
- 3
- 4
- 5

NORTH

Deep-sky objects

Galaxy

Globular cluster

Open cluster

Diffuse nebula

Planetary nebula

Date	Std Time	DST
October 1	11 pm	Midnight
October 15	10 pm	11 pm
October 30	9 pm	10 pm

WEST

SERPENS CAUDA

OPHIUCHUS

AQUILA

Altair

SAGITTA

Vega

Albireo

VULPECULA

M27

LYRA

Epsilon Lyrae

DELPHINUS

EQUULEUS

CYGNUS

Deneb

Cygnus Rift

AQUARIUS

LACERTA

PEGASUS

Great Square of Pegasus

DRACO

Delta Cephei

Zenith

20°S

CEPHEUS

Horizon 20°S

ANDROMEDA

PEGASUS

PISCES

CETUS

Polaris

Horizon 0°

CASSIOPEIA

Horizon 40°S

M31

TRIANGULUM

869
884

ARIES

Pleiades

Ecliptic

CAMELOPARDALIS

PERSEUS

TAURUS

Hyades

Aldebaran

ERIDANUS

Capella

AURIGA

ORION

M38

M36

EAST

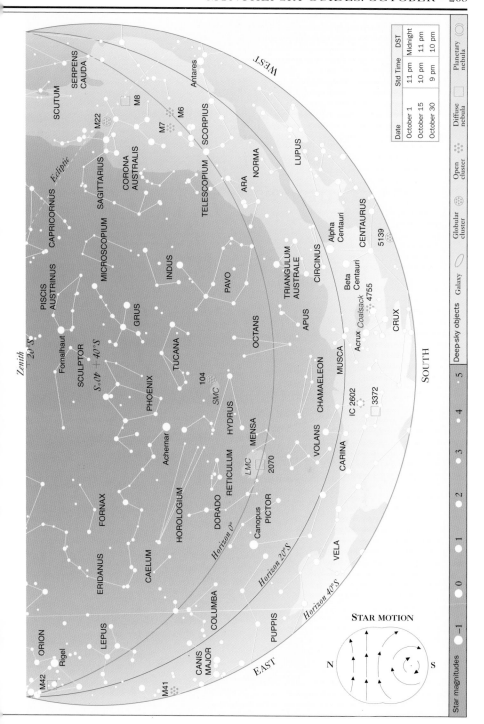

Date	Std Time	DST
October 1	11 pm	Midnight
October 15	10 pm	11 pm
October 30	9 pm	10 pm

STAR MOTION

Star magnitudes: −1 · 0 · 1 · 2 · 3 · 4 · 5

Deep-sky objects: Galaxy · Globular cluster · Open cluster · Diffuse nebula · Planetary nebula

NOVEMBER

A LL THE constellations named after characters in the story of Perseus and Andromeda are on view this month – Perseus and Andromeda themselves, Cassiopeia and Cepheus, her parents, and Cetus, the sea monster from which she was saved by Perseus. In northern latitudes, daylight savings time is at an end.

SUNRISE AND SUNSET ON NOVEMBER 15

Latitude	Sunrise	Sunset
60°N	08:00	15:30
40°N	06:50	16:40
20°N	06:10	17:20
0°	05:40	17:50
20°S	05:10	18:20
40°S	04:40	18:50

| November 1 | Std time 🕐 DST 🕐 | November 15 | Std time 🕐 DST 🕐 | November 30 | Std time 🕐 DST 🕐 |

NORTHERN LATITUDES

• **LOOKING NORTH** The Milky Way (see pp.206–207) arches overhead from west to east. Perseus, Andromeda, and Cassiopeia are high up, with Cepheus beneath them. Auriga, with its brightest star Capella, is high in the northeast, with Gemini below it. The Summer Triangle of Vega, Deneb, and Altair is now low in the northwestern sky.

• **LOOKING SOUTH** Cetus lies due south, flanked higher up by Aries and Andromeda. Pisces, Pegasus, and Aquarius dominate the sky to the west. The stars of winter are rising in the east, among them Orion and Taurus, which contains red Aldebaran and the Hyades and Pleiades clusters (see p.207).

Zenith 20°N
LOOKING NORTH

SOUTHERN LATITUDES

• **LOOKING NORTH** Cetus is almost over-head, with Pisces and Aries below it, while Perseus, Andromeda, and Cassiopeia are close to the northern horizon. Pegasus, with its Great Square, occupies most of the northwestern sky. In the northeast, Taurus is climbing into view, with Orion farther east, a sign of approaching summer.

• **LOOKING SOUTH** Achernar is due south, with the Large and Small Magellanic Clouds (LMC and SMC, see p.209) below it. There are few noticeable stars near the zenith, but Sirius and Canopus, the two brightest stars in the sky, stand out in the east and south-east. Fomalhaut is high in the west.

Zenith 40°S
LOOKING NORTH

THE LARGE MAGELLANIC CLOUD Lying mostly in Dorado, this is the larger, brighter, and closer of two small galaxies that accompany our own. It appears to the eye as a long, hazy patch like a detached part of the Milky Way, while binoculars show a host of star clusters and nebulae.

Star magnitudes ● –1 ● 0 ● 1 • 2 · 3

WHOLE-SKY CHARTS

NOVEMBER FEATURES

☐ **NGC 2070 (DORADO).** The most prominent object in the Large Magellanic Cloud is a diffuse nebula visible to the naked eye and through binoculars. It is popularly known as the Tarantula Nebula because of its spidery shape, which is particularly noticeable on photographs. It is about 50 times larger than the famous Orion Nebula (M42) in our own Galaxy. See also p.91.

ALSO VISIBLE
◒ M31 (p.199)
✷ M36, M37, and M38 (p.211)
✷ M41 (p.151)
☐ M42 (p.145)
✷ NGC 869 and NGC 884 (p.199)
✷ NGC 2244 (p.151)
● The Hyades and Pleiades (p.211)

LOOKING SOUTH

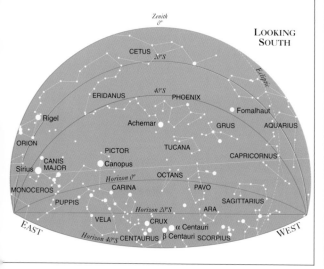

LOOKING SOUTH

NOVEMBER METEORS

THE TAURIDS. Starting in late October and continuing for a month or more, the Taurids reach a sustained peak in the first week of November. Activity is no more than 10 an hour, from just south of the Pleiades, but Taurid meteors are striking because they move slowly and are often bright.
THE LEONIDS. This shower radiates from the head of Leo around November 17. Activity is normally only about 10 an hour at best, but it can surge sharply at 33-year intervals when the parent comet, Tempel–Tuttle, returns to the Sun. A Leonid storm occurred in 1966, and similar activity is expected in 1998 and 1999.

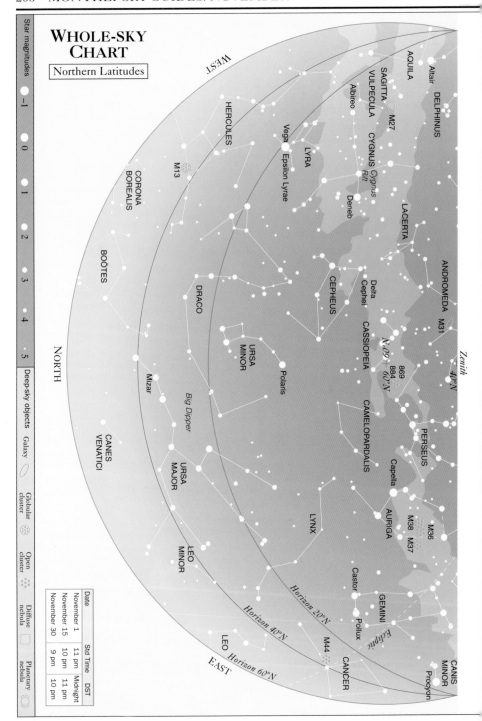

WHOLE-SKY CHART

Northern Latitudes

Star magnitudes

- ● −1
- ● 0
- ● 1
- ● 2
- ● 3
- • 4
- · 5

NORTH

Deep-sky objects

Galaxy	Globular cluster	Open cluster	Diffuse nebula	Planetary nebula
◯	✺	⬡	▢	◎

Date	Std Time	DST
November 1	11 pm	Midnight
November 15	10 pm	11 pm
November 30	9 pm	10 pm

WEST

AQUILA
Altair
DELPHINUS
SAGITTA
VULPECULA
Albireo
M27
CYGNUS Rift
HERCULES
LYRA
Vega
Epsilon Lyrae
Deneb
LACERTA
CORONA BOREALIS
M13
ANDROMEDA
M31
BOOTES
DRACO
CEPHEUS
Delta Cephei
CASSIOPEIA
N.00
884
869
60°N
40°N
Zenith
URSA MINOR
Polaris
CAMELOPARDALIS
PERSEUS
Capella
Mizar
Big Dipper
AURIGA
M38 M37
M36
CANES VENATICI
URSA MAJOR
LYNX
Castor
GEMINI
Pollux
LEO MINOR
Horizon 20°N
M44
CANIS MINOR
Procyon
CANCER
Horizon 40°N
Ecliptic
LEO
Horizon 60°N
EAST

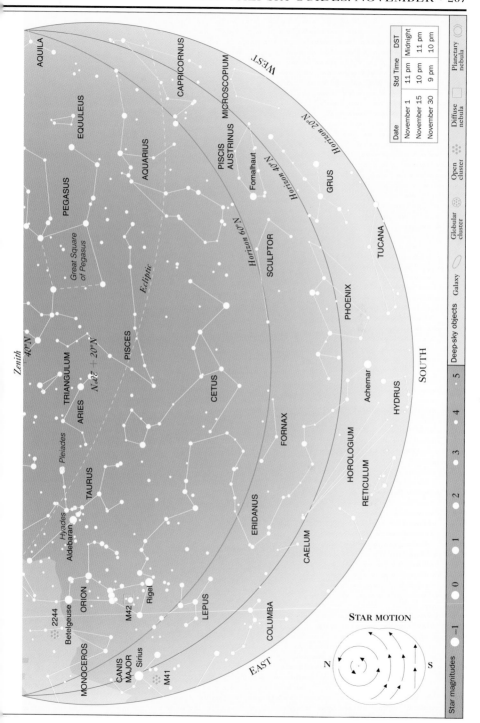

Date	Std Time	DST
November 1	11 pm	Midnight
November 15	10 pm	11 pm
November 30	9 pm	10 pm

STAR MOTION

Star magnitudes

−1   0   1   2   3   4   5

Deep-sky objects

Galaxy   Globular cluster   Open cluster   Diffuse nebula   Planetary nebula

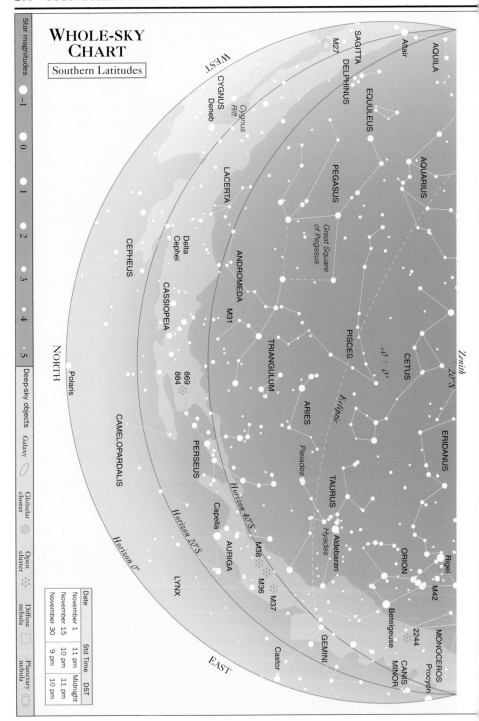

WHOLE-SKY CHART

Southern Latitudes

Star magnitudes

-1
0
1
2
3
4
5

Deep-sky objects Galaxy Globular cluster Open cluster Diffuse nebula Planetary nebula

NORTH

WEST

EAST

Zenith

Polaris

CEPHEUS

CAMELOPARDALIS

CASSIOPEIA

LACERTA

CYGNUS

Deneb

Cygnus Rift

SAGITTA

M27

DELPHINUS

EQUULEUS

AQUILA

Altair

Delta Cephei

ANDROMEDA

M31

869
884

PERSEUS

PEGASUS

Great Square of Pegasus

AQUARIUS

PISCES

CETUS

ERIDANUS

TRIANGULUM

ARIES

Pleiades

TAURUS

Aldebaran

Hyades

ORION

Rigel

M42

Betelgeuse

2244

MONOCEROS

Procyon

CANIS MINOR

GEMINI

Castor

AURIGA

Capella

M38

M36

M37

LYNX

Ecliptic

20°S

0°

0°

Horizon 40°S

Horizon 20°S

Horizon 0°

Date	Std Time	DST
November 1	11 pm	Midnight
November 15	10 pm	11 pm
November 30	9 pm	10 pm

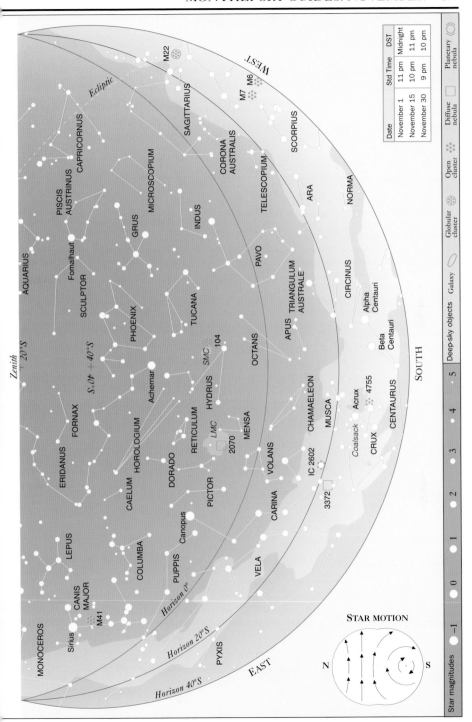

Date	Std Time	DST
November 1	11 pm	Midnight
November 15	10 pm	11 pm
November 30	9 pm	10 pm

Deep-sky objects

Galaxy · Globular cluster · Open cluster · Diffuse nebula · Planetary nebula

Star magnitudes: −1 · 0 · 1 · 2 · 3 · 4 · 5

STAR MOTION

N   S

WEST

SOUTH

EAST

Zenith

Ecliptic

20°S

S∘0t + 40°S

Horizon 0°

Horizon 20°S

Horizon 40°S

SAGITTARIUS
M22
M6
M7
SCORPIUS
CORONA AUSTRALIS
TELESCOPIUM
ARA
NORMA
CIRCINUS
Alpha Centauri
Beta Centauri
4755
Acrux
CRUX
Coalsack
CENTAURUS
MUSCA
CHAMAELEON
IC 2602
3372
VOLANS
CARINA
VELA
PYXIS
PUPPIS
Canopus
COLUMBA
PICTOR
DORADO
LMC
2070
MENSA
RETICULUM
HOROLOGIUM
CAELUM
HYDRUS
SMC
104
OCTANS
APUS
TRIANGULUM AUSTRALE
PAVO
INDUS
TUCANA
Achernar
ERIDANUS
FORNAX
LEPUS
CANIS MAJOR
Sirius
M41
MONOCEROS
PHOENIX
SCULPTOR
Fomalhaut
PISCIS AUSTRINUS
AQUARIUS
CAPRICORNUS
MICROSCOPIUM
GRUS

DECEMBER

NIGHTS ARE AT THEIR LONGEST and days at their shortest in the Northern Hemisphere, and vice versa in the south. Much of the sky as it appears in the far south is occupied by constellations that were never seen by the astronomers of ancient Greece. A bright meteor shower radiates from Gemini in mid-month.

SUNRISE AND SUNSET ON DECEMBER 15

Latitude	Sunrise	Sunset
60°N	09:00	14:50
40°N	07:10	16:40
20°N	06:30	17:20
0°	05:50	18:00
20°S	05:20	18:40
40°S	04:30	19:20

December 1 Std time 🕐 DST 🕐 | December 15 Std time 🕐 DST 🕐 | December 30 Std time 🕐 DST 🕐

NORTHERN LATITUDES

• **LOOKING NORTH** Perseus is almost overhead with Capella and the other stars of Auriga to its right. Gemini is farther east, with Cancer rising beneath it. On the northeastern horizon, Regulus leads the stars of Leo into view. In the northwest are Cassiopeia and Cepheus, with Deneb closer to the horizon.
• **LOOKING SOUTH** Taurus is high in the south, ideally placed for observing the Pleiades and Hyades clusters (see p.213). Eridanus is beneath it, while to its lower left Orion is still rising, followed by brilliant Sirius and Procyon. Cetus can be seen in the southwestern sky, with Pisces and Pegasus visible progressively farther to the west.

Zenith 20°N

LOOKING NORTH

SOUTHERN LATITUDES

• **LOOKING NORTH** Eridanus, the celestial river, meanders overhead. Taurus is below it, with the Hyades and Pleiades (see p.214) ideally placed and Orion high to its right. Auriga and Perseus are near the northern horizon, with Gemini in the northeast. In the northwest, the Great Square of Pegasus is setting, followed by Pisces.
• **LOOKING SOUTH** Achernar and Canopus lie to the right and left of center. In between them, slightly lower down, are the Large and Small Magellanic Clouds (LMC and SMC, see p.215). Sirius is high in the eastern sky, and Vela and Puppis are rising in the southeast. Fomalhaut is setting in the southwest.

Zenith 40°S

LOOKING NORTH

THE HYADES AND PLEIADES (TAURUS)
The stars of Taurus depict the top half of a bull's body. The large, V-shaped Hyades cluster (to lower left) outlines the face, and the red star Aldebaran represents one eye. The Pleiades cluster (top right) lies on the bull's back. See also panel, right.

Star magnitudes ●−1 ●0 ●1 •2 ·3

LOOKING SOUTH

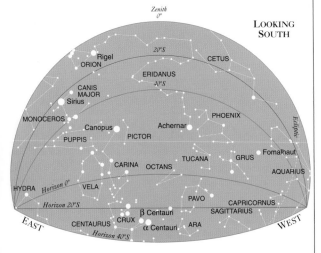

LOOKING SOUTH

WHOLE-SKY CHARTS

DECEMBER FEATURES

❖ **M36, M37, AND M38 (AURIGA).** In the Milky Way star fields of Auriga, a crooked line of three open clusters can be seen through wide-field binoculars. M37 is the largest of them, while M36, in the middle of the line, is the smallest but also the easiest to resolve into individual stars with a small telescope. See also p.69.

● **THE HYADES (TAURUS).** This large, bright open cluster, the closest such cluster to Earth, contains more than a dozen stars visible to the naked eye. See also pp.132–33.

● **THE PLEIADES (TAURUS).** At first glance, this open cluster appears as a hazy cloud, but a closer look reveals several individual stars. Although the cluster is also called the Seven Sisters, normal eyesight shows only about six stars. People with exceptional vision can see several more, and binoculars bring dozens of stars into view. See also pp.132–33.

ALSO VISIBLE
❖ M41 (p.151)
☐ M42 (p.145)
❖ M44 (p.157)
☐ NGC 2070 (p.205)
❖ NGC 2244 (p.151)

DECEMBER METEORS

THE GEMINIDS. The second-best shower of the year radiates from near Castor, in Gemini, reaching a maximum on December 13, when as many as 100 bright meteors an hour may be seen. Lower rates of activity occur for several days either side of the maximum.

WHOLE-SKY CHART

Northern Latitudes

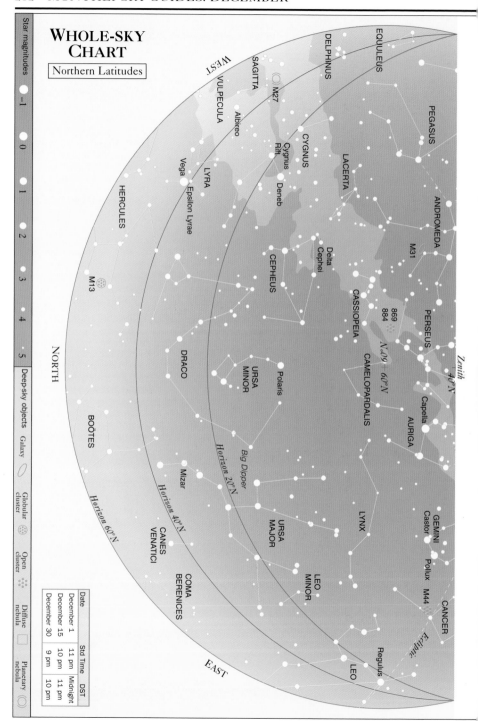

Star magnitudes

- −1
- 0
- 1
- 2
- 3
- 4
- 5

Deep-sky objects

Galaxy

Globular cluster

Open cluster

Diffuse nebula

Planetary nebula

NORTH

WEST

EAST

Zenith 40°N

40°N + 60°N

Horizon 20°N

Horizon 40°N

Horizon 60°N

Ecliptic

DELPHINUS
EQUULEUS
PEGASUS
SAGITTA
VULPECULA
M27
CYGNUS
Albireo
Cygnus Rift
Deneb
LACERTA
ANDROMEDA
M31
Vega
LYRA
Epsilon Lyrae
HERCULES
CEPHEUS
Delta Cephei
CASSIOPEIA
PERSEUS
869
884
CAMELOPARDALIS
Capella
AURIGA
M13
DRACO
URSA MINOR
Polaris
LYNX
BOÖTES
Big Dipper
GEMINI
Castor
Pollux
M44
Mizar
URSA MAJOR
CANCER
CANES VENATICI
LEO MINOR
COMA BERENICES
Regulus
LEO

Date	Std Time	DST
December 1	11 pm	Midnight
December 15	10 pm	11 pm
December 30	9 pm	10 pm

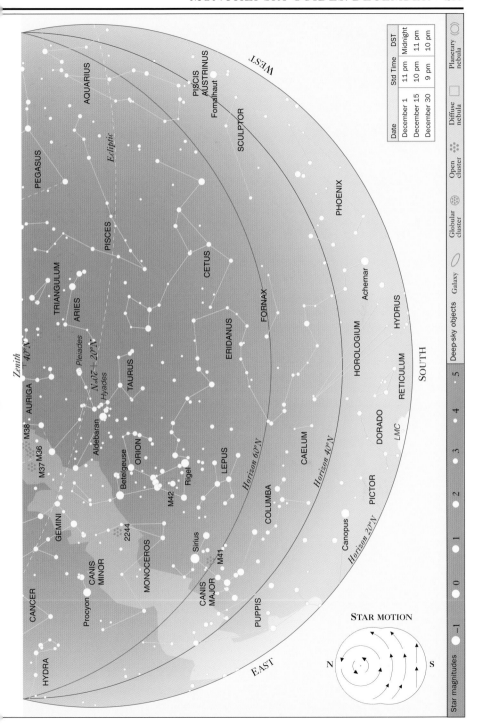

Date	Std Time	DST
December 1	11 pm	Midnight
December 15	10 pm	11 pm
December 30	9 pm	10 pm

STAR MOTION

Star magnitudes

Deep-sky objects: Galaxy · Globular cluster · Open cluster · Diffuse nebula · Planetary nebula

WHOLE-SKY CHART

Southern Latitudes

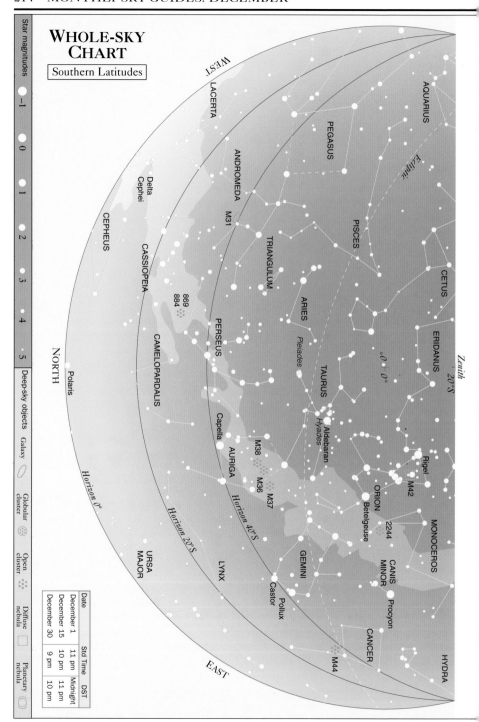

Star magnitudes

- −1
- 0
- 1
- 2
- 3
- 4
- 5

Deep-sky objects

Galaxy

Globular cluster

Open cluster

Diffuse nebula

Planetary nebula

Date	Std Time	DST
December 1	11 pm	Midnight
December 15	10 pm	11 pm
December 30	9 pm	10 pm

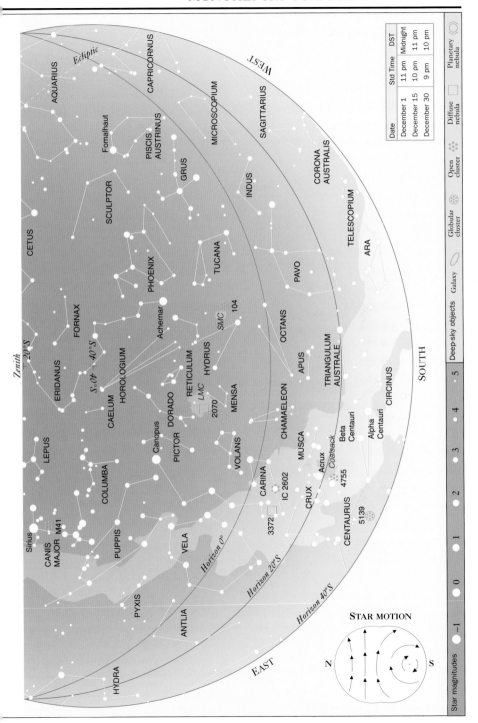

Date	Std Time	DST
December 1	11 pm	Midnight
December 15	10 pm	11 pm
December 30	9 pm	10 pm

Deep-sky objects   ◯ Galaxy   ⊛ Globular cluster   ⋮ Open cluster   ▢ Diffuse nebula   ◎ Planetary nebula

STAR MOTION

N   S

Star magnitudes   −1   0   1   2   3   4   5

GLOSSARY

WITH THE EXCEPTION of words in regular use, words that are defined elsewhere in the glossary appear in **bold** type.

• **ABSOLUTE MAGNITUDE**
A measure of the true luminosity of an object, defined as how bright it would appear if it were at a standard distance from the Earth, chosen to be 32.6 **light-years**.

• **APERTURE**
The diameter of the light-collecting lens or mirror of an astronomical instrument.

• **APPARENT MAGNITUDE**
The brightness of an object as seen from the Earth. It is affected by the object's distance from us.

• **ASTERISM**
A pattern formed by stars in one or more **constellations**. Examples are the Big Dipper (or Plough), which is part of Ursa Major, and the Great Square of Pegasus, formed by stars in both Pegasus and Andromeda.

• **ASTEROID**
A small, rocky body, also called a minor planet, orbiting the Sun.

• **AXIS**
An imaginary line about which a celestial object rotates.

• **BINARY STAR**
A pair of stars linked by gravity, orbiting around a common center of mass. *See also* **Eclipsing binary**, **Spectroscopic binary**.

• **BLACK HOLE**
A volume of space in which gravity is so great that nothing can escape, not even light, although objects can fall in. Black holes are thought to form when massive stars collapse.

• **CELESTIAL OBJECT**
An object in space, such as a star, planet, or **galaxy**, that appears in the Earth's sky.

• **CELESTIAL EQUATOR**
The celestial equivalent of the Earth's equator, lying on the **celestial sphere** directly over the Earth's equator.

• **CELESTIAL POLES**
The celestial equivalent of the Earth's poles, around which the **celestial sphere** appears to turn each day.

• **CELESTIAL SPHERE**
An imaginary sphere of infinite size around the Earth, on which celestial objects appear to lie. *See also* pp.16–17.

• **CEPHEID VARIABLE**
A type of **variable star** that pulsates regularly in size, every few days or weeks, with a period that is linked to its average luminosity.

• **CHARGE-COUPLED DEVICE (CCD)**
A light-sensitive silicon chip used in place of photographic film to record images of celestial objects.

• **CIRCUMPOLAR STAR**
A star that is above the horizon all night, as seen from a particular location on the Earth. Instead of rising and setting, the star appears to circle one of the celestial poles.

• **COMET**
A ball of frozen gas and dust on a long orbit around the Sun.

• **CONJUNCTION**
An occasion when two bodies in the **Solar System** (usually the Sun and a planet) line up as seen from the Earth. *See also* **Inferior conjunction**, **Superior conjunction**.

• **CONSTELLATION**
An area of sky, originally a star pattern, but now defined as the area within boundaries set by the International Astronomical Union.

• **DECLINATION (DEC.)**
The angle between an object and the **celestial equator**. Declination is the equivalent of latitude on the Earth. It is measured at right angles to the celestial equator, from 0° on the equator itself to 90° north or south at the **celestial poles**.

• **DEEP-SKY OBJECT**
A term applied to star clusters, **nebulae**, and **galaxies**.

• **DIFFUSE NEBULA**
A bright cloud of gas, illuminated by stars within it.

• **DOUBLE STAR**
Two stars that look close together as seen from the Earth. *See also* **Binary star**, **Optical double star**.

• **ECLIPSE**
An occasion when one celestial object cuts off some or all of the light from another.

• **ECLIPSING BINARY**
A pair of stars in orbit around each other, in which one star periodically passes in front of the other as seen from the Earth, cutting off its light.

• **ECLIPTIC**
The plane of the Earth's orbit around the Sun, projected on to the **celestial sphere**. The Sun appears to move along the ecliptic, but this is in fact due to the Earth's motion around the Sun.

• **ELONGATION**
The angle between a planet and the Sun, or between a moon and a planet, as seen from the Earth.

• **EQUINOX**
The occasion when the Sun lies on the **celestial equator**. This occurs twice a year, around March 21 and September 23. At an equinox, day and night are roughly equal in length everywhere on the Earth.

• **GALAXY**
A mass of stars, numbering from millions to billions, all linked by gravity. Galaxies range from about a thousand light-years to hundreds of thousands of light-years across.

• **GIANT STAR**
A star that has become bigger and brighter in the late stages of its development.

• **GLOBULAR CLUSTER**
A ball-shaped group of stars, about 100 light-years across, with tens of thousands to hundreds of thousands of members. Such clusters contain some of the oldest stars known.

• **INFERIOR CONJUNCTION**
The occasion when either Mercury or Venus lies between the Sun and the Earth.

• **LIGHT-YEAR**
A unit of distance. It is the distance a beam of light covers in a calendar year, or 5,878,600,000,000 miles (9,460,700,000,000 km).

• **LOCAL GROUP**
The cluster of about 30 **galaxies** that includes our own.

• **LUMINOSITY**
The inherent brightness of a light-producing celestial object.

• **MAGNITUDE**
The brightness of a celestial object, measured on a numerical scale on which bright objects are given low

or negative values and faint objects have high values. The brightest stars are termed first magnitude, fainter ones second magnitude, and so on. In general usage, an object described as being of, for example, fourth magnitude has a magnitude between 3.5 and 4.49. *See also* **Absolute magnitude, Apparent magnitude**. *See also* p.18.

• **METEOR**
A streak of light in the sky, caused by a small particle burning up in the Earth's atmosphere.

• **METEORITE**
A fragment of an **asteroid** that has fallen to the surface of a planet or its satellite.

• **MILKY WAY**
The hazy band that can be seen in the sky on dark nights, composed of billions of distant stars in our own **Galaxy**. It is also a popular name for our Galaxy as a whole.

• **MIRA VARIABLE**
A red **giant** or **supergiant star** that pulsates in size over a period of months or years, varying in brightness by as much as 11 **magnitudes**.

• **NEBULA**
A cloud of gas and dust, usually found in the spiral arms of a **galaxy**. *See also* **Planetary nebula, Diffuse nebula**.

• **NEUTRON STAR**
A small and highly dense star consisting of the atomic particles known as neutrons and thought to be the remains of a massive star that has exploded as a **supernova**.

• **NOVA**
A star that erupts temporarily in brightness by many thousands of times. Novae occur in close **binary stars**, one member of which is a **white dwarf**. Gas flows from the companion star on to the white dwarf, causing a small explosion which leads to the brightening.

• **OPEN CLUSTER**
An irregularly shaped group of dozens or hundreds of relatively young stars, usually found in the spiral arms of a **galaxy**.

• **OPPOSITION**
The occasion when a body in the **Solar System** appears opposite the Sun, as seen from the Earth, and is hence visible all night.

• **OPTICAL DOUBLE STAR**
Two stars that appear close to one another in the sky but in fact lie at different distances from the Earth.

• **ORBIT**
The path of an object that is moving through space under the gravitational influence of another body of greater mass.

• **PARALLAX**
The change in position of an object when seen from two different locations. How much the object's position changes depends on its distance and the separation of the observing locations. Nearby stars show a slight parallax shift as the Earth orbits the Sun, from which their distances can be calculated.

• **PHASE**
A fraction of the illuminated disk of a planet or moon, as seen from the Earth.

• **PLANET**
A relatively large object that orbits a star and does not emit light.

• **PLANETARY NEBULA**
A shell of gas thrown off by a star late in its development.

• **RADIANT**
The point from which the **meteors** in a shower appear to diverge.

• **REFLECTING TELESCOPE**
A telescope in which light is collected and focused by a mirror.

• **REFRACTING TELESCOPE**
A telescope in which light is collected and focused by a lens.

• **RETROGRADE MOTION**
Movement from east to west (or clockwise as seen from above an object's north pole). This is opposite to the general direction of motion in the **Solar System**.

• **RIGHT ASCENSION (RA)**
A coordinate on the **celestial sphere**, the equivalent of longitude on Earth. It is measured in hours (one hour being equivalent to 15 degrees) from the point where the Sun crosses the **celestial equator** in March.

• **SOLAR SYSTEM**
The Sun and the various bodies in orbit around it. These include the nine planets and their moons, as well as **asteroids, comets**, and smaller pieces of debris.

• **SOLSTICE**
The occasion when the Sun reaches its farthest point either north or south of the **celestial equator**. This happens around

June 21, the longest day in the Northern Hemisphere, and December 22, the longest day in the Southern Hemisphere.

• **SPECTROSCOPIC BINARY**
A pair of stars so close together that they cannot be separated with any telescope. The fact that the star is a **binary** is revealed only when its light is studied with a spectroscope.

• **STAR**
A ball of gas that generates heat and light as a result of nuclear reactions at its core.

• **SUPERGIANT STAR**
A star at least ten times as massive as the Sun, and which has become bigger and brighter in the late stages of its development. Supergiants can be hundreds of times the diameter of the Sun and tens of thousands of times as bright.

• **SUPERIOR CONJUNCTION**
The occasion when Mercury or Venus lies on the far side of the Sun, as seen from the Earth.

• **SUPERNOVA**
An explosion in which, for a few weeks or months, a star brightens by millions of times. Only the most massive stars become supernovae.

• **UNIVERSE**
Everything that exists, including all matter, space, and time.

• **VARIABLE STAR**
Any star that appears to change in brightness. This is usually due to pulsations in the size of the star, but some variables are actually close **binary stars** in which one star periodically **eclipses** the other. *See also* **Cepheid variable, Mira variable**.

• **WHITE DWARF**
A small, dense star with a mass similar to that of the Sun, but only about 1 percent of the Sun's diameter.

• **ZENITH**
The point in the sky directly above an observer.

• **ZODIAC**
The band of sky either side of the **ecliptic** through which the Sun and planets move. Although there are 12 **constellations** of the zodiac dating from ancient times, more recent changes in constellation boundaries mean that the Sun and planets also pass through a 13th constellation, Ophiuchus.

INDEX

ACKNOWLEDGMENTS

THE AUTHOR AND PUBLISHER would like to thank the following people for their invaluable help: Robin Scagell for advice on photography; the staff at Her Majesty's Nautical Almanac Office, Cambridge (particularly Steve Bell, David Harper, Catherine Hohenkerk, and Andrew Sinclair) for their work on the star charts and planet location diagrams; and John Woodruff for proofreading and indexing.

DORLING KINDERSLEY would also like to thank: Broadhurst, Clarkson and Fuller Ltd (63 Farringdon Road, London) for supplying telescopes; Lynne Marie Stockman for reference material for the inset chart of the Pleiades on p.133; Nick Stevens for the photographs used in the illustration of moon phases on p.40; Giles Sparrow for checking the constellation figure artworks; and Lesley Riley for editorial assistance.

ILLUSTRATION CREDITS
All star charts and planet-location diagrams plotted by Her Majesty's Nautical Almanac Office, Royal Greenwich Observatory. Solar System locator illustrations by Rob Campbell. Illustrations of the internal structure of the planets and the rings and moons of the gas planets by Luciano Corbella. Tilt, rotation, and orbit illustrations and pie-charts of atmospheric composition by Martin Cropper. Constellation figure illustrations by Gavin Dunn.
 Other illustrations are by the following artists/organizations: Julian Baum 14 (b), 26 (all), 29 (c), 32 (c), 38, 41 (c), 42 (cl & cr), 46 (c), 50 (c), 51, 54 (c), 56 (c), 58 (c), 59 (t), 60 (t), 61. Richard Bonson 12 (c), 13 (all), 14 (t & c), 19 (bl), 23 (all). Rob Campbell 12 (b), 27 (c). Luciano Corbella 9 (b), 19 (br), 34 (cl), 44 (cr). DK Cartography/ Planetary Visions Ltd (London) 36 (c). DK Cartography 142 (t). John Egan 16 (all), 17 (all), 53, 60 (bl). Helen Taylor 15 (tr, bl, & br), 18 (b), 20 (b), 21 (all), 33 (c), 36 (b), 39 (c), 40 (t), 43 (c), 44 (cl), 47 (t), 59 (c). King and King 28 (all), 40 (b), 62.

PHOTOGRAPHY CREDITS
The following pictures were provided by Galaxy Picture Library: Robin Scagell 12, 17, 22 (all), 27 (clb), 30 (tr), 33 (tr), 43 (tc & tr), 47 (cl), 51 (tr), 60, 64, 67 (both), 68, 69, 70, 72, 78, 81, 85, 86 (tr & bl), 87 (all), 88 (both), 90 (cr), 93, 95, 96, 97, 99, 103, 105, 108, 121, 124, 126, 133, 137, 138 (both), 145, 157, 163, 169, 175, 187, 199, 211, jacket back flap; Stan Armstrong 28 (tr, cr & tc); Howard Brown-Greaves 28 (c); Adrian Catterall 108 (br); Stephen Fielding 129; Chris Floyd 127 (br); Bob Garner 43 (c), 47, 51 (cr); Gordon Garradd 30 (tl), 74, 76, 77, 79, 91, 94, 106, 114, 116, 122, 127 (bl), 134, 139, 151; Maurice Gavin 33 (c), 41 (b), 47 (cr), 51 (c), 107; Y. Hirose 40; Eric Hutton 115 (tl inset); JPL 31 (r), 35 (all), 45 (all), 48, 49 (all); Chris Livingstone 205, 193; Rob McNaught 181; Brian Manning 90 (br); Michael Maunder 28; Stan Moore 111; Bob Mizon 141; NASA 53 (br), 311 (Calvin J. Hamilton), 41 (l), 53 (cl), 57; Terry Platt 137 (tr); Pedro Re 99 (tr), 100, 113, 117, 130, 140; Royal Observatory, Edinburgh and Anglo-Australian Observatory (©) 1982 10 (both); Trevor Searle & Phil Hodgins 137 (bl); Charles Smith 22 (br); Michael Stecker 13, 64, 66, 73, 77, 89 (tr), 110, 115, 115 (br), 118, 125 (all), 127 (tl), 128, 131, front cover (br); Nick Szymanek/Ian King 83, 89 (bl), 120, 132, 137 (br); STScI 10, 59, 131 (tr); US Geological Survey 39.
Pictures from other sources: Anglo-Australian Observatory: 9 (all), 13 (c), 135. Corbis: Roger Ressmeyer 8–9 (t). Andy Crawford 20 (all), 21, 22 (cl), 23 (all), 24 (all), 143. Dave King 22 (cr). Science Photo Library: NASA/GSFC 37; Hale Observatory 27 (tr); Frank Zullo 2.

Jacket design by Sharon Spencer

KEY TO PICTURE CREDITS
a=above, c=center, b=below, l=left, r=right, t=top

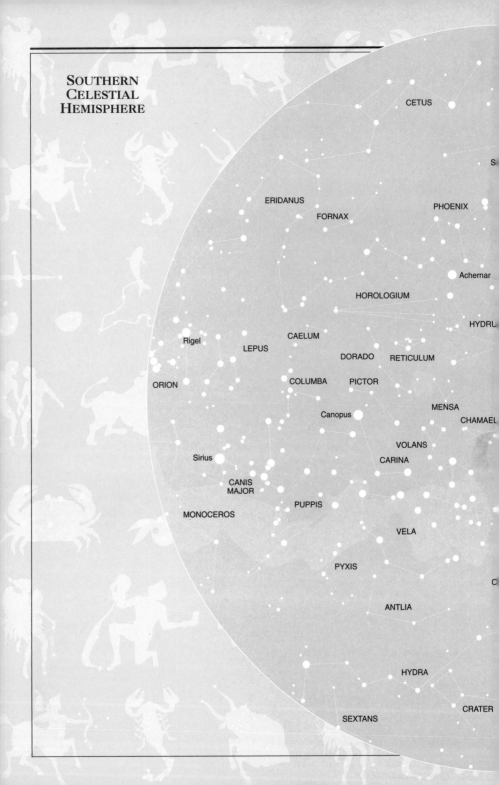

SOUTHERN CELESTIAL HEMISPHERE

CETUS

S

ERIDANUS

PHOENIX

FORNAX

Achernar

HOROLOGIUM

HYDRU

CAELUM

Rigel

LEPUS

DORADO

RETICULUM

ORION

COLUMBA

PICTOR

MENSA

Canopus

CHAMAEL

VOLANS

CARINA

Sirius

CANIS
MAJOR

PUPPIS

MONOCEROS

VELA

PYXIS

C

ANTLIA

HYDRA

CRATER

SEXTANS